THE
CARDINAL

Stephen Fermoyle had wanted to be a priest ever since he could remember. The son of a working-class, Boston-Irish Catholics, he was destined to rise above his brothers in Christ to become the Cardinal. His story is a testament to the faith of one young man and the strength he was to find in his Church, his God, and in himself.

The Cardinal depicts the spiritual yet profoundly human growth of Father Fermoyle against the backdrop of a world at war, a Vatican in conflict with twenty million loyal American Catholics, the daily struggles and earthly temptations of the entire Fermoyle family, and Stephen's confrontation with the love of a beautiful woman.

Whether portraying the inner working of the Holy Roman Apostolic Church, or the constant self-appraisal of a young man's dedication, the depth and power of *The Cardinal*—the saga of holy men and their fellow men of the world—is a triumph of faith.

FOR
Cecile and Joseph Forman

AUTHOR'S FOREWORD

A novelist may, if he chooses, disclaim all resemblance between the characters in his story and actual persons living or dead. While I am prepared to make such disclaimers for many of the people in The Cardinal, *I cannot pretend that Stephen Fermoyle is wholly a product of my imagination. It would be truer, I think, to say that he is a composite of all the priests I have ever known—and particularly those priests who left mysterious imprints of their sacred office on my youth.*

To these indelible traces, deeper and fresher now than when they were first made, I owe whatever insight I may have into the priestly life. Upon such seemingly frail foundations, buttressed by conscious study and mature observation, I have sought to build the many-chambered temple of Stephen Fermoyle's character. Some may think the attempt presumptuous. "How," it will be asked, "dare a layman approach the altar as celebrant, enter the confessional as a looser of sins, wield the crozier, and don the red hat reserved for Princes of the Church?" Granting that the sacerdotal soul is a secret place, I feel, nevertheless, that the ecclesiastic life offers the novelist a genuine challenge in a much neglected field.

The reader may be interested to know that I am, and always have been, a Roman Catholic. Whether or not I am a "good" Catholic is surely a matter between me and my Creator. I never aspired to be a priest. As a writer, I was struck long ago by wonder and awe at the priest's function. In The Cardinal *I have attempted to express these feelings by describing a*

AUTHOR'S FOREWORD

gifted but very human priest fulfilling his destiny as a consecrated mediator between God and man.

Some readers may find my hero too-improbably virtuous; others may complain that in certain episodes he forgets, momentarily, his divine calling. With no desire to disarm such criticism beforehand, I ask only that Stephen Fermoyle be judged (as all men must) not on the testimony of single incidents, but on the manifest intention of his entire life.

The Cardinal is neither propaganda for nor against the Church. Most emphatically it is not a theological treatise or a handbook to history. It is a purely fictional tale, a story to be read as a narrative woven by a watcher of our world, who believes—in spite of evils fearfully apparent—that faith, hope, and compassion animate men of goodwill everywhere.

HENRY MORTON ROBINSON

WOODSTOCK, NEW YORK
JANUARY 19, 1950.

E LA SUA VOLONTATE È NOSTRA PACE

—THE PARADISO, Canto III

Q. Why did God make you?

A. God made me to know Him, to love Him, and to serve Him in this world, and to be happy with Him forever in the next.

—Lesson First: A CATECHISM OF CHRISTIAN DOCTRINE

The
Cardinal

PROLOGUE

𝖔𝖓 𝕿𝖍𝖊 𝕳𝖎𝖌𝖍 𝕾𝖊𝖆𝖘

LIKE MANY A FLORENTINE before him, Captain Gaetano Orselli, master of the luxury-liner *Vesuvio*, was inordinately fond of jewelry. As a younger man he had not wholly resisted the temptation to overload his person — especially his hands — with costly stones; but now in his meridian forties a purer taste was asserting itself. The gem for its own sake had become a canon with Captain Orselli. He contented himself with wearing a single ring at a time, and exercised his really superb sense of ritual by selecting precisely the right stone for the occasion.

Tonight Captain Orselli was choosing his ring with particular care. In a few minutes he would make his appearance on the bridge of the *Vesuvio* to point out sidereal wonders — stars, planets, constellations — to a small group of saloon passengers gathered there by special invitation. He hovered over his ring-case, hesitating between a cabochon emerald and a Burmese ruby. The Captain owned dozens of rings and might have owned hundreds of them, were it not for his incurable habit of giving them away to women — preferably Northern women with wheat-colored hair, deep bosoms, and blue eyes. Deciding in favor of the ruby, he slipped it ceremoniously over the polished nail of his right index finger, and pressed it down to the knuckle. With a perfume atomizer he sprayed his de Reszke beard, adjusted his gold-embroidered hat to the precise slant of the *Vesuvio's* smokestacks, then surveyed the effect — front, back, and profile — in a three-paneled, full-length mirror. Where others would have seen merely a handsome dandy, Captain Orselli saw the truer reflection of a Renaissance magnifico smiling back at him ironically from the glass.

The Captain nipped an English-market cigar between his fine teeth and went on deck. The night was moonless, clear; acid stars etched brilliant geometric patterns in the heavens. Orselli glanced at the sea and sky — a mariner's glance that established the position of the *Vesuvio* almost as accurately as a sextant and chronometer. By Polaris and Boötes the Captain knew that his ship was traveling on the northwesterly Atlantic course assigned to full-powered steamers, and that Cape St. Vincent, the southwesternmost jut of Europe, must be fading somewhere off his starboard beam. Two and one-half days out from Naples, the *Vesuvio* had traversed the Mediterranean, slipped through Gibraltar, and, Boston-bound, was now approximately fifty miles out on the Great Circle of the Atlantic.

Clustered electric lights, spraying downward from the midship rail, illuminated the large Italian flags painted on either side of the vessel — royal notice to U-boats that the *Vesuvio* was the property of a neutral nation. Privately, Captain Orselli expected no danger from submarines. In April, 1915, with Germany urging Italy to line up with the Central Powers against France and England, U-boat commanders were being tenderly respectful to Italian vessels. No such respect could be guaranteed, however, from the random mines swirling about in this part of the ocean. Yesterday the British auxiliary *Frobisher* had struck a mine; the day before, a French destroyer had gone down. Because there simply was no insurance against these spiky, drifting terrors — you could hit one at eight or eighteen knots — Captain Orselli's standing order was "Continue speed."

At twenty knots the *Vesuvio* plowed through the North Atlantic.

On the bridge, darkened save for a gleam from the compass binnacle, a small company of saloon passengers was gathered; the Captain himself had selected them for reasons balanced somewhere between policy and pleasure. First in the Captain's interest was the Swedish-American mezzo-soprano with the Brünnhilde bosom and the pale-gold Psyche knot worn low at the nape of her neck. Professionally known as Erna Thirklind, she was, according to the steamship's publicity department, returning to her native America after wild scenes of acclamation at Milan, Rome, and Naples. Captain Orselli doubted the acclamation story, but was finding other interesting aspects to Erna Thirklind's character and accomplishments. Bending over her hand, he addressed her now as

"Diva," and was not in the least perturbed by her temperate response. Gaetano Orselli was a man of patience.

Next to be greeted was Cornelius J. Deegan, occupant, with his wife and retinue, of the Ildefonso Suite on A deck. Mr. Deegan, whose fortunate brick and gravel contracts with the city of Boston had made him a millionaire, was returning from Rome, where he had recently been inducted into papal knighthood because of his generous interest in restoring the Irish abbey of Tullymara. The redness of brick dust was in the Knight's hair at sixty, and the hardness of brick was still in his freckly hands. Sir Cornelius was accompanied by his wife, Agnes, a grayish woman of no importance to anyone except her husband, her seven children, some fifteen assorted Catholic charities, and a hundred or more poor relatives.

Captain Orselli conveyed to the Deegans just that measure of indifference which a famous portrait painter might bestow on a couple of bourgeois sitters. And to the Reverend Stephen Fermoyle, the sparely built young priest in the Deegan entourage — newly ordained, by the austere look of him — the Captain gave that special inclination of the head which no Catholic, however anticlerical, can withhold from the priesthood.

To the others on the bridge — an attaché of the Italian embassy and his handsome wife, a British banker seeking a fresh Admiralty loan in New York, and a Chicago specialist in canon law who was getting strictly nowhere with the Rota in an annulment case — Captain Orselli made salutations. Then with a brief explanation of celestial mechanics, he began to point out the stars that for centuries had been the guides and familiars of men.

Orselli's interest, like that of any transatlantic navigator, lay to the north. "Regard the Bear," he said, pointing to the great constellation that blazed like a crystal bonfire overhead. "It pivots around the North Star, as if the Bear were being whirled about by its tail. At the tip of the Bear's nose you see Algol, beloved of camel drivers. And those golden streamers between the Bear and the Plow are known to the poets as 'Berenice's Hair.' Yes, a woman's tresses beautify even the heavens. Shall I tell you how it came about, this myth of much charm?"

To the passengers gathered on the darkened bridge, Captain Orselli's dandyish index finger, scented beard, and lyric vocabulary were as bewildering as the stars he was pointing out. The type was new to most of them. That the commander of a 25,000-ton vessel should drive his ship at full speed through mine-strewn waters, yet find time to oil his beard and discourse poetically on the stars, was completely baffling, for instance, to Mr. Cornelius Deegan. Long before his induction as Knight Commander of the Order of St. Sylvester, Mr. Deegan had been a pillar of morality. He struck the moral note now, in muttered undertones to his wife.

"I don't like it, Agnes. With all those U-boats prowling around outside, this fellow ought to be tending more to business."

Aware but contemptuous of the Hibernian's disapproval, Captain Orselli continued to drive his ship at twenty knots and to rub up the rest of his audience with the oiled pumice of his charm. He struck his poet-navigator stance and strummed *dolce* on his lyre. In telling this Berenice story, he had a message to convey. Everyone knew by now that he was a bold shipmaster, and his handsome shoulders suggested certain powers attractive to fully grown women. The Swedish-American soprano with the blonde Psyche bun felt these things as well as anyone else. Captain Orselli knew she felt them. But he wanted her to know also that wheat-colored hair excited him beyond the love of rubies, and that if he might enjoy the one, he would — if pressed — part with the other. Especially on a night of stars.

"Berenice was an Egyptian queen surpassing in beauty," he began. The Captain would have preferred to work in Italian, but to show his virtuosity as a linguist, he spoke in English. "When her husband carried a dangerous expedition to Syria, Berenice cut off her golden hair" — Orselli's wrist made a sickle motion suggestive of wheat shorn close to the root — "and laid it on the altar of Amen-Ra. Do such women exist today?" Shaking his notched beard with ever so slight a melancholy, Captain Orselli pointed at the constellation. "To reward such sacrifice, the god displays Coma Berenices in the sky. And that is for why [the idiom momentarily slipped away

from him] navigators and lovers see on spring nights the glory
of her tresses in the heavens."

The reception was only fair. Cornelius Deegan grunted that
it was getting chilly, and the American nightingale wrapped
her boa tighter around her throat. Long experience in treading his starlight stage had led Captain Orselli to expect a
warmer hand. It occurred to him that he should have worn
the emerald. He was about to launch into his Andromeda
routine when a baritone voice inquired:

"*Qual' e Lucifero?*" The question had edge, timing, and
intent.

In the darkness Captain Orselli felt the attack. He could
not see his questioner but he recognized the Roman accent —
ecclesiastic, acquired. That would be the voice of the young
priest in the Deegan suite. The Captain decided to have a
little quiet fun with this bantling curate.

"Lucifer? The fallen angel? Why do you wish to locate him,
Father?" The questions jockeyed a laugh from the audience.
"You fear his fate?"

"I fear, you fear, we fear." The voice in the darkness was
good-natured, humorous. "No, Captain, I'm curious about
Lucifer because, like his namesake, he travels under so many
aliases."

Captain Orselli liked both the temper and matter of the
young priest's presentation. A whipmaster himself, he enjoyed
a punishing flick from another. "You are perfectly right,
Father. The star has been known by many names — Lucifer,
Phosphor, Hesperus. But they are always one and the same."
The Captain's finger pointed to the western horizon. "And
there it lies, dusky-red, fallen, but still proud."

The ruby on Orselli's index finger, catching the red glow
of his cigar, duplicated the precise color of the planet.

"The oddest part of the story," he continued, "is that this
very star will rise from the sea tomorrow morning, blonde
and golden, under the name of Venus. Is it not wonderful,
this alchemy of the night?"

The question, a mixture of rhetoric and innuendo, neither
required nor expected an answer. The stargazing party began
to break up.

Captain Orselli moved among his guests, Thespian foot

forward. The brush with the young priest had heightened his exhibitionistic mood. Pinked unexpectedly, Orselli covered the small hurt with Tuscan exaggerations of speech and gesture. His good-night bow to the Deegans was a mock obeisance, and his tone to Stephen was that of a champion swordsman congratulating a novice on a lucky thrust.

"Your wrist is supple, Father. You reached me nicely with your conjugation of *timeo: I fear, you fear, we all fear*. Ha! How true! Pride, captain of the capital sins, is ever the undoing of the great ones. 'That last infirmity of noble minds,' as your Milton says. Or do I misquote?" He turned solemnly to Cornelius Deegan. "We must speak by the book here, else we are ruined."

The Knight's honest and utter confusion tempted Orselli beyond bounds of courtesy. "Shall we continue in my cabin, Father? Tuscan honor demands satisfaction, and the stars say it is yet early. Your friends will not mind?"

Agnes Deegan felt heat waves radiating from her husband's neck. That danger signal she knew well. It meant that Sir Corny was doubling his freckled fist and in another moment would be throwing his applesauce punch at the Captain's fine medieval nose.

"Go with him, Stephen," she said. "Cornelius and I are tired, anyway. We'll be going to bed." Her eyes considered the heavens, as though she had never seen them till now. "Ah! 'Tis a beautiful night for an argument."

Stephen hesitated. The flattery of Orselli's invitation was not lost upon him, and he longed for a tussle at close quarters with this arrogant dandy. But the slight to the Deegans was inexcusable. The young priest must make a choice; he would either surrender to the charm of this worldly, fascinating man or declare his deeper loyalty to Corny and Agnes Deegan. Much as he wished to know Orselli, Stephen declared for the stronger loyalty.

"I'm afraid you'd have a drowsy opponent tonight, Captain. I couldn't risk being cut to ribbons in my sleep. Will you make it another time?"

Out of the tail of his eye, Orselli saw the British banker making up to Erna Thirklind. The danger from the English quarter outweighed the two rebuffs that this independent young priest had given him. He lifted his gold-embroidered hat. "At any time, Father. But the voyage is short, remember. We have only seven more days to grapple for each other's soul." He exposed his handsome teeth to the Deegans. "*A domani.*"

"*A domani,*" said Stephen, wondering, as he strolled toward the Deegan suite on A deck, When and where have I ever met such a thoroughgoing and magnetic rascal?

THE DEEGAN SUITE was a baroque version of the luxury expected by Americans on an Italian liner in the second decade of the present century. Much-tapestried and ornately gilded, it befitted the new-made Knight of St. Sylvester as he sat down on a rococo armchair, hoisted his feet (large feet that had climbed many a ladder, with many a hod of cement) onto a spindly taboret, and delivered himself of strong feelings about Captain Orselli.

"The man galls me, Stephen," he said. "His whiskers, the stuff he sprays them with, and that guff about the stars. They're bad enough." Corny's agitation seemed to shake brick dust from his hair. "But what I cannot *stand* is a man who wears a ring on his forefinger."

Stephen Fermoyle considered the justifiable state of his older friend's feelings. How much could Sir Cornelius stand — or understand? The past forty-eight hours had put a trying strain on the Deegan system of values. But then again, Stephen's own patience was beginning to chip at the rim. Loyally, he took up his burden.

"Wearing a ring on the index finger is merely an old Italian custom, Corny. Every Renaissance gentleman from Lorenzo down wore one. It's all part of a very great tradition."

"About that I wouldn't know," said Mr. Deegan, rooting desperately for expression in his one-syllabled vocabulary. "But I still don't like the fellow. That big fat pride he has — it rubs me the wrong way, Stephen."

"I know what you mean." The young priest was noncommittal. He understood very well what Cornelius Deegan meant, but as a guest he didn't feel like disagreeing with him further.

"And was I proud of you, Stephen, when you knocked him

off his perch with that Lucifer comeback." Cornelius Deegan's
cheek glowed with pleasure. "The Cardinal will hear of it
from my own lips when I pay my respects to him in Boston."

"Please, Cornelius, no," begged Stephen. "Promise me you
won't mention it to anyone — particularly the Cardinal."

"And why not?" The Deegan wind was rising again.

"The fact is, Corny, I'm a little bit ashamed of that business
on the bridge."

"Ashamed? Here you turn the laugh on an Italian show-off,
and make him treat you with the reverence due a priest.
What's to be ashamed of in that?"

Stephen was finding it increasingly hard to explain certain
things to his host. For a moment he regretted joining the
Deegans. But no — they were goodhearted, generous folks.
He must try to make his position clear.

"Listen, Corny," he said, "when I asked, 'Which is Lucifer?'
I was inviting trouble. I meant the question to be a kind of
lunge at the man's vanity. He felt the attack, and, naturally
enough, parried it by turning the laugh against me." Stephen
paused. "And of course I was showing off a bit myself when
I put the question in Italian."

"It's his own language, isn't it?" asked Agnes Deegan.

"But he was speaking English at the time," Stephen pointed
out.

Cornelius Deegan shook a puzzled head. "You certainly
figure things funny, Steve. Not like an American at all. Did
they teach you to think that way in Rome?"

Stephen traced with his finger the ornate pattern of an
inlaid table. "It's not any particular thing they teach, Corny.
But after you've lived in Rome awhile, you begin to see and
feel a richness of design — the mosaic on this table is as good
an example as any — that you don't encounter anywhere else.
Take this Captain of ours. I don't blame you for being irritated at his self-conceit. But you must realize, Corny, that
Gaetano Orselli is a remarkable specimen of a culture that we
can't grasp, much less duplicate, in the United States."

"Remarkable? Would you be specifying now?"

"I would. Over and above Orselli's accomplishments as a
navigator and shipmaster, he's a linguist, a poet, a gourmet —
it was a joy to watch him eat that plover tonight — as well as

a connoisseur of wines, gems, cigars, and" — Stephen sounded them to see if they had caught the mezzo-soprano overtones — "the opera. He probably can sing, or at least hum, every important aria in Wagner, Puccini, Verdi. . . ."

The Deegans were dumfounded. How should a priest — and a young priest — be knowing about these worldly matters? And not only knowing about them, but including them in a litany of high regard.

Stephen sensed their disapproval. "Oh, I suppose Orselli is a villainous agnostic, a rabid anticlericalist, and a man of no morals. I'm not defending him, Corny. I'm only saying that there's something about these Italians that awakens the memory of a dream that's pretty well faded from the Western world." With fresh enthusiasm Stephen went on:

"You'll laugh when I tell you, Corny, or get angry maybe, but at Rome I had a professor of sacred theology, Monsignor Alfeo Quarenghi, the most ascetic, the most scholarly man I've ever known — ringless, unscented, utterly unselfed by prayer and abstinence. Yet somehow these two men, so utterly different, resemble one another. I'll put it this way: Quarenghi — elegant, fascinating, unforgettable — is the spiritualized counterpart of our captain."

Cornelius Deegan thought that the cooling time had come for such warm comparisons. Linking a Monsignor with Orselli? Why, if Father Stephen went any further, he'd be dabbling in heresy! Sir Corny grasped the moral bell rope and chimed ponderously.

"Background they may have in common, and a way of policy such as we don't come by in America. But take my word for it, Father" — Cornelius Deegan permitted his opinion to ring out loud and clear — "take my word for it, this Captain Orselli is naught but a windbag. No moral fiber. Put on the pressure, and he'll crack wide open."

Stephen nodded. "You may be right, Cornelius." The folly of contesting with the stubborn contractor-Knight made him feel more than slightly ridiculous. Smiling, he held out a good-night hand to his host.

Something about Stephen's gesture of surrender soothed Cornelius Deegan; the gruff pomposity of the Knight evaporated, and the parochial self-esteem of the contractor vanished quite away. All that remained on his face was the broad County Wicklow smile that he had brought to America forty years ago in the steerage of a twenty-day ship from Queenstown.

"Steve," he said, grasping the young priest's hand, "you've got quite a touch of the Italian about you, yourself. You know when to hang on and when to give in. It's a trick your father never learned. I'm wondering now what Dennis Fermoyle — Dennis the Down-Shouter we used to call him — will be saying when he finds himself crossed in argument by his Rome-educated son?"

The proud edge of Father Steve Fermoyle's intellect was blunted by the question. "I'll never cross him, Corny. He can win every argument he starts with me. That great fist of his pounding the table and the gun-flint anger snapping in his blue eyes are the things I've missed most these four long years. God make me worthy to be his son."

"GOD *make me worthy to be his son.*"

Stephen Fermoyle knelt beside a gilt chair in the solitude of his stateroom, bowed his head, and humbly meditated on the unbelievable wonder of being a priest. No prayer could frame his joy; no spoken words were strong enough to bear the tribute of love and thanksgiving that he wished to offer God the Father. For many minutes he was silent, then with his mind and heart at full stretch he said the Our Father very slowly, praising with every syllable His Name, His Kingdom, and His Will.

Stephen now opened his breviary and read Matins and Lauds in anticipation of the morrow. First he said the prayer before Office:

"Open, O Lord, my mouth that I may praise Thy Holy Name; cleanse my heart from all vain, perverse, and distracting thoughts; enlighten my mind and inflame my heart that I may pray this Office worthily, attentively, and devoutly, and that I may deserve to be heard in the presence of Thy divine Majesty, through Christ our Lord, Amen.

"O Lord, in unison with that divine intention with which Thou, whilst on earth, didst Thyself praise God, I offer Thee this Hour."

Into the spiritual world of the Office, contrasting with the vain contentions of the world of men, Stephen entered. As he read Matins and Lauds, the strength and purity of his vocation was renewed; the essential nature of his drive toward the priesthood became clear to him, as it always did when he knelt in prayer. Stephen Fermoyle's relationship to God was as direct and immediate as the relationship of a well to a spring. In him throbbed no mystical desire to lose his identity in the Father; instead, almost overwhelming in its intensity, Stephen felt the need of declaring himself as an outflow of the Source. As a son and lieutenant, he again resolved to bespeak and represent God the Father among men.

"Father they call me. Father I will be," he vowed. "To the Blessed Virgin and to Mother Church, all loyalty and devotion I shall give. But expressly to you, First Person of the Trinity, do I dedicate my being."

His Office over, Stephen rose from his knees and went out into a night of stars. He leaned over the rail and gazed into the mysterious beauty of the sea. A line from Keats swam into his memory:

> *The moving waters at their priestlike task*
> *Of pure ablution round earth's human shores . . .*

Priestlike task. Ever since Stephen Fermoyle could remember, he had wanted to be a priest. The call had come early — he was barely fourteen when he first knew that his heart was in the sanctuary. Stephen was one of those fortunate souls, not uncommon among Americans of Irish parentage, on whom the Holy Ghost had descended surely and soon. All through high school and college, the sacerdotal imprint had been clear. Inwardly consecrated, yet without excessive piety, he had been at twenty-two an outstanding candidate for special training at the North American College in Rome.

In four years, Stephen had grown to love the Holy City. Its tide rip of past and present — of Trajan, Bramante, and Canova, of Hildebrand, Sixtus, and Michelangelo — had stirred in him a profound sympathy with the grandeur and timelessness of Rome. Its temporal monuments had fascinated him — but more fascinating than the architecture, more permanent and abiding than the cathedrals, was the Roman mind itself.

The Roman viewpoint! What was it exactly? Stephen had tried to label the thing, but failed, as others have failed, in the attempt to characterize this compound of universal awareness and calm assumption of centrality. The intuitional scope of the Roman mind! How he admired its ability to operate like a piece of weatherproof mechanism in all latitudes! From one teacher in particular, Monsignor Quarenghi, he had drawn the universal wisdom of the Church — a vision that he had not previously imagined and could not wholly grasp even now. In Quarenghi's elegant voice and hands, in the ascetic planes of his forehead, jaw, and shoulders — high narrow shoulders, straight as the hilt of a Toledo blade — Stephen had found his model of the priesthood. The axle of the cosmos seemed to pass through Quarenghi's mind. Knowledge of this world, political insight, and social vision were matched only by his attachment to the Church. Part diplomat, part teacher, and all priest, this remarkable man had been the chief influence on a young seminarian.

Other memories, unconnected with human personality, rushed into Stephen's mind as he gazed into the dark sea below. His progress through the minor orders of the priesthood were spotless stones marking his approach to the fulfillment of ordination. The chrism, the words of the ordaining bishop, "Thou art a priest forever" — and the concelebration with others of the priestly ritual — these had left indelible imprints on Stephen Fermoyle's soul.

And now he was on his return to America to take up his duties as a parish priest. Normally he would have sailed second class with a band of fellow students; but on the eve of departure Corny Deegan had appeared at the seminary, resplendent in a morning coat and striped trousers that contrasted hugely with the overalls in which Stephen had remembered him. As an old friend of the family, Corny had requested that he be allowed to take the newly ordained priest home on the *Vesuvio*. Corny Deegan's standing as a papal knight had not been without weight. The request had been granted, and instead of sharing a berth with a fellow seminarian, Stephen Fermoyle was now occupying a state-

room in the Ildefonso Suite, homeward bound to America.
He was twenty-six years old, strong-bodied, proud in spirit.
Too proud, perhaps, for the humbling labors that lay ahead.
Quarenghi's last words came to him now. "Be careful,
Stephen, of the First Sin — Pride, that greatest of temptations
to the intellect. Make your stature small before men that it
may be greater in the eyes of God." Quarenghi had pointed
to the crucifix hanging by a silver chain on his breast. "This
act was the final abnegation of self. By it, the Son is made
worthy of the Father."

Made worthy of the Father!

"Grant," prayed Stephen for the second time within the
hour, "that I may be made worthy to be His son."

THE PARALLEL BARS clewed to the deck in front of Gaetano
Orselli's cabin trembled under the assault of the Captain's
hundred and ninety-eight pounds. Sweat dripped from his
beard as he thrust his feet skyward in a handstand, then
lowered himself with a slow bulge of deltoids and biceps.
With a graceful shoulder roll, he somersaulted off the end
of the bars and landed on the balls of his feet. It was the
maneuver of a practiced gymnast; very dangerous to the neck
if it didn't come off.

Basking in a deck chair, Stephen struck his palms together
in mock exhaustion. "Another workout like this, Captain, and
I'll be worn out. You asked me up to play *Mühle*, remember?"

Orselli snatched up a towel, blotted the runlets of perspiration streaming from his face and chest. It pleased him to display his physical prowess before this young American priest.
Like all exhibitionists, Orselli needed an appreciative audience, and Stephen had unexpectedly supplied him with the
knowingest mixture of discernment and irony that the Captain had received in many years. The attraction was mutual;
for three days now the two men had promenaded, dined,
debated, played handball and *Mühle* while the *Vesuvio* cut
a white furrow across the Atlantic.

"So you want another 'licking,' as you call it, at *Mühle*.
Good. There is just time for me to trounce you before luncheon. Step into my parlor, Messer. This sun deck is much too
warm for anyone but thin-blooded Englishmen."

Stephen entered Orselli's cabin. He liked this horseshoe-shaped, glassed-in compartment permitting vision from all points of the compass. Mahogany, brass, and Burgundy-hued leather struck the correct masculine tone set for the Western world by Edwardian clubs. A gimbal lamp swinging from the ceiling and a long spyglass on a fixed tripod supplied the only marine clues. The walls of the cabin were covered with autographed photos: Orselli standing beside ambassadors, presidents, royalty, actresses. Stephen examined them. A letter from Victor Emmanuel. A snapshot of Theodore Roosevelt, his arm around the Captain's shoulders. *After a bully crossing.* A studio photograph of the Divine Sarah was signed *À Gaetani Orselli, mon Capitaine favori, Bernhardt.* A company of handsome women, unknown to Stephen, completed the gallery.

Orselli was placing the *Mühle* board on a little table. "My sorrow is, Father, that your vows of poverty do not enable you to play for stakes. What a murdering I could make on this voyage!"

At *Mühle,* a combination of chess, checkers, and ticktacktoe, Captain Orselli was adept. The trick of the game lay in outguessing and outfeinting one's opponent at least three moves in advance. They played two games. Stephen lost both of them, then pushed the board away.

"I don't give you much competition, Captain. Something in the game eludes me."

"*Mühle* is very old, very European," consoled Orselli. "Your American mind does not grasp its central idea. You are too transparent; you expose yourself. There are no shadows in your thinking. Well, in another hundred years perhaps, you will learn the value, the necessity, of shadows."

Stephen gazed through an open window at the sparkling sea. No shadow there — only sunlight breaking in galaxies of diamonds against a sapphire swell. The beauty of sky and ocean sponged him with contentment. He had no desire to argue with Orselli about the function of shadow in life and art; he only knew that this was the most perfect day that had ever been made, and that he was both the laziest and most sentient part of it.

"*Fa bella,*" he murmured.

"*Fa bella,* indeed," said the Captain. "No weather is more beautiful than the Atlantic in spring. Too bad" — he waved at the horizon — "that it does not lie in the public domain."

"What do you mean?"

Orselli's voice distilled rancor. "Haven't you heard? It is the private property of the British Navy. We sail on it only by their leave. Ha! Have you never heard the story about His English Majesty's bos'n?"

"Never."

"A bos'n was being court-martialed for striking a captured U-boat commander. His defense was a classic." Orselli turned on a Tuscan conception of a cockney whine. " 'I didn't mind when this 'ere blighter tried to torpedo us, sir. And I took it as a matter o' course when 'e refused to answer our Capting a civil question. But when e' spit in our ocean, sir, *then* I let 'im 'ave it.' "

Stephen laughed at Orselli's crossing of Florence with Houndsditch. "My father would enjoy that story, Captain. He still thinks of the British as the oppressor under Cromwell."

"Cromwell, Clive, Rhodes," said Orselli gloomily. "What does it matter? The oppressor is always British."

"Yet if Italy goes to war, it will surely be on the English side."

Orselli fingered his beard thoughtfully. "My country's best interests would be to stay out of this war. She is not prepared, either in material or ideas. War will be fatal to her. Yet it is only a question of days now." He patted his midriff. "Did you think I was sweating over those parallel bars for fun? When Italy declares herself, the officers of her Naval Reserve must not be lard barrels."

Italian contempt for other nations warred with Orselli's realization that Italy's great age lay behind her. "When we enter the war, we shall lose — in addition to prestige and territory — the one institution that lifted the world out of barbarism."

"What is that?"

Orselli broke into Italian. "The idea of *l'uomo unico* Man, unique and glorious, the creature who came to life in Florence in the thirteenth century. Man the artist, the city-maker, the poet, the fame-hungerer — man the paradise-stormer and celebrator of this world's beauty. The mold was made in Italy; the original stuff was poured in the city of my birth and spread northward. But nowhere was man ever so flowering, so complete, so universal, yet so individualized as in Italy." The Captain's voice saddened. *"L'uomo unico* was our glory. Today it is our tragedy. There are so many unique men in Italy, partisanship is so violent, the counsels so divided, that no clear voice can be heard."

"I agree with you about *l'uomo unico*," said Stephen. "He existed once. He doesn't now. But he may again. And when he reappears, his wealth and weapons won't be temporal."

"Prove it." Orselli's cynicism was almost hopeful.

"I'll give you the case of Gioacchino Pecci, Leo XIII, that is. When the Pope lost his temporal dominions in 1870, many people thought that the papacy was dead. Actually it was reborn under Leo. His army consisted only of the household guard carrying halberds. But Leo's moral energy was something new in the world. By his encyclicals he demonstrated that when a man of moral integrity appears, all other forces crumble under his pressure. Pecci insisted that . . ."

A JUNIOR OFFICER was saluting. "Sorry to interrupt, sir, but the bridge reports a British cruiser off the port beam. She's displaying international flag signals, 'Stop immediately.'"

Captain Gaetano Orselli was on his feet. Binoculars at his eyes, he confirmed the second officer's report. "Here comes Britannia," he murmured. "See how she churns His Majesty's waves. Tell the bridge to take off speed, Lieutenant." Orselli turned to Stephen. "This will be worth dressing for. No, don't go away, Father. I may need some of that Leo XIII moral force you've been describing. Here, take a look while I dress."

Stephen trained the binoculars on the approaching warship. He saw the gray hull, the embodiment of physical force as it towered up into a complex superstructure, gaining rapidly on the *Vesuvio*.

L'uomo unico won't have much chance, he thought, viewing the long guns trimmed fore and aft from their turrets.

Captain Orselli was spraying his underarms with a perfume atomizer. "Break out my Bond Street whites and London boots," he cried to his dresser. "For this encounter we must be garbed correctly. *L'Inglese* will reek with protocol. We will give him protocol and something else besides." He darted to his cabin phone, called the bridge.

"Drop the pilot ladder and meet our visitors with all courtesy at the companionway."

Stephen saw the British cruiser, her decks alive with men, slide alongside. A whaleboat swung out from davits; eight oarsmen, blades aloft, took their places. Two officers stepped into the stern. The whaleboat struck the water. Lofted oars fell into rowlocks, swung in unison toward the *Vesuvio*.

The *Triton's* whaleboat was a dozen lengths from the ladder when Captain Orselli appeared on his sun deck. He was superbly dressed in an English-made uniform of white linen; an English-market cigar was between his teeth, and a magnificent diamond glittered on the little finger of his right hand.

"I know what they want," he said quietly to Stephen. "Come, Father, watch me meet them on the solidest ground in the world — the bridge of my own ship."

"Wouldn't you rather carry on without me?" asked Stephen.

"On the contrary. It will be valuable to have an American witness of what may be an international incident. And if my English fails," Orselli smiled, "I may call upon you to translate."

On the *Vesuvio's* bridge, a group of Italian officers saluted their captain. "Relax, gentlemen," said Orselli. "Have a stenographer ready to take down the conversation." He savored his cigar and promenaded like a man in the foyer of La Scala during the entr'acte of an agreeably light opera.

Up the companionway came the Englishman, impeccably formal and imperially slim. On his sleeve he wore the three stripes of a commander in the British Royal Navy; his cap had the grommetless, bashed-in appearance affected the world over by deep-water sailors. The energy of a perfectly conditioned thirty-year-old man was in his step, and the fatigue of a three-week Atlantic patrol was in his eyes. Behind him, ruddy and insolent, came a bos'n's mate, and behind them both rose the invisible trident of England's sea power.

The Englishman brought two fingers to the visor of his salty cap. "I am Commander Ramilly of His Majesty's ship *Triton*," he announced in the manner of a viscount laying a gold piece on a tobacconist's counter. "Captain Nesbitt desires me to thank you for responding so promptly to our signal. We regret any inconvenience we may have caused you."

"It is as nothing, Commander. When you return my compliments to Captain Nesbitt, please say that the heart of every seaman on the *Vesuvio* throbs with pleasure at the honor His Majesty's Navy does our ship. . . . Will you smoke, Commander?"

The Englishman considered the strings attached to the cigar and murmured, "Thank you, no." Whereupon Captain Orselli put his gold cigar case into his pocket and waited for the British Navy to make known its business on board the *Vesuvio*.

The tactic of silence put Commander Ramilly slightly off balance. He had hoped for something more in the way of oral squirming. While the Englishman gazed about the bridge as if he expected to see a dust pile swept into a corner, Orselli continued to relish his Havana in silence.

It's the old game of *Mühle*, thought Stephen. The odds on *l'uomo unico* went up slightly.

Not until Orselli walked to the rail of the bridge, and flicked his cigar ash in the general direction of the Atlantic, did the Englishman speak.

"You have among your crew a stoker shipping under the name of Matteo Salvucci," he said in a bored, declarative tone. "Please be so good, Captain, as to ask him to come to the bridge with his papers."

"On what grounds do you make this request?" asked Orselli.

The Englishman was either very tired or very patient. He closed his eyes wearily. "That will be made clear after my examination."

Captain Orselli briefly considered the move. "Bring Salvucci here," he ordered.

The guns of the *Triton* rose ominously on six ocean swells and were sinking into the trough of the seventh when Matteo Salvucci climbed onto the bridge. From his soot-streaked bald head, which he was still wiping with a wad of cotton waste, to the dirty-nailed toes that poked out of his broken shoes, he was the original coal-hole Giuseppe — haggard, red-eyed, sweat-out, and characteristically unnerved by the idea of sunlight.

"Are you Matteo Salvucci?" asked Orselli in Italian.

The man nodded and automatically handed his passport to his questioner. Orselli glanced at the document briefly, then relayed it to the British.

Commander Ramilly riffled the pages of the passport in the manner of a proconsul about to exercise his double power of accusing and judging inferior people in a language not their own.

"Where were you born, Salvucci?"

"Napoli."

The proconsul of Empire apparently had never heard of the place. From a letter case carried by the bos'n's mate he drew out a photograph and held it up as Exhibit A.

"This picture was made in Hamburg six months ago," he recited. "It is the picture of a German national named Rudolf Kassebohm. Do you deny that this is a picture of you?"

Orselli's translation met a violent cataract of Italian from the stoker.

"He denies it," said Orselli. "He denies it in a Neapolitan dialect with no trace of a German accent. Moreover, may I point out, Commander, the resemblance between this man and your picture is not at all convincing."

"The British Admiralty must be the judge of that." The evidence being in, and objections having been heard, sentence was now pronounced. "I am sorry, Captain, but I must take your stoker to London for further questioning."

Gaetano Orselli flung the butt of his cigar past Commander Ramilly's nose into the Atlantic. Stephen saw the English officer dodge and the bos'n's neck veins bulge with anger.

"I, too, am sorry, Commander," said Orselli, "but I cannot permit you to take this man off my ship."

Ramilly chose five frosty words. "You have no choice, Captain."

"No?" The Italian's inflection was humorous. "I have a great many choices, Commander. My first choice is to declare a moment of silence in which we can all hear your bos'n strangling his rage more audibly. And my second choice is to escort you to your whaleboat and proceed on my voyage."

Commander Ramilly murmured that the latter course would unavoidably cause pain to all concerned. He buttressed his remarks with a half glance in the direction of the British cruiser.

"I am aware," said Orselli, "that cruisers of the *Triton* class carry twelve nine-inch and ten six-inch guns. A single shell could shear off my rudder or explode my boilers. But let us talk rationally, Commander. Even a British naval officer should know something about the posture of world affairs at this moment."

Orselli's tone contained a grain, or possibly less, of pity for this slender victim dangling on the hook of ignorance. "You probably realize Mr. Ramilly, that while we exchange pleasantries here, English diplomacy is — how do you say — 'panting' to win Italy to her side in this unfortunate war. How would it look to your admirable Prime Minister, Mr. Asquith, and your estimable Lord Grey — a headline in the London *Times:* 'British Warship Fires on Italian Liner'?" Orselli wagged his beard gravely. "And how — I put it to you, Commander — how would such a headline look in the Italian papers? These political embarrassments must be considered, must they not?"

If only Corny Deegan were here, thought Stephen.

The Englishman took a dogged turn. "Your political views are interesting, Captain. But the fact remains that the *Triton* has Admiralty orders to take this man. The order must be carried out."

Nelson glared at Lorenzo, and Lorenzo smiled back.

"But must it?" asked Orselli. "I suggest to you, Commander, that your Admiralty based its order on a certain premise. That premise was that no order issued by the British Royal Navy is ever resisted. It is the old story. British search and seizure, British bullying on the high seas, have always succeeded in the past. The order was issued on the assumption that they would succeed again."

Dignity and contempt husbanded for six centuries rode the Italian's words. "But now I, Gaetano Orselli, a Florentine, do resist that order. I resist it politically and morally. The English bluff has been called. The only course open to you, Commander, is to wireless your Admiralty that Gaetano Orselli, Captain of the neutral vessel *Vesuvio,* will *not* hand over one of his stokers." Orselli lowered his voice confidentially. "I predict that you will get this reply: 'Permit the *Vesuvio* to proceed unmolested!' And that reply will be signed, 'Churchill.'"

Commander Ramilly suddenly felt the need for consultation with his superiors. "I must report your position to Captain Nesbitt. Stand by for further orders."

"No," said Orselli, "as soon as I have escorted you to the companionway, the *Vesuvio* will take on speed. The *Triton* may, if she wishes, follow at a respectful distance until the Admiralty order calls her off. And now, Commander"—Orselli produced his diamond-studded cigar case — "will you be so kind as to present this to Captain Nesbitt as a memento of my esteem. It is not of itself greatly valuable but it contains a half dozen of your excellent London-market cigars."

The English officer had a tradition of sportsmanship to maintain, and he almost maintained it. "Captain Nesbitt will probably enjoy your cigars much more than my report." He saluted, turned to go. "And may I add, Captain, chiefly for my bos'n's benefit, that if I were in command of the *Triton,* I'd straddle your vessel at two thousand yards with a most persuasive weight of metal."

"*Giovanezza,*" laughed Orselli. "Youth, impulsive youth. When you are old enough to command a cruiser, Mr. Ramilly, you will be cooler in judgment."

He bowed the Englishman to the companionway, then turned to the deck officer. "Put speed on the ship," he ordered.

From Orselli's officers burst a triumphant shout as they rushed toward their captain. They pummeled him, hugged him, kissed his cheeks and neck with unashamed emotion. "*Bravo,*" they cried. "*Viva Orselli, Viva Italia, Viva Vesuvio!*"

Viva, thought Stephen, *l'uomo unico.*

Later he grasped Orselli's hand. "You were magnificent," he said. "What a show! The finest piece of diplomatic sleight of hand I ever saw. The Englishman never knew what hap-

pened to his guns. They simply vanished." He wrung the
Captain's hand in admiration. "How did you do it?"

"You might say that I caught *l'Inglese* between his political
wind and water," laughed Orselli. "I was fortunate in having
the necessary information at just the right time. If the whole
British Navy had been bobbing alongside the *Triton*, their
guns would have been powerless against the international
levers now in play."

"There's more to it," insisted Stephen. "You were on top
of him politically, of course. But your real strength lay elsewhere . . . in your moral courage, and your faith in *l'uomo
unico*."

Orselli was curiously humble. "Is that so strange in an
Italian? Have you forgotten your little homily on Gioacchino
Pecci and the wonders he accomplished with a handful of
halberdiers? 'All weapons are not temporal,' you said. Well"
— laughter bubbling out of his great throat — "after my little
encounter with *l'Inglese*, I'm beginning to believe it myself.
Come, let us promenade."

Together they strolled toward Orselli's cabin, and from the
vantage of his sun deck watched the battle tower of the
Triton swaying like an inverted pendulum across the horizon.
Orselli pulled out his watch, and waited exactly twenty minutes before he spoke.

"We are now beyond the range of the Englishman's guns,"
he said. "In six centuries no Florentine has been happier than
I am at this moment."

As the Captain spoke, Stephen saw on the deck below a
man and a woman walking arm in arm. The woman was Erna
Thirklind, and the man leaning attentively toward her was
the English banker. A *tailleur* suit of navy-blue flannel accen-
tuated the soprano's full figure and set off her creamy skin
and wheat-gold hair. Pink excitement heightened her make-
up. For a reason he could not explain, Stephen hoped that
Orselli would not notice the pair.

But he did. For a long moment he regarded the strolling
couple. Then his shoulders went up in a very Tuscan shrug,
and his forked beard went down like a semaphore announcing the end of a race.

"One is never," he remarked wryly, "quite beyond the range of the English guns."

ON THE LAST NIGHT of the crossing, just after the *Vesuvio* had picked up Minot's Light, Orselli knocked at the door of Stephen's cabin.

"I've come to say good-by, Father. Tomorrow morning will be a time of bustle and confusion. Of meetings and partings. your family will be on the pier to greet you?"

"I expect so, Captain."

"You will go home with them?"

"No. My orders are to report immediately to the Chancery of the Archdiocese. Headquarters, you know. There I'll receive my faculties — a kind of ecclesiastical license to practice my profession. After that, if I'm lucky, I'll be assigned to one of the parishes around Boston."

The Captain laid his hand on Stephen's shoulder. "It will be a lucky parish that gets you. May I make a prediction? You will go far in the Church."

"I have no desire to go far. My only ambition is to be a good priest."

"You will be that, of course. Nevertheless, you will go higher. And do you know why?"

"Why?"

"Because," said Orselli, "you are not afraid of worldliness. I do not mean that you are worldly. Far from it. But you have a talent for being all things to all men — a talent not common among Americans, if I may say so. I have watched you handle your honest friend Deegan; I felt your sympathy go out to me" — Orselli affected a schoolboy sheepishness — "in the affair of the blonde nightingale. Trifles maybe, but they reveal a humanity that the Church will put to good use."

Orselli dipped his fingers into a small fobbed pocket of his jacket, drew out a gold ring, and held it between his thumb and forefinger. "It is a Tuscan sentiment to make gifts of value when parting from a dear friend. Will you do me the honor to accept this token of remembrance?"

Stephen examined the jeweled gift. An oblong amethyst, deeply beveled and edged with seed pearls — all set in massive gold. His first instinct was to refuse the costly present

"This is a beautiful ring, Captain. I value the feeling that goes with it. But how can I accept it? In America, a parish priest could never wear such a ring."

"It is not the ring of a parish priest," said Orselli. "It is a bishop's ring." He closed Stephen's fingers over the amethyst. "Keep it, my boy. Lay it away, forget it for the present. But when you finally put it on, say a prayer for the anticlerical Florentine who gave it to you."

"I began praying for him a week ago," grinned Stephen.

Shrill toot of a steam siren. "We're picking up the pilot," said Orselli. He grasped Stephen's hand. "The *Vesuvio* will not be coming to Boston again for a long time. But when she returns . . . Remember, we were made to see each other again. Good-by, Father."

"Good-by, and God bless you," said Stephen.

In the middle of the night watch the *Vesuvio's* great propeller stopped churning, and her hoarse booming invited the little tugs to take over. At dawn they were still shunting and worrying the great liner into her berth at Commonwealth Pier. Stephen was shaving when he felt an almost imperceptible bump. The ship had touched the shores of America. He was home.

Walking down the gangplank with the Deegans in the April morning sunlight, he saw his father and mother waving among the crowd at the pier. Tears started from his eyes when the walrus mustaches of Dennis Fermoyle pressed his cheek. And they mixed with the tears cascading down Celia Fermoyle's face when she lifted her arms around her son-priest's neck. A slender, dark-haired young woman said, "I'm Monica," and Stephen could not believe that this was the little sister he had last seen in pigtails. Bernard and Florrie were there too, hugging, exclaiming, pulling out handkerchiefs.

So much love, so much human longing in the world. So good to be a part of it. For the next couple of hours Stephen Fermoyle forgot that he was an anointed priest, and became the human son and brother, loving his own people greatly, and greatly loved by them in return.

BOOK ONE

The Curate

CHAPTER 1

WHAT VEHICLE, bottle-green in color, arkish in shape, cranky in motion, and dilapidated in repose, was a familiar feature of the Mystic River flatlands between Boston and Medford during the early years of the present century?

That's easy! Trolley No. 3, of course — a four-wheeled drudge that had lugged some six million passengers, at a nickel a head, to their clerkish warrens in the morning and back to their suburban hutches at night. The strain had taken its toll. No. 3 may have been a mechanical marvel in her youth, but by the year 1915 she was a balky shrew with a notable slippage of her trolley, an incurable slappage of her brake shoes, a profound weakness in her rheostat, and a proneness to fuse-box trouble on cold mornings and hot afternoons. How she found courage to start, stop, grunt, and start again was a mystery to the repair crew at the Medford carbarns where No. 3 lay nightly at her siding like a spavined cab horse gathering heart for the next day's run.

The theory advanced by Bartholomew ("Batty") Flynn, chief dispatcher and carbarn metaphysician, was that No. 3 must be held together by a pure act of faith on the part of her motorman, Dennis Fermoyle. To state the proposition in Batty's own words: "Reason fails us here. Din's car should now be the fragment of a figment. But faith is beyond reason. *Ergo*, No. 3 is held together by faith rather than reason, or," he always added slyly, "good works."

None of this quiddish logic went on in the hearing of Fermoyle. Din's feelings on the subject of No. 3 were well known. His walrus mustaches would stiffen into tusks at the suggestion that No. 3 be junked in favor of the newer, handsomer, sixteen-wheeled air-brake job that his seniority rated. Devotion to Din, or possibly fear of his stern mustaches, kept superintendents docile and repair men gagged. Not even suffering passengers who hung to No. 3's tired leather straps

26

dared voice the hope that she would blow up, or fall apart, or be put decently out to pasture.

On a spring evening late in April, 1915, No. 3 was lumbering along at its top speed of nine miles an hour toward the Medford carbarns. With Din Fermoyle at the controls, and conductor Marty Timmins on the rear platform, it rounded the Highland Avenue curve with a banshee screech of wheels and plunged down the gentle grade near the end of its suburban steeplechase. As No. 3 careened past the center door of the Immaculate Conception Church, Dennis lifted his right hand from the brake and doffed his motorman's cap. No perfunctory touching of hand to visor. This was a real off-the-head obeisance to the Presence that dwelt — Dennis Fermoyle could not tell you how — in the tabernacle on the high altar within. He had made this obeisance a dozen times today: six times on the inbound run to Boston and six times on the outbound run to the carbarns. Yesterday, and the day before yesterday, he had raised his hat twelve times. For twenty-five years — ever since the tracks were first laid — he had been raising his hat as he passed the center door of the church. And if the varicose veins in his right leg didn't murder him entirely, Dennis Fermoyle hoped to keep on repeating the gesture of devotion and respect for twenty-five years more. Well, fifteen maybe. By that time he would have eight service stripes on his coat sleeve. One life, one job. . . .

To accompany the hat-raising ritual, Dennis always added an aspiration. His favorite was "Blessed be the Holy Family," but he often varied this with sentiments appropriate to his state of mind or body. If the deep veins throbbed in his leg, as they did now, he would murmur, "Blessed be the wounds of Jesus." Or if his throat was parched, as it always was, come evening, he would say, "Blessed be His Holy Thirst." The whole business took but a second and was immediately followed by an uprush of well-being that burst geyserlike into song.

In a true-keyed but husky baritone Dennis now gave off with the first stanza of "The False Bride of O'Rourke," a ditty of his youth in Cork. The weary passengers smiled as they heard the Celtic melody rise above the clatter of car wheels; they winked at each other knowingly, as characterless people do when confronted by a character. Even "Greasy" McNabb, the company spotter who was dying to nail Marty Timmins in the act of knocking down a nickel, had to wink and smile. He was sure that Marty was knocking down plenty of nickels and professionally resented the veteran conductor's skill at masking his larcenies. But the sweet contagion of Din Fermoyle's song soothed the spotter's rancor, transported him to the wattled glens of Connaught, and caused him to wink knowingly at the very man he was attempting to catch.

A black Protestant should have this job, thought Greasy, unscrewing the wink from his eye.

In mid-melody Dennis Fermoyle shifted his hundred and ninety pounds onto his good left leg, tapped his right toe gingerly against the gong button on the floor, and let his car glide into the network of trackage and switches in front of the carbarn. He had mastered the art of the jerkless halt and now gave a virtuoso performance unnoticed by anyone but Marty and himself. The forlorn passengers streamed palely into the lengthening April sunlight. Two bells from Marty. *Ding-ding!* Then the slow entry into the long cool carbarn, sliding under the very guns of the big sixteen-wheel jobs, to the special corner that was No. 3's berth.

Dennis removed the control handle, smooth from long contact with his cotton glove, and slipped it into the side pocket of his blue brass-buttoned coat. Tomorrow at seven A.M. he would fit the handle onto its square spindle again. Till then, none could start Dennis Fermoyle's car. Or would want to. A poor thing but very much his own.

He walked through the empty car to the rear platform, where Marty Timmins was peering with bloodshot eyes at some figures on the clocklike register above his door. Baggy at the knees and saggy about the coat pockets, Marty was of the pint-sized defenseless breed that juries take pleasure in finding guilty on sight. His mildness would be mistaken for weakness, his timidity interpreted as guile. Thin stubble covered his rabbitish chin, and a perennial drop hung from the tip of his nose. He jotted down a figure on his tally book and snapped it shut before Din reached him.

"Everything even, Marty? All regular and even?"

The conductor scruffed at his nose drop with the back of

a dirty hand, and nodded. Wordless rather than silent, Marty Timmins had no language to express the bewildered, lonely dumbness that had come over him in the past year. Ever since he had lost his wife Nora after her sixth baby and third miscarriage, there were only two things that consoled the terrible desolation of his days. One was whisky; the other, Din's great hand on his shoulder. The hand was on his shoulder now. He would have the whisky later.

A fine delicacy prevented Din from mentioning Greasy McNabb's presence in the car. Nor could he bring himself to lecture Marty now or at any time about the booze. Thick fingers squeezed thin shoulder; calloused palm patted bent spine.

"Good night, Marty. Go straight home now."

"Good night, Din. I will."

Trolley mates. The miles of their common voyaging on No. 3 would have put ten girdles around the earth.

At a little wicket near the gates of the carbarn Dennis Fermoyle thrust his walrus mustaches close to an iron grille. "Would you be having a little something for me, Angus?"

The man behind the grille riffled through a small box of envelopes, and shoved one under the wicket. Din felt the flat fold of bills and the hard half dollar inside the envelope. His weekly pay, $27.65 — forty cents an hour for an eleven-hour day, six days a week, plus a bonus of twenty-five cents for each of the diagonal gold service stripes on his coat sleeve. He thrust the envelope into his pocket and faced westward into the salmon-colored rays of the six P.M. sun. With the stiff-legged gait of a man who stands in one place all day, he trudged along a muddy unpaved sidewalk fronting straggly three-story houses and vacant lots. To let the cool spring air sponge his forehead, he pushed back his motorman's cap. A deep red stripe, cut by the sweatband, lay across his forehead. The true service stripe, the wound of vocation.

A lance of pain traveled up his leg from ankle to groin. Din quickened his pace; movement seemed to help a little, speeding sluggish blood through knotted veins. The pain would be all right, it would go away, as soon as he sat down in his kitchen rocker and hoisted the leg onto another chair. Thoughts of coming good sustained him as he turned up an inclined side street, the gentle gradient of Woodlawn Avenue. The best of the day lay just ahead: the bottle of beer that Celia would pluck dewy cold from the icebox when she heard his step on the back porch; the fine fat cod stuffed with bread crumbs that was browning right now in the kitchen oven; the oval supper table, the faces of his children, grown-up now, but still making reasonable concord when he breathed upon them.

"Blessed be the Holy Family."

Tonight the family music would have a special quality. There would be clean napkins all around, a fresh jar of piccalilli from the cellar, a deeper glow in Celia's dark eyes. Stephen was coming home for dinner. Stephen the dedicated priest, Steve the proud-walking one, the eloquent first-born of Dennis and Celia Fermoyle; Stephen the motorman's son who had led his class for four years at Holy Cross. Steve would be at dinner tonight for the first time since arriving home from the North American College in Rome.

They had seen him for a moment when he came off the liner, but that glimpse had been too brief, too full of gulped excitement. Tonight Din would savor his son's quality in more leisurely fashion, strike the spark of an argument maybe, and come over his son's elegant learning with a nimble brick-bat of his own. He hoped, with all his Irish love of disputation, that Steve would not be too proud to grapple with him in debate.

Din's soul magnified the Lord as he reached the last house at the top of the street. Boxy, brown, and graceless with its ugly front stoop, 47 Woodlawn Avenue was a whole house, not a flat, and after living in it for almost twenty-five years, Din almost owned it. By scrimping and denial, by putting a dollar a week into the Building and Loan Bank for fifteen years, he had laid eighteen hundred dollars on the line. There was still a twelve-hundred-dollar mortgage. Easier for a camel to enter a needle's eye than for a motorman with seven children to get title free and clear to his own home.

He entered his house, workingman fashion, by the back door. Odors of baking fish, gingerbread, and damp mops in the back closet told him that he was home. Celia at the stove gave a half turn, a half smile, a half kiss that struck the air in the general direction of her husband's bent-down face. Comely buxom at forty-nine, a trifle gone at the middle and not too tidy about her graying hair, Celia Fermoyle was still airy on her feet. She had been a tireless dancer, the belle of many a Hibernian ball in her day. Now, knowing exactly where she stood with her man and her children, she was a confident woman without a fear in the world.

She held out her hand expectantly. Dennis Fermoyle drew his pay envelope from his pocket, and placed it in her outstretched palm. Celia tucked the envelope into her bosom, then in place of spoken thanks she gave her husband something much better — a bit of wifely service.

"I'll fetch your beer in a jiffy, Din. Let me clear the sink for you first." Celia Fermoyle was a good cook and a thrifty manager, but she did not place a high value on neatness. Her kitchen was a clutter of pans, dishes, pails, and unironed clothes. Now she made an open space among her saucepans in the sink, put a tin basin under the hot-water faucet, tossed a sliver of yellow soap into it, and gave the roller towel a swish to bring a reasonably clean sector into view. "There now, Din."

"*Lavabo,*" intoned Dennis Fermoyle. He hung his hat and coat on his regular hook, rolled up his sleeves, and with narwhal sputterings washed his face and hands. While he dried himself on the roller towel, Celia flipped off the cap of a beer bottle and set it on the kitchen table. She had never learned to pour beer to Din's satisfaction. He poured it to his own taste now, drained a tumblerful, rubbed the back of his hand across his foam-flecked mustache, and picked up his *Globe.*

In the manner of an appellate judge reviewing a weighty case he surveyed the news. "Ho-ho, Celia — look at this," he roared, reading aloud the streamer headline:

BRITISH REEL BACKWARD TO CHANNEL PORTS

"Von Falkenhayn has the lobsterbacks on the run, Ceil, with their teacups and shooting boxes and all. Right into their precious Channel he'll push them — wait and see."

To Din, the British Army was still the oppressor of Irishmen and the historic despoiler of their religion, homes, and children. But to Celia, born in Boston, the feud between lobsterback and bog trotter had no such pulsing immediacy. Other matters — her backward oven, for instance — claimed the front of her mind just now. She pushed her stove dampers this way and that with the preoccupied briskness of a stage manager on a first night.

"Read to yourself, Din, if it's all the same to you, because I've got nothing else to do for the next half-hour but cook a dinner fit for Stevie in a slow oven that won't heat up because the coal is slaty and the flues need cleaning."

Piano chords and a tenor voice drifted into the kitchen. Din cocked a critical ear. "Bernie has a new ballad," he said placatingly to no one in particular. "This I must hear." He limped into the dining room and ducked under a beaded valance that separated it from the parlor. At an upright piano tucked into the aperture of a bow window sat an overfed young man with hair parted in the middle, wearing a pinch-back suit, chamois-topped shoes, and the high starched collar of the period. Bernard, Din's second son, a song plugger — and not too good at it if the truth had to be told.

With beer and paper Din sat down in a leatherette arm-chair and listened as one who reserves judgment, till the singer ended his performance on a true-toned high C.

"New, Bernie?"

The young man nodded. "It's Chauncey Olcott's latest, 'Ireland Must Be Heaven, For My Mother Came from There,' " he warbled. "They'll be crazy for it at the Gamecock."

"The Gamecock? That wouldn't be the fancy house on Washington Street, Bernie?"

"Cabaret, Pa," corrected Bernie. "I'm getting a tryout there tomorrow night. If I connect, it's two weeks at twenty dollars a week."

If I connect! Accent on the *if*. That was Bernard for you. Din hoisted his leg onto a carpet-covered hassock. "Give us the 'Fingarry Christening' like a good boy now."

"Sure, Pa." Always obliging, Bernie threw back his pom-aded head of hair and gave off with the opening verse of a ballad that dealt with the vagaries of certain elegant Celts at the christening of an infant referred to only as "sweet

Dennis the boy." The first stanza was vague in Bernie's memory, but his mind cleared at the second:

> All the aristocracy came to the party,
> Bold McCarthy, hale and hearty,
> And Bridget Bedelia Fogarty,
> 'Twas the French (so she said) for her name.

Din's glass of beer touched him off. He joined his son in song:

> Then they all went into the luncheon,
> There was such munchin' and much crunchin'
> While the christeners went about punchin'
> On coffee, tea, whisky, and wine.

Their harmonizing, and the peace that rises therefrom, was broken when the front door opened, and a young woman, big of hip and heavy about the lower part of her face, entered the parlor. Florence Fermoyle resembled a not-too-modish policewoman. At twenty-five she had little lightness of mind, manner, or body. For six years now she had been working as a bookkeeper in an automobile office, and her wage was as large as her father's. In a few months she would pass him as the chief earner at 47 Woodlawn.

"Stephen here yet? Who's helping Ma in the kitchen? Where's Mona?" The questions came in a staccato jet as Florrie pulled the pins out of her hat with disapproving truculence at the sight of males lounging in the parlor. Not too subtly she conveyed the feeling that nothing ever got done unless she did it herself. Bossy was the word for Florence. No wonder, thought Din, that she scares the men away.

"You got the chamois tops, I see, Bernie." she said, edging around to get a side glance at her brother's feet. "That ten dollars I gave you was for a pair of 'good substantial shoes,' and now you turn up with these 'Pretending Percy' numbers. What's the idea?"

"Well — mm — you see, Florrie, I needed something a little bit dressy for my tryout." To nip off further debate, Bernie made a run with his left hand, and soared into song.

> *In the midst of the feasting, Mike Cronin,*
> *Mighty Cronin, without groanin'*
> *Downed a pound of pâté de foie gras*
> *Made of goose livers and grease —*

Again the harmony was shattered by Florrie's top-sergeant voice calling up the front stairs: "Mona . . . *Mona*. Come down here and set the table. Ma's breaking her back in the kitchen, and Father Steve'll be here any minute. Come down right away."

Monica came down. At sixteen she had a fragile porcelain beauty — a doll's face linelessly smooth, but pouting now with discontent. She had been washing her hair, drying, combing, and pinning it this way and that for the past two hours, and now it lay in a lustrous blue-black aureole around her head. Snatched from her favorite occupation of gazing into the mirror, she half expected her father to defend her against Florrie's barging. To win him, she planted a kiss on his cheek, then sat kittenlike on the arm of his chair. He put his forefinger under her chin and tickled it as though she were still an infant.

Something about the armchair tableau sent Florrie into a tantrum of anger. She had a barb to throw. She had planned to save it till later, but now she let Mona have it right up to the feather.

"What's this I hear about you walking round the Reservoir last night? You were supposed to be at Sodality."

Maiden skill at dissimulation failed Mona completely. Her cheeks were bloodless china. "Who — who said I was walking around the Reservoir?"

"Oh," sniffed Florrie, "she takes a questioning tone."

"For heaven's sake, Florrie," said Bernie, "quit nagging the kid."

"I'll quit nagging her when she stops sneaking off into the woods with Ikey Rampell."

Mona turned defiant. "His name isn't Ikey, it's Benny."

"Ikey or Benny, what's the difference? Aren't there enough Catholic boys in the parish without you running around with a ragpicking Jew?"

Mona sprang from kitten to full-clawed cat. "Benny isn't a

ragpicker. He's the smartest boy in high school and he's going to be a dentist." The futility of defense broke over her; Florrie the prosecutor had her down. Mona burst into tears and fled upstairs.

Vexed by the undaughterly scene, Din lifted voice in reproof. A good drag-down and knockout argument on politics was all very well, but female bickering was something he could not tolerate. "I want no more of this wrangling, do you hear, Florrie? You'll drive your sister away from you by your barging."

"It's for her own good, Pa."

Blue anger sparked in Din's eyes. Florrie might contribute as much as he to the family purse, but Dennis was still master in his own house. "Let your mother and me decide what is good for our children," he thundered, then clamped down on his temper as though he were braking his trolley car. "Stephen must not find us quarreling. Go cool your face with a wet towel, Florrie. You'll feel better. Bernie, play the piano."

"Sure, Pa. Want to hear 'Too Much Mustard'?"

"I'll listen to anything that'll drown out the sound of contention in this house."

Bernie jammed his chamois-topped boot onto the forte pedal, and bore down on the keys till the upright trembled under the attack. He raced through "Too Much Mustard" (not a vocal number), vamped the first bars of "I Didn't Raise My Boy to Be a Soldier," and broke into a refrain:

> I didn't raise my boy to be a soldier,
> I brought him up to be my pride and joy,
> Who dares to place a musket on his shoulder
> To shoot some other mother's darling boy?

"Louder, Bernie," advised a quiet voice in the front hall. "They can't hear you down at the carbarns."

Bernie whirled round on the piano stool; Dennis dropped his *Globe*. "Steve," they cried with one voice, both moving toward the young priest in the doorway. Spare he was, built like the ideal miler — narrow in the hips, long in the thighbones, broad and easy in the shoulders. He had Celia's lightness of stance and Din's commanding head carriage, but his coloring was his own. A blackness of hair and eyebrows made white drama of his face. Thin-walled nostrils gave the ascetic clue, heightened by the good forehead climbing straight above blue-black eyes. There was a collectedness about him that one sees in the concert pianist sitting down to his instrument. All of which was laid aside now in the excitement of greeting his father and brother.

"St. Dennis forever," he cried, producing a red tin of smoking tobacco. "Here's something for your old dudeen." Stephen was up to his old habit of making little presents. He handed Bernie a pack of cigarettes, surveyed his brother's pinch-back suit and chamois-topped shoes with humorous approval.

"Dazzling, Bernie — especially the footgear. It wouldn't be quite the thing for a young curate" — Steve put a well-shined oxford through the beginning of a heel-and-toe routine — "but in show biz . . ."

"That's it," echoed Bernie eagerly. "In show biz you've got to dress this way. Classy! People expect it."

Celia coming out of the kitchen saw her first-born through the bead-fringed valance. Involuntary tears welled into her eyes. Having grown accustomed to Steve's being away, Celia must now get used to having him home again.

"Stevie," she said, holding out her arms in the not-to-be duplicated manner of mothers. The compass of those arms was too small now; willingly she let herself be encircled by Stephen's embrace.

"Got something here for you, Mother." He lifted the cover of a tiny pasteboard box, revealing a delicately embroidered *Agnus Dei*. "It's from the Cenacle of St. Theresa, and it's blessed by the Pope himself."

"By the Pope himself," Celia repeated in awed accents, showing the imprinted wax disk to her husband. "I'll put it away."

Father Steve looked at Din; both laughed. Celia's habit of "putting things away" was an old joke in the Fermoyle family. Tablecloths, sheets, towels, china, silverware, glasses — everything was "put away" for a future that never quite arrived. It was part of her hoarding instinct, a hangover from the poverty of her childhood.

"Why put it away?" asked Steve. "Use it for a place mark

in your missal and pray for your son every time you see it."

"Ma!" Florrie's voice came from the kitchen. "The cod's all but done."

"Merciful Mary, I forgot the cod. Go upstairs, Son, and get washed. Here, let me give you a towel." Celia darted toward the sideboard drawer where she had "put away" her best linen.

"I can find a clean place on the roller, Ma."

The idea of an ordained priest using a roller towel violated Celia Fermoyle's sense of the decencies. "You'll do no such thing," she said, handing him an embroidered guest towel she had won fifteen years before at a parish whist party.

"There is laughter from certain quarters when I put something away," she said, looking at her husband, "but the laughter freezes when they see what I put it away for."

Towel maniplewise on wrist, Steve passed through the kitchen on his way upstairs. Florrie, flushed from the hot stove, was peeling jackets from boiled potatoes preparatory to mashing them. Competent, on-the-job Florrie. Steve hugged her with one arm. "Hello, Steve," she said, going on with her work. A rivalry, or offishness rather — chiefly on Florrie's side — had always lain between them. Should I soften her now, thought Steve, with the little phial of perfume in my pocket? No, that was for Mona.

"Be down in a jiff," he said, climbing the back stairs two at a time. The same old linoleum was on the steps, the same cracks were in the plaster. Had nothing changed during his four years in Rome? Not, at any rate, the plumbing fixtures at 47 Woodlawn! The same slow trickle of water from the thin faucets, the same zinc bathtub with the cast-iron legs. The permanence of impermanent things! Stephen lathered his hands on a curled chip of blue soap, splashed some water onto his face, then dried himself on the linen towel. He felt hungry, glad to be home, eager for family food and talk.

Familiarity woven of a thousand boyhood yesterdays lay over the back of the house. Here was the brown patternless wallpaper, grease-smudged and peeling at the baseboard; the bedroom doors with their cocoa-colored knobs; the frayed runner of carpet — how elegant it had seemed to his bare feet when it was first laid! And over everything the indefinable smell of one's own family.

Here at the left was Ellen's room, unoccupied since she had gone away to the Carmelites to live out as a garbed nun the dream of mystical love that had possessed her since childhood. Through the closed door shone the radiating purity of his sister's life. How could so frail a taper burn with such an energizing ray and still not consume itself to ash? The secret fuel of the heart . . .

Across the hallway, a flight of steps mounted to the attic bedroom that Stephen had shared with his brother George. Some impulse bade him climb the stairs and see again the garret room — "the boys' domnitory," as Celia called it — where he had slept and studied till he was eighteen years old. The garret was neater now; a student lamp, a new armchair, and rows of lawbooks told him that his brother George used it as a study. But the dormer window looking out upon the roofs and rhubarb gardens of Woodlawn Avenue revived in Stephen emotions deeper than recollection. It was in this room that he had decided to become a priest. Beside this lumpy bed he had knelt in prayer, dedicating his life to the service of the Master who had beckoned with an imperious finger, "Rise, clasp My hand, and come!"

He knelt again now, lightly, momentarily, on one knee in a genuflection of gratitude, then left the attic room and hurried downstairs.

A snuffling sobbing sound caught his ear as he passed Mona's door. Tears? He tapped gently, turned the knob, and saw his youngest sister lying face downward on her single bed, weeping. Silently he sat on the bed beside her, put his hand into the hair at the nape of her neck.

"Monny darling" — it was his special name for her — "it's me, Stevie. What's the matter, Monny?"

Mona kicked her toes in a small fury against the foot of the bed. "That Florrie! She's hateful."

"Florrie's tired, upset about something. She doesn't mean the things she says."

"She's *spiteful*, that's what she is." Mona pressed her tear-stained face into the pillow "She treats me like an infant."

"A most beauteous infant," said Steve. "Here, roll over, and let me see you."

Lying on her back, Mona gazed up at her brother. Tears, like drops of belladonna, had made her eyes lustrous and dark.

"Do you really think I'm beautiful, Steve?" Vanity, catching her halfway between child and woman, snatched at this almost unknown man looking down at her.

"As beautiful as one of Raphael's angels. No one should be as beautiful as that — but you are. Don't all the boys rave about your dark eyes and black hair?"

"I wish I was a blue-eyed blonde," sighed Mona.

"A blonde? Blue-eyed? Ridiculous. I guess you never heard what a pretty good poet said about his Dark Lady."

"What did he say?"

"What *didn't* he say! He practically rifled the language, looking for similes in praise of black. Images of pearl and gold were tossed into the wastebasket — nothing but ebony damask and ravens' wings would suit him when he wrote about his mistress' hair and eyes."

Stephen couldn't quite decide how much emotional pressure Mona could stand. He didn't want to frighten her by plumping out the sonnet in all its glorious rhetoric — but anything that would soothe her grief was worth trying. He'd give her the opening lines for a sample. Muting all but the barest note of tenderness, he recited the first quatrain:

> Thine eyes I love, and they, as pitying me,
> Knowing thy heart torments me with disdain,
> Have put on black, and loving mourners be,
> Looking with pretty ruth upon my pain.

Magnetized by language she did not understand, spoken in a tone she had never heard before, Mona lay silently looking up at her priest-brother. She had neither curiosity to ask the name of the poet who had written the lines nor the intelligence to make any comment on their substance or quality. All that she conveyed to Stephen was a kind of astonishment that such words should exist, or that a priest should utter them.

Stephen changed the note. "Got something here for you,

widgeon." He pressed the little phial of perfume into her damp palm. "The drugstore man said to use it with caution. Up you come now — they're waiting dinner for us downstairs."

"You're awful sweet, Steve," said Mona. She wanted to add that somehow, in a different way, of course, he reminded her of Bennie Rampell. But the moment passed. She rose, dabbed at her eyes with Stephen's clean handkerchief, and with his arm around her went downstairs to dinner.

DINNER at the Fermoyles' was strictly a one-dish affair, a solid workingman's meal with no date-and-nut nonsense about it. Barely had Father Steve finished grace when Celia began heaping the first plate with cod, mashed potatoes, a cascade of egg sauce, and a big spoonful of piccalilli for color and relish. In this home Din was always served first; even now with her priest-son at the table Celia gave her husband precedence.

"A hungry man is an angry man," she said, passing Din his laden plate. Without waiting for the others, he fell to his food with zesty trencherman manners.

"Do you know, Steve," he said between forkfuls, "things haven't changed much around here. There's still nobody that pours tea like Florrie. She makes it hot, black, and strong" — he held out his cup to his oldest daughter — "the way I like it."

"Pa's tea blarney" was a remnant of the time Florrie was a little girl with the privilege of snuggling into Din's lap as he read his *Globe*. Ousted from this seat of affection by later girl babies, Florrie had kept some part of her emotional security by taking on certain semiwifely duties. Pouring her father's tea was the sole reminder of the earlier father-daughter love that had existed between them. Steve remembered the violent quarrel that had once broken out when his sister Rita had attempted to pour the tea. Now as he watched Florrie perform the vestal role unchallenged, he knew he was watching a devotional rite. That flush of pleasure on her cheek — the first, the only relaxation of her face that evening — told Steve more than he could understand about Florrie's thwarted love for her father, her tension, and her bad temper.

"How do you like Monaghan, your pastor, Steve?" Din was asking.

"I've only been at St. Margaret's a day or two," said Steve, "and the rector hasn't yet invited me into his private parlor. As a matter of fact, he was pretty gruff when he greeted me. I guess he didn't like the Italian Line stickers on my suitcase."

"You'll soften him up." Celia's confidence was magnificent, airy.

"I hear he's one of the biggest money raisers in the Diocese," said Din. Only a very good Catholic had the right to say anything like that, and Din, a man of great piety but little reverence, was always the one to exercise his rights freely.

"Father Monaghan's not exactly *El Poverello*," laughed Steve. "But when you consider that he's putting up a new school, and plans to build a parish house when the school is finished — why, I'd say he has plenty of need for money."

"That parish house at St. Margaret's must be ninety years old," said Celia, who knew every church in the Diocese. "It ran down terrible under Father Ned Halley, sainted man. The threshold was worn hollow when I went there to stand up for Delia Doherty's second child Annie, in May, 1907, it was, eight years ago. Has anything been done since to it, Steve?"

"It's still pretty much of a barracks, but Father Monaghan has made a lot of improvements, I hear. Painted it up and put in some new plumbing. He's quite a manager."

"Managed himself a new Packard last week," observed Florrie. "Paid cash for it, too."

"The pastor of a big parish needs a good automobile," said Father Steve stoutly.

"Father Halley before him had no automobile," said Celia. "He made his sick calls on foot — ankle-deep in slush he walked — all over the city of Malden and without rubbers either. He'd give them away to the first poor man he met, so they say."

Stephen Fermoyle looked at his mother curiously. "I've heard that about Father Halley." A special interest in the last end of priests prompted his question: "Whatever became of him?"

"Oh, he was bundled off to a poor place somewhere near Taunton — I forget the name of it now — with a lot of French Canadians for parishioners. Delia Doherty went to see him there, and came back with some story or other about his church falling apart. She sent him a dollar for Christmas once, then she lost track of him."

With the deft step of one who knows dangerous ground when her feet are on it, Celia changed direction. "And how do you get on with the other curates in the house?"

"I'm going to like both of them, I think. Especially Father Paul Ireton. He's a handsome, quiet priest, doing a grand job as assistant pastor. I — I rather get the feeling that he'd like to have a church of his own."

"He's got a long wait ahead of him," said Din. A truculent preargument jut stiffened his jaw. "If the Cardinal in the augustitude of his wisdom would only break up the big parishes and squeeze some of the lard out of a few old pastors I could mention, then the young priests could have churches of their own in jig time." His eye was hopeful. Would this elegant son of his, with the fine top-lofty brow, snap at the bait of argument?

It was Celia who snapped. "When His Eminence wants advice about laying out new parishes, he'll come down to the carbarns and ask for it," she said, peppering her cod so violently that she burst into a fit of sneezing. "Forgive me, Son. My pepper hand slipped. What about the other curate?"

"The other curate" — a half smile laid hold of Steve's mouth — "is a gentle, pious chap called 'Milky' Lyons. He's interested in Gregorian music and wants to start a plain-song choir, but" — Steve's black eyebrows went up in sympathy for a hopeless cause — "Monaghan will have none of it."

"Why do they call him 'Milky'?" asked Monica.

"Because his skin and voice have all the resplendent color of a glass of milk. Either he's genderless or — " Father Steve's answer was interrupted by a voice of great carrying power ringing through the house.

"Stephen . . . Stuff . . . you're here!" George Fermoyle, a full-grown man at twenty, flung an armful of books onto the sideboard and came toward his older brother, both hands outstretched in greeting. They hadn't seen each other for four years. Now they embraced, pounding each other like football players after a touchdown. Then they stood off to appraise each other.

"Where did you bury that pimply kid?" asked Stephen, taking in George's breadth of shoulder, long jaw, and clear skin.

"The same place you buried that pie-faced seminarian. Why, Stuffy, you're bigger, better-looking. Rome's marshy, I mean martial, air must have agreed with you."

"It did, Gug. Sit down, eat some of Ma's patented cod — it's wonderful — and tell me all about yourself."

"Haven't got much time, Stuff." George craned his neck to get a look at the kitchen clock. "My class in 'Bills and Notes' starts at eight. But I had an hour after work, so I thought I'd run out and see you." George sat down at the place Celia and Florrie fixed for him and began on his cod.

"You've changed, Gug," said Steve. "When I slept with you on that three-quarter bed in the attic, you wouldn't even move over. And now you go five miles out of your way just to see me. *Ego te absolvo . . .* How do you like the law?"

"She's a stern mistress, Steve. As Cicero said, '*Advocati nascitur non fit.*'"

"*Advocatus*, George. In Latin, as in English, subject and predicate must always agree in number."

"You see what happens" — George appealed to the table — "in the case of Upside-Down Collar vs. Gentleman and Scholar. The defendant — me, the gentleman Latiner — hasn't got a chance against a professional. Stuffy, remember the time you sat up all night coaching me for my Latin entrance exams at Holy Cross? Showed me just what verbs to study and what syntax to bone up on? Well" — George drew his listeners into the magnetic realm of his anecdote — "when I got the examination paper next day, I could have sworn that Stevie must have snitched it in advance. Every detail. Come clean, Steve, how'd you know those questions ahead of time?"

"I didn't know the questions, George. But I *did* know the questioner — Lawrence Burke, S.J. A merciless Jebby. So I figured out what a merciless Jebby would ask — "

"And bejabbers, the Jebby asked it," said Bernie, screwing up his features in mimicry of a vaudeville Irishman. The

crude caricature was good enough to make everyone laugh.
Din, well pleased by his three sons tossing the ball around,
caught Celia's eye. "Ours," the glance said. The moment was
one of those perfect gifts which only family life at its best
can offer. It swelled for a slow second of ripeness, then Din
held out his teacup again to his eldest daughter.

"More of the same, Florrie." Tea drops clung to the ends
of his mustache. Steve watched Florrie as she leaned toward
her father, napkin in hand, to wipe the drops away. Love and
criticism were in the gesture. Poor Florrie.

"Tell us about the Holy City, Son," Celia was saying. "Is
it so wondrous as I've heard? Full of shrines and cathedrals
all blazing with candles, and services going on at every hour
of the day and night?"

Stephen swallowed a mouthful of salty cod and sweet
bread crust. How convey in a few dinner-table sentences the
grandeur and timelessness of Rome, its temporal monuments
and abiding purpose — all in words that Celia could understand? He must try.

"Rome is even more wonderful than you've heard, Ma.
Time runs both ways there — backwards to the beginning of
history, and forward to — well, a promise of something world-
wide, universal." He geared his description closer to her needs
and understanding. "You should see the churches, hundreds
of them, named after saints we never hear about in America
— Apollinare, Filippo Neri, Cosmas and Damian — every one
a hymn in a different kind of stone."

"Did you make visits to all the churches, Steve?"

"Many of them, Mother."

"And the Holy Father — have you seen him, too?"

"Many times. When Benedict XV was crowned, all the
seminarians lined the aisles of St. Peter's. What a procession!
Golden candelabra flaming like the tongues of the Paraclete;
music brought down straight from the choirs of seraphim, and
cardinals of all nations in their great purple copes all swinging censers as Benedict approached the Fisherman's throne."
Stephen paused to let the color run. "And right in the midst
of all this grandeur, what do you suppose happened?"

"What happened, Son?"

"Just when the ritual was becoming almost unbearable, a

cowled monk stepped in front of the Pope and halted the whole procession by holding up a little twist of smoldering oakum — a half inch of burning rope."

Celia's mind couldn't grasp the symbolism. "Why did he do that, Stephen?"

"The twist of oakum represented the temporal glories of the world, destined to pass away, burn to ashes in a tick of time."

Celia sighed. " 'Tis wonderful, Son, how you explain things. You always had the gift. Once when you were a little boy you told me how lightning rods work — all so clear that I never forgot it. And do you know," she added, "I've never been afraid of lightning since."

"That's because you were well grounded, Ma," said George. Only Steve got the pun. Bernie, mystified, found solace in buttered gingerbread, and longed for the simplicity of sheet music.

"What do you make of the war, Steve?" asked Dennis. Maybe this fine talker would make a false move. Then the battle could begin.

"We'll be in it sooner or later," said Stephen calmly. "American loans to the English are too big, too binding. We can't let our dear British cousins down, you know."

Din's gingerbread stopped halfway to his mouth. "American loans to — to *who* did you say?"

"To the English. A billion dollars. Don't they know about it yet in Boston? Isn't it in the *Globe?*"

"It is not. And where did you hear this monstrous business?"

"I heard it first from Monsignor Quarenghi, my professor of sacred theology, way back last fall after the British defeat at Mons. It's his belief that Wilson is being led down an alley by the Morgans, and won't be able to turn back." Steve looked around the table. "It's common talk in every chancellery of Europe. 'Wilson's pickle,' Quarenghi called it — meaning the grim cleavage between the President's ideals and the position he's being forced into by the international bankers. Surely I'm not telling you anything new."

"It's news to me," said George.

Steve could see that it was news to Din, too. The idea that

America was lending money to the hated lobsterbacks took
the starch out of the Fermoyle mustaches, dampened the
flints in his eyes. His great fist did not pound the table in
rebuttal. Steve's news had subdued him quite, though how
his son could have information not found in the columns of
the *Globe* was something of a puzzler. Din munched his gingerbread, a temporarily broken man.

"Any news from Ellen, Ma?" Steve's question was the
gesture of a duelist firing into the air.

Celia Fermoyle fished in the pocket of her apron and
pulled out a letter. "This came in the afternoon mail, Steve.
Your father hasn't seen it yet. Read it out loud to us, Son."

Steve drew a single sheet of dime-store paper from its envelope and gazed for a moment at his sister Ellen's familiar
handwriting — ethereally light, almost floating, as though the
writer were too gentle to bear down even on the nib of a pen.

DEAREST MOTHER AND FATHER, BROTHERS AND SISTERS:
    I know you will all share my great joy when I tell you
that I am preparing to take my first vows in a few days.
With the permission of my Superior, I have chosen the
name Humilia Theresa, the first to signify my lowly
unworthiness and the second in honor of the Great Soul
who founded our Order. I ask you all to pray for my
special intention so that my own poor pleadings will be
supplemented by your loving devotions.
    My heart is overflowing with mixed feelings of fear and
delight as I approach this great moment in my life. Please
believe, dear earthly loved ones, that I think of you constantly, but I want you to know also that I am never lonely
in the service of One who possesses all my heart. With
increasing devotion through Him, to you, I am
                        Your loving daughter and sister,
                                        ELLEN

In every member of the family Ellen's letter struck a private chord of feeling. In Dennis Fermoyle it awakened the
old unhappiness his daughter had caused when she first
entered the convent. It had meant that he was losing her forever; the rule of her order decreed that its members should
leave the world behind, never see their families again. It was

bitter to lose Ellen's gentle presence; Din had never reconciled himself to the parting. As for Celia, she worried constantly about Ellen's weak lungs. How could such a sickly girl stand up under the stern Carmelite regime? Florrie, though she couldn't admit it, had experienced a definite feeling of relief when Ellen left for the convent; it meant that another rival for Din's affection was out of the way.

Stephen caught the note of ecstatic rapture rising from the cheap gray paper. Here, authentic and rare, was the voice of the true mystic whose goal was to lose her own identity in a larger Being, to become a drop of water in the vaster sea of God's love.

"I hope her health holds out," Celia was saying. "Walking without shoes on those cold floors. And the long fasts they go on, too."

Steve comforted her. "Don't worry, Ma. The genuine mystic is the toughest thing in the world. Why, St. Theresa practically never ate — but listen now to what she did." Father Steve launched into a description of St. Theresa's life and achievements. "She reformed the Carmelites, built convents, found time to write her autobiography, and all this, mind you, while she was in such bodily agony that they had to carry her around in a sheet."

"She must have been a very holy woman," said Celia.

"She was more than a holy woman. She was a saint. A genius, too. Sanctity is only part of the secret. Theresa was a creative artist as great as Raphael, Shakespeare, Dante, or any of those fellows who moved the world."

The names meant nothing to anyone but George. Only Celia's desire to hear her priest-son keep on talking prompted her question, "We don't seem to have any saints these days. Why not, Steve?"

Celia could always bring out the exhibitionism in her oldest son.

"Well, Ma, it seems that sainthood as a career fell off rather sharply, oh, around 1400. Plenty of reasons why. For instance, when Petrarch stood tiptoe on a little hill and conceived the notion of dedicating his poems to Laura — an earthly mistress instead of a heavenly one — a different set of values began to prevail. Geocentric, earthbound values, reflected in the paintings of Giotto and Masaccio. That's odd, too, when you come to think of it, because very soon afterwards Galileo clearly demonstrated that the earth wasn't the center of the universe at all."

For a moment Steve glimpsed the lean brown profile of Monsignor Quarenghi nodding encouragement; this was the kind of thinking his teacher liked. But the vision faded as Steve felt his immediate audience falling away from him. Ashamed of his intellectualism, Father Stephen subsided. He was not talking to Quarenghi now, but to some rather ordinary people that he happened to love very much. This was no time for showy learning. His words and thoughts from now on would have to be those that simple minds and hearts could understand. The winged horse of speculation must put on the harness of the parish hack.

"Let's have a little music, Bernie," he suggested.

"A God-marked and constructive idea," said Din.

George peeked at the kitchen clock. "I've got to be ducking out, Stuffy, or I'll miss my class. Sorry to bust this up." He kissed his mother, swept up an armful of books. Steve followed him to the front door. "Let's see a lot of each other, Georgie," he said, shaking his younger brother's hand.

"As much as you can take, Father." He put his arm affectionately around Steve, then ran down the front stoop.

RITA, with Dr. John Byrne behind her, came in around nine o'clock. Dark like the rest of the Fermoyles, she was slenderer than Florrie, not so fragile as Ellen or so beautiful as Mona. But of all Steve's sisters she was his favorite, his counterpart, and his emotional equal. A public-school teacher, Rita struck the good balance between sense and sensibility not uncommon among American girls of the middle class. Pleasure rayed from her face and voice as she threw her arms around her brother in a full-sized hug.

"Stevie . . . it's so good to *feel* you. You're so handsome. The girls of St. Margaret's will be *mad* for you."

"That's what you tell all the young curates," laughed Steve. "Hello, John." He held out a cordial hand to Dr. Byrne, tall, bony, and too pale with the labors of internship; the seal of undramatic honesty was on Dr. John's forehead. A good man to have in the family.

"Nice to have you back again, Father Steve." Having said so much, Dr. Byrne quietly sat down on the sofa in order to give the highly charged Fermoyle current a freer opportunity to flow about the room.

The current leapt in polar exchange from Rita to Stephen. There was no rivalry between these two; each supplemented and advanced the other without competitive tension. She showed Steve her engagement ring, a thin gold circlet with a tiny chip of a diamond clutched in a Tiffany setting. Stephen had never seen a smaller stone. He thought of the old wheeze, "Love is stone-blind," but could not mar Rita's happiness by repeating it. "It's beautiful," he murmured.

"We're getting married as soon as John finishes at the Maternity."

Steve addressed himself to Dr. John. "Isn't that one of the best internships in Boston? I thought the Back Bay Brahmins kept those jobs for themselves."

"They can't turn down brains," said Din. A cramping pain passed upward from his swollen leg veins, pinched his mouth into a grimace. It occurred to him that he had better get into bed before Dr. John's professional eye could focus on him too closely. He lowered his leg from the chair and started to rise. Something about his eggshell manner caught Dr. Byrne's diagnostic eye.

"Veins still troubling you, Mr. Fermoyle?"

"A mere whinge of a twinge now and then."

Celia, sensing the presence of allies, put in a word. "May the Holy Ghost forgive you, Dennis Fermoyle, for the lie you've just spoken." She turned to Steve. "Lumps big as eggs stand out on his legs, and he'll do nothing about it."

"Lumps big as eggs, is it?" said Steve. "If we had a doctor in the house — "

Dr. John Byrne gravely caught the ball. "Varicose veins can be dangerous, Mr. Fermoyle." He put his hand on Din's shoulder. "Let's go upstairs and have a look."

No escape for Din now. Cross as a mustached bear, he limped upstairs with Steve and Dr. John behind him.

"Get undressed and into bed," said Dr. Byrne. A moment

later his bony fingers and impersonal eyes were moving clinically up and down Dennie Fermoyle's right leg, noting the blue distended veins, knotted and ugly-looking. He turned Din's foot this way and that, bent it gently at the ankle, pressed his finger under the arch of Din's knee.

"This has been neglected too long. You need surgical attention, Mr. Fermoyle."

"In a hospital?"

"You'd get better care in a hospital, Mr. Fermoyle. There's really not much to the operation. The Mayo brothers report success with it — and I've had good results with a few cases myself." Dr. Byrne was one of those surgeons who believed in explaining things to a patient. "We excise, that is, cut out the damaged vein, and keep you in bed till the circulation finds its way back to the heart through smaller veins. The whole business won't take more than two weeks."

"Two weeks!" Violent agitation seized Dennis Fermoyle. He tried to rise from his bed. "No, no, I couldn't stay away two weeks."

Steve pressed a restraining hand against his father's chest. "Look at it this way, Pa. It's either two weeks now — or," he turned to Dr. Byrne for confirmation, "or a permanent lay-up with open sores and crutches maybe. You can't run a trolley car on crutches. Which'd you rather be, a martyr or a motorman?"

Din temporized. "There's a cost to these things," he mumbled.

"The hospital bed will be two dollars a day," said Dr. Byrne. "You'll get no bill from me."

"That's kind of you, Doctor. But" — Din struggled to get off the surgical hook.

"But *what?*" asked Steve. He sensed that something other than the expense was troubling his father. Something as yet unstated, and not plain stubbornness, either.

"How about an elastic stocking?" The craft of the devil was in Din Fermoyle tonight.

Dr. Byrne wasn't the man to talk a patient into an operation. "In my judgment your leg has passed the elastic-stocking stage. Still, if you want to try one" — he unclipped a pen from his vest pocket, wrote a name and address on a card —

"go see this fellow McGuire. He'll fit you." Dropping the card on the bureau, Dr. John left the room.

Alone with his father, Steve boiled over. "Pa, you're as stubborn as O'Shaughnessy's pig. What's all this nonsense about elastic stockings and expense? Tell me now, what's really holding you back?"

Dennis Fermoyle grinned up at his son. "Is it in the confessional we are?"

"The confessional of father-and-son confidence. What *is it*, Pa?"

Dennis took his son's fine hand between his calloused palms. "Sit down on the bed, Stevie, and listen to what I'll be telling you. It may be that you won't understand — though it's no fault in a young man, even though he's a priest, to lack understanding. That comes only with age."

Din hesitated. "The fact is, Steve, that Marty Timmins, since his wife passed away, has taken to knocking down company nickels."

"What's this got to do with your varicose veins?"

Din gazed at the ceiling. "You don't know, Son, the thing that grows up between men who've run the same car for a million miles. They lean against each other. Even dumb animals pulling the same beer wagon know the feeling. Well, as long as I keep my eye bent on Marty, he runs straight and honest. But if I were to leave him alone a couple of weeks, he'd begin knocking down company nickels, and get caught at it. Lose his job. They'd send him to prison. That's why I must stay on the job with him, Steve."

"You've talked to Marty about all this — warned him what will happen?"

"Many times. He weeps, promises he won't even let himself be tempted. Then next day he comes and tells me that he's tempted again. It's a running fight, Steve, and Marty may fail in the battle. It gives me the good feeling, Son, to help him over the bad places."

A muteness came over the ready tongue of Father Stephen Fermoyle. What could he say to this large stubborn man on the bed? No counsel would solve the problem of Marty's temptation, or free Din from his duty to support a stumbling friend. He wondered what Monsignor Quarenghi would have

made of the problem? Was there anything in Aquinas or
Liguori applicable to the case? Steve's glance traveled about
the shabby room and came to rest on the small ebony crucifix
on the faded wallpaper above his father's bed.

"We'll try the elastic stocking for a while," he said.

He might be able to tell this man many things about the
British war loan, the influence of Petrarch on Western thought,
and the chitchat of European chancelleries. But there was
nothing he could add to Dennis Fermoyle's understanding of
the Sermon on the Mount.

He said good night to his father and closed the door of the
stuffy bedroom very softly.

A ten-o'clock hush lay on the lower floor as Stephen went
down the backstairs to the kitchen. Bernie had gone to the
Gamecock. Florrie and Mona were in bed; Dr. Byrnes and
Rita were making the most of the poor privacy of the living
room. In the kitchen Celia Fermoyle was kneading dough,
tossing it lightly from hand to hand before putting it in the
baking pan. The maker of daily bread gazed up at her son
with a matter-of-fact affection. Loving she could be, mawkish
never. Her concern now was for her husband.

"What did Dr. John say about Pa's leg?"

"He advised an elastic stocking."

Celia patted an oval loaf into its pan. "Lizzie Gillen says
hers gives her great comfort. Sit down now, Stevie, and have
a piece of bread and molasses before you go."

"Will it make my hair curly, Ma? You used to tell me it
would."

Stephen sat at the kitchen table and watched his mother
set out the bread and molasses. Her hair had become disarranged during the evening, and the dark pigmentation of her
skin was purplish under the shadeless electric bulb. The
knuckles of her hands were red and cracked, her nails unat-
tended. As she moved about the kitchen, it seemed that she
had lost something of the tireless resiliency Steve remembered
as a boy.

"You must be tired, Ma."

"No," she said cheerfully. "I was tired an hour ago, but I'm
all right now, Son. Florrie did the dishes, and baking a batch
of bread is no work at all. A good night's sleep will fix me fine."

The old bounce! An inheritance more valuable than gold.

Celia cut bread, poured molasses into a saucer, then sat down opposite him. Her forearms, still plump and shapely, lay on the figured oilcloth; her eyes, brown as the liquid she had just poured, were fixed on her priest-son as he mopped up molasses with a slice of homemade bread.

"Remember how I used to *wade* through this stuff?" he asked.

"I remember everything about you, Son. The magic-lantern shows you were always giving in the dark pantry, the printing press down cellar, the telescope in the attic, the rabbits in the back yard, the mandolin in the parlor, the candy-making in the kitchen, the baseball in summer and the hockey in winter, the tap dancing, the yodeling, and that time you tried to be a ventriloquist. I remember the wet battery you made for the front doorbell, the bobsled you almost killed Mona on, taking her down Crescent Hill, and the string telephone you rigged up in the back yard. I remember every bit of it, Son — including the girls you were wild about, not to mention the ones that were wild about you."

Celia paused in her nostalgic cataloguing, a question in her eyes.

"There's something I've always wanted to ask you, Steve, ever since you told me you had a vocation. Maybe I won't get the answer I expect. But tell me, Son — tell me truly — did my wanting you to be a priest make you decide to be one?"

Stephen pondered the answer he should give his mother. Dare he reveal the hard truth that his love for her, great as it was, could not be compared with the mightier devotion that had drawn him, and now bound him, to the priesthood? How could he tell her that the depth and power of this greater love was immeasurable, that it filled and dominated him, that it was stronger than any love a son could feel for a mother?

He spoke as honestly as he could to the tired woman opposite him. "No, Mother, your wanting me to be a priest didn't make me one. I used to wonder about it when I was younger. But now I know I'm a priest because there's nothing else on earth that I want to be. It's as simple as that, and it will never change."

The worn corners of Celia Fermoyle's mouth trembled

slightly. "That's the answer I hoped for, Steve. I've known mothers who were forever at their sons to be priests, and because the sons loved them, or were weak, they sometimes mistook that love for a vocation. Unhappiness is their lot afterwards."

Courage and good sense, plenty of both, were in Celia's voice. But Stephen felt that his answer had somehow disappointed her. Well, he would try to make it up to her in a thousand loving ways. He started to say, "I'm offering my first Mass for your intention tomorrow," when he glanced at the kitchen clock.

"Ten-thirty! Monaghan will murder me. I'm supposed to be in before eleven." He snatched his black hat from its hook and bent down to kiss his mother's cheek.

"Give me your blessing, Son."

He made the sign of the cross above her bowed head. "Give me yours, Mother. It's worth more."

He could still feel her thumb-cross on his forehead as he walked swiftly down Woodlawn Avenue to the carbarns. The lightest of spring rains was falling. An indescribable joy, an exuberant sense of work ahead, made Stephen feel like running. And when he saw the headlight of the trolley leaving the carbarn. he *did* run, and leapt aboard it sure-footed.

As the car jolted toward Malden Square, Stephen read the Office for the Time, then closed his breviary with the echo of Matins in his ears.

"I am the true Vine," the echo said, "and you are the branches. He who abides in me bears much fruit, Alleluia, Alleluia."

A few minutes later, Stephen Fermoyle let himself into the parish house of St. Margaret's, and started to tiptoe up the thin-carpeted stairs. He heard the chime of a clock striking in Father Monaghan's room, and saw the pastor's door open slightly.

Then at the head of the stairway appeared an apparition of great bulk — the towering figure of William Monaghan himself.

"Are these your usual hours, Father Fermoyle?" the rector was inquiring in a sarcastic, bullying tone.

CHAPTER 2

IN OTHER TIMES and places, had he not been a priest, William Monaghan might have been many things: centurion under Pompey, the master of a clipper ship, or the general manager of a Bessemer steel mill. He had the physical bulk of an Olympic hammer thrower and the vocal cords of Michael the Archangel, roughened, it is true, by long misuse in a large church with poor acoustics. His complexion was of the meaty red rightly associated with choler, and his curly gray hair, which he combed in a roach, would tighten like individual watch springs when his choler rose. Neither curate nor layman dared cross him: he ran the parish of St. Margaret's as a veteran conductor runs a crack train, responsibly and hard, along the steel tracks of pay-as-you-go discipline.

The city of Malden, in which St. Margaret's lay, was wedged like a slice of suburban pie, five miles north of Boston, between the Saugus marshes on the east and a woody, undeveloped section of Medford to the west. The place had been settled in 1631 by a shipload of dour Dissenters; in 1915 the tone of the city was still puritanical and Protestant. Socially, the best people attended either the Baptist church, with its really magnificent cast of bells, or the Episcopalian St. Jude's that rose in an ivied Gothic pile on Pleasant Street. Numerically, however, William Monaghan's congregation was the largest in the city. Upwards of four thousand devout worshipers surged in and out of the three Masses said at St. Margaret's every Sunday — an edifying spectacle from any point of view, except possibly that of the Protestant divines, who pursed their lips enviously as they thought of the bright silver clinking into the collection boxes of St. Margaret's fifty-two Sundays a year.

The wittiest and least envious of these divines, Dr. Arthur Lethbridge, D.D. (Oxon.), had punned rather brilliantly, so he thought, on the name of William Monaghan. "Dollar Bill," he had called him at a smart, very Anglican luncheon at the

Kenilworth Club shortly after his arrival at St. Jude's. But the wheeze was already ancient among Father Monaghan's parishioners. They had nicknamed him "Dollar Bill" ten years before, when, on taking over the pastorate of St. Margaret's, he had baldly declared that pennies and nickels were fit coinage for gum slots only.

"Green in any denomination is a color most pleasing to the Lord," he was quoted as saying. A canard, probably — yet even the Cardinal had laughed when he heard it.

If the fiscal part of William Monaghan's soul was somewhat over-developed, this could be traced to realistic causes. As a youth he had felt hunger to the marrow of his large leg bones; but even more painfully he had felt the hatred and contempt in which his unpropertied kind, the South Boston Irish, were held by Boston Brahmins. Muckers, Micks, Harps, they were called, and their lot was to dig in the streets, drive garbage carts, or tend bars. Gradually he had seen his people climb the economic ladder to become policemen, firemen, motormen, and — after decades of struggle — lawyers, teachers, and doctors. They had moved away from South Boston, migrated to Dorchester and Roxbury, gained title to houses of their own. If Father Monaghan overvalued property, it was because the society in which he lived overvalued it, too. Ownership of something — that was the badge of membership. A house was a physical monument built on the rock of social acceptance. And a well-constructed church of Quincy granite or a prosperous parochial school of fine brick was an outward sign of substance that could not be blown down or whirled about by winds of prejudice.

That was why William Monaghan valued the dollar and drove hard for it.

The Cardinal, knowing all this about Father Monaghan, had called him in, one day back in 1906, and handed him two slips of paper. On the first piece was written: "Dedham, Parish of St. Jerome. No church debt, a new parish house, a nine-grade school." On the other: "Malden, Parish of St. Margaret. $30,000 church debt. Rickety parish house, no school."

"Take your choice, Father," the Cardinal had said.

"I'll take St. Margaret's, Your Eminence."

"Thanks, Father." Whereat "Your Eminence" evaporated,

and a grateful administrator held out a very human hand. "Good luck to you, Bill."

In ten years, William Monaghan had wiped out the $30,000 church debt, and was now incurring a bigger one — with his Cardinal's consent, of course — for the new parochial school. Meanwhile he dwelt with his three curates in a time-stained wooden structure, and let his mind leap forward to the day when this tumble-down ark would be supplanted by a modern parish house of brick and granite. As a reward for his labors in this once arid vineyard, the Cardinal had conferred upon him the coveted honor of the P. R. — permanent rector — with life tenure on a tough job.

The toughness of the job alarmed William Monaghan not at all, but he had been somewhat dissatisfied of late with the curates sent out to assist him. They were not the men they used to be. They lacked ruggedness and push; there was no jump to them. One and all, they were too much concerned with liturgical niceties and all manner of clerical bric-a-brac. But at the drudgery of parish work — they were no good at all. Take Father Lyons, for example. "Milky," they called him, and a blind man could see the reason for the name. Why, if a cupful of rain fell on Milky Lyons while making a parish call, he would rush back to the house in mortal fear of pneumonia. And forever talking about Gregorian music, he was. With two hundred housebound invalids in the parish, all needing the comfort of a priestly voice and hand, why should a curate always be harping on Palestrina?

And this new chap Fermoyle, the fine imported article from Rome. A theological disputant, no doubt, a learned wrangler on canon law, with a varnish of Italian and a lively admiration, like as not, for the sound of his own voice box. The Reverend William Monaghan had never been to Rome, but he had seen plenty of young curates fresh from the North American College there, and they were all cut from the same bolt: "All finish but no fabric," he grumbled to his fellow pastor, Flynn of Lynn. "Their feet are too small, Gene, for the heft of their ideas." A Hibernicism — but one that found ready understanding in the crypt of the Flynn ear.

Peevishness heated William Monaghan's red neck as he paced his study on this rainy April evening, dreaming of the ideal curate with big feet and tireless hands. Other matters, too, were putting a tighter curl in his roached hair. Italians in great numbers were flooding into the parish of St. Margaret's; the whole region west of the B & M tracks was swarming with Neapolitans — noisy, wine-drinking brawlers, quick with their steel but slow with their silver. True, they were Catholics, and therefore welcome in God's sight. But in the sight of William Monaghan, who was not God but merely the rector of a self-sustaining parish, they were definitely *not* welcome. And for two reasons: first, they didn't support their rector generously; and second, he didn't know how to get along with them. They were excitable, superstitious, dirty, and cynical, not in the decent fashion of Celts, but in some outlandish manner of their own. To put it briefly, they were not Irish. Worse yet, they were pushing out the Irish! The fine old names of Finan, Finnegan, and Foley were giving place, on the baptismal roster, to Castelucci, Foppiano, and Marinelli. Unless Michael the Archangel or some other Saint Militant defended Bill Monaghan in the battle against his Latin parishioners, St. Margaret's was doomed.

Saint Militant? Pastor Monaghan would have settled for a good curate.

The ormolu clock with the fine Waltham movement chimed ten-thirty, and a deeper burn of irritability reddened the pastor's neck. Where was this new curate Fermoyle at such an hour? Monaghan glanced at the Mass schedule for the week, written out in Father Ireton's tall clerical hand. Praise be for Paul Ireton, a steady priest and a fine assistant. Plain as day the schedule showed that Father Stephen Fermoyle was assigned to the six-thirty A.M. Mass tomorrow morning and that Jimmy Splaine was to be his altar boy. Wouldn't you think now that a young priest, on the eve of celebrating Mass in his first parish, would be in his room, on his knees, preparing himself by prayer and meditation? But where was Father Fermoyle? Ah, yes, this elegant limb was at home visiting his parents in West Medford, regaling them no doubt with marvelous stories about his doings in Rome — how he saw Cardinals Vannutelli and Merry del Val just leaving the Vatican arm in arm with His Holiness on their way to sing High Mass in St. Peter's. Or some such sculch.

Monaghan's wrath climbed with the rising minute hand as it swept toward eleven o'clock. This night-owl business must be checked. The ormolu clock was chiming the hour when the front door opened and the new curate came tiptoeing upstairs. Bill Monaghan jacked his huge body out of its pastoral armchair and started for the brown crockery knob of his study door. The whole duty of pastors being to discipline and regulate curates, Monaghan was about to tear the door off its hinges and do his whole duty, when his ireful blue eye alighted on a small photograph in an oval silver frame.

The photograph was of a young priest with roached hair and a square, cleft chin. The eyes of the young priest were neither raised to heaven nor cast down to earth. They were level with hope, steady with purpose. The photograph of Father William Monaghan was taken the day after his ordination. How proud his father and mother had been of that picture. They had placed it in the silver frame and kept it on the parlor mantelpiece in South Boston till they were both dead and gone. A long while now. Neither they nor William Monaghan had ever realized that this photograph was a composite picture of all the big-footed, capable-handed curates that had built the Archdiocese of Boston, a brick at a time. Pastor Monaghan had no such notion even now. The picture merely reminded him that most young curates have parents somewhere, and that no great harm comes to the priestly cloth when stroked by a mother's admiring hand.

The thought did not entirely blunt his intention to give Father Fermoyle a good dressing down. He jerked open the door and, in the manner of a clipper-ship captain asking a second mate why in God's name the vessel wasn't getting anywhere, queried:

"Are these your usual hours, Father Fermoyle?"

A soft answer, thought Stephen, is indicated here. "I'm sorry if I'm late, Father. It won't happen again."

"See that it does not." Monaghan was about to close the interview and his door when he noticed that the hair of this long-legged young priest was slightly shower-sprinkled, as though he had been walking in the rain. In contrast to Milky Lyons' dread of dampness, this sign of hardihood in a curate was almost endearing. Certainly a matter to be investigated.

"Step into my room, Father Fermoyle." Monaghan's crafty eye estimated the probable amount of water glistening in Stephen's hair. He ventured a testing remark. "I see you're not afraid of a little rain."

"I like rain," said Steve.

"Sit down," said Monaghan.

Into a sag-bottomed Morris chair Stephen sank unevenly, and gazed about the room. Study, office, bedroom, Monaghan's lair had the incoherent no-period look that only a hard-working celibate can give a place. Nothing matched anything else. An ancient roll-top desk of fumed oak, its pigeonholes crammed with envelopes, ledgers, blueprints, and canvas coin bags, clashed with a surly black walnut bookcase full of unread religious periodicals. The lumpy four-poster bed disagreed with the brass hatrack on one side of it and an oleograph of St. Cecelia playing the organ on the other. A mangy carpet covered the floor; from the ceiling hung a crystal chandelier of the Welsbach gas-mantle era, now wired for electricity. The crystal pendants of the chandelier carried on the feud by jangling noisily whenever a streetcar rumbled past.

Does it have to be as dreary as this? thought Steve. He remembered Quarenghi's study: white-walled, bare except for a flat table, a hard chair, a shelf of books in red and gold. The cell of an anchorite. But this room — what was it trying to say about the man who lived in it?

Collarless, carpet-slippered, hands locked behind his back, and his great meat-colored face thrust forward, Monaghan began pacing the track between window and door. He was trying hard not to glance at something — and that something was his curate's feet. The attempt failed. Monaghan left off his pacing, and stared point-blank at Stephen's shoes.

Ten B's. H'mm, y'mm . . . a touch on the narrow side. Will broaden a width or two, maybe. Must recommend ground-grippers with vici-kid tops. . . . Later. . . .

"Arches ever trouble you?" asked Monaghan.

"Never." What's he getting at? Steve wondered. Monaghan's gait and posture reminded him of a huge ox dragging a remorseless plow. The pastor made another furrow to the window, peered through the lace curtains.

"I hope," he said, "that you don't come to St. Margaret's

all burthened with — attitudes." (He pronounced it "atti-chudes.")

"Attitudes? What kind of attitudes?"

Monaghan flung out a heavy arm like a man knocking clutter off his workbench. "Oh — stained-glass attitudes, Gregorian attitudes — the niminy-piminy attitudes they try to come over you with at Rome."

Stephen mastered everything but puzzlement. "I don't understand, Father. All that I feel or know about the Church goes much deeper than 'attitude.'"

"We weren't talking about the Church," snapped Monaghan. "We were talking about curates. Rome-cured curates, that is."

Fuses of anger crackled along Stephen's spine. Rome-cured! So that was Monaghan's idea of a body punch, was it? — a coarse, punning attack on the system that produced men like Pecci, Rampolla, Merry del Val — scholars, diplomats, princes of the Church. He wanted to retort with scathements beginning: "Listen, Ox-neck — " But he closed his teeth on these Din-the-Down-Shouter locutions, and what he said was quiet but stubborn.

"No one in Rome tried to 'come over me' with anything. I merely took the regular course of studies offered at the North American College."

"Aha!" said Monaghan in a "now-we're-getting-at-it" tone. "And would you mind running over the list of those studies for me?"

Stephen decided to keep cool and impersonal. "Not at all. We studied sacred theology, canon law, moral philosophy, and had some special lectures on ecclesiastical diplomacy. Then, of course, there was the usual work in hermeneutics — "

"Herman *who?*"

Steve disregarded the Weber and Fields clownery. "Herme-neutics," he repeated, "the science of interpreting the Scrip-tures." He let fly at Monaghan's big jaw. "We compared St Jerome's translation of the New Testament with the Aramaic and the Greek." *Bang*, that should fix him!

"Did you so?" Unshaken, Monaghan nodded at the silver-framed photograph as if to say, "See the training a curate gets nowadays." "And what else did they teach you at Rome?"

"During the last year, some emphasis was laid on liturgy and rubrics."

Gleefully, like a prosecutor who hears a witness convicting himself out of his own mouth, Monaghan rubbed his hands together. The mass of mixed evidence pleased him. Father Fermoyle's fondness for rain and his reasonably large feet were more than outweighed by the fanciness of his education. More testimony must be gathered.

"In the course of your elegant education, Father Fermoyle, did you ever" — he paused with forensic intent — "did you ever drive a milk wagon?"

Stephen conveyed large uninterest in his "No, I never did."

"Well, there, at least, my experience cries on top of yours. For in my youth I drove such a wagon. In those days we poured the milk from open cans into such household containers as dippers, or pitchers, or whatever our poor Mick customers might have handy. But I will pass over that part of my story and come to the advantage enjoyed by those who have driven a milk wagon over those who haven't." Pastor Monaghan rubbed a didactic paste into the palm of his left hand with the pestle of his right forefinger. "That advantage lies in being able to tell a good milk-wagon horse ten blocks away. Do you take my meaning, Father?"

"As a kind of homely parable, yes."

"My parable goes on to say, then, that many a fine-spirited animal breaks down between the shafts of a milk wagon. Not gaited to the task. Another breed, of still higher mettle, tries to run off with the milk cart as though it were a tallyho or rubber-tired vehicle of some kind — which, as you can see, Father — "

"It is not," murmured Steve.

"No resemblance. Not the faintest. Now, what is needed on a milk wagon, Father, is a docile, steady creature who can carry the load up hill and down dale, start at a cluck, and stand without hitching. Which, to drop the parable once and for all, is what the work of a curate amounts to here at St. Margaret's."

Stephen's nostrils flared, but he kept the good silence.

"This disturbs you, Father Fermoyle?"

"A little." Rising from the sag-bottomed chair, Stephen

unconsciously put his feet in the furrow worn by his pastor, and paced off the width of the room. "I know, of course, that a curate is not a steeplechaser, and that my job at St. Margaret's is no rubber-tired sinecure. I expected drudgery. I welcome it. But" — a trolley car rumbled past, and Stephen waited for the crystals in the chandelier to stop jangling — "but do you have to be so horribly explicit about the milk wagon?"

"Vagueness," said Monaghan, "would be no help at St. Margaret's. Better to be clear — explicit, as you say — at the beginning than to lallygag around with attitudes."

For God's sake, Stephen wanted to cry, stop using that word. So I'm a milk horse. Fine. I'll start at a cluck, and clop about the parish till I'm a wind-broken old hack like yourself. But, meanwhile, what about scholarly exercise of the mind, personal dedication to God the Father, spiritual fellowship with the saints? Are these unavailing at St. Margaret's?

The questions surged toward utterance, but went unspoken as Stephen gazed about the dreary room. How could he convey himself to the heavy-footed man who inhabited it? How breach the ghastly wall of Monaghan's parochialism?

Tr-ranggg!

Someone was yanking hard at the front doorbell. "I'll answer it," volunteered Stephen. He flew down the rickety stairs and opened the front door. A breathless little man, with the flannelette collar of a nightgown showing under his jacket, and deathbed news in his eyes, began to gasp out a telegraphic message:

"Mrs. Fitzgerald . . . sinking fast. . . . Dr. Farrell says for Father Monaghan . . . come right away "

The pastor's hoarse voice rumbled down from the head of the stairs. "Would that be Annie Fitzgerald of 14 Brackenbury Street?"

"It would," said the flanneletted messenger. "This is me, Owen Fitz, her husband. Come quick, Father, please."

"I'll be there in five minutes," said Monaghan.

In a double bound Stephen was up the stairs. "Let me go, Father," he pleaded. "I'm dressed." He could not bring himself to add, "I'm younger . . . my arches are springier than yours."

"Dollar Bill" Monaghan, buttoning on his rabat, shook his head. "Thank you, Father Fermoyle," he said, "but this call I must take myself. Annie Fitzgerald has lived in pain for three years, and the dear woman wouldn't know how to die without me now." He pulled on his No. 13 vici-top shoes with the elastic inserts. "But if you'll be so kind, Father, just run down to the sacristy — the key is hanging on the bulletin board — and fetch me up the case of holy oil. Mrs. Annie Fitz will be needing the last sacraments tonight."

Stephen ran. When he returned with the case, William Monaghan was backing his new Packard out of the garage. "Get a good night's rest, Father Fermoyle," he advised. "You're saying your first Mass at St. Margaret's tomorrow, and nothing gives greater scandal to our Saviour than the sight of a priest yawning and gawping all over the altar. You take my meaning, Father?"

"I do," said Stephen. He stood bareheaded in the driveway till the crimson flicker of Monaghan's taillight disappeared in rainy darkness.

IMPARTIALLY gilding objects sacred and profane — the cross on the pinnacle of St. Margaret's and the ugly brown cylinder of the municipal gas tank behind it — a May sun was well sprung from the Mystic Flats when Father Stephen Fermoyle in cassock and biretta, breviary in hand, came down the three steps of the parish house next morning. His chin glistened from the razor as he inhaled the fresh spring air and breathed it out again in a canticle of thanksgiving to the Maker of Days in general and this spring day in particular. For on this day, indeed in a few minutes — at six-thirty A.M., to be exact — Father Stephen Fermoyle would enter into the special glory of a priest's life. He would celebrate his first Mass as a curate in the parish of St. Margaret's.

He crossed the narrow strip of brick courtyard between the parish house and the church, unlocked the door of the sacristy, and let himself in. Odors of myrrh and spikenard lay on the almost chilly air; in the ruby flicker of the sacristy lamp he saw the high, broad chest containing the vestments of his priestly office. Stephen was glad that the Sexton Val McGuire had not yet opened the basement chapel, and that the altar boy hadn't yet arrived. The young priest wanted to be alone while he prepared himself for the central act of his being, toward which he moved now with secret exultation and almost tremulous joy.

He knelt at the worn *prie-dieu,* bowed his head, covered his face with his hands, and inwardly supplicated the Divine Father to make him a worthy priest. This private devotion over (he kept it brief to avoid sentimentality), Stephen offered up the Mass for the special intention of his mother. Arising, he washed his hands, murmuring the humble *"Da, Domine,"* as he did so. Then he laid his biretta on the *prie-dieu* and approached the vesting bench to attire himself for his office as celebrant.

Stephen Fermoyle had received his instruction in rubrics — the prescribed rules for the conduct of sacred ceremonials — from that great perfectionist, Guglielmo Zualdi, S.J. Under Zualdi's tutelage, Stephen had acquired a full and intimate knowledge of the august tradition surrounding the solemn sacrifice of the Mass. Exactness and reverence, combined with a high degree of esthetic sensibility, were focused now in the clear white flame of the celebrant as artist. Every inflection of voice, every movement of head, hands, and body, would be perfectly executed in this first essay of his priesthood.

Stephen placed the fine linen amice over his shoulders, and arranged the alb evenly, so that it fell chastely white to his ankles. He girdled himself with the cincture, saying in Latin as he did so, "Engirdle me, Lord, with the cincture of purity, and extinguish in my bowels every libidinous desire, that I shall be filled with the strength of continence and chastity." Taking up the maniple, he kissed the cross in the center and placed it on his left forearm as the symbol of the worldly sorrows the priest must bear. Then taking the stole in his two hands, he said, "Give back unto me, Lord, the stole of immortality, lost by the sin of our first parents." He was about to place the sacred vestment around his neck when the sacristy door burst open, and a breathless small boy rushed past the *prie-dieu*, knocked Father Steve's biretta to the floor, picked it up again, and stood panting in the middle of the sacristy floor.

"All right, Jimmy," said Father Steve without turning his head. "Get your surplice on."

In the act of crossing the stole on his breast, Father Stephen looked around and saw a nine-year-old boy unwashed and uncombed, covered to his knees by an emerald-green coat-sweater buttonless and clasped at the middle with a horse-blanket safety pin.

"I'm not Jimmy," panted the youth. "I'm Jemmy."

"Jimmy was sick last night," gasped the boy. "He threw up twice all over the bed. Pa said it was the pig's knuckles Ma gave us for supper, and they had a fight, but anyway Jimmy told me to come down and be the altar boy this morning."

Jemmy looked in amazement at the biretta he had picked up. "Must've knocked it off," he volunteered.

Father Stephen tried not to be unduly distracted. "Put it on the *prie-dieu*, and get into your surplice, Jemmy. You'll find it in that closet by the door." Calmly Father Steve put on the chasuble, passed the strings behind his back, and tied them inside on his breast.

Out of the corner of one eye he saw Jemmy Splaine fighting his way out of the oversized sweater. Behind him he heard Sexton Val McGuire peeping into the sacristy to see what was holding up the Mass. Annoyance began to gather between Father Steve's eyes. But he let none of it appear in his voice as he addressed his young server. "You know the responses, of course, Jemmy?"

"Pretty good, Father."

A dubious instrument, thought Steve. "Hand me my biretta, please."

He took the chalice in his left hand, placed his right hand over the burse and veil, and held the sacred vessel in front of him, neither touching his breast nor far removed from it. Motioning to Jemmy to lead off, then falling in behind the boy, Father Stephen walked gravely toward the altar, his mind fixed on the sacred ritual of the Mass.

Scarcely had he uttered the *Introibo ad altare Dei* when the quality of Jemmy's Latin was revealed as something less than elegant. For the first two responses, Jem's memory served him moderately, but at the *Quia tu es Deus*, it began to crack, and long before the *Introit*, the substitute acolyte was floundering hopelessly. As the Mass progressed, the boy's responses, his mismanagement of his feet, hands, and tongue, became pitiful. A minor catastrophe occurred while he was transferring the missal from the Epistle to the Gospel side: ascending the steps of the altar, he stumbled, and only Father Steve's outstretched hands saved Book and boy from an ignominious tumble.

A tide of anger rose in Father Stephen Fermoyle as he saw his first Mass being ruined by this mumbling, stumbling clown. The spiritual work of art was being daubed by dirty paws; the oblation conceived as a masterpiece of rubric, and offered up with purist punctilio, now lay hacked to pieces around his feet.

Desperately Father Stephen fought to ignore the distractions arising from the sorry movements of his altar boy. During the Canon of the Mass, he strove to forget all else but the Host that he held in his hands. Secretly, and with particular attention, distinction, and reverence, he uttered the five words, *Hoc est enim corpus meum,* from which the mystery of the transubstantiation radiates into the lives of men.

Mercifully, Jemmy did nothing to destroy the moment, but later at the Communion he again disgraced himself by failing to extend the paten while Father Steve placed the sacred wafers on the tongues of the few early communicants.

So exasperated was Father Steve as he left the altar at the conclusion of the Mass that he yearned to plant his boot squarely in the seat of Jeremy Splaine's corduroy pants. As he entered the sacristy, sharp words of rebuke sprang to his lips. But he choked them down, placed the chalice on the sacristy altar, and began taking off his sacred vestments. At first his wrath could barely consume itself, but as he removed the handsome garments — the brocaded chasuble, heavily embroidered with gold and silver, the rich satin maniple, and the alb of fine linen — a strange realization came over him.

He saw that he had put on these garments not in humility but in pride, and that he had approached the altar in a spirit of haughty elegance fatal to the fulfillment of his priestly function. From a complete display of vanity he had been saved by Jemmy's uncouth stumbling. Unconsciously the boy had stretched his frail body like a living bridge across the pit of arrogance that had yawned at Father Stephen's feet.

"Jemmy, come here."

With uncombed head bent in consciousness of failure and disgrace, Jemmy obeyed. He had removed his surplice, and had not yet donned the sweater of emerald green. His upper body, thin as a picked pullet, was covered by a torn and dirty undershirt; a piece of clothesline, in lieu of a belt, held up his corduroy pants.

Vestments of a kind they were — vestments not spiced with myrrh and spikenard, nor stored away in the cool precincts of the sacristy, but worn next to sweating, corruptible flesh in the heat and dust of common day.

Stephen put a consoling finger under the boy's peaked chin, lifted the large head with its wild shock of hair, and gazed into the tear-streaked face.

"That was a pretty bad performance all around, Jemmy."

"Yes, Father."

"But before we're through, Jem, you'll be a better altar boy" — salt dimness blurred Father Stephen's eyes — "and with the help of God, I'll be a better priest."

EXACTLY what it was that Sexton Val McGuire whispered into William Monaghan's ear, no one will ever know. But somehow or other Sexton McGuire conveyed the impression that the new curate didn't know how to celebrate Mass properly.

That noon the rector sat down to the luncheon table, hungry for his meat and potatoes. He cut a large triangular wedge of veal from the cold joint and turned the silver-plated Lazy Susan till he came to his bottle of caper sauce. "I hear," he said, not using his Arcturus-blue eyes on anyone in particular, "that the six-thirty Mass this morning was turned into a circus." The pastor sliced his veal slowly. "But with this difference" — he shot out his indictment — "*that a circus starts on time!*"

Father Paul Ireton, having slept until seven that morning, said nothing. Just an innocent bystander, not even in the line of fire. Milky Lyons put on a brightly surprised expression as if to say, "Can such things be?" The silence left Father Steve exposed on both flanks, a position especially reserved for new curates in Monaghan's house.

Yesterday in the lustihood of his young powers, Steve might have offered half a dozen parries. Even now he was tempted to say: "So, we have talebearers at St. Margaret's?" Instead, he looked quietly at his pastor. His tone was apologetic as he said:

"There *was* a bit of delay, Father. I wasn't quite familiar with the vestment racks."

Pastor Monaghan was out for a disciplinary ride that noon. "How about the antics with the Book? I hear" — it was a favorite elocution with him — "that you and your server were practically juggling it between you. Is that the latest thing with the American College crowd at Rome?"

Paul Ireton came to the rescue. "It was the altar boy's fault, Father. Jimmy Splaine got sick last night and had to send his young kid brother as a last-minute substitute. I got the whole story, along with several yards of other material, from Mrs. Splaine in the Square this morning."

This information, instead of salving the Monaghan burn, only scraped more flesh off. "So Jimmy Splaine gets sick and the Mass is disrupted. In the name of God, have we but one altar boy in the parish? Can't some of you curates organize the altar service — teach half a dozen kids how to serve Mass?"

Monaghan's irritation, Steve felt, had a measure of reason. Hip-deep in parish finances, the pastor might fairly expect one of his assistants to take over the training of altar boys. Steve wanted to volunteer then and there — but now Frank Lyons was making a pallid gesture.

"I'd like to instruct some boys in plain chanting."

The proposal infuriated Monaghan. "There'll be no plain chanting in St. Margaret's. This is a parish church, not a — a basilica." He pronounced the word as though it were the name of a disease.

Father Lyons sipped weakly at his glass of milk. Stephen stepped into the breach. "I'll train some altar boys, Father."

"The job is yours. And no fancy stuff, mind you. Just the responses in decent Latin, and some sense of respect for what they're supposed to be doing up there on the altar. You understand?"

"I understand, Father."

Pastor Monaghan said grace hastily and rose from the table, eager to get at the cigar that he kept locked in a humidor in his room. The three curates sat silently looking at each other.

"What's he got against plain chanting?" the milky one asked petulantly. "It's very beautiful. And important, too. Piux X wrote a *Motu Proprio* about it, you know."

"So he did," said Steve. "Isn't that the one where he says that mechanical instruments are no substitutes for the glories of the human voice?"

"That's it," said Milky eagerly. "The Sovereign Pontiff urges upon all Catholic pastors the importance of training choirs of children in plain chanting. Furthermore" — evidently Father Lyons had the document by heart — "he inveighs against the laxity of responses from the congregation and says that — "

"Listen, you-two," put in Paul Ireton. "Consider the facts surrounding the writing of that *Motu Proprio*, will you? In the first place, Piux X was a Patriarch of Venice. Remember Venice, the place that held the glorious East in fee? No motorboats in the canals, no electric lights — just a lot of gondolas, singing boatmen, palaces on stilts, and all that. Fine. That's the tradition Pius X was working in. But now you get a man like our *pastoricus* here, a gadget-loving Westerner who doesn't know a square note from a round, living in an industrial town where electricity is cheap. Why in heaven's name should he prefer plain song to the nice ten-thousand-dollar electric organ he's just installed?"

"But plain singing is a heritage from the earliest Church," said Milky. "It has centuries of medieval tradition behind it."

"Plus three centuries of British — that is to say, Anglican — tradition," said Paul Ireton. "You wouldn't expect a man sprung from landlord shooters to embrace the practices of the landlord, would you?"

"You're being rather parochial," sniffed Milky.

"You mean," corrected Paul Ireton, "I'm being rather Boston-Irish."

Steve sipped his coffee, reserving judgment. He had always wondered what curates talked about; surely it couldn't always be as good as this. Both sides of the argument were familiar to him: Father Ireton was only repeating parochialisms of Din

Fermoyle, Corny Deegan, and Monaghan himself, while Father Lyons was pleading, ineffectually enough, for the universal viewpoint that Stephen had acquired at Rome. Could the two ever be fused? Would America ever grasp the larger meaning of the Holy Roman Apostolic Church — an organization transcending national tongues, arts, and boundaries? And would Rome ever appreciate the peculiar vigor and quality of the transatlantic Church?

Father Paul Ireton stuffed his napkin into an imitation-bone napkin-ring with the finality of a man who'll argue no more that day. Stephen felt a quickening admiration for this sober, scholarly priest who knew all the arguments but refused to be drawn into speculative debate.

Paul Ireton lifted a beckoning finger to the new curate.

"Confessions this afternoon," he said. "We'll start you off with the kids. Take the box on the west aisle at four P.M., and be ready to hear the quaintnesses that spring *ex ore infantium.*"

A TREMOR such as he had never felt before seized Stephen as he opened the door of the confessional and sat down in semi-darkness. He made his final plea to the Confessor of Saints and Angels. "Let me not judge harshly, Lord, as in mercy Thou has not judged me." He pushed back a small sliding panel, covered his eyes with his hand. Stephen Fermoyle's work as a looser of sins began.

Through the fine-meshed screen came the hasty, almost inaudible murmur of a twelve-year-old girl: "Bless me, Father, for I have sinned. It's a week since my last confession. I went to Holy Communion and said my penance." Then she poured out a little throatful of venial sins. "I talked in church three times. I got angry with my sister when she took my stockings. I slapped my brother once, no . . . twice. I answered my mother back when she told me to do something, and I was vain in front of the mirror while dressing." A pause. "I . . . sinned against purity . . ."

"In what way?" asked Stephen gently.

"Playing post office — at a party — I let a boy kiss me on the mouth." A little sigh. Glad to have it over and done with. "For these and all the other sins I may have committed, I ask forgiveness, Father."

In a minute the child had unreeled the commonplace scenario of her life. The slaps and bickerings, the budding female vanity at the mirror, the adolescent rebellion, the first kiss clumsily given, awkwardly received — Stephen saw them all. How comment on these undistinguished faults? — not faults even, for the word was too strong to characterize the things the child had done. What counsel could he offer this innocent soul? Vanity at the mirror gave Stephen a clue.

"These little misdeeds of yours are like-tiny flaws in a beautiful complexion," he said. "When the Blessed Mother gazes into the mirror of your heart, will you try not to have even the slightest blemish there?"

"Yes, Father, I will try."

"For your penance, say three Hail Marys. And now make a good act of contrition." He lifted his right hand in the gesture of absolution.

For two hours Father Steve heard the confessions of children — a monotonous catalogue without variation or enormity of any kind. "I lied, I swore five times, I had impure thoughts twice, I peeked at my sister while she was dressing." And so forth, in the manner of earth's newest angels, *in saecula saeculorum.*

At six P.M. Father Steve emerged from his box, blinking like a mole as he stepped out into the late afternoon sunlight. There, pacing up and down in the bricked courtyard, was Father Paul Ireton, taking a breath of air before supper.

Father Paul was in a twitting humor. "Ah, the young curé of souls, fresh from the Children's Hour."

Steve fell into step beside Father Ireton. "If this afternoon is any example, the kids of Malden, Mass., are a fairly undistinguished bunch of sinners."

"It's a sort of merry glissando compared to what you'll hear tonight." Paul looked at his watch. "We've just got time for six fast turns before supper. Come on, let's step out."

Seven-thirty found Steve back in his box for the evening stint. The first half-dozen penitents were pious married women who repeated, on a slightly more adult level, the trivial offenses of their children. "I gossiped twice; I envied my neighbor the new piano she got on installments; I was late for Mass once, but I could have got there if I got up in time. I ate meat on Friday because nothing else was in the house but eggs. I took sixty-five cents from my husband's pocket and lied about it afterwards. I — I refused my wifely duty to my husband on two separate occasions, because . . ."

Stephen found that the women were more apt to extenuate their offenses than the men. The men would come right out with it: "I committed adultery four times." But the women would beat about the bush with all manner of fancy locutions. Stephen was beginning to think that something about the feminine soul made plain statements difficult.

Just when he was feeling secretly complacent about his handling of things in general, Stephen got his comeuppance. As he opened the slide to his left, a faint attar of good perfume — vaguely carnation — struck his nostrils. The delicate voice of a young woman began a pianissimo recital of the usual minor offenses. Intelligent, a trifle sulky. After the briefest of hesitations she said with neither shame nor pride:

"During the past six months I've had sexual relations with a man. Many times."

Steve asked the natural question. "Why don't you get married?"

"He's a Baptist. My family doesn't want me to marry outside the Church."

"Have you asked him to become a Catholic?"

"I've begged him to turn, Father. But he hates the Church. He says terrible things about it."

"Yet you continue to go with him."

"Yes, Father." She made a stubborn declaration. "I love him very much." Then the fabric of her stubbornness gave way, and she uttered a miserable, "What shall I do?"

The classic Montague and Capulet dilemma, complete with sectarian complications.

Stephen wanted to rise, walk about while he thought out an answer. But motor release was denied him; he must sit still. And not only must he remain inside the physical boundaries of the confessional. More important yet, he must remain within the doctrinal bounds of his faith. In advising this erring daughter of the Church, his plain duty as a confessor was to set forth some well-established truths. Tenderly he began his instructions.

"Hard though it is to break your relationship with this man, you must give him up. There is no other way to lasting happiness for either of you. If you marry him outside the Church it means a lifetime of spiritual grieving, not to mention the emotional antagonisms that mar so many mixed marriages." Stephen paused. "And of course you must stop this business of illicit relations. It is dangerous, immoral — cheap."

Unsubmissive, the young woman lifted her chin. "It isn't cheap at all, Father."

"But you intend to stop?"

The girl shook her head. "I can't."

"In that case," said Stephen, "it is not within my power to grant you absolution. You cannot receive the sacrament of penance until you have made a firm resolution to give up your sinful way of life."

The girl rose from her knees. "Why did I come here anyway?" she murmured angrily. "I might have known." Leaving behind her a scent of carnation, she flew from the confessional.

Stephen's instinct was to run after her, catch her by the arm, beg her to be patient with the Church and himself. But he could do none of these things. He knew he had been technically correct in refusing absolution, but he knew also that he had been too brusque, too unbending, not tactful enough. His want of skill had caused a troubled soul to slip through his fingers. He scarcely heard what the next few penitents were saying.

"*I slapped my son in anger . . .*"

"*I refused my wifely duties . . .*"

"*I was slothful about the house . . .*"

He was jerked out of his daze by a sourish, stale reek of alcohol, the aftermath of prolonged and excessive drinking. The man kneeling in the penitent's booth was so large that sheer bulkiness brought his head and face close to the screen. A hangover breath, and a bad one, assailed Father Stephen's nostrils. He drew out his handkerchief, held it to his nose. The man was sober enough now, but desolation and remorse were in his bent head and discouraged voice.

"I broke my pledge again, Father," he announced in a mumble of self-loathing. "It started last Saturday . . . a week ago."

More cautious now, Father Steve waited.

"I spent my pay, and gave my wife the back of my hand when she asked me where it all went. She cried bitterly, not at the blow so much, but the sight of me lying drunk in front of my children, with no job left and a broken pledge besides." He breathed heavily. The flood of self-pity subsided.

"Where do you do all this drinking? Malden has no saloons."

"I go to Boston. Around Dover Street mostly."

Stephen knew the region — a sink of derelicts. "Why do you pour this terrible poison into your body, made in the image and likeness of God?"

The big man shook his head hopelessly. "I don't know, Father. If you asked me, like you are now, I couldn't tell you. I don't mean to get drunk. I don't want to. But I do."

Just like that. No convivial glass lifting, no cheerful clink to the accompaniment of song. Only a compulsive alcoholic, fumbling for the neck of his bottle. Stephen, helpless, without answer, almost overpowered by the man's breath, begged inwardly for a spark of God's grace to fall on him.

"How old are you?" Stephen sparred for time. This one must not get away.

"Forty-one."

Still no spark. Instead, physical nauseating revulsion. "What's your job?"

"I'm a stonemason, Father. A good one. I can always get work when I'm sober."

The odor was making Stephen ill. In another moment he would have to break out of his box and run for the fresh air in the bricked courtyard. St. Stephen, the patron saint of stonemasons, must have seen his namesake twirling a withered branch of helplessness — for the spark *did* fall. The glimmering of a plan.

"Come around to the parish house tomorrow afternoon," said Stephen. "I'll have a talk with you. Perhaps I can find you a job helping Father Monaghan on the new school. Then you wouldn't have to pass all those swinging doors on Dover Street."

"Would you do that, Father?"

"We'll see. Now make an act of contrition and ask God to have mercy on you and your family."

Wretchedly, the last confession heard, Father Stephen stumbled out of the box at ten-thirty P.M. Every muscle in his body was aching, every nerve taut and exhausted. His head was split by an ax of pain, his cheeks were flushed, the membranes of his throat dry as old flannel. And his spirit, which had soared with exaltation at suppertime, was now flat in the dust.

Dizzily he straggled into the open air, strode up and down the strip of bricked courtyard.

"I never knew. I never knew," he kept saying to himself. "God forgive me. I never knew."

Paul Ireton fell into step beside him, solicitous but silent.

"No one ever told me, Paul."

"It can't be told," said Father Ireton.

Steve's finger pressed his throbbing temples. "In all the books," he said, "sin was an abstraction, a remote depersonalized theory about man's failure to realize God's will. But here it's an ulcer burrowing in the flesh, a rage in the blood, a mortal itch in man's brain, a rank wind in his belly."

"Bend with that wind, Stephen, or it will knock you over."

"I'm not thinking of myself, Paul. It's the people, with their dirty laundry bag of little sins and the cancerous burden of the big ones. How can anyone help them?" Stephen's grief was half guilt, half sweating sorrow for his fellow men. "What does one do?"

"Got you down, has it?" said Father Paul.

"Flat on the ground."

Paul Ireton put his arm around the young curate's shoulders. "There's this much to be said for the horizontal attitude, Steve. It has a long tradition behind it. Don't ever forget that Christ, too, spent a bad night flat on the ground, under some olive trees a long way from Malden, Mass."

They took a few turns up and down the brick areaway. "Come into the house," said Paul Ireton. "I'll give you a couple of aspirin."

CHAPTER 3

THE RECORDER of minor annals, lay and ecclesiastic, making his entries for the Archdiocese of Boston as of Sunday, May 2, 1915, would have had a full but mixed book by sundown.

HOLLOWED-EYED Filomena Restucci, kneeling at the shrine of the Virgin in the basement of St. Margaret's Church, fixed her eyes on the lily-fringed heart of the Madonna and lighted a candle for the speedy recovery of her sweetheart, Victor Provenzano. If Victor hadn't been stabbed twenty-four hours ago in a knife fight, he would have married her this day. Now, two months pregnant, Filomena wept natural tears and beseeched a miracle. "Let my Vittorio live, Madonna of Sorrows. Stop the blood coming from his mouth, and I will make to you a perpetual novena of my life."

She lifted her eyes to Mary's statue, and screamed as she saw blood dripping from the Madonna's flower-crowned heart.

ASSISTANT Manager R. W. Bailey of the Boston Streetcar Company strode up and down his office, addressing a small audience of common *mozos* variegated in height, size, and demeanor, yet all sharing a certain ferretish aspect of nose and eyes. Assistant Manager Bailey, eligible as a case history in any textbook on peptic ulcers, was now giving his listeners some ulcers of their own.

"Conductors all over Boston are getting away with grand larceny," he screamed. "Unless you spotters bring in a dozen of these dirty-fingered bastards next week, I'll see to it personally that you're all fired." He waved a sheet of paper at them. "These figures show that the company is losing five hundred dollars a month in knocked-down nickels. That figure must be reduced to zero. Zero, you hear?"

Manager Bailey's tone and manner changed from nagging to suspicion. He pointed a nicotine-yellow forefinger at his huddling listeners. "There's a law that takes care of spotters in cahoots with crooked conductors. Now get the hell out of here, all of you, and prove that you're on the level. Go on . . . get out. . . ."

MONICA, loveliest of the Fermoyle clan, walked nervously to a scheduled part of Forest Dale cemetery to meet her sweetheart, whom she was not allowed to invite to her home. A thin, good-looking Jewish boy stepped out from behind a copper beech and said, "Darling, I thought you'd never get here." Thereupon he took her arm and led her to a still more secluded part of the cemetery where they sat on the grassy knoll, talked, kissed, and kissed again till dark.

SPIRIDION LARIOS, proprietor of the Gamecock Café, peeled a ten-dollar bill from an indecently large roll, and handed it to a stoutish young man in an ascot tie and chamois-topped shoes. "Go 'way," said Larios. "You giva my customers earache. Pipple say, 'Mr. Larios, you got nize place here, but who tol' that Irish Thrush heza piccola-player?' "

Larios laughed at his own misrendering of the old joke and poured himself a giant thimbleful of Metaxa brandy.

HIS EMINENCE LAWRENCE CARDINAL GLENNON sat at one of the three ebony Steinways in the magnificent study of his episcopal mansion, repeating contemplatively eight sedative measures of Bach. To facilitate the fingering of this passage, which in the Cardinal's opinion contained the whole secret of counterpoint, he removed the massive sapphire from the third finger of his right hand, and laid it on the music rack. He solved the passage, and, moving on to the next invention, raised his large hazel-gray eyes to an early Mantegna that was gathering to its umbers the last golden rays of an afternoon sun. Tranquillity lay at least epidermis-deep upon the Cardinal's domed forehead, and softened the diagonal gash of his large mouth. But the involuntary twitchings of the trigeminal nerves, running from the lobe of his ear to the sole (so to speak) of his heavy but not fat chin, would have revealed to any member of his retinue that Number One was about to blow off. No member of the retinue was in the study at the time; they had all taken to their quarters and were busy battening down the hatches in preparation for the coming storm.

The Bach-Mantegna medicine lulled Lawrence Cardinal Glennon for about twenty minutes before he remembered why he was dosing himself. Abruptly now it all came back to him. He rose from his piano stool and jammed the sapphire ring back onto its official finger. He snatched irritably at a copy of *The Monitor,* the Catholic weekly published under his direction, took a brief vexed glance at its front page, then slapped it against the polished surface of his pearl-inlaid desk.

"Is there no priest in this Diocese who can write English with a bite to it?" he bellowed.

No answer forthcoming, he jerked at a brocaded bell rope. His secretary appeared with Japanese celerity, pencil poised, pad in hand. "Scour every parish in New England for an editor who'll get some crunch into this paper," said the Cardinal. "Meanwhile send Monsignor O'Brien in to me. I want him to write a ringing editorial against the murders going on at the Boston Maternity Hospital. Crushing babies' heads, are they? I want every doctor in Boston to know just where the Catholic Church stands in this matter."

He ground his massive ring into the palm of his left hand as if sealing the doom of baby-killers. "Send O'Brien in to me."

IN THE KITCHEN of their five-room railroad flat on Tileston Street, Malden, large, suety James Splaine, stonemason, talked hopefully to his wife. "Julie," he said, "that new young priest is a saint. He talked to me for an hour when I went to see him this evening. Not a word of religious guff. He says to me, 'Jim, if you had a job in Malden here, a job that didn't take you past all those swinging doors on Dover Street, do you think you could stay sober?' 'Why sure, Father,' I said. 'It's the whiff of the stuff coming out of those places that makes it so hard.' Then he says, 'I've put in a word to Pastor Monaghan for a job on the foundation of the new school. You can walk to work and home again without ever passing a barroom. The rest is up to you, Jim.' "

Julia Splaine, stringy-haired, greasy-wrappered, put in a

word. "Is it true now what he said about me collecting your pay?"

"True as true, Julie. Every Saturday you just go down to the priest house and get my envelope from Father Fermoyle himself."

Blessed be the mother who bore him, thought Julia Splaine; she must be a wonderful woman.

THE REVEREND WILLIAM MONAGHAN unloosed the three center buttons of his cassock, stretched his large legs under the roll-topped desk in his room, and lighted his evening cigar. His favorite dinner of barley soup, roast beef, and boiled potatoes lay just behind him, and an evening of "counting up" — the happiest time of the week — lay just ahead. In the top drawer of his desk were four canvas bank bags, three of them fat with bills and coins collected at the nine-, ten-, and eleven-o'clock Masses that Sunday; the fourth bag held the miscellaneous coins, mostly nickels and pennies taken that week from the poor boxes, the votive-candle offerings, and the pamphlet racks.

He was halfway through his first cigar when he started counting; his third cigar was a cold stub when the last penny had been tallied. He added up his jottings: $1156.44. A creditable sum. Deduct the tithes he must forward to the diocesan treasury, and there would still be more than a thousand dollars left to carry on the work of his parish. A payment on the new electric organ, the salaries of his curates, the upkeep of the parish house. Not to mention a little sum that must be set aside for the repair of the church furnace and the steam pipes, long overdue.

Not to mention the new parochial school.

The pastor drew out a small deck of bankbooks, unsnapped the elastic band holding them together, and studied the figures therein: Malden Savings Bank, $5500; Malden Trust Company, $3500; First National of Boston, $11,000; Medford Savings Bank, $4200. He totaled them: $24,200. His glacial blue eyes thawed when he saw that his cash position amply warranted the start of the much-needed parochial school.

From the altar at High Mass that morning he had made his announcement to a crowded upper church. "Dear Parishioners," he had said in his hoarse pulpit voice, "by virtue of God's grace and your generosity, we will start digging tomorrow on the new school. Ten long years — years of bountiful giving on your part and stewardly saving on mine — have brought us to this propitious time and place. But though a beginning will be made, 'tis only a beginning. The school will cost three times as much as we have on hand, and though the local banks have promised to see us through, this means, my dear people, that you must continue to give, and I must continue to save. Meanwhile the regular expenses of the parish do not — y'mm — decrease. This church in which you now worship needs new heating equipment; the furnace and the pipes are almost beyond repair. And the house in which your pastor and curates live needs tearing down completely, it's that old. How often I've been stopped on the street and had people say, 'Father Monaghan, when are you going to build a new parish house for St. Margaret's? The old one is a disgrace.' And my answer always is, 'St. Margaret's will get a new parish house after the parochial school is built and paid for.' Meanwhile don't worry about me or the curates. None of us will be rained on in our beds — you can be sure of that. I will now read the Gospel for this Sunday. But before that, I want to make one more announcement. If any among you are looking for jobs on the new school, don't come to me. McBurney Brothers, the well-known contractors, are in charge. See them. I'm running a parish, not an employment agency. The Gospel for this Sunday . . ."

From a pigeonhole in his desk Father Monaghan drew a tube of blue-prints, spread them out lovingly, and gazed at the plans of the new school. Three stories high, faced with finest Quincy granite, thirty classrooms, a gymnasium, a recreation hall, a chapel for the nuns. All modern, fireproof, up-to-date. It would be called the Cheverus School, in honor of that long-dead fighting missionary bishop of Massachusetts, Louis Cheverus. The Cardinal himself had chosen the name.

Outside Pastor Monaghan's window rose the clatter of voices, shrill, foreign-sounding, hysterical. He glanced at his watch: nine-forty-five P.M. What tumult was going on at this hour? Monaghan flung up his window and saw a throng of people milling about in the bricked areaway at the entrance

to the basement church. Unseemly. Disorderly. Must be
stopped. Pastor Monaghan stepped to his door and called in
a shipmaster's voice: "Father Fermoyle."

Steve appeared at his own doorway. "Yes, Father."

"Go down into the areaway and see what all that shouting
is about. Sounds like a lot of Pastafazoolis drunk on dago red.
Get them out of there. Do you hear?"

"Right away, sir." Steve clapped on his biretta and slipped
downstairs. At the edge of the bricked areaway he heard cries
of, *"Miracolo! Miracolo! . . . La bella Madonna ha fatta uno
miracolo."* Steve shouldered his way through the mob till he
saw Val McGuire braced against the door of the basement
church.

"What's going on here, Val?"

Whey-faced, the sexton explained. "They say a miracle
has happened, Father. Some girl came in here this afternoon,
lit a candle in front of the Blessed Mother. Then she went
home and found that her boy friend, good as dead from a
stiletto stab, was sitting up in bed, asking for his spaghetti.
These wops have been flocking up in droves here ever since.
I'm trying to get them out so I can lock up."

A woman, shawled, with an infant in her arms, pushed
toward Father Stephen. "My baby vomiting these-a three
days," she cried. "The Blessed Madonna will make him keep
milk down."

"Wait, little mother," said Father Stephen. "We'll go in
together." Facing the crowd, he lifted his voice and addressed them in the language they knew best.

"Children of the Miraculous Queen of Heaven," he cried in
the declamatory style matching their mood, "listen to your
priest."

"We listen. Speak to us, Father."

"The Virgin has performed a deed of great wonder here
today. You, her children, weeping and wailing in this valley
of tears, wish to honor this most tender of advocates. You come
to light candles, to pray, to ask her intercession. That is most
pleasing to her. But all this must be done in the spirit of
orderly devotion. I will lead you. Follow me, in reverent
silence, to the feet of the Madonna."

Sexton McGuire tugged at Stephen's elbow. "But it's ten

o'clock, time to lock up," he protested, pulling out his watch.

"Come on, Val, put that ticker in your pocket. Miracles don't happen by the clock. Help me form them into a single line now, that's the good man."

Into the dimly lighted church, down the side aisle to the Virgin's statue, Stephen led the hushed throng. They packed the pews nearest the shrine, overflowed into the aisle, buzzing like excited hornets. Stephen approached the triple tier of candles blazing in fiery apostrophes before the little niche sheltering the figure of the Virgin. It was a tawdry chalk statue in the style prescribed by local taste and tradition. A gilt-pronged crown sat on the Virgin's head; beneath a face of serene purity, she held the nestling Infant in the hollow of her right arm, while her left index finger pointed toward the apex of her lily-crowned heart. Kneeling at the shrine, Stephen gazed upward at the statue.

Blood-red drops falling from the Virgin's heart were splashing in a tiny pool at the base of the statue.

"If I could only dip my finger into that stuff," thought Stephen. But a buzz like the flight of asthmatic hornets rose behind him. No time for scrutiny now. Emotions were bubbling dangerously. He must drain them off somehow. How?

By prayer. What prayer? The Rosary, of course.

Stephen turned to the people. "This is the first Sunday of May," he said. "The month of Mary song." The feeble wail of a retching baby was the only sound in the church. "Let us garland her with flowers — the flowers of the Five Glorious Mysteries of the Holy Rosary."

Father Monaghan, storming into the basement to find out for himself what was going on, saw five hundred bent heads, and heard his curate's clear voice uttering the first part of the Angelical Salutation:

"Hail Mary, full of grace, the Lord is with thee, blessed art thou amongst women, and blessed is the fruit of thy womb, Jesus."

To which five hundred voices responded:

"Holy Mary, Mother of God, pray for us sinners now and at the hour of our death. Amen."

Father Monaghan tiptoed out of the church. "He's sure got a way with these wops," he murmured.

Father Stephen Fermoyle said the Rosary five times before the crowd was completely calm. Meanwhile the drops continued to fall. There was awe in the eyes of the Italians as they filed singly past the Virgin's statue on their way out. The last to leave was the woman with the retching baby. "Look," she said to Father Fermoyle, peace in her voice and eyes, "he has not thrown up since Rosary began."

It was one A.M. before the church was empty. "Now," said Father Steve, "we'll see what goes on." He opened the gate before the Virgin's shrine, came close to the statue, and reached out to touch the crimson heart with his finger. As he did so, a soft red splash fell on his fingernail.

He looked upward into the ceiling shadows, high above the Virgin's head. Rusty water, falling from a steampipe, was leaking down, a drop at a time, onto the heart of Mary! It struck the cheap brilliant color in a solvent splash and continued falling to the floor.

"Wait till Dollar Bill hears this," said Father Steve.

"The Miracle of the Leaking Steampipe," as Paul Ireton called it, was nipped early next morning by a crew of plumbers. Under the sound of their hammers the mystical music died, but its echo lingered on. It lingered in the heart of Filomena Restucci, who was married to her Vittorio a few days later at a nuptial Mass celebrated by Father Stephen Fermoyle. It lingered in the heart of the shawled woman whose baby died of an intestinal obstruction. And especially it lingered in the memory of Pastor William Monaghan.

"I've got myself a curate at last," he told his crony, Flynn of Lynn. "A funny combination he is, too. A proud-walking American — if carriage is any sign, Gene, he'll end up with a miter at least — and sprung from good Irish stock, the Fermoyles of Medford. His father is on the cars, I hear, and he has a sister with the Carmelites. But the luckiest part of it, Gene" — Pastor Monaghan put it to his colleague as one Leinster man telling a tale of wonder to another — "the luckiest part of it is . . . he knows how to get along with those Eyetalians."

HAVING GOTTEN HIMSELF a curate, Father Monaghan now proceeded to put him to work. There was plenty for Steve to do.

With his priesthood honing in him like a trident, he waded chin-deep into parish waters. He celebrated Mass daily, alternating with Father Lyons at the six-thirty A.M. service. He baptized babies, and was quite expert at soothing their shrieks after the holy water had been poured over their soft pink heads. "Where'd you learn that trick, Father?" asked an admiring young mother after Stephen had hushed her squalling infant.

"Had plenty of practice as a kid," said Steve, laughing. "I played first base with a baby in my arms till I was fourteen years old. It's all in the jounce. Here, let me show you. No, not straight up and down — babies like the horizontal jounce, stomachside up. But when you *bubble* them, lay them over your shoulder — like this."

On three evenings a week he stood house watch, patiently listening to the troubles of garrulous old women who came in to have a medal blessed, then launched forth upon the unselected details of their life. Getting them out the front door with their tale still in the telling was a triumph of tact. Observing Steve's manner with these "old biddies," Monaghan promptly made him spiritual adviser to the Married Women's Sodality.

"But what'll I say to them?" Steve was genuinely puzzled.

A cheerful grunt rumbled out of Monaghan's chest. "Your mother and father had a big family, didn't they?"

"Yes."

"And when your father came home from work, your mother had a hot supper ready for him, didn't she? Night after night, no matter what else happened, there was the supper, and he always got served first, didn't he?"

"Why, yes, he did. She always used to say, 'A hungry man is an angry man,' as she handed him his food."

"A smart woman. And when supper was over she washed the dishes while he read the paper in his stocking feet, didn't she?"

"Usually."

"Then they had a few words, maybe about money or the children, sometimes pleasant, sometimes not so pleasant — which might have ended in a family brawl if one of them hadn't given in to the other. Isn't that the way it was with them?"

"Just about," said Steve.

"Then around nine or nine-thirty your father went to bed while she worked around the house, darning socks or making a batch of bread while she spoke with her children. And when it was all done, she went upstairs, or wherever their bedroom was, and laid her tired head on the pillow beside him." Pastor Monaghan's blue eyes sought confirmation in his young curate's face. "Isn't that about the way things went, Father Fermoyle?"

Stephen nodded. Justness and knowledge, uncolored by sentimentality, were in the picture that Dollar Bill had drawn.

"I think now," said Monaghan, "you'll have no trouble in saying the few words required of you at the Married Women's Sodality." The tight curl in the pastor's hair seemed to loosen a trifle. "In my judgment, Father, the best training for the priesthood is to be brought up in a big family by a good father and mother. The values are sound. They can be applied anywhere. And were I the Pope, writing an encyclical, I'd say that these values are the hope of the world."

Stephen did not tell his pastor that a great Pope had already written such an encyclical. Monaghan wouldn't have read it, anyway. He wouldn't have to, thought Steve. Thereafter, when the new spiritual adviser to the Married Women's Sodality lacked material for his homilies, he merely tapped the gusher of his old knowledge of Celia and Dennis Fermoyle.

BY LONG TRADITION, the supervision of Sunday school was automatically taken over by the junior curate. Every Sunday afternoon Stephen heard children lisp, stammer, or reel off the answers to questions in the blue-green catechism. (Q) Who is God? (A) God is the Creator of heaven and earth and all things. (Q) Why did God make you? (A) God made me to know Him, love Him, and serve Him in this world, and to be happy with Him forever in the next.

How simply the penny catechism stated the essential terms of the covenant between God and man! In its taut counter-point of question-and-answer Stephen heard echoes of Aquinas the Angelic Doctor thundering out his divinely inspired propositions. And here, seven hundred years later, those propositions, unchanged and unimpaired, were being given new utterance in a Western tongue of whose existence Aquinas had never dreamed. Might it not come about that these same questions and answers would one day be recited in languages yet unformed on the tongue of man?

Stephen found special delight in examining his Sunday-school pupils on points not covered by the catechism. One Sunday afternoon he propounded a puzzler to a class of thirteen-year-old boys:

"Can Protestants go to heaven?" he asked.

Young faces, blank, bewildered, gazed up at him. What kind of trick question was Father Fermoyle pulling? Stephen saw a bright talkative boy, Charlie Boyle, holding up his hand.

"Well, Charlie, can Protestants go to heaven?"

"Of course not, Father," said Charlie. "Everyone knows" — his voice broke in a comical adolescent croak — "that only Catholics are let in."

Father Steve nodded solemnly at the upturned faces. "Do you all believe what Charlie says?"

"Yes, Father," came the obedient chorus.

"Sorry," said Steve, "but you're all wrong. No matter what you've heard elsewhere, the Catholic Church teaches that *anyone* — Protestant, Jew, or Mohammedan — who sincerely believes in his own religion, and who lives up to its teachings, can get to heaven."

He let this astounding fact sink in, then continued: "It is true that God has given special blessings to the Catholic Church and has made it the divine instrument of salvation. But wouldn't it be hard to believe that the same God who loved mankind well enough to send them His Son would turn His face away from billions of His children?" Stephen paused, wondering how much their young minds could absorb. "We must honor the religion of our neighbor just as a great modern missionary, Cardinal Lavigerie, honored the Mohammedans he went to convert. He sought earnestly to win them to the Catholic faith, but so great was his respect for their religion that whenever he passed a mosque, he alighted from his carriage and *walked!*"

The boys heard what Father Fermoyle said, and they saw

that he meant it. But they were still unconvinced. After he had gone, Charlie Boyle spoke for the lot of them by mumbling: "If it's true like he says — that any old hard-shell Baptist can get into heaven — what's the use of going to all this trouble to be a Catholic?"

ONE OF Monaghan's insistencies was the "house call" — that constant round of visits to every home in the parish. "Look to your flock" was a cardinal point in his pastorate; as a younger man he had been a tireless roundsman of the Lord, ringing doorbells or knocking at doors without bells. But he had long ago delegated the chore of parish visitation to his curates, requiring from them a weekly list of the homes they had entered and a general report of the conditions they found there. One day he called Stephen into his study and instructed him on the art of the house-to-house visit.

"You're familiar with the chief spiritual works of mercy, Father?" Dollar Bill began.

"Of course."

"Run over them, just to refresh my mind."

Stephen felt like one of his own catechism scholars. "The chief spiritual works of mercy," he replied, "are seven: to admonish the sinner, to instruct the ignorant, to counsel the doubtful, to comfort the sorrowful — "

"That's fine," interrupted Monaghan. "Now look you, Father, these spiritual works are prescribed for the layman, which is not to say that they don't apply to a priest. The best means of practicing them — far and away the best — is the house-to-house call. It's an institution with us here at St. Margaret's. No special hours or days are set apart for it, but whenever you've got an afternoon that you don't know what to do with, or a morning that hangs heavy on your hands, just devote it to the honor and glory of God by making a few parish calls."

"I'll do so, Father." Stephen started to go, but Monaghan recalled him with a pastoral finger.

"After you've admonished, instructed, or just listened to troubles as the case may be, you will be offered a bit of refreshment in the way of tea or coffee, bread and butter. This I would strongly advise you *not* to accept. First, because often enough it'll be a drain on their pantries. And in the second place, the drinking of tea and the munching of cakes may lead to — y'mm — relaxations of tongue and mind that don't always turn out to a curate's advantage — if you take my meaning, Father."

"I do," said Stephen.

"And one last thing, Father Fermoyle. These poor women — and they'll be mostly women you'll meet — will be forever trying to press a little money into your hand as you take your leave. They'll say, 'This is for yourself, Father,' or, 'Here's a little something for your special charity.' It's their good heart prompting them to piece out the meager pay they know a curate gets."

Dollar Bill weighed his next words as if measuring out his own blood. "You're under no obligation to take this money, Father; and oftener than not, the poor souls who offer it need it more than you. But if you *do* take it" — and here Monaghan spoke with the force of a man who had thrown the devil of indecision over a cliff — "*I want all such money turned over to me!* It belongs to the parish. If you weren't a curate at St. Margaret's, you wouldn't be getting it. Is that clear?"

"Quite clear," said Stephen. He closed the door and went to his own room to sort out the curiously mixed instructions his pastor had given him. What a marvelously consistent piece of work the man was! A true shepherd of his flock, a master in the niceties of official conduct, a veteran calculator of probabilities, and the unrelenting collector of the coin of parish tribute.

From these pragmatic woolgatherings Stephen was aroused by the knock of Bridget Loonan, the housekeeper. In the unenthusiastic voice reserved for new curates she said, "Your sister Rita phoned while you were in with him." (Mrs. Loonan always referred to her employer by the third-person pronoun. "'He' wants to see you" . . . "The Cardinal is begging 'him' to take a bigger parish.") "Your sister says to call her right away at Beacon 1218."

Stephen called the unfamiliar number. Rita's voice, tremulous with anxiety, was saying, "Steve dear, I'm at Dr. John's, 12 West Newton Street. Can you get over here this evening? John's in trouble."

"What's he done?"

"It's what he *hasn't* done. Oh, Steve, they want him to kill babies with forceps or some such thing. If he doesn't promise to kill them, he'll lose his appointment, and we won't be able to get married." Rita checked her panic. "Please come over, Steve. Dr. John'll explain it all to you."

"I'll be there at eight." Steve made his calculations to get out of house duty that evening. Would Milky Lyons stand in for him? No, the Milky one couldn't — he was playing whist that evening at the home of Annie K. Regan, chiropodist and arbiter of the medium-high social circle of Malden. How Milky was permitted to spend so much time munching cakes and relaxing his mind was something Stephen couldn't quite understand. Distracted, Steve turned to Paul Ireton for help.

"Sure, Steve. I'll take over for you. Say nothing about it to Monaghan. What he doesn't know will never hurt him."

A few minutes after eight o'clock Steve rang the doorbell of a shabby brownstone house on West Newton Street — a region of Boston almost entirely taken over by medical students and interns. He climbed three flights of dark stairs, saw the crack of light at an open door. There was Dr. John Byrne, paler, gaunter than ever, greeting him. Rita, in tears, arose from a lumpy horsehair sofa and threw her arms about Stephen's neck.

"What's this I hear about killing babies?" asked Steve.

"Sounds ridiculous, doesn't it?" said Dr. Byrne. "But it's true. If you can bear hearing another man's troubles . . ."

Stephen loved him for that. He sat beside Rita while Dr. John got into the middle of things.

"As you know, Steve, I'm beginning my last year of residency at the City General. It's a fine appointment. Among other things, I see a lot of obstetrics, rare cases that would baffle the average practitioner. Of course, most births are normal, but in the past month we've run into an unusual series of big-headed babies — so big-headed (to keep it non-technical) that they just can't get through the birth canal."

"I thought they performed Caesareans in such cases."

"Smart, foresighted doctors who take measurements in time can perform a Caesarean. But a great many mothers never go near an M.D. till the day a child is born. Then it's too late for measurements. If the birth is started, and the infant's skull gets wedged in the pelvis" — Dr. John's hand closed over Rita's — "then you've got something serious. And that's exactly what's happened three times in the past month."

"What do you do about it?"

"Routine practice among non-Catholic doctors calls for a craniotomy — that is, the crushing of the infant's skull."

"But that's murder," said Stephen.

Dr. John Byrne sat dejectedly on the edge of his desk. "I know. That's why I refused to perform one yesterday. The mother died." Memory racked him. "Her husband made a terrible scene. Took a punch at me. I don't blame him much. Now he's suing the City General. In self-protection the hospital will hereafter require every intern to sign a paper saying that he'll perform what's known as a 'therapeutic abortion' when, as, and if the situation demands."

"And if you don't sign?"

"I'll lose my appointment."

Stephen knew that to toss away a residency at the City General was to ruin all prospects of advancement among the surgical elite of Boston. The Harvard crowd that controlled the best hospitals might occasionally admit an Irish-Catholic of unusual promise — as they had admitted John Byrne. But if for any reason he lost his place, it meant a second-grade career, the rat race of minor surgery: tonsils, hemorrhoids, fifty-dollar deliveries, with an occasional hernia or appendix as the ultimate top. No chance at the nice thyroids, bowel resections, or end-to-end anastomoses. You stepped aside, even in the Grade B hospitals that took you in, and watched a man from City General coolly enter a belly, and considered it a wonderful break if he asked you to sew up after him.

Obliged by every canon of faith to uphold the commandment "Thou shalt not kill," Stephen could not bring himself to exert pressure on a good man faced by such a choice

"When do you make your decision?"

Dr. John Byrne gazed at his scrubbed bony hands as though apologizing to them for the hack work that stretched ahead. "I've made it already, Steve. I told Dr. Kennard this morning I couldn't sign."

Rita's full fresh lips pressed against Dr. John's cheek. "My man's no baby-killer," she said.

Stephen was wrothy. "You can make an issue of it," he flared. "If the Cardinal knew that murder was now mandatory at the City General, he'd break the thing wide open. The more I think about it, the madder I get." He seized John's high bony shoulders. "How about my nailing this right onto the Cardinal's door as a test case?"

Dr. John shook his head. "No — that's not the way to handle it, Steve. You'd only get a name for meddling in affairs beyond the jurisdiction of a curate. Besides, I happen to know that the attitude at the Chancery is 'hands off.' There'll be a ringing editorial about it in *The Monitor*, but as for interfering with the internal management of the City General, well — Number One is too smart for that."

John Byrne's diagnostic turn of mind let him see the other side of the case. "I can understand why, Steve. To the lay mind, the Church's position in this skull-crushing business is a nasty one to defend." He hooked a long arm around Rita's waist. "Most men, myself included, feel that a living wife is more valuable than a dead baby."

Watching Rita's head find a natural place under Dr. John's collarbone, Steve understood very well. "What's your next step, John?"

Humor too grim for smiling, too controlled for bitterness, played through John Byrne's reply. "Oh, I'll open up shop in South Boston and write prescriptions for people with sniffles and hangovers. I may even get some life-insurance examinations at a dollar apiece. And don't forget, I'm supposed to be an obstetrician. People in South Boston have a lot of babies, and at the last minute they'll be asking Dr. Byrne to kindly step around with his little black bag, and please bring his own soap because the rats ate the last piece in the house. There'll be plenty to do, once I get started. Meanwhile, Rita and I — well, I guess we'll just keep on waiting."

For the first time in his life Stephen wished that he had a great deal of money. He would say to this wonderful pair: "Look, you two. Here's twenty-five thousand dollars. Get married right away and buy a house in Brookline, with enough room for five or six kids. Then you, John, set yourself up on

Commonwealth Avenue, with waiting rooms, receptionists, and nurses — out-Brahmin the Brahmin doctors at their own game of high-priced surgery."

How childish! No, salvation didn't come that way to people like John Byrne and Rita Fermoyle. Steve said the thing he really believed. "I'm glad you made the decision, John. It's tough — but there's nothing else you could have done."

He kissed Rita, shook hands with Dr. John, and felt his way down the dark, banistered stairs. He knew that as soon as he closed the door, Rita's consoling mouth would be under her John's. The knowledge brought only gladness. In a world of grief, frustration, and loneliness, when men and women kissed and clung to one another for mutual support, Stephen felt neither alone nor unsupported.

A sea of greater love buoyed him; he floated on its sustaining wave.

Yet as he reviewed John Byrne's decision, Stephen saw quite clearly that God's weather was not always halcyon. The sea of faith could buffet as well as sustain. To accept its salt chastisement without whimpering required extraordinary self-discipline and perfect trust.

"When my test comes," prayed Stephen, "grant, Lord, that I shall not murmur against the rigors of Thy love."

CHAPTER 4

IN TRAINING the new crop of altar boys, Stephen crashed into unexpected trouble.

A peculiar situation, of long standing and not wholly intelligible to Steve, had developed in St. Margaret's: a mysterious young man named Lewis Day had installed himself as a combination of sacristan, verger, and personal acolyte to Pastor Monaghan, and devoted himself so single-heartedly to assisting him at High Mass that the pastor nourished the illusion that his curates were as well served as himself. Actually there was a grave shortage of altar boys, and the quality of their performance was unforgivably poor.

Lew Day, in addition to being the perfect acolyte, had gradually taken over complete care of the altar Its linen,

candles, and flowers were in his charge, and he performed
his duties so scrupulously that he could (and did) beat off
all attempts of well-meaning female parishioners to share his
labors as sacristan. Lew had gone even further; he had fitted
up a little room off the sacristy as a workshop, and in this
monastic cubbyhole he polished candlesticks, filled the sanctuary lamps, and exercised his talent for painting on parchment.
The illuminated altar cards in the upper church were Lew's
handiwork, and he had also painted in crimson and gold the
Latin inscription invoking a gift of purity in body and soul.
This he had hung over the sacristy washbowl:

> *Da, Domine, virtutem manibus meis ad abster-*
> *gendam omnem maculam, ut sine pollutione*
> *mentis et corporis valeam tibi servire.*

More recently Lew had begun to mend and repair the
sacred vestments belonging to St. Margaret's. At his own
expense he purchased gold and silver-thread, and by skillful
use of his embroidery needle kept many a brocaded garment
in service long after its time. All this he did so quietly and
self-effacingly that it was difficult for Sexton McGuire, or
anyone else, to lodge a complaint against him.

Such was the situation when Father Stephen undertook to
reorganize the altar-boy system. At various times he had seen
Lew Day gliding like a wraith into his cubbyhole, or kneeling
with bowed head within the sanctuary, but Steve had always
hesitated to break in on the young man's work or devotions.
Puzzled by the air of mystery hanging about this shy soul,
Stephen applied to Father Paul Ireton for information.

"What's the story on Lew Day?"

"A sad one, Steve. But there's no secret about it. When he
was seventeen or thereabouts, Lew went away to one of the
monastic orders. You can see why. There's not a trace of the
secular in him. Well, just before he took his final vows" —
Father Ireton wasn't being his usual outspoken self — "they
discovered that his nervous system wasn't — quite strong
enough. His heart's locked in the sanctuary, but they won't
let him be a priest. So he takes it out by being just about the
best acolyte that ever assisted at the altar." Father Ireton

turned his gray eyes full on the younger priest. "Handle him gently, Steve. He bruises easy."

"Should I ask him to help me with the new altar-boy setup — or go around him entirely?"

Paul Ireton pondered the question. "No matter how you handle Lew, he's going to be hurt. Everything considered, perhaps it might be better to tell him what you're planning to do."

Tact was uppermost in Stephen's manner as he approached the brooding young man in his little workshop. Lew Day was about twenty-three, frail-boned, with thin, silky hair baldish at the crown, as though nature had given him the tonsure that the Church withheld. Steve found him sitting on a high stool, diligently rubbing metal polish into a massive candlestick. Some reticent dignity about this strange young man kept Steve from being too brisk as he outlined his plan.

"Lew, I turn green with envy every time I see you assisting at High Mass. Do you suppose you could help me train a few kids in the lost art of serving properly?"

Eyes downcast, Lew applied metal polish to the base of the candlestick. "How can I help?" he asked. Undertone of self-pity added, "An ordained priest doesn't need help from a poor reject like me."

Temperament, thought Steve. Mr. Lew Day is touchy, all right. Aloud he said: "I can put the kids in shape for Low Mass, Lew — but I'll need someone to help me while I'm getting them ready to serve at a Solemn High." Steve let his enthusiasm ride. "You and I, celebrant and deacon, will run through the Mass for them on the sacristy altar. When they see how Mass should be served, it may mean the start of a new tradition here at St. Margaret's. What do you say?"

Conflict agitated the frail verger. He saw clearly enough that his monopoly of the high altar must now be divided among a herd of young ruffians. A galling surrender. Yet here was a sympathetic and very pleasant priest inviting him to take part in a project that might lead to a — a friendship that a soul as lonely as Lew Day's could not afford to reject. The struggle showed outwardly in his almost hysterical rubbing of the candlestick with a piece of chamois. Finally the passive part of his nature asserted itself. He laid down his polishing cloth and said submissively, "I'll do whatever pleases *you*, Father."

The emotional note, underscored by a timid lifting of the eyelids, surprised Steve. Embarrassed by Lew's capitulation — sudden, personal, and complete — he found himself talking too rapidly. "There won't be much to it . . . a couple of sessions should whip things into shape. Some of those kids will take on a high polish. I mean . . ."

The tension was broken by a sound like a herd of yearling bulls all trying to push through the sacristy door at the same time. It was the new crop of altar boys, brash, clumsy, and un-Latined, reporting for their first drill. Father Steve closed Lew's door behind him and stepped out into the sacristy to take command. He lined the boys up and proceeded to forget all about Lew Day as he gave the jostling, undisciplined youngsters the settling treatment of his voice and eyes.

"Boys," he began, "from now on, you're going to have privileges denied to all but special servants of God. You'll be allowed inside the altar railing; you will ascend the steps of the altar. You will be close to sacred vessels; and the Mass Book will be entrusted to your hands. It's important, therefore, that your hands be clean."

A sudden thrusting of hands behind backs. "We'll spend the next fifteen minutes at the sacristy washbowl," said Steve. "Small boys first. And don't spare the soap."

Afterwards, hands scrubbed, hair combed, and faces two or three shades cleaner, the boys lined up again.

"That's fine," said Father Steve. "Outwardly, you're in prime shape. Now the next thing is what we call 'interior preparation.' Before anyone, priest or server, approaches the altar, he must spend a little time in prayer and meditation. Anyone here have a prayer to suggest?"

Silence complete and paralyzing.

Father Steve saw Jemmy Splaine wearing his green sweater with the horse-blanket pin. "Jemmy," he asked, "what's the one prayer that's always acceptable?"

Jemmy made a lunge into the unknown. " 'Our Father'?"

"Perfect. St. Augustine himself couldn't have given a better answer. Now let's kneel and go through it together, very slowly and distinctly, as if we were saying it for the first time."

Scuffling, they knelt. Steve then led them through the great prayer, making it a lesson in diction and reverence. At the *Amen* he nodded approvingly. "On your feet now. Next time we'll say it in Latin."

They chattered like delighted monkeys. "Latin? Yeh. Pig Latin? No, real Latin . . . He says next time we'll say it in Latin."

"Can anyone tell me," asked Steve, "why the Mass is said in Latin?"

No immediate takers. Then the tentative hand of Andy Curtin, a stutterer.

"Well, Andy?"

"The M-Mass is said in La-Latin so that p-people w-won't know wh-what you're s-saying."

One for the eternal book, thought Steve. He remembered his own childhood puzzlement at the strange cadences falling from the priest's lips. Belief that the language of the altar must be bound up with some incomprehensible secret had troubled him until the day he had assisted at Mass for the first time. Father George O'Connor of the curly brown hair and conse-crated hands — young, smiling, newly ordained — was the celebrant. Burning with boyish love for his hero-priest, Stephen had watched him turn to the congregation, open angelic arms, and utter the ancient greeting, "*Dominus vobis-cum.*" "Why, that means, 'The Lord be with you.' " Stephen had told himself in astonishment. And when he heard his own piping voice respond, "*Et cum spiritu tuo,*" all strangeness vanished. The timeless greeting, understood and answered, had made him an initiate in the sweet fellowship of the Mass.

And now, twenty years later, he was initiating others. From lip to lip the fire of the unchanging Word would always pass.

"No, Andy," he explained gently, "it's not that the priest wants to make a mystery of what he's saying. Just the oppo-site. He wants everyone, in all ages, everywhere, to understand exactly what he's saying. The Mass is said in Latin because no other language — except Hebrew, perhaps — is so universal and changeless. When we say '*Dominus vobiscum*' today, it still means 'The Lord be with you,' just as it meant twenty years — or twenty centuries — ago. Now say it after me."

"*Dom-i-nus vo-bis-cum.*"

He fed the syllables to them one at a time, as a bird feeds bread crumbs to its young.

"*Dom-i-nus vobiscum,*" they repeated.

"*Et cum spiritu tuo.* That means, 'And with your spirit.' "

"*Et cum spiritu tuo,*" they piped in ragged chorus.

"See," said Steve, "you're really talking Latin now."

He drilled them in the opening words of the Mass, coached them in the management of their hands and feet as they approached the altar. At the end of an hour they were bowing like grave little bishops, and at the end of two weeks they could perform quite creditably the not-too-difficult task of serving at a Low Mass. Steve knew, however, that they could not yet undertake the more complicated ritual of High Mass sung at eleven A.M. on Sundays.

Once more he tapped on the door of Lew Day's cubbyhole. "I'm looking for a deacon," he said pleasantly. "Could you spare a few minutes this afternoon, Lew?"

Lew Day lifted his spectacled eyes from the vestment he was embroidering. He had been sewing rapidly, and the exacting needlework had puckered his forehead into squinting wrinkles. At the sight of Father Stephen, some of the tension disappeared from his taut lips, and his narrow shoulders relaxed as though the burden of waiting had been lifted.

"I'm ready."

A nameless embarrassment unsettled Steve. Lew's trick of tendering more than was asked, his emotional jostling, warned Stephen that he must handle the suggestible young man with extreme caution. To jockey the conversation away from personalities, he picked up the embroidery hoop lying on the workbench. A green satin maniple was stretched across the hoop, and a needle filled with gold thread pierced the cross that Lew had been embroidering. Stephen saw no point in withholding his admiration.

"This is beautiful, Lew!"

"Are you — surprised?"

"Not at all. Why should I be? Every medieval monastery had an artist who did nothing else but design and repair vestments. I remember seeing a fourteenth-century Cluny chasuble, a masterpiece of jeweled brocade, all amethysts and seed pearls. The man who did it must have been a great craftsman." Stephen knew he was laying on the butter, but continued. "Then there was Cellini, who did the papal cope for Clement VII."

"Cellini did only the button for the cope," said Lew quietly. His correction was a warning: "Don't try to push me around with flattery." And the prissy fix of his lips said, "I may be emotionally docile, but I'm no intellectual pushover."

Stephen felt like a man walking through a patch of cockleburs. He was glad to hear scuffling in the sacristy. "Here they come, Lew."

Part drill sergeant, part wet nurse, Steve marshaled his Low Mass veterans at the end of the sacristy farthest from the altar. Then he addressed them much as Caesar might have addressed his legions on the eve of their departure for Gaul:

"Boys, today we'll attempt a very beautiful and complicated ceremony of the Church — High Mass. I've asked Lew Day to help us, and I want you to do and say exactly what he tells you. Now I'm going to assign the various parts to boys who've shown up well during the past few weeks. Jemmy Splaine, you be thurifer, Andy Curtin and Charlie Boyle can be acolytes, and the rest of you fall in behind.

"High Mass starts as a solemn procession to the altar," Father Steve went on. "First comes the thurifer swinging the censer — that's you, Jemmy — followed by the cross-bearer with the acolytes behind and on either side. Then comes the main body of altar boys followed by Lew as master of ceremonies, and last the celebrant — that'll be me."

Father Steve surveyed the line-up critically. "Lengthen out a bit — you're all bunched up in a huddle. Ready, boys? No shoving now. Step off slowly on your left foot. There'll be music to this. Hey, Jemmy, that's not a lariat you're swinging. It's a thurible, full of smoking incense. Keep it down!"

At the sacristy altar the procession halted while Father Steve and Lew Day regrouped the boys in their proper positions. Steve read the Introit and Kyrie at the Epistle side of the altar; after the *Dominus Vobiscum* and its hearty answer from the boys, he read the Collect.

While teaching the boys the art of serving, Lew's Latin was a model of cleanliness and articulation. His demeanor, priestly perfect, touched Stephen's sense of pathos. So much devotion, so genuine a calling! What pity that the intended vessel should contain a secret flaw!

Stumbling and bumping into each other, the boys floundered through the complex ceremony. In rehearsal fashion Father Stephen moved through the Gradual and Gospel, his back to the fledgling mob. Desperately, Lew Day was acting as a whipper-in, bringing up the stragglers, prompting them with word and gesture. The carnage was fearful, but somehow the great drama went forward and its dignity rose above the stumbling.

Three weeks later the new crop of altar boys assisted Father Monaghan at High Mass. Jemmy Splaine swung the thurible with notable restraint. Andy Curtin managed the bells beautifully. It was a distinguished performance all around. William Monaghan glowed with pastoral pride, and even that sensitive plant, Lew Day, managed a smile when Stephen thanked him after Mass.

AUGUST HEAT simmering over the Mystic River flatlands broiled the asphalt pavements and shingled roofs of St. Margaret's parish. Babies died, houseflies multiplied, the beaches were jammed, and Stephen Fermoyle lost fourteen pounds from a frame already perilously spare. He was working too hard; there was no doubt about it. Celia Fermoyle, heaping his plate with Friday-night codfish, warned him that he was too pale — and Dennis of the walrus mustaches seconded the "take it easier" theme.

"What's this new color you're going in for?" he asked. "Is it green trying to be white? Ecclesiastical pallor is one thing, Steve, but the hue of a corpse is another. Be like Bernie, now. Go out to the ball park, sit in the bleachers, and tone up that mushroom complexion."

Green trying to be white . . . ecclesiastical pallor . . . mushroom complexion. Din Fermoyle's pungent phrases ran like a fugue through Stephen's weary mind as he drove himself to his parish duties. He was fagged and he knew it. Too thin maybe, too pale perhaps — but because the first rapturous gale of his priesthood had not yet blown itself out, Stephen crowded on more canvas and prayed for the coming of cooler weather.

As the summer wore on, a curious depression and loneliness settled over him. He missed Rome! He missed the magnificent architecture of stone treated by generations of builders who had lifted marble and travertine infinitely higher than the surrounding hills from which they were quarried. By contrast, the poor New England Gothic of St. Margaret's with its red brick veneer, its trim of Quincy granite, began to seem cheap and ugly to him. What would the great Bramante, designer of St. Peter's, say of this edifice? Would Michelangelo smile patronizingly at the chalk statue of the Virgin in the basement? Stephen knew in his heart that altars of jasper and columns of finest *cipollino* marble were no essential part of the covenant between God and man. Nevertheless, he longed for them.

But more than these, he missed the Roman point of view, the Roman passion for world affairs, that he found not at all in the lives of the people, Catholic or Protestant, he met in his parish rounds.

A great war grinding deeper into its second year of military deadlock and diplomatic impasse had already stripped the delicate gears of Western civilization. Stephen knew that in Rome everyone, from the Pope down to the humblest *minutante,* was devouring hourly dispatches from a score of chancelleries, weighing and interpreting every shred of information for its bearing, in all latitudes, on the Roman Catholic Church. Eagerly Stephen scrutinized the Boston papers, hoping to catch some emergent hint of America's role in the struggle. But aside from the military communiqués, played up with anti-British emphasis to please Irish readers, he found nothing. On the day that Nuncio Pacelli carried Benedict XV's peace proposals to the Kaiser, *The Boston Post* carried head-lines "Two-Headed Squash Grown by Weymouth Farmer." Of the million Catholics in the Archdiocese of Boston (and the three million Protestants in the same area) few — as far as Stephen could discover — knew or cared about the larger implications of the European struggle.

The Boston Red Sox, hot as pistols, were the focus of attention that summer. Led by dauntless Bill Carrigan, catcher, the Red Sox looked like pennant winners. The Detroit Tigers, sparked by the great Ty Cobb, were the team to beat. Now in August, 1915, a mortal feud existed between Bill Carrigan and Ty Cobb. Carrigan publicly announced that he would block home plate with his two hundred and twelve pounds of bone and sinew every time Cobb attempted to score. Cobb responded by vowing that he would massacre Carrigan with his spikes if he blocked the base line. To the delight of the customers the feud went on all summer. Sometimes Carrigan's massive bulk would cut off Cobb at the plate; anon Cobb's flying spikes would slide around, over, or across Carrigan's shins, for a score. While Cobb and Carrigan made baseball war, the tireless missions of a lanky Cardinal to Germany and Austria, England and France, went notably unrecorded by the Boston papers.

If only I could sit down with Orselli, thought Stephen, he could tell me in ten sentences what's going on in the world. But since his farewell to the Florentine dandy on the deck of the *Vesuvio,* Steve had heard from Orselli only once — a brief note saying: "Italy now fights on the side of the stronger diplomacy. Am in command of an auxiliary cruiser in the Mediterranean. Had a good laugh with Ramilly at Genoa last week. Dear friend, preserve yourself for the joy of our many meetings after the war. Meanwhile write me of your apprentice labors in the vineyard. Affectionately, Gaetano."

No news from Quarenghi. Stephen had written twice, but either the war mails were slow or his old teacher had forgotten him.

Hungry for Roman intelligence, Stephen sounded off to Father Paul Ireton after luncheon one sweltering Thursday. Heat-laden dust from Main Street sifted through the screened windows of the dining room; a cracked hurdy-gurdy unrolled its melancholy program amid the desolation of suburbia. Not eager to pick up the labors of the long afternoon ahead of them, the two curates lingered over some iced coffee and a plate containing six ginger snaps.

Stephen stirred the thin, sweetish liquid with peevish energy and was off:

"Paul, how'd you like, just for a change of pace, to find out what's going on in the world? What's *really* going on, I mean. Not what Annie Regan said about Lizzie Gillen while paring Agnes Doyle's corns, or how Bill Duffy figures the

Red Sox chances for the pennant. But just as a novelty, a mature, world's-eye view of the world?"

Paul Ireton dipped a ginger snap into his coffee. "I don't get the importance of it, Steve — this hankering of yours for European information. Suppose a private wire to the Vatican were plugged in beside your bed. So before you fell asleep tonight you'd hear that Nuncio Ragazza had, or had not, just concluded a three-hour audience with Prince Manglewurzle of Trans-Bavaria." Father Paul lifted the dripping cookie to his mouth. "What could a shavetail curate like yourself do about it?"

"*Concedo*. Nothing. Don't misunderstand me, Paul. It's not that I want to be privy to a lot of palace gossip. But what I *do* miss here in St. Margaret's is the sense of being in at the pivot of things — a feeling I had every minute in Rome. Something streams out of the stones there — political awareness, diplomatic insight — call it what you please." Steve drained the sweetened coffee dregs from his glass. "What I feel is that hardly anyone around here has the slightest notion of what's going on in the world."

One of Paul Ireton's ironic smiles, the equivalent of a guffaw from anyone else, loosened the corners of his mouth. "What you're really grumbling about, Steve — forgive my saying it — is the obscure little part the Church is asking you to play. Shush now! Hear me out. While the chamberlains curtsy and the amethystine nobility tread the center of the stage" — unexpected acid dripped from Paul Ireton's words — "poor, abused Father Fermoyle frets at his menial task and fears that his chance will never come. He's ambitious, is Fermoyle. Oh, most vaultingly. After a short three months on the milk route, he chafes for private advancement, and would reorganize the Archdiocese of Boston to get it."

"It's not true, Paul. I won't let you twist my words like that." Fatigue and heat made Stephen irritable. "Is it ambitious to think of the priesthood as something more than a milk route? Am I a menace to St. Margaret's because I point out the Church is Roman Catholic — Catholic meaning universal, and Roman meaning Rome?"

Half hearing, Paul Ireton batted down a housefly. "Coast awhile, Steve." He had the knack, often found in strong-

charactered priests, of consigning intellectual problems to a
cool limbo located somewhere between indifference and
mañana. "Let Rome take care of itself. It's been doing all
right for several centuries. They've got a good man in charge
there, I hear." He dropped his cavalier tone and became
a solicitous sub-master advising an overstrained student. "Play
hooky this afternoon, Steve. Go see the Red Sox rip the hide
off Detroit. It'll do you more good than all the spiritual self-
floggings from here to Compostella."

"The rude cries of the bleacherites would be too much for
me, Paul. Besides, I'm way behind on my milk route. I've got
some parish calls to make — and today is the God-marked time
for making them."

Father Paul Ireton wiped the sweat from the blue-black
bristles of his cleft chin. "Well," he shrugged ironically, "if a
curate wants to get a world's-eye view of the Church, there's
no grimmer way of getting it than by making parish calls on a
blood-hot August afternoon."

IT WAS two P.M. when Father Stephen Fermoyle began his
parish rounds on Wigglesworth Street. Named after Michael
Wigglesworth, a colonial Protestant minister, the street was
now a stagnant backwash of working-class Irish. Beyond it
lay the city dumps and the Mystic Marshes, the latter traversed
by a meandering stream in which Father Fermoyle could
see boys bathing. No. 44, the last house on the left, was a
creosoted barracks with a flat roof and three crazy verandas
sagging from its blistery brown façade. Father Steve entered
its cracked, plastered vestibule; a penciled legend over a door-
less letter box read: J. FALLON — TOP FLOOR. He climbed
steeply, passed a gloomy little boy and girl, patted their heads,
then climbed again. Without pausing for breath, he knocked
at a scratched door on the third story. Slippered steps shuffled
down the hallway; the door was opened an inhospitable two
inches.

"Who is it?"

"I'm Father Fermoyle from St. Margaret's. I was just going
by — and thought I'd drop in on you."

Kate Fallon, completely gone about the teeth and middle,
but with her hair up, opened the door with decent courtesy.

"Come in, Father. The hallway is dark, and look out for the cot where my Perley sleeps, but come in. I'm just giving Jerry his soup."

Down a corridor stale with bedclothes, disinfectant, and the mingled odors of cabbage, fish, bacon, and cauliflower, Father Stephen followed her into the living room. Sun beating down on the flat roof made the room roasting hot, yet all the windows were closed. By a cluttered table sat a gaunt man, rigid as a mummy, clothed only in a suit of long underwear commonly known as balbriggans. In his left hand he held a funnel attached to a rubber tube. The other end of the tube disappeared through a little hole just below his Adam's apple.

The man did not rise or speak.

"Jerry, this is Father Fermoyle," announced Kate with considerably more cheerfulness than the situation warranted. "He's come to make us a little call. Sit down, Father, and I'll go on giving Jerry the rest of his dinner."

Father Steve sat down on a broken-bottomed cane chair and watched the strange ingestive process going on before his eyes. Kate Fallon took the funnel from her husband's hands, raised it slightly above the level of his mouth, and carefully ladled into it a tablespoonful of beef broth. She waited two or three seconds for the soup to gurgle down, then poured another tablespoonful into the funnel. "Tastes good, eh, Jerry?" She turned to Stephen. "He had an accident ten years ago," she explained. "One of his great thirsts came over him in the middle of the night, and he got up for a hair of the dog, you might say, but instead of putting his hand on the right bottle, he put it on the wrong one, and swallowed down almost a pint of sulpho-naphthol."

Father Steve cringed. Sulpho-naphthol was a cleaning fluid, caustic as carbolic acid. "Merciful God!" he exclaimed at the thought of the damage Jeremiah Fallon must have done to the membranes of his throat.

"Merciful God indeed," said Kate. "We're lucky Jerry's alive. It's only through God's mercy that he pulled through. His throat's closed up entirely, and he can't say a word for himself; but thanks be, Dr. Farrell cut a little hole just like you see, and now Jerry does his eating through a tube."

Father Steve fanned himself with his black hat.

"It's warm, I know, Father," said Kate, "but we can't open the windows because Jerry might get a draft, and if he catches cold Dr. Farrell says there's no hope for him." She switched the conversation to Steve. "You're the new curate just out of the seminary at Rome, I hear."

"Yes, Mrs. Fallon." Rome had never seemed farther away. Nor could he devise any conversational link between the Eternal City and the top floor of 44 Wigglesworth Street. He sat there sweating, lost for the little parish chitchat that Kate Fallon was longing to hear. Fumbling for a peg on which to hang one rational remark, he found it in an unframed photograph of a boy and girl tacked to the wall. "Are those your children, Mrs. Fallon?"

"Yes, that's Perley and Mamie taken twelve years ago, the day they were confirmed by Bishop McArdle. They're twins. Mamie's married these five years and lives in Roslindale. Four children she has, counting the baby that's just come. Perley works in the rubber factory. He's a fine boy, Father. Without his wages I wouldn't know where to turn." Kate gazed unbelievingly at the picture. "Twelve years ago. That was before Jerry drank from the wrong bottle, and a year before Father Monaghan came to St. Margaret's."

"You must have known the old pastor, Father Halley."

Kate's eyes went to the ceiling as if following the gown of an ascending angel. "How well I knew his sainted ways! Holiness breathed out of him like air breathes out of you and me. 'Twas a pity he had to be sent away. What became of him I don't know." She recovered the present. "Can I be making you a cup of tea, Father?"

Stephen rose hastily. "Thank you, no, Mrs. Fallon. I must be on my way. So many calls to make this afternoon." He laid his hand on the balbrigganed shoulder of the voiceless man sitting rigidly in the armchair. A clammy dampness, smelling of death, exuded from the nightmarish figure of Jeremiah Fallon.

The corporal works of mercy . . . visit the sick, bury the dead.

"God gives us strength to bear the crosses He lays upon us, Mr. Fallon," said Stephen.

Jerry Fallon's eyes, glazed like those of a codfish in the

bottom of a dory, stared unblinkingly at the young priest.

Kate Fallon was fumbling in the depth of a black handbag. Now it was coming. Steve turned his face away.

"Here's a little something for your private intention, Father," said Kate, holding out a half dollar.

"No, no, Mrs. Fallon. Really — I can't. Buy something for Mamie's baby." Over her protests, past her shapeless bulk, he was down the dark hallway. "Good-by, Mrs. Fallon. I'll remember your husband in my prayers." He stumbled over Perley's cot, found himself on the landing, and ran down three flights of stairs. The little boy and girl were sitting silently where he had last seen them. Without stopping to pat their heads, Stephen tumbled into the streaming sunlight of Wigglesworth Street.

A terrible revulsion gagged him. Was this the high calling to which he had dedicated himself? Were these the labors that he must carry on till the end of his days? A distaste for the whole business of the priesthood overcame him; he felt hot, nauseated, unclean. Useless now to tell himself that the two people in that suffocating, mean room were gentle, uncomplaining souls, bearing their grief with heroic fortitude and mutual love. The gurgling of the soup down that horrible rubber tube, the codfish stare in the eyes of the afflicted man, and the odor of encroaching death rising like a grave motif from unlovely flesh — these swept over Stephen Fermoyle in an hour of desperate fatigue and drenched him with loathing and disgust.

Utterly lost, and desperately in flight from the realities of his vocation, he stood under a grocer's awning at the corner of Wigglesworth and Main Streets. He wanted to get far away from the smell, feeling and remembrance of the Fallon nightmare. But where could a young priest go, what could he do on a broiling August afternoon? It was still early; many parish calls might yet be made — but Stephen lacked the will to make them. Should he return to the dim sacristy of St. Margaret's, fling himself down at the altar, acknowledge the sin of overfastidiousness, and pray humbly for a renewal of strength and love? The idea oppressed him. For the first time since his ordination, he had no wish to lift up his heart in prayer. Worse, he feared that if he asked for succor, only a vast deafness would hear his plea.

An open trolley car, orange-colored, bearing the sign WAKEFIELD COMMON, clanged toward him. Stephen knew Wakefield slightly — a semi-rural hamlet at the extreme northern end of the trolley line. He had played baseball there occasionally while in high school, and recalled a small lake, scarcely more than an ice pond, that bordered the town. I'll ride out to Wakefield, he thought. The open country will do me good. He swung aboard the nearly empty car, found a seat on the shady side, and gratefully let his sweating face be sponged by the little breeze whirled up by the car's motion.

Wakefield Pond, once a rendezvous for canoeists and picnickers, had long ago fallen prey to the weedy ills that afflict small bodies of fresh water. Rushes and pond lilies rimmed its banks; the stilts underneath the dock of the canoe livery had snapped with rottenness, and the chute of an abandoned icehouse was overgrown with creepers. Stephen circled the lake to its farthest tip, sat down on a patch of pebbly sand, and gazed dejectedly at the brownish water. A lethargy, physical and spiritual, crushed him. He took off his shoes, shed his coat and Roman collar, and lay on his back, gazing up at the midsummer clouds drifting like fleecy spinnakers across a blue sea. For a long time he watched them sail high-piled, weightless, uncontaminated by the sick griefs of earth.

"Happy as a lark," "free as the wind," "lonely as a cloud." How tempting for distracted human beings to wish themselves into the condition of natural objects! The poets were always doing it. He smiled a little at the sentimentality of poets, closed his eyes, dozed lightly. Into the shallows of his nap fell a splashing pebble of sound: Stephen sat up just in time to see a veteran pickerel leap out of the pond lilies, snatch at a waterfly, and dart back into the protective forest of reeds. The grace and surety of the pickerel moved Stephen to a kind of admiration; the fish suggested an unconscious metaphor too elusive for his tired mind to grasp.

Absently he began taking off his clothes, and stood for a moment contemplating the unusual sight of his own body naked in the sunlight. From a frame already too bony, he had lost fourteen pounds in the first three months of his curateship; his skin was colorless — "green trying to be white" — and the great extensor muscles of his arms and legs ached with fatigue. Unbidden, two lines from Baudelaire sprang to Stephen's mind:

> *O Seigneur, donnez-moi le force et le courage*
> *De contempler mon corps et mon coeur sans dégoût.*

Baudelaire! How, thought Stephen, do I happen to be quoting Baudelaire? Then he remembered where he had first heard the lines. He was in Rome; it was his third year as a seminarian. Monsignor Quarenghi was lecturing on mysticism, explaining the painful steps of the illuminated soul in its progress toward God.

"At first, all is warmth and light," said Quarenghi. "The soul, rejoicing in its loverlike kinship with God, traverses a luxuriant, flowering terrain. Suddenly the landscape changes, becomes an arid desert. God's presence is withdrawn. A sense of bereavement and emptiness assails the heart. Joy turns to dust, the salt of prayer loses its savor. It is indeed the dark night of the soul."

The burning brown eyes had closed, as if drawing Quarenghi into a remembered darkness. "Such, my friends, is the classic pattern repeated over and over again in the lives of every great mystic — and every priest. A truly illuminated soul persists in its search, but the weak and malformed spirit, overcome by world-weariness and corporal disgust, sinks into despair.

"Consider the case of Baudelaire, an imperfect mystic whose fastidious senses, outraged by appearances of ugliness and decay, deceived him into morbid self-loathing. Few poets have ever been more talented — or more pitiful. It is as though our Lord, having fallen for the first time, had permitted Himself to be overcome by the futility of His travail, and never risen again to bear His cross."

By the edge of this New England ice pond, overgrown with weeds and rushes, Stephen heard Monsignor Quarenghi's elegant Tuscan syllables: "You will all be assailed, my dear friends, by the very real temptation to believe that you have been forsaken by God — that your priesthood is in vain, and that the weight of mortal grief and sin is more than you can bear. In the midst of your anguish you will ask of Him

a sign, some visible ray of His unchanging light in a world of
hideous darkness. I am sorry to say that this visible sign will
rarely be given. The burning bush of Moses, the jewel-
encrusted dove of Theresa, the *Tolle lege* of Augustine —
these are no longer the style, as in the simpler days of saint
and prophet. The light will be interior; you must look for it
within."

But here there is no light, thought Stephen. Disconsolate,
he waded into the lake across a sharp-pebbled beach, and the
stones hurt his feet. He saw an island of pond lilies in the
center of the lake and swam toward it. The entangling stems of
the lilies grasped at his ankles as he circled the floating garden
and inhaled the special perfume that rises from water flowers.
He floated face toward the sky, and this time the sight of the
sailing clouds filled him with peace. Stephen was not a pan-
theist, accustomed to finding God in dells and birch groves,
but was it not a kind of worship to exalt the Creator of natural
beauty in slow rhythmic strokes through water scented by
sedge and lilies?

Filled with a new tranquillity, he turned toward shore. Face
buried in the water, he moved in leisurely strokes, diamonds
dripping from his arms, and when he turned his head to
breathe, each intake of air was an act of praise. His eyes were
closed now, the better to enjoy the embrace of so much sweetness. Once more he felt the pebbly beach beneath his feet,
and this time its stones were marvelously smooth.

Stephen stood knee-deep in the lake, and opened his eyes
on a world curiously transformed into greenness and beauty.
Who is the patron saint of little ponds? he wondered. And it
was then that he saw the pond lily clinging maniplewise to
his wrist.

The sign! Natural and miraculous, the stem of the lily lay
across his forearm like an emerald ribbon, reminding him of
the labors and burdens of the priestly vocation.

"Load me more heavily with Thy secrets, Lord," he murmured, and bent his head to kiss the dewy blossom.

At five o'clock, refreshed and strengthened, he put on his
clothes and walked toward Wakefield Common. An open car
marked MALDEN was standing at the end of the trolley line.
He got aboard, and as the conductor gave the two-bell start-

ing signal, Stephen slipped his hand into the pocket of his
black coat, pulled out his breviary, and read his Office for
the Time with serenity and devotion.

CHAPTER 5

WITH FEAST, fast, and changing color of vestments, the
ecclesiastical year wore on. September brought crisper weather
and the Nativity of Our Blessed Lady. October slipped past in
an ocher haze: All Souls' Day trod upon the eve of All Saints';
the long Pentecostal cycle drew to a close, and the blessed
season of Advent began. With purple vestments the coming of
the Infant was celebrated — the beginning of a new cycle of
joy to the world, and the Incarnation of new hope for man.

How frail that hope seemed under the assault of war! From
the Baltic to the Mediterranean, men faced each other at
bayonet length. In Flanders, the poppy fields ran red before
their season; in the Masurian Lakes, armies perished. The
trenches grew longer; the deadlock of Europe dragged on.

In blood-red vestments, on December 26, Stephen celebrated the feast of his name saint, Stephen the first martyr.
The Epistle for the day recounted the age-old story of that
earlier Stephen who, full of grace and fortitude, saw the
heavens open and the Son of Man standing on the right hand
of God. But even in that younger age, when the personal
splendor of Christ still illuminated the world, men could not
sustain the vision. They ran violently upon Stephen, stoned
him to death. He fell asleep in the Lord, forgiving his perse-
cutors in words of loving severity. And then, from the Gospel,
Father Stephen read Christ's lament: *"How often would I
have gathered together thy children, as the hen gathereth her
chickens under her wings, and thou wouldest not?"*

Smiling at the homely tenderness of the hen-and-chicken
simile, Stephen was unvesting after Mass, when young Jeremy
Splaine came up. Jeremy had become Stephen's favorite altar
boy. Nothing clownish these days about Jeremy's handling of
the Book and bells. He was a little master of liturgy now, and
a daily joy to Stephen at early-morning Mass.

There was a troubled query in Jeremy's blue eyes, and one

of them was black. "Father," he began, "is it true like it says in the Collect for today that we should love even our enemies?"

"That's what it says, Jemmy."

"Does that mean I ought to love some Episcopal kids that make fun of the skates my father gave me for Christmas?"

"I think it includes Episcopalians, Jem. But why should anyone make fun of your skates?"

"Because they've got straps," said Jemmy.

"And what," inquired Steve, "do other skates have?"

Jemmy burst forth. "These sissy Episcopals have aluminum skates that fasten right onto their shoes. The blades are hollow — they go like blazes. Well, yesterday afternoon me and some other altar boys went up to Spot Pond to play hockey, and these St. Jude kids — they've got a choir team — began to laugh at my skate straps . . ."

"That got your Irish up, eh?"

"It sure did. But I came right back at them. 'My skates ain't screwed onto my shoes,' I said, 'but me and my brother and Dave Foley here, we'll beat you playing hockey.'"

"You played them?"

"Yeh, we played them all right, Father."

"And," suggested Steve, "they beat the pants off you. Those St. Jude sissies skated all around St. Margaret's tough guys?"

Jeremy Splaine nodded. "They goose-egged us, fourteen-nothing."

Stephen pretended to mull over the tragedy. "Did you have a little disagreement afterwards?"

"Well, we sort of threw snowballs" — Jeremy hung his head — "with rocks inside."

Still stoning each other, thought Stephen. Aloud he said, "Fourteen-nothing is quite a trimming. Still, it's not a matter for a religious war. Seems to me that what St. Margaret's needs is a little coaching."

"Yeh, I guess we could use some, Father. Dr. Lethbridge, the Episcopal minister, coaches *his* kids."

The Groton touch. "Well," said Stephen, "I haven't been on skates for four or five years. But when I played forward for Holy Cross — "

"You played for Holy Cross! Geez, Father. I mean gee, Father — would you coach us?"

"I'd do anything to back up that Collect for St. Stephen's Day. Get your gang up at Spot Pond this afternoon at three-thirty. I'll be there with skates on."

The next month was one of the happiest times in Stephen Fermoyle's priesthood. Full of grace and fortitude, he did great wonders among the skaters of St. Margaret's. He showed them how to nurse a puck across the ice in the crook of a hockey stick, how to pass the hard-rubber disk in team play from man to man instead of dashing down the pond with it alone. The boys took on style — but no amount of style could keep their cheap strap skates from falling off at critical times. Stephen dreamed of fitting out his squad with hollow-tubed shoe skates; he priced these desirable items at Troland's Sport Shop, and found that six pairs of shoe skates would stand him two weeks' salary. Whereupon he called up Cornelius J. Deegan and said to that knightly gentleman:

"Corny, I need thirty dollars to buy shoe skates for six little hockey-playing demons."

"Shoe skates, is it? When your dad and me were boys, we slid across Liffey ice on the seat of our pants."

"I know, Corny. But my altar boys are playing the Episcopal hockey team."

"Episcopals!" exploded Corny. "Why didn't you say so in the first place?"

The next day St. Margaret's swarmed onto the ice in aluminum shoe skates, while the Knight of St. Sylvester stamped up and down the edge of the pond warming himself with the fire of Irish pride. The ragged jackets of Stephen's boys troubled Corny. "You'll be needing sweaters with a big gold *St. M.* on the breast of each and every one," he burst out — and straightway the team had sweaters.

"Arrange the game, Jemmy," said Stephen, after two weeks of practice. "St. Margaret's as ready as she'll ever be."

The game was played on a day of iron New England cold. Sharp skates rang against blue ice as hard-muscled boys, inheritors of the world's toughest tradition of play, struggled against each other. It was strictly a North American clash; as Stephen watched the two teams play he knew that no Greek or Italian boys had ever moved so rapidly or with equal grace. With the score 6-6 and a minute to play, Stephen saw Jeremy Splaine snatch the puck from a scuffle of hockey sticks and streak down the pond like a zigzag wind. But now the St. Jude captain, a long-shanked blond youth, shot in obliquely, hooked the puck away from Jemmy, and was off toward St. Margaret's goal for a heartbreaking score.

Episcopals, 7; Catholics, 6.

But no religious war broke out. When the game was over, Jeremy Splaine shook hands with the St. Jude captain. Even Corny Deegan, setting up hot chocolates for both teams at Morgan's Drug Store, had to admit that the Protestant lads had an honest bit of an edge somehow.

Dog-tired when he went to bed that night, Stephen turned back the pages of his Missal to the Gospel of St. Stephen's Day. "*How often,*" he read, "*would I have gathered together thy children, as the hen gathereth her chickens under her wings, and thou wouldest not?*"

Would it ever be otherwise? Would men one day drop the stones of hatred, forget the names of sect and nationality, and join in praising one Name forever and that Name alone? Stephen Fermoyle doubted that they ever would, but the last image in his mind before he fell asleep was that of a red-cheeked Jeremy Splaine extending his hand in a sportsman's embrace to the St. Jude hockey captain.

PILL HILL is the irreverent name given to a steepish incline in the heart of South Boston. It is a street of doctors; every door sports a medical shingle, and the higher a patient climbs, the larger the fee he pays. Major surgeons crown the hill; halfway down are the consultation rooms of well-established general practitioners; clustering at the base of the slope are the dingy offices of physicians young in reputation, green in judgment, or shady in practice.

On a shabby door at the foot of Pill Hill hung a sign bearing the simple legend: *John Byrne, M.D.* By Dr. Byrne's location, medical bargain hunters knew that his fee was one dollar. In the year since the sign had gone up, an increasing number of patients with or without a dollar bill (mostly the latter) had passed through the paintless portal into Dr. Byrne's office, where they received as thorough a going-over and as thoughtfully written a prescription as could be had all up and down the hill. John Byrne's fame was growing and if his income would only grow in proportion, all would go well with Dr. John and his newly taken wife, Rita, born Fermoyle.

It was nine thirty-five, one April evening, when Dr. Byrne closed the door behind his last patient, a Mrs. Julia Twombly who suffered from dropsical legs and a chronic tanning of her liver, brought on by drinking twenty cups of tea a day for thirty years. Julia Twombly also suffered from another long-standing ailment, lack of cash. She tendered Dr. Byrne a coin characterized by her as "my last half dollar in the entire world, except one." By pressing the coin back upon her, John Byrne had kept his evening receipts just under four dollars. He had seen fifteen patients and had collected a total of $3.85.

He walked through the railroad flat to the kitchen, where his wife sat having an aftersupper visit with her priest-brother, Stephen Fermoyle. The men greeted each other affectionately. "Don't see you often enough, Steve," said John. He kissed his wife, then handed her the little wad of money he had taken in that evening. Rita counted the bills and silver, then helped her husband out of his white surgical jacket.

"Your coat's the wrong color, darling," she teased. "It should be black like Steve's here. Then you could work for nothing all week, but drag down a swalloping big collection on Sundays."

"A percentage player," said Stephen. "What do you *do* with all the money your husband gives you?"

From a shelf over the kitchen table, Rita took down a red spice tin marked *Cinnamon* and popped a dollar bill into it. "In this house," she announced to Stephen, "*Cinnamon* means Rent. Whereas *Clove*" — she took down a yellow tin — "means installment on office equipment." Rita put a dollar bill into the yellow tin. "And *Nutmeg* means baby clothes." She dropped the loose change into the nutmeg tin. "Which leaves a dollar for food and other unnecessaries" Rita waved the remaining bill triumphantly.

"What's John's share of all this?" asked Stephen

Dr. Byrne's arms were around his wife "Ever hear of *Allspice*, Steve? That's what *I* get." He kissed Rita twice. "It's a rather unbalanced diet! How about some quick carbohydrates as in Shredded Wheat?"

Stephen had never seen his brother-in-law in such buoyant

spirits. Marriage had brought color to his sober personality. Now as they sat around the kitchen table, eating cereal from blue-ringed bowls, John impersonated one of his dead-beat patients reading a list of symptoms from a slip of paper.

"Oh, Doctor" — John mimicked the whiner's recital — "I suffer pangs from green and yellow spots before my eyes, a mortifying drip from my nose, a knifelike pain between my shoulders, and an empty, gone feeling in the pit of my stomach. I have a strain at stool; hot urine in the morning, and a bathing, cold sweat at night. I need a little something for a general weakness in front and a rash behind — not to mention the carbuncle big as an egg under my right knee, the torments of rheumatism in my left big toe, and a twinge of numbness in the soles of both feet." John Byrne grinned. "Can you imagine trying to diagnose a case like that in twenty minutes?"

The patient's mixed bag of ailments somehow reminded Stephen of the hopeless catalogues he so often heard in the confessional. How did a medical man handle such cases? "I'd be interested to know what you did for him," he said.

"What could anyone do? He was a malingerer with alcoholic complications — broke, undernourished, and determined not to work. I lanced his carbuncle and wrote him a shotgun prescription — strychnine, caffeine, and cascara — which ought to hit everything but the numbness in the soles of his feet."

So much doldrum misery in the world — stagnant grief that neither medicine nor religion could move. Sometime, thought Stephen, I'll explore the matter with John Byrne. For the present he was content to keep the conversation on a shop-talk level. "How's the surgery coming, John? Getting your share of gall bladders and appendectomies?"

"Haven't opened a belly for three months, Steve. You'd think at least *one* derelict would collapse on my front stoop with perforated ulcers — the stuff they drink would burn holes in a tin roof. But no such luck. I open my office door hoping to see a nice thyroid or emergency hernia — and what flashes before me? Running noses and numbness in the soles of both feet." John's grin was on the rueful side. "I guess the story's got around that I'm strictly a pill-and-powder man."

"Don't believe a word of it, Steve," protested Rita. "Make

him tell you about the new outpatient clinic he's just started at St. Joseph's Hospital, and the wonderful surgery he's doing there, free."

John was his old sober-sided self again. "Rita makes it sound too altruistic. The fact is, Steve, that the better-known surgeons on Pill Hill — like anywhere else — hog the major operations for themselves. It's next to impossible for a new man to get a bowel resection or even an appendix. The only things left are the minor specialties." John Byrne crunched another Shredded Wheat into his bowl. "That's why I've gone in for peripheral vascular surgery."

"What would that be?" asked Steve.

"Varicose veins, mostly. It's a wide-open field. The big fellows aren't interested, and the quacks murder people. But new surgical techniques are coming along fast, and I'm practically the only man in South Boston that knows about them."

"Where does the free clinic at St. Joseph's come in?" asked Steve. "Aren't you doing enough charity work right here in your own office?"

John Byrne explained, "Surgeons need hospital connections, Steve. They can't work without a hospital any more than a priest can function without a church. But here's the catch — most surgical staffs are full up. A newcomer has to win a place for himself. Well, I made my varsity try about a month ago by suggesting to Sister Domenica — she runs the show at St. Joseph's — that her hospital needed a free varicose-vein clinic, and that John Byrne was the man to run it."

"He got the job," said Rita. "Three mornings a week, no money, but plenty of operating. See how a surgeon gets his knife inside the door, Steve?"

Stephen regarded his sister and brother-in-law with new admiration. Yokemates, eager to make the hard, rugged climb together. "You two can't miss," he said.

Pill Hill was dark when he came down Dr. John Byrne's stoop, a few minutes later. The patients had all gone home; the diagnosing and prescribing were over till tomorrow. As Stephen climbed the steep ascent, his mind was filled with cheering thoughts of men and women paired for love and work, fulfilling themselves in daily acts of human goodness and mutual consolation. What though the world be plagued by physical disease and its spiritual counterpart, sin? While people like John and Rita Byrne loved each other, the forces of hell could not prevail against them or the world in which they lived.

The important thing, Stephen saw, was not to be oppressed or deceived by the multiple symptoms of evil, but to search beneath these appearances for the divinely implanted realities of courage, faith, and charity that throbbed in the heart of man.

It was well past eleven P.M. when he entered the parish house in Malden. A letter and a package were lying on the table in the front hall. They were postmarked ROMA and addressed to the Reverend Stephen Fermoyle. He snatched them off the table, bounded up to his room, and read the long-awaited letter from Alfeo Quarenghi.

CARISSIMO STEVE: [the letter began]
Did you think I had entered the order of *Sepulto Vivo* and taken vows of eternal silence? I would not blame you, dear friend; your Roman correspondent has indeed been remiss. Yet I speak truly; not until this hour of snatched pleasure have I had a free moment to answer your letter, so kindling with news and warmth that it makes a little glow among the dreary tundra of papers on my desk. I envy you, Stephen. All that you tell me about St. Margaret's and your incomparable Monaghan makes me realize that a priest's greatest happiness is found in parish labor. Whence, curator of souls, springs my joy at your good fortune, and my longing someday to taste a crumb of that priestly fortune myself. I pray only for a swept room, a small altar, the faces of my people. *Deo volente*, the day will come.

But it will not be tomorrow. I had hoped, after ten years of teaching (not altogether barren if they helped bear fruit such as you, Stefano), for an assignment to parish work. But war comes, and in the search for men who can pass muster as linguists, I am combed out of pedagogy and pressed into service as a *minutante*, a kind of upper clerk in the Vatican Secretariat of State. The Holy See maintains diplomatic relations with forty countries. Even in peacetime this calls for an enormous amount of correspondence, but

I really can't describe the avalanche of detail that has fallen upon us since the war began. As a *minutante*, I spend sixteen hours a day working up the raw material of notes and dispatches to French, German, and English ambassadors. I then hand my scrivenings up to my immediate superior, a diplomatic genius, Monsignor Eugenio Pacelli. He gives my clumsy phrases the gloss of diplomacy, then presents them to our overworked Secretary of State, Cardinal Giacobbi, a tireless Titan who hurls Vatican bolts in the name of our Holy Father.

These bolts have, of course, no temporal power, yet they *do* have an effect in the realm where politics touches upon morals. Let me cite an example. Last week His Holiness protested to General von Falkenhayn that the German treatment of Belgian noncombatants was needlessly cruel. Monsignor Pacelli delivered the note in person to von Falkenhayn, and absorbed the usual amount of Prussian bullying. Finally our Nuncio told von Falkenhayn that if Germany persists in its inhumanity to defenseless women and hungry children, it will forfeit the moral support of the Christian world. A weak argument? It *worked!* Might not one recast the wisdom of Archimedes: "Give me a moral lever, and I will move the world?"

Stephen remembered a similar lever in the hands of another Italian. A gray battleship, bristling with guns, rising and falling in a North Atlantic swell. What force could oppose its temporal majesty? Then Orselli's innocent question: "How would it look in your London *Times* — 'British Warship Fires on Italian Liner'?" *That* lever had worked, too. Yes, undoubtedly a power existed above and beyond the temporal. If one only dared use it to its full, thought Stephen.

The saddest part of the Vatican's position [the letter went on] is this: No matter what truth the Holy Father utters, it is distorted and misinterpreted. If he says: "Loving all our children equally, we must by necessity and logic remain neutral when they quarrel" — then the British press abuses him for not condemning Germany! Does he beg for disarmament? He is accused of mouthing pieties! Yet when he

offers his very practical and impartial skill as a mediator, he
is warned not to meddle in matters that do not concern him.
The Holy Father was shocked — *stricken* is a better word —
to learn that the secret treaty between England and Italy
the very treaty which won Italy to the side of the Allies)
contains a clause barring the Vatican from any part in the
peace negotiations. Is it not ironic that the voice whose only
plea is *Pax* should be excluded from the shaping of the
peace prescribed by Christ, and longed for by man?

But enough of this dismal strain. In your last letter you
asked what progress I was making with my volume of
essays. I can report that the Speranza Press has just published it under the title *La Scala d'amore*. I send you a copy
with this letter. What I've tried to do in this thoroughly
unimportant book is to show the various rungs of mystical
experience, — some orthodox, others not quite so sanctified
— recorded by souls in every age and climate. We Catholics
are apt to think of mysticism as our monopoly. But witness
the case of E. Swedenborg, or again, the strange experience
of your Mormon-founding American, Joseph Smith. Where-
in does his vision of the "two glorious personages" who
accosted him differ from those of Theresa or Augustine?
Don't answer till you've waded through the book, Steve.
Then tell me what you think. It will give this mumbling
cogitator fresh courage if, far off in a country I have never
seen (but someday hope to see), a priestly colleague is
mulling over the awkwardly set down conclusions of *La
Scala d'amore*.

So late the hour, so drugged with sleep the world! Soon
the first day-shallows of the sun will lap at the turrets of
the Leonine Wall, and new clamors of diplomatic and
military strife will begin again. Forgive me if I sound
weary-hearted. Really I'm not, Steve. Just weary-headed.
I shall fall asleep now, trusting as always that our days are
in His hands. Good night, dear friend. Write soon and
fully to

> Yours devotedly in Christ,
> ALFEO QUARENGHI

Stephen let his breath escape in an exhalation of delight.

By some epistolary sleight, Quarenghi had conveyed his heart
and mind to the heart and mind that needed them most. He
smoothed out the letter, and started to read it again. "Carissimo Steve . . . this hour of snatched pleasure . . . I envy
you . . . a priest's greatest happiness is found in parish
labor . . . I pray only for a swept room, a small altar, the
faces of my people."

Pious clichés dispensed for the benefit of the lower orders?
On two counts, no. Quarenghi's patrician soul could distill
no untruth. And odd though it seemed, Stephen realized that
this distinguished scholar-diplomat, destined to glorious preferment in the Church, was somehow being deprived of his
birthright as a priest.

Would I change places with him? thought Stephen.

He read the letter three times before unwrapping the
package that accompanied it. *La Scala d'amore* (The Ladder
of Love) was an octavo volume of 168 pages, wide-margined
and beautifully set in Aldine type. Eagerly Stephen riffled
through the pages, snatching a title here, a sentence there.
One essay, "The Pears of Augustine," particularly fascinated
him. He read the opening paragraph, translating freely from
Quarenghi's flexible Italian. The essay told of Augustine's
boyish prank — how, with a band of "lewd companions," he
pillaged a pear tree in his native village, took great loads of
fruit, and flung it to the hogs. Normal enough for boys in
any climate, comments Quarenghi. But thirty years later the
saint is still lamenting the theft of those pears. "O Lord, my
God, I inquire what in that theft delighted me," he cries
over and over in his *Confessions*. And now Quarenghi begins
unraveling a skein of fine argument. "Augustine's rapined pear
tree and its penitential aftermath cut to the very quick of the
saint's character, and reveal in a blossomy flash the psychic
travail of all who climb the ladder of love."

Emphatically not to be gulped down, thought Steve. He
spent that evening and the next reading in Quarenghi's
book. Then late in the third night, he came to a decision.

"I will translate *La Scala d'amore* into English," he said
aloud and quite suddenly. He had no other motive than the
literary challenge of rekindling in his own language the ardent
flame of Quarenghi's thought. He seized a pencil, began trans-

lating the title essay, "The Ladder of Love." To render its precise color and meaning was like trying to pick up globules of quicksilver between thumb and forefinger. At the end of two hours, Stephen had an imperfect page — the beginning of an affectionate labor that went on in his room every night after the work of the day was done.

ON A particularly handsome June afternoon in 1916, Dennis Fermoyle stared open-eyed at the ceiling of the operating room of St. Joseph's Hospital while Dr. John Byrne excised the ulcered saphenous vein of the motorman's right leg. The vein had ruptured that morning, and Din had been rushed to St. Joseph's for an emergency operation. The pain was nothing to the elder Fermoyle. His physical safety was in the hands of an able son-in-law, and his spiritual well-being had long ago been consigned to the care of the Holy Family. Nevertheless, Din had a worry, and it was this worry that he now communicated to his priest-son, standing beside his bed.

"Watch over Marty Timmins," was Din's injunction to Stephen. "Like a good boy now, Steve, see that he doesn't knock down any company nickels."

Din enjoined in vain. Two days later the heavy hand of Greasy McNabb fell on Marty Timmins' thin shoulder. "Come along," said Greasy, with the spotter's relish at having finally caught his man. "Manager Bailey's waiting to see you. Like myself, he's been waiting a long time."

They clapped Marty in jail on a charge of grand larceny, and fixed his bail at twenty-five hundred dollars. Stephen carried the bad news to Dennis Fermoyle.

"Go down and plead with Bailey," Din urged his son. "Explain the cause of Marty's little slip-up and say that I'll guarantee his behaving when I get back on the job."

Stephen got a fairly accurate notion of what was in store for him when General Manager R. W. Bailey kept him waiting forty minutes in his anteroom. Mr. Bailey did not rise or greet the young priest by word, sign, or even a grunt when he was finally admitted into the presence. As a free-thinker and stanch follower of Ingersoll, Mr. Ralph Waldo Bailey had two ideas about the Romish clergy: (1) maidens

were ravished in the confessional by priests; (2) maidens were
ravished by priests. Mr. Bailey furthermore resented the fact
that Father Fermoyle would take up much valuable time
pleading for that sniveling, pint-sized nickel thief, Marty
Timmins, who was now languishing without bail in the local
dungeon, and could languish there, for all Mr. Bailey cared,
until the grand jury met in September.

"I've come to ask what can be done in the case of Marty
Timmins," Stephen began.

"Wasting your breath," snapped Mr. Bailey.

"The facts surrounding this case are worth considering,
Mr. Bailey. Marty is an old employee, and this is his first
offense."

"The man's been knocking down nickels for years," countered Bailey. "We've just caught up with him, that's all. The
company intends to prosecute to the full extent of the law.
Nothing you can say or do will get this man off."

Stephen caught the implacable note of hatred in the
manager's voice. "You're pretty sure of that, aren't you, Mr.
Bailey?"

"*Dead* sure," said Bailey. He slapped some papers on his
desk. "And now, sir, I'm a busy man. Good day."

In the street, Stephen boiled over. "Mr. R. W. Bailey isn't
going to get away with this!" All very fine and indignant —
but how begin to euchre the highhanded Mr. Bailey, who held
all the cards and Marty, too?

For the first time in his life Stephen felt bewildered by a
set of facts. Here was a man in jail: exactly how did one go
about getting him out? The ground was unfamiliar; the pro-
cedures new and strange.

I need advice, thought Stephen. A lawyer might help. Do I
know any lawyers?

Georgie! George Fermoyle, the night-school lawyer who
worked by day on the fish pier. George should know something
about these matters. Half an hour later Stephen Fermoyle
was picking his way among the lobster pots on Long Wharf,
looking for his younger brother. He found George, stripped to
the waist, repacking and icing a shipment of Maine lobsters.
Independent, hard-working George! Another year on Long

Wharf, another year of night school, and he would take his bar exams.

"*Salve, advocate!*" cried Stephen.

"Stuffy!" exclaimed George. "What are you doing down here? Anything wrong with Dad?"

"The old boy's fine. It's his side-kick Marty that's in trouble. I need some legal advice, Gug." Stephen told of Marty's dereliction and Manager Bailey's hard heart. "Now just where do I begin, Counselor?"

George Fermoyle tossed a chicken lobster into a barrel, covered it with a scoopful of cracked ice. "Easy. First you bail your man out — "

"Wait a minute. By canon law, priests aren't allowed to go bail for anyone."

"Interesting idea." The student in George was wondering how *that* got started. "Then get someone else. Bail commissioners do it for a fee."

"Fine. Except for twenty-five hundred dollars, we've got Marty bailed out. What happens next?"

With judicial detachment, George packed some seaweed into the barrel. "Next, he comes before the grand jury for indictment. And make no mistake, he'll be indicted all right. Every member of the grand jury probably owns stock in the Boston Streetcar Company."

Stephen's spirit was damper than the seaweed in his brother's hand. "No way to stop the indictment?"

"Tamper with a grand jury? That's *bad,* Stuffy." George tossed in another lobster. "Now the way *I'd* handle it if it were my case, I'd let the grand jury indict. Then after that august body had expressed its property-holding indignation, I'd work a little psychology on the D.A."

"Psychology? D.A.?" Stephen was floundering in strange waters.

"Sure. No district attorney likes these public-utility cases. You can see why — big corporation bears down on little runt to get nickel back. Doesn't *look* good." George went on scooping ice and seaweed. "Whereas if all this were set in a favorable light before a smart prosecutor, he might never bring Marty's case to trial." Doubt beset George at this point. "Still, with a guy like Launceford Chalmers pressing the case . . . "

"Who's Launceford Chalmers?" asked Stephen.

"A big mogul in the Streetcar Company . . . a tough man to shave."

More ice, more lobsters, more seaweed. And Marty still in the toils, unbailed, his case studded with legal quiddities and contingent ifs, ands, and buts. All very chilling.

"So that's what they call 'due process of law,' " murmured Steve. "I never realized the ins and outs of it before. Well, thanks for the legal advice, George. Now that I know where we stand, I'll rustle around for Marty's bail."

George Fermoyle's sea-blue eyes read the concern in his brother's face. "There's another way of handling it, Stuff. You could save yourself a lot of wear and tear by mentioning the case to a certain friend of yours."

"Who?"

"Cornelius J. Deegan."

"Corny? What can he do about it?"

George started icing another barrel of lobsters. "What couldn't he do? Next to Number One himself, Corny has more political say-so than anyone in Boston. D.A.'s, mayors, even street-railway lawyers are but clay in his hand."

"No!"

"Ask anyone. Better yet, ask Homomagnus Deegan himself. Here's a nickel. There's a pay station at the end of the wharf."

In a daze Stephen called Corny's number. The contractor-Knight himself answered.

"I want to see you, Corny," said Stephen.

"And what's to prevent? Come right over, Father."

CORNY'S HEADQUARTERS in Pemberton Square was a ground-floor layout so accessible to the street that it seemed to Stephen — and indeed was — little more than a vestibule off the sidewalk. The outer office had the look of a public waiting room; a stale brown smell hung on the air, and high brass cuspidors quivered under a steady drumfire from the legmen, bagmen, and camp followers of Cornelius J. Deegan, Knight of St. Sylvester, Boss of Bosses, and contractor with full portfolio to the city of Boston.

There was a momentary cessation of spitting as Stephen entered. Regard for the cloth caused some of the men to reach for the brim of their hats; more could scarcely be expected, since the hats were of the iron-pot type which, once jammed on in the morning, could not be removed till the wearer lay down to sleep at night. Stephen approached a purple-faced, sergeant-at-armish fellow leaning against a door on the further side of the room.

"Is there something I can do for you, Father?" asked the man, getting his suety shoulders respectfully off the door panel.

"Please tell Mr. Deegan that Father Fermoyle is here."

A business of opening door slightly and thrusting derby through crack reminded Stephen of the quick-change vaudeville act in which the head goes in Bill Sykes and comes out George Washington. But the purple face that went into the crack came out unchanged.

"The boss'll see you." He flung open the door a full eighteen inches, and Stephen squeezed through into the presence of Corny Deegan.

The contractor-Knight, sitting comfortably in two chairs, arose as Father Stephen entered. His freckled hod of a hand was out, and his face glowed like a kiln-fresh brick. It glowed with good reason — two good reasons. First, he was seeing Stephen (almost pleasure enough for one day), and second, the city council had just accepted Corny's $900,000 bid for the paving of Causeway Street with granite cobble-stones. "Accepted" was scarcely the word; Corny had snatched the contract bald-headed from a New York paving company that had neglected the little matter of getting a pocket majority in the city council.

News of Din's operation had already reached Corny. A bonfire of candles lighted by his own hand was blazing at this very moment before the shrine of St. Anthony in the Cathedral; and on a more material level, tins of pipe tobacco, fine cut-plug, and boxes of cigars were making the journey from S. S. Pierce's humidors to Din's bedside.

"He'll have the leap of his old hurling days in that leg when he gets up again," said Corny reassuringly. "So rub the worried look off your high forehead, lad."

"It's not Din that's worrying me. It's Marty Timmins." Briefly Stephen told of Marty's unbailed plight. "Din said something about the Whiteboys of Hoodie Head marching against the Orangemen."

"March, they shall," said Corny. He bellowed the single word "Hector" into a side office about as big as a butler's pantry, where a pallid hare of a man sat on a high stool, scratching away at a ledger. The man hopped down off the stool and came running as though the beagles were after him.

"Hector, this is Father Fermoyle." Corny inserted a foot-note of explanation: "Hector's a hard-shell Baptist, Father, but more to the point, he's the best double-entry bookkeeper in Boston. Double entry, ha-ha . . . eh, Hector?"

Hector scrunched up his high shoulders in appreciation of a good thing often said. What's Corny got on this fellow? thought Stephen. Embezzlement at least, the way he hops. Stephen's speculations were interrupted by a businesslike change in the Knight's manner.

"Hector, what mortgages have we on hand?"

"Residential, city of Boston and suburbs, seventeen parcels totaling $195,670," recited Hector. "Business properties, Boston proper, eight parcels amounting to $210,500."

"Pick me out a nice $5000 residential, top cut," said Corny. Hector darted into his office and reappeared with a warranty mortgage in his hand.

"Best bail in the world." Corny tapped the document as though it were a sovereign cure for all ills. "Ask Joe Faye to step in here."

Joe Faye turned out to be the suety twin of the doorkeeper. Same iron hat, sliding manner, and blue veins on bulb of nose. A type.

"Joe, there's a friend of ours — Father Fermoyle's and mine — lying in the Suffolk County lockup," said Corny.

"The one we supplied gravel for?" asked Joe Faye, a kind of horror in his voice.

"The same. They've trumped up a charge of larceny against him. Marty Timmins is the name. One of our own." Corny held out the mortgage bond. "Trot down to the clerk of the court and post this bail for the dear man. Find out if he needs any small thing, some groceries, or a pint maybe, to cheer him up when he steps out onto the hot street. And tell him that the Whiteboys said not to worry."

Joe Faye stowed the bond into the inner breast pocket of his cardigan, buttoned it to his neck, and was off.

The whisking celerity of the business amazed Stephen. "Corny, you're a *deus ex machina*, a 'god from the machine,' as the Greeks used to say."

Corny's hair crackled with pleasure at Stephen's praise. "In Boston we give it a shorter name, Stevie. The 'fix.' Watch me now, while I pin a large farewell bow on the case of Marty vs. the knocked-down nickel."

Corny unlocked the top drawer of his desk and consulted a small black book, too confidential, apparently, for Hector's double-entry gaze. "Tackle we have for every fish, Stevie. I'll bait this hook myself." He thumbed through his private directory. "Ah, here's the speckled beauty we're looking for. . . ."

The Knight of St. Sylvester popped a black cough drop into his mouth. "Sweetens the pipes," he explained, reaching for his phone.

"This is Cornelius J. Deegan," he announced clearly after getting the number. "I'd like to speak to Mr. Launceford Chalmers."

Stephen recognized the name, unfamiliar to him an hour ago, as that of the Streetcar Company's official. A large fish indeed. What kind of a hook would Corny be baiting for him now?

"Top of the afternoon to you, Launce." Corny's tongue was pivoted in the middle and greased at both ends with butter. "I have news for you, news cheering in nature, I think you'll say." Corny let his voice find a confidential level. "The city council has just voted a new ten-year issue of paving bonds, par 100 to yield 7.3. We're letting a few of our old friends in at 65." Corny paused to let the good tidings resound. "Write you down for the usual? *Double* the usual? A pleasure, Launceford."

Corny grimaced at Stephen, made a hooking motion with his forefinger. "And while I've got your ear, Launce . . . there's an unfortunate case . . . my old friend and countryman, Martin Timmins . . . conductor for twenty years on your Medford run . . . seems to be in a bit of a jam . . . I think your Mr. Bailey can tell you the whole story. Mrs. Deegan and

myself would take it as a personal favor if the company . . .
Oh, restitution, of course. Thank *you*, Mr. Chalmers."

Corny hung up. "Well," his grin asked, "and what do you
think of us now?"

Stephen shook his head in puzzlement and distaste. "Is —
is this the way things are done in Boston?"

"It's the way they're done the world over, Steve," said the
contractor cheerfully. "Boston, Washington, Rome — anywhere you go."

The Deegan formula for universal fixery brought a protest
from Stephen. "I don't like it, Corny."

"*What* don't you like?"

Stephen had some trouble stating the precise nature of his
scruples. After all, he had come here for the express purpose
of getting Marty (an acknowledged thief) out of jail. And
now, mission accomplished, he was suffering moral qualms.
Why?

"I think what bothers me most" — Stephen tried hard to put
his finger on the sore spot — "is the bribe you offered Launceford Chalmers just now."

"Bribe is too harsh a word, Steve. In politics we call it 'a
little favor.' Three little favors gets you one big one." As if to
apologize for his thick-skinned realism, Corny spread his
hands, palms upward, across the desk. "Calluses are nothing
to be proud of Steve, and they'd be out of place on the hands
of a young priest. But in a life of toil and battle, ordinary men
sometimes develop them. They're the mark of Adam, you
might say, and I don't know that they'll ever disappear."

Corny wound up his little homily by pulling a fat butter-
gold watch from his pocket. "Come along, Father, hop into my
new Caddy, and we'll drive over to see Din the Down-
Shouter while he can't lift hand or foot against us."

DIN'S LEG healed, but the leap of his old hurling days never
came back into it. And when he returned to duty, his beloved
No. 3 was no more. They gave him a brand-new, sixteen-
wheeled monster, a one-man job fitted up with a mechanical
contrivance for taking nickels at the front door. With Marty
gone (Corny Deegan gave him a berth as timekeeper — no
money to handle, out of temptation's way), Din's voice was

not the joyous organ it had been. He continued to sing "The False Bride of O'Rourke," but pianissimo and sadly, as if commenting on the passage of temporal loves. Yet, he still lofted his hat proudly a dozen times a day as he passed the center door of the Immaculate Conception Church, where, on the high altar within, dwelt the Everlasting Presence — Dennis Fermoyle could not tell you how.

CHAPTER 6

FLYING LOW across the Archdiocese of Boston early in February, 1917, the Angel of the Lord might have remarked the following not-unrelated events.

ALDEN P. KIMBALL, president of the Malden Trust Company, and a fine old cravatted specimen of the McKinley school, rose to greet the maker of the ninety-day note that lay on his desk. The note, in the amount of $7500, was due tomorrow; the signature on the note was that of William J. Monaghan, and the stated purpose of the loan was to pay for the plumbing of the new parochial school. Banker Kimball half expected Pastor Monaghan to ask for a renewal, and was fully prepared to accommodate him. ("With *that* signature, gentlemen," he pointed out to his directors, "how can we go wrong?") He was not surprised, however, when Dollar Bill tendered him a perfectly good check for $7500 drawn on the Old Colony Trust Company of Boston.

"Done is done," said A. P. Kimball, returning the note to its maker. "The only question, Father, is — how do you do it? The man before you — Haley, Hawley? — what was his name? — wasn't quite up to it."

Dollar Bill tucked the canceled note into his wallet. "The name was Halley — Edward Everett Halley," he said distinctly, as if unwilling to slur over a precious syllable of it.

"Ah, yes . . . E. E. Halley. His signature didn't mean much in this shop."

"St. Francis' signature wouldn't have meant much, either," grunted Monaghan. With a that's-neither-here-nor-there wave of his hand, he came down to cases. "I've a bit of a favor to ask, Mr. Kimball. Next Monday we dedicate the Cheverus School. His Eminence Cardinal Glennon will be the guest of honor, and it's my hope that some of our local personages will, ah — ornament the platform." Dollar Bill laid his blue eyes on the president as a carpenter lays his spirit level on a joist. "Will you represent the banking fraternity, Mr. Kimball?"

A. P. Kimball was on a bit of a hook. Father Monaghan was a good customer, but several of the Malden Trust Company's directors didn't quite approve of parochial education. True, it took a load off the public-school tax (and that was desirable) — but then again, these R. C.'s were coming *might*-ty fast. Too darn fast, if you asked Mr. Kimball. He tugged at his cravat.

With no design in the world other than to take A. P. Kimball off an embarrassing hook, Pastor Monaghan said casually: "I suppose you've heard that His Eminence is making large deposits of diocesan funds in some of the better-grade suburban banks?" Dollar Bill had no need to add that one hand washes the other. But at the dedication of the new parochial school, Banker Kimball was on the platform to greet His Eminence. They seemed to get on together. Anyway, $40,000 from an entirely new source was deposited in the Malden Trust Company a week after the Cheverus School opened its doors.

Lew day sat in his sacristy cubbyhole trying to gather courage for the thing he must now do. Lew's job as sacristan was over; henceforth his duties would be performed by others. With the completion of the new parochial school, a community of nuns had come to St. Margaret's; they would teach in the school, and, as the sweetest part of their prerogative, take charge of the altar. Monaghan had broken the news a month ago. This was the last day of grace. Lew must go.

Lew began packing his few belongings: spools of colored thread, embroidery scissors, some assorted needles, and various remnants of material left over from the repairing of priestly vestments. Scarcely an armful all together, yet that armful embraced everything that had kept Lew Day alive since his rejection from the seminary. An old red chasuble, too shabby for repairing, hung from a hook; Lew folded it reverently, placed it in the suitcase. "Clothe others, Lord, in shining garments," he murmured, "but for Lew Day, only shreds and patches."

A bit of metal polish remained in a can. How use it most fittingly? Lew went to the cabinet where the sacred vessels were kept, and removed the chalice. Returning to his high stool, he spread the last of his metal polish over the golden vessel, and rubbed it with a worn piece of chamois until the chalice gleamed like a king's cup.

Occasionally he paused as if listening for footsteps outside his door. If only Father Fermoyle would walk in with supporting courage and a touch of heart-strengthening love! But Father Fermoyle was away, making a spiritual retreat with the Cistercians; he would be meditating in his cell now, or joining others at Compline. Lew Day stopped listening with his ears for Father Fermoyle's footfall. In his heart he had stopped listening long ago.

The metal polish was all gone now; no brighter glow would ever be rubbed into the vessel's golden cheek. Like a child trying not to cry, Lew sat for a long time with the chalice in his hand. Twilight was wrapping the sacristy in violet gauze when he carried the sacred goblet back to the cabinet. This final service completed, Lew stood at the bottom stair of the altar in the manner of a priest about to commence Mass.

"*Introibo ad altare Dei,*" he murmured. "I will approach the altar of God."

It was dark when Lew stole out of the church, carrying all he owned with him on his one-way journey. Next morning they found him hanging in the coalbin of his mother's rooming house, attired in the vestments worn by a priest while celebrating Mass. The vestments were old, shabby, and red (the hue of martyrs), and they had been terribly slashed by small, sharp embroidery scissors held by rejected, self-loathing hands.

BURNING with mystical devotion and tuberculosis, Ellen Fermoyle was carried up the steps of 47 Woodlawn Avenue on a stretcher. The mother superior of her order had made a wise and humane dispensation in Ellen's case. "To our beloved novice and spiritual sister, Humilia Theresa, now in the last

extremity of illness, we grant permission to return to the home
of her earthly parents." No surer death warrant could have
been written; its date, stamped on the flaxen parchment of
Ellen's body, was short.

Dennis Fermoyle took one fiercely proprietary look at his
daughter, and determined to tear up the contract between her
and death. Single-handed, Din was powerless. But connections he had. The best. He decided to use them shamelessly.

"Celia," he said to his wife, "our plea must be lifted to the
Virgin herself — then handed up, wet with her tears, to Him
who cannot refuse His Mother anything she asks in the name
of love."

Kneeling together in their bedroom, they stormed heaven
with the Litany of the Blessed Virgin. Din led off; Celia
responded. Their voices echoed through the house.

> Lord have mercy
> *Christ have mercy*
> Christ hear us
> *Christ graciously hear us*

They beseeched the Virgin most prudent, venerable, and
renowned; they pleaded with Mary, Queen of Angels, Queen
of Apostles, Queen of Martyrs; they begged Mary — Mystical
Rose, Morning Star, Tower of Ivory, Health of the Sick, and
Comforter of the Afflicted — to intercede for their child Ellen
at the throne of Her Son.

The Virgin did not intercede in vain. Ellen hung on, sank,
burned, sank once more, and hung on again while Din's pre-
posterous plea and Celia's unflagging antiphon rang through
the house:

> Mirror of Justice,
> *Pray for us*
> Cause of our joy,
> *Pray for us*
>
> Singular Vessel of Devotion,
> *Pray for us*
> Mystical Rose,
> *Pray for us*

The Litany, repeated every night — supported by the medical skill of Dr. John Byrne and Celia's heroic nursing — began to justify Din's celestial connections. At the end of February, Ellen was still alive. Death's chattel mortgage had been torn up, dissolved, abrogated, and spat upon by Dennis Fermoyle.

Stephen, bringing his sister the spiritual comfort of the Eucharist, marveled at the flaxen stem that had refused to wither in the fires of tuberculosis. An unbelievable victory. At what point, he wondered, did Ellen's spirit make its unconquerable stand against the awful batteries of disease and death? And what had supported her in the battle? Only to hear Din's voice ringing through the house, and one knew the answer. Din might call it faith, and faith indeed it was. But Stephen felt that love was also having its way here — a love so God-partaking in its authority, so steely terrible in its Father-resolve — that neither flesh, nor hell, nor death could prevail against it.

Lacking such love, Lew Day had killed himself. Possessing it, Ellen Fermoyle could not die.

Yet, as if undecided about which sphere she inhabited — the world of mystical dream or fleshly reality — Ellen developed strange symptoms of somnambulism. She lived, but became a sleepwalker. Once Celia found her kneeling before the statuette of the Holy Family in the living room.

"Ellen dear, come back to bed," said Celia softly.

"Yes, Mother. But let me venerate the three of us before I go."

"What three, darling?"

"Stephen, me, and Father. See, Father carries him so lamb-like, Stephen, I mean. But his other arm supports me, too."

"*Jesus, Mary, and Joseph protect us,*" said Celia Fermoyle, chilled with fear at the very names she uttered.

THE KETTLEDRUMS of war were really thundering now. Every day brought a new crisis: an American merchantman *spurlos versenkt,* a larger loan to Britain, a more agonized plea from France. All Woodrow Wilson's diplomacy had failed to shackle the U-boat; fresh atrocities and galling ultimatums incensed the American people. Events stood in a narrow place when the President read his fateful message to Congress on April 2, 1917.

Stephen heard the news as he came out of the sacristy into the bricked areaway between the church and the parish house. Aloysius Quinn, the waddling youth who delivered the *Globe*, thrust the paper into Steve's hand and was off again without touching the visor of his cap. Father Steve was about to call Aloysius back and give him a brief lecture on manners when his eye fell on the streamer headline: WILSON ASKS CONGRESS FOR WAR. Transfixed, Stephen read the President's message:

> The world must be made safe for democracy . . . right is more precious than peace, and we shall fight for the things we have always carried nearest our hearts — for democracy . . . for the rights and liberties of small nations, for universal dominion of right by such a concert of free people as shall bring peace and safety to all nations.

Stephen paced up and down the bricked areaway, studying the periods of the noble stylist whose idealism had set the tone of American war-thinking. Moving though the message was (and beautifully timed to coincide with the peal of public opinion), Stephen saw that it lacked the one element which alone could bring peace and safety to the world. That element? Recognition of God's primacy in the affairs of men. Nowhere was that primacy mentioned. Democracy, the rights of small nations, peace, safety, and freedom — all good and desirable in themselves — were merely parts of a vaster whole which had somehow escaped the notice of President and people. Stephen Fermoyle was neither a cynic nor a pessimist, but he shook his head with foreboding of disaster yet to come.

He entered the house, folded the *Globe* in the special way that Bill Monaghan liked it folded, and wedged it between the doorknob and jamb of the pastor's door. Then he went into his own room and looked up a passage in his breviary:

Come, behold the works of the Lord . . . He maketh wars to cease; unto the end of the earth; he breaketh the bow, and cutteth the spear in sunder; he burneth the chariot in the fire.

Be still, and know that I am God; I will be exalted among the heathen, I will be exalted in the earth.

Four days later, the American nation was at war.

MILITARY ENGINES began to grind out the materials and per-

sonnel of war; the newly discovered art of propaganda became
a bellows that fanned America's temper to martial heat. Four-
minute men, editorial writers, cartoonists, and song pluggers
transformed the war into a crusade. To insure adequate
marchers in the crusade, a compulsory draft became operative
on June 5, 1917. Almost ten million Americans registered, and
the mass trek to training camps began.

Bernie Fermoyle's flat feet kept him out of combat duty,
but his honey-boy tenor got him employment as a camp entertainer. George Fermoyle didn't wait to be drafted. He went
into one of the first overseas detachments and got his second
lieutenancy at once. Stephen waved him off at a Commonwealth Pier debarkation to the mingled tunes of "Washington
Post March" and "Over There."

The single greatest surprise was Paul Ireton's volunteering
as a chaplain. He knocked at Stephen's door late one night
and announced quite simply, "I'm going away with the
Twenty-sixth Division tomorrow, Steve. May I come in and
say good-bye?"

"Come in, Paul. Take my chair." Stephen sat on the bed
and waited for his friend to open up. Paul Ireton was a man
you didn't catechize; he either disclosed the springs of his
action, or he didn't. Usually the latter. But tonight his reserve
was broken by a deeply charged impulse to talk.

"Quick-change Ireton, they'll be calling me," he began,
"out of the cassock and into the tunic. Different uniform, but
same old discipline. 'Right by squads . . . forward, *march!*'
I'll catch on quickly, don't you think?"

"No doubt of it." (What's he so bitter about? Steve wondered.) "If you can think up some deathless phrase like 'Fire
when ready, Gridley,' you may go down in history as the 'Cast-
Iron Chaplain.'" Steve tried to keep it light. "What rank are
they giving you?"

"Captain." Paul Ireton's false zip fell away. "I suppose you
wonder why I'm going?"

"Other than patriotism, I can't think of any reason a thirty-
nine-year-old priest should be dashing off to the wars."

" 'Sweet and fitting it is to die for one's country,' as Horace
says. But that's not my real reason for going, Steve. You came
nearer it when you mentioned my age. In a few months I'll be

forty. You can't imagine what it feels like to be pushing forty
— and still without a parish of one's own."

Father Ireton must have remembered his earlier strictures
on the subject of priestly ambition, for he burst out, "It's not
a big church that I'm after, Steve. I'd gladly take the meanest
ark in the diocese, sleep on the ground beside it, if I could only
call it mine."

"I understand, Paul. It's the Jacob in you, craving a flock of
his own. But here in St. Margaret's the flock happens to belong
to another Biblical character named Monaghan."

"And what a grip he keeps on his shepherd's staff! He'll be
pastor here for another thirty years." Ireton rubbed his blue-
black chin ruefully. "Let's see — that would make me his
assistant till I'm seventy."

"Will marching off to war speed things up any?"

Paul Ireton had evidently asked himself that very question;
he laid down his answer like a well-considered card. "Maybe
it sounds calculating, Steve, but I figure that after the war
there'll be a big shake-up in this diocese. It's got to come. The
present pastors are holding on to their parishes like baronial
fiefs. They're getting too — too *proprietary*. It's my hunch that
the Cardinal is just waiting for the right moment to split the
old parishes in half, and give the younger men a chance to
build new churches."

This passion for building! Stephen had yet to feel it, but
sooner or later every priest was consumed — as Paul Ireton
was now — by the need to build a church.

"If ever a man deserved the opportunity to put up a church,
it's you, Paul. And if I were Number One, I'd stick a pin in
the toughest spot on the diocesan map, and bellow: 'Build it
there, Father.'" They both laughed at Stephen's fantasy.
"Wait and trust, Paul. When the flag-waving is all over, your
day will come."

Paul Ireton put out a hard-palmed hand. "Good-by, Steve.
You'll pray for me?"

"In all my orisons."

Four hands were clasped now, around, above, and below
each other in the wordless supporting embrace that close
friends often use in parting.

PAUL IRETON'S going away left an empty place in St. Margaret's — and in Stephen's heart. Thrown together oftener now with Frank Lyons, Stephen discovered that Milky, despite a pallid complexion and fear of rain, was quite up to carrying his full share of parish burdens. Though Father Lyons was not (as Monaghan put it) "the discoverer of dynamite," he was zealous and hard-working in the discharge of his priestly office. There hung about him, however, a certain air of immaturity that caused Stephen to withhold the final measure of confidence and affection.

Other than music, Father Frank Lyons had few internal resources. The only book he ever read was his breviary. Ideas of more than parochial scope terrified his inexperienced soul. He spent most of his free evenings visiting the homes of a select group of parishioners, where he made himself welcome by his willingness to play the piano and be a fourth at whist. It was all innocent enough, though Bill Monaghan might have been somewhat disedified if he could have heard his curate splashing about sentimentally on the best parlor uprights of the parish.

Milky kept begging Steve to join him in his forays among the whist-playing nobility. Busy with translating Quarenghi, Steve cut him off several times. "I don't play whist well enough, Milky. Let me off this time, will you?"

Milky would take the rebuff as though he expected it, and Stephen would turn once more to his task of translating *The Ladder of Love*. The deeper he plunged into the work, the more he discovered that it was not a mere literary exercise nor a theological treatise. Instead, it was a celebration of love, a new *Convivio* investigating the mysterious relationship between body and soul. Which dominated which? Where in man's clayey tabernacle did the soul reside, and was it master or tenant in the house? Quarenghi, mystic and realist, sang the triumphs and limitations of life as men actually lived it. Clear and warm, the stream of his thought glided between banks of flesh and spirit, touching both affectionately in the passage.

Perfect love, Quarenghi said, was that divine infusion which inclined men to cherish God for His own sake — not as a source of help, or reward, or propitiation, but as an infinite good in itself. Such was the mystical love of Bonaventura, Theresa, and Bernard. But Quarenghi knew also that other kinds of love existed; that human hearts hungered, pitiful hands reached out, and voices pleaded for the mutual consolation that the children of earth are commanded to show each other.

"Yet this consolation," wrote Quarenghi, "sweet though it be, is but a human accident of love, and not to be compared with Love itself. As neither the color nor the perfume of a rose is the Veritable Rose, but merely suggests the perfect flower, so the mortal aspects of love serve only to remind us of Love's immortal splendor."

Stephen was meditating one June evening on Quarenghi's definition of love, when Milky Lyons popped into his room waving a pair of theater tickets like a conductor's baton. Theater tickets were enough of a rarity in Stephen's life to warrant a decent curiosity.

"Where'd you get them?" he asked.

"Luck of the Irish," exclaimed Milky. "I just dropped in at *The Malden News* with a sodality announcement, and Leo McKinnon, the city editor, asked me if I could use a couple of passes for tomorrow night."

"You *are* in luck. What's playing?"

"A revival of Victor Herbert's *The Only Girl*. Gorgeous melodies." Milky started to hum "When You're Away, Dear," the hit song of the show, accompanying himself on an imaginary violin. "Listen" . . .

> *When you're away, dear*
> *How weary the lonesome hours!*
> *Sunshine seems gray, dear!*
> *The fragrance has left the flow'rs!*

Stephen smiled leniently at the sentimental lyrics . . . springes to catch woodcocks. "Whom are you taking?"

Milky dropped his airy fiddle and pointed the tickets straight at Stephen. "Who but *you*, Father Fermoyle?"

"N-nuh." Stephen rumpled the manuscript on his desk. "I've got my work cut out for me here, Milky. This Italian prose is music enough for me. Try someone else."

Frank Lyons let his temper flare. "Now look, Steve," he protested, "you just can't keep on refusing civil bids from a pal. You'll either come with me tomorrow night or — I'll tear up these damn tickets right in front of you." Milky held them aloft in the manner of a man about to keep his word. "Are you coming?"

Steve wished that Milky Lyons would stop using the word "pal," and stop waving invitations at him. Still, he hadn't been inside a theater since his seminary days . . . it might be fun. . . .

"Don't be sacrilegious, Milky. I'll come.".

Next evening two expectant curates were sitting in row C, center aisle, when the orchestra struck into the lush overture of *The Only Girl*. Settling back in anticipation of the delightful sights and sounds ahead, Stephen forgot that certain eyebrows in the audience were raised askance at the Roman collars in the third row. Steve's conscience was clear. He had his rector's permission, and was in the decent company of a fellow priest. If a grown man couldn't withstand the impact of some oversweet music! . . .

Milky, however, was in a lyric heaven. Things musical affected him much as a plumber's torch affects solder. At the end of the first act he was an unprotected, fluxing rod of sensation. Milky had never seen a musical comedy before; the standard libretto of lovers, romantically plighted and tragically parted, struck him with the raw force of novelty. But the book was merely the first rung on the ladder of Father Frank's delight. The many-throated orchestra, now breathing tenderly with muted reeds, now swelling into bosomy yearning from the strings, transported him into a world of emotion never previously entered by the pallid curate. The frou-frou costumes and bare shoulders of Andrea Ferne, the prima donna — a really handsome girl — added the final intoxicating elements to Father Frank's glass of experience.

During the intermissions, Stephen noticed Milky's agitation, but chose not to comment on it. Even an inexperienced curate had a right to his private state of feeling. Father Frank would snap out of it in the open air. As for Steve himself, he felt a lulling overhang when the play was over. The music had seeped into his nerves, and visual images of the handsome prima donna moved delightfully through his mind. Refreshed, he stepped out onto Boylston Street as though returning from a long vacation in some never-never land of fantasy.

"Feel like walking home?" he asked Milky.

"Five miles?"

"Do us both good. Let's hit across the Common."

Milky had no objections. Something was on his mind, and a long intimate walk with Stephen would give him a chance to blow off some emotional steam. The two struck out across Boston Common; its summery foliage dimmed the city lights and spread a turfy enchantment across the grass. Stephen felt wonderfully elated.

"What a performance!" he exclaimed. Romance sprayed by a full orchestra in music sugary but hummable. " 'When you're away, dear, how weary the lonesome hours,' *da-da dum de-de* — how does the rest of it go, Frank?"

No answer from Milky. At the bottom of his adolescent soul he was framing an overwhelming question. Walking beside Stephen on this summer night, he wanted desperately to bring the conversation around to the important half of creation that had always baffled and bothered him. Girls! Milky made a timid opening move.

"What did you think of Andrea Ferne?" he asked.

"Eye-filling. A positive beauty. What else could I think?"

They walked under three elms in silence. Time for another try. "I wonder what they're like, Steve."

"What who's like?"

The risk of offending Stephen was great, but Milky took it. "Girls," he said compulsively.

Stephen caught the green-sick odor, unpleasing in any grown man. He felt sorry for Milky, ashamed of himself for his cavalier comment on Andrea Ferne. Pity, and refusal to develop the theme further, were in his reply.

"There's quite a literature on the subject, Frank. Experts from Ovid to Dante have described women in all moods and tenses."

A park lamp obscured by an elm trunk threw a corona of light over Milky's tormented face. "That's not what I mean, Steve. Books don't tell me what I want to know. But hearing that girl sing tonight, looking up at her bare shoulders" — and ague shook him — "believe it or not, Steve, that's the

most I've ever seen of a woman — filled me with a, a — misery
that I never felt before." Frank's voice was charged with
loneliness and longing. "Why should I feel this way, Steve?"

Surprised by his own question, Frank Lyons stood still;
tears, blue under the park lamp, streamed down his cheeks.
Until this moment he had slipped through nearly thirty years
of life, scarcely aware that women were in the world. Taken
young by the seminary, he had been shielded from the polar
currents flowing between the sexes. Milky's experience with
women was simply nonexistent; he had never danced, played
tennis, or swung in a hammock with a girl. He had never
touched or kissed one. His only emotional release, other than
a genuine devotion to the priesthood, was music. And now,
suddenly, the power and mystery that streams from women
had struck at him, and the hurt — shafted with Andrea Ferne's
voice — was twisting in his nervous system.

"Do you feel the way I do, Steve?"

"No," said Stephen honestly.

Stephen Fermoyle was neither afraid nor ignorant of
women. This evening he had looked with enjoyment upon
Andrea Ferne and seen her exactly as she was — a delightful creature gifted with feminine graces of voice and body.
Happy for the world that such women existed! And happier
yet for Stephen Fermoyle that their existence did not seriously disturb his greater love.

But here was Frank Lyons tangling himself into emotional
knots about the newly discovered wondrousness of women.
Steve recognized Milky's problem as one of those personal,
never-quite-to-be-resolved matters that every man (priest or
no) must solve for himself. The belated ferment now bubbling in Frank would doubtless make him a maturer person,
and therefore a better priest. Yet right now, crossing Boston
Common, Milky needed a bit of emergency treatment; Steve
decided that the treatment of choice was to let his colleague
talk freely till the throbbing pressure of his curiosity was
reduced.

In another setting, Stephen's decision might have been wise.
But around them on the darkened Common the night air
reeked with aphrodisiacs of turf and summer. Human forms
were stretched on the grass; lovers embraced on every bench.

Stephen himself began to feel the earthly contagion of the place.

"Let's get out of here, Frank."

He struck westward, setting a rapid pace toward the Charlesway. His new plan was to walk Frank Lyons into sheer breathlessness, and for fifteen minutes Steve set such a clip that Milky was tagging half a length behind in a desperate attempt to keep up. Now they were stepping it out heel-and-toe, following the car tracks across the Mystic marshes. This was familiar terrain to Steve; he felt secure here. Over these steel tracks, glistening under carbon arc lights, his father had driven Trolley No. 3 (curious, that Triune number) for a quarter of a century. As a boy, Stephen had often stood beside him at the controls; now his thoughts followed Din as an obedient obbligato follows a soloist. Memories of Din the Down-Shouter, Din the table-pounder, the no-sayer, the Lawgiver, the God-surrogate, filled his mind. Lighter, more laughing memories flocked, too. Din's love of song and prayer, his old-fashioned wit and fondness for puns and wordplays came to mind. Steve remembered his father's favorite conundrum, a kecksy-whimsy straight out of Dublin. He tried it out on Milky:

"What opera reminds you of a trolley line?"

"Give up," gasped Milky.

"*Rose of Castile.*" Stephen laughed aloud, more in remembrance of Din than at Milky's puzzlement. "*Rows of cast steel — get it?*"

The pun was doubly unfortunate because it brought up both the name of a woman and a musical performance. Milky snatched at it eagerly to reopen the conversation. Anything would have served; itched by devils of pruriency, he dug his fingernails into the theme once more.

"Don't you think, Steve, that priests should have — more firsthand experience of women?"

"Why should they?"

"Well, in order to understand them better."

"A sophist's argument. You might as well say that a physician must have heart trouble himself before he can diagnose or treat it in others."

The road narrowed as they crossed a drawbridge over the

Mystic. "Let's lean on the rail a minute," said Milky. "I'm too out of breath to think."

They leaned over the iron railing of the drawbridge, gazed down at the black tide slipping out to sea. A marshy smell, oldest of aphrodisiacs, rose from the brackish flatlands, assailing the membranes of their nostrils with associations more ancient than man. Frank Lyons struggled in vain against the suggestions of the primal odor. Then the inevitable question. "What are women really like, Steve?"

The point-blank anguish in the question saved it from being a piece of outrageous impertinence.

"I could give you half a dozen answers to that question, Milky. But none of them would have any bearing on the matter that's really troubling you."

"Why not? If a pal won't tell me anything about women, how am I ever going to know about them?"

The hateful word "pal" irritated Stephen. Annoyance edged his voice. "Are you sure it's women you want to know about, Frank? Aren't you itching with curiosity about something else?"

"What else? What else could it be?"

Straight from Quarenghi's pages, the answer came. "Love," said Stephen, "and the need to love."

Milky was more puzzled than before. "But aren't love and women the same thing?"

"Not necessarily. Women are the usual objects of love — wonderful and essential objects to most men. Women have the power of reminding ordinary men that love exists. That's as God intended it to be. But as priests, Frank, we are moved by another power — not the physical accidents of love, but Love itself."

They were walking again now. Frank Lyons, struggling to keep pace with Steve's longer strides, was silent. Inside his narrow rib cage, his lungs and heart were gradually stretching to unaccustomed fullness as Stephen went on:

"You said back there, Milky, that poets couldn't tell you what you wanted to know about women. You're wrong. Poets and artists have the remarkable power of changing love from flesh into idea. El Greco does it in paint; Dante in poetry — yes, and whoever wrote the Litany of the Virgin was flaming with love when he invented those glorious names for her: *House of Gold, Morning Star, Mystical Rose. . . ."*

"Tower of Ivory, Singular Vessel of Devotion," added Milky, realizing for the first time how beautiful the names were.

"The artist is always part saint, part proselytizer for the ideal. In the *Paradiso,* Dante's love for Beatrice is consummated, not in sweaty grapplings such as we saw tonight on the Common, but in a blinding vision of light. In that vision Beatrice appears to him as a petal of the Sempiternal Rose. And Dante, who had loved her and longed for her all his life, cries out:

> *By virtue of love's power*
> *From servitude to freedom thou hast drawn me.*
> *Preserve in me thy pure magnificence,*
> *So that my spirit, cleansed of all desire,*
> *May, thanks to thee, be loosened from my body.*

The difficulties of coming back to earth, of refraining from comment that would sound priggish or patronizing, were not lost on Stephen. He saw the dangers of descending into preachment and parable, but the fisherman's net placed in his hands at ordination (or at birth) had already closed around Frank Lyons. Steve drew him in without a struggle.

"Is not this the ideal to which we are both dedicated, Frank? Tonight you were reminded of it, if not for the first time, then more powerfully than ever before, by sensual beauty and music. No man is immune to such reminders. Count yourself lucky to have felt them this night. But remember, Frank, that these are the fleshy accidents of love, and not the Love which is our special study and pursuit."

Around a bend of the tracks, the lights of the Medford carbarn glinted. Bells clanged. "If we run, we'll catch the last trolley to Malden Square," said Steve. They caught the moving car, swung aboard pantingly. Frank Lyons fell onto the cushion, mopped his forehead, and smiled weakly at his companion.

"The long-walk part of the treatment was fine," he said.

"Wait till you try the cold shower," grinned Steve.

They had a tall orange phosphate, double strength, at

Morgan's Drugstore, and reached the parish house just as the clock on Monaghan's mantelpiece was striking twelve. At the top of the creaky stairs, Milky held out a frail hand.

"Thanks, Steve, for helping me over a spot." There was nothing mawkish about his gratitude.

Alone in his room, Stephen stripped off his clothes, showered, and sat by the open window of his room to relax and cool off. But now the mixed tensions of the evening began to put in their delayed claim. The spiritual tourniquet, tightly applied for Frank's benefit, was slowly released; a mortal tide flowed back into Stephen's limbs and organs, bringing unbearable pain. Andrea Ferne's wonderful shoulders and seductive voice, the sweethearts sportive on the grass of the Common, the lofty (perhaps too lofty) discourse on Love — all these began to tumble and churn in Stephen's blood stream. A persistent fugue, the theme song from *The Only Girl,* whirled through his brain:

> *When you're away, dear,*
> *How weary the lonesome hours!*

How lonely, indeed, the uncompanioned hours of a priest's life! — hours that most men solaced with common love. All very well to fix one's gaze upon a petal of the Veritable Rose, but meanwhile, what of the summery earth night and the flowers of here and now?

> *Sunshine seems gray, dear!*
> *The fragrance has left the flow'rs!*

What flowers? Elbow on sill, Stephen gazed out upon Main Street; there, in full bloom under dreary arc lights, he saw a gray stretch of car tracks. *Rows of cast steel.* Unperfumed flowers of duty and obligation!

Over the municipal gas tank climbed the pale profile of a new moon. Stephen remembered that moon climbing from another part of the heavens, gazing at another part of the earth. A *fête de bal* in the gardens of the Conte Falerni, a Roman nobleman. Ghislana, his wife, herself a noble beauty. Stephen remembered her gardenia-fleshed shoulders, bare against green chiffon. He had walked barely thirty yards with her down a formal garden path fringed with ilex. What was he then? A young cleric in minor orders confiding to an older woman (two years older, maybe) his hopes and dreams. She had listened . . .

> *Ever I hear you in seeming,*
> *Whisp'ring soft love words to me . . .*

She had looked at him, and her eyes had filled Stephen with knowledge of an unsayable loneliness.

A thirty-yard walk. An answered look. No more. But now in his cell-like room, images of Ghislana Falerni, the only woman who had ever disturbed Stephen's priestly ideal of love, wove through the melodies of *The Only Girl*.

Stephen lay down to sleep. The melodies became a dream. Not a dream of platonic conversings, but of Ghislana Falerni moving toward him unshod across the grass.

> *Ah, if I knew t'were but dreaming*
> *Ne'er to be!*

From this happy-companioned sleep, Stephen Fermoyle was awakened by the wheels of the five A.M. trolley rattling across the tracks beneath his window.

CHAPTER 7

CAPTAIN GAETANO ORSELLI, commander of the Italian cruiser *Garibaldi*, locked the door of his cabin, spread an armful of newspapers on his bunk, and wept impotent tears of grief and shame.

Caporetto . . . Catastrophe on the Isonzo . . .

Orselli read the frightful details. Out of an Alpine mist, a mist made denser by clouds of poison gas, the Germans had struck a supposedly impregnable flank of the Italian 2nd Army on October 24, 1917. Within forty-eight hours the break-through had become a streaming rout. Twenty-five divisions of Italians — General Capello's entire corps — threw down their weapons and fled into the interior of Italy. With drawn pistols, agonized Italian officers tried to stem the flight. But before Generalissimo Cadorna could reorganize his broken lines, the Germans had captured two hundred thousand prisoners, eighteen hundred guns, and millions of rounds of ammunition.

Caporetto . . . the greatest military disaster of modern times.

Gaetano Orselli set his handsome teeth into the gold braid on his forearm and ripped the insignia of his rank off his fine London-made uniform. In frenzy he pulled the glossy curling hair of his beard out in handfuls. Here he was, anchored at Malta, cribbed and cabined in the obsolete *Garibaldi*, a cast-iron ark built in 1905 — the single Italian component of a British-commanded Mediterranean patrol. To the proud Florentine it was agony enough that his countrymen were giving the world an example of poltroonery that would make Caporetto a reek forever in the nostrils of men. But unbearably worse were the sneering condolences of the damned *Inglese!*

"Fortunes of war, old fellow . . . might happen to almost anyone."

Orselli's tongue was bleeding, his face gray with humiliation, as he stared again at the newspaper accounts of the lost battle. It had come true, the thing he had always known: Italy would gain nothing from this war, neither territory nor power. And now, not even honor. Too many factions in politics, and in the army a divided command. Cadorna the Freemason had not admitted Capello the clericalist into the full confidence of his larger strategy. Generals at swords' points: dissension, subversion, open mutiny in the ranks. And in Parliament too many parties sapping a government already rotten at the core.

So many parties, and every party had its own press. Orselli gazed at the dozen journals spread under his gloomy eye. Left, right, and center, they all agreed as to the scope and horror of the catastrophe, and disagreed as to its cause and cure. In one of the journals a stentorian editor bellowed: "The scattered spears of Italian power must be grasped in a single strong fist, and bound together into an unbreakable sheaf of fasces. . . ."

Orselli nodded. "It is the only way." The paper was the *Popolo d'Italia* and the name of the bellowing editor was Benito Mussolini.

UNDER the oriental lanterns of the Dreamland Dance Pavilion,

Mona Fermoyle dipped and hesitated with Benny Rampell across a waxed half acre of paradise. In the violet glass mirrors that ran along three sides of the hall she could catch ecstatic glimpses of herself floating in Benny's arms to the heavenly music of Mack Hallette's Syncopators. And when Mack himself stepped into the orange glow-light and lifted his saxophone in a special arrangement of "Beautiful Ohio," Mona, forsaking all others, clove unto Benny alone.

"If it could always be like this," she whispered.

"Darling, it can. It will. Always."

"But you're going to be drafted."

"Not till next summer. Dentists get exemptions till they finish their course. The war may be over by then." His lips found her ear. "Darling, I'm crazy for you."

"Me too."

"Let's get married before I go."

"Sweet, I want to. So much." Mack Hallette's music faded, disenchantment of reality set in. "But what would I tell my family?"

"Tell them anything. Say a justice of the peace married you to a Jew. If that's too brutal, tell them nothing. Only marry me."

Pure masculine plea for the thing most wanted was met by feminine tactic of delay. "Wait a little longer, Benny . . . just a little while till I figure out a way. . . ."

Mack Hallette's sax took it on the upbeat again. Once more forsaking all others, Mona Fermoyle dipped and hesitated across a waxed half acre of heaven with Benny Rampell. Nothing ever got decided, but everything was all right as long as she and Benny could catch glimpses of themselves floating together in the violet-colored mirrors of Dreamland.

As a CHRISTMAS PRESENT befitting duties of a curate in the North Temperate Zone, Corny Deegan gave Father Stephen Fermoyle a pair of four-buckled arctics with heavy rubber soles. Thus shod against the terrible winter of 1917-18, Stephen stepped out on his ceaseless round of parish duties. To the sick and the housebound, he brought the Eucharist in its golden pyx, and on many a night of falling snow he car-

ried the case of holy oil down unplowed streets to anoint the
eyes, lips, and limbs of the dying.

Sheer routine, most of it, yet a touch of drama colored
Steve's priesthood now and then. Early in January, he climbed
a swaying extension ladder to hear the confession of Fireman
Miles Harney, trapped under a fallen girder in the Commercial
Warehouse fire. While men worked frantically with hacksaws
to cut Miles free, Stephen lay down on the scorching floor,
placed his ear to the doomed fireman's lips so that a little tent
of privacy would cover his final act of contrition.

"Better get going, Father," gasped Miles, "the walls will
be buckling any minute." Three minutes after Stephen went
down the ladder, the warehouse wall caved inward.

By Ash Wednesday, which came early that year, the heavy
soles of Corny's gift overshoes were worn through.

At about the same time, Stephen completed his translation
of *The Ladder of Love*.

Not once during his labors had he given a thought to publishing Quarenghi's essays. The work had been a challenge
and a delight in itself. But now that two hundred pages made
a thickish sheaf on Steve's desk, a natural desire to give the
work an audience began to ferment in his mind. He tested the
idea on Milky Lyons, who became greenishly pale at his
confrere's audacity.

"Publish a book?" he gasped. "Why . . . why . . . Steve —
curates can't *do* that."

"You mean there's a papal decree against it?"

"No, but" — the idea of printing anything was too much for
Milky — "what will Monaghan say?"

"I'll certainly have to get his permission. If he says 'no' —
then it's no. But after all, I didn't *write* the book, Milky. It's
only a translation, you know."

"Better pick a good time to broach it to him," was Milky's
timid and very sound advice.

It was after an excellent dinner of barley soup and roast
beef that Stephen laid the manuscript before his rector. Monaghan had never seen a book manuscript before. "What's
this?" he asked testily, fingering it as though it were a specimen in alcohol.

Briefly, Stephen explained the nature of Quarenghi's book.

Dollar Bill lighted one of his special Havanas and examined the title page.

"Hmmph . . . *The Ladder of Love*. In plain English, what would be the meaning of that?"

"Well, Father, you know how the angels are ranged in heavenly choirs — cherubim and seraphim nearest the throne, and the others taking their places lower down?"

"Yes, yes." Happy to show that he was up on such matters, Monaghan puffed his cigar like a robed theologian. "They sing *Hosanna in excelsis* all the time."

"That's it. Now the author of this book suggests, inferentially, of course, that similar rungs of spiritual experience exist on earth. Each of us sings, so to speak, in a different choir."

Monaghan looked up sharply. "Did anyone ever doubt it?"

"No, I suppose no one ever really did."

"And we all try to sing the same *Hosanna in excelsis*, each in our own way, don't we?"

"Yes . . ."

"Then what's all this grand wordage about?" asked Monaghan, riffling the pages of the manuscript.

Stephen, considerably cooled down, tendered his ace.

"Would you like to read it and find out?"

"God forbid. I'll take your word for it. But you came in here to ask me something, Father."

"I want your permission to hand this manuscript up to the diocesan censor. If he approves, it will then go to the Cardinal for his imprimatur."

Monaghan considered the matter from the only viewpoint that really concerned him. "Will this . . . ah . . . little typing item . . . be getting the parish into trouble with Num — I mean His Eminence?"

"I don't think so. The Cardinal might even regard it as a fine compliment to Rome."

"He might. Then again — but I wouldn't presume to be reading the thoughts of a Cardinal." Monaghan looked up at Stephen with paternal fondness. "It's a risk you're taking, Steve. His Eminence is a great hand for letting one know who's the cook and who's the potatoes. If you want to take the chance of being boiled in your jacket, and if you assure me that this book contains no scandalous or heretical matter, why, yes — you have my permission to hand it up to the diocesan censor."

"Thank you, Father," said Stephen. That very night he mailed *The Ladder of Love,* together with the original much-annotated volume of *La Scala d'amore,* to Monsignor Linus Sully, *censor librorum* for the Archdiocese of Boston. It was April 20, 1918, almost three years since he had taken up his work at St. Margaret's.

THREE YEARS had wrought changes in the Fermoyle household at 47 Woodlawn. The welt in Din's forehead, the wound of vocation cut by his motorman's cap, was deeper; the bison hump of his great shoulders more pronounced. Since the operation his leg pained less, but still it pained, and he dragged it coming home from work. Much of the bounce had left Celia's step, too. Nursing Ellen meant running up and down the back stairs twenty times a day; the preparation of special meals (Ellen's dishes and laundry had to be kept separate to protect the rest of the family) meant double duties at the stove, sink, and washtubs. There was an increasingly blue discoloration of Celia's hands, and her upper teeth had been replaced by a dental plate. Because the plate was uncomfortable she seldom wore it during the day; as a result her upper lip had sunken, and the robust beauty of her late forties was, at fifty-three, quite fled. Yet since Celia Fermoyle was a woman who never looked at herself in the mirror, her only inkling of change was the dragged-out feeling that a good night's rest — when she got it — could no longer banish.

Even with George away at war, the house was packed to the eaves. Ellen's return from the convent and Florrie's marriage to Al McManus (she had insisted on bringing her husband home with her) had filled the second-floor bedrooms. Bernie, chronically jobless, was crowded into the attic. "A temporary arrangement till Bernie finds something permanent," was Celia's way of putting it. But the temporary arrangement had a terrible permanency that Bernie was unlikely to disturb. He slept till eleven every morning, ate the hearty breakfast that Celia cooked for him, borrowed a half dollar from her, and disappeared till dinnertime. Promptly at six P.M. he would come whistling up the front stoop, kiss his mother, go to the piano, and literally sing for his supper.

This placid, if somewhat overcrowded, domestic hive, with its workers, drones, and sick queen upstairs, was a happy enough home except for the goading fury in the breast of Florence Fermoyle. Marriage to Al McManus had not soothed that fury. To tame Florrie would have required the imagination, nerve, and whip hand of a Petruchio, but if Al had possessed these qualities Florrie would never have married him. Al belonged to the weakfish species that most women contemptuously throw back into the sea; tepid good temper and a mild interest in baseball, bowling, and Kelly pool were his only visible assets. Merely looking at him seemed to irritate Florrie.

If Al irritated her, Mona drove her quite mad. The wrangling between the sisters had deepened into a feud. Possibly Mona's stemlike fragility and camellia complexion heightened Florrie's awareness of her own coarse-pored skin and piano legs. Mona's unwillingness to help in the kitchen, her slack habit of leaving her bed unmade while she primped and adorned her person, were tormenting burrs under Florrie's heavy girdle. But the chief source of contention was the fact that Mona, despite a hundred family scenes, still "went around" with Benny Rampell — a non-Catholic, a Rabbi's son, a Jew.

Coming home for dinner one Friday in April, Stephen felt the tensions reverberating through the house. As he took his place at the table, it seemed that everyone was eating off a drumhead. How different his home-coming dinner three years ago! Then, all was promise; the Fermoyle wave was still creaming to a peak. Now, the moment of promise had passed. Din running down, Celia wearing herself out with overwork, Ellen ill upstairs, Bernie a jobless sponger, Florrie a hippish shrew. And Mona? Stephen looked at his sister's face, dewy, lineless, pretty as a violet — what about Mona? Too often, Steve observed, she was sullen, rebelliously withdrawn, ungiving either in word or manner. Over her blue-black eyes she had pulled a visor — not the gay domino that questing maidens wear, but a stubborn mask of hostility. Sometimes Steve could coax her to lift it; any talk of dancing would bring her around

(wasn't she Celia's daughter?) and once, after he had brought
her an Irene Castle dance record, she had put it on the phonograph and floated about the room petaling with laughter.

"That's what I'd really like to be," she breathed in confidence. "Not a stenographer in a plumber's office, but a ballroom dancer." She drew him behind the green portieres
between the living room and front hall. "No one home here
knows about it, but Benny and me won a contest a couple
of weeks ago."

"What kind of contest?"

"Oh, for amateurs. At Dreamland. Benny'd be a wonderful
dancer if he didn't have to study so hard about teeth and
things."

The old difficult subject of Benny once more. Steve had
hoped she would go on, and was at the point of asking her to
let him meet Benny sometime. But Florrie had come in just
then, and the visor had dropped over Mona's eyes again.

It covered them now. Stephen tried to catch her interest
by tricking out the table talk with bright pennons of anecdote.
But on this listless air, no flag could flutter. Celia was tired
to the bone nursing Ellen, Din was silently holding out his
teacup to Florrie for "more of the same." And Florrie, wiping
the tea drops from his graying mustache, nagged, "Be more
careful, Pa." Al McManus, a chin-in-plate eater, was putting
away cod and potatoes with two hands. Florrie signaled him
to lift his face a little. Al obeyed. Then, as Mona rose from
the table, the storm broke.

"Where're *you* off to?" challenged Florrie.

"Shh-sh," warned Celia. "Ellen must not hear you quarrel."

"I don't care who hears me." Florrie jabbed her fork bellig-
erently at Mona's back. "She's going to help with the dishes
tonight for a change."

Mona whirled, small infantile teeth parted, a kitten become
cat. "You and your old dishes," she screamed. "I'm sick of
you, them, and everything in this house."

Florrie split her with a deliberate shaft: "You'd rather go
dancing with your sheeny boy friend, I suppose."

The gibe goaded Mona to frenzy. On a small table beside
her stood a chalk statue of the Holy Family. She picked it up,
and using the venerable head of St. Joseph as a handhold,

flung the statue at her older sister. Aimed in rage, the image of the Holy Family struck the platter of codfish. Statue and platter broke, sending fragments of crockery, fish, and chalk flying across the table.

A piece of the broken statue struck the red welt on Din's forehead; from the wound of vocation a red drop fell. He sat dazed for a moment, then in awful anger lifted his great hand to strike Florrie, author of the quarrel. If the blow had fallen, it would have broken her neck.

The blow did not fall. Self-mastering forbearance held it off. "Jesus, Mary, and Joseph forgive us," said Din in the frightened whisper of a man who has seen the Adversary coming in the front door.

Having once escaped the wrath, Florrie tempted it a second time. "Let's have a showdown on this," she screamed. "Either Miss Fancy-pants stops running around with a Jew, or I walk out of this house — salary, bag, and baggage."

Stephen was tempted to say, "What a blessing!" But the contentious words were checked by a voice, near at hand but far off, familiar yet terribly strange, drifting in from behind the green portieres. It was the voice of an exorcist, a mingling of incantation and lament:

"Hail Holy Queen, Mother of Mercy, our life, our sweetness, and our Hope . . ."

Through the green portieres glided the figure of Ellen Fermoyle, barefooted, wearing only a nightgown of unbleached cotton. Her hands were clasped like a bride carrying a wedding bouquet; the waxen pallor of long illness lay on her forehead. Is she awake or asleep? Stephen wondered. He could not tell. Ellen's eyes were open, and she appeared to be searching for something.

"What are you looking for, dear?" asked Celia with the tenderness a mother uses on a sick child.

Wandering puzzlement crossed Ellen's face. "Where has the statue gone?" she murmured.

"What statue, darling?" asked Celia.

"Don't you remember, Mother? The statue of the Holy Family that used to stand on this little table. Has someone taken it away?"

No one answered. Mona stood chilled with fright. Florrie's

face was in her hands. And from Din's downcast forehead trickled a dark ooze of blood.

Celia was at Ellen's side, gently urging. "Come back to bed, dear. We'll find the statue again."

Ellen's voice lost its exorcist quality; she became again the Fermoyle daughter. "Let me stay downstairs a little while, Mother. It's so lonely up in my room when I hear you talking and laughing around the supper table," she said. "So often in the convent I remembered our happiness together. More than all my other memories of home. Tonight, Mother, I had to see the faces of my brothers and sisters once more."

She called them each by name, characterizing them by their nobler parts. "Florrie, responsible and hard-working. Be patient with us, Florrie. Mona, pleasure-loving and beautiful. Beauty must be generous, Mona. Sweet-tempered Bernie, lover of song; never change, dear Bernie. And Stephen" — she turned to her priest-brother — "fisher of souls; one of the divining few. Ah, such a chant of praise should go up from this home!"

Bewilderment puzzled her again. "Perhaps if we all looked for the statue, we could find it." She approached the table as if to begin the obsessional search anew. "Look!" She pointed to a sharp fragment of blue plaster, a portion of the Virgin's robe lying in the platter of codfish. "There's a piece of it now." Ellen's hand went to her mouth as if to suppress the utterance of reality. "Oh."

The glaze of half-dream slowly left her eyes as they traveled around the disordered table, gathering up, in fragments of blue, white, and gold, the awful meaning spread before them.

Stephen prayed that she would not notice the blood on Din's brow.

His prayer went unheard. Ellen was awake now. On her father's face she saw the crimson evidence; by the immortal act of Veronica she acknowledged it. Taking a napkin from the table, she pressed it with maternal pity against Din's forehead. Her gesture seemed to say: "Only believe, dear Father, that this blood has not been shed in vain." What she actually said, Stephen could not hear. For Ellen's lips were buried in Din's grizzled hair, and he was pressing her close to him.

"I will carry you upstairs myself," said Din, lifting Ellen

in his powerful arms. A beatific smile lighted her face. At this moment she was not the rejected spouse of the Mystical Bridegroom, but the much-loved daughter of Dennis Fermoyle.

FLORRIE cleared away the dinner-table debris, and Bernie sat down at the piano. In the everyday manner of mortals, the Fermoyles were attempting to forget the wretched quarrel that had marred the evening. By a sleepwalking miracle, Ellen had temporarily stripped the poisonous leaves from the vine of family dissension. But Stephen knew that it would flourish again, break forth in new strife between Florrie and Mona, unless the roots of the trouble were torn out.

Celia knew it, too. Sitting on a low chair beside her priest-son, she laid a bluish worn hand on his knee. "Stephen," she asked, "will you do a great deed of kindness for your mother this night?"

Stephen knew what was coming. "I'll do anything you ask, Mother."

"Go to Mona. Urge her to give up this boy. Plead with her, Stephen, while she is torn by grief for the sorrow she has caused us. Speak to her heart, Son, speak as a priest and brother. Wring the promise out of her — for my sake and her own."

Stephen dreaded the ordeal that his mother proposed to him. His sympathies were all with Mona; even her unforgivable hurling of the statue was the result of Florrie's nagging. To interfere with the emotions of others, to tamper with their private concerns, was distasteful to him. But with Celia's hand on his knee, he had no alternative. Heavyhearted, he mounted the front stairs, knocked at Mona's door.

"Monny dear; it's me, Steve." In the darkness he stroked her forehead. Mona's muscle tensions told him that the dark visor of her rebelliousness was down and that her small, infantile teeth were tightly set against him. How, either by logic or love, could he reach her?

Logic was out. Love, then, it must be. Tears sometimes came with love, and if one could get tears . . .

"Monny darling." His lips were close to her ear as he

struggled for her soul in the darkness. "Put your arms around me, Monny."

No response from Mona's rigid body.

"Remember the bear hugs you used to give me when I'd take you down Crescent Hill on my double runner? Before we'd start I'd show you how to wrap your arms around me. I'd say, 'No matter what happens, just hang onto me.' And you'd say" — Stephen mimicked the high-pitched trustingness of that little hugger — " 'I'll hang on, Steve.' "

Without encouragement from Mona, he placed her rigid arms around his neck. "Hang on again, Monny. Trust me once more."

He waited till her arms tightened in an embrace that said, "I'll always trust you, Stephen." Now that he had softened her, he could proceed. "You know, Monny, you were a naughty girl tonight."

"It was Florrie's fault. She nagged me into it. If she'd only move out, there wouldn't be any more fights about me and Benny."

"That's not the answer, Monny." Stephen couldn't bring himself to say, "You must give up Benny Rampell." Instead he asked, "Why don't you let me meet this boy? Maybe he'd want to become a Catholic. Then you two could be married."

"He'll never turn, Steve."

"Why not?"

"Because his father's a rabbi. It would kill him, Benny's father, I mean, if his son turned Catholic. They've got their pride, too."

No escaping it now! "Have you ever thought of breaking up with Benny?"

"Breaking up? Why, Steve, we're in love with each other. How can you break up with someone you love?"

Stephen remembered another such conversation. His first evening in the confessional; the stubborn girl with the faint scent of carnation in her hair. "You must give up this Protestant," he had said. And the girl's reply: "I can't. I love him very much."

By his dogmatic insistence, he had driven that girl from him unabsolved. Ah, the futility of dogma to sweep back the tides of the heart. The heart! "Speak to her heart," Celia had advised. . . .

Fowler to thrush he was now. "But if loving a boy leads to family quarrels . . . hurting your father and mother? Don't you see, Monny, you can't go on wounding others, making them suffer."

Like a captive bird, Mona struggled in her brother's arms. She was caught in a net of affection and authority that she lacked the strength to break. "I can't give him up. I'll die if I do," she wept. But Stephen felt the weakening flutters of her resistance. He pitied the frail child, but Celia Fermoyle's voice was at his ear. "Wring the promise out of her — for my sake and her own."

"Say that you'll give him up. Promise me, Monny."

In a burst of weeping, Mona tore the promise from her heart.

Celia was waiting at the bottom of the stairs when Stephen came down. "She's promised, Mother," he said.

"God will bless you for this, Son."

But as Stephen walked down Woodlawn Avenue that night he doubted that God's blessing or any other good would flow from the violent wound he had inflicted on his sister's soul.

SCARCELY two weeks after mailing off *The Ladder of Love,* Stephen was summoned into the Cardinal's presence.

The summons came in the form of a three-line note:

You are requested, on receipt of this information, to present yourself at the Cardinal's residence in connection with a manuscript sent to this office.

Very truly yours,
MONS. DAVID J. O'BRIEN,
Secretary to the Cardinal

Monaghan grunted when Stephen showed him the note. "The tone of it — if anyone should step out from behind a lamppost and ask me — is not exactly warm." With a Pilate-like dusting motion, he brushed some dandruff off his cassock and handed the note back to Stephen. "Better hop over there."

"When should I go?"

"Early this afternoon. I hear His Eminence gets broodier as the day wears on."

Muted chimes from the depth of a Flemish clock bonged two as Stephen entered the Cardinal's antechamber — a high-ceilinged room of squeezing narrowness. Against a black walnut wainscot, shoulder-tall, stood tapestried chairs, high-backed, armless, and so widely intervaled that conversation was impossible. Stephen took the edge of an isolated chair and scrutinized the other people in the room. A mendicant friar, sandaled, sat gazing at the shovel hat on his lap. A puffy secular priest — a rector, judging by his flesh and years — nervously opened and shut the gold cover of his hunting-case watch; the clicking, which seemed to reassure him, increased in tempo whenever a member of the Cardinal's retinue entered. Two or three other people were at the far end of the room. Stephen had the feeling that everyone on the coldly formal chairs was expecting summary judgment to descend in awful form very soon.

A prelate with the purple touch of a monsignor at his throat opened the door of the Cardinal's sanctum and beckoned to the puffy pastor.

"His Eminence will see you now, Father Boylan."

Giving his watch cover a final click for courage, Father Boylan slid into the presence. When he came out five minutes later, he was wiping his eyes with a handkerchief.

"Friar Ambrose . . . this way please."

The sandaled monk arose, passed through the door. In seventy seconds he emerged again with the precipitate, singed look of a man who has taken a loud, round "no" for an answer.

What in God's name does he do to them? Stephen wondered. He rose from his chair and was gazing out the nearest window when he heard his name uttered with the exaggerated vocalism of a man in love with his own larynx.

"Stephen Fermoyle," the voice said. "It's been years!"

Steve knew that voice. It belonged to his Holy Cross classmate, Dick Clarahan — formerly "Dicky the Tonsil" — but now the Reverend Richard Clarahan of resounding pulpit fame and a member of the Cardinal's palace guard.

"Hello, Dick." Stephen held out his hand. He saw no harm

in being cordial to an old classmate, even though they had disliked each other in college. "It's a pleasure to see an old H. C. face in these high chambers." Stephen smiled. "Oh, I almost forgot. You *work* here."

On Dick Clarahan's unquestionably fine forehead three lines appeared: two were deprecatory, and the third underscored the others with sheer self-esteem. "In a semiattached way, yes. I deliver the High Mass sermon at the Cathedral on alternate Sundays. People seem to like it."

"So I hear. They tell me you take your audience right up the face of the purgatorial cliff — then drop them into burning brimstone a thousand feet below."

"Rank hyperbole. Still I wish you could hear me sometime. Benefit no end by your criticism. Where'll you be next Sunday at eleven A.M.?"

"Deaconing at St. Margaret's, probably."

"St. Margaret's? That's in Malden, isn't it?" Dick Clarahan managed to convey the idea that Malden was somewhere east of Tibet. Creepers of association began to cross his fine marble forehead. "Say, you aren't the chap who handed up those, ah — Italian translations for an imprimatur, are you?"

"That's me."

Clarahan puckered orator lips in a low whistle, then motioned with his head toward the Cardinal's door. "Monsignor O'Brien tells me His Eminence has been in a viceregal pet ever since he laid eyes on your manuscript. What's it all about, Steve? Don't tell me you're still dabbling in mysticism?"

"In a semiattached way. I can't seem to escape from such God-bitten characters as Augustine, Bernard, and Bonaventura."

"Number One won't like *that*," said Clarahan.

Monsignor Secretary O'Brien was announcing, "His Eminence will see you now, Father Fermoyle."

"*Dominus vobiscum*," murmured Dick.

"*Morituri te salutamus*. Keep the brimstone burning, Dickie."

Stephen followed the Cardinal's secretary through an iron-hinged oaken door, climbed a spiral stone staircase, and entered the hexagonal chamber known as the Tower Room. The dominant motif here was military-ecclesiastic. Mullioned windows, spandrel ceiling, and arras-hung walls made the room seem precisely what Lawrence Cardinal Glennon wished it to seem: the tribunal of a Templar general in the era of the Crusades. Cardinal Glennon had other rooms for other moods, but when he wanted to chill and paralyze a man he chose the Tower Room.

Across a floor of bare masonry Stephen advanced toward the refectory table where Lawrence Cardinal Glennon, Archbishop of Boston, sat nursing a chronic wrath.

The causes of that wrath were as numerous and as sharp as the colored glass pushpins sticking in the large wall map behind the Cardinal's chair. The map represented the Archdiocese of Boston, an area of 2465 square miles in eastern Massachusetts, one of the most thickly populated regions of the United States. More than a million Roman Catholic souls lay in Glennon's spiritual keeping; the churches they attended were represented by 452 green pins. The ninety-eight blue pins were parochial schools with an enrollment of 86,000 children. The thirty-six red pins stood for charitable institutions — hospitals, orphanages, houses of shelter and mercy, their inmates numbering 40,670. Other pins told the Cardinal that his Archdiocese sheltered communities of Jesuits, Augustinians, Redemptorists, Oblates, and Franciscans, not to mention 1100 secular priests and 1676 nuns gathered together in some thirty different orders of the Sisterhood. All these must be co-ordinated, disciplined, made to function and prosper, which, under the administrative genius of Lawrence Cardinal Glennon, is exactly what they did.

To the spiritual cares and mental irritations of administering the second richest Archdiocese in the world, this prince of the Church could now add a fleshly ailment, recently diagnosed. Only last week his physician had pronounced the dread word "hypertension" to explain the maddening headaches of his distinguished patient. The state of medicine being what it was in 1918, not a great deal could be done about the Cardinal's blood pressure. It was his cross, and for the most part he bore the cranial agony with toughhearted contempt. But today the headache was unbearable, and the Cardinal's temper was that of a bear pursued by remorseless hornets.

In addition to these personal and administrative griefs, His

Eminence was carrying a still heavier sorrow. To put no fine point on the matter, he was not hitting it off with Rome. Or more particularly, with Pietro Cardinal Giacobbi, the papal Secretary of State. The feud between Giacobbi and Glennon, ancient and unrelenting, had broken out shortly after Pius X had ascended the papal throne in 1903. At a Vatican musicale, Lawrence Glennon — at that time merely an attaché of the Propaganda College — had improvised on a theme from Scarlatti. His inventions had been unusually rich and pleasing, but Pietro Giacobbi, the sheepherder's son, who disliked both music and Americans, had taken the opportunity to whisper loudly: "This Monsignor plays the piano like a North American cow."

At the time Giacobbi's contempt had meant nothing, politically speaking, to Lawrence Glennon. His chariot was hitched to another star — the brilliant, well-born Merry del Val, then papal Secretary of State. Merry del Val was a lover of music, an adept with foils and horses, and, oddly enough, a superb rifleshot. A deep and lasting friendship had sprung up between Glennon and Merry del Val — a friendship that had flowered long after Glennon returned to the United States. Many favors flowed between Rome and Boston during those years. At the peak of the wave Pius X had placed the red hat of a Cardinal on Glennon's head and hung a pectoral cross of diamonds around his neck.

Then in 1914 Pius X died, and Glennon journeyed to Rome for the election of a new pontiff. What more human than to hope that his beloved Merry del Val should wear the triple crown? In this hope, Glennon and God did not see eye to eye. The conclave of cardinals chose a Genoese noble — Benedict XV — as Keeper of the Keys. And then the fearful blow fell. The new Pope selected Pietro Cardinal Giacobbi as his Secretary of State, and straightway all warmth evaporated between Boston and Rome. The scalar chain of authority was of course unbroken, but it clanked dismally. Glennon's more than generous contributions to the Holy See were coldly acknowledged or received as a matter of course. With Merry del Val in retirement, Glennon had no influential friend at the papal court. A new crowd was in power; the old basking days were over, and Lawrence Glennon felt chilly, out of things, alone.

"Father Fermoyle, Your Eminence," Monsignor O'Brien was saying.

The Cardinal looked up with weary uninterest at the young priest advancing toward him. Ah, yes, this would be the translator of those elegant and perfectly useless essays on mysticism. His Eminence felt no particular ill will toward mysticism; it merely had no bearing on his problems, could not help him in his administrative labors. And with so much financing and organizing to be done, why did young curates complicate matters with their private urgencies to explore and translate the emotions of mystics long dead and buried?

Stephen genuflected to kiss the beveled sapphire ring that the Cardinal extended and then snatched away. His Eminence was in no mood for ecclesiastical homage; he wanted to get down to cases, particularly the case of the manuscript on the table before him. He signaled Stephen not to stand around calfishly, but to take a chair, *that* chair, for the critical scrutiny about to begin.

From the infallible side of the table His Eminence appraised the young priest opposite him. Forty-two years of professional experience were in Glennon's fine hazel eyes — eyes that gazed with a single query at the endless line of priests bending and bowing before him. Like any other administrator of large affairs, Glennon was sorely pressed for capable lieutenants. His first inquiry — frankly explicit by now — was: "How can I use this man?"

Fingering his pectoral cross, Glennon assayed Father Fermoyle. Physique and carriage excellent; grooming impeccable (Glennon despised slouchers with dirty fingernails, imperfect teeth, and poor skin). Demeanor reserved, with just the proper touch of dedication. Outward markings favorable. Interior gifts? Glennon's clairvoyant glance uncovered in Stephen the spiritual glow so essential to a priest during the earlier phases of his career. And the manuscript (which Glennon had carefully read) revealed an undoubted stylistic grace. Barring the subject matter of the essays, it appeared that the Archdiocese of Boston could use a man with this talent. Not particularly in its present form, of course, Father Fermoyle would have to come off his mystical perch, descend to terra firma. But after all, *The Ladder of Love* was merely a translation. This good-looking curate might be persuaded to lay the subject matter aside, and, after a season of tempering and growth, who could foretell the uses to which his maturer pen might be put? Why, he might even become editor of the archdiocesan organ, *The Monitor*.

His Eminence permitted none of these favorable judgments to appear in his face or manner. There was yet another test to be made — a test that took the form of a standing question: "What is this man's weakness?" Is he vain, stupid, greedy, or spineless? The Cardinal intended to discover whether the curate now facing him was underboweled or overweening, too stubborn for handling or too easily led by the nose. Glennon had his own techniques for exposing hidden defects of character. He picked up *The Ladder of Love*, showed it to Stephen as Exhibit A, and asked:

"Did you make this translation?"

"Yes, Your Eminence."

"Why?"

"The original appealed to me as a work of great power and beauty. I put it into English so that it might be enjoyed by others."

"What others?" snapped Glennon.

"Anyone who — who takes pleasure in exalted thought and feeling."

"Ah, the lofty type. Not interested in muckers, grubbers, and such small deer, eh?"

Stephen flushed at the libel. "I wouldn't put it that way, Your Eminence."

"But your book puts it that way." The Cardinal ran a finger down the table of contents. "Listen to these titles: 'The Fallacy of Occam's Razor,' 'Alighieri and the Sweet New Love,' 'The Pears of Augustine.' You haven't the gall, Father — in spite of your highflying fancies — you haven't the gall to say that these essays could give any help on earth, or hope of heaven, to ordinary men or women?"

A tart rejoinder sprang to Stephen's tongue. He might point out that Quarenghi's work, despite its literary flavor, was actually an ideal extension of the First Commandment: "*Thou*

shalt love the Lord thy God with thy whole heart and soul."
Were "ordinary men and women" exempted from obedience
to this commandment? And where, if not in God's love, should
one seek hope of heaven or help on earth? Wisely, Stephen
suppressed these replies. He knew that the Cardinal would
only be irked by such rebuttals. Submissively he bit his
tongue.

Submission was no new thing to Glennon; he exacted it
from everyone, and usually required that it be accompanied
by a certain amount of cringing. In Stephen's silence he was
keen enough to detect no trace of terror. A golden mark went
down in the Cardinal's book: here was that rare creature, a
curate who could be obedient without cowering. Yet scarcely
had the golden mark been recorded when a strange part of
Glennon's character asserted itself. It was habitual with him,
after testing a man and finding him serviceable, to become
suspicious of his motives. Suppose this gifted young curate
were outflanking him with calculated self-restraint? Might not
obedience be the mask worn by a climbing fellow bent on
personal advancement? The Cardinal decided to cross-examine
further.

"What are your relations with the original author of this
work?"

"He was my professor of moral theology at the North
American College in Rome."

Rome. Hm. The beanstalk of suspicion grew rapidly in
Glennon's mind. "Were you on terms of special intimacy with
him?"

"I could not use so warm a phrase, Your Eminence. I
admired him immensely, and he was generous enough to
show me some personal kindnesses."

"Such as? . . ."

"Lending me books. Inviting me to accompany him on a
holiday walking trip in the Campagna." This niggling line of
inquiry puzzled Stephen, but he continued: "On two or three
occasions I visited him in his quarters, where we talked of
literature and philosophy."

"Politics too, perhaps? *Ecclesiastical* politics?"

What is the man driving at? thought Steve. "Only in a
general way, Your Lordship."

"Have you heard from this, ah — Monsignor Quarenghi since your return from Rome?"

"I've had three letters." A desire to make the whole matter perfectly clear led Stephen to add, "In one of them, Monsignor Quarenghi mentioned that he had been transferred, because of wartime urgencies, from teaching to the secretariat of Cardinal Giacobbi."

The lobes of Glennon's ears turned scarlet. The very uttering of Giacobbi's name sent his blood pressure soaring; an ax of pain split his domed forehead, and a flood of jealousies poured into the cleft. So! His suspicions were well founded, after all. While Lawrence Glennon twiddled his cardinalatial thumbs in outer darkness, this scheming curate was inching his way toward the central chandeliers of light. A wretched satisfaction at having foiled this backstairs plot prompted Glennon's sarcastic cut:

"I daresay, Father Fermoyle, that you baited your Vatican hook with the promise of American publication?"

The malignant unfairness of the charge touched off Stephen's anger. His Fermoyle-blue eyes met Glennon's hazel-irised attack without flinching. "I baited no hook, Your Eminence. I made no promise of publication. As a simple curate, how" — the sheer absurdity of the idea bewildered him — "how *could* I?"

"A simple curate might well ask that question," said Glennon. "But I detect in you, Father Fermoyle, such a lack of simplicity as I have rarely encountered in all the years since my ordination. I charge you with being that most unthinkable of creatures — a self-seeking priest."

Head bowed at the injustice, Stephen was silent. There was nothing he could say.

His Eminence continued: "I could forgive your literary pretensions, your two hundred pages of mystical moonshine, if they were not aimed at such an obvious target. There is an ugly word for this kind of thing — a word I've never had occasion to use before." Glennon brought the whip down hard. "I put it to you bluntly, Father Fermoyle: you are a toady, a foot-swallowing toady, and your mystical *Ladder of Love* is nothing but a — a handbook for climbers!"

Hell might freeze over, but no one could talk like that to a

Fermoyle. Pallid with anger, Stephen rose. "You must allow me to go, Your Eminence. My priesthood will not permit me to listen to such indignities."

"Will not permit?" Glennon's wattles went turkey-purple. "Sir, your priesthood will listen to what my cardinalhood tells it. *Primo:* I will not grant the imprimatur you came here to get. Write your fine Vatican friend, say that the whole business is off."

His Eminence rose from the table and straightway lost precious inches of stature. Massive above the waist, his short thighbones cruelly robbed him of height and reduced him to a squat, bald man, fifty pounds overweight. "*Secundo,* I hereby remove you from the parish of St. Margaret's. You need seasoning, Father Fermoyle, and I think I know just the brine to pickle you in."

He whirled to the archdiocesan map, pointed to an isolated pin at the northernmost tip of his domain. "As of next Monday you will be curate at Stonebury — and a moldier vat of obscurity I cannot imagine. The parish is called St. Peter's — a touch of irony that will not be lost on a man with your ambitions, Father Fermoyle. You will serve as assistant there to the Reverend E. E. Halley, a conspicuous failure as a pastor. I wish you joy of each other."

Stephen genuflected in silence as the Cardinal concluded: "Possibly — though I doubt it, Father — Ned Halley can educate you in humility." An unwonted melancholy banked the hazel fires raging in Glennon's eyes. "For if the meek and the poor are really with us, you are about to make the acquaintance of the meekest spirit and the poorest administrator in the Archdiocese of Boston."

BOOK TWO

The Rector

CHAPTER 1

THE NASHUA DIVISION of the Boston & Maine was, in 1918, the dreariest stretch of track in New England. Leaving the black mills of Litchburg behind, it wound across a wasteland of scrub timber and unscrubbed towns, then plunged into a desolate terrain of fern swamps, rocky farms, and abandoned granite quarries stretching to the New Hampshire border. This was the land of the Pilgrim's pride, a land that the sons of Pilgrims had long ago deserted for the more bountiful prairies of the West. Never gracious, the region was now haggard and exhausted as it waited to sink back into its pre-Pilgrim state of flint, fern, and pine.

Elbow on a sill of No. 64, the one-coach local making all stops between Litchburg and Nashua, Stephen Fermoyle laid against his heart the loneliness of the countryside. An April downpour was grooving rivulets through the sooty murk on the car window. Stephen watched the raindrops run their compulsive races to the bottom of the pane. Pathetic fallacy or no, these obscure tricklings might almost be symbolic of the vain courses of men. Grass would wither, raindrops would slide down a dingy window, and men would break their hearts in banishment. Meanwhile the seraphim would continue to circle about the throne, singing *Gloria in excelsis*.

It was this latter perspective that Stephen proposed to himself as he gazed out upon the gloomy landscape. He had not the slightest intention of feeling downcast by his transfer to Stonebury. His Eminence might fulminate like an archdiocesan Thor, but Stephen could not persuade himself to feel frightened or guilty, as the bolts of demotion whistled past his ears. A want of humility? Perhaps. But one had only to watch the raindrops jostling each other down the windowpane to realize that sooner or later they would all reach the sea.

He had felt some natural pangs at leaving St. Margaret's. The parting with Monaghan had been particularly painful.

170

Dollar Bill, trying to be noncommittal, had succeeded only in being hoarser than usual. No Polonius advice, no counsel to be a good soldier. His gift of a new valise with a blunt, "You'll be needing this in your travels, Father," almost brought tears. His "Good-by, God's blessings on you, Steve," *did* bring them. At the door of the parish house he handed Stephen a letter. "Give this to your new pastor." The frog in Monaghan's throat had a strange croak. "And don't make the mistake of judging him by his surroundings."

A pursy conductor wearing a Masonic emblem on his watch chain punched Stephen's ticket as though it had personally affronted him. Catholic priests did not often travel on the Nashua division; even this one-man Romish invasion was something to get suspicious about. The conductor went back into the baggage compartment the better to brood over men with reversed collars, and stuck his head through the door only to announce a succession of local stops.

"Stonebury, Stonebury," he cried at last, making the name a reproach to right-thinking Protestants everywhere. Steve gripped the handle of his new valise, and swung off the car steps onto the platform. The baggageman, gingerly assisted by the conductor, rolled a paunchy keg onto the station platform. Then the wheezy engine snorted asthmatically toward New Hampshire, leaving the keg and Stephen alone in the drenching rain.

The station door was locked. Stephen peered in the telegrapher's window, saw a Morse key, a half-empty ticket case, and a spindle jammed with faded yellow dispatches. Of recent human activity there was no sign. He was about to start walking along the muddy road when a hammer-headed horse pulling a one-seated vehicle known as a "democrat" clopped up to the platform. Over the driver's head sagged a tattered umbrella, once orange-colored, still bearing a hay-and-grain advertisement. From the washed-out horse and faded umbrella all pigments of energy had been drained; the spidery rig was a paradigm of decay.

Then the driver leapt from his seat and the whole picture changed. Stephen had never seen a fellow with so many springs in his arms and legs; his agility was a combination of fox, hawk, and jumping jack. A brown wiry man he was, with skin the color of strong tea and eyes black as coffee jelly. Copious jets of tobacco juice spurting from his mouth had made brown blotters of his oversized mustache. He wore logging boots, patched butternut jeans, an oilskin jacket, and a hat that might have been stolen from one of the region's scarecrows.

The man saw the priest's collar and touched his hat. Of all the salutations Stephen Fermoyle would ever receive, this crude obeisance was the most welcome. The brown man must be a Catholic. Stephen returned the salute. "Can you tell me how to get to St. Peter's?"

"Bes' way, hop on rig. I drive you pas'." No mistaking that dialect. Pure Canuck.

Stephen started to put his suitcase behind the seat of the democrat, but the brown man held up a semaphore paw. "She go in front. Bar'l go in back." He darted up the platform toward the fat keg and rolled it lightly toward his rig. With the exhibitionism of one who knows his own strength, he spat confidently into the palm of his left hand, rubbed it across his right, then seized the barrel at both ends, got his knee under it, and tossed it like an eiderdown pillow into the cart. As the springs of the tiny wagon flattened under the weight, the horse's ears went up.

"Napoleon, by gar, he tink oat tas' good aft' he pull me, you and bar'l two mile."

Horse blanket over his knees, the hay-and-grain umbrella shedding some of the rain, Stephen felt wonderfully expansive as the rig drove off. Soon they were passing through a valley of stone. Granite was the ground motif of the region; it cropped out in quartz ledges and lay heaped in enormous dumps rimming abandoned quarries — deep ugly gashes that men had blasted in the granite hills. He wanted to ask his driver the story of these desolate workings, but waited till the brown man's sidelong glances mounted to a query of his own.

"You com' for help Fath' Hallee?"

"Yes," said Stephen. "I'm his new curate. My name's Father Fermoyle. What's yours?"

"Hercule Menton." Hercule tickled Napoleon's rump with a broken whip. "Fath' Hallee wan ver' good man. But tired mebbe, like Napoleon here."

The whole countryside looked tired to Stephen. "What do people do for a living around here?"

Hercule pointed his whip at the gaunt mast of a derrick. "When Merlin quarry cut beeg stones, everywan have good job. No more stone now."

The nostalgic sadness in his voice prompted Steve to ask, "Were you a quarryman, Hercule?"

"Bes' goddam dynamiter you find." The artist was speaking now. "I drill deeper holes ev' drilled in Merlin — thirty, forty hole same time, ha! Open dynamite with teeth, by gar." The mimic in Hercule made him enact everything in motor detail. Now he chewed the waxed paper off imaginary dynamite sticks. "Then I tap heem into hole." Hercule made pounding motions with his fist. "I wire all hole together per*fect*. Then I push blast handle down — wa-y down. Mountain say, 'Hercule, why you do zis to me?' Then she break like cider jug on stone floor." Hercule's coffee-colored eyes surveyed the broken fragments at his feet.

Stephen had to laugh at the mimicry. "You blasted yourself right out of a job. What do you do now?"

"Mak' fiddle sometimes." Hercule shook his head dolefully as if to say, "People don't appreciate violin making in these parts." He bent over and drew an ax helve from under the seat. "W'en fiddle trade slow, I carve bes' goddam ax han'le you buy in store."

Stephen balanced the ax helve in his hand. The thing curved like a snake standing on its tail. "Why, this is a piece of fine wood carving, Hercule. But what do you do about axheads?"

Hercule spat over his shoulder at the barrel flattening the springs of his rig. "Buy wholesale, fi' dollar a dozen from Boston." In humorful mimicry he went through the motions of fitting a forty-cent axhead onto a homemade handle, then handed the imaginary product to Stephen. "Wan dol*lar*," he said, merriment bubbling out of him as sap pours from a maple.

"Cheap at double the price," laughed Steve. He had the good feeling that this ex-dynamiter, luthier, and axmaker would make a valuable companion either on a desert island or in a broken-down parish.

Now they were clopping through Stonebury Center, a juncture of three roads that had long ago forgotten why they crossed each other. On the rain-swept village green a latticed bandstand was flanked by two Civil War cannon. The tallest structure in town was a two-story building with the gilt letters I.O.O.F. in an upper window. Bearing right, Hercule drove down a gantlet of boxy houses, mustard-brown and too high for their width. New England at its seediest. Puritanism needing a coat of paint.

It was almost twilight when Hercule pointed with his whip to a gray pile perched on rising ground a mile beyond the town. "San' Pierre," he announced, bringing his rig to a halt. "I t'ink hill too steep for Napoleon wit' bar'l on."

Stephen leapt down from the democrat. "Napoleon is excused. He's already given me the ride of my life. Thanks, Hercule." Stephen held out his hand. "God bless both of you."

"Merci, mon père. Giddap! . . ."

Climbing the rain-swept hill, Stephen braced himself for his first view of the church. Built of granite, St. Peter's could not tumble down for another five centuries. But its very durability gave it the sadness of sub-eternal things. Stephen walked around the church like a man inspecting a ruin. Cascades of water streamed from broken gutters. Panes of stained glass were missing, and an arm of the cross atop the squat bell tower was gone. Stooping to inspect the cornerstone, Stephen saw the Roman numerals MDCCCLXXII. And in smaller letters the Latin for: "Thou art Peter. On this rock I will build my church."

Buoyed by the stubborn grandeur of his tradition, Stephen walked toward the parish house, a stone dwelling some hundred feet away. Chilled, hungry, he knocked at the door. A hot supper would fix everything. He knocked again. No answer. He pushed open a creaking door, and entered a musty front hall.

"Father Halley," he called . . . "Father Halley."

Still no answer. Through unaired rooms Stephen penetrated to the kitchen. The housekeeper must be very deaf. But the unpolished stove, curtainless windows, and bare table told him there was no housekeeper.

A nickeled alarm clock over the sink said six-five, and was still ticking.

Someone must live here; someone had wound the clock. Stephen washed his hands at the iron pump, then reconnoitered for something to eat. Church mice would have scorned the pantry. After much searching he found a tablespoonful of tea, a piece of smoked fish, and the heel of a rye loaf. He kindled a fire, boiled some water in a saucepan, swallowed two mugs of scalding tea, and gnawed at half of the rye heel. The fish he did not eat.

The hands of the alarm clock were crossing each other at six-thirty when Stephen heard the front door open. He stood up expectantly to greet his rector. Quiet feet came through the house. The kitchen door opened, and Stephen Fermoyle saw Ned Halley in the flesh.

There was little flesh to see. The aged priest weighed scarcely a hundred and twenty pounds, including the water in his overcoat and the mud on his shoes. White-polled he was, and toothless or nearly so. His lips had sunk into an oral hollow, deeper than the sockets of his still-burning eyes. He raised his white eyebrows in courteous apology that seemed to say, "Excuse me, whoever you are, for — for" — a fluttering motion of his hand included the poverty of the entertainment, his own fatigue — "for everything."

Ned Halley stood near the stove, treating his hands to the luxury of unaccustomed warmth. "A fire is cozy, of a March evening," he murmured absently. That a stranger had built the fire and was now pouring tea for him seemed not at all odd to the old priest.

"Here, Father," said Stephen. "Sit down and drink this tea. It'll take away the chill." He helped the old priest out of his sodden coat, then sliced the remnants of the rye loaf. Ned Halley sat down at the table, murmured grace before food, and lifted the steaming cup to his lips. Because the bread was too hard to chew, he soaked small pieces of it in his tea before putting them into his mouth.

"Would you like some fish, Father?" Stephen almost said *the* fish.

"No, thank you; this is quite enough. I eat my heavy meal

in the middle of the day. But, if *you* would like the fish, Father — "

"No, no." Stephen stoked the fire while Ned Halley finished his supper and crossed himself in thanksgiving. They sat in silence. Steve couldn't decide whether the pastor was too courteous to ask, "Who are you?" or whether he knew already, and was past caring. Either his spiritual detachment was great or his fatigue was heavy. He dozed by the fire.

When Ned Halley awoke, Stephen handed him the envelope containing his credentials and the letter from Pastor Monaghan. The old priest glanced briefly at both, then gave proof that his faculties were alert.

"My old friend William Monaghan says in his note that you are an extremely able curate. Flattery is not a weakness with William. Therefore I can believe you are everything he says." Having completed this perfect syllogism, Ned Halley rose. "Welcome, Father Fermoyle, to the parish of St. Peter's in Stonebury." He walked unsteadily toward the kitchen door. "I insist that you eat the fish, Father. You must be hungry after your long ride."

Rolling sleeplessly on a stiff straw mattress, Stephen could barely wait for daybreak. So much to be explored in the parish. So much to be understood about his pastor. Stephen had half expected to find in Father Halley one of those unfortunate "whisky priests," a man whose secret tippling had barred him from advancement. But this frail priest was no tippler; the acid of abstinence had gouged away everything but the luminous core of his spirit. He didn't even eat! Stephen twisted on the coarse mattress, ravenously hungry, his thoughts circling around the strange phenomenon of Ned Halley. How had he incurred the Cardinal's wrath? And what was the cause of his strange detachment from reality, which he carried to the point of neglecting health and appearance? Some defect in intelligence? No. His precise appraisal of Monaghan's letter ruled that out. From what character malady was the man suffering, and what in life would be its cure? Stephen turned with his own questions, famished for food, awaiting the first gray announcement of morning.

At six he arose, doused himself with cold water, and hastened toward the church. His plan was to offer Mass, then slip into town for groceries, and make breakfast for the pastor and himself. But when he opened the sacristy door, he saw Ned Halley already at the vesting bench, robing for Mass. Wordlessly Stephen took up the humbler office of acolyte, led the way to the altar.

He was shocked, entering the body of the church, by its pitiful state of disrepair. Walls and ceiling were cracked, splotched with rain streaks and patches of mold. Many of the pews were broken; the stations of the cross, poor wooden things, hung askew. Two posts were missing from the altar rail, and the sanctuary carpet was in tatters. The altar itself needed a new coat of paint and urgent replacement of worn linen. The sacred vessels were tarnished, and the leather covers of the Mass book were curling with age.

Yet, assisting Ned Halley at this shabby altar was one of the richest experiences that Stephen ever had. The frayed vestments and tarnished chalice were miraculously transformed when the old priest lifted his thin arms at the *Introibo*. Flesh of earthly defeat became radiant as Ned Halley humbly united himself with the Victim in the mystical re-enactment of Calvary.

Afterwards, he acknowledged Stephen's assistance with gentle detachment. "Thank you, Father," he said simply. "Now I will assist you."

Held in the magnetic field of Ned Halley's saintliness, Stephen walked slowly back to the house with the old man. A protective instinct filled him with a yearning to lift the physical burden of parish duties from his frail shoulders; he hoped that the pastor would give him instructions, assignments to duty. But at that hour Ned Halley was eager for only one thing — the meditation which is the special joy of those who have just celebrated Mass. He entered his study, knelt at the worn *prie-dieu,* and covered his face with blue-veined hands.

Ravenous hunger was consuming Stephen. The fish! He must have his half of it now. He opened the pantry door, and there on a little shelf he saw not one, but two smoked perch. Two chunks of a *habitant* rye loaf lay beside them. And on a piece of brown paper was a little mound of coarse-ground coffee.

The loaves and fishes. Coffee, too. *Miracle du jour!*

Stephen made coffee, set the table for two, and waited for Father Halley to join him at breakfast. The pastor, long at prayer, finally emerged from his study and sat down at the kitchen table like a toothless Elijah accepting heaven-descended food as a matter of course. Stephen waited till the rector's coffee-soaked crust had disappeared, then ventured to ask:

"Would you mind, Father, if I took a walk around the parish?"

"Not at all. Feel free to come and go as you wish." Ned Halley paused for a moment. "I'm afraid, though, that you may have some difficulty locating our parishioners."

"You mean they're scattered all over the countryside?"

"No," said Ned Halley, "they're all in one place. But that place is rather hard to find."

"You make it sound mystifying."

"It *is* a little puzzling at first," agreed the pastor. "Officially the parish of St. Peter's coincides with the town borders of Stonebury. But actually you'll find most of our people clustered in a rock hollow called L'Enclume."

"An odd name."

"It's French for 'anvil.' " The rector, who could talk as well as another when the vein was flowing, continued: "Twenty years ago, in the great days of the Merlin quarries, a forge and a tavern prospered there. Oxcarts drawing heavy blocks of granite to the railway siding in Stonebury would stop at L'Enclume for repairs and — ah — refreshment. Fire has long since razed the tavern, and no axles are straightened now at the forge. But the French Canadians who worked the quarries — they're all Catholics, of course — still cling to its exhausted flank."

"What do they do for a living?"

"Not a great deal. The chief industries hereabouts are blue-berry-picking in summer and ice-cutting in winter. Some of the men chop wood."

Steve began to understand why St. Peter's was in such a state of disrepair. "How do I get to L'Enclume, Father?"

"I'll show you." Ned Halley led his new curate to the back door of the parish house and pointed across a deep, tree-filled valley. "L'Enclume lies on the other side of this gorge," he said. "I myself never take the short cut through the valley; it is a swampy treacherous bog. You will do better if you take the macadam road that passes the front of our house, and follow it for three quarters of a mile. Turn left down a sloping dirt road, and stay on that till you strike a burned forge. Then, by the complexion and language of the people, you'll know you're in L'Enclume."

"I'll find it," said Stephen confidently.

"I have no doubt that you will." Ned Halley fingered his lower lip thoughtfully. "My only suggestion — and I offer it merely as a suggestion — is that you do not enter the houses of these people unless they invite you to do so. Their poverty is extreme, and when a priest comes knocking at their door" — the old pastor phrased his meaning with oblique delicacy — "well, you can imagine what they're apt to think, Father."

"I can well imagine," said Stephen. His thoughts were divided between Monaghan's theory of parish visitation and Cardinal Glennon's description of Ned Halley as a "conspicuous failure." In their own way, both might be right. But in another way — a sensitive way that neither Glennon nor Monaghan could conceive — Ned Halley was right, too.

STEPHEN found L'Enclume after a brisk fifteen-minute walk. Following the macadam road, he passed huge derricks with broken booms, old donkey engines, their boilers rusty from exposure, clinging to the rim of abandoned pits that once rang with drill and hammer but were now filled with stagnant pools.

What had happened here? How long ago? Who could tell him the story of these desolate quarries, and the fate of the men who had once worked them? Unconsciously Steve turned his head, hoping to see Hercule's spidery rig clopping down the road. But behind and ahead the road was bare. Where are all the people? he wondered, gazing about the strangely unpopulated countryside.

He dipped left down the dirt road as Ned Halley had directed, and came to the first landmark, the burned-out forge. Its tall stone chimney was still standing, and the huge anvil that had given the place its name lay overturned amid a heap of debris. Inanimate things are the most desolate of all, thought Stephen. Then another fifty paces, and he stepped from the inanimate desolation of the forge onto the stage of a vast amphitheater teeming with life.

In front of him a steep hill fanned out on three sides; terracing its slopes, somewhat like benches in a stadium, were the tar-paper shacks of L'Enclume. A midmorning sun touching the scene with the first warmth of spring had tempted the inhabitants out of their mean dwellings. Shawled women with clothespins in their mouths were hanging poor garments on sagging lines. Men smoked black clay pipes at broken gateways or climbed makeshift ladders to nail pieces of tin or wood to leaking roofs. Pigs, hens, dogs, and children issued from winter's pen and raced over the muddy slopes of the hill. Stephen felt as though he were viewing a mammoth anthill from its base.

No one paid the slightest attention to him as he climbed up and down quagmire lanes, making a point-blank appraisal of L'Enclume's houses and people. A taxgatherer would have turned away hopelessly; revenue from these people was unthinkable. They seemed alien in spirit too; impenetrably hostile in alien, suspicious ways. The men did not touch their hats, the children darted away as Stephen approached. L'Enclume certainly was not the picturesque tableau of song and story — the village padre surrounded by his respectful flock offering the first fruits of their husbandry. No, this was something else again — a reality meaner, more terrifying than Stephen had ever imagined.

The full weight of his exile settled upon his shoulders. Here among unfavored strangers, he must beat out his salvation — and theirs, if possible — on the anvil of ugly reality. How and where should he begin? Trained in the Monaghan school of house-to-house visitation, Stephen yearned to knock at the doors of these people, break down their resistance with acts of service and love. But he was under other orders now; he must not embarrass the inhabitants of L'Enclume by entering their homes. If only he could come upon Hercule Menton, the brown, mischievous man might advise him how best to win the hearts (or at least the friendly smiles) of these suspicious natives.

At a thicket of R.F.D. mailboxes he saw a knot of men puffing at their pipes. "Could you tell me where I can find Hercule Menton?" he asked.

The men exchanged sullen glances, warning each other to silence, then started to drift away. Angered by their sheer incivility, Stephen was about to seize one of them by the shoulder when he heard the ringing of an indecently loud bell. He turned and saw, in the middle of the quagmire road, a curious cart, once white, but now streaked with mud and time. A black-letter legend, VICTOR THENARD, MEATS AND PROVISIONS, was painted on its side. At the tail of the cart stood a man in a bloodstained apron, wielding his cleaver with the butcher's professional disregard for thumbs, as he hacked at a quarter of ancient beef. Stephen came close to the cart; tripes and loops of foreign-looking sausages hung from iron hooks. The man finished hacking, picked up a bell, and rang it town-crier fashion, bellowing, *"Viande de boucherie, bas prix."* At the sound of his bell and voice, the women of L'Enclume came running out of the tar-paper shacks. With black shawls flung over their heads they gathered at the cart tail, pulling at scraps of meat as they gabbled to the butcher and each other. The gabbling of the women and their wheeling motions about the butcher's cart gave the scene a nightmarish quality, part witch dance, part adoration of some tribal totem.

Shocked, almost frightened, Stephen hastened away from the butcher cart. He knew that he must resist the temptation to overfastidiousness, but this cackling tug of war for scraps of spoiled flesh challenged his ideal of human behavior. As he climbed the hill he realized how heavily the souls of men were freighted by fleshly ballast — imposts of passion and appetite that must be accepted as part of the human luggage. At the top of the hill he gazed backward and saw a scene of Breughelish activity below; the inhabitants of L'Enclume were performing the mixed duties of life — banal, sorrowful, compulsive. "What did I expect of these people?" he asked himself. "Urbane deportment, intellectual discourse, picturebook piety? Absurd." Sympathy and understanding claimed him. Whatever approach he would make to these strange souls must be made on the basis of mortally limiting facts.

Turning, Stephen saw the steep gorge that Ned Halley had

pointed out; on its farther rim stood the blocky edifice of St. Peter's. Despite the pastor's warning, he decided to take the short cut through the valley. A narrow road, scarcely more than a trail, led him down the bushy descent into the swampy lowland, past ruined trees half submerged in pools of stagnant water. The pools gradually became a bog filled with a kind of white moss, half lichen, half peat. Stephen stooped, tried to pull up a handful, and was amazed at the stubbornness with which the moss roots clung to damp soil. The tenacity of earth-sprung things! Yet examining the moss, he found it to be a delicate interlacing of tendrils finer than the work of a crochet needle. He held the moss to his nose; its odor was a mixture of death passing into life, the primal smell of nature.

Now the ground rose slightly; the bog gave way to a stand of dark pines — majestic first-growth conifers, huge-boled and heavy-boughed. As Stephen entered the wood, the light grew dimmer, greener, pierced only by an occasional broadsword of sun. Stephen was familiar with the allegories that men of all ages have hewn from forests. It pleased him now to ask, "What forest is this?" Not the dark wood in which Dante encountered the antique guide that led him through Hell and Purgatory. Not the tarn forest of Grendel nor the tangled grove guarding the Jason fleece. Stephen rejected these as too lofty, too remote. The great pines in the hidden gorge between L'Enclume and St. Peter's held a meaning more immediate and personal, yet plaguingly concealed.

Standing on a carpet of springy needles and brown pine cones, he gazed up through the great branches spreading like massive candelabra above. Whatever the secret of these trees might be, he knew that he would come here often and alone to read his Office, to forget his human isolation, and to remind himself of his spiritual destiny as a priest.

Following the path through the forest, he climbed a steep slope and came out of the gorge at the back door of St. Peter's. He had traveled a full circle across his parish. He had encountered poverty, decay, desolation, and indifference. He had discovered the anvil of his fate and welcomed the falling sledge of experience that would beat him into tougher, more tempered steel.

CHAPTER 2

THE POVERTY at St. Peter's was grimmer than Stephen had imagined; the people of L'Enclume hadn't enough money to support themselves, let alone their pastor. No one paid pew rent; the standard contribution at Mass was a penny, and one rainy Sunday in April the basket yielded only ninety-two cents. God himself couldn't run a parish on that! And on the day that Father Halley pleaded for special generosity in the matter of Peter's pence — the annual collection for the Supreme Pontiff at Rome — the parishioners responded with $1.85. To this amount the pastor gravely added such odd coins as he had on hand, and asked his curate to send a postal money order for $2.50 to the archdiocesan treasurer.

Father Fermoyle took private pleasure in writing the money order. He pictured the Cardinal running his finger down the list of pastoral contributions and coming to the item: *St. Peter's, Stonebury, Mass., $2.50.* Probably His Eminence would have a cerebral hemorrhage. . . .

Stephen had to marvel at the pastor's genius for operating without ready money. Somehow, he managed to survive on the crumbs brought in by his parishioners — an egg from Berthe Crèvecoeur, a smoked perch or a heel of *habitant* bread from Agathe d'Éon. The heavy meal of the day was a bowl of pea soup placed unobtrusively on the pantry shelf by the Mesdames Bouchard and Leblanc. The old man could subsist on this meager diet, but roaring hunger drove Stephen to the grocer in Stonebury, where he laid out his last twenty-five dollars on a hoard of basic eatables: coffee, rice, canned goods, potatoes, and condensed milk. What he would do when these supplies ran out was a matter that Stephen preferred not to think about.

Desperately he canvassed ways and means of jacking up parish revenues. The usual methods of raising funds — a whist party or church bazaar — were out of the question. No one in L'Enclume played whist or had any cash to purchase the frosted cakes, raffle tickets, or secondhand knickknackeries generally on sale at a bazaar. For a moment Stephen considered sending out a humorous SOS to Corny Deegan: "Save Our Souls (with Cash Contribution)." But he remembered that the contractor-Knight was on a mixed jaunt to Dublin and Rome — restoring broken abbeys in the one place and repairing ecclesiastical power lines in the other. Whatever begging Stephen would have to do must be done in humbler ways.

A letter to Bill Monaghan asking for discarded altar linens and vestments brought a bundle by express, together with a twenty-dollar check for Father Halley's "special intentions." Stephen had nearly persuaded the pastor to spend the money patching the church roof when a mendicant monk (the very Friar Ambrose that Stephen had seen in the Cardinal's antechamber) wandered past, sandal-shod. Ned Halley endorsed the check over to Friar Ambrose, "to help the good man," as he timidly explained to Stephen, "carry on his work in Upper Nigeria."

Against such innocence, protests were unavailing. Besides, twenty dollars would never solve the economic problem of St. Peter's. The pastor needed a regular income, no matter how small; but before he could obtain such an income, the people of L'Enclume must have steady employment. To provide such employment Stephen had turned over in his mind a dozen projects. It occurred to him that the huge quarry dumps lying about the countryside might be converted into crushed rock for road building. But inquiries soon showed that Stonebury had neither the capital to set up a rock crusher nor any need for broken stone. Net: zero. Once while tramping across a rocky hillside he saw some glossy-leafed mountain laurel and recognized it as the stuff that florists used for wreaths and festoons. He picked an armful, and brought it hopefully to a wholesale florist in Litchburg. The florist said the laurel was excellent and in great demand, but that a recent state law forbade picking it for commercial purposes.

All Stephen's efforts to uncover new sources of parish revenue amounted to nothing. Meanwhile, as Sunday contributions dropped even lower, he learned that until the blueberry-picking season started, the population of L'Enclume would be on short rations. Then, at a time when hope, cash, and groceries struck new lows, he stumbled over a nugget of what seemed to be pure gold.

Returning from a long, fruitless walk around the parish, he descended into the deep gorge between L'Enclume and St. Peter's, picked his way across the peaty bog, and came to the grove of dark pines. At the edge of the wood he heard a metallic tattoo of ax strokes falling in double tempo. He entered the greenwood dimness and, standing under the branches of a majestic pine, saw two men swinging axes as only French Canadians can. They worked beaverishly at a great tree; two other trees lay felled in a small clearing, and a small portable sawmill stood near by.

As Stephen stepped into the clearing, one of the men uttered a cry and plunged like a deer into the green cover of the forest. His companion looked up in surprise, then, seeing the priest, fell upon his knees and began beating his breast in a terrified *mea culpa*.

The man on his knees was Hercule Menton.

"*Pardonn' un pauvr'* woodcutter," implored Hercule as Stephen approached. "Eet ees only t'ird wan we chop. Forgive, Seigneur."

"Why ask *my* forgiveness?" Stephen was puzzled. "Get up, man, don't kneel to me."

Mustaches drooping with guilt, Hercule arose.

"Do you own these trees?" asked Stephen.

Hercule shook a vigorous "no."

"Who does?"

"*L'église* . . . she owns."

"You mean this forest belongs to the parish of St. Peter's?"

Hercule nodded. "Twenny year ago Vince Trudeau lef' all zese trees — to parish." Hercule put in an extenuating bid for sympathy. "I tell Fath' Hallee las' year pine board wort' t'irteen cent a foot in Litchburg."

"I suppose you were going to saw up these trees, sell the lumber, and hand over the money to Father Halley?"

At this convenient contrary-to-fact interpretation, Hercule grinned cheerfully.

"*Oui,* just what I t'ought I do."

"Well, hold off your philanthropy awhile," advised Steve.

"I'll have to get Father Halley ready for the shock." Calculation of the revenue to be had from one hundred thousand feet of pine board at thirteen cents a foot was making Steve tolerant of this wood-poaching, fiddle-making ex-dynamiter. "Say nothing about this to anyone, Hercule. I think we can put all the able-bodied men in L'Enclume to work for the first time since Merlin closed."

That very evening Stephen broached the subject of the pine forest to Ned Halley after they had finished their usual supper of bread, tea, and smoked fish.

"I was told in the village today," he began, "that the parish owns quite a stand of pine trees."

"Pine trees?" The pastor's inflection was that of an invalid trying to remember when he had last taken his medicine.

"Yes, down in the gorge, you know."

"I think I remember the place. At Christmas we get evergreen there. The trees are very handsome."

"Handsome *and* valuable. Do you realize, Father, that there's about ten thousand dollars' worth of timber in that grove?"

"Well, well, I had no idea."

You're going to get the idea, vowed Stephen. "I've taken the liberty, Father," he went on, "of going into the matter with one of our parishioners, Hercule Menton."

"Ah, Hercule. A dear charitable friend. He has been kind enough to keep our wood box filled on occasion."

"Hercule assures me," Stephen improvised, "that with the help of a few other — um — dear friends, he could cut down several hundred dollars' worth of timber during the next month."

Ned Halley felt disposed to keep his new curate happy, but cutting down pine trees was not quite in his line.

"Why," he asked mildly, "should we go into the lumber business?"

"Why?" Stephen almost lost his temper. "Why?" To get enough money (he wanted to say) to make our dilapidated old church a decent habitation for the Blessed Sacrament. To help us carry on our work among the sick and poor of this parish. To put bread in the pantry, meat on the table.

Against Monaghan's alligator hide he could have hurled

these fighting arguments, but the self-naughting serenity in Ned Halley's faded eyes tempered Stephen's enthusiasm for the lumber business.

"I merely suggested it as a source of parish revenue," he said. Anything further would have been an attack on Ned Halley's stewardship.

"Thank you for the suggestion, Father." Nothing more. No sarcastic hint, "I'm running this parish." No abstract theorizing on the virtues of poverty. No apology for the shabby past or hand-to-mouth present. Just the placing of a period at the end of an impossible proposition.

The gentle manner of that placing taught Stephen a deeper spiritual truth than he had ever learned from St. Francis or Alfeo Quarenghi. He saw that this obscure priest possessed a serene and literal trust in goods that thieves could not steal nor rust corrupt. Ned Halley did not quote Matthew on the subject of keeping no purse about one. He merely was the purseless man, fearlessly refusing to encumber his soul with perishable treasures.

Ned Halley's fearlessness made Stephen fearless, too. After that supper of bread and fish he stopped worrying about money. He found out that one could live without money, or at any rate without being over-anxious about it, and that much of the energy he had spent in casting about for revenue had been a sheer waste of spirit. Faith that money would come in somehow, or that if it didn't why, that would be all right too, supported Stephen Fermoyle for the rest of his life.

He staved off Hercule Menton's queries about the pine forest, and took up his true work in the parish of St. Peter's.

STEPHEN's first care was to tighten up the somewhat relaxed teaching and practice of religion among the people of L'Enclume. He scraped together a first-communion class of girls and boys, drilled them in the simple theology of the blue-green catechism, and incidentally gave them lessons in English reading and diction. He instructed a group of the more promising lads in the proper serving of Mass, with accompanying homilies on the function of soap, water, brush, and comb. On Friday nights during Lent he took over that solemnly beautiful devotion, the Stations of the Cross, symbolizing the Passion of Christ. The pump-organ was irreparably broken; Stephen taught his acolytes the words and music of the sorrowful *Stabat Mater*. At first their thin voices echoed through an empty church, but gradually the elders drifted in to watch the symbolic procession and to lift their broken French responses in the Five Sorrowful Mysteries of the Rosary. Stephen carefully refrained from taking up the collection that usually concluded these services.

In preparing his Sunday sermon, Stephen modeled himself as closely as possible on Father Halley. The pastor had little apparent flair for preaching; he exhorted not, neither did he scold nor pass moral judgments in matters of drunkenness, unchastity, or missing Mass. He neither wept over his parishioners nor endowed them with feelings that they did not possess. Stephen soon realized that such seeming laxity was wisdom of a very special order, perfectly geared to the spiritual understanding of his people. Avoiding all pretensions to rhetoric, Stephen spoke simply and briefly to his unschooled listeners, never laying upon them more than their emotions could bear.

Gradually he came closer to the people of L'Enclume, and found them — except for their rude poverty — not unlike the families of Irish and Italian descent he had known at St. Margaret's. These exiled French Canadians were not quite so cheerful or outgoing as the Irish and not so quick-witted as the Italians. They were immature, superstitious, fearsome of strangers, and evasive as small furred animals when one approached them too suddenly. But they had a childlike gaiety and a gift of dramatic exaggeration (Hercule Menton was a perfect example) that easily led them into boasting and outright lying. What seemed like laziness was a philosophic acceptance of their high-and-dry helplessness. Watching a group of men lounging in pipe-smoking attitudes against a stone wall reminded Stephen of stranded dory men waiting for a tide to float them off.

Everyone whittled in L'Enclume. Stephen decided to take advantage of this local skill in carving and joinery. He persuaded Alphonse Boisvert to repair the broken cross on top of the church. Boisvert did the job skillfully, then mended and varnished the rickety pews that had caused Stephen so much pain. Lest Hercule Menton feel slighted, Stephen asked him to freshen up the neglected Stations of the Cross. When the job was done, Hercule could stand outside the church after Mass on Sunday and boast to his circle of admirers, "Bes' goddam Stations you buy in store, by gar." And Stephen could honestly add, "You're right, Hercule. Excepting the goddam part, they are."

Weeks passed, and as yet Stephen had not crossed a threshold in L'Enclume. Patiently he waited for an invitation into one of the mean shacks, but none came. Ned Halley made all the sick calls, and the old man would come tottering home covered with dust or mud after trudging on foot about his parish. Stephen begged for the privilege of relieving his rector, who always put him off with the same gentle excuse. "The people are used to me. Your chance will come, Father."

Stephen's chance came on Friday noon in mid-May. He was leaning against a stone fence in L'Enclume, discussing with Roy Boisvert the repair of a church window, when he saw Hercule Menton's wife ascending the hill. At fifteen Adèle Menton had been a buxom Nova Scotian belle, but twenty years of poverty and childbearing had filed her down to spindle thinness. She was wearing a faded calico wrapper, not too clean, and her mouth had the desperate pinch of chronic fatigue. The only remnant of her beauty was her bun of braided hair, still black, held in place by a cheap barrette. Stephen raised his hat, smiled good morning, but no spark lighted Adèle Menton's agate eyes. What she needed (Stephen felt) was not the time of day from a young curate, but a few dollars to buy soap, food, a new comb for her hair, and some cotton dresses for her children. Through a screenless doorway she disappeared into the shack — a worn-out woman trudging beside a jobless man.

Stephen had just concluded his talk with Boisvert when Adèle Menton darted out of the house. "Hercule chop hees foot," she screamed. "Com' queek."

Stephen bounded across the road and entered the shack. The place was buzzing with flies, an undiapered baby was playing on the floor, and the scraps of many meals lay on a clothless table. A black iron sink was cluttered with dirty pans and dishes, and a wash boiler stewed on the sheet-tin stove.

In a corner of the room stood an iron bedstead, and on its bare mattress Hercule Menton lay gasping while jets of blood spurted from his ankle.

Stephen's knowledge of first aid was slight, but he knew enough to clamp both hands around Hercule's lower leg. He saw the throbbing artery, looking very much like a piece of sliced spaghetti, and squeezed harder with his thumbs. The crimson jet still spurted; loss of blood was sending Hercule into shock.

"Get me something to tie around his leg," said Stephen. "Tear up a sheet, a pillowcase, anything."

Adèle Menton had no sheets or pillow slips to tear up. The nearest piece of cloth was the calico dress on her back. She was about to rip it from her skinny body, when she realized that she would be standing naked before a priest. Instinct, primitive and female, instructed her now. She pulled the comb from the coiled bun on top of her head, seized a pair of iron shears, and slashed off a braid of her black hair.

"Will zis do?"

Stephen seized the rope of hair, bound it above the severed artery; using the shears as a purchase, he twisted the braid of Adèle Menton's hair until it garroted Hercule's foot. He was still twisting the improvised clamp when Barbe Leblanc, the local veterinarian, bounced into the room.

"Nice emergency work, Father," said Barbe approvingly. The vet scrutinized Hercule's wound. "Another quarter inch, and he'd have opened up real trouble. But we can fix this with a stitch in time." He pulled a needle and thread from his instrument bag and neatly sewed together the edges of the artery.

"I don't suppose you've got any bandages in the house," he asked, in the tone of a man expecting a negative answer.

A toothless beldame stepped forward with a basket filled with sphagnum moss, white and damp. "Better than bandages," she said, thrusting a handful of it at Barbe with the confidence of the midwife offering a sovereign remedy.

"Have to do for now," muttered Barbe, molding handfuls of the absorbent moss onto the wound. He loosened the hair tourniquet and ordered Adèle Menton to make a pot of strong tea for her husband.

"He's going to live," said the veterinary. In fulfillment of the prophecy Hercule opened his eyes.

Seeing Stephen, Barbe, and a roomful of neighbors, he remembered what had happened. "Goddam ax, she slip," he murmured apologetically. "Holy *Vierge*. I have bad luck because I eat rabbit on Friday."

"Don't worry about it," consoled Stephen. "Right now the job is to lie quiet and get well." How one could do either in this crowded dirty room was a problem that must be solved by a higher intelligence than Stephen's. Evidently Hercule was acquainted with such an intelligence.

"Get Lalage," he said to his wife, as if asking her to summon a sublime personage.

"Who's Lalage?" asked Stephen.

"My bigges' girl, nurse in Litchburg. When t'ings march crooked" — he made a zigzag line with his finger — "Lalage make t'ings march straight."

"Quite a talent," observed Stephen. His eyes traveled slowly around the mean room. If Lalage could straighten out this confusion she must be a remarkable girl. He patted Hercule's shoulder reassuringly and turned to Adèle Menton standing at the foot of the rumpled bed.

"Poets say that hair is a woman's crowning glory. You proved it today." As both a man and a priest Stephen took the chance that Adèle Menton would understand at least a part of what he meant.

WHEN he came back to see Hercule next day, *chez Menton* was a much-changed shack. No dirty dishes in the sink; floor scrubbed, and the small children glistening like newly soaped angels. Hercule was sitting up on two chairs with a clean gauze bandage skillfully bound from knee to ankle.

"Who made all this miracle business?" asked Steve.

Hercule smiled at the curate's surprise. "Lalage, she com' rat away when I call. All las' night she feex — feex t'ings all over." He lifted his voice, "Lalage! Com' meet Father Fermoyle."

Stephen turned his head to see a young woman entering the room. She was the nut-brown maid, the ballad come to life. She wore a nurse's uniform, crisp and white as a fresh

carnation. He acknowledged her smiling, vital presence with
deserved praise.

"Your patient looks much better. You've done wonders
already."

Pleasure at the compliment brought a russet flush to
Lalage's cheeks. "Thank you, Father." As if recognizing a
hazard, she avoided giving Stephen the full power of her
voice or eyes. She busied her hands with pillows and blankets,
deftly bringing order to whatever she touched.

Stephen valued the girl's detachment. "Will you have Dr.
Jennings over from Stonebury?"

"Not unless infection sets in. That awful moss was loaded
with all sorts of things that shouldn't be put on a wound. But
I cleaned it up last night." Lalage made no mention of the
overhauling she had given the house. "I think everything will
be all right — if Dad will stay put for a week or so."

"I stay put so long you stay put," bargained Hercule. The
pure sadness in his voice reminded Stephen of Dennis Fermoyle's way with Ellen.

"I'll stay a week," she said, "if you'll promise to carve a fiddle top while you're laid up. Rafe can help you." She turned to
Stephen. "With two luthiers in the house, a violin ought to get
finished once in a while, don't you think?"

"I *do* think so. Definitely."

Lalage's offer and Stephen's approval touched off the
luthier's pride. "Tell Rafe bring me maple block from top shelf.
Chisel and whetstone *aussi*. I show you who fineesh bes' goddam fiddle you buy in Boston."

Lalage was off in a rustle of starch. She returned with her
brother Rafael, a youth of sixteen who looked like an apprentice version of Hercule. Curly shavings, insignia of the wood
carver, clung to Rafael's denim jumpers and black hair. In one
hand he carried a slab of maple, in the other an assortment of
gouges and chisels.

"Here you are, Dad, the three-year-old maple you asked
for."

Hercule seized the slab, waved it at Stephen. "T'ree year
zis wood has wait." His finger pointed at the wavy curl of the
wood. "*Voyez la flamme*. Bes' *flamme* in Nort' America."

"By *flamme* he means the grain," explained Lalage. "Here, I'll show you."

A wisp of Lalage's glossy hair brushed Stephen's cheek as she bent over the block to trace with her finger the wavy grain so prized by fiddle-makers. "This makes the violin sing," she said. "Dad and Rafe found the maple tree themselves, cut it down, then let it season. And now"—she handed the block back to Hercule—"they're going to begin carving it."

With Rafe's help and much running back and forth for calipers and tools, Hercule began the delicate task of cutting a violin top. For nearly an hour Stephen watched miniature chisels paring smooth golden ringlets. While father and son were leaning over the block, absorbed in their craft, Lalage put a finger to her lips, smiled at Stephen.

He smiled back at her, disposed to believe by everything he knew of her that Lalage Menton was without exception the most deviceful, courageous, and charming of all the daughters of Adam. And as he walked home through the gorge it occurred to him that with a single exception she was also the most beautiful. It was then that he recalled his first emotion on seeing her.

"Why," he asked himself, "should I feel sorry that Lalage Menton came home?"

Puzzled by his feelings, Stephen decided to see no more of this charming young creature. He stayed away from the Menton shack for nearly a week, and when he dropped in again, Hercule was hobbling about on homemade crutches. Adèle had a new calico wrapper, and Lalage was gone.

SUMMER dragged on. A letter from Paul Ireton told of American arms victorious at Belleau Wood. "Our bayonets are locked for the show-down," wrote Paul. Early in August another letter came from Quarenghi. "*Carissimo* Stefano: The end is in view . . . Berlin is sending out peace feelers. Write me in detail of your new parish . . . Affectionately *in Cristo*, Alfeo. P.S. Do not grieve, dear friend, about the fate of the translation. Our works, as well as our days, are in His hand."

Stephen dropped his replies into the Stonebury mailbox as though he were dropping pebbles down a well. Life in the parish of St. Peter's made the outer world seem far away, a stage seen through reversed opera glasses. The activities of that world failed to touch him. Sometimes of an evening he would pick up *The Monitor* and read of diocesan events as though they were happening on some distant planet. "Thirty Carmelites Take Final Vows at Holy Tree," "Cardinal Lays Cornerstone of St. Bonaventura Orphanage," "Mons. James MacWilley Celebrates Golden Jubilee as Priest." Expenses up, collections down, coughing all over the sanctuary. As it was in the beginning, is now, and forever would be, Amen. . . .

One sultry midsummer night, when the air was full of insect music, he picked up his translation of *La Scala d'amore*. He had not looked at it since coming to Stonebury, and now he read it as one might read a manuscript found in a bottle. The ideas and diction were those of a sensitive, educated man framed in the exalted discipline of the mystical life. Stephen could not change a single sentence in his translation of Quarenghi's work. Though lofty, *The Ladder of Love* was neither rhetorical nor pretentious. And yet with new-gained vision Stephen saw that the book had at best a limited appeal. Glennon's angry accusation, "Not interested in muckers, grubbers, and such small deer, eh?" rang in his ears.

"I'd scarcely put it that way," murmured Stephen to himself, but he could appreciate now, as never before, the Cardinal's exasperation.

He put the manuscript in the bottom drawer of the rickety commode that held his personal belongings. As he started to close the drawer he saw a small oblong case that he had quite forgotten. He opened the case and there, nestling in a crease of white velvet, a ring gleamed in the lamplight. Beveled amethyst framed with seed pearls. Orselli's ring. A bishop's ring. "You will go far," the Florentine had predicted. But as Stephen put the ring away he knew that he had passed beyond hope or even desire that Gaetano Orselli's prophecy should come true.

THEN Ned Halley fell ill. The pastor had been failing visibly all summer. Gray marks of exhaustion lay on his lips and eyelids. The fine tremor of head and hands had grown more pronounced; his thumb and forefinger were those of an ancient apothecary rolling pills. The drag in his left leg became heavier; his gait and stance were unsteady to the point of being disordered. One night, rising from his supper of bread and tea, the old pastor staggered, then gripped the back of his chair for support.

"Just a touch of dizziness," he said as Stephen settled him on the horsehair sofa in his study. The touch of dizziness came back next day. "I see two of everything," the pastor murmured, passing his hand over his eyes.

Steve was alarmed. "We must get a doctor."

"No, no, it will pass. Tomorrow I'll be all right."

When tomorrow came he was not all right. He could not rise from his bed. The local doctor, a general practitioner who knew a sick animal when he saw one, was unable to put a name to the pastor's illness. "Something's wrong with his nervous system: I think you should get a neurologist up from Litchburg."

"How much would it cost?"

"A good man like Dr. Sylvester would come for twenty-five dollars."

"I know a good man who'll come for nothing," said Steve. That night he called up Dr. John Byrne and described the pastor's symptoms over the phone.

"You say he staggers, sees double?" Dr. John Byrne was weighing the diagnostic evidence. "How old is he?"

"Around sixty-five. Looks eighty."

"Hmm. Could be any one of a number of things. I'd have to see him. Tell you what, Steve. I could drive up Saturday afternoon. If it's what I think, it's serious, but not urgent. Keep him in bed till I get there."

"I hate to have you make this long trip, John. But we're broke."

"Forget it, Steve. I'll be there late Saturday afternoon."

At five o'clock on Saturday Dr. John was going over his patient with a diagnostic fine-tooth comb. He peered into the old man's eyes with an ophthalmoscope, tested his reflexes, and searched every inch of withered nerve and muscle for clues. He made him reach for a spoon, carry it to his mouth. Finally he finished his examination, patted the old priest on the hand. "We'll make you comfortable, Father, if you'll just take it easy."

"I'll take it any way God sends it," said Ned Halley.

Outside the sickroom, Dr. John spoke gravely. "It puzzles me a little, Steve. In a man of advanced years with the signs and symptoms of your pastor, we usually say 'hardening of the arteries' and let it go at that. Such a diagnosis readily accounts for motor difficulties and dizziness." Dr. Byrne was up to his old trick of explaining things. "But your man here has something else again. Did you notice how his hand trembled when I asked him to reach for that spoon?"

"It trembles that way when he reaches for anything," said Steve.

Dr. John nodded. "We call it 'intentional tremor.' The hand trembles *before* it picks up an object—say a spoon or a cup—then firms perceptibly as it carries the object to the mouth. I'd say your pastor was in a late stage of multiple sclerosis, Steve."

"What does it mean?"

"Degeneration of certain centers in the spinal cord. In words of one syllable, your pastor will be less and less able to take care of his bodily functions. Fortunately—or perhaps not so fortunately—his mind will remain clear." Dr. John Byrne was putting his stethoscope back into his bag. "How long have you known this man?"

"I never actually saw him till six months ago, but I've heard of him for many years."

"And what was it that you heard?"

"Everyone spoke of him as a saint."

"Did anyone ever remark his lack of energy?"

"I always got the impression that he was frail, not actually sick, mind you, yet somehow lacking in physical vigor."

"That clinches it," said Dr. Byrne. "Multiple sclerosis in its milder forms and earlier stages is hard to diagnose. It sets in quite early in life and sometimes goes away again, always taking a fraction of the victim's physical and nervous strength."

"Could you say," asked Stephen, "that he might have been sick for many years?"

"I could say that."

Mixed emotions of pity and relief surged through Stephen. Physical illness explained a great deal about Ned Halley's deficient energy.

Dr. John was writing out a prescription. "There's nothing we can do except administer supportive drugs and give him good nursing." He eyed Steve questioningly. "You'll be able to get a nurse, of course?"

"Not if they cost money."

"Then look here, Steve, the Diocese ought to take charge of him. Send your pastor to a nursing home or hospital where he'll get good care. Take my advice, Steve. Report the case to your Dean."

Fermoyle stubbornness stiffened the curate's neck. "I can't do that, John. Ned Halley's been kicked around all his life. He's been a failure, a clerical outcast. I can't send him away from St. Peter's. If he's going to die, he's going to die in his own bed as pastor of his own parish."

"Admire your loyalty but can't agree with your judgment." Dr. John wrote out two prescriptions. "Give him these as directed. One lucky thing, there'll be very little pain. It'll be harder on you than on him."

On the porch of the parish house Stephen and John stood shoulder to shoulder, two thoughtful men of comparable age, similar in build and temperament, one ministering to the corporal, the other to the spiritual needs of their brothers. Recognition lay between them, a recognition approaching love.

"Good-by, John. Give my best to Rita and the baby."

They shook hands. "Call me if he gets worse. I'm afraid you've got a sick man on your hands."

To his duties as curate Stephen now added the burden of nursing Ned Halley. As the disease invaded the old man's nervous system, he had to be washed and fed. The services of a practical nurse were needed, but because the parish treasury was bare, the hour-by-hour mechanics of handling the pastor fell upon Stephen. Sometimes he was spelled by Berthe Crèvecoeur or Agathe d'Éon. But the awful responsibility of nursing an incurable old man settled chiefly on Stephen's shoulders. At first the physical contact was revolting; the details of bedpan and urinal, of washcloth and towel, gagged Stephen to nausea. He closed his eyes while rubbing Ned Halley's wasted flesh with alcohol; he stopped breathing when odors of the sickroom assailed his nostrils. But this phase passed. Revulsion became pity, and pity changed to wonder at the patience and dignity of the fleshly tabernacle that housed Ned Halley's many-splendored soul.

ONE STEAMING Saturday in August, Stephen had a visitor. Answering a knock at the rusty screen door, he saw a thin, freckled boy standing on the porch. Stephen would have recognized those freckle patterns anywhere.

"Jeremy," he exclaimed. "Jemmy Splaine. How'd you get here?"

"Hitched, Father."

"Come in where it's cooler. You're melting too fast, there won't be anything left to talk to. I'll get you a drink." Stephen fetched a brimming tumbler of water from the kitchen pump.

"How's everything at St. Margaret's?"

"Fine, Father."

"Remember that first Mass you served for me? The juggling act we did with the Book?" They both laughed. "What's happened to Milky — I mean Father Lyons?"

"He's still around. He drills the parochial school choir now in plain chants. Boy, does he *drill* us." Jemmy changed the key. "The fellows miss you a lot, Father."

"I miss them too, Jemmy. They were my first boys."

"How are the kids here? Any teams?"

"No, we haven't any teams, Jemmy. The boys here are mostly French Canadians. They'd rather fish and trap than play baseball. Ought to make good hockey players, though. How about some blueberries and milk for lunch, Jemmy?"

"Sounds great, Father."

Jemmy ate two bowlfuls of blueberries, then laid his spoon down on the bare table. If he thought the diet thin, he gave no sign. Something else was on his mind—something more serious than gossip of the good old days at St. Margaret's. Stephen sensed what was coming, waited for the boy to speak.

"Father," said Jeremy, "I want to be a priest."

Shy utterance of the call, proud acknowledgment of the sacerdotal gift! Stephen remembered his own shy, proud declaration in another room, long ago, and the question from Father O'Connor: *"How old are you, Stephen?"*

"Fourteen going on fifteen, Father."

Transition and full turn. "How old are you now, Jeremy?"

"Almost fifteen, Father."

"And how long have you wanted to be a priest?"

"Ever since that morning I spoiled your first Mass."

Stephen knew the sequence. Hero-hungry boy sees prancing cavalry troops on parade. Longs for epaulets of command. Carries Mass book from Epistle to Gospel side of altar, while richly vested celebrant recites Gradual. Boy aspires to role of celebrant. Oldest story in the world. Youth always tracing figures of high romance. More to it, though. Must scrutinize.

"Let's walk around, Jemmy. I want to show you our church."

Down an alley of maples almost submarine in cool greenness they walked toward St. Peter's. A robe of ivy covered its granite ribs and gave it an illusion of pastoral peace.

"What's your idea of a priest's life, Jemmy?"

With adolescent brush Jeremy Splaine began sketching a picture for his hero. "Well, a priest is sort of—sacred."

"Why sacred?"

"Because he touches the Body of our Lord every day in the Blessed Sacrament, and that makes him want to be like our Lord—that is, as much as he can."

"Then a priest is an imitation of Christ, would you say?"

"I don't like the word 'imitation,'" said Jemmy. "*Like* is better."

"A nice distinction. And in what does this likeness consist?"

"In loving people, forgiving them."

"Forgiving them? For what?"

Jemmy's theology flashed, true-tempered. "For offending God and making Him suffer."

"Hold on a minute, Jemmy. God the Father, being perfect and omnipotent, can't suffer."

"But His Son suffered. When He became man, He suffered plenty."

Jemmy had touched the central mystery of the Incarnation, the act by which Pure Being uniquely manifested itself in the flesh. Stephen was moved by this freckle-faced aspirant's recognition of the divinity and humanity of Christ. The lad was all right.

They were at the door of the sacristy now; they entered the gloom within. At the altar rail they knelt. Jeremy made a secret wish, then gazed about the church. Accustomed to the substantial fittings of St. Margaret's, he seemed bewildered by the threadbare poverty of St. Peter's.

"It looks so poor," he said when they left the church.

"Would you be ashamed to serve God in a poor parish?"

Jemmy considered the question. "No, I don't think so."

Stephen was curious to know how much the boy could stand. "Would you be willing to leave your family, friends, and go wherever the Church sent you? You must think about these things, you know."

"I've thought about them already, Father."

A final test. Cruel perhaps, but it must be made.

"I want you to meet Father Halley, our pastor," said Stephen. "A very great man."

Stephen knocked on Father Halley's door. "A visitor from Malden, one of your old parishes, Father. May we come in?"

Into the shabby bedchamber, odorous of senescence and disease, young Jeremy entered. He saw the ugly accouterments of the sickroom, the lumpy brass bed, and a toothless old man propped up on pillows. At his side Stephen was saying, "Father Halley, this is Jeremy Splaine, one of my first altar boys."

The old priest mumbled a courtesy. From his mouth, saliva drooled. Stephen, wiping it away with a towel, watched Jeremy assembling his nerve under the triple shock of smell, sight, and sound. The boy was trembling, his freckles the color of saffron dough. Was it unfair, a mistake in judgment, perhaps, to let the beginning see the end? If by some awful prescience a young lover could foresee his beloved in the final phase of fleshly decay, would he have the heart to go on loving? Or would some ghostly finger of the spirit beckon encouragement and affirmation from the almost spectral clay?

Ned Halley answered the question by lifting a withered hand. "You have a vocation." His voice was a clairvoyant declaration, the joy of a sentry recognizing a friend. "It is a shining one. May God bless you." The old priest made the sign of the cross. "*In nomine Patris, et Filii, et Spiritus Sancti.*" It was both benediction and countersign.

Advance, friend, the blessing said. Advance confidently, praising as you go.

CHAPTER 3

THE STAR Sirius glowed in the mouth of the Great Dog, and the population of L'Enclume turned out to harvest high-bushed blueberries ripening in the August heat. Because Berthe Crèvecoeur and Agathe d'Éon were out all day picking berries, the burden of nursing Ned Halley fell on Stephen alone. House cleaning and sickroom duties nearly crushed him; dishes piled high in the sink, domestic clutter slipped beyond his control. Stephen understood better now the domestic grind that kept Adèle Menton (and millions of other women) in a state of chronic fatigue.

To escape from the cruel routine of kitchen and sickroom, he descended into the gorge one mid-August evening and walked through the grove of pines. Cool sanctuary! Yes — but also standing cash! If cut down, the pines would give employment to the jobless men of L'Enclume, bring much-needed revenue to the parish. Should I disregard Ned Halley's counsels, thought Stephen, and convert this greenwood chancel into commercial lumber? The old question of values. How solve it? Probably the answer would never leap, clear and sustaining, from the springs of mortal economy. Always the partial solution, the dusty, running compromise. Yet for this twilight hour at least, the problem of values was solved for Stephen Fermoyle. He ascended the hill, refreshed, quieted, unquestioning.

A light was burning in the kitchen. Perhaps Berthe Crèvecoeur was treating the littered house to a whisk of her broom. Stephen opened the back door, and there at the sink, elbow-deep in dishwater, stood Lalage Menton.

"Hello," she said, scrubbing at a pan with steel wool and soap powder.

Stephen's first impulse was to send her away. Quite all right for dumpy matrons to work in a priest's house. But this heart-faced young creature bursting the seams of her cotton dress sang in quite a different choir. Yet, as she scraped and

201

scrubbed without looking at him, Steve's accent on propriety gave way to curiosity.

"Where'd you get that stuff you're rubbing on the pans?"

"Brought it along." Her airy drollness came straight from Hercule.

"That was thoughtful of you." Stephen despised the priggish note in his voice, but didn't know what other note to strike. Lalage struck it for him.

"You needn't pay any attention to me, Father. I've just come home for a couple of weeks' vacation, and my mother told me you were doing all the work up here yourself." Sudsy platter in hand, she faced him squarely: "You don't *mind* my helping, do you?"

"Not at all. In fact, I'm grateful."

"That's all settled then. Have you had supper?"

"Yes, thank you."

"And him?" Lalage's chin indicated Ned Halley's room.

"I gave him some tea around six. He's in for the night."

Lalage appraised the disorderly kitchen in terms of work to be done. "It'll take me about an hour to straighten things up here."

Her natural acceptance of the Martha role in this untidy house reconciled Stephen to her presence. His task, he decided, was to match her generosity of spirit; any other attitude would be a confession of prudishness and mean regard. He tried to convey all this in his casual "Good night."

Next morning, wearing her white nurse's cap as a passport, Lalage invaded Ned Halley's sick chamber. She gave the bed and room a thorough cleaning, sponged the old pastor with alcohol, and varied his luncheon with a bowl of soup. Stephen almost laughed at the startled look on Ned Halley's face as he felt himself tenderly bounced around like an infant in the hands of a capable mother.

"Who— is *she?*" he asked once, when Lalage left the room.

"A professional nurse. Daughter of Hercule Menton, the fiddle-maker. Shall I tell her to go away?"

Ned Halley's perplexity shifted to alarm. "No, no. Don't send her away. She seems very—competent."

"Probably the most competent female now alive," said Stephen. He was glad to have his pastor's approval of Lalage;

it cleared him with himself, stilled lingering scruples of propriety. On the practical side, Lalage's competence relieved him of a hundred household duties, freed him to think his way out of the deep financial morass into which parish affairs were sinking. But most important of all, she made Ned Halley's last days comfortable.

Stephen spent longer hours now reading or talking to the old priest. Mostly the pastor was silent, but occasionally he would emerge from enveloping shades to speak of the past, much as a retired clipper-ship captain might speak of youthful voyages to China and Ceylon. He knew well enough that he had not been a successful voyager. Instead of bringing home rich packets, he had always returned with an empty hold, or with goods not particularly in demand. He would tell Stephen of his failures at this parish or that, making no attempt to gloss the record, yet regretting, as only a sensitive lieutenant can, that he had not succeeded in discharging his mission.

"Something always balked, betrayed me," he told Stephen. "What was it?" he went on, interrogating the nature of the betrayal. "What was it that failed me when I stepped out of the simple office of the priest— saying Mass, hearing confessions, visiting the sick—and tried to take on a pastor's problems of organization and finance?"

Would it be an act of mercy to tell this dying priest that the only betrayal had been the mysterious canker of disease that had spoiled his middle years? Stephen tested him with a question.

"Did you sometimes feel—not physically well or strong?"

"There were such times. A lassitude—a fatigue when faced by responsibility." He smiled wanly. "But no, I must not accuse the flesh. Perhaps it was only that I had a poor brain or no brain at all for administrative affairs." He pondered his record of failure. "For myself I would not care so much. But when I remember the chances that His Eminence gave me . . ." Ned Halley's voice was fluttering in his throat. "Ah, I have displeased His Eminence many times."

"Did you know him personally?"

"Know him? Larry Glennon and I grew up together. I used to call him Larrybuck; his name for me was Nedboy. We were ordained on the same day. As ordinands we lay prostrate on the floor, side by side; trembling with joy and fear, we were bound and blessed by the same bishop, rose and embraced each other as brothers in Christ."

The priest's sunken eyes traveled inward, backward. "Larry was a fine, able priest. The chancery welcomed his talents, advanced him rapidly. While I was still a curate, Larry was a monsignor. As auxiliary bishop he gave me my first pastorate. St. Anselm's in Stowe. A small church—like so many others—with a big mortgage."

His tired shoulders were back in Stowe, trying to lift the mortgage. They tensed for the effort, then gave up. "I could not lift it. Larry sent me to Needham, a prosperous parish with money in the bank. I ran Needham into debt. His Eminence warned me, sent me to Malden, to Taunton, Ipsfield — always lower in his great favor until there was no more favor. Only disappointment and bitterness at my"—tears streamed down Ned Halley's cheeks like raindrops down a car window—"at my failures."

"They were not failures," said Stephen gently, wiping the old man's eyes and mouth. "Many in those parishes remember your goodness. And in his heart of hearts, the Cardinal knows you to be a just and holy priest."

The rector of St. Peter's smiled feebly. "It is kind of you, Father, to comfort an old man. But I know how His Eminence prizes success—and I have not been successful." A leaf of yearning trembled. "I wish I might see Larrybuck once more. Would he but come, call me Nedboy, forgive me my failures, I could die in peace."

Across Ned Halley's yearning fell the obscenely loud voice of Victor Thenard. "*Viande de boucherie, bas prix . . . ,*" he cried from the seat of his filthy meat wagon drawn up at the front door of the parish house. He rang his bell noisily; its metallic clatter broke in with tidings of man's mortality. "Cheap meat, cheap meat," the bell and voice were crying. Father Halley opened his eyes, smiled a little at Stephen bending over him. There were gleams of irony, humor, and self-recognition, but not a trace of self-pity in the old man's glance.

THE FINANCES of St. Peter's grew more and more desperate. Ready money was needed to pay for Ned Halley's medicines, the soap that washed him, and the special foods that sustained his ebbing strength. Because John Byrne could not always be driving up from Boston, Stephen sometimes had to call in Dr. Sylvester. The Litchburg neurologist reduced his fee to fifteen dollars, but wanted it in cash. To meet these demands, Stephen sent begging letters to his family and friends. The responses were prompt, but pitifully thin; at the end of August Stephen was down to his last two dollars. Whether he wanted to or not, he must seek help from ecclesiastical quarters.

The nearest and properest quarter was Monsignor Andrew Sprinkle, pastor of St. Jerome's in Litchburg, and head of the local deanery. Monsignor Sprinkle was a provincial cleric who had forgotten nothing and learned nothing since coming to Litchburg thirty-five years before. Now he sat in his shabby deanery snuffling (he was a martyr to hay fever) as Stephen told him of Ned Halley's illness and the fearful pinch for cash at St. Peter's.

The latter part of the tale was an old story to Andy Sprinkle. He made a temporary clearing of his inflamed nasal membranes, and launched into a worried homily. "Frankly, Father, St. Peter's has been a question mark in this deanery for many years. I am surprised that the Cardinal keeps a resident pastor there at all. In my judgment, the best course would be to close the church up, write it off as a dead loss."

"But there are still two hundred Catholics in St. Peter's," argued Stephen. "At least forty of them are children, needing the sacraments and religious instruction. You just can't shut the door on them."

Monsignor Sprinkle was unimpressed. "All such matters could be easily handled by a mission priest sent out from Litchburg on Sundays. I shall—*ha-choo*—recommend the mission idea to the Cardinal in my next report." The Dean made a note on his memo pad. "Meanwhile, what about Father Halley? From what you tell me, he's not long for this world."

"It's a matter of weeks — maybe days."

Andrew Sprinkle made a magnanimous offer. "I can get him a free bed in our hospital here. The Benedictines are in charge. He'd get good care."

Stephen wanted to ask, "How would you like to be snatched from your pastoral berth to die on a charity bed?" But cash urgency made him tactful. "Both Father Halley and I would prefer that he stay where he is." Stephen measured his man for the touch. "What I came for specifically, Monsignor Sprinkle was to request an advance from deanery funds."

Andy Sprinkle, having expected the touch, now turned it down with measured regret. "The deanery has no authority to advance money in such cases, Father. As you may or may not know"—he settled back for a disciplinary lecture—"the Cardinal expects every parish to be self-supporting. When a pastorate ceases to stand on its own feet financially—as is the case with St. Peter's—reorganization is—ah, overdue."

Monsignor Sprinkle dabbed his handkerchief at his nose. "Mind you, Father, I make no charges against your pastor. His personal piety is known to us all. But I am very much afraid that his lack of physical energy puts him at a disadvantage as an administrator." The Monsignor concluded his homily on parish management with cold finality. "Officially I cannot advance you a single penny on such a poor risk as St. Peter's."

Stephen rose despondently, his ambassadorship a failure. What had he expected? Showers of bank notes, a letter of credit? His hand was on the doorknob when Andy Sprinkle said in unofficial tones:

"But as a private matter. Father—a personal gift—would twenty dollars help?"

"It would help a great deal, Monsignor."

From a green tin box Andy Sprinkle counted out four five-dollar bills and handed them to Stephen. "From one priest to another," he said not unkindly.

"Thank you, Monsignor." Stephen was genuinely grateful. "And as a special request, will you please postpone your report to the Cardinal until—?"

Andy Sprinkle nodded sympathetically. "Very well, Father. But you understand that sooner or later something—um—constructive must be done about St. Peter's."

"I understand perfectly," said Stephen

FIFTEEN PRECIOUS DOLLARS slipped away when Dr. Sylvester made his third visit. Within forty-eight hours Stephen was again down to loose change. Sleepless, cornered for cash, he lay on his straw mattress, figuring ways and means of raising quick money. What did other people do in similar pinches? They begged, borrowed, stole, sold or mortgaged household furniture, pawned jewelry. . . .

Jewelry? Orselli's ring was jewelry! It might have a pawning value. Stephen leapt from his mattress, lit the kerosene lamp, and rummaged in the drawer of the commode where he had last seen the bishop's ring. Its cool amethystine beauty reassured him. He had no idea of its value, but estimated that the gem and the exquisite workmanship of its setting might be worth one hundred dollars.

It was two-thirty A.M. when Stephen decided to take the milk train into Boston. Exactly eight hours later he walked into the pawnshop of Susskind and Flatto, 8 Scollay Square. Stephen had never been in a pawnshop before, but he knew the right question. "How much will you give me on this?" he asked, laying the ring on the marble-topped counter.

Moe Susskind fixed a dubious eye on the amethyst ring, then picked up his jeweler's glass to scrutinize the bezel of seed pearls around the violet-colored stone. Hmm . . . Florentine work. His glass magnified the name *"Dolcettiano": Firenze* —a rare hallmark in goldsmithery. Moe Susskind had seen that mark only once before. In Dresden, as an apprentice jewelsmith. Mr. Susskind never forgot a hallmark, but he had no interest now in the handiwork of Messer Dolcettiano. Nor would his clientele be likely to bid it up if the piece went unredeemed. Moe laid the ring on the worn marble counter.

"Pawn value, five dollars."

"I had expected more."

"Sell outright, you get more."

"Fine," said Stephen. "I'll sell it to you."

"By police regulations, pawnbrokers cannot buy. But there is yet a way, Father."

"Let's keep it legal," said Stephen.

"*Ja*, legal. Forty years in Scollay Square. *Immer* legal." Moe Susskind scribbled a name on a piece of paper. "Brothers Karaghousian . . . you should find them by Marliave Court, Number Twelve."

"Much obliged," said Stephen. At the Marliave Court address, a region of curio dealers, he found the shop of the four

Karaghousians. Three of the brothers were elsewhere at the moment, but Nicolaides Karaghousian sat amid his rugs, laces, clocks, ceramics, jewelry, and silverware equally poised to buy, sell, or swap. The blood of the entire Levant—Armenian, Greek, Turkish, and Syrian — throbbed through Mr. Karaghousian, putting him under constant and intense pressure to do business at any margin of profit between a hundred and a thousand per cent.

By temperament Mr. Karaghousian preferred not to buy anything unless he knew beforehand where he could sell it. Temperamentally, therefore, he was much pleased by the Dolcettiano ring. He knew exactly where he could dispose of it, and how much he could get.

"For a defective specimen like this," Mr. Karaghousian began, "I make a final one-price offer. Thirty-five dollars."

Stephen had never haggled for anything in his life, but the wine of Karaghousian's personality was heady with possibilities of a dicker.

"Seventy-five dollars," said Stephen, trying hard to act as though he meant it.

"I must think of my brothers. Forty."

"Sixty or I go next door." Stephen had no notion of who or what he would find there, but evidently the menace was real to Mr. Karaghousian. He examined the ring again.

"My regard for the priesthood moves me." He crossed himself like a pilgrim at a shrine. "Forty-five . . ."

"Fifty and done." Stephen held out his hand. The dealer unsnapped a rubber band from a thick bundle of bills, peeled off two twenties from the outside, and nine ones from the inside, then put the bundle back in his pocket. "Appraisal fee, one dollar," he said, handing Stephen the forty-nine dollars. "Now, write me a bill of sale, full name and right address."

Stephen made out the bill of sale, hastened away from Marliave Court, swallowed a cup of coffee in the North Station, and was back in Stonebury by suppertime.

THREE DAYS LATER the ladies of St. Elizabeth's Guild were holding their annual garden party at broad-lawned Fenscross, the Auburndale estate of Cornelius J. Deegan. The contractor-Knight, newly returned from successful missions in Dublin and

Rome, sauntered genially among the tables set up beneath the
fine magnolias that had once sheltered the Protestant Froth-
inghams. Corny had snapped the place up for a song, a mere
sixty thousand dollars, and had placed title in the name of his
wife Annie, "just in case." Today might well be the peak of
Annie's social career, because His Eminence Lawrence Cardinal Glennon was due to arrive any minute now, retinue and all,
in public recognition of the fine charitable work performed by
the Guild among the deserving poor of Boston and environs.

Behind tables laden with every conceivable knicknack, gew-
gaw, bauble, gaud, and wearable, including lace blouses,
hand-knitted sweaters, castoff furpieces, outmoded *gilets,* or-
gandy jabots, bone-supported lace collars, strips of ruching,
and hand-me-down scarves, stood the ladies of the Guild. Because the lady presiding over each table was in competition
with every other lady to secure the largest possible amount
of cash, each eagerly cried her wares.

For three years now, the lady amassing the largest receipts
had been Mrs. Daisy Lamping-Boland, a convert and widow,
who spared neither energy nor expense in rounding up what
she called *articles de vertu* for her table. Daisy Lamping-
Boland had a natural flair for collector's items, which she in-
dulged with a ready checkbook. She specialized in such objects
as gold chatelaines, enameled pillboxes, jeweled lorgnettes,
mother-of-pearl opera glasses, diamond-crusted combs, and
the usual line of brooches, pins, pendants, and lavalieres. She
had a reputation to maintain and was quite willing to lay herself out to maintain it.

A hum of chitchat, first-name calling, and high-keyed ex-
clamations of delight at snatched bargains rose above the five-
piece stringed orchestra playing behind the shrubbery. The
buzz mounted to a sudden crescendo. "The Cardinal is here."
Then it died away entirely as the Cardinal stepped out across
the lawn. Attired in a scarlet cloak and biretta, attended by
numerous clerical aides and secretaries, all with a touch of
purple, he swept across the sward, this prince of the Church,
prepared to spend, say, half an hour and half a thousand dollars, in honoring one of his favorite charities.

Graciousness poured from his smile, gestures, gait, and
purse as he stopped at the various tables to make the pur-

chases expected of him. The Cardinal would select an object, then at a signal Monsignor Dave O'Brien would step forward with a privy pocketbook and pay for it. His Eminence stopped now at the table of Daisy Lamping-Boland, received her curtsied genuflection, and gazed at the *articles de vertu* spread tastefully on folds of black velvet. The Lamping-Boland wares always brought out the connoisseur in His Eminence. His large hazel eyes traveled appreciatively from brooch to buckle and hovered with genuine delight over an amethyst ring framed in a bezel of seed pearls. He leaned forward, picked the ring up to examine it.

"A bishop's ring," he exclaimed. "A really superb specimen of Florentine work. How in the world did you come by it?"

Daisy Lamping-Boland laughed like the rich and roguish widow-convert that she was. She had no intention of exposing her sources of supply to the other ladies of the Guild, and was not above twitting a man as distinguished as the Cardinal.

"One of your bishops must have been in financial straits," she said. "You should pay them a higher salary, Your Eminence."

His Eminence disliked twitting, and it occurred to him now that he disliked Daisy Lamping-Boland. He scrutinized the bauble in puzzlement. A genuine Dolcettiano, a bishop's ring in the great Florentine tradition. Whose was it? Glennon had only one bishop under him, Mulqueen, his auxiliary; and he himself had given Mulqueen a bishop's ring when consecrating him. This Florentine article certainly was not Mulqueen's. But who in the Diocese would be trafficking in bishop's rings?

Glennon had ways of finding out such things. He proceeded with tactful directness.

"May I ask the price of this ring, Mrs. Lamping-Boland?"

"Two hundred and fifty dollars, Your Eminence."

The Cardinal signaled O'Brien, who counted out gold notes for the amount.

Two hours later His Eminence was giving explicit instructions to Inspector Hugh Shea, chief of Boston detectives.

"Hugh, I want you to get the whole story of this ring. Who sold it in the first place, how much he got, and all the rest of it. I don't think it's a criminal matter, you understand. I merely want to find out what's going on, and who's behind it."

"A short horse is soon curried, Your Eminence," said Inspector Shea. "I'll go to work on it myself."

The currying of this particular horse required a scant twenty-four hours of routine investigation among the Boston hockshops. At the end of that time Hugh Shea was reporting to Number One in person.

"A young man dressed in the habit of an R. C. priest tried to pawn the ring at the shop of Susskind and Flatto, 8 Scollay Square," recited Shea. "Susskind sent him to the shop of an Armenian Greek, Karaghousian by name, who gave him forty-nine dollars for it. Karaghousian brought it straight to Mrs. Daisy Lamping-Boland and sold it to her for a hundred and fifty. That's the whole story, Your Eminence."

"Did you get the name of the priest?"

Shea consulted his notebook. "He gave the name Stephen Fermoyle, and put down his address as Stonebury, Mass." The inspector's discretion was notorious. "I didn't want to check further without your permission, Eminence."

"Quite right, Hugh. Many thanks. Send your man around when you're taking up the Police Welfare Fund."

Reverently, the Inspector genuflected and retired.

Glennon closed his fist over the Florentine ring in the manner of a boy with a grasshopper in his hand. He might almost have been murmuring the childish abracadabra: "Grasshopper, grasshopper, give me some molasses, and I'll let you go." The molasses was there all right, but how guarantee the maximum quantity? Should he call for his black Daimler, whirl up to Stonebury, and hold a drumhead court of inquiry in the parish-house parlor? The dramatic possibilities of dropping on Father Fermoyle as a red-winged hawk drops on a frightened rabbit appealed to His Eminence. It amused him to think of the scurrying that would go on in that shabby parlor. . . .

Other considerations moved him, too. Intangible considerations, blent of guilt and nostalgia for the sight of a white-polled head with a thin gold aureole of saintliness shining above it. How pleasant it would be to sit down with Ned on the old equal terms of fellowship and talk of that sweetest form of death-in-life, the days that were no more!

How sweet—and how impossible! Freighted with consciousness of a hundred failures, Ned Halley's head would be bowed. Apology would hang weights on his tongue. The old laughing comradeship of the seminary was dead beyond recall. Foolish to dream of reviving it now. .

His Eminence pulled a brocaded bell rope. Monsignor O'Brien appeared. "Take a telegram," said Glennon. He dictated:

REVEREND STEPHEN FERMOYLE
ST. PETER'S CHURCH
STONEBURY MASS
IMPERATIVE YOU PRESENT YOURSELF AT CARDINAL'S
RESIDENCE TOMORROW AT 2:30 P.M.

"Sign it and send it off at once, Dave. I want to get to the bottom of something."

THE TELEGRAM CAME at a critical time. Ned Halley, sinking like a broken ship, might go under at any moment. Stephen hesitated to leave the old man even for a few hours. His first impulse was to wire Monsignor O'Brien, stating the facts and requesting a postponement of the interview. But a second look at the "Imperative you present yourself" changed his mind. This was a command. He must go.

Leaving the pastor in Lalage's care, Stephen took the morning train to Boston. At two-fifteen he was sitting in the Cardinal's wainscoted antechamber, on a high-backed armless chair, awaiting the summons into the Presence. Why had the Cardinal wired him? What did His Eminence have in mind? Good or bad, it made little difference to Stephen. Six months in Stonebury had armored him against the darts of political fortune. Lower in station it was impossible to go. You couldn't fall out of bed when you were already on the floor.

Monsignor O'Brien was beckoning. Stephen passed through the oaken door, mounted the spiral staircase, crossed the masonry floor of the Tower Room, and approached the refectory table where Lawrence Cardinal Glennon sat in his curule chair. The curate genuflected without flutter, kissed the Cardinal's sapphire, and stood silent as a tall schoolboy waiting for the stern headmaster to speak.

The Cardinal wasted no time in preliminaries. He produced

Orselli's amethyst, set it down on the table. "Have you ever seen this before?"

A classic star-chamber opening. Truth was the best, the only defense. "Yes, Your Eminence," said Stephen. "Until a few days ago I owned it. I sold it last Monday to a curio dealer in Marliave Court."

This open admission cut the prosecutor's case off at the knees. His Eminence had expected something more in the line of dissimulation—a bit of startled quibbling, at least. He took refuge in sarcasm.

"So you've given up writing mystical essays and gone in for peddling ecclesiastical jewelry, eh?"

"I'd scarcely call the sale of one ring 'peddling,' Your Eminence."

"Whatever you call it," snapped Glennon, "such traffic brings the clergy into disrepute. I'll not permit it in my Archdiocese, you understand, Father Fermoyle."

"It won't happen again, Your Eminence." Stephen's irony was lost on his superior.

Glennon picked up the ring, regarded it with a connoisseur's curiosity. "How did you come by this?"

"It was a gift from a friend, Captain Gaetano Orselli of the Italian Line."

"You seem to have quite a way with these Italians," said Glennon dryly. "Why did you sell it?"

"For private reasons, Your Eminence."

Hedging answers always stirred up Glennon's wrath. "Between a curate and his archdiocesan superior, there can be no 'private reasons,' as you call them, Father Fermoyle. I demand that you tell me why you disposed of this ring."

Very well, thought Stephen. You're asking for it. "I sold the ring to pay the medical expenses of Father Edward Halley."

"Medical *what?*" The Cardinal's tone was that of an incredulous patrician hearing that an old club member was in straits. "Is Father Halley ill?"

"Dying, Your Eminence."

"Ned Halley *dying?*" Terror and remorse struggled for possession of the Cardinal's throat. For a moment he was speechless; then indignation had its habitual way. "Why wasn't I told of this earlier, Father Fermoyle?"

Through the Cardinal's broken defenses, Stephen saw his opening. A pawn sacrifice that might lead to an ultimate check. Shrewdly he invited attack: "I presumed that Your Eminence would be uninterested."

Lawrence Glennon bought the gambit. "Presumed?" He bounced the heel of his hand off the table. "Your presumption passes belief, Father Fermoyle. How could I be uninterested in Ned Halley? He is one of my senior pastors, a fellow seminarian, a boyhood . . ."

Lawrence Glennon started to say "friend." Then in mid-sentence he realized that Stephen had lured him into a fool's mate, and that the frosty blue eyes of this extraordinary young curate were now gazing at him as a humorous chess master might gaze at a tyro.

His Eminence sat down in his curule chair, not as a Cardinal celebrant settling back to hear a *Gloria* at High Mass, nor yet as a Cardinal judge about to expound a point of canon law. His sitting down was the resigned performance of a faded beau who has unexpectedly caught a daylight reflection of himself in a full-length mirror. Or more exactly, the tired surrender of a man who knows he has made a poor showing in a life-insurance examination.

Life insurance?

Lawrence Glennon knew well enough that neither his scarlet sash nor pectoral cross could help him pass even the kindest scrutiny of stethoscope or blood-pressure machine. It occurred to him that organically he had exchanged a spleen for a heart, hypertension for a soul, and power for friendship. A dull deal all around. Why, even the edge of his mind was becoming dull! Thirty, twenty, even ten years ago, he would not have snapped at the intellectual bait that this stripling Fermoyle had dangled before him.

But here he sat now, his paunch touching the edge of the table, his heart crushed between the steel jaws of memory. Ned Halley dying! Scenes, cracked and damaged like an old motion-picture film, unwound before him. Ned Halley, golden-haired, a shining circlet of purity above his head, stood smiling across the desk.

"I'm sending you to Stowe, Nedboy. Your first pastorate, a great chance."

The film darkened as Ned Halley reappeared. "I'm giving you a fresh try at Needham, Ned."

The images were snowy, defective now. Malden, Taunton, Ipsfield, God knows where, the parishes always meaner, Ned Halley's hair no longer gold, his teeth going, body shriveling, a chaplet of failures dragging his bent neck lower. But always that circlet blazing above his head. Then the parish of dead hope—Stonebury. Buried alive in uncomplaining silence beneath an abandoned quarry dump. The reel flickered out.

For the first time in many years Lawrence Glennon permitted himself to ask a question in a natural tone. "How is he?"

"He is very low," said Stephen. "I think he may die tonight."

"Is someone in attendance?"

"A registered nurse. The daughter of a parishioner." (How inadequate a description of Lalage Menton!)

Cardinal Glennon's hazel eyes rested on Stephen for support. A patriarchal shepherd-king, leaning on the shoulder of a young herdsman. "Will you give Father Halley a message for me?"

"Gladly, Your Eminence. A word from you will make him very happy."

"Tell him that I . . ." Like a man on a winter seashore trying to choose a handful of shells that would convey the depth and salt music of a June ocean, Lawrence Glennon tried to choose words.

"Say that I . . ." The shells slipped through his fingers. The things he must say to Ned Halley could not be carried by a messenger. The Cardinal rose from his chair. He would go to Ned himself, tell him what should have been told long ago. He pulled the bell rope.

"The Daimler," said His Eminence when Monsignor O'Brien appeared. "Have a police escort to take us through traffic." Again his patriarch glance rested on Stephen, and this time it was the eye of a stricken shipmaster appealing to a dependable first mate.

"We should be there in ninety minutes," he said.

WITH LIVERIED TOM KENNY at the wheel, the black Daimler made it in eighty-seven minutes. Not a word was uttered. Deep in puce-colored cushions, the Cardinal gazed through plate-glass windows for thirty miles. Then he pulled out his breviary and like any other priest read his Office for the day. Stephen did likewise. It was the Feast of St. Joachim, the father of Mary; over and over through Matins, Lauds, and Vespers the Office repeated the moving lines of Ecclesiastes: "Blessed is the man that hath not gone after gold, nor put his trust in money, nor in treasures. *Who is he?* We will praise him, for he hath done wonderful things in his life. His goods are established in the Lord, and the Church of the Saints shall declare his alms."

Breviary still open, the Cardinal leaned toward Stephen. With his index finger he pointed to the three-word question, "*Who is he?*"

Voiced acknowledgment was unnecessary. The Cardinal had recognized the picture, too. Somehow, twenty-four hundred years ago, Ecclesiastes had drawn a pen portrait of Ned Halley. The two men sitting on the puce-colored cushions smiled at each other.

As they left the black mills of Litchburg behind, the Cardinal spoke for the first time.

"Short end of the brisket, eh, Father?"

"Certainly not the fancy end, Your Eminence." Inwardly Stephen praised Victor Thenard and his butcher wagon. Without them he would not have known what the Cardinal was talking about.

As the Daimler climbed the rising ground of St. Peter's, Stephen had his first worries about protocol. How did one treat a visiting Cardinal? Did host or visitor take command? Protocol vanished when Lawrence Glennon said, "Tom Kenny will take care of me, Father. You get things ready inside."

Lalage Menton greeted Stephen at the door. "You're just in time, Father—he's sinking rapidly."

"Is he still conscious?"

"His mind is very clear."

"Thank God!" Stephen barely had time to set a small table bearing the holy oils of Extreme Unction beside the pastor's bed, when the Cardinal entered.

"*Pax huic domui,*" said Lawrence Glennon.

"*Et omnibus habitantibus in ea,*" replied Stephen.

The Cardinal came forward, not with the assurance of a

great prince, but hesitantly, on tiptoe, like an intruder in sacred precincts. At the bedside he gazed down at Ned Halley's face, shining with the preliminary phosphorescence of death. Gone was all likeness to the face he had known in youth. Only hollows remained, and the graying ash of Ned Halley's eyes were banked by heavy lids.

"Ned," whispered the Cardinal, "it's me, Larry."

Ned Halley opened his eyes. "Eminence," he murmured.

"No Eminence, Nedboy. No Eminence now." The Cardinal dropped to his knees. "It's Larry—Larrybuck, remember?"

"Larrybuck . . . I knew you'd come. I lived till you came."

Tears streamed down the Cardinal's face and fell on the atrophied hand he held between his own. "I should have come sooner, Nedboy. Forgive me, I always meant to come."

"You were busy with high deeds, Larry. High deeds in high places. I did not deserve your remembering."

"Gentle Ned, you deserved more than I ever gave. I should have made you my confessor, and lighted my path by the shining circle above your head. Instead, I saddled you with pack-horse assignments, mortgages, broken parishes." The Cardinal buried his face in the torn quilt. "Forgive me, Ned."

"Forgiven, Larry . . . all . . ."

Lawrence Glennon turned to Stephen. "He's going. Bring the holy oils for Extreme Unction."

Stephen brought out the little table, set it at the Cardinal's right hand. His Eminence dipped his thumb in the sacramental oil and carried it to Ned Halley's eyelids. He anointed those eyelids in the form of a cross, saying in Latin as he did so:

"Through this holy unction, and of His most tender mercy, may the Lord pardon thee whatsoever sins thou has committed by sight."

What sins could they be? thought Stephen.

Gently the Cardinal anointed the ears, nostrils, lips, and hands of his boyhood friend. Then he motioned to Stephen. "Lift the quilt so I can anoint his feet," the gesture said. Eyes blurred with tears, Stephen did not spring quickly enough to execute this last service for his dying pastor. It was Lalage

Menton who exposed the ghostly feet for their drop of sacred
oil.

The Cardinal's thumb made the sign of the cross on Ned
Halley's wasted instep. "Through this holy unction, and of
His most tender mercy, may the Lord pardon thee whatsoever
sins thou hast committed by thy footsteps. Amen."

Like a thin veil, Ned Halley's lifelong expression of ineffable
courtesy dropped from his face. Eyes, ears, lips, and hands
were freed from their sensual burdens. Feet that had never
walked in any way but righteousness became clay. Ned
Halley's soul rose from the menial ash of body and leapt in
flame to join the fellowship of saints, martyrs, and confessors.

CHAPTER 4

NOVEMBER WINDS pierced the flimsy shacks of L'Enclume.
Stephen hugged the wood fire in Ned Halley's old study, and
bent over the litter of invoices, time sheets, and bills of lading
on his desk. Midnight found him adding a long column of figures; pleased at the total, Stephen picked up his pen and began his report to the Chancellor of the Archdiocese:

RT. REVEREND MONSIGNOR:

I have the honor of transmitting to your office a complete
account of the St. Peter's lumbering operations, together
with all financial records pertaining thereto.

Acting under pastoral powers conferred upon me by the
Cardinal on August 18, 1918 . . .

August 18 . . . the day of Ned Halley's burial. Gazing into
the ruby embers, Stephen relived the events of that day. In
a summer downpour, Lawrence Glennon had led the funeral
procession from church to cemetery. As the earth fell on Ned
Halley's coffin, the Cardinal murmured a last *requiescat*,
blessed the kneeling mourners; then, leaning on Stephen's arm,
had returned to the parish house for a supportive cup of tea.

"Oolong, hot and strong, with plenty of sugar," was his
only command. But even a third cup of the heart-building
brew failed to sponge away the Cardinal's melancholy. His
secretary loitered in the hallway, wondering how long His

Eminence would mourn, yet not daring to approach the brooding prelate who sat in an armchair, sipping the black tea that Stephen kept pouring for him. Silence, and a kettleful of boiling water, was the treatment of choice; if liberally administered (Stephen reasoned), the grieving Cardinal would soon enough regain his spirits.

Other more opportunistic calculations were churning, however, in the soul of Monsignor Andrew Sprinkle. He was, after all, head of the local deanery, and his office laid upon him certain responsibilities. With the Cardinal's edge temporarily dulled, now was the time for all good men to broach the subjects closest to their hearts. Andy Sprinkle glided into the study, stirred the cup of tea that Stephen handed him, and made a cautious beginning:

"For many years, as Your Eminence well knows, the parish of St. Peter's has had slight function — and no revenue. Might it not be the part of prudence, Your Lordship, to close its doors at this time?"

In his temperless state, Glennon would have nodded assent, but Stephen's quick-taken breath caused him to turn a querying head. "You hold another view, Father Fermoyle?"

"I do, Your Eminence."

"State it."

"With all deference to Dean Sprinkle, I disagree that the function of St. Peter's is slight. Your Lordship saw its people kneeling at the grave today. Their number is upwards of one hundred and fifty. Thirty children of Sunday-school age, are being prepared for first Holy Communion. I cannot believe that their spiritual needs would be best served by closing the church."

Studying his tea leaves, Andy Sprinkle saw a dark young man crossing his path. Because the Dean saw no money in the young man's hand, he cheerfully waited for Glennon to roar, "What about parish revenues?" Within two sips of oolong, the Sprinkle prophecy was half fulfilled: Glennon clicked cup against saucer and asked:

"What about parish revenues?" The words were strong, but the roar was weak.

"Revenues could be found, Your Eminence," said Stephen.

"Where? How?"

Short questions requiring a long answer. From a drawer in Ned Halley's desk, Stephen drew forth a pen-and-ink map of the parish, unrolled it on the table, and placed his finger on the gorge. "This valley," he said, "belongs to the parish. It was deeded to the church twenty years ago, but the title has never been recorded."

Lawrence Glennon examined the map. "What makes the property of special interest?"

"A forest of prime timber, Your Eminence. Some twelve hundred first-growth pine trees. By cutting only three hundred of them — a fourth of the existing stand — I estimate that we could net thirty-five hundred dollars."

The Dean contributed a typical Sprinklerism: "Canon 142 of the *Codex juris canonici* expressly states: *'Prohibentur clerici mercaturam exercere'* — in plain English, priests may not engage in business."

"I am familiar with the canon, Monsignor," said Stephen. "But our lumbering operation would not be conducted by a priest."

"By whom then?" asked Glennon, faintly alarmed.

"It would be a joint undertaking, Your Eminence . . . somewhat on the pattern set by the Canadian fishing parishes. In Nova Scotia, pastor and parishioners share the fishery profits on a co-operative basis. Here in Stonebury, our local unemployed would perform the actual labor of chopping and sawing. Their wages would be paid from the sale of the lumber, and the remaining sum would accrue to the owner of the trees — namely, the parish of St. Peter's. Both parties would benefit, and" — Stephen bowed respectfully to Andy Sprinkle — "canon law would not be infringed."

The Dean shifted his ground. "Apart from canon law," he said, "is it the function of a parish to make economic arrangements for its people? We are interested in their spiritual welfare, yes. But I fear we shall find ourselves in deep and dangerous waters if we begin looking after their material prosperity."

Glennon was relishing the debate; his silence gave Stephen permission to rebut.

"May I remind the Dean of Aquinas' aphorism: 'A certain minimum of material well-being is essential to the good life'?

And may I point out that the whole weight of Leo XIII's social encyclicals is on the side of a wider, more equable distribution of wealth?" The absurdity of the term "wealth" struck Stephen. He turned to the Cardinal. "The cutting of these trees would mean the bare difference between unrelieved poverty and a fighting chance to get our people through the winter."

Monsignor Sprinkle had saved his best argument till last. "The logging interests of Litchburg would quite properly protest if the parish of St. Peter's began competing with them in the production of lumber."

"That might be true," said Stephen, "if any logging interests were left in Litchburg. But the industry abandoned this area twenty-five years ago. The Litchburg dealers are mere jobbers; their interest is to buy semi-finished lumber. I've gone into the matter with them, Monsignor. They are eager to pay nine cents a board foot for all the pine they can get."

Glennon's hazel eyes rested appreciatively on Stephen. "Your plan has a certain short-range ingenuity, Father Fermoyle. But what about next year, and the year after that?"

"Careful cutting and systematic replanting of seedlings would guarantee a small permanent income to the parish, Your Eminence. And that's all we need to keep St. Peter's open." Stephen was pleading now. "The people of L'Enclume are thrifty and industrious. If we turn our backs on them, they will be economically stranded. But with the few dollars earned from the cutting of this lumber, they can be saved, both as citizens and Catholics."

Stephen's challenge was the whetstone that Glennon's steel needed. "There is merit in your plan, Father. I never like to close a parish, and I am quite willing to give St. Peter's another chance. That is" — he turned with a fair imitation of deference to Monsignor Sprinkle — "that is, if the Dean has no objections."

Studying the tea leaves in his cup, Andy Sprinkle now saw the money in the hands of the dark young man. "I have no objections, Your Eminence."

"Good." The old edge of authority was in the Cardinal's voice. "You have my permission to give this project a trial, Father Fermoyle. Your authority will be that of rector here." The glow of being in business once more suffused His Eminence. His circulation quickened. Life could go on, and Lawrence Glennon suddenly decided that it should.

"I must be getting back to Boston," he said, rising from the armchair that had been his melancholy throne. "Have Monsignor O'Brien put my bags in the car." On the front porch he extended three fingers of farewell to Andy Sprinkle, then peered with exaggerated concern at a world of falling rain. "Is there an umbrella in the house, Father Fermoyle?"

Stephen rummaged about in the front hall closet, found a venerable umbrella, and held it protectively over Lawrence Glennon's head. Escorting him to the car, Stephen was obliged to curve his arm around the Cardinal's massive person. At the feel of the lean extensor muscles against his back, Glennon gazed up at the strong-boned face above his own.

"You are not afraid of me, Father Fermoyle?" His observation was half question.

"Afraid? Not at all."

"Most people are. Why aren't you?"

"I've never thought about it. But now that you've asked me" — Stephen assessed the problem objectively — "I'd say it's because you remind me of my father."

"Do I resemble him in build or features?"

"No. The resemblance isn't physical." Stephen tried to isolate the single characteristic that linked Lawrence Glennon to Dennis Fermoyle, and smiled when he discovered it. "It may help if I tell you that my father was sometimes called 'Din the Down-Shouter.' He roared a great deal, and pounded the table with his fist when he wanted to make a point."

"Did none of this frighten you?" asked Glennon.

Stephen shook his head. "No matter how much Din roared or pounded, he always gave me the feeling that he loved me."

"He must have been a remarkable father. Is he still living?"

"Very much so. But his voice and drive are beginning to fade."

Beginning to fade mused Glennon. The male voice crumbling at the edge . . . the power drive sifting downward through the hour-glass. . . . "It happens to all of us," he murmured. "First we fade, then we fail." The Daimler slid alongside; Glennon roused himself. "Finish up this job here,

Father Fermoyle. Be pastor to this rural flock. I shall watch with interest."

Stephen's arm lowered the older man into the puce-colored cushions. "Felling lumber is a far cry from translating mystical essays, my son," said the Cardinal. "But there is a place in the Church for both." He raised his hand with an affectionate gesture, part blessing and part farewell.

ALL DURING OCTOBER, axes rang in the gorge of L'Enclume. Tall pines swayed and crashed; nimble woodsmen lopped off boughs, fed the trunks to Hercule Menton's improvised saw-mill, then loaded wide boards onto trucks of the Litchburg Lumber Company. Under Stephen's direction the St. Peter's Lumbering Association — the first organization of its kind in the Archdiocese of Boston — was converting parish pines into employment and cash.

And now, on November 2, the operation was successfully over. Stephen's figures astounded him; after deducting all expenses, there would be a clear profit of $3680.24. More than two thousand dollars would go to the twelve axmen who had cut the trees down; each worker would receive $204.10 for six weeks' labor — the highest wages ever earned in L'Enclume.

Stephen finished his report to the chancery and looked unbelievingly at the staggering sum of $1131.04 credited to the parish of St. Peter's. "What will I *do* with so much money?" he asked the graying embers in the fireplace.

Then the answers began coming in. . . .

Stephen's first care was to mark Ned Halley's grave with a stone. In a creek bed he found a huge granite boulder flecked with feldspar, and asked Hercule Menton to search it for flaws. With his quarryman's hammer Hercule tested the boulder for secret defects. "She ring solid" was his final verdict. Leaving the other planes rough, he polished one face of the stone, and on this quartz-gleaming surface, Stephen bade him carve the simple epitaph:

IN MEMORIAM
EDWARD EVERETT HALLEY
JUNE 10, 1855 — AUG. 16, 1918
"A PRIEST FOREVER, ACCORDING TO THE ORDER OF MELCHIZEDEK"

Carting, polishing, and carving Ned Halley's headstone cost Stephen sixty dollars.

Next he bought seedlings for the pine forest and set them out between the stumps of the felled trees. Three hundred seedlings and the labor of planting them came to one hundred dollars — an investment that would be returned fortyfold in twenty years.

The bulk of the money went into repairing the church. Its interior was plastered and painted, the front doors were re-hung on new strap hinges of wrought iron. For the sanctuary and altar steps Stephen bought a new burgundy-colored carpet. A decent armchair for his study and a new cotton-tufted mattress for his bed took a quick fifty. And after much poring over catalogues from ecclesiastical supply houses, Stephen ordered some new vestments and a gold-plated chalice at a cost of two hundred dollars. He paid himself two months' arrears in salary (one hundred dollars) and bought a ready-made suit of clerical broadcloth — the first since his ordination — for thirty-five dollars. By this time the parish bank account was down to three hundred dollars and the young rector began to think of putting on the brakes.

But it was impossible to stop short. He took cross-eyed nine-year-old Angela Boisvert into Boston for a delicate operation that centered the child's eyeballs and transformed her squinty face into confident prettiness. On the day that he fetched Angela home from Boston, Stephen dropped into a small book-shop and permitted himself the luxury of an hour's browsing. In a heap of secondhand tomes he discovered a copy of *L'Art des luthiers italiens*, containing many full-page illustrations of violins made by the Cremona masters. For five dollars he bought the book and presented it to Rafael Menton on the lad's seventeenth birthday.

Rafe was making better fiddles than Hercule now — rugged instruments with a voice big enough to sing above the stomp-ings of country square dancers. Though Rafe's violins were selling locally for twenty-five dollars apiece, the young violin-maker had no illusions about their quality. "Crates," he called them contemptuously and kept on trying to turn out more graceful instruments. But the mysteries of design and con-struction, the secrets of glue and varnish, eluded him. Hercule could teach him no more; short of studying with a new master, *L'Art des luthiers italiens* was the most encouraging gift Rafe could have received.

Laying the book on his workbench, he turned its pages with devotional wonder. "Do you think that violins as beautiful as these will ever be made again?" he asked Stephen one day.

"I do, Rafe." Stephen said the thing he believed. "American artists will produce works — violins among them — that the ancient masters never dreamed possible. No valuable part of tradition will be lost, but we will add New World accents and fresh strength to the old designs."

Rafe lifted his eyes from the colored plate of a glorious, golden Amati, and gazed at the clumsy contours of the maple block he had been carving. "I know you mean what you say, Father. But right this minute" — he hefted the inert maple as though it were lead — "it's awful hard to believe."

THIS was the happiest time of Stephen's life. The war to end war was over; the jubilant Armistice rocket that filled the sky with sparks of golden hope had not yet come down a dead stick. Into his pastorate Stephen poured the vigor of his young thirties, an inexhaustible flood of love and energy. The winter set in bitterly cold, and Stephen shuddered at the thought of the hardships that the sale of the pine trees had averted. On his parish rounds he noticed the good effects of the little cash earned by the axmen of L'Enclume: a new rocking chair in the Crèvecoeur living room; fresh tar paper on the d'Éon roof; a nickeled parlor stove here, a square of carpet there. The children went shod in stouter shoes, and housewives burgeoned out in cheap calico dresses, and Adèle Menton wore a new tortoise-shell comb in her hair.

Daily he explored the full possibilities of the priestly life. He attended the sick, counseled the discouraged, and solaced those who came to him with human cares. For relaxation he would skate, far up Spectacle Pond, where the men of L'Enclume were cutting ice. Through winter twilights he skated home, tingling with cold, happily aware (like that earlier poet-skater) of a Presence in the leafless wood, and happiest when, like him, he cut across the reflex of a star.

Contact with the outer world was scant. He rarely left

Stonebury and seldom heard from anyone but his family or a few old friends. Occasionally a letter came from Quarenghi telling him of diplomatic adventures or some canonical crux; at wider intervals, a postcard from Orselli promising a renewal of their loves when the postwar Atlantic passenger runs began again. "Are you a bishop yet?" the Captain scribbled, and Stephen smiled as he recalled Orselli's hopes for him. Far away and long ago . . . echoes from another sphere. . . .

Into this obscure Eden, the serpent crawled — a buxom, good-looking serpent named *la veuve* Agneaux. Stephen began hearing whispers about *la veuve* — the Widow — who lived in a substantial farmhouse just across the New Hampshire border and wove spells for a not-too-select clientele. The spells were usually woven on a cash basis, but often — cash being scarce — her customers paid for her favors in day labor. *La veuve* had the best-tilled fields and the highest woodpile in the surrounding countryside.

Occasionally her business judgment wavered. Like the Wife of Bath, she had a weakness for men "meek, young, and fresh abed." And it was this weakness that caused *la veuve* to burn, by no means hopelessly, for Rafael Menton. She had met him at a barn dance, liked the music he made in her blood, and promptly took him home for a command performance, the first of many.

Stephen learned of the affair from Rafe's mother. Shawled and grieving, Adèle Menton came into the parish house one snowy afternoon. "I am worried about Rafe, Father," she began, then very simply told the story of *la veuve's* blandishments. "Speak to him, Father," she pleaded. "Warn him against this woman. Tell him of the great danger . . ."

Stephen could agree that Rafe was in danger — but not chiefly from *la veuve*. Sooner or later, Adèle must realize that the lifeless quarries of Stonebury, the stagnant air of L'Enclume, were the real threats to her craftsmanly gifted son. He sat down beside the grieving mother and tried to buoy her with knowledge of God's secret way with His chosen ones.

"It would be easy for me to read Rafe a lecture — urge him to avoid this woman. At the proper time I may do so. But *la veuve* is only a part of Rafe's trial. He must struggle with a still heavier burden — the development of the luthier's skill breathed into him by the Holy Ghost."

The idea that *le Saint-Esprit* had anything to do with Rafe's fiddlemaking was entirely new to Adèle. She checked her tears as Stephen went on. "Rafe should get away from L'Enclume. He needs better instruction in the art and practice of violin-making. Offhand, I can't tell you where he'll find the right master. But he'll find him.

"Meanwhile, be loving with your boy. Say nothing about *la veuve.*" Stephen smiled down at Adèle Menton's tearful face. "Loosen your hand a little — as God does sometimes. Rafe will not stray far. Be confident, as I am, that the son of those tears can never be lost."

FROM CHILDHOOD, the crèche (or manger) had always seemed to Stephen an essential part of Christmas. The humble tableau of the Holy Family surrounded by the Magi and dumb kine never failed to renew in him fresh wonder at the mystery of the incarnation. All children, he knew, loved that scene in the stable, and this year Stephen determined to satisfy their longing with a real crib.

Early in December he set the whittlers of L'Enclume to carving the conventional figures of wise men, shepherds, and oxen. To Hercule Menton he assigned the carving of Mary; Alphonse Boisvert undertook Joseph; to Rafael went the coveted honor of whittling out the Babe. For two weeks cunning jackknives flashed in the lamplight, and the more the soft pine wasted, the more the figures grew.

Now the painting began. Stephen distributed tiny cans of precious vermilion and crimson lake. Gilt dust was mixed with banana oil for the gold crowns of the three kings. The Virgin's robe was traditionally blue; Joseph's tunic came out a yellowish brown (too much gamboge), and the Infant's cheeks were the rosiest pink that ever glowed in a stable. Stephen had to smile when he saw that Rafe had given the Babe brown eyes.

Individually the pieces were excellent, but when Stephen set about arranging them he found that they did not combine well. Was it their newness? Perhaps. "They aren't used to each other yet" was Rafael's way of putting it. Stephen tried to conceal his disappointment at the stiffly formal atmosphere of the crèche. Several times he tried rearranging the figures, but finally resigned himself to the fact that the manger was not a success.

Late one afternoon, a couple of days before Christmas, he entered the church, thinking to make a happier arrangement of the crèche. In the crimson light flowing from the sanctuary lamp he saw a young woman bending over the crib; her posture was that of a mother putting a child to bed, and she murmured softly as she tucked and patted the figures in-the manger. At her feet was a pile of hay.

Only one woman in the world could bestow such comfort and order with her bare hands.

"Lalage!"

The girl turned. Wisps of hay were in her chestnut hair. The hay was timothy, and its perfume hung field-sweet above Lalage Menton's face.

"I hope you don't mind what I'm doing to your crèche," she said.

"What *are* you doing?"

"Just making it into a stable. It *was* a stable, remember? With hay." She stuffed handfuls of fragrant clover under the oxen, making them appear to be munching contemplatively at the wonder before them. Lalage tucked more hay about the kneeling figure of Mary, softening the edges of her blue robe and bringing her an inch nearer the Child. "There — she looks more comfortable, don't you think?"

"Yes, she does." Stephen marveled at Lalage's way with things living or inanimate. "But what's that you're putting on St. Joseph?"

"It's chilly in here," said Lalage, "so I made a little sheep-skin vest for him." She slipped the garment over the carpenter-saint's shoulders, kissed the back of his patient neck. "All we need now is a bellyband for the Infant."

Stephen found himself vetoing the bellyband. "I'm afraid," he said, "that a touch like that would make things too — too naturalistic. After all, the crèche is intended to suggest what happened that first Christmas night. The hay helps carry out that suggestion — it was just the thing we needed. But if we get too realistic — with a vest for Joseph, and a bellyband for the Christ child — we're apt to lose sight of what the characters stand for."

Lalage gazed at the three principal figures as if trying to grasp a meaning beyond them. "I forgot they stood for anything," she said. "I keep thinking of them as people in a cold barn."

Lalage Menton's ideas about the Incarnation might bring smiles or even frowns to a synod of bishops, but Stephen realized that she was the bearer of something much more important — the special love that is the monopoly of women.

Droll defiance was in her face as she looked up at Stephen. "I wish I'd been around to help Mary that night. I'd have pinned a nice warm bellyband on her Baby, no matter *who* He was."

"Pin it on Him now," said Stephen. And as he watched Lalage's capable fingers bind the swaddling cloth around the figure of the Babe, he had the feeling that any mother would have welcomed such help on a cold night in a drafty stable.

They left the church together, Lalage carrying the remnants of her hay in a clovery bundle. "I promised Napoleon I'd bring back all I didn't use," she explained. Outside the sacristy door she inhaled the fragrance of her timothy bouquet. "Mmm — it's soaked with summer." Artlessly she lifted her armful of hay to Stephen's face. "Doesn't it make you think of August?"

The scented grass awoke memories in Stephen — the summer night he had found Lalage straightening out his kitchen; the day her hair had brushed his cheek as they bent over Hercule's fiddle top. Irritably he wondered how any woman could be so honest and provocative at the same time. Lalage's mixture of outgoingness and coquetry — her fearless and disarming advances — were these the marks of childlike innocence or feminine design? Stephen had never been able to decide. He could not decide now.

They walked through the winter dusk toward the road that Lalage must take to L'Enclume. It would be a lonely walk; Stephen wanted to go with her, but prudence advised no personal involvement with this affectionate girl. He was about to bid her good night when Lalage said:

"My father tells me he sees you skating sometimes on Spectacle Pond."

"Yes, I often go there."

"Will you skate with me there tomorrow night?"

The invitation was guileless as a snowflake, but Stephen held off his acceptance. Lalage put a special plea in her voice. "It'll be the last time I'll ever skate on Spectacle — and I want it to be with you."

"What do you mean, 'the last time you'll ever skate on Spectacle'?"

Lalage's inflection was matter-of-fact. "The day after Christmas I'm going away to the Geraldines."

"The Geraldines! The nursing sisterhood?"

Breathing at her clover nosegay, Lalage nodded. "I've always wanted to go, ever since I was a little girl. That's why I studied nursing."

"But the Geraldines! They take only incurables into their hospital. Hopeless t.b. cases, last-stage cancer — and all that." Stephen couldn't reconcile Lalage's brimming health with the death-in-life duties of the Geraldines. "It's the grimmest kind of burden."

"It's the one I was born to carry," she said simply.

If her simplicity was a rebuke, it was also a revelation. So this was the secret of Lalage's wide-open heart, her mystifying habit of walking up to life with outstretched arms! Stephen understood now the hidden source from which her actions bubbled. Strong in vocation, dedicated to purity, she could pour affectionate strength over everything she encountered: a braggart father, a spavined horse, a whittled wooden figure of Joseph, a fellow creature wasting incurably to death — or a priest, endangered, perhaps, by a too-stuffy reading of his role. All needy things claimed her, and she responded in proportion to their want. Everything Lalage Menton did or said was only a manifestation of the thing she was.

Standing beside her in the snowy road, Stephen realized that anyone fortunate enough to be the object of this girl's love should count himself the recipient of a special grace. Could he not match that gift with a generosity of his own?

He would try.

That night Stephen searched his emotions concerning

Lalage. Honestly he put the question, "What do I feel about this girl?" Without equivocation he could answer: "She is the most natural and unspoiled woman I have ever known. Out of a surplus of human affection (which cannot be disregarded) she has asked me to go skating with her on the eve of her departure for the convent. To refuse would be churlish; to accept would give me pleasure and make Lalage happy."

"I will go skating with her."

But he did not go.

When the next evening came, etched blue with winter stars, Stephen could not give himself permission to keep a rendezvous with this girl who would never skate again. There was nothing wrong about meeting Lalage on a sheet of wind-swept ice. They would join hands as skaters do, and glide up the pond together under a tall sky. Coming back, they would joyously surrender themselves to the goad of a December wind. All very innocent and harmless. But Stephen knew that some pleasures, innocent though they might be, were not for him. The knowledge gave him no feeling of elation or virtue. Actually, he felt rather ignoble at being unable to match the yes-saying generosity of Lalage Menton's heart.

IRON WINTER merged into the rigorous season of Lent — then as if tired of severities, spring took Church and nature by the hand and led them both into the warmth of April. Again L'Enclume became a scene of crackling activity: clotheslines flapped in the breeze; shawled women gathered at the tail of Victor Thenard's meat wagon, while their husbands lounged with blunt, brown pipes against sunny walls. Nothing had changed — yet everything was different. And the difference, Stephen realized, sprang from his sharing of human hardships and triumphs with those people. They had come through a year together. They had survived winter, and now were quickening into a new cycle of hope.

It was the third Saturday after Easter when Corny Deegan drove up from Boston in his black Cadillac. After an admiring inspection of Stephen's refurbished church, the papal nobleman accepted an invitation to supper. The one-dish meal of spareribs and cabbage cooked and served by Agathe d'Éon was settling pleasantly while Corny — a mouse-colored

Corona in his hard, red fist — talked about Rome (from which he had just returned), Vatican politics, and a dozen other matters. Clearly the papal Knight had something more than his elbow up his sleeve, but exactly what it was, Stephen could not determine. At last he broke in on Corny's detailed account of the Cardinal's plan for a new cathedral:

"Cornelius, what in heaven's name are you being so canny about?"

"Can't an old friend pass the time of day?"

"The time of day and all night, too. It's a joy to have you and to hear of your missions in high places. But every so often you start to grin like a man who knows something. What is it, Corny?"

Cornelius came down to cases. "Do you remember holding an umbrella over the Cardinal's head on the day of Ned Halley's funeral?"

"I do."

"Well, his Eminence remembers it, too. Spoke of it this morning. He was much moved by the fact that you weren't afraid of him — that you dared put your arm around his exalted person. But the thing that struck him most was the reason you gave for your fearlessness."

Stephen laughed. "I told him that he reminded me of Din. It's true, Corny; he does. Glennon is a peremptory man with a stiff Irish neck. But Din's that way, too. He's a perfect father — and Glennon, somehow, seems to fit into that pattern."

Cornelius, the father of five girls and a hard-drinking son, was meditative. "Every man dreams of having a son who loves him without fear. Would it surprise you to know that the Cardinal has such a dream?"

"Not at all. Even God had it. But what's this mystery prologue leading up to? Does His Eminence plan to adopt me?"

"Adoption isn't the word for it, Steve. But he'd like to have you around him. In fact — to stop all this beating about Paddy O'Houlihan's barn — Glennon's decided to make you his secretary."

Astonishment whirled Stephen to his feet. Three times he paced diagonally across the study, then halted in front of the contractor-Knight. "Have you been up to your old fixing tricks again?" he demanded.

Corny raised a solemn, red-freckled hand as if taking an oath of innocence. "It's no doing of mine, Steve. Number One picks his own peppers. And out of the whole bushel, he's picked you. Somehow I had the idea that this news would be pleasing to you."

"A year ago, it would have been wonderful. But right now I want to stay at St. Peter's. I suppose I could say that my work here isn't finished yet — not even begun. But the honest truth is, Corny, I like it here."

The papal Knight held the fire — or more accurately, the blackthorn — of his sarcasm. He loved Stephen too much to bring that heavy bludgeon down with, "Oh, the wee man likes it here, does he? He wants to stay in his nice broken-down parish and be a brushwood saint to a tribe of Canuck woodcutters." Even to twirl such a shillelagh in Stephen's presence was dangerous. Corny was silent for the length of a Hail Mary; then he spoke with all his forthrightness.

"Once I thought you were ambitious, Stephen. I see now that the fire of the Holy Ghost has burned that ambition right down to cinders. But did you know" — there was a cheerful upturn in Corny's voice — "that cinder blocks make the best building material? Stuff that's passed through fire to ash can't be burned by anything else. Master contractors know that. Glennon knows it. That's why he's chosen you for his purpose."

The contractor-Knight laid a hodlike hand on his friend's shoulder. "The days of your initiation are over, Stephen. Now the real work begins. For the next forty years you've got to be the toughest, tenderest, *damnedest* priest of your generation — a son worthy of the father — a chip off that old cinder block, Din the Down-Shouter."

BREAKING pastoral ties, Stephen discovered, was like breaking the point off his heart. He made his final rounds of L'Enclume, entering low-roofed homes once peopled by strangers. Now, just as these strangers had begun to think of him as their champion and friend, he must tell them that he was going away. Scrawny women, whom he had first seen gabbling around the butcher wagon, held greasy aprons to their eyes when they heard the news. Men who had sullenly drifted away from him a year ago now wrung his hand in dumb puzzlement. "Why you leave us, Father? You come back to see us sometime?" they asked. And to these unanswerable questions Stephen gave the most cheerful replies that he could summon. He entered the pine forest in the gorge and, standing under massive boughs, recaptured for a moment the sorrow of banishment breathing through the theme poem of this sacred wood, *The Nut-Brown Maid*. No longer exiled, elected to preferment, he could say now:

> *I need not to the greenwood go,*
> *Alone, a banished man.*

But the triumphant finale was mixed with a motif of mourning. The persons associated with the ballad — Ned Halley, Hercule Menton, and the Nut-Brown Maid herself — had passed, or were passing, from his life. The tears of everchanging things. He fingered the pine seedlings between the giant stumps of their predecessors; during the hard winter the young trees had taken root, and were an inch prouder in height than when he had planted them.

For the last time he visited the burned-out forge and laid his hand on the legendary anvil that had given his parish its name. *L'Enclume!* He knelt amid the cobwebbed debris and briefly praised the Maker of symbols so meaningful and lasting on the tongues of men.

Stephen said his pastoral good-by from the altar on the fourth Sunday after Easter. The church was filled. In the front rows sat his first-Communion class; the girls flowercrowned, white-veiled, on one side of the center aisle; on the other, little boys in patched serge suits and white silk ties. Behind these scrubbed first communicants sat their fathers and mothers — the men weather-scarred and ageless, their wives aged too early by poverty and domestic toil. Gazing into the familiar faces, Stephen saw the indestructible toughness that is the preserver and guarantor of life; a more reassuring vision, no lover of humanity could ask to behold.

He read the Gospel for the fourth Sunday after Easter. It was from John XVI, verses 5-12, and began: "At that time

Jesus said to his disciples, 'I go to him that sent me.'" He finished reading Christ's last discourse to His disciples, laid aside the Book, and spoke to his people.

"My dear friends: For the past few days we have been saying good-by to each other. In your homes or along the roadside, we have clasped hands as friends do in parting, and bid each other farewell. Though there has been much sadness in these farewells, we have tried to keep them as cheerful as possible, saying to each other, 'After all, Boston is not so far from L'Enclume. We will be running into each other all the time. You will visit us, we shall visit you. Let us say, then, *au revoir*. Good-by until we meet again.'

"I heartily wish that my going was merely a matter of *au revoir*. Even more heartily, I wish that I might never go away at all. If I could spend my life among you, baptizing your children, preparing them for Communion, bringing you the sacraments, and growing ever closer to you in friendship and love, this I would choose to do."

Stephen paused. "But to a priest, such dear and human happiness is not permitted. Lest we become attached to mortal friendships and thereby forget the immortal love of Him to whom we are dedicated, we learn to say not *au revoir* but *adieu*.

"*À Dieu*. To God. Your native language, in its ancient wisdom, instructs us in obedience to His will, His work, His plan.

"Together we have come through many hardships. During the rigorous seasons of winter and Lent we have measured and sustained each other. Spring and Easter have given us victory over cold and death. We have had other victories, too: I see it in the faces of the boys and girls who today will receive our Lord for the first time. I see it in your gentleness to one another, husband to wife, father to son, neighbor to neighbor. I feel it in the ties of mutual trust and love that were beginning to bind us together. But now these ties must be broken.

"I have told you why.

"In the Gospel for today, Christ says to His disciples, 'I have yet many things to say to you, but you cannot bear them now.' I do not know exactly what our Lord meant by these words, for the promise contained in them is fearful and great. But I think He meant that we should ready ourselves for the gifts of suffering and joy He holds in store for us" — Stephen spoke very slowly — "and accept obediently whatever burdens, sorrows, and commands He lays upon our lives.

"It is in this spirit of obedience that I say to you now, *'Adieu, mes amis.'*

"It is in the spirit of acceptance that I say, *'Adieu, mes frères.'*"

Stephen opened his arms as if to embrace the people of L'Enclume. "I have called you friends and brothers. You are more. The priest whom you call 'Father' echoes your love with a still dearer name. *My children all!* Till the day when we are gathered up into the arms of the eternal Father, I give you that tenderest of farewells. *'Adieu, adieu, mes enfants . . .'*"

He raised his right hand to bless them in the name of the Father, and of the Son, and of the Holy Ghost.

BOOK THREE

The Touch of Purple

CHAPTER 1

THE CATHEDRAL OF THE HOLY CROSS, episcopal seat of Lawrence Cardinal Glennon, had been in its day an architectural marvel. Cruciform in shape, built of Roxbury pudding stone, and covering an area nearly as great as that of Notre-Dame de Paris, it was considered in 1875 — the year of its consecration — the handsomest church between Baltimore and Montreal. But the luckless truth about the Cathedral was this: in selecting its site, the builders had guessed wrong! Scarcely had the glorious edifice been erected in the quiet purlieus of the South End — at that time the most substantial section of Boston — when one of those unforeseen population shifts that plague property owners and city planners took place. Tall green waves of Irish immigration began to flood the port of Boston, foamed southward past the Cathedral, and flattened out in the unstylish backwaters of neighboring Roxbury. To meet the rapid-transit needs of these newcomers, the elevated railway thrust an unsightly double track along Washington Street, and at the turn of the century a noisy procession of elevated trains began roaring past the Cathedral's enormous rose window at three-minute intervals. The intolerable clatter marred the dying fall of pulpit oratory, broke in on prayer, and destroyed meditation. Worse, the el drove the more prosperous people away from the neighborhood. Into the vacuum of run-down dwellings and lowered rents rushed a poorer and even poorer tenancy, until the noble buttresses of the Cathedral were surrounded by a wasteland of cheap lodginghouses, huddling shops, and dingy taverns.

The Cathedral's location secretly troubled Cardinal Glennon, but in public he made eloquent rationalizations of the matter. Many famous cathedrals, he was fond of pointing out, bordered on the poorer sections of their cities. Even St. Peter's in Rome rose out of the squalor of the Borgo slums. It was fitting and proper, declared Glennon, that the feet of God's loftiest temples should be laved by streams of the living poor.

These high pulpit utterances had not prevented His Eminence from diligently canvassing possible sites and probable costs of a new cathedral. Tucked away in his confidential files were sketches of a structure that would dwarf the poor dimensions of Chartres and Strasbourg, not to mention Manning's Anglican effort on Morningside Heights.

The cost of such a temple would run into millions of dollars. Estimates varied: Cornelius Deegan's figure of fifteen million was conservative; the Cardinal himself, specifying the finest of Rutland marble and twin spires fifty feet higher than Bunker Hill Monument, believed that the cost might be nearer twenty. But whatever the new cathedral might cost, the money could be had. Two millions in cash were already on deposit in various Boston banks; another four million lay in gilt-edged securities registered in the name of the Archdiocese of Boston, a corporation sole. Assuredly, it was not lack of cash that stayed the builder's hand. No, there were other brakes that operated powerfully whenever the Cardinal's fancy played wantonly among the groined ceilings, Gothic lily-work, and soaring spires of his marble dream.

The nature of these brakes was demonstrated one March afternoon in 1920 as his Eminence presided at a meeting of the Congregation for Archdiocesan Affairs. Privy and high, the council was being held in the directors' room of the Cardinal's residence. At the head of the long mahogany table sat Lawrence Glennon in the cassock of a working priest; at the Cardinal's right hand was the Most Reverend Vincent Mulqueen, Auxiliary Bishop of Boston (sometimes mentioned as the Cardinal's successor), a man of glacial mien whose temperature had been known to rise from zero to freezing point during a particularly warm discussion. At Glennon's left sat Monsignor Timothy Blake, Vicar-General of the Archdiocese, a sanguine, hearty cleric onto whose shoulders the Cardinal slipped many an administrative burden. And beside the Vicar-General sat Chancellor Michael Speed, as efficient an executive as ever escaped the clutches of corporate big business. These three acted as archdiocesan consultors to Glennon in matters of large policy; by canon law they possessed an ancient, inalienable right to be heard. The Cardinal in turn was obliged to listen and give proper weight to their opinions.

But the final decision always rested with the Cardinal alone. From his person, and his divine office of Bishop, emanated supreme authority in all matters affecting the Archdiocese of Boston.

Down the table, four other clerics ranged themselves according to rank. And at the foot of the table, reading the minutes of the last meeting, sat the Reverend Stephen Fermoyle, secretary to His Eminence these last ten months or more.

"Any objections to the minutes as read?" asked Glennon with nice parliamentary deference. There being no objections, the Cardinal swung his head on the pivot of his short neck and addressed his Vicar-General. "Have you anything ready for us on the college business, Tim?"

"I think Father Gorman's report will cover the matter, Your Eminence."

Halfway down the table, a priest with the cheekbones of an ascetic unlimbered a sheaf of notes. David Gorman, president of Regis College, was by temperament a scholar (he had studied philosophy under Mercier at Louvain). Events had placed Father Gorman at the head of a Catholic college in an era of physical expansion. The task of raising a huge building fund lay like a galling yoke on shoulders too delicate, perhaps, for the job. But implicit obedience to the rule of his superior denied David Gorman even the luxury of a wince. He began speaking now in longish periods as though translating from a rather dull passage in Cicero.

"Our estimates, based on the bids of primary contractors, and augmented tentatively by the addition of figures from subcontractors, indicate that our envisaged program of erecting two new buildings at Regis College — a library and a science laboratory — will require a sum not less than one million, nine hundred thousand dollars, and not greater than" — Father Gorman consulted an outlying note — "two million, one hundred thousand dollars."

The Cardinal nodded approval. "The figures seem not unreasonable, Father Gorman." (Good-by to lily-work dreamery a while, thought Glennon.) "And how do you propose to raise the money?"

Father Gorman took a header into another Ciceronian

period. "Recognizing, as we do, that the public has become indifferent if not calloused to campaigns for large sums we — our committee, that is — nevertheless see no alternative to launching another drive, provisionally to be known as 'A Greater Boston Fund for a Greater Regis College.'" Father Gorman took a breather. "With the aid of the Knights of Columbus and other Catholic organizations we propose to raise half the money in this manner."

"And the other half?" asked Glennon.

Father Gorman dropped his translator's manner. "Frankly, Your Eminence, we are counting upon your personal interest in the College for the rest of the money."

Glennon frowned. "You are quite right, Father, in counting upon my personal interest in Regis College. It nourished my early studies, bent my youth towards the priesthood. More importantly, the college carries on the most essential of activities — Catholic education." The Cardinal paused in the manner of a judge setting a respected barrister to rights on a point of law. "But these are not reasons for saddling the arch-diocesan treasury with obligations of a million dollars. I think you must raise your campaign sights, Father. The college has many wealthy alumni. Reaching them is merely a matter of organization."

The educator shook his head doubtfully. "It would be overoptimistic to expect our volunteer committees to raise more than a million, Your Eminence."

"Then call in professionals. We must make use of all available means to raise at least four fifths of the money by popular subscription." Glennon's tone was absolute. "You may count on me for a balance not to exceed four hundred thousand."

"Thank you, Your Eminence," said David Gorman with an exhalation of mixed relief, gratitude, and obedience that Stephen could not translate into the minutes.

The Cardinal turned again to his Vicar-General. "What progress on the children's wing of St. Joseph's Hospital?"

"Slow but sure, Your Eminence." The Vicar-General's heartiness evaporated somewhat as he explained the "slow" part of the progress. "Looking back on it now," he concluded, "I think we counted rather too heavily on local support."

"What do you mean by 'local support'?" asked Glennon. "You didn't expect contributions from China, did you?"

"I should have said 'nonsectarian support,' Your Eminence. Since St. Joseph's takes in patients of all creeds, we had hoped that a larger share of the money would be forthcoming from Protestant and Jewish sources."

"The Protestants won't give it, and the Jews take care of their own," said Glennon. "But what about the South Boston rectors themselves? Why don't they run bazaars, raffles? Sixty thousand is not an impossible sum to get from two prosperous parishes."

Vicar-General Blake put a frank face on the matter. "The truth is, Your Eminence, a feud is boiling up between the two South Boston pastors. McConickey of the old Sacred Heart claims that Melanson of the new Star of the Sea is drawing people away in droves. . . ."

"Which is precisely the reason I put Melanson there," barked His Eminence. "Tell McConickey for me that unless he simmers down — and *comes across* — there'll be a scrawling of transfer papers and much loud gnashing of dental plates in outer darkness. How much have they actually raised over there?"

"Twenty-five thousand, give or take a few hundred."

"Build a fire under them, Tim. Get some steam up. Advise McConickey and Melanson that I'm giving them thirty days to collect the rest of the money." Glennon consulted a small calendar at his elbow. "Tell them I'll lay the cornerstone myself on April fifteenth."

His Eminence was really administering now. In quick order he pulled the Cathedral Home for Foundlings out of the red by making a personal contribution of ten thousand dollars; displaced an incompetent supervisor of the Working Boys' Institute; gave his permission to use photographs in *The Monitor* (quite a departure), and assigned Bishop Mulqueen to inspect the new convent of Poor Clares in West Newton. "Rake it from attic to cellar, Vincent; I want the whole story on the furnace, plumbing, and kitchen facilities. Piety isn't enough; we've got to be sure that these nuns take care of their health."

The agenda seemed clear when Chancellor Michael Speed

lifted a document rolled up like a diploma. "Another petition from the Sons of Assisi," he said.

"The old tune?" asked Glennon.

Chancellor Speed nodded. "With a couple of new verses." Pretty scurrilous."

"Read it. No never mind. I can give it to you backwards: 'We, the undersigned Italian Americans known as the Sons of Assisi, hereby protest for the twenty-fifth' — or is it the thirty-fifth? — 'time against the high-handed attitude of Lawrence Cardinal Glennon in refusing us permission to hear Mass on the premises of 25 Prince Street, a decent edifice purchased by the above-mentioned Sons of Assisi.' " The Cardinal's diagonal mouth slipped into a wry grin. "Isn't that the way it runs, Michael?"

"To the dotting of the i's, Your Eminence. Except that they've added a couple of new threats about taking the matter directly to the Minister-General of the Franciscans."

"Let them take it to the Holy Father himself," snapped Glennon. "They'll get no permission to hear or celebrate Mass at 25 Prince Street until they hand over the property — lock, stock, and warranty deed — to the Archdiocese of Boston." His forefinger shot out in a directive to Stephen. "Write their president, that troublemaking malcontent, Bozzi; send him a stiff letter. Draw his attention to our previous correspondence and state that our position is unchanged."

His Eminence circled the table with querying eyes. "Is there any further business?" No one spoke. The Cardinal got up, inclined his head; the members of the Congregation for Archdiocesan Affairs rose, bowed back. Stephen opened the door.

"No appointments for the next hour," said the Cardinal. "I shall be in my chapel."

In the archiepiscopal stall of his private chapel, Lawrence Glennon knelt gratefully. He was not praying; he was not meditating. The mere act of kneeling always soothed him, relieved the high blood pressure generated by executive tensions. Refreshed by ten minutes on his knees, he sank back into his cushioned stall, cinctured his large abdomen with plump hands, and gave himself up to the sweet sedative thoughts of an American Chartres built on a commanding promontory (exact site unknown), with twin spires higher than Bunker Hill Monument.

Yesterday he had seen the tops of those spires quite clearly, but today a cloud of mist enwound the upper part of the structure — and somehow it seemed a little further off. Then too, other buildings had sprung up in front of it — a library, a hospital wing for children, a science laboratory, a convent heated by a modern furnace — buildings lower in stature but more pressingly needed by the Archdiocese.

The Cardinal picked up his crushed-morocco Douay Bible and turned to the Old Testament. He was looking for a certain passage in the Book of Kings, and when he found it, the words were strangely comforting.

And it came to pass . . . that Solomon began to build a house to the Lord.

And the house which King Solomon built to the Lord was threescore cubits in length, and twenty cubits in breadth, and thirty cubits in height.

And the house when it was in building, was built of stones hewed and made ready, that there was neither hammer nor axe nor any tool of iron heard in the house while it was in building.

So he built the house and finished it; and he covered the house with roofs of cedar.

And the word of the Lord came to Solomon saying:

This house, which thou buildest, if thou wilt walk in my statutes, and execute my judgments, and keep all my commandments, walking in them, I will fulfill my word to thee . . .

In the quiet of the chapel, the promises of the Lord seemed very real to His Eminence. He nodded, dozed, dreamed of a temple with ceilings of beaten gold and lily-crowned columns of rich jasper. He snored a little, and was still snoring when Stephen woke him up an hour later.

DAILY, Stephen's education went forward. As secretary to the Cardinal, he gained a knowledge permitted to few men: the inner workings of a great archdiocese, and the complex operations of Lawrence Glennon's mind.

The Cardinal's day began at seven-thirty with Mass in his

private chapel, followed by a substantial breakfast of fruit, eggs, toast, marmalade, and coffee — during which His Eminence riffled through the Boston *Globe* and *L'Osservatore Romano,* the official Vatican newspaper. At nine, Stephen brought in the mail, already opened and sorted according to Glennon's stated preference. Contributions, if any, came first; a check for five thousand dollars was a pleasant eye opener; anything larger meant a delightful day. Next came letters from personages lay or clerical. Stephen always tried to top this department with a laudatory puff from some senator or college president, felicitating His Eminence on a nice turn of phrase in a recent episcopal utterance (Glennon, a brilliant pulpit orator, was humanly fond of praise). Official correspondence with rectors and congregational heads came next in order. To some of these Glennon might dictate detailed replies; usually, however, he indicated the line to be taken and let Stephen frame the actual letter. The Cardinal's rule was that every piece of mail must be acknowledged on the day of its arrival — a task that often kept Stephen and two typists at their desks till late in the evening.

Appointments and conferences began at ten A.M. and went on till four P.M., with a brief halt in mid-flight for a cup of bouillon, a cracker, and an apple. The dark-wainscoted antechamber was always full of pastors, architects, contractors, politicians, erring curates, and assorted favor beggars. It was Stephen's job to shuttle them tactfully in and out of the Tower Room or the study with the two pianos, depending on the Cardinal's mood or the nature of the interview.

Stephen discovered that His Eminence kept three moods in fairly constant rotation. His prevailing tone was abrasive — gritty enough to flick a chunk of skin off an unlucky victim. In this mood, usually induced by high blood pressure, Glennon addressed Stephen as "Father Fermoyle," and put a caustic edge on the title. ("Your thumbs are curiously prominent today, Father Fermoyle.") The Cardinal's second manner was impersonally executive: at such times he called Stephen "Father." ("Search the archives, Father, for the records of that nineteen-ten Diocesan Synod.") The third and deepest layer of Glennon's temperament was fatherly affection, indicated by the use of Stephen's first name. ("Get me a couple of tickets, Stephen, for the Kreisler concert next Monday. We'll take a night off together.") Sometimes His Eminence was jocular. ("Cast your eye over this menu, Stephen," he would say. "Lowell of Harvard is dining with me tonight. Do you think that *escargots à la marseillaise* and a filet of sole *amandine* will persuade the Prex that our custom of not eating meat on Friday has its advantages?")

It was at dinner and afterwards that Glennon laid aside his official personality and emerged as the man of taste, lover of high company, and amateur of the arts. His Eminence had a gourmet's palate that he gratified not too sparingly at his evening meal. Sometimes he dined alone at a long table gleaming with silver and napery. Two or three times a week he would invite dinner guests — a visiting governor or bishop, a novelist on a lecture tour of New England, the publisher of the *Globe* or *Herald,* a soloist appearing with the Boston Symphony — or just an assortment of old friends and clerical colleagues. After the pleasures of table and cellar, His Eminence would lead the way to his music room, where, with little or no encouragement, he would sit down to one of his Steinways and play Bach and Beethoven with the flair of a superb amateur.

Stephen's notes, personal observations, and the carbons of his letters might have served as source material for a diocesan history of this period. Boston was expanding, and the volume of Glennon's affairs was expanding with it. His huge building program was merely one aspect of the ecclesiastic province that he administered with viceregal fidelity to Rome. Yes, to Rome, for despite Glennon's personal differences with the papal Secretary of State, he preserved a broad outlook on the Universal, Apostolic Roman Catholic Church ruled by the Sovereign Pontiff, Christ's Vicar on earth. In conformity with the new Codex of Canon Law promulgated by Benedict XV, Glennon had established in Boston a complete Curia modeled on the Roman design. The Archdiocesan Chancery handled matters legal and disciplinarian; the Marriage Tribunal was a first-rate domestic court; the Bureau of Charities, the Auditing Division, and the Office for the Propagation of the Faith — though cut on the Roman pattern — were oriented to American needs and tempo. Only gradually did Stephen realize how vast, intricate, and efficient was the ecclesiastical machine that Glennon kept in motion.

Currently, the Cardinal was breaking up the big parishes around Boston. One after another, sleek suburban rectors were summoned into his presence to hear that a third or a half of their domains were to be shorn away from them and given to younger men. The shearing followed a pattern, tactful but firm. His Eminence, seated in the Tower Room with a map of the Diocese before him, would stretch out a hand to his visitor. "Sit down beside me here, Father Tom" (or John, or Bill), he would say cordially, "and have a look at this map."

A bit of exposition was now in order. "These crosshatch-ings," Glennon would explain, "show density of Catholic population. You can see for yourself, Tom, that your parish is solid black, which means a population upwards of three thousand per square mile." The Cardinal would lay his pencil tip on the parish under discussion. "And along this eastern edge here, the Melfield section is building up very rapidly."

Then the rector, who knew what was coming, might say: "Thus far, Your Eminence, we've had no trouble handling the increased population. Sure, the church is crowded on Sunday mornings, but what's more cheerful than nice full pews and people standing in the back? If I could have an extra curate, and brighten up my basement church for the overflow, I'm sure we could accommodate everyone."

"I'm sure you could, Tom — for a year or two. But have you heard that Henry Ford is putting up a new assembly plant right on the border of your parish? When *that* goes up, you'll be overrun entirely. Now here's what I've decided to do." Pencil in hand, Glennon would indicate a dotted line. "I've taken the eastern quarter of your parish and the western half of St. Vincent's, and combined them into the makings of a new pastorate. Beginning next month . . ."

For a few minutes Father Tom would be sullen, crestfallen, angry, or whatever else he dared be. But in the end it always came out on Glennon's dotted line, and the pastor would walk out resigned to the partitioning of his parish. Sometimes he might even be grateful for relief from a burden becoming too heavy for his aging shoulders. Somerville, Newton, Lynn, and a dozen other overgrown parishes were divided in this way.

Under the Cardinal's scheme of reorganization, new churches were springing up all around Boston.

Among the yet undivided pastorates was the Medford domain of the Right Reverend Patrick Barley — the Immaculate Conception parish, an ecclesiastic barony, huge and old, and immoderately ripe for pruning. Glennon's pencil had often skirmished along its eastern marches, making a sally here, a foray there, yet never quite daring to invade the baronial holdings of Pastor Barley. Rumor said that His Eminence stood a bit in awe of Pat — and rumor spoke with a half accent of truth. Pat Barley, the oldest pastor in the Diocese, was already a cast-iron fixture when Lawrence Glennon came to Boston as Bishop in 1905. Father Barley's memory ran back to the days when the United States was a missionary country, and the powers of individual pastors were virtually unlimited. Stubborn in the face of change, the Right Reverend Patrick Barley had clung to those powers. When, for example, Glennon installed a uniform system of bookkeeping for the entire Diocese, Father Pat had openly rebelled. "I'll keep my books the way I've always kept them — in the crown of my hat," he announced. It took Glennon five years to persuade Barley that he should keep a set of ledgers and send in monthly financial reports like everyone else.

At eighty-two, Pat Barley was a grumpy old tyrant — a terror to curates and parishioners alike. Stephen knew him well. Father Barley had baptized him, and on many a frosty dawn Stephen had run all the way from Woodlawn Avenue to serve Father Barley at early-morning Mass — a service that had been an act more of fear than of love. Age had not softened the pastor; full of years and contending diseases — of which arthritis and a double cataract were the most crippling — he stood his ground against innovation and authority, defying anyone but death to budge him from his pastoral seat. Small wonder that Glennon hesitated to trim down the Barley holdings.

Yet trimmed they must be. In the past decade the Catholic population of Medford had nearly doubled; the Immaculate Conception Church was no longer big enough, nor was Pat Barley strong enough, to care for the needs of the Medford flock. New parish lines were imperative, and Stephen happened to be present on the day Glennon drew those lines.

The Cardinal and Chancellor Mike Speed were bending over a map like a pair of artillery officers when Stephen entered with the afternoon letters. Glennon's pencil was tracing creatively. "With the Medford carbarns as a hub," he said to his Chancellor, "we'll describe a flat circle along Barley's eastern boundary." At the mention of "Medford carbarns" Stephen pricked up his ears. "Pat can keep the rich residential core of the old Immaculate Conception," continued Glennon, "and we'll give the poorer outlying section to the new parish." The Cardinal completed his dotted line. "What do you think of it, Mike?"

"I think Pat'll bell like a beagle when he hears the news."

"Let him. His belling and bawling have gone on long enough. The thing I'm worried about is finding a man capable of handling the new parish. Whoever goes in there will run smack up against the loyalties of old-timers — plenty of them — who were christened and married, shriven, yes, and shorn by Pat Barley. They'll resent a newcomer, no matter who he is. And when they remember the money that old Pat Barley shook out of them (what a man he was with the collection box!), they won't like the idea of digging down for a new church."

Chancellor Speed grasped the complexity of the problem. Part of his strength with the Cardinal was his unwillingness to minimize difficulties. "We're running low on first-class administrators, Your Eminence," he warned. "I'll begin combing the Archdiocese for the best we have."

"Do so, Mike," said Glennon thoughtfully, as Stephen left the Tower Room. "We won't make a move until we find just the right man."

FOR A YEAR NOW, shiploads of khaki-clad heroes had come straggling home from war. At first, civic committees greeted them with boutonnieres, oratory, and brass bands; fresh from the awful crossroads of the Chemin des Dames and the carnage of Belleau Wood, the homecomers were harangued as national saviors by many a fulsome tongue. But gradually the welcoming committees mislaid their boutonnieres and lost their tongues; the brass bands forgot to go down the harbor on tugboats, and by the spring of 1920, incoming transports were docking like any other cargo vessel. Rumpled and sea-sick, the debarkers told bitter tales of year-long waits at Brest for westward passage across the Atlantic. Some of these tales got into the papers. Congress investigated, Pershing pleaded, and the Boston *Globe* ran a streamer, BRING OUR BOYS HOME. But the country was thinking about something else. America, like the rest of the world, was emerging into the common light of postwar day.

On a June morning in 1920, Stephen Fermoyle, coming out of the chancery office with his brief case full of documents for the Cardinal's signature, saw the military figure of Paul Ireton ascending the steps. Still in his chaplain's uniform, with a major's oak leaf at his shoulder, Paul was grayer, older-looking than his forty-three years. The cleft in his blue-black chin seemed deeper, but the severity in his eyes lightened as he grasped Stephen's hand.

"Why the delayed homecoming, Paul? Where've you been?"

"At Brest, where the paths of glory end in duckboards. A couple million Americans happened to be waiting there at the same time." Paul's voice lost color, like a phonograph record running down. "Some of them are still waiting."

Stephen could make no comment on the tragedy of those waiting men. He hedged with the standard question: "Is the mud as bad as they say?"

"It isn't the mud. It's the idleness and desperation. No one can describe it, Steve. I won't even try. All I want is a nice dry parish and work enough for three men. Say, where do I report for assignment around here?"

"I'll show you." They were at the very door of the Chan-cellor's office when a brazen idea leaped fully armed into Stephen's mind. "Could you postpone reporting for duty till this afternoon?" he asked.

"I guess the Diocese could struggle along without me till then. But what's up?"

Stephen's idea was generating arms, legs, and a wonder-fully smiling countenance. "Don't cross-examine me now, Major. But be at the Cardinal's residence at two P.M. today. That'll give me a couple of hours to get the big wheels turning."

When Paul left him Stephen darted into a room off the

Chancellor's office and walked down an alley of steel filing cabinets. He opened a file, ran his finger along an index until he came to the folder containing Paul Ireton's record as a priest. Under a twenty-five-watt bulb Stephen studied the dossier. There it was, the whole story of Paul's life and achievements, meticulously detailed, and very impressive.

"If Number One isn't convinced by this, he's no judge of dossiers," murmured Stephen.

At two o'clock, with the antechamber full of suppliants — Paul among them — Stephen entered the Tower Room and plunged *in medias res.* "There's a returned army chaplain, Major Paul Ireton, outside, Your Eminence."

Glennon looked up skeptically. "What does he want?"

"He's awaiting assignment to parish duties," said Stephen, trying to remain impersonal. But the attempt failed, and the Cardinal's secretary became a special pleader for his friend. "Paul Ireton is the best priest I know. He's forty-three years old, was assistant pastor for ten years at St. Margaret's, and has a brilliant record of overseas duty. . . ."

"What's the drift of this unsolicited panegyric, Father Fermoyle?"

Stephen flushed. "I respectfully suggest to Your Eminence that Paul Ireton be assigned to one of the new parishes."

Glennon's sarcasm cut like a carborundum wheel. "Thanks for your suggestion, Father. And have you selected any particular spot for this priestly paragon?"

"Yes. The toughest, unlikeliest-to-succeed."

"We've got plenty of those. Where's his dossier?"

"I have it here." Stephen spread the confidential record of the Reverend Paul Ireton on the table. The Cardinal's suspicion that jobbery was afoot led him to examine the papers with more than usual care.

"Let's see, now. Ah, yes. Paul Ambrose Ireton, ordained Brighton Seminary, nineteen-five. Tenth in a class of twenty-six. Hm—m, not precisely a prodigy. Curate four years at Wakefield. Moderate praise from pastor. Transferred to St. Margaret's, nineteen-nine. Ha, let's see what Dollar Bill says about him." His Eminence pored over Monaghan's letter. "Father Paul Ireton, a priest of unusual caliber . . . high spirituality . . . exceptional devotion to parish duties. Wholly dependable in financial and administrative matters . . . judgment conservative but sound . . . sorry to lose him."

"Why did he go away to war?" asked Glennon suddenly.

"I think, Your Eminence, that Father Ireton should answer that question himself."

"Bring him in."

Introducing Paul Ireton to the Cardinal was one of the happiest offices that Stephen ever performed. He was proud of Paul's unflustered genuflection and soldierly mien as Glennon dissected him with a surgeon's eye.

"Sit down, Father Ireton," Stephen heard Glennon say as he closed the oaken door.

Half an hour later Paul Ireton came out of the Tower Room, a smile quivering on his face. Seemingly he was tongue-tied.

"Well?" Stephen shook him by the arm. "Well, what happened?"

Paul Ireton's voice was that of a man recounting hallucinations. "He's sending me to Medford."

"To set up shop next to Pat Barley? What a location!"

Paul was still in a daze. "He says I'm to build a church there. . . . He's given me a start financially."

"He *has!* That's most unusual, Paul. How much?"

Paul Ireton opened his hand. There in his palm lay a worn Libertyhead nickel. "Carfare to my new parish. Oh, Steve . . . it's come true." The muscles of Paul Ireton's throat contracted as he gulped down a rising lump.

When His Eminence opened the door a moment later, his fine hazel eyes witnessed the extraordinary scene of two grown men, one in black, the other in khaki, pummeling each other about the head and shoulders. It occurred to His Eminence that jobbery had indeed been done, but on re-examining the papers in Paul Ireton's folder he could not decide offhand who was jobbing whom.

CHAPTER 2

LIKE MANY A FLORENTINE before him, Captain Gaetano Orselli enjoyed making an entrance. Whether into a boudoir or harbor, he relished the drama of the *entratura* and had lifted it to the condition of a minor art. At the moment, he was looking forward to taking his ship into Boston Harbor for the first time since the Armistice. Off his starboard bow stood Boston Light, and a more welcome beacon the Captain had never seen. There had been times during the voyage when the *Vesuvio's* tired engines and rusty plates had seemed no match for the Atlantic combers. But now the hazards were over; Orselli felt the slackening pulse of the *Vesuvio's* engines as she reduced speed for the pilot boat, tossing like a chip at the foot of Boston Light. Down went the rope ladder; up scrambled the pilot with the speed of a frightened cat. The Captain's responsibilities were over, and he could now yield himself up to the acclamation that an ocean liner receives on entering a friendly port.

In his cabin, Orselli arrayed himself in his London-made uniform — a trifle easy around the waist after four Spartan years of war — adjusted his gold-embroidered hat to the precise angle of the *Vesuvio's* smokestacks, and surveyed in a triptych mirror the total effect of glistening beard, broad back, and conquistador profile that never failed to please him. It did not fail him now. At forty-eight Orselli looked a robust forty-two, and thanks to the kindness of a certain *donna generosa* on B deck, he felt an eager thirty-nine. From his jewel box the Captain chose a gold snake ring, a fat python with emerald eyes, and slipped it onto his little finger. He was running low on jewelry, and because he would never wear this particular ring again he pressed it to his full lips in regretful farewell. "She has been deserving of you," he murmured. Then nipping an English-market cigar between his handsome teeth, Gaetano Orselli went on deck.

April sunlight, brilliant but not warm, broke into aquamarine splinters as it struck the channel. The fanfare of welcome was exploding all around the *Vesuvio:* sirens zoomed, flags dipped, and a cratelike airplane made a near miss as it attempted to drop a bouquet on the liner. At Fort Banks, international signals at the mast of the flagship officially spelled out "Welcome, *Vesuvio*," while an irreverent noncom at the foot of the mast wigwagged *"Viva Spaghetti."*

Pleased by the reception, Orselli mounted to the bridge and began pointing out marks of interest to a group of dis-

tinguished passengers. The company was sparse: a four-star
American general returning from the peace conference; a
British banker-diplomat seeking a lower rate of interest on
the new American loan; and a representative of a German
cartel who had hoped to regain certain important factories
from the alien property custodian. Lastly, there was Archbishop Lodovico Rienzi, the Apostolic Delegate, veteran of
many an embassy to the chancelleries of Europe, but now
seeing for the first time the shores of the New World.

The Archbishop, despite his diplomatic missions, was not
a worldly man. His field was canon law, and his present assignment was to bring the structure of the great American sees
into conformity with the Roman Curia. And because the
Supreme Pontiff was scraping the bottom of his coffers for
such poor coins as might be found, the Apostolic Delegate
also hoped to speed the flow of New World contributions to
the papal treasury. The Archbishop could smile approvingly,
therefore, at the massed shipping, the crowded steel
piers, and other signs of material prosperity in this teeming
port.

He gazed about the harbor in astonishment. "It is as large
and almost as colorful as Naples! I confess I am much surprised."

"You will have many such surprises in America, Excellency," said the Captain. "It is a country of unbelievable
magnitude and resources. Raw, perhaps, and without patina.
But a century from now it will be challenging Italy's culture,
and — am I being heretical? — even the spiritual authority of
Rome."

Orselli disregarded the Archbishop's politely pitying smile,
and pointed to a huge, round-sterned vessel berthed at a new
concrete pier. "That is the *Leviathan*, which was once queen
of the Hamburg-American run. She was seized by the United
States at the outbreak of the war, converted into a transport,
and ferried half a million American soldiers to Europe."

"A monument to Teutonic stupidity." Choosing not to
offend the German openly, the Apostolic Delegate spoke in
Italian.

"You may well say so, Excellency," said the *Farbenindustrie*
man. But you may count upon us not to make the same mistake

again. The new Germany will make no mistakes. And as for luxury liners" — he beamed complacently at the company — "we shall have them, too."

"*Aber natürlich,*" said the English banker. "Everyone will have luxury liners again."

Orselli knew this to be true. Even now in the great ship-yards of Ostia a new superliner was being built for him. As senior captain of the Italian Line he would tread its bridge and command its Italian crew. But ownership of the vessel would rest in foreign, which was to say, British, hands. Orselli permitted a jet of lava to erupt from his Italian soul.

"Yes, magnificent new vessels will sail the seas again. But no matter what flag they fly, or where they are built, a British board of directors will control them."

"That is undeniably true," said the Englishman.

"But where will *l'Inglese* get the money?" asked the Arch-bishop a bit anxiously.

The English banker-diplomat relished the innocence of the query. "Where does anyone else get it?" he murmured in French.

Everyone laughed except the American general. At West Point in his time, no one had bothered to study French.

Six rope-nosed tugs began nudging the *Vesuvio* into her berth. By now the ring on Orselli's little finger was a burning band. There would be at least an hour before the American husband could come aboard. "You must excuse me, gentle-men," he said. "The business of docking grows complicated." He lifted his gold-fringed hat to the group, and made a special bow to the Apostolic Delegate. "May Your Excellency enjoy full success in your mission."

"And you in yours, Captain." The Archbishop had strolled often enough on the B-deck promenade to know that a per-fumed wind was blowing from that quarter. The New World might teach His Excellency many things, but it could scarcely tutor him in the poignard art of irony.

From the *Vesuvio*'s bridge an hour later, Gaetano Orselli watched his passengers debark. Through marine binoculars he saw the American *donna generosa* give the seacomer's kiss to her husband. "Lovely, treacherous creatures!" mur-mured the Captain compassionately. He focused his glass on the airplane swooping overhead, and made out the message painted on the underside of its wings. "*Sons of Assisi?*" The Captain wagged a puzzled beard. In Italy the children of St. Francis walked unsandaled across the earth. In America they flew madly about in airplanes. Shifting his glass, Orselli picked up the figure of a somewhat bewildered Archbishop descending the gangplank, and watched a dark-haired young priest advance to meet him with a respectful but quite American obeisance of knee and head. No mistaking that high-shouldered carriage or the expression of filial welcome on the priest's face as he rose to greet the papal envoy. Only one man in the world could combine so much ecclesiastic punctilio with such independence of spirit. Orselli seized his megaphone.

"Stefano!" he shouted.

Above the tumult of sirens and clamoring voices, Stephen heard his name. His eyes traced the bellow to its source — a bearded man was waving a megaphone from the Captain's bridge. The niceties of protocol forbade shouting back, and the immediate business of herding the Apostolic Delegate and his little retinue across the pier was too pressing for a quick dash up the gangplank. Stephen did the best he could in a hasty pantomime with an imaginary knife and fork.

His gestures conveyed to Orselli: "I received your wireless and will meet you for dinner at the appointed place."

The Captain's glistening beard bobbed joyous confirmation. He laughed at the gay telegraphy, but his laughter changed to admiration as he watched Stephen shunt his charges past photographers and ship reporters to a pierhead court, where Lawrence Cardinal Glennon advanced with open arms to greet the emissary of his Sovereign Pontiff, Benedict XV.

Arrayed in his best clerical broadcloth, a ten-dollar hat, and a pair of excellent black oxfords on his feet, Father Stephen Fermoyle walked eagerly along Prince Street to his rendezvous with Captain Orselli at the Café Torino. Prince Street, if not the heart of Boston's Little Italy, is one of its principal arteries. Long before the Italians came, America's earliest great — James Otis, the first Adamses, and Paul Revere — had trod this narrow thoroughfare. From its solid burgherish homes and mercantile establishments, the fledgling murmurs of American independence had issued. But the high tide of Colonial fame had long ago ebbed from this historic region, and latter-day waves of immigration had flooded it with newer, swarthier Americans from Naples and Sicily.

A heavy shower had fallen that afternoon, mud and garbage from swollen gutters flooded across the pavement, and eddied around Stephen's polished boots. No matter. More significant currents were swirling along Prince Street. Stephen heard a soapbox agitator flogging his listeners with foam-flecked protests against the recent arrest of Sacco and Vanzetti. The pair had been charged with the high crimes of murder and armed robbery. "But their real offense," cried the orator in Italian, "is their heroic opposition to capitalistic oppression." The crowd roared approval. Stephen passed on.

In front of a steamship agency, an ecstatic group of Italian Americans were waving handfuls of paper money at each other. "Ponzi, he will make us rich," they cried. "Ponzi will break the bankers' stranglehold on the throats of little people."

Stephen was dubious about that. He knew the Ponzi system; its fame was flying all over Boston. You gave Ponzi a hundred dollars, and in three months you got back a hundred and fifty. According to Ponzi, he used your money to buy Italian lire, and made a handsome profit on the difference in exchange. Clearly, the little Sicilian was suffering from fiscal dementia. Sooner or later his mansion of finance would crash, and the little people would lose their money. Meanwhile they hymned his name, and cursed the banks that paid a mere three per cent.

Are the times out of joint? Stephen wondered. He crossed a plank trestle and gazed into a deep excavation running parallel to the sidewalk. A water main had broken, and gangs of men were laying a new conduit in the shadowy trench lighted by bomb-shaped flares.

From the window of Torino's café an amethyst light was shining. The source of that light was an electric light bulb in a bunch of alabaster grapes held in the bronze uplifted hand of a Neapolitan youth at the expectant moment of crushing the luscious fruit to his lips. The statue was not merely the bush of the Torino establishment; to the proprietor it was

a lively memento of his own boyhood in the vineyards of
Naples. It symbolized carefree enjoyment of two excellent
things — youth and wine — both gone now, the first *de facto*,
the second *de jure*. About his departed youth Torino could do
nothing, but about the wine he took specific measures. He
made it himself on his farm in Sudbury and sold it, *de jure*
or not, by the glass or bottle to the regular patrons of his café.

Tonight, Virgilio Torino was readying three bottles of his
best purple wine for the palate of a distinguished guest. Captain Gaetano Orselli would pay for two bottles; the third
would be on the house. A *fricassea di pullo* was gently stewing
in bay leaves for the Captain; his table was laid for two in a
curtained booth; Torino's little fountain splashed among its
pebbles. The first bottle of wine lay in a wicker basket. *Tosto*,
the good things of life would begin.

A priest entered. "Is Captain Orselli here yet?"

"No, but *bene*, soon. Will the Father sit down, have a glass
of wine while waiting?" Stephen sat down, but took no wine;
anticipation of meeting Orselli had lifted his spirits high
enough already. He stretched his long legs under the table,
listened to the splashing fountain, saw the wine bursts of
light gleaming through the alabaster grapes, munched a
plump olive from a heaping *antipasto*, and wondered when
and where Americans had lost the secret of enjoying life.

At a long table near the window a society of some kind
was beginning dinner. The chairman, bushy-haired, tub-
chested, was proposing the first toast. Stephen could not
catch his solemn words.

Of a sudden the fountain splashed higher, the light inside
the alabaster grapes gleamed a richer purple, and Gaetano
Orselli came through the door. The art of the *entratura*
reached a minor peak as he handed his gold-leafed hat to
Torino and strode, arms extended, toward Stephen.

The gift of glad greeting was in this man. "*Furfantino!* You
ecclesiastical rascal! It is good to touch you again." The Captain's beautiful hands grasped Stephen, then passed upward
to wrists, elbows, biceps, and shoulders before holding him
off for appraisal. "You look heavier, handsomer, *Stefano*."

"You look leaner, as handsome as ever, Captain."

Orselli gazed about for a mirror to confirm the compliment,

found none, then exposed his fine white teeth in the physical delight of smiling. "*Lusingatore . . .* you flatterer! We Florentines yield to the Irish in the courts of blarney. Torino, the corkscrew! We have only a few hours. We must drink as we talk." Orselli poured two goblets of the Sudbury wine, lifted his glass connoisseurwise to the light, and found in its deep color the inspiration for a fitting toast.

"To the purple." Pleased by the wordplay and the wine itself, Orselli drained his glass. "Purple? What am I saying? I expected you to be at least a monsignor already, Stefano. What has held up the procession? Tell me everything without benefit of chronology." Orselli speared a slice of salami. "Serve it forth all at once, like this excellent *antipasto.*"

Between mouthfuls of pimento, anchovies, and pickled mushrooms, Stephen told of his curateship with Dollar Bill Monaghan; the *minestrone* found him describing Ned Halley's saintliness and poverty. Orselli was finishing the first bottle of wine as Stephen recounted the saga of the Dolcettiano amethyst. At its happy ending the Captain burst in with admiration and delight.

"Either the Holy Ghost guided you — or you have the trick of landing on your feet. In a world off-balance, one gift is as valuable as the other. Who knows? They may be identical. . . ."

Torino was uncovering an earthenware casserole. "In all Italy, the Captain will find no plumper chicken than this," he assured Orselli. "Even the King does not dine as well tonight."

"Nor for many nights," said the Captain. "No one dines well in Italy any more." He drew the cork from the second bottle of wine. "Let us drink to happier days for the Italian nation."

Stephen touched the wine to his lips. "Tell me about Italy, Gaetano. We get no reliable news of what's happening there."

"It is not a joyful tale," said Orselli. "My country is like a man with boils, sitting on a dung heap of confusion and dismay. The war gave us a bayonet wound here" — pointing to his midriff — "but the peace has dismembered us entirely." Orselli made chopping motions at his own arms and neck. "At Versailles your Mr. Wilson with his Fourteen Points —

God Himself had only ten — treated us like an enemy rather than a faithful ally."

"What about the League of Nations?"

"League of robbers!" Orselli spat out a chicken bone. "We have already lost Dalmatia and Fiume. Japan receives mandates that should be ours. But we have only ourselves to blame. We are disunited in our councils, broken at home, powerless abroad. In a world of whirling chaos Italy will be destroyed unless a strong man arises to bind the broken rods of authority into a firm bundle. . . . What's this, Torino?"

Torino's head popped apologetically through the curtains. A flask of liquor was in his hands. "I deliver compliments from an old friend of yours," he said to the Captain. "Messer Arnoldo Bozzi sends you this bottle of *grappa* in the hope that you are still able to drink his health."

"Bozzi! Is that sheep poisoner still alive? Tell him to come to the bridge at once. The Captain will gladly match thirsts with him."

As Torino darted away, Orselli explained to Stephen, "In my youth I had the honor of not marrying this Bozzi's sister. Since then he is compelled to admire my judgment. Other than that, Messer Bozzi is as illustrious a rogue as ever fled the Italian police. He has the soul of a true Florentine conspirator. Ah, here's the conspirator now . . . Arnoldo!"

A man of vast girth — the frizzled-haired toastmaster that Stephen had noticed on entering the café — filled the entrance to the booth. He and Orselli gripped hands with exclamatory warmth, each standing off to appraise the other — as if hoping to find a broken tooth, a balding scalp, or other evidences that the years had been unkind.

Bozzi glanced inquiringly from Orselli to Stephen.

"You are surprised by the honest company I keep, Arnoldo. Meet my dear friend, Father Fermoyle, Secretary to His Eminence the Cardinal. Stephen, this is Arnoldo Bozzi — a whited *carbonaro*."

Stephen remembered the name. "I have often heard of Mr. Bozzi. He is president, I believe, of the Sons of Assisi."

"A crew of counterfeiters, no doubt," said Orselli. "Well, Torino, do not stand there smirking like an innkeeper. Brandy glasses are what we need. Sit down, Arnoldo, if you can crowd that belly of yours into a small space."

Bozzi sat down and lifted his glass of *grappa*. "*Sempre!*" he toasted, his index finger erect. This, the favorite toast of the *Bersaglieri,* was a studied insult to the celibate priesthood. Stephen did not raise his glass.

"Well now, and what is this Sons of Assisi business, Arnoldo? Was it your airplane that almost knocked off the funnels of my ship this afternoon? What have I done to deserve a bouquet that missed my deck by a hundred meters?"

"The bouquet was for Archbishop Rienzi, the papal delegate, who comes to straighten out the ecclesiastical mess here in Boston."

Stephen's smile said: "Go ahead and be as bad-mannered as you please. This is my night off." His smiling challenge drew a direct question from Bozzi. "Are you really the Cardinal's secretary?"

"I am."

"Then you know of our plea for an Italian church in the North End?"

Stephen nodded, "I am familiar with the correspondence."

"In God's name, what's all this about?" asked Orselli. "Don't tell me you've become a champion of religion, Arnoldo?"

"A champion of Italian Americans, rather," said Bozzi. He launched into a partisan explanation for Orselli's benefit. "Three years ago the Sons of Assisi bought and decorated a church for our neglected countrymen. We imported a good and holy Franciscan priest from Italy, and all we ask is that he should say Mass in our church. We have petitioned the Irishman Glennon for permission to conduct holy services — but His Lordship refuses to hear our plea." Bozzi turned to Stephen with a flattering "you're-an-intelligent-fellow" expression on his heavy face. "You have read our petition. What is your opinion of it?"

"My opinion," said Stephen, "is expressed in the last letter from the Cardinal."

Bozzi sneered. "You see, Captain, they all hang together, these Irish-American priests. Well, let them hang." The Sons of Assisi president took a new tack. "Would it surprise you to learn that the Pope himself is behind us, and that your Irish

Cardinal will find himself overruled by our infallible Italian pontiff?" Bozzi was gibing at Stephen now. "He *is* infallible, you know."

"About the Pope being behind you, I wouldn't know," said Stephen. "But as to his infallibility — well, there's the famous story told by Cardinal Gibbons. When someone asked the old Cardinal, 'Do you believe the Pope is infallible?' Gibbons laughed and said, 'All I know is that when he last addressed me, he called me *Jibbons*.'"

Orselli's laughter broke the tension. "'Jibbons'! Ha-ha. Come, Arnoldo, smile, my friend. This is not a consistory." He poured more *grappa* for himself and Bozzi.

Bozzi tossed off the powerful distillate, but refused to be placated. He was one of those intensely individualistic rebels who resist any form of authority. Sincerely enough, Bozzi believed in a return to the simpler religion of St. Francis. And now, with his followers behind him (the entrance to the booth was packed with the Sons of Assisi), he determined to give this cool cleric a thrashing.

"In every letter to us the Cardinal says: 'Hand over the deed to your church property, and I will give you permission to say Mass there.'" Hired-hall truculence and too many liters of alcohol were in Bozzi's question, "Why is this?"

The old proverb, "Never argue with a drunk or a zealot," warned Stephen against entering the debate. But the man was entitled to an answer, and of the many possible replies, Stephen sought the one best suited to his audience. With Orselli gazing at him confidently, and Bozzi sneering like a chess player who has just checkmated a king, Stephen began:

"You must understand, Signor Bozzi, that the constant and unchanging objective of the Church is the care of souls. It was for this purpose that Christ founded His Church and made it the divine instrument by which man might gain eternal union with God." Stephen waited for this basic proposition to sink into the minds of his hearers, then proceeded. "The Church is the source of the sanctifying grace that enables man to achieve this end. And it is also the guardian of the inspired truths that Christ revealed to men."

"One knows all this from the catechism," said Bozzi. "But what has it to do with the ownership of Church property?"

"I might make the point," said Stephen, "that a synod of American bishops has decreed that all Church properties must be owned by the diocese in which they are located. I might go into the history of that decree, and describe the confusion, the schismatic dangers arising from the lay-trustee system that preceded it. But with your permission, I would rather attempt to explain the doctrinal concepts underlying the diocesan ownership of Church property."

Bozzi turned to his followers. "We must watch out for this *argomentatore clericale*, else his priest talk will lead us astray."

Stephen let the laughter subside, then resumed the high ground of his original argument. "The Church," he said, "is not only the mystical body of Christ: it is also a tangible earthly organism — a society formed of living men, a structure clearly manifest to the world in its ceremonial observances, its laws, and administrative offices. It has its visible head, the Pope, who as Christ's Vicar speaks with infallibility" — Stephen loaded his words for Bozzi's benefit — "*in the sphere of faith and morals*. From the Pope, or as some theologians contend, from God Himself, this authority descends to the bishops, who guard, define, and teach Christ's sacred truths within their diocesan limits. The bishops must be watchful lest errors of doctrine or practice creep into the Church. Cardinal Glennon, in the discharge of his sacred office, is the guardian, definer, and teacher of Catholic truth for the Archdiocese of Boston."

"Guardian of truth, maybe," said Bozzi. "But does his guardianship include title to all real estate?"

"According to Church law, it does."

"Then Church law is ridiculous," shouted Bozzi. "God does not care who holds title to a brick building."

"If God does not care," said Stephen quietly, "why should you?"

"*Bravissimo!*" roared Orselli. "Are the Sons of Assisi more property-minded than God?"

Bozzi thrust his enraged bulk across the table and poured a torrent of abuse over Stephen. "Your soapy words will not clean the face of the matter. Put it as you please, the truth is that your American Church is nothing but a big corporation, always stretching out greedy fingers for more holdings. From the Cardinal down, it has forgotten the simple teachings of Christ, and thinks only of revenues and property."

"Shame, Arnoldo," cried Orselli, tugging at Bozzi's shoulder. "Father Fermoyle has tried to demonstrate the matter fairly. I will not permit this attack on my guest."

"Let him speak," said Stephen.

Grappa and anger swelled the veins of Bozzi's forehead. "Thank you, Reverend Broadcloth, for your kind permission. You may take this message back to your Cardinal: tell him that when the Sons of Assisi find a priest who will bring religion to the poor — a priest who will come to us barefooted and garbed in rags as St. Francis did — when we find an American-Irish prelate who will forget property claims and humbly bring the sacraments to my neglected countrymen — *then*" — Bozzi turned his bushy head to the Sons of Assisi as if asking approval for the proposition he was about to make — "*then* we will sign over our title deed to the Cardinal. Is that fair?"

"Fair enough," said Stephen. "And if you walk through the streets of Boston you will find a hundred such priests eager to meet the conditions you have laid down. But no, you would not recognize them." He turned to Orselli. "Come, Captain. Let's get out of here. It would take a miracle to convince this man."

Stephen shouldered his way through the hostile crowd; Torino, all apologies, followed them to the door. On Prince Street oil flares from the excavation sent up a greasy light, and the odor of stagnant water hung corpse-heavy on the evening air. Silent and depressed, Stephen and Orselli walked southward, crossed the improvised trestle over the broken water main.

"What a stupid exhibition that was!" said Stephen. "I should have known better than to dispute with such a man in public."

"You had no choice," consoled Orselli. "Bozzi pressed the quarrel upon you. I must say that you managed the whole business with dignity and reason. Does it matter to you if a pig wishes to wallow in the mire of ignorance?"

"I should have handled him more skillfully. But I was so bent on winning an argument that I lost an opportunity to make a convert."

An ambulance clanged along Prince Street and pulled up with a brake-screeching stop. Two white-coated interns jumped off and began questioning some laborers along the edge of the ditch. The men pointed into the muddy trench, and one of the interns ran back to the ambulance for a stretcher. Policemen began swinging their sticks at the gathering crowd. Stephen spoke to a tin-hatted workman climbing out of the excavation.

"What's going on?" asked Stephen.

"All hell's broke loose, Father." The foreman pulled a bandanna from his hip pocket and wiped a mixture of sweat and mud from his face. "We're layin' a new water main when a cloudburst falls on us and blocks the new pipe with a lot of silt and stuff." The man seemed eager to absolve himself from blame. "Well, I send Joe Salvucci in there — he's the skinniest man we got — to clean the stuff out. Just then a truck backs up to the edge of the excavation, and the whole wall caves in, truck and all, right on top of the pipe where Joe's working." More bandanna work. "He's a goner, sure."

"Is he still alive?" asked Stephen.

"Mashed like a cockroach, but we can hear him groaning inside."

The crew of a wrecking crane were trying to fasten a block and tackle to the foundered truck as a preliminary to rescuing the buried man. "Hoist away," came the cry. Windlasses strained, the truck moved about a foot, then slid back with a grunt onto the galvanized pipe. It was like hitting a baby on the head with a flatiron.

I can't stand here watching, thought Stephen. He pulled off his coat, handed it to Orselli, and jumped into the ditch.

"Hey, you, get out of there," shouted the leader of the wrecking crew.

On his hands and knees Stephen crawled under the truck and tapped on the dented main with a piece of stone. No response came from Joe Salvucci. Stephen pounded harder, laying his ear to the galvanized main. From the trapped man inside the pipe came a feeble knocking made by a desperate knuckle.

Joe Salvucci was still alive! How can I reach him? thought Stephen.

He crawled along the section of galvanized pipe till he came to its open end, the same dark orifice that Joe had entered a few minutes before. A noxious sewery stench struck Stephen's nostrils as he peered into the death canal. A tight fit! Off came his Roman collar and silk rabat, off came his broadcloth trousers. In cotton undershirt and shorts, he thrust his head into the galvanized main, and inched his way through its mucky ooze. The terror of narrow places almost suffocated him. The slime lubricated his body, permitting it to slip along the inside of the pipe; he found that by lying on his side he could hump along on his shoulder.

It seemed to Stephen that he had crawled an oozy mile before he heard a man's low groaning. In the darkness Stephen reached out to touch Joe Salvucci's face. The man was lying on his back, his lips moving piteously.

"Can you hear me, Joe?"

"Who you?"

"A priest — Father Fermoyle. I've come to hear your confession."

A note of wild beatitude entered Joe Salvucci's voice: "I thanka God you come, Father." Joe's breath was being choked off by the weight of the truck as he began his confession. "I make Jesus name in swearwords . . . hundred times a day. Everything I say is Christ-a this, Christ-a that."

"That shows how near He always is. What else, Joe?"

"I get drunk. I go to bad house. Afterwards I go home and kick my wife."

"Yes, my son."

Accents of fierce regret were in Joe Salvucci's dying words. "I have been bad to my children. I drive my son Vittorio from the house. I tell God I am mos' sorry for that."

"God understands, Joe. In His misery He forgives you, and all the poor trapped men who will come after you, forever and ever. Is there anything else now?"

"One more thing, Father." Consciousness was slipping away, and with it slipped the language of Joe's adopted country. He began murmuring in Italian. "I say many times that priests are not good men, that they think only of money, their robes, their belly. I say many times that priests do not love their people . . . I take back those lies now, Father."

A fierce joy burned in Stephen as he put his lips as close as possible to Joe's ear. "Make a good act of contrition, my son."

Joe Salvucci's voice came gaspingly. "*Signore, io detesto tutti i miei peccati, perche sono vostra offesa e mi rendono indegno di recevervi nel mio cuore . . .*"

"Go on, Joe, finish it."

"*. . . e propongo con la vostra grazia di non commetterne più per l'avvenire, di fuggirne le occasioni, e di farne la penitenza . . .*"

At the end, Joe's lips were barely moving, Stephen felt an ominous tightening of the pipe; he wriggled backward through the constricting dark. There was a grinding wrench as the full weight of the truck descended.

Covered with filth, Stephen crawled out of the pipe. Half naked, dazed, and heart-stricken, he lay in the mud, the words of Joe Salvucci's confession ringing pitifully in his ears.

"You all right, Mac?" asked one of the workmen.

"I'm fine," said Steve. "Just throw a couple of buckets of water over me, and I'll put on my clothes." He tried to get up, staggered, and would have fallen again. But Orselli's powerful arms were around him, Orselli's perfumed beard was in his face. "You were magnificent, Stefano," the Captain murmured, covering Stephen's nakedness with his London-made coat. "Help me lift him into the ambulance," he snapped at the gaping interns.

"No ambulance, please," begged Stephen. "Just take me home in a cab, Gaetano."

THE BOSTON PAPERS were full of it next morning. Placing the Cardinal's mail beside his plate, Stephen tried to leave the room quickly.

"Not so fast, Father," said Glennon. He picked up the *Globe*, and read the headline aloud. " 'Priest Risks Life to Hear Confession of Trapped Laborer' . . . I see you covered yourself with mud — and publicity — last night."

The Cardinal sipped his coffee. "You realize, Father Fermoyle, that I do not ordinarily approve of such melodrama. It tends to create a false impression of a priest's daily routine." He spread marmalade on buttered toast and munched awhile. "There are in this case, however, extenuating circumstances."

More marmalade, more munching. "It may interest you to know that a man named Bozzi came here in person last night."

"Oh?"

"He had his crowd with him — the Sons of Assisi. Excitable fellows. At the time I didn't quite understand what all the jabbering was about — especially the reference to St. Francis walking barefooted through . . . ah . . . mud. But the *Globe* clears the matter up nicely. I hope you suffer no aftereffects from your plunge into the primal ooze."

Stephen gazed at the tips of his second-best shoes. "Only the loss of a broadcloth suit and a pair of new oxfords, Your Eminence."

"The archdiocesan treasury will replace them, Father. But to get back to Bozzi. He seemed apologetic about an argument he had had with you. His apology took a rather handsome form — *very* handsome, I may say. He presented me with a document — I think I have it on me now. Yes, here it is — a warranty deed to the Prince Street property in the North End."

A smile slanted across the Cardinal's large mouth. He rose from his chair and slapped the document exultantly against the breakfast table. "We made it, Stephen!" he laughed, holding out a congratulatory hand. "My heartiest thanks, Father. The whole affair was a masterpiece of priestly behavior and perfect timing."

The Cardinal lowered his voice confidentially. "Rienzi, the Apostolic Delegate, was much impressed. He had instructions to straighten out this sticky Sons of Assisi business, but when that wild-eyed delegation came in last night and voluntarily surrendered title, Rienzi did the handsome thing and distributed medals blessed by the Holy Father himself. Everything, including the honor of the Archdiocese, had a bright burnish around midnight."

Glennon's mood of jubilation ebbed. Laying aside the warranty deed that meant so much to him as an administrator, His Eminence became a priest again. "Tomorrow morning, I'm saying a funeral Mass for Joe Salvucci at the Prince Street Church. I'll be greatly pleased and honored, Father Fermoyle, to have you assist me as deacon."

CHAPTER 3

MONA FERMOYLE pitched her toque at the bedroom bureau, kicked off her pumps, and flexed her slim body restlessly on her narrow bed. She had come home from work, entered the front door without a word of greeting to her father or mother — and now Celia was at the foot of the bed, unpacking a heartful of mother-hen questions. "Would you like a little supper in bed? Have you got a headache, darling? Do you know that Emmett's coming tonight?" Mona's replies were undaughterly. No, she didn't want any supper in bed. Yes, she knew that Emmett Burke was coming. No, she didn't have a headache — headaches weren't due for a week yet. Yes, no; no, yes. "Ma, for heaven's sake lay off me, will you? I'm frazzled. Maybe it's the job, maybe it's the weather. I don't know. It's something. Shut the door."

As Mona sat up to unfasten her garters, the tangled nature of that "something" flattened her out on the bed once more. Something? Everything! Job, Church, family, Emmett Burke, respectability, life in general. The plumbing-supply office with the Sani-enamel bowl in the window beside her typewriter; the bickering with Florrie; Celia's solicitous clucking, the Thursday-night meetings of the Unmarried Women's Sodality — and Emmett. His breathlets, speckled neckties, weekly haircuts, and monotonous monologues about K. of C. politics, and firing pins.

If he talks about firing pins tonight, thought Mona, I'll throw his three-sixteenth-carat diamond on the sidewalk, and stamp on it.

Mona was engaged to Emmett now; at Christmastime he had given her the smallest possible yellow diamond, and received the smallest possible kiss in return. In certain quarters Emmett was considered a catch. Caramel-faced Lucy Curtin paled for him; Celia Fermoyle saw valuable deposits of piety and regularity in his chunky person; and Sister Bernadine, who had taught Emmett commercial geography in high

school, was on record with the statement that he was the finest
young man in the parish, and would have made a noble priest
if only he had had it in him to learn just a noseful of Latin —
which noseful Emmett could not acquire. So, on his return
from war he was cast as a stanch lay pillar, and went to work
in his father's grocery store for nineteen-fifty a week.

Of this princely wage, Emmett deposited twelve dollars
every Friday night in the Medford Co-operative Bank; when
he had saved five hundred dollars he and Mona Fermoyle
would get married. Emmett had it all figured out. "We'll
furnish a flat with that Four-Room $298.89 Love-Nest Spe-
cial in Caldwell's Furniture Store . . . Groceries won't cost
anything. The old man will come across with a five-dollar raise
the day we get married, and off we go to Providence for our
honeymoon, with a hundred biscuits in the old haversack.
Register at a hotel and everything . . ."

At the prospect of her nuptial flight, now alarmingly near,
Mona rolled over and punched her pillow. Tonight Emmett
would claim a small advance in the shape of a good-night
kiss, and the taste of Sen-Sen would be on her lips afterwards.
Strange, if you loved someone, you didn't care what his kisses
tasted like. And no tightening up, either. You just laid your
head back, and waited with your mouth quiet till it was covered, then sank into the bottomless dream, murmuring — or
sometimes only thinking — "Benny darling . . . it's been so long."

At seven o'clock Mona sipped the cup of corn chowder that
Celia brought up. She said "yes, no; no, yes," to her mother's
questions, then listlessly began dressing. Her midweek date
with Emmett being strictly nonfestive — a movie and sundae
afterward — it didn't make much difference what she wore.
The navy gabardine suit and batiste blouse would be good
enough. At seven-twenty-nine she heard Emmett's familiar
ring, a long and two shorts, kept him waiting about six minutes, then came clicking down the front stairs.

There stood Emmett in the parlor, barbered to the nines,
wearing his brown suit (the blue serge came out on Sunday
evenings), a fig-speckled tie, shoes shined with ox-blood polish, a new round hat in his hands, and a box of candy under
his arm.

"Hi, Mona," he said, in the too-eager way of a roulette

player who doubts that his luck will hold. With clumsy carelessness he proffered the candy.

"Cavalier Brand, all cream centers," he announced. "A special at Morgan's."

"Oh, chocolates. Thank you, Emmett." Without looking at the box, Mona laid it on top of the piano.

"Where're we stepping tonight?" Emmett's question implied a boundless variety of entertainments — dancing on the Westminster roof, the floor show at Sirocco's. But financially these were out of bounds. Emmett had exactly a dollar to spend, and Mona knew it.

"What's down at the Alhambra?" she asked with no salt in the question.

"Vilma Vale in *Canyon Love*."

"I hear that's good," said Celia, who had opened the box of candy and was munching a cream center.

"*Canyon Love* it is, then. Good night, Ma."

With such *non sequitur* counsels as, "Have a good time," "Be a good girl," and "Get home early," Celia Fermoyle put the sign of the cross on their young backs as they went down the front steps. "Jesus, Mary, and Joseph protect them," she breathed, watching them through the curtained window. "Emmett's a good boy, Emmett is. He deserves a good, home-loving wife. It'll be a happy day for me when Mona's safely married to him."

Mona, knowing that her mother was mumbling pieties behind the curtain, and realizing that the whole population of Woodlawn Avenue was peeping through similar curtains, wanted to smash Emmett's new round hat over his ears, and run shrieking down the street.

She wanted to go dancing with someone she loved, but that being impossible, she walked circumspectly through Medford Square with Emmett holding her by the arm as though he were a sheriff, telling her all about the firing pin on the Springfield rifle — what a good long, strong, classy, nifty, pip of a firing pin it was. And once, when his stream of small-arms enthusiasm slackened for a moment, he promised that he'd take her to Rappaciutti's after the show and buy her a banana split.

Canyon Love was no masterpiece, but at least it brought

tears, and when you get tears, you get a very good thing. Streaming from his blue eyes, Emmett's tears were a delicious solvent to delivery-wagon cares and the pangs of underprized love. In the warm lassitude of the darkened theater his hand closed wistfully over Mona's fingers. She did not object, and Emmett sat choking with weepy bliss until the organist, with a good-night fillip, crashed into *The Sheik of Araby*. The house lights flashed shamelessly on, and the dream collapsed.

"Geeze," said Emmett (whose single vice was that one interjection of familiarity with the name of the Second Person of the Trinity), "that was a good show. Always get a good show at the Alhambra. Better'n the Plaza, but the ventilation's not so good. They got the best organ, though. Some organ. I hear it cost ten thousand bucks. . . ." He lingered in his seat, for although the lights had forced him to drop Mona's hand, he was still glowing with the treacly warmth of *Canyon Love*. The theater was emptying rapidly, and Mona prodded her escort.

"Let's get going, or we'll be locked in for the night."

"That wouldn't be such tough luck, would it?" This was the most suggestive thing that Emmett had ever said, and because Mona made no answer, he considered himself rebuked for his "freshness." He was about to apologize, when he remembered that he still had the big gesture of the evening ahead of him . . . the banana split. He waxed resilient, big.

"Well, let's gumshoe over to Rappaciutti's and line up for the banana split I been promising you. . . ."

Again Mona failed to blow back the feather of repartee; again Emmett was disconcerted. She could put him out of gear so easily, with or without a word. Everything would be rolling along beautifully, then, with no preliminary flutter, the illusion of companionship would crackle and fade. And always Emmett would suffer in puzzlement before making the fatal mistake of asking:

"What's the matter with you, anyway, Mona?"

Mona couldn't have told him, because she didn't precisely know. She only knew that the organ music and picture had twisted her up into a taut E string yearning for excitement and novelty. She wanted to be taken somewhere (not to Rappaciutti's) in a rolling limousine; she wanted to sink back into upholstery, or perhaps into the arms of — well, certainly not Emmett Burke — and be helped out at a café where a canopy ran from the curb to the front door. She wanted to be led through a roomful of brilliant and beautiful evening creatures to the edge of the wide dancing-floor by a Benny Rampell whom she could never stop loving, no matter how hard she tried.

Actually she said: "You give me the heebie jeebies, asking all the time 'What's the matter?' Nothing's the matter. Everything's the mat — Oh, let's get over to Rappaciutti's. . . ."

"Yes, we better go there. They got better banana splits than the Palace, too. That's what you wanted, wasn't it . . . a banana split?"

Rappaciutti's was a combined fruit store and ice-cream parlor, with little half booths in the rear. Mount Vesuvius erupted blotchily on your left, and gondolas plied traditionally on your right. As they entered, a player piano with a violin attachment whirled wirily through *Dardanella*. The booths were filled, so they took a table beside the mechanical violin. Privacy — try and get it, thought Mona. But suppose you did get it, what then? Meanwhile Emmett, luxuriating in the role of free spender, was sounding off to the waiter.

"Bring us two of the biggest banana splits in the place. Vanilla and ice cream for me, with lots of goo. What kind'll you have, Monny?"

"The same, without the goo."

Dreading the silence of Mona's face, Emmett gazed about the room, spotting acquaintances at every table. A red-haired blade in the furthest booth shouted, "How'd you like that last clinch?" and Emmett shot back, "Eva, burn my shoes!" A general laugh confirmed Emmett's private opinion that he could be a riot if he set his mind to it. Only Mona's rigid mouth troubled him. When the sticky sundaes were brought, he ate his hurriedly, scraped the dish, and said with openhanded largeness:

"Guess I'll try another. How 'bout you, Mona?"

"No more for me. Let's get out of here."

The walk home was not a success. Emmett tried hard, but the thing eluded him. Even a skillful, humorous articulate man would have found Mona difficult, and Emmett Burke was none

of these. Down the tree-shaded vista of Maple Street he spoke
of the new pool table the K. of C.'s had just installed. Passing
lilacs in bloom, he described a tenth-inning rally that the Red
Sox had made last Saturday in Cleveland. The blue arc light
at the corner of Highland Avenue blinked unpityingly down
on a stocky young man trying to explain the bolt action of a
Springfield rifle to a slender young woman who was thinking
of someone else.

Crunching up the gravelly walk to the Fermoyle back door,
Emmett furtively popped a Sen-Sen into his mouth, in preparation for the good-night kiss. Mona dreaded the stiff embrace, and yet she wanted to be kissed. Not by Emmett or anyone else in Medford, but by a splendid lover on a wide silk bed
— a lover who would not take breathlets or talk eternally about
firing pins and K. of C. politics. When he spoke, his conversation would come nearer to herself, the lovely center of romantic imaginings. It would flutter about her on soft wings, strok-
ingly, caressingly, as fantasy lovers should. He would be a
master of illusion, himself an illusion, lost now, relinquished
forever by her promise to Stephen.

In the shadow of the back porch, Emmett nerved himself
for the climax of the evening. Expectant, long patient, he
was about to claim his goodnight kiss. As Mona reached down
for the key under the door-mat, his lavender-scented breath
caught her full on the mouth. She took it passively. A fellow
deserved something for the money he'd spent and the good
time he'd been trying to give you. She heard Celia wheezing
asthmatically at the window above them. Love's young dream?
Scarcely. With a strained good night Mona opened the back
door and let herself into the kitchen.

She heard Emmett shuffling down the gravel walk in
dejected perplexity.

It isn't his fault . . . altogether, she thought as she was
climbing the back stairs. But it's no use. I can't stand it any
longer. I can't marry him.

She flung her hat down and sat on the edge of her narrow
bed. She had tried so hard to follow Stephen's advice! "Pick
out a fine young Catholic and go steady with him," Stephen
had counseled. For more than a year Mona had "gone steady"
with Emmett Burke, and now she knew that she hated

Emmett and everything else in Medford. Job, Church, family,
life in general. "I've got to get away from here," she said to
the small oval face in her mirror.

She rummaged in the top drawer of her bureau for a piece
of paper and a pencil stub. Words did not come easily to
Mona Fermoyle. She had so few of them. On the piece of
paper she scrawled two lines: "Dear Mother and Father: I'm
going away. Please don't try to follow me. Mona."

She packed her bag, waited till the house was asleep, then
stole down the stairs, and took the last trolley into Boston.

MONA'S DISAPPEARANCE was a mortal blow to Din and Celia.
At first they put hopeful ads in the papers: "Mona, come
home. We are all grieving." At the end of three months Din
took upon himself the shame of reporting her to the police as
missing. Novenas were made for her return, but neither the
police nor the loving prayers brought her back. Celia waited
for the letter that never came; at every footstep in the front
hall she would start up from her chair or turn expectantly
from her tasks. In the evening Din's voice and movements,
subdued by grief, ended in silent staring at his aftersupper
Globe. Even Bernie's warblings took on a soft melancholy;
night after night he rendered pianissimo the theme song of the
household:

> *The chairs in the parlor all miss you,*
> *The folks ask me why you don't call,*
> *The whole house is blue,*
> *We miss you, only you,*
> *But I miss you mo-st of all.*

"For God's sake, Bernie, play something more cheerful.
What is this, a morgue?" That would be Florrie, barging and
nagging more shrewishly than ever. Secretly, she blamed herself for driving Mona from the house, but because open
acknowledgment of guilt was impossible, Florrie scourged
everyone else, especially Al McManus, with the whip of her
own remorse.

Though she and Al slept in the same bed, Florrie had not
spoken to her husband for three months. In a flight of financial
wizardry, Al had withdrawn eight hundred dollars from their

joint savings account and given it to Ponzi for a quick profit.
A week later, Ponzi's paranoid mansion of finance crashed.
But the more dreadful crash came when Florrie landed both
physically and verbally on her husband. Locking him in their
bedroom, she belabored his cowering body with her feet and
fingernails, then let her tongue cut to ribbons all that was left
of his manhood. All night long she raged; with morning came
a cold, contemptuous silence that she had not broken since.

As a filial chore Stephen went home on his nights off, but
all joy had been squeezed from the visits. His only escape from
the gloomy downstairs tensions was in the quiet refuge of
Ellen's room. Here, as if in a sanctuary, Ellen had fortified
herself against the assault of illness and the still more harrowing knowledge of family unhappiness. Slowly her strength was
coming back; for an hour or two every day she could sit by her
window overlooking the fences and rhubarb patches in the
back yards of Woodlawn Avenue. But her vision was not outward; prayer and contemplation made her life a sequence of
ecstatic stillnesses. In her conversations with Stephen she was
cheerful, even optimistic, as tubercular patients often are. She
would make brave small plans for the future: visits to neighboring churches when she grew a bit stronger, some launder-
ing of sacristy linens perhaps. No task was too humble if
offered in His name.

Ellen loved poetry and would sometimes read to her priest-
brother from the small collection of volumes beside her bed.
Donne, Crashaw, and Francis Thompson were her favorites; a
flawless critical taste prevented her from falling into the sentimental errors of "devotional" verse. One evening she stretched
her hand across the coverlet and picked up a volume of
George Herbert.

"Do you know Herbert's *The Elixir?*" she asked Stephen.

"I think I do. But read it to me."

Ellen read the exquisitely simple poem until she came to
these stanzas:

> *All may of Thee partake;*
> *Nothing can be so mean*
> *Which with this tincture, "for Thy sake,"*
> *Will not grow bright and clean.*

> *A servant with this clause*
> *Makes drudgerie divine;*
> *Who sweeps a room as for Thy laws*
> *Makes that and th' action fine.*

Ellen laid the book down; her eyes, lifted to Stephen's, were like leaf-brown pools catching the reflection of cloudless skies. "Nothing can be truer than that," she said.

"Nothing is," added Stephen.

Leaving Ellen that night, he could not help comparing her with Lalage Menton. Both were teeming with dedicated love, but where Lalage's physical strength enabled her to pour her love fearlessly over humanity, Ellen's frailty was like a burning glass that focused the rays of divine energy with an intense inwardness. If Lalage reminded him of a glowing monstrance, Ellen was an alabaster vase lighted by an unextinguishable flame.

At the memento of the Mass next morning, Stephen prayed that Ellen's love might sometime pierce the walls of her room and bring its special illumination to the world of common men.

GEORGE FERMOYLE'S RETURN from war somewhat lightened the gloom at 47 Woodlawn Avenue. He came out a good-looking Captain with a medal for valor at Chateau-Thierry, a shrapnel wound under his right collarbone, and some seventeen hundred dollars saved from his military pay. George's viewpoint on the postwar world was moderately cynical, as he remarked to Stephen: "The brotherhood of man, like the fatherhood of God, is a notion too radical for our age." Without wasting any time worrying about the future of the world, George took up his law courses again. No more drudgery on the Fish Pier; his savings would easily see him through law school. He spent a couple of hundred dollars fixing up the attic bedroom, bought himself a good armchair, and bent over the lawbooks that were meat and drink to his famished legal mind.

Some of the best talks Stephen ever had were in George's attic study. Other than law, politics were George's main interest. To Wilson's international idealism George added social and economic ideas quite in advance of the time. A wave of strikes was spreading across the country, and George interpreted them as the opening action in a long struggle between capital and labor.

"Our national wealth must be more evenly distributed, Stuffy, with the workers getting an ever-increasing share in the form of higher wages. Imagine it! Steelworkers in Pittsburgh are getting only twenty dollars for a seventy-hour week. I don't want to sound like a Socialist, but doesn't it seem that American potentialities are being selfishly exploited for the benefit of a few rich men?"

"You sound like Leo XIII's social encyclicals," said Stephen. "If you want to find chapter and verse for everything you've just said, read Leo's *Rerum novarum,* written in 1891."

"Find me a copy in English," said George. "The trouble with you churchly oysters is that your pearls are always in polished Latin."

Then George would puff at a bos'n pipe, and urge his priest-brother to implement with action the social theories of the Church. The argument might go on till midnight, but always across the fascinating themes of law, religion, and social reconstruction fell shadows of the grief hovering over the Fermoyle household. Invariably the sessions ended with talk of Mona.

"Are you satisfied that we're doing all we can to find her?" asked Stephen one night.

"I don't quite know, Stuffy," George tamped a fresh load of Burley into his pipe. "Sometimes I think we ought to take a more positive line of action. The police aren't really interested in these missing-persons cases. Perhaps we should go after Mona with private detectives. They're a rum-dum lot, but sometimes they get results."

"That would run into money, wouldn't it?"

"A minimum of twenty dollars a day, plus expenses. . . ."

Stephen shook his head. "No one in this family could afford that kind of thing."

George fingered the buckram cover of Wharton's *Bills and Notes.* "I could, Stuffy. You see, I saved most of my pay for three years. I've still got almost fifteen hundred dollars in cash."

"But that money must see you through law school."

"I could go back to my old job on the Fish Pier. And I'd do it in a minute, Stuff, if it would put the skip in Celia's step and the roar in Din's voice again."

All for love, thought Stephen. "We couldn't ask you to spend your money that way, George. It might be as useless as throwing it out the window."

"I've got a hunch it wouldn't be, Stuffy. I'll look into it anyway."

At noon the next day, George Fermoyle was engaging the confidential ear of Lloyd C. Brumbaugh, proprietor of the Acme Detective Agency. The shell of Mr. Brumbaugh's ear was as bloodless and hard as any clam dug in the flats of his native Cape Cod, but he was an experienced operator and knew exactly what questions to ask. Weight, height, color of hair, eyes, complexion, and the etceteras of Mona's anatomy; her men friends, favorite forms of recreation, out-of-town acquaintances — the whole story was jotted down on Mr. Brumbaugh's pad.

"Acme investigators will begin looking for your sister at once, Mr. Fermoyle. Naturally, I can guarantee nothing — but we have our methods. The fee will be six hundred a month, payable in advance."

From his wallet George drew six one-hundred-dollar bills, handed them to Mr. Brumbaugh. A month passed. No trace of Mona. George paid out another six hundred. He was back at his old job on the Fish Pier now, working all day, attending law classes at night. Toward the end of the second month he got a letter from the Acme Detective Agency, and rang Stephen at once.

"News, Stuffy! Brumbaugh thinks he's located her."

"Where?"

"In Wilkes-Barre. Meet me in front of the B. U. Law School at ten tonight. I'll give you the details."

Shortly after ten P.M. the brothers Fermoyle were sitting in a one-arm lunchroom on Boylston Street. Stephen read the typewritten report of the Acme Agency:

Our operative has located a young woman who fits the description of Mona Fermoyle in all but one detail. Age twenty-one or thereabouts; height 5 ft. 6 in., weight approx. 118 pounds, dark blue eyes, fair complexion. The single point of difference is *color of hair*. This woman has blond hair, which could easily be caused by bleaching.

Stephen remembered Mona's desire for golden hair, wistfully expressed on the day of his return from Rome; Brumbaugh was probably right. Stephen raced on:

The person located by us is traveling under name of Margo LaVarre, and is accompanied by a Spanish-type male, early thirties, known as Ramón Gongaro. Sometimes claims to be a medical doctor, but earns living as a professional dancer. Billed as Gongaro and LaVarre, this man and your sister gave exhibitions of ballroom dancing in small towns on the dime-a-dance circuit. Have worked recently in Newport News, Wilmington, Wheeling, Scranton, and Altoona. Appeared two nights last week in Wilkes-Barre. Present whereabouts uncertain, but will probably show up in New Jersey or New York.

Please advise us as to course of action, and kindly remit check for $600 for development of further information.

Sincerely yours,

L. C. BRUMBAUGH

P.S. If desired, charges might be brought against Gongaro for violation of Mann Act.

The sheer ugliness of the business! Stephen looked across the table at George sipping his coffee. There was only one thing to be said, and George said it.

"Just when we locate her, the money runs out." He slid his bankbook across the table. "There's only two hundred dollars left, Steve. Do you suppose Florrie would pitch in with four hundred more?"

Stephen stirred his coffee despondently. "I'd hate to ask her, George. There was always a bickering between Florrie and Mona. And after that Ponzi episode I don't think Florrie's in the mood to hand out any cash."

"She couldn't do any worse than refuse."

"I wouldn't want to put Florrie or anyone else in that position."

George understood the charity of Stephen's attitude. "Corny Deegan might help us," he suggested.

"No doubt he would. He'd tear off a dozen blank checks and say, 'Come back for more if you need it.' But this is a family affair, George. We can't ask Corny to shoulder the private troubles of the Fermoyles."

"What'll we do? We can't risk losing track of her now."

Calculations long as a column of ledger figures were going on in Stephen's mind. "If we only dared wait."

"Wait for what?"

Stephen's finger was at the list of towns in the typewritten report. "Look, George, it's as clear as a plotted graph. Mona's heading north. Virginia, Delaware, Pennsylvania, New Jersey. Brumbaugh says she'll probably turn up next in New York." Stephen's excitement mounted. "It's the homing instinct. I bet she'll be back in Boston within a month."

"We can't hang around dance halls every night waiting for her to show up."

"*We* can't," said Stephen, "but Bernie can. From now on, Bernie's going to be Operator Fifty-nine, attached to the dance-hall district. And with the help of a few well-directed prayers I'll be surprised if we don't catch up with Gongaro and LaVarre within the next few weeks."

STEPHEN'S PREDICTION came out with adding-machine precision. He was returning one night to the Cathedral rectory when the curate on duty said, "Your brother's waiting for you in the reception hall." There was Bernie, packed sausage-tight in a pinchback green suit, wearing an Ascot tie, narrow high-cuffed trousers, and suède-top shoes. The rig was a vaudevillian's dream, but Bernie's double chin was sunk to his Ascot.

"I've just seen Mona," he announced.

"*The homing bird!* Where?"

"At the Metro Dance Pavilion, a dime-a-dance place on Tremont Street."

"How does she look? Did she speak to you?"

Tears slid down Bernie's chubby cheeks. "She looked all right. But she wouldn't speak to me."

"Was she alone?"

"No, a guy was with her."

"What kind of a guy?"

"One of them patent-leather Spanish dancers. He shoved me away."

Mona was back in Boston, Gongaro was with her. "You say they're at the Metro Dance Pavilion?" asked Stephen. "Let's get right down there."

Twenty minutes later, Stephen was following his brother into the butt-strewn lobby of the Metro Dance Pavilion, a second-floor layout on lower Tremont Street. Knots of young men, many with padded shoulders and pomaded hair, were taking a quick drag of cigarettes between dances. Stephen had borrowed a flashy handkerchief from Bernie and tied it Ascot-fashion around his Roman collar. They climbed the stairs. Suppose Mona weren't there! Or suppose she were! Halfway up the stairs Bernie stopped at a little booth. "Ten tickets please," he said and handed the box-office man a dollar.

The dance floor was fenced off by a waist-high railing, broken by a turnstile. Hostesses lolled on settees waiting for customers, while some two hundred couples were fox-trotting to the strains of *Margie,* brassily rendered by Dinger Doane and his Jazz-bo Babies. A dim orange light made it difficult to see a face clearly.

Stephen searched the floor for a glimpse of Mona. "Do you see her?" he whispered to Bernie.

"Here she comes now, with that guy in the tan suit."

Stephen saw the couple. The man had an arrogant talent for dancing. He was wearing a cocoa-colored jacket and purple shirt; high-heeled shoes added to his height. In agony Stephen watched Mona dance past, her head thrown back, her delicate body floating petallike in her partner's arms. She was undeniably lovely; her blondined hair, which at first shocked Stephen, added a theatrical touch to her beauty. She was wearing a pink ball gown glittering with sequins and silver lace; her costume and dyed hair expressed with painful emphasis Mona's notion of herself as a queen among taxi dancers.

A deadly emotion gripped Stephen. "Let's walk out there and take her away from him," he said to Bernie.

"We can't do that, Steve. Bouncers are all over the place. They'd throw us downstairs."

The music stopped, the lights went up, and the dancers streamed through exit gates. The floor was empty now save for a man who held up a hand for attention. Unable to get silence, he signaled the drummer, who tore off a mama-papa flam ending in a *boom-boom*. The master of ceremonies began talking with the false elegance of a prize-fight announcer.

"La-deez an' gennelmen! Tonight with your kind permission we offer for your ennertainment a re-fined exhibition of sussiety dancing in the final innerstate a-liminations for a silver loving cup. Your applause will decide the winnah . . . thank you one and all." His finger shot a directive at the band leader. "Perfessor Doane will take it from here."

The band blared into *Dardanella,* and two couples glided toward the center of the floor. Stephen had no consciousness of the other dance team; he saw only Mona and Gongaro. He knew little about dancing, but recognized the professional touch that Mona and her partner gave to the showy steps. As the exhibition progressed, partisan applause grew louder. The rivalry between the couples was high; each tried to surpass the other with fancy variations. Mona and Gongaro did a hesitation dip to handclapping and shouts of "Attaboy, Ramón." The other couple countered with a reverse pinwheel, and took their meed of applause. Then Gongaro let Mona spin free for a solo whirl and caught her in mid-flight with heel-clicking precision. What hurt Stephen most was the Spaniard's command over Mona's person. Gongaro's preening self-esteem said: "Alone, this girl is nothing. But with me — watch now."

The music stopped, and the two couples stood in the center of the floor while the master of ceremonies approached them, loving cup in his hands. A barrage of applause rattled across the hall as he held the cup over Mona and Gongaro. An equal barrage was let loose when the trophy rested over the heads of the other couple. Again and again, the test was made, till at last, with the cup over Mona's head, the roof went sailing away.

Gongaro accepted the prize and strutted ahead of Mona toward a side door.

"Come on, Bernie," said Stephen.

They circled the edge of the dance floor and pushed open the door through which Mona and Gongaro had disappeared. In a bare greenroom the dancers were being paid off by the master of ceremonies. He was handing Gongaro twenty-five dollars when he saw Stephen and Bernie.

"What you guys want?" he challenged.

"We want to speak to our sister," said Stephen.

Mona looked up in terror, saw Stephen, and tried to run from the room. In three quick steps he had her by the wrist. "Monny darling . . . please. . . ."

Gongaro stepped forward. "What's the big idea?"

"The big idea," said Stephen, "is that we haven't seen our sister for quite a while, and we want to talk with her."

The dancing man shrugged a padded shoulder: "From where I stand, she don't look like she wants to talk to you."

It was true. Mona's eyelashes, beaded with mascara, were lowered. Her visor of defiance was down. "Take me out of here, Ramón. These men are bothering me."

Gongaro had no intention of getting his neck broken. "I'll get The Bite." He darted out and returned with a stocky musclebound character — an ex-wrestler, to judge by his necklessness and gorilla-length arms.

"Who's causin' the trouble here?" he demanded.

"Him." Gongaro pointed to Stephen. "He won't let go of my partner."

"Oh, yes he will," said The Bite. "Leggo of the lady's arm, mister." He shot out a heavy paw, grabbed Stephen by what seemed to be an Ascot tie (a favorite hold with bouncers), and jerked. The silk handkerchief came off, revealing the Roman collar underneath.

"Geeze, he's a priest." Having broken the taboo against striking a clergyman, The Bite's poor brain collapsed in apology. "I didden' mean nothin', Father. Honest, I didden'."

"Don't worry about it," said Stephen. "Everything's going to be fine if you'll leave me alone with my sister here for a little talk."

"Sure, sure, Father. Breeze, everybody." The Bite pointed at Bernie. "Who's he?"

"My brother." Stephen spoke to Bernie. "Get George over

here on the double." Glad to avoid the scene about to take place, Bernie vanished.

Alone with Mona in the bare room, Stephen loosened his grip. "Forgive me, Monny; I had to hold onto you. Tell me, darling, where've you been?"

Silence, stubborn and willful, was Mona's answer.

"Please, darling." Stephen tried to put his arms around his sister, but she flung his hands down, the flares of her nostrils dilating.

"Don't try being a big brother any more. It worked last time. But it won't ever work again. Ever, ever, do you hear?"

"I hear you, Mona."

"Oh, you hear, all right. But you don't *understand*. How could you?" Contempt and anger quivered in her throat. "*You* don't know what love is."

The hopelessness of convincing Mona that he knew the power of love overcame Stephen.

"You mustn't say that, Mona," he pleaded.

"I'll say anything I damn please. I'm through with you, and all the mealymouthed things you stand for. Let me go to hell in my own way, will you?"

"But this isn't your way, Mona. I watched you dance to-night. I saw how happy you were, and what a gift you have. That gift shouldn't be wasted on cheap exhibitions. Dancing is one of the arts, and you could make a career of it."

"I don't want a career."

"What do you want, Mona?"

"I just want Benny Rampell," she said obstinately.

"Come home with me tonight," bargained Steve. "I'll help you get him."

"No one can help me get him now. It's too late." Grief at irrecoverable loss shook her. "He married someone else."

Thundering against the walls of the bare greenroom, mourning above the cheap rhythms of Dinger Doane's music, Stephen heard the echo of Job's mightiest voice. "*No man can deliver his brother unto God.*" The folly of interfering with other people's lives, the awful presumption of touching with one's finger the valve of another human heart brought Stephen to his knees beside his sister. What could he say to undo the wrong he had done her? Small comfort now to offer Mona the solace of religion or to explain that he had acted in accordance with the dictates of his Church. He spoke humbly, his forehead against her shoulder.

"No one can unmake the past, Monny, or strike out human errors of judgment. It was a mistake on my part, a terrible mistake that will leave marks of grief on both of us for the rest of our lives." His lips touched her cheek. "Next to your suffering — and Benny's perhaps — mine will be greatest." He was pleading now. "Celia's courage is failing; Din mourns for you. Can you keep on hurting them, Monny?"

Ferments of filial love and self-destruction worked in Mona's heart. Stephen let them rise in silence, then made the absolute minimum request.

"Come home tonight just for a visit, Monny. You won't have to stay. We'll say you've got a grand job in New York."

The conflicting ferments in Mona's soul almost neutralized each other. Then the urge to self-destruction triumphed. "You might as well get off your knees," she said. "I'm not going home with you. I was a fool to come back to Boston. This time I'm going away and won't ever be back."

She walked to the door of the greenroom and opened it. Outside, Ramón Gongaro was waiting.

"Come, pigeon," he said masterfully. "We will dance."

CHAPTER 4

PAUL IRETON'S NICKEL was soon spent.

He swung off the trolley at the Medford carbarns and from military habit surveyed the terrain. He knew he was standing midway between two of the largest parishes in the Diocese — St. Vincent's to the west and the Immaculate Conception about a mile to the east. Somewhere between the two, and within the dotted lines drawn by the Cardinal's own hand, Paul Ireton must organize a parish of his own. By a series of diplomatic and financial maneuvers he must wean some two thousand Roman Catholics away from deep loyalties to their old pastors; he must persuade them to attend services in temporary quarters and, lastly, he must gently extract from them funds to build a new church. Because any man in his right mind would be slightly apprehensive about such operations, Father Ireton spent a bad sixty seconds wondering where and how to begin.

The month was June; a summer sun poured straight down on Father Ireton standing amid the network of car tracks, and dabbing with his handkerchief a drop of sweat in the cleft of his blue-black chin. The light breakfast he had eaten five hours ago was quitting on him. As a minor ascetic gesture, Paul had intended to eat no lunch; but a swallow of liquid, he decided, would vastly benefit the parched membranes of his throat. Across the street he saw a row of stores; a barbershop, its red and blue pole symbolizing arterial and venous blood; an apothecary with red and blue vases symbolizing the same thing; a chain-store grocery, a bakery, and a fruit stand shaded by a wide-striped canvas awning. The shrill whine of a peanut roaster came pleasantly to Father Ireton's ear. He crossed the car tracks to the fruit stand, stood in the grateful shade of the awning, and delivered up all his senses to the wares spread before him.

Oranges were piled in pyramids, bananas hung ripely; figs, tamarinds, dates and lemons tempted his taste buds, and a jar of pickle limes started the saliva in his dry throat. He was taking a bag of peanuts from the copper roaster when he heard a clinking of ice against glass in the cool interior of the fruit shop.

The proprietor, in a dirty Panama hat, was ladling lemonade into a green-glass pitcher held by a customer wearing the uniform of the Boston Streetcar Company. The ladler was Nick Papagyros, and the pitcher holder was Bartholomew ("Batty") Glynn, chief dispatcher of trolleys and theologian at large to the Medford carbarns.

"Six for the price of five, Nick?" Batty was asking.

Nick laughed at the whimsy of the thing. Old joke from old customer. Seeing the priest, Batty Glynn raised his hat with easy respect. "Five for the price of six would be cheap for Nick's lemonade, Father. It's the best tipple this side of Raingpouria."

"I'll have a glass," said Paul.

Mr. Papagyros poured a tall one for his new customer. Paul lifted the sweet citrus juice toastwise to the dispatcher, who responded with a gigantic tug at his green-glass flagon. Cool lotion of ice in his mouth, Paul nodded appreciatively. So much nice gulping pleased Mr. Papagyros. A modest man, he wished to assign credit where credit was really due. He picked up a lemon, bit into it and smacked his lips appreciatively.

Paul Ireton was not an easy mixer, but after such pleasures some talk was bound to follow. He handed Mr. Papagyros a quarter and asked:

"Do you happen to know of any vacant stores around here?"

Hairy fist in change bag, Nick shook his Panama doubtfully. "No stores empty. Business too good for vacancies," he explained.

"A hall then?"

"How big a hall would you be looking for, Father?" asked Batty Glynn.

"Oh, something big enough to accommodate three or four hundred people at Sunday Mass."

"Sunday, *what?*"

"Mass," said Paul quietly. "I'm starting a new parish here."

Batty Glynn's eyes popped like grapes. This was the weirdest heresy since the days of the Albigensians. Strict orthodoxy prompted his next question. "Does Pat Barley know about it?"

"Yes. He'll announce it from the altar next Sunday."

While Batty Glynn marveled into his flagon, Mr. Papagyros came up with a suggestion: "What's that place — Mattakeesis — how you say it? — Mattakeesis Hall?"

"No, no," said Batty decisively. " 'Twouldn't do."

"Why not?" asked Paul.

Ever the purist, Batty set forth his objection. "A colored congregation used to meet there, Father. The police had to clean them out."

Paul gave proper weight to Batty's piece of information. "I'd like to see it anyway. Would you mind telling me how to get there?"

"Your request," said Batty solemnly, "has the force of an edict, Father." With his toe the dispatcher-theologian started to draw a diagram in the sawdust on Nick's floor. Then he had a better idea. He consulted the butter-gold watch that had never lost more than two seconds a week for twenty years. "I'm on my lunch hour, Father. I'll take you there myself."

My first convert, thought Paul. If this pompous ox could be led, others would follow.

A short walk brought them to a three-story building, bearing the legend MATTAKEESIT 1886 on the crest of its lugubrious brick façade. Long ago, Mattakeesit Hall had been the bon-ton thing in Medford — the smart rendezvous for social affairs, top-cut weddings and dances. Until 1910 it had served the K. of C. as their meeting place, but when they moved to their new home, Mattakeesit Hall had been cut up into offices for chiropodists, dollar-a-filling dentists, fortunetellers, and similar gentry. Holy Rollers had held services on the top floor until their noisy rituals attracted police attention. And it was this top floor — dusty, littered, and long unused — that Sol Seidelbander, the renting agent, now showed to Father Ireton.

A glance told Paul that it would do. Having said Mass in trenches, tents, garages, and at the tailboard of commissary trucks, he felt no queasiness about celebrating it in Mattakeesit Hall. The dirty floor and grimy windows could be cleaned; the taint of Holy Rollerism (if any) could be removed by blessing. After all, it was the Mass that mattered. Where Batty Glynn's eyes saw only dirt and debris, Father Ireton beheld a well-swept upper room and the faces of his people.

"What rent are you asking, Mr. Seidelbander?"

"With heat in winter, twenty-five dollars a month."

Paul gave Mr. Seidelbander the full treatment of his severe gray eyes. "I'll take a year's lease . . . on one condition."

Sol Seidelbander, who hadn't had a penny from the hall in five years, said he'd listen to any reasonable proposition.

"The proposition is this," said Father Ireton. "Instead of paying the first month's rent in advance, I'll give you my note for thirty days."

The renting agent knew a customer when he saw one. "Why bother about notes, Father? The word of a Catholic priest is good enough for me."

BATTY GLYNN put the news on the grapevine. Every trolley that left the carbarn carried headlines, full reportage, and editorial comment supplied by Eyewitness Glynn. He told his story a dozen times that afternoon, larding it imaginatively until his hearers might have thought that Batty Glynn himself was the Cardinal's right-hand bower. His best and final version was reserved for the ear of Motorman Dennis Fermoyle as the latter sat down for a pipe and chat after stabling his sixteen-wheeler for the night.

"Courteous and reserved he was," said Batty, "as he lifted his glass of lemonade to me, and I drank back at him, without the faintest notion of who he was or what he was doing in Nick's shop, except that I could see that he had ecclesiastical business uppermost in his mind. Well, Din, when the nature of that business came out you could have knocked me over with the fumes from your pipe. 'I'm looking for a place to say Mass,' he said. 'Say *what?*' I asked. 'Mass,' he said, 'and would you be knowing of any vacant stores or halls in the vicinity?' Then before I knew it I was leading him down to Mattakeesit Hall, telling him at every step what a bad name it had. But when he saw it — I was standing right behind his shoulder — a kind of determination stiffened him, and he said to Seidelbander, 'I'll take it.' " Batty paused in his circumstantial narrative: "Then came the queerest part of all. He didn't have the first month's rent in his pocket, so he had to throw himself on Seidelbander's mercy for thirty days' indulgence, as you might say. Can you tell me now why a rich diocese obliges a new pastor to start off penniless?" The question being rhetorical, Batty continued without waiting for an answer. "Anyhow, that's the way it happened, Din. Beginning next Sunday we'll all be hearing Mass in a former den of Holy Rollerism. Off with the old, on with the new. Barley must be bitter about it."

Dennis Fermoyle brought the news home to Celia, who straightway carried it upstairs to Ellen.

"The Cardinal has split Monsignor Barley's parish at last," said Celia. "There's a new priest named Father Ireton down at Mattakeesit, fixing up a temporary church."

A private excitement took possession of Ellen when she heard the news. Fearful currents stirred within her; prayer did not quiet them. Like a distracted girl who knows that she is being challenged by womanhood, Ellen paced her room in agitated colloquy with herself.

"Have I the strength to undertake this long-awaited labor? Physical strength, yes; I am well enough to perform light tasks. It is courage of soul that I lack. Courage to leave this sheltered room, and pick up the strands of life that I laid down — where? — why? — how long ago?"

What am I afraid of?

Sleepless that night, Ellen could not answer these questions. When morning came, she arose and went to her window. Over fences and clotheslines, over the domestic gear and straggly vegetable gardens, a new day was beginning. Another day in His eternal cycle — a day that would be filled, like all His days, with a meaning above and beyond the commonplace appearance of things. Unbidden came the lines:

> *Teach me, my God and King,*
> *In all things Thee to see*
> *And what I do in any thing*
> *To do it as for Thee.*

"I will go forth this day and accept whatever task He assigns me," said Ellen.

After breakfast, while Celia was busy in the kitchen, Ellen stole out of the front door and walked rapidly down Woodlawn Avenue. She passed the carbarns and after a few moments came to Mattakeesit Hall. Some remnant of terror counseled, "Turn back," but a deeper instruction said, "This is the time and place." She climbed the dark stairway, opened the door of the upper room, and saw a man in a white collarless shirt swinging an awkward broom at the dirty floor.

> *Who sweeps a room as for Thy laws*
> *Makes that and th' action fine.*

Billows of dust whirled out the open windows; the sweeper sneezed, blew his nose in a handkerchief. Ever conscious of her lungs, Ellen wanted to say, "You should sprinkle first. No one dry-sweeps any more." Actually she said, "I'm Ellen Fermoyle, one of your new parishioners."

"Ellen Fermoyle? Not Steve's sister?"

She nodded timidly. "And you're Father Ireton. Stephen has told me a lot about you. He says you're the best priest he knows."

"I'll go Steve one better. He's the best priest there is."

In the littered hall they stood wordlessly recognizing each other. Paul Ireton saw the invisible nimbus over Ellen's head. And in the ascetic jut of Paul Ireton's chin Ellen saw the man become priest. The covenant between them was instant, unbodied, and binding.

"When do you plan to say your first Mass here?"

"I wanted it to be next Sunday," Paul waved a dubious broom at the floor. "But that'll take a miracle."

"Four days is time enough for a *small* miracle." Ellen's brown eyes surveyed the black hall, ticked off the necessities. "You'll need some kind of temporary altar, with linens, of course. I'll manage that if you'll let me."

"*Let* you? My dear girl . . ."

"How about vestments?"

"I've been promised the loan of some from Monsignor Barley — of all people. The things I haven't got, and can't seem to borrow, are a chalice and a Mass book. I guess some ecclesiastical supply house will have to extend me credit. If Seidelbander can do it, others can, too."

"Then all we'd need right now is a pail of water, a mop, and some soap powder." A proprietary glow flushed Ellen's cheek. "We'll make it shine, Father."

Almost, they did make it shine. Paul Ireton scrubbed the floor while Ellen washed the windows. Sometimes they forgot each other's presence, then remembering, they would look up, smile at each other, and fall to work again. All day they scrubbed and scoured; Ellen went home exhausted and fell asleep on a short prayer.

Next day she persuaded Celia to hand over a damask tablecloth won ten years ago at a whist party and still lying unused in the bottom of the linen closet. Ellen cut the prized fabric in two pieces, and hemmed them on the sewing machine. Laundered, they made acceptable altar cloths. The altar itself was improvised from a dry-goods packing case that Ellen found in the Fermoyle cellar. Bernie lugged it on his back all the way to the hall, then gave it two coats of flat white paint. Candlesticks, a pair of cut-glass cruets for wine and water, and three linen napkins were contributed by other parishioners. By Saturday noon Paul had completed his credit arrangement and appeared with a gold-plated chalice and a new Mass book.

Together they dressed the altar. "It's beautiful," breathed Ellen. "Nothing was ever so beautiful. The people will love it."

At ten o'clock on Sunday morning two hundred people climbed three flights of stairs to attend Father Ireton's first Mass in Medford. They sat on chairs loaned by Tim Noonan, the undertaker, and saw their new pastor, an austere, gray-eyed priest in his early forties, emerge from behind a screen in borrowed vestments. They felt the loving severity of his manner, and when they heard his first announcement from the foot of the improvised altar, they knew he meant business.

"In this upper room," said Father Ireton, "we begin a shared adventure in the new parish of St. Stephen's. The Cardinal has laid upon us — upon you as well as me — the responsibility and privilege of starting a new parish. To me it means the opportunity that every priest longs for. To you it means the severance, painful perhaps, of old loyalties and the shouldering of fresh burdens. But I can assure you that those burdens will be divided between us. I shall hold my steward-ship strictly accountable to you in all things. In return, I shall expect your help and confidence. Though our financial needs are pressing, we must not permit ourselves to be overborne by them, or forget the purpose of our work here. That work is primarily of the spirit, and as long as I am rector of St. Stephen's, it shall remain so. I shall now read the Gospel for the day . . ."

LAWRENCE GLENNON's faculty for surprising people who thought they knew him was a character trait that gave the Cardinal some of his best effects. As Chancellor Mike Speed put it to Stephen (in a figure borrowed from baseball), "Just when you're saying to yourself, 'Well, I've solved the man's fast ball,' he fools you with his knuckler."

Soon after this, the Cardinal's knuckle ball caught Stephen flatfooted. In the middle of a routine morning, His Eminence looked up casually and asked: "Father, do you remember a manuscript that you left in my keeping after our first inter-view?"

"*The Ladder of Love?*"

Glennon nodded. "I happened to glance through the work last night and discovered a certain literary elegance about it." Recalling his earlier strictures on the subject of "mystical moonshine," Glennon had the good taste to cough. "You'll find the manuscript on the refectory table with my imprimatur written on the title page. I suggest, Father Fermoyle, that you start looking for a publisher."

FINDING A PUBLISHER for *The Ladder of Love* proved to be a fascinating but somewhat thorny business. Though Glennon's imprimatur was canonically essential, it did not, of itself, guarantee an interested body of readers. Stephen sent his manuscript to a couple of Brahmin firms on Beacon Hill and promptly received courteous letters of regret from editors who expressed themselves as being personally anguished because they "could not see their way clear at this time to bring out a volume so patently limited to a special audience." Reardon & O'Neill, the Catholic publishers, were eager to get the manuscript, but Stephen had no intention of seeing *The Ladder of Love* lumped together with a basketful of devotional tracts and hortatory pamphlets. As he explained to Chancellor Mike Speed: "Quarenghi's work deserves literary treatment. I'll shop around till I find a publisher willing to handle it on a belles-lettres basis."

This shopping around ran into months of correspondence with various publishers. It was Mike Speed who finally brought the manuscript to the attention of Whateley House, a New York firm with a reputation for doing good things with essays and poetry. Whateley House offered Stephen a modest contract calling for a two-hundred-dollar advance against ten per cent royalties on the first twenty-five hundred copies; twelve and one half per cent thereafter. Stephen signed gladly and in due time received from Whateley House two sets of galley proofs in Caslon Old Style, a pleasing though conservative type face. He mailed one set of proofs to Quarenghi, accompanying it with a brief note:

MY DEAR ALFEO:

At last I have found an American publisher for *La Scala d'amore.* Your light still shines through my opaque journeyman translation. I think you need not be afraid of the reception your book will receive from readers and critics. Please go over this set of proofs, making any changes that occur to you, and mail the galleys back to me as quickly as possible. Too much time has passed already; Whateley House wants the book to be on their spring list, and if we move rapidly I think we can make it.

Love and homage to you,

STEPHEN

Quarenghi sent back the galleys without a single correction and a letter that said in part:

. . . I am deeply touched, Stefano, by your kindness and persistence in bringing about American publication of my work. Do I say "my work"? You have succeeded, dear friend, by the elegance of your translation, in making *The Ladder of Love* your own. Be the bearer of my heartfelt thanks to your Cardinal for his gracious imprimatur. And for yourself, Stephen, choose for permanent lodgment the innermost chamber of my heart.

Affectionately *in Cristo*,

ALFEO

The Ladder of Love, published in April, 1921, received glowing notices in the literary and religious press. A two-column review in *The New York Times* linked Quarenghi's name with that of Santayana and Ortega y Gasset; not forgetting to give the Reverend Stephen Fermoyle a puff for his polished translation. The staid *Boston Transcript* went into critical dithyrambics: "Here at last is a writer who combines mystical insight with the too-long-neglected art of the essay. It is as though St. Bonaventura and Agnes Repplier had joined forces to produce a work of authentic spirituality — and impeccable taste."

Catholic reviewers were unanimous in welcoming the book. The official journals of Dominicans, Benedictines, Jesuits, and Paulists assigned their sternest writers to the task of appraising the literary form and theological content of Quarenghi's mysticism. No flaws of doctrine or lapses of style were uncovered. Stephen breathed freely when a Jesuit critic commended

The Ladder of Love for having avoided "the pitfalls into which well-meaning but weakly endowed mystical essayists sometimes stumble."

The sweetest triumph of all was the feature article appearing in *The Monitor*, the home paper of the Archdiocese of Boston. In this article Quarenghi's career as a savant and diplomat was colorfully handled; Boston readers might easily have got the impression that Monsignor Quarenghi was a privy councilor to the Sovereign Pontiff himself, and an alter ego to Cardinal Giacobbi, the papal Secretary of State. This exalted prelate was on terms of closest intimacy (the story ran) with Cardinal Glennon's secretary, the Reverend Stephen Fermoyle, a local boy from Malden who had studied under Quarenghi in Rome. *The Monitor* then went on for several paragraphs describing Father Fermoyle's arduous labors of translation, and ended on a note of gratitude to Lawrence Cardinal Glennon for having recognized the outstanding merit of the work.

Reading the article, His Eminence beamed.

Felicitations poured in on Stephen like spring rain. At the May meeting of archdiocèsan consultors, Chancellor Mike Speed gave him a hearty clap on the back — and even Auxiliary Bishop Mulqueen thawed out long enough to shake Stephen's hand. Mulqueen hadn't read the book and didn't wholly relish Father Fermoyle's success. Dick Clarahan was *his* fair-haired boy; privately Mulqueen wished that his protégé might be wearing the literary laurels that bound Stephen's brow. The Bishop coolly minimized the whole business and continued to plump for Clarahan whenever comparisons were made between the talents of the promising pair.

Among the congratulatory letters that Stephen received were warm notes from Dollar Bill Monaghan, Milky Lyons, and Paul Ireton. The warmest note of all came from Dick Clarahan — who could well afford to step aside momentarily while Stephen took the plaudits of the crowd. "May I use your charming chapter entitled 'The Pears of Augustine' as material for my sermon next Sunday?" wrote Dick. To this sincerest form of flattery Stephen replied, "You may add your luster to any of the poor pearls you find in my book, but I

warn you I'll be in one of the back pews when you cast them
forth in your sermon."

Stephen kept his promise. He sat in the rear of the Cathedral the following Sunday and heard Clarahan spin an opulent
web of rhetoric that delighted every listener. Afterwards in
the sacristy, Stephen showered praise upon the oration and
was somewhat surprised when Clarahan seemed avid for
more.

"Did you think my style too ornate?" he asked eagerly.

"Rich but not indigestible," was Steve's comment.

"I wish," said Dick, "that you could hear one of the lectures
I'm giving Wednesday evenings at Boston College. The series
is called 'False Prophets of Modern Materialism.' Not quite so
florid as my Sunday stuff. More matter with less art, you
know."

"What's your subject next Wednesday?"

"I'm taking Darwin apart for the multitude."

"I hope you're not saying that it's an insult to God and man
to believe that *Homo sapiens* once lived in trees?"

"You don't think he did, do you?" asked Clarahan.

"All the evidence isn't in yet. I'm reserving judgment. But
supposing man *did* swing from a branch at one time or
another. He could still have had an immortal soul, couldn't
he?"

Clarahan took the whole thing as a tease. "Perhaps you'd
better not come next Wednesday. You might taint the atmosphere. But I think you would be interested to hear what I'm
saying about Freud the week after next."

"Freud? That *does* interest me. I'll be there."

In 1921 a lecture on Sigmund Freud was something of a
novelty in Boston. True, *The Introductory Essays* translated
some years back had long been discussed in the Harvard
graduate classes that Clarahan attended. Stephen, fairly familiar with Freud's general theories, realized that Clarahan was
giving an index of alertness by preparing a talk on the subject.

One of the smaller halls in Boston College was three quarters filled by Catholic intellectuals on the night of the lecture.
Stephen, accompanied by Dr. John Byrne, slipped into the
back row. After a longish introduction by Bishop Mulqueen,

who referred to the speaker as the "bright particular hope of Catholic thought in America," Clarahan began his address. His platform manner was flawless; he possessed an exceptional voice — an instrument of many stops and colors — a ranging vocabulary, and a Jesuit-trained gift of organization. His exposition of Freud's theory of the unconscious was, as far as Stephen could judge, accurate and well knit. Not until Clarahan came to the contents of the Freudian id did he really cut loose.

"We are asked to believe by this self-styled scientist (who, incidentally, began his career as a dabbler in hypnotism) that the basic drives of the human soul — prepare yourself for a shock, gentlemen — are *incest, cannibalism,* and *murder.* Yes, these are the ingredients of the Freudian psyche. From infancy our only motives are three; to achieve sexual congress with our mother, murder our father, and devour whosoever prevents us from attaining our objectives."

Clarahan paused to let the horror travel about the room. In perceptible shivers, it did. "But the common observations of mankind," he continued, "prove that these monstrosities do not in fact occur. To account for this discrepancy between fact and fancy, Freud advances another absurdity: the theory of repression. He concedes that the individual learns to suppress his frightful urges toward incest and murder, but at what a cost! Crowded to the bottom of the psyche, these urges crop out, says Freud, in the masked forms of dreams, anxiety states, and neurotic disturbances.

"Catholics will ask, 'But what of free will?' In Freud's structure, free will — the keystone of moral choices — is abolished. Man is a creature of will-less compulsion, driven by sexual gases, so to speak, rising from the psychic cesspool that Freud would substitute for the soul."

Clarahan pulled out the deepest stop of his voice box. "Can such things be? In place of St. Thomas Aquinas' testimony concerning the divine origin and nature of the soul, must we substitute the Freudian nightmare of libido and repression?"

Clarahan warmed to his peroration. "We shall be increasingly urged in the years ahead to teach these infamous doctrines to our students. At this moment, in a lay university not a thousand miles from here, professors are attempting to dissect the soul as though it were a mass of pathologic tissue. I urge you, as educators faced by the responsibility of training young Catholic men and women, to extirpate from Catholic schools and colleges the works of Sigmund Freud."

Enthusiastic applause greeted this close. In the question period that followed, not a great deal of new material was brought out. Few of Clarahan's hearers were equipped to make a critical analysis. Stephen wished to inquire into the relationship between Aquinas' "concupiscence" and Freud's "libido," but knew that Mulqueen would mark him as a heretic for even suggesting the comparison. It was a nameless priest who asked the most perceptive question of the evening.

"What distinction might be made, Father Clarahan, between Freud's id, with its predispositions to lustful violence, and the Catholic doctrine of original sin? Does not each attempt in its own way to account for the hereditary stain on the human soul?"

With Mulqueen's admiring eye on him, Clarahan was all unction. "A searching question, Father. Both Freud and Catholic theology do take into account man's tendency to evil. But need I point out to you, Father, that according to Catholic doctrine, original sin is at bottom nothing more than a withholding of God's sanctifying grace—a condition that can be remedied by baptism? Whereas Freud would have us believe"—Clarahan's timing and intonation were perfect—"that the condition can be remedied only by psychoanalysis."

Laughter greeted this clever hit. The questioner sat down.

As the meeting broke up, Stephen congratulated his old classmate. "A clear and reasoned presentation, Dick. I'd like to talk further about this id business. Can't we all ride downtown in my brother-in-law's car?"

At a lunchroom in Copley Square they had crackers and milk. Dr. Byrne ventured the opinion that Freud would one day be valued by physicians and clergy alike for the light that his theories threw upon the dark crevasses of the soul. When Clarahan vehemently opposed the notion, Stephen asked:

"Why are you so afraid that Freud will get into general circulation?"

Clarahan attempted to make an honest answer. "It's not so much his stressing of sex, though he does terribly overdo that part of it. No, it's the emphasis Freud places on sheer pathology. After reading him, one gets the impression that the human soul is a poor sick thing. I claim that the nature of the soul cannot be learned from a study of its diseases."

John Byrne interposed quickly: "I don't know that I agree with you about that, Father. In medical school our basic courses are two: biology, which concerns itself with healthy tissues; and pathology, which treats of morbid ones. From my experience as a surgeon and physician, I've found that one learns as much about the body from disease as from health."

"But we aren't talking about the body," said Clarahan. "I thought we were discussing the soul."

Stephen was happy when John Byrne replied: "I know, Father. Man is a creature composed of body and soul. But for the life of me, I couldn't tell you where the body ends and the soul begins. I wouldn't go so far as to say with Walt Whitman: 'The body *is* the soul' — but they're wonderfully and fearfully connected somehow." John Byrne expanded his thought. "Patients come to my office with bodily symptoms caused by obscure psychic troubles. There is a host of ills — drunkenness, for example—that penalize the body for some defect in the soul."

John Byrne, a sound Catholic and a thoughtful healer, went on: "The day will come, Father, when doctors and priests may be obliged to regard alcoholism, sexual perversion, and certain chronic illnesses such as tuberculosis — not to mention insanity, suicide, and other less obvious forms of self-destruction—as self-inflicted wounds, wrought upon the body by the revengeful soul."

"I can't follow you that far, Doctor," said Clarahan.

Long after Stephen went to bed that night he thought of John Byrne's ominous suggestion that man might be a self-destroying animal. What lay at the bottom of the soul's impulse to harm the body? And did the body in turn have power to stunt and deform the soul?

He fell asleep thinking of Mona.

CHAPTER 5

THE ESTABLISHMENT kept by Señora Guiomir ("Gussie")
Lasquez at 5 Stanhope Lane was too shady to be a lodging-
house and too grim to be a brothel. The sinister façade was
pockmarked by grimy windows in which roller curtains of
green scrim were drawn day and night. Rusty cast-iron bal-
ustrades flanked its brownstone stoop, and above the dangling
bell pull the sign No VACANCIES. The sign told a literal
untruth, because many rooms in the house of Señora Lasquez
were unoccupied. But because the place was an abortion
mill, Gussie could not risk opening her door to room hunters
who might turn out to be police. Bolted and chain-latched
from the inside, the front door was opened only to admit a certain type of caller — desperate young women with fifty dollars
who could utter the password, "Dr. Ramón sent me."

Fifty dollars would move Señora Lasquez to exercise her
skill with rare herbs and ingenious packs—or, if all else failed
— blunt instruments not unlike knitting needles. The herb-
and-pack method took a little time—three or four days, perhaps—and during this curative interval Gussie lodged and fed
her customers according to their ability to pay. The fee for
her front parlor was a straight two dollars a night, but third-
floor rooms could be rented for as little as $2.50 a week. Meals
extra. No plumbing or heat went with these quarters, but
inmates of the Casa Lasquez, gazing through the unwashed
windows on the top floor, could get an excellent view of Boston's South End, with the spires of the Cathedral in the near-
to-middle distance.

On a sheetless mattress in one of these upper rooms lay
Mona Fermoyle, approximately eight and a half months along
in pregnancy. She had come to 5 Stanhope Lane three weeks
ago, much too late for the exercise of Señora Lasquez's principal art. But because she showed splendid credentials, and
because she had twenty dollars in her pocketbook, Gussie had
consented to don the Samaritan mantle of midwife and give

the pale, terrified girl refuge. She took Mona's twenty dollars, assigned her to the third-floor back, and fed her patient whenever she remembered to do so.

Mona lay on the sagging cot and traced with her eyes the gaping crack in the plastered ceiling. She did not know enough about the rivers of the world to realize that the crack bore a striking resemblance to the Amazon. She knew only that her baby might come any time now. It thumped inside her like a rabbit trying to escape from a snare drum. Each percussion shook Mona with guilt and terror. Guilt, because her body gave swollen proof of what she had done; terror, because she was ill, penniless, and alone.

Of a certainty, ill. Not quite penniless though, because she still had a dime in her pocketbook — the remnant of two dollars a pawnbroker had given her for her coat. And not wholly alone either, because by twisting her head more, she could see the paired spires of the Cathedral. For three weeks now, ever since her creeping, compulsive return to Boston, she had drawn from those upraised arms some childhood recollections of protective comfort. In the fading light of a January afternoon, Mona levered herself onto an elbow and gazed at the symbols of goodness and security she had willfully left behind. A wild longing claimed her childish soul. If only she could snuggle back into the safety of those arms. Regret squeezed full tear glands. Like an exile dreaming of home, or a small girl waking fearfully in the night, Mona wept.

The tears, as tears will, purged away her accumulated anxieties. For the first time in many months, hope made a pattern, a plan, in a patternless world of guilt and misery. Mona rose from the cot and looked into her purse to be sure the dime was there. Feverishly she brushed her hair, dirty gold at the ends, ebony-black at the roots, where no bleach had been applied for weeks. Then, bareheaded and coatless, she felt her way down the dark, uncarpeted stairs, noiselessly unhooked the chain latch on the front door, and slipped out of Señora Lasquez's house into a world of falling snow.

At first the cold braced her, but by the time she reached the Spanish Pharmacy at the corner of Washington Street, she was chilled and spiritless. The drugstore had a soda fountain; to revive her strength, Mona ordered a cup of hot chocolate, the first nourishment she had taken in twenty-four hours. She slid her dime onto the marble slab; a splotch-aproned proprietor shoved a nickel back. The coin of her salvation! Mona sipped the sweetish liquid slowly, trying to summon up courage to enter the phone booth at the end of the dark shop.

As she passed the rubber-goods showcase, a thin icicle of fear pierced the inner membranes of her heart. Who would answer the phone? What would they say when they heard her voice? At the cosmetics counter she wavered. The salesman eye of Mr. Hernandez passed over her coatless figure, lighted hopefully on her two-toned hair. He wiped his hands on his splotchy apron. Perhaps he could sell her a bottle of peroxide. No sale, he concluded, as he watched her move heavily toward the pay station. When a woman lets her hair go like that, she no longer cares.

Coin clutched in her thin hand, Mona entered the telephone booth and closed the door behind her. The dimensions of the box, its darkness and stuffy air, reminded her of — of what? The confessional! Soon a little panel would slide back; she would hesitate for a moment, take a deep breath, and say: "This is Mona, Father. I want to come home. . . . *Forgive me, Father, for I have sinned.*"

Oh, impossible declaration! Guilt too great for absolving! Yet of necessity the confession must be made. With trembling fingers Mona dropped the nickel into the coin box and gave the operator the number of the telephone at 47 Woodlawn Avenue. She heard the muffled brr-r, brr-r of the little bell under the mission-oak table in the Fermoyle front hall. Long ago, Florrie had stuffed the bell with a piece of cotton because it jangled too loudly. Brr-r, brr-r. Now the sound was echoing through the chenille portieres into the living room where Bernie would be playing the piano while Din raised his voice in accompaniment of song. At the kitchen stove Celia would hear the brr-ring and hope that someone less busy than herself would answer the phone. Upstairs in her quiet sanctuary, Ellen would hear the bell, too. . . .

Clickingly the receiver came off its hook. Then Mona heard the gruffest, sternest voice in the world—the male voice that had filled her childhood with the thunder of its authority. The voice of Dennis Fermoyle said, "Hello."

Mute fear paralyzed Mona's tongue. It would not make the words that must be made: *This is Mona, Father. I want to come home.*

"Hello, hello," Din was saying, "who is it?"

Shaken by old fear and sin too shameful for utterance, Mona hung up the receiver. She waited till her knees were strong enough to bear her, then wavered from the booth, and clung for a moment to the cosmetic showcase. Unsteadily she walked out of the drugstore and stood on the freezing pavement of Washington Street.

Swollen with the wickedness thumping inside her, where could she go? To whom could she turn? This troubled, foolish girl had never heard the trusting cry of the Psalmist: "If I make my bed in hell, behold Thou art there. If I take the wings of the morning and dwell in the uttermost parts of the sea, even there shall Thy hand lead me, and Thy right hand shall hold me." She had never read a book in her life, and she could not know the promise of the poet's line, "Fear wist not to evade, as love wist to pursue." But better than familiarity with poet or Psalmist was Mona's recollection of the comforting Presence streaming from the altar. Remembrance of that Presence drew her toward the steps of the Cathedral. Into its tenebrous silence she entered now, knelt in a pew at the back of the church, and gazed down the long vista of the center aisle where the sanctuary lamp glowed in crimson comfort above the altar. She felt neither ecstatic nor pious. An emotion older than these cradled her. She felt safe.

A pyramid of candles with flames like fiery apostrophes burned before the shrine of St. Anthony. Mona could not remember when she had last lighted a candle, but she could never forget the first one. It had been lighted to this very saint — the patron of lost things. Her mother had sent her downtown to buy a flatiron holder, and on the way home Mona had stopped to play jump rope with some girls on Maude Street. When it came time to go home, Mona could not find the flatiron holder. "Why not light a candle to St. Anthony?" suggested Kathleen O'Donnell. "I haven't got a nickel," sobbed Mona. "Oh, he'll trust you," soothed Kathleen. "I owe him a dime already for two things I've found." At the head of a party of supplicants Mona had walked into the church, lit the can-

dle to St. Anthony, said three Hail Marys — then suddenly
remembered that she had left the holder on the counter at the
hardware store.

O marvelous St. Anthony, patron of lost things! Would
another candle, lighted on credit, solve the woman's problem
as easily as it had solved the child's?

He'll trust me, thought Mona as she approached the rail of
the shrine. With a taper she lighted the highest candle in the
pyramid, then, kneeling before the dusky statue of the saint,
watched her candle flicker timidly on its prong. The flame
caught hold, and when she saw it burning as fierily as the
others, Mona said three Hail Marys. For the first time in all
her vacant years, the prayer was not a jumble of nothingness.
Her specially tuned ear caught the central phrase 'of the
Angelic Salutation, "Blessed is the fruit of thy womb, Jesus."
The words supported her like a prop under a laden bough, and
the splendor of bringing forth new life warmed her with a
proud fire.

Twilight was a purple veil dotted with snow when Mona
left the Cathedral. She stretched out her hands, palms upward
to catch some falling flakes, then, happier than she had been
for a long time, trudged past the pharmacy of Señor Hernandez, turned left, and disappeared into the shadows of the
South End.

Her pains were beginning as she reached the cast-iron stoop
at 5 Stanhope Lane.

IN THE MAGISTRATE'S COURT at Roxbury Crossing, the usual
number of Monday-morning drunks, streetwalkers, and sneak
thieves were on the receiving end of justice as dealt out by
Judge Peter J. Stranahan. His Honor had a bad head cold, and
he sniffed angrily at a menthol inhaler that was doing him no
good at all. Calendar and courtroom were overcrowded; nothing marched right, and as the day grew longer Judge Stranahan's patience grew shorter. At 3:22 P.M. he listened irritably
to the evidence given by Patrolman No. 677. "The defendant
was found lying in a hallway at 10 West Springfield Street in
a state of alcoholic intoxication injuced by a bottle of Jamaica
ginger discovered on his person."

"Guilty or not guilty?" asked His Honor, and, on hearing the answer, pronounced irreversible judgment, to wit: "Ten days on Deer Island. . . . Next case."

"The next case," explained Assistant District Attorney Schultz, his eye on the court clock, "involves the theft of a bicycle from the premises of Ignatz Lazlo, repairman, 1144 Washington Street. The defendant, James T. Splaine, a minor with a record of delinquency, admits taking the bicycle without permission of the owner and selling it for four dollars."

"Is Splaine represented by counsel?" asked the judge.

"Yes, Your Honor. The Catholic Charities Bureau has engaged . . ."

"Skip the details," snapped Stranahan. "Put the defendant on the stand."

The defendant turned out to be a gangling, scab-complexioned youth in need of a necktie, a haircut, and a month of good meals. Examined by District Attorney Schultz, he sullenly admitted the charge as drawn, then gazed piteously at a sunken-eyed woman on a front bench as if to say, "Honest, I .didn't mean to cause you no more trouble, Ma."

Counsel for the defense, a fledgling barrister named George Fermoyle, began a gentle cross-examination. "Where do you live, Jimmy?"

"Twenty-two High Street, Malden."

"Who lives there with you?"

"My mother." Jimmy motioned with a dirty knuckle at the haggard woman with the sunken blue eyes.

"Where's your father?"

"Dead. Got killed in a barroom fight three years ago."

Magistrate Stranahan sniffed at his inhaler. "Counsel will please not range all around O'Houlihan's barn, or we'll never get out of this court tonight. What do you intend to show by this line of questioning?"

"I intend to show the family background of this boy, Your Honor. He is the product of a home invaded by death and economic want. His mother works all day as a domestic servant. I hope to demonstrate that the defendant is a virtual orphan who needs social care and psychiatric guidance."

Stranahan could scarcely credit his ears. "What *kind* of guidance, did you say?"

The Fermoyle temper exploded in Stranahan's face. "I said

'psychiatric guidance,' Your Honor. If this boy were physically ill he would get free medical care. Yet now, during critical formative years . . ."

"Critical formative rats," scoffed Stranahan. "He stole the bicycle, didn't he? Sold it, didn't he? Spent the money too, heh?"

"We admit all that, Your Honor. But . . ."

"But now you ask this court to coddle him." Justice Stranahan dropped his inhaler, snatched up his gavel, and banged twice. "What this young thief needs is not coddling, but discipline. If you've finished your argument, Counselor, the Court will pronounce judgment. Six months in the Concord Reformatory. Court adjourned till tomorrow."

Tears coursed down Julia Splaine's cheek.

"Better luck next time, Counselor," said the assistant D. A. "Even Rufus Choate didn't win his first case. But seriously, Fermoyle, don't try to pull that psychiatric line on P. J. Stranahan."

"It's not a line, it's the dreary truth," said George. He stuffed his papers into his brief case and turned to the melancholy business of consoling Julia Splaine. "It's lucky that Stranahan didn't send Jimmy to State's Prison," he told her. "They'll teach him a trade at Concord. He'll be a credit to you yet, Mrs. Splaine."

"It's the kind heart of the Fermoyles that makes you say that, George, but my boy's a stray, and I know it now." She shook her gray hairs in bewilderment. "The question I'm asking myself is why should my Jimmy be so bad, and my Jemmy so good?"

Having no offhand answer to this classic problem, George patted Julia Splaine's bony shoulder and walked out into the gloom of a snowy twilight. Roxbury Crossing was an X-shaped traffic tangle; trolleys, trucks, and pedestrians crawled in slow motion across slushy cobblestones. While George waited for the Park Street trolley that would take him back to his office, he bought the *Globe* and scanned its headlines. "Pope Benedict Sinking"; "New England Battens Down for Hurricane"; "Italian Superliner Enters Boston Harbor on Maiden Voyage." With the ominous expectancy that always accompanies a falling barometer, George Fermoyle found a seat in the warm streetcar, and settled himself for the ride to his office.

"So that was due process of law," he murmured, gazing out the car window at the mean shops along Washington Street. Anger at Stranahan's stupidity flared once more, then lost its heat in a cooler tide of reflection. Julia Splaine's question, "Why should my Jimmy be so bad, and my Jemmy so good?" provided more meditative fare. Sons of the same parents; products of the same environment — and here was Jemmy heading for the priesthood and Jimmy heading for the penitentiary. If you threw Jeremy Splaine overboard in mid-ocean, he'd strike out for heaven's beach — and make it, too. Whereas if you tossed Jimmy into a horsepond he'd sink without a struggle into the muck at the bottom.

Strange.

Along Washington Street, bums with a dime were already gathering in gaslit speakeasies, and bums without a dime were standing in hallways or shuffling along on snowy sidewalks. This was the South End, the terrain of down-and-outers, the irrevocably lost. At the stop nearest the Cathedral, the trolley halted to take on a passenger. *Ding-ding.* As the conductor gave his go-ahead signal George Fermoyle saw his sister Mona standing on the steps of the Cathedral. By the sputtering blue glitter of a street lamp, he could see that she was coatless, hatless, pregnant. And she was holding out her hands to catch a flake of falling snow.

George plunged through the crowded aisle, shouting, "Stop the car!" By the time the conductor pulled his bell rope, the trolley had traveled fifty yards. George raced back to the Cathedral where he had seen his sister standing in the snow. She was gone.

"Mona, Mona," he shouted. "Where are you?" He dashed into the church, ran irreverently up and down the aisles, then found himself again on the steps of the Cathedral. At the corner he saw a shop bearing the sign, "Farmacia Española." He burst through the door and interrupted the proprietor in the act of compounding a prescription. "Have you seen a girl— a woman with black hair—no coat or hat—around here?"

Mr. Hernandez remembered the girl. "Fifteen, twenty minutes ago, she had a hot chocolate here. But her hair was not black."

George accepted the correction. "Blond, then?"

"Say half and half. At the tips blond, at the roots black."

"Do you know which way she went? Where she lives?"

The pharmacist's shrug said, "One knows nothing about such matters in South End. Excuse me, *Señor*—my customers."

Mona's nearness had the almost palpable quality of a person seen in a dream. By closing his eyes George could feel her presence; opening them was to grasp at shadows. And he fumbled among these shadows until he struck the solid idea: *Call Stuffy*.

From Hernandez' pay station he phoned the Cardinal's residence, asked for Father Fermoyle. A clerically modulated voice said: "Father Fermoyle has just left his office. You'll be able to reach him at the Cathedral rectory before dinner."

George caught Stephen entering the rectory, looking very handsome in a white muffler, black overcoat, and suède gloves. "*Salve, advocate*," cried Steve. "But prithee why so pale, young sinner?"

George laid an arresting hand on his brother's arm. "Stuff, I've just seen Mona."

Stephen's forward motion ceased. "Where?"

"On the steps of the Cathedral, standing in the snow. I caught a glimpse of her from the trolley car. She had no coat on, and she's pregnant."

Stephen pulled his brother into the reception room. "Begin at the beginning—tell me everything." George told the whole story, ending with Hernandez' comment on Mona's partly bleached hair.

"That clinches it, George. It's Mona, all right. We'll find her if we have to knock on every door in the South End."

STEPHEN'S FIRST MOVE was to request the Cardinal for a leave of absence, and he decided to make the request in person. He found Glennon finishing a solitary dinner of pressed duck and a bottle of his favorite Château Cos d'Estournel. The Cardinal was in one of his lonely moods. "Join me in a thimbleful of this," he said, pointing to the vintage bottle. "It's the last of its kind. There'll never be another red Graves year like '81."

"I'm afraid it would be wasted on me, Your Eminence."

"A sip of port then. Try a glass of that Alto Douro on the sideboard. Product of Portugal. Tawny, very dry. . . . What's the trouble, my boy?"

Stephen had not intended to drag His Eminence into the domestic affairs of the Fermoyles. He had hoped that the simple explanation "family crisis" would be enough. But Glennon's lonely mood drew him in, and while the Cardinal finished off his wine, Stephen recounted Mona's unfortunate history.

"How do you propose to locate her?" asked Glennon.

"My two brothers and I will make a house-to-house canvass of the South End. She's hiding there, frightened and ashamed. We'll knock on every door between Tremont Street and the New Haven tracks till we find her."

The Cardinal shook his head with "that-won't-do" emphasis. "I'm afraid you don't know the South End, Stephen. It's a Sargasso Sea—stagnant, chartless. In half an hour you'd get lost among its alleys and dead-end courts." Large sympathy was in Glennon's hazel eyes. "Why not call in the police?"

"I wanted to keep the matter as quiet as possible. Can't you imagine the headlines: 'Sister of Cardinal's Secretary Sought by Police'?"

"Discretion is an excellent medicine, Stephen. But don't take an overdose of it. I suggest that we get in touch with my friend Inspector Shea. Phone him at police headquarters and say that the Cardinal would like to see him at once."

The Flemish clock in the front hall was bonging eight when Hugh Shea, hard hat across his knees, sat down on a gilt chair in the Cardinal's music room. He heard Father Fermoyle's story, then massaged the nap of his derby before venturing comment.

"Searching for your sister in the South End," he began, "will be like trying to find the proverbial needle's eye. A mixed metaphor, you'll say, but it's exactly what I mean. There are forty thousand people down there — floaters and drifters most of them — as nameless, faceless a population as ever slipped through the fingers of the law." Shea rubbed up his hat as though currying a fine horse. "The region is a jungle of abortion mills, out-of-bound apothecaries, and fake doctors, all operating together. The drugstores sell morphine, cocaine, ergot, and cantharides — the latter, begging Your Lordship's pardon, better known to the trade as 'Spanish fly.' "

"A pharmaceutic dangerous to health as well as morals," observed Glennon.

Hugh Shea affirmed the Cardinal's opinion with a vigorous rub at his derby. "But the drug traffic is merely a twig on the tree, Your Eminence. The phony doctors are the root we're striking at. With neither diploma nor license they practice their murderous trade on ignorant girls drawn from the brothels and cheap dance halls in the neighborhood."

Stephen shuddered at the Inspector's unconscious description of Mona. Shea went on. "The Mayor has given orders to crack down on the whole business, and I've detailed six of my best men to the task of collecting evidence. Much of it will be petty stuff, but if we could lay our hands on the rascal who calls himself Dr. Panfilo Echavarría"—the professional man hunter's glint lighted Shea's eye—"I'd feel that the campaign was a success. He's the prince of tomcats . . . the master abortionist of them all. Police from Richmond to Montreal are looking for the knave, but he travels fast and has a bagful of aliases." Shea exhaled fervently. "I'd give a year off my pension to nab the fellow."

The Inspector rose from the edge of his gilt chair and turned to Stephen. "Rest easy, Father. I'll instruct my men to keep an eye peeled for your sister. We'll search till we find her."

"Thank you, Inspector," said Stephen. "You won't object if my brothers and I make our own search at the same time?"

Hugh Shea permitted himself a policeman's paraphrase of St. Paul: " 'The harvest is large, but the workers are few.' If you had a hundred brothers, Father Fermoyle, they wouldn't be too many. . . . Keep in touch with me for the next few days."

With lay piety Shea began a genuflection—an obeisance that Glennon staved off with a man-to-man handshake. "Thanks, Hugh," he said gratefully. "Do what you can in this matter. It is close to my heart."

With the Cardinal's blessing on his back, Stephen went straight to the Cathedral rectory, where George and Bernie awaited him. In the bare reception room they mapped out their campaign. Dividing the South End into three roughly equal parts, they each took a section and pledged themselves to make searching inquiries at every house in their district. The rectory was to be field headquarters, and the brothers agreed to meet there every four hours for interim reports and conferences.

"Don't you think we should cross Hernandez' palm with silver?" suggested George. "Mona might show up there again. If she does, our Spanish friend might get her address or even detain her."

"We've got to stop thinking of Hernandez as a friend," said Stephen. "From what Inspector Shea tells me, none of these Spanish pharmacies are above suspicion. Still, you've got a point there, George. A five-dollar bill might keep him on our side."

It was ten o'clock on the evening of January 18 when the three brothers plunged into the tideless swamp of Boston's South End. Stephen took the area between Canton and West Concord Streets—a sieve through which a mixed population of Spaniards, Puerto Ricans, and Negroes drained into an anonymous sewer of poverty. He knocked on the doors of fifty-cent lodginghouses and basement speakeasies, always asking the same question: "Have you seen a young woman, twenty-two years old, about to have a baby, around here?"

Five hundred assorted negatives answered his query. Along wretched streets, up and down unlighted stairways, he tramped for two days and nights. Of drunks, derelicts, panderers, prostitutes, stew bums, and panhandlers he saw thousands. But never a trace of Mona.

George and Bernie were equally luckless; faithful as retrievers, they combed their districts and turned up not a single clue. Nor did Shea's men do any better. They dragged in a dozen girls, some far gone in pregnancy, but none of them was Mona Fermoyle.

"We need a break," said the Inspector to Stephen. "And I define a break as something that comes after you've sawed through ninety-nine strands in the hundred-wired cable of difficulty. Let's keep on sawing." Shea assigned another half-dozen detectives and twenty extra patrolmen to the district, while he himself concentrated on the illegal traffic in abortion-inducing drugs. Three pharmacists were arrested in the act of selling ergot without a prescription, and seven phony doctors were rounded up. All of which enhanced Inspector Shea's reputation and provided several heartening columns in the Boston papers—without turning up a single trace of Mona Fermoyle.

STEPHEN'S LEAVE OF ABSENCE had been twice extended. On the fourth night of the search he decided that in fairness to the Cardinal he could not remain away from his secretarial post much longer. He was a haggard, discouraged priest as he finished a midnight cup of coffee with George and Bernie. Red-eyed with fatigue, George was scanning the *Globe*.

"Your friend Orselli sails tomorrow at eleven A.M.," he reported.

Orselli! Was the Italian Captain still in the world? "I forgot all about him," said Steve listlessly. "I didn't even phone him. His Florentine pride will be hurt, I'm afraid."

"His Florentine intelligence will understand when you tell him what you've been doing," said George. "Well, men, I'm going to get my daily dose of 'No news, Señor' at Hernandez' drugstore. Anybody coming?"

They walked along Washington Street to the Spanish Pharmacy. "I need a pack of cigarettes," said Bernie. "I'll go in with you."

Weary to exhaustion, Stephen leaned against the corner lamppost. Bones, muscles, and brain cried out for rest. He was in the act of making a solemn vow to the Blessed Virgin that he would abstain from meat for a year if he could find Mona, when Bernie joggled his elbow.

"Hey, Steve . . . Take a peek through the window. A friend of ours is inside."

Peering through the dirty pane of Hernandez' drugstore, Stephen saw Ramón Gongaro. High-heeled, wax-mustached, very spruce in his chesterfield and velvet fedora, the dancer was engaged in a confidential business with the proprietor. A doctor's instrument bag lay on the showcase beside him. Stephen watched Gongaro stuff some phials into the bag, pass Hernandez some money. Then with a *caballero* farewell, Gongaro started for the door of the pharmacy.

Literally he walked into the arms of the three brothers waiting at the door.

Stephen laid a hand on the shoulder of the dancing man's chesterfield. "We want to talk to you, Gongaro. You'd better come quietly."

Gongaro put up a show of indignation. "Let me go . . . I'll tell the police."

"You'll tell us first," said Stephen.

They led the terrified dancer down a side street and turned into an alley near the railroad tracks. George and Bernie pinned his wrists and shoulders to the brick wall of a warehouse. Stephen did the talking.

"Where's Mona?" he began.

The Spaniard's teeth chattered like dice in a cup. "I don't know. I haven't seen her since two months."

"Where did you see her last?"

"In Troy. We — separated there."

"You mean you abandoned her because she was going to have a baby."

Hidalgo honor stiffened Gongaro. "I asked her to have an abortion." His professional vanity betrayed him. "I offered to do it myself."

George Fermoyle's arm went back at full cock. "You bastard!" His fist exploded against the Spaniard's jaw. The blow bounced Gongaro's head off the wall, and he slumped to the ground.

"A pretty business," said Stephen. "Our chief witness is now out cold."

At the entrance to the alley, silhouetted against the arc light, appeared the bulky form of a patrolman, night stick raised.

"What's going on here?"

Stephen stepped forward, all his teeth in a smile, his Roman collar gleaming. "Our friend is a bit under the weather, Officer. You know how it is — spirit willing, flesh weak."

At the sight of Stephen's Roman collar, the cop grinned. "Some can take it, Father; some can't. Could I be getting your friend a cab?"

"That would be kind of you, Officer."

The patrolman was turning away when he remembered something. "I suppose you've heard the news?"

"What news?"

"The Pope is dead. Passed away an hour ago. May his soul rest in heaven tonight."

Above the patrolman's pieties, Stephen could hear Glennon roaring: "Where's Father Fermoyle? The Pope dies, Peter's throne stands empty, cardinals from all over the world start their journeys to Rome. Bags must be packed, steamship tickets bought—and my secretary is lally-gagging around the South End. Fetch him, I say. Bring him here within the hour."

Angels and ministers of grace defend me! thought Stephen. But I must find Mona first. . . .

He ran back to his brothers standing helplessly over the unconscious dancer. "Search him," said Stephen. "He may have papers that will tell us something."

George thrust his hand into the inner pocket of Gongaro's coat and drew out a wallet and a small red address book. In the wallet were some obscene photographs, several hundred dollars, and a collection of business cards. Among the latter Stephen found a dozen bearing the legend:

DR. PANFILO ECHAVARRÍA

SPECIALIST

(By Appointment Only)

Ramón Gongaro and Panfilo Echavarría were the same man! "Poor Mona."

George was examining the red notebook containing names and addresses from all parts of the country. "It would take six months to check these," he said gloomily.

"Look through his bag. There may be something there."

The professional bag was stuffed with gaudy shirts and neckties, some unmarked phials of medicine, and a mixed clutter of surgical instruments. Shea would be glad to have them as evidence, but they were valueless to the brothers Fermoyle.

"Here's a letter," cried Bernie. "I found it in his overcoat pocket, all crumpled up as though he meant to throw it away. It's written in some foreign language."

Under the arc light Stephen read the illiterate scrawl: "*No puedo darle comida a la paloma si no manda viente pesos.*" The letter was signed "G. Lasquez."

"What does it say, Steve?"

Stephen translated: "I cannot feed the pigeon any more corn unless you send me twenty dollars."

"A 'pigeon-fancier," said George disgustedly.

"Pigeon!" Excitement mounted in Steve's voice. "That was Gongaro's pet name for Mona. I heard him call her 'pigeon' in the dance hall. Was this letter in an envelope, Bernie?"

"Yes." Bernie handed his brother an envelope addressed to Dr. Panfilo Echavarría, General Delivery, Boston. Hopefully Stephen looked for a return address on the back flap. Not a line. The writer of the letter had been too shrewd for such an obvious giveaway.

"Another dead end," said Stephen. "Extract of nothingness, triply compounded."

"Wait a minute, Stuff." George was piecing together the tags of evidence in his hand. "That pigeon letter was signed 'G. Lasquez.' Now if we could only find a 'G. Lasquez' in the red address book . . ." His finger ran down the L's. "'Labbiano, Albany, New York . . . Langenstein, Richmond, Virginia . . .' holy mackerel, here's a Lasquez, first name 'Guiomir.'"

"Any address?"

George snapped the book shut. "5 Stanhope Lane . . . *Boston!* It's a chance, Stuffy."

A taxi horn tooted at the mouth of the alley. "You the guys that want a cab for the drunk?"

"Coming," cried Stephen. The three brothers lifted Gongaro from the ground, and bundled him into the taxi. "Five Stanhope Lane," Stephen directed the driver.

The jolting of the taxi stirred Gongaro into consciousness.

"Where are you taking me?" he jittered.

"To the Casa Lasquez," said Stephen.

"And if that's not the place" — George belted Gongaro in the short ribs — "we'll start all over again."

At the last house in a forbidding court the taxi halted. "This is the dump," said the driver, "and I mean dump. How long's this gonna take?"

"Wait for us," said Stephen.

George and Bernie dragged Gongaro from the cab. Holding him hostagewise in front of them, they mounted the cast-iron stoop while Stephen jerked at the bell pull and pounded on the door.

"*Quien está?*" demanded a woman's voice.

George's knee went into Gongaro's rump. "Speak up," he whispered.

"It's me, Dr. Panfilo," said Gongaro in Spanish.

"Ah, Doctor," Señora Lasquez fumbled at the latch chain. "Am I not glad you have come." She opened the door a crack's width. "Something is very wrong with the pigeon . . ."

Her words were drowned under an avalanche of strange men crashing through her door. Señora Lasquez saw two of the strangers hurl Dr. Panfilo to the floor and sit on him, while the third stranger, wearing the collar of a Catholic priest, grasped the yoke of her frowsy flannel nightgown and asked in a terrible voice, "Where is the pigeon?"

"Third-floor back," choked Gussie.

Up the uncarpeted stairs Stephen leapt four at a time, "Monny, Monny!" he shouted. "Where are you, darling?"

At the third landing he listened in a darkness seemingly composed of carbolic disinfectant hiding the odor of death. At the end of the hallway he heard a woman groaning. Stephen pushed open a door, and there on a filthy cot, half naked in a cold, stench-filled room, he saw Mona. She was panting like a wounded animal exhausted by a long chase, and her head moved from side to side in a delirium of pain. He was at her side, his arms around her. "Monny darling, it's me, Stephen. Everything's all right now."

The grinding of her teeth told him more than her agonized plea: "Stevie, it's awful. Take me out of here."

He lifted Mona in his arms, caught up a torn blanket, and wrapped it around her. "Hold on tight, Monny. We're getting out fast." Through the reeking dark he felt his way down the stairs to the front hall.

George and Bernie were over them like a wave, hugging Mona, thumping Steve, gloating and sobbing with joy at having found their sister. Weakly she smiled at her brothers as they kissed her lips caked with dry saliva.

"I knew you'd find me," she said, then buried her face in Stephen's shoulder when she saw Gongaro and Gussie.

"Turn that pair over to Shea," Stephen said to George. "I'll take Mona to the hospital."

Exultantly the brothers carried Mona down the front stoop, helped lift her into the cab.

"City General," cried Stephen. "Step on it, driver."

THE RIDE to the hospital was joyous and terrible. Stephen held Mona close, murmuring her name in an attempt to soothe her physical agony. Through an isolating mist of pain Mona's words came wanderingly. At times she knew Stephen's arms were around her; again the mists would rise, and her voice would trail off into childhood rememberings. Crescent Hill . . . the double runner . . . *I'll hold on tight, Teevie* . . . jump rope on Maude Street . . . the lost flatiron holder. *Dear St. Anthony, let me find it.*

The childish mists unwound. "Stevie," she said timidly. "You know the statue of St. Anthony in the Cathedral?"

"Yes, dear, what about it?"

Mona snuggled into his shoulder. "I owe him a nickel for a candle. Pay him, will you, for finding me? . . . Promise?"

Stephen promised. His lulling caresses soothed her. Mona was calm but not lucid as Stephen carried her up the steps of the hospital.

"Name and address of the patient?" asked the intern on duty, preparing to take down the usual case history. "Primipara or — ?"

Stephen snatched the form from the intern's hand. "Call the resident physician and get this woman up to the delivery room." The frightened intern set in motion the brisk mechanism of a modern hospital. An attendant wheeled Mona to the elevator. At the maternity floor, an intelligently cheerful nurse appeared.

"We'll take care of her, Father. Don't worry. Everything's going to be all right."

Stephen sank into a white iron chair in the corridor and lifted inward paeans of thanksgiving.

A doctor slightly older than Stephen came out of the delivery room. From his neck hung a stethoscope; his white shoes, starched coat, and the aloof carriage of his head stamped him as the prime product of a Class A hospital.

"I'm Dr. Parks, the attending physician," he said. "Is this woman a relative of yours?"

"My sister."

Dr. Parks, obviously Harvard, put no gloss on his speech. "My examination shows your sister to be in grave condition. Apparently she has been in labor for several days. Unclean hands have made repeated attempts at delivery. I am not surprised that these attempts have failed" — the physician paused to choose language for his disclosure — "because on the basis of sheer mechanics, normal delivery is impossible in this case."

"Why impossible, Doctor?"

Lay explanations were distasteful to Dr. Parks. How could one express obstetrical mysteries to the uninitiated? He made the effort. "Your sister's pelvic structure is small, almost infantile. The baby's head is unusually large. In addition, we are confronted by what is known technically as a 'brow presentation.'"

Stephen thought he had the picture. "Can't you perform a Caesarian?"

Dr. Parks shook his head. "Your sister comes too late. She is already in shock from loss of blood. Her heart tones show extreme exhaustion, and the kidney function is gravely impaired. Surgical intervention at this point would be fatal."

"What do you advise?"

The resident measured Stephen with blue Anglo-Saxon eyes. "Termination of labor by means of a craniotomy."

"But that's murder!" said Stephen.

Nettlement rasped Dr. Parks's voice. "I am not Catholic. I am under no obligation to take your view of the matter, Father. I realize the frightful choice that you must make. But unless you give me permission to destroy the fetus, nothing can save your sister. It's her life against that of an unborn child."

Stephen gripped his chair. *"Jesus, Mary, and Joseph help me!"*

His ejaculation struck the ceiling of the hospital corridor

and then rebounded in the words of the Fifth Commandment: *Thou shalt not kill.* God's explicit injunction, binding upon all — physicians not excepted. No room for private judgment here, and no bargaining about the comparative worth of one life as against another. In the Creator's eye, the value of human life did not depend on its phase of development. Mother and unborn child were equal in His sight. No man had the right to decide that one should be sacrificed for the other. To make such a decision would be usurping a prerogative belonging only to God.

Dr. Parks glanced at his watch. "You must make up your mind at once, Father."

A drench of anguish sapped Stephen's will. For support he grasped at rebel fantasies — matchwood temptations whirling down the wind of despair. Was it thinkable that he should let Mona die, when a single word — a mere nod of assent — might save her? Had human love, with its pitiful intertwining of nerve roots and memory threads, no right to plead for special mercy? Would it be presumptuous to pray: "Lift thine ordinance, *this once*, Lord?"

"Well?" Dr. Parks asked again.

The iron fall of the question brought Stephen back to reality. His training as a priest, his consuming faith in the Catholic Church bent his whole being to a submissive trust in an all-wise, all-knowing, all-merciful God. Stephen bowed his head; he yielded to the divine will expressed in the Fifth Commandment and reiterated in the canon law of the Church.

"I have no authority to permit murder," he said.

Dr. Parks had the good taste not to say what he was thinking: You Catholics baffle me. Aloud he said, "Would you like to see your sister?"

In the delivery room, Stephen bent over Mona's sheeted form. Her face was a purple, toxic bloat, and her breath came pantingly between small teeth. Her once-glossy hair was a tangled mat — dirty-gold on the pillow, blue-black at the roots. She was sinking now; prolonged labor had flogged her almost to unconsciousness.

"Oxygen," said Dr. Parks quietly to the nurse. His code bound him to sustain the life of the body as long as possible, and by every means at his command.

Stephen, too, was bound by a code — a solemn code looking beyond bodily death to the everlasting life of the soul. The thorn of personal sorrow, the lance of private remorse, must not prevent him from discharging his final obligation as a priest. He brought his head close to Mona's.

"Make a good act of contrition, darling," he whispered.

Mona looked up at her brother, tried obediently to speak. Her lips moved without sound.

"Trust me, Monny. I won't let you down. Try hard. Say it after me."

The essential words came. "Most heartily . . . sorry . . . for having offended Thee," breathed Mona. Stephen was giving her absolution when Dr. Parks' stethoscope caught the last flutter of her exhausted heart.

The obstetrician leaped to his instruments. "I've got exactly three minutes to save that baby," he said. "You'd better get out of here, Father. It's not going to be pretty."

Outside the door, Stephen leaned against the corridor wall. He had scrupulously fulfilled his sacerdotal contract, and now payment was due in terms of mortal anguish and physical collapse. He wanted to lie down on the floor and beat his head against the uncaring wood. Gross forms of human lamentation beckoned to him. His lips were shaping desperate words when he heard a thin wail — a trumpet pitiful and piercing, the announcement of a new life entering the world.

A nurse appeared in the doorway, holding something in a delivery blanket. "It's a little girl!" she said. "Dr. Parks says the baby is going to live."

CHAPTER 6

IN AN UPPER CHAMBER of the Vatican Palace twelve kneeling cardinals of the Roman Curia intoned the *de profundis*. At the end of the majestic psalm a prelate, whose hawk beak and saddle-brown coloring proclaimed his Sicilian lineage, rose heavily from his knees and approached a canopied bed. In his right hand he held a silver mallet; with decent hesitation he lifted the mallet and gently tapped the lifeless forehead of Benedict XV.

"Giacomo," he murmured, calling upon the Pontiff by his baptismal name. Thrice he tapped with the silver hammer, repeating the name each time. Receiving no answer, the hawk-beaked prelate turned sorrowfully to the company of cardinals.

"Most Reverend Lords," he announced, "the chair of Peter is vacant. Of a certainty, the Pope is dead."

A Prothonotary Apostolic drew up the official certificate of Benedict's death and submitted it to the assembled cardinals for their signatures. First to sign was the hook-nosed prelate, Pietro Cardinal Giacobbi, who, as Camerlengo, assumed virtual control of Vatican affairs until a new Pope should be elected. Entrusting the papal apartments to a platoon of Noble Guards, the Camerlengo withdrew to an adjoining chamber where, in the presence of witnesses, he broke Benedict's ring and seals. These high symbolic actions duly performed, the Camerlengo notified cardinals in all parts of the world that the Supreme Pontiff was dead, and summoned them to meet in solemn conclave to choose his successor.

Among the prelates to receive the Camerlengo's notification and summons, none was more disturbed than Lawrence Cardinal Glennon. His personal grief was not beyond control, for he scarcely knew the deceased Pontiff. Nevertheless, Glennon was deeply moved. To soothe his agitation he withdrew to his private chapel and gave himself up to prayer and meditation. The prayers were moderately comforting, but the meditations were immoderately bitter. From old knowledge and grim experience the Cardinal knew that a painful inequity was about to be suffered by the Catholics of the United States. Within the next ten days a new Pope would be elected, and in this election some twenty million American Catholics, Glennon among them, would be coolly neglected by the Roman See.

Narrow patriotism, Glennon could agree, was no ground for electing Christ's Vicar; the Holy Father, as head of the Universal Church, must transcend national boundaries. But if the Church were truly universal (and this is what bothered Glennon), why should America have such meager representation in the approaching conclave? Of the sixty cardinals accredited to the Sacred College, at least thirty-five would be Italian — and only two American. The proportion was grievously unfair, but a still more grievous unfairness would be perpetrated. The conclave would take place before the two American cardinals could reach Rome!

It had happened before, and Glennon saw that it was about to happen again.

By a provision of the Apostolic Constitution, the conclave must begin on the evening of the tenth day after the Pope's death. Rarely were American Cardinals able to cross the Atlantic in time to cast their votes. Though Glennon loved Rome with the genuine and profound love of his Catholic heart, the recurring injustice of the conclave galled him. Not that any protest had ever escaped his lips! For years he had choked down his choler. But the fact was clear: America, the country that made the heaviest material contribution to the support of the Holy Father, was in practice barred from the spiritual privilege of voting for him.

Glennon's superb Catholic faith caused him to believe that divine intention, operating through the College of Cardinals, would be expressed perfectly (though perhaps inscrutably) in the naming of Peter's successor. No matter who wore the triple crown, he would be God's choice. Lawrence Glennon's acceptance of this truth did not oblige him, however, to become feebly docile about it. As a Cardinal-elector he rated himself on a par with any Italian as a spokesman of the Lord. And because he was theologically entitled to regard himself as an instrument of God's will, His Eminence held very definite views about the next occupant of the Fisherman's throne.

The Cardinal's favorite candidate was his old friend, Merry del Val, former Secretary of State. What a Pope Merry del Val would make! Glennon snatched a fantasy of himself at the conclave discreetly canvassing suffrages for his favorite. The French, Irish, Spanish,. and South American delegations were being persuaded; segments of the Italian ring began to crack. Glennon started counting votes on his fingers.

At the thumb of his left hand, the absurdity of the whole business struck him. There he sat electing a dream Pontiff in Boston when he should be packing his trunks for Rome. Ridiculous! But a goose chase across four thousand miles of ocean, only to arrive as the conclave ended — wasn't that ridiculous, too?

Humility beckoned Glennon Romeward; dread of humiliation held him back.

The Cardinal emerged from his chapel more disturbed than when he went in. Entering the Tower Room, he saw his secretary sorting an unusually heavy mail. Stephen's chalky pallor was frightening . . . looks like St. Anthony coming out of the desert, thought Glennon. Taking his sister's death hard. Blames himself, no doubt. A cruel option, but how else could he have solved it? Caroming off the side wall of Glennon's mind, these thoughts promptly disappeared into the limbo of things that can't be helped. Other more pressing matters were forward.

"Tell the Vicar-General and Chancellor Speed to come here at once for a conference," he said to Stephen. "I want you in on it too, Father Fermoyle."

It was ten o'clock when the Cardinal's diocesan consultors ranged themselves around the refectory table. "I see you've read the sad news," Glennon began, eying the folded *Globe* in Mike Speed's hand. "Benedict is dead. God rest his soul. The Camerlengo's cablegram makes it official. The throne of Peter stands vacant, and most of my colleagues are already on their way to Rome."

Like any troubled executive, the Cardinal wanted the opinions of his advisers; like any other advisers, the priests around the table wanted a clearer idea of the advice expected of them. In silence they waited till Glennon spoke again.

"The privilege of taking part in a conclave is the highest prerogative of a Cardinal's office. Dearly would I love to exercise this privilege" — Glennon was being purposely oblique — "yet I am of two minds about making the journey."

"Why does Your Eminence hesitate?" asked the Vicar-General.

Not even to trusted subordinates could Glennon acknowledge hint or tint of disloyalty to Rome. He chose instead to state the problem in terms of time and space. "The conclave opens in ten days. Rome is four thousand miles distant. The question is this — how can I get there in time to cast a ballot?"

Stephen, trying to consider the immutable facts, found his brain fuzzy. No bounce, no *lift* to it. Grief, the great fogmaker. He heard Mike Speed suggesting: "Your Eminence might cable the Camerlengo, asking for two or three days of grace."

The Cardinal was tart. "A feasible idea — *if* the Camerlengo were anyone but Giacobbi. Unfortunately, the relations between the Lord Camerlengo and myself are marked more by coolness than cordiality. If I asked for an extension, he'd reply as he did at the last conclave. Giacobbi was Camerlengo then, too. And do you remember what happened?" Glennon jabbed his thumb over his shoulder like an umpire calling a base runner "out." "They held the election without me."

Memory of the old affront broke loose in Glennon's blood stream. "Do you wonder that I hesitate to race across the Atlantic — *and* the Mediterranean — only to hear Giacobbi's scornful 'You come late, Lord Cardinal,' as I stagger into the conclave?"

A tradition of secrecy made it undesirable for Glennon to reveal, outside the conclave, his cherished hopes for Merry del Val's candidacy. It was his strongest motive, but he could not mention it. He drummed the table testily. "Can any of you advance a reason why I *should* go to Rome?"

Chancellor Speed took it upon himself to utter the forthright speech the Cardinal wanted to hear. "The journey will be strenuous, and Your Eminence will probably arrive late. You may even be exposed to the Camerlengo's derision. But these painful facts do not, in my opinion, outweigh your obligation — both to your sacred office and twenty million Americans — to make the journey."

"Brave words, Michael." Irony masked Glennon's appreciation of his Chancellor's honesty. "Now that you've pointed out my duty, can you devise some mode of getting me to Rome? Shall I fly through the air in a Zeppelin or be translated as a pure spirit to the Eternal City?"

"Seagoing vessels still sail from Boston, Your Eminence." Mike Speed opened his *Globe* and turned to the shipping page. "Outbound steamers . . . let's see. The *Norumbega*, flagship of the Atlantic Line, sails tomorrow at noon."

"I know the boat," snapped Glennon. " 'Tis little better than a raft. Thirteen days to Naples. No, thank you, Michael. If I must be late, I prefer to be late in comfort."

The Chancellor lifted humorous-regretful eyes. "Too bad

you missed the *Stromboli*. She sailed at eight-thirty this morning."

Through a cottony fog Stephen heard a familiar name. "The *Stromboli*? That's Orselli's new ship."

"And who," asked Glennon, "might Orselli be?"

"An old friend of mine. He just broke the Atlantic record — ten days from Naples to Boston."

"Ten days?" Hope kindled the Cardinal's voice; reality doused it. "Ah well, he's sailed already."

Stephen got his brain turning at three-quarter speed. "If we sent Orselli a wireless — he might hold the *Stromboli* for Your Eminence."

"Has a captain the authority to do that?" asked Glennon (significantly, he stressed the word "authority").

"We can ask him." Stephen was on his feet. "Shall I try?"

A gambler's chance that an American cardinal might reach a conclave in time brought Glennon up fighting. "Try," he urged. "Try with everything you've got, Stephen. Beg your friend Orselli to stand by. No need for him to turn back — we'll catch up with him somehow."

The prospect of outfacing Giacobbi in conclave lifted Glennon to field-marshal stature. He spun to his aides. "You Mike, take care of my credentials and diplomatic passport. Get five thousand cash and a letter of credit from the bank. Vincent, pack my regalia in a single trunk. *Cappa magna,* rochet, and mozzetta are all I'll need. I can borrow the rest from Merry del Val. Stephen, stick to that phone till you get a wireless through to the *Stromboli*. Then pack a bag for yourself. I'm taking you with me to Rome as my conclavist."

Five hours later — five hours of the most brutal tension that Stephen had ever endured — the U.S. revenue cutter *Dolbear* drew alongside the *Stromboli* as she idled off the tip of Cape Cod. From the deck of the Coast-Guard cutter, skippered by Lieutenant Commander "Cuffy" McCrear (whose brother was a curate in West Newton), the side of the *Stromboli* sheered upward like a portholed cliff. Before Glennon could ask, "How'll we ever make it?" a boom swung outward from the top of the cliff, and a bos'n's chair came plummeting down like a spider on a slender thread.

Glennon gingerly inspected the apparatus. "A practical-looking device," he said. "Who goes up first?"

"By marine usage," advised Lieutenant Commander McCrear, "the highest in command is the last one off the ship."

"I like your sea rules," said Glennon. "But wouldn't it save time if" — he looked appealingly at Stephen — "if we went up together?"

And that was the way they went, the Cardinal sitting like a great bald-headed baby in Stephen's lap as the bos'n's chair swung over the *Dolbear's* side and was reeled skyward by an electric winch "like a fish in a basket," as Glennon said.

Captain Orselli greeted them at the companionway. "*Furfantino*," he exclaimed, wringing Stephen's hand. "Five days I wait in Boston to see you, then on the sixth you have a sudden whim." Orselli surveyed Stephen's gaunt pallor. "What have you been doing to yourself? No matter. Our Mediterranean sun will cure it."

The Captain's gold-embroidered hat came off in a sweeping arc when Stephen presented him to the Cardinal. "Honored to have you aboard, *Eminentissime*." Glennon extended his hand in frank gratitude. "You are most kind to stand by for us, Captain." As Orselli bent to kiss the Cardinal's ring. His Eminence forestalled that gesture of respect by twisting the diamond-crusted sapphire from his finger and thrusting it into Orselli's hand.

"A token of my appreciation, Captain Orselli. The Holy Father himself shall hear of your graciousness to the Archdiocese of Boston."

The Florentine's experienced eye told him that the Cardinal's ring was the most magnificent piece of jewelry he could ever hope to own. He murmured an astonished, "Thank you, Eminent Lord," then glancing up from the princely sapphire, his eye caught Stephen's. Neither the Captain nor the priest thought it fitting to share their private joke with the Cardinal.

TO MAKE UP for lost time, Orselli really tested the *Stromboli's* power plant. Twenty-four hours off Cape Cod the liner's patent log recorded the record-breaking distance of 661 nautical miles. To the Cardinal's query, "Do you think we'll reach the conclave in time?" Orselli confidently replied: "Either Your

Eminence will cast a vote in the Sistine Chapel, or the *Stromboli* will burst a boiler."

That was before the storm struck.

An Atlantic gale shrieking out of the northeast quadrant of the compass buffeted Orselli's nine-hundred-foot vessel like a fisherman's dory. Mountainous combers piled across the *Stromboli's* bow, their foamy crests flecking the Captain's beard with spume as he sought an opening through the impenetrable windwall. A merciless shipmaster, Orselli was taking no unnecessary chances. Even half speed meant risking the *Stromboli's* spine under the weight of those giant rollers. Moreover, the freezing spray on his beard suggested icebergs in the vicinity. Reluctantly Orselli set the bridge controls at "slow," gulped black coffee, and decided to enjoy the ordeal by hurricane.

He was confident that his new ship would ride out the storm. But every wallow and side slip of the great liner threatened the fulfillment of the Florentine's pledge. Should the hurricane last more than twenty-four hours, the *Stromboli* would steam into Naples too late. Therefore, the Captain fumed into his freezing beard and blasphemed the luck that was robbing his vessel of three hundred miles a day.

An officer in yellow oilskins handed Orselli a weather report: "Gales of hurricane velocity expected to continue for the next forty-eight hours. Icebergs reported south of fiftieth latitude. Clear and calm east of Azores."

Orselli tore the report into four pieces and threw them, one for each quarter of the compass, into the air. "What is this nonsense — 'calm east of Azores'?" he cried. "East of purgatory it is calm too, no doubt. Does that help us in this inferno of wind and iceberg?" A wave, ominous as a Doré engraving, rose off his port quarter. "Aiee-ee! *Un cavallone!*"

Up the cliff of a gigantic sea the *Stromboli* climbed. Orselli felt his ship obeying the laws of buoyancy her designers had built into her. Up, up she went like a steel kite. At the ridge of a wave, just short of the sky, she flattened out and hung suspended in middle air while her four bronze propellers, indecently exposed, spun against nothingness. A terrible shiver racked the vessel until her propellers engaged the water again. Then she plunged hissingly downward, nose into the trough of the wave, just as her designers had planned.

The performance of his ship filled Orselli with tenderness. *"Che bella cosa!* You beautiful thing," he murmured. "A creature so well made deserves to be well manned." For the next twenty-four hours, watch in, watch out, he remained on the bridge. So engrossing were his attentions, so sensitive her replies, that Orselli forgot he had a Cardinal on board. Only when the hurricane had cracked its cheeks and skulked away exhausted did Orselli discover that his ship was two days behind schedule on its pilgrimage to Rome.

Race as he might, not more than one of those days could ever be recaptured.

THE HURRICANE'S ILL WIND blew the grief from Stephen's heart. For three days he lay in his cabin, physically unable to stand. During an earlier phase of the blow he had managed to open the door between Glennon's stateroom and his own, but a forlorn wave of the Cardinal's hand told him that His Eminence was past caring for secretarial service. Back in his own bunk, Stephen surrendered to the torments of seasickness — and remembrance.

Images lurched past like figures in a migraine dream: Mona writhing in the filthy room at 5 Stanhope Lane; sheeted on the delivery table; washed and decently laid out in her casket. The despairing hunch of Din's shoulders at the cemetery; the rosary beads dangling from Celia's numbed hands — round and round whirled the fantasies on a carrousel of anguish. Above the shrieking wind rose mixed echoes of accusation and remorse: *Take me out of here, Stevie . . . A nickel for St. Anthony . . . I advise immediate termination of labor . . . foetus humani abortum procuraverint . . . Trust me once more, Monny . . .*

Most heartily sorry.

While the cabin bounced like a cube tumbling down a rocky hillside, Stephen clung to his berth, sick beyond sorrowing. To pray, weep, or even groan was impossible. Physical wretchedness filled him.

Odors assailed the membranes of memory: the carbolic stench of Gussie Lasquez' stairway; the pomade on Gongaro's hair; carnations withering in the funeral wreaths on Mona's casket; the closet staleness of Celia's ratty fur collar as she clung to him at the open grave — these surged up from his diaphragm in awful convulsions. Misery emptied him.

When the storm had spent itself, Stephen came on deck more haggard-green than ever. But violence of grief had spent itself too, and he was ready to let sun and sea caress him with forgetfulness. Dozing in a deck chair under a blue-silk sky, Stephen's strength and spirits rose. The *Stromboli's* prow cut the calm sea like a diamond, and as the lengthening wake healed the scar — first with foam, then in seamless peace — Stephen felt his own wounds healing, too.

His principal chore was to keep Glennon occupied — a task that would have taxed the resources of an entertainment bureau and the patience of a governess handling a refractory child. Anxiety about getting to the conclave had turned Glennon's soul into a weathervane pivoting on pure mercury: ceaselessly he boxed the emotional compass with fresh tantrums, and his fretting distrust of Giacobbi bordered on the irrational. Twenty times a day he would teeter along the edge of his monomania, then slip into a tirade against the Sicilian whom he regarded as the source of all his woes.

To check these outbursts, Stephen laid out a full-time program. Every morning he assisted Glennon at Mass in the *Stromboli's* exquisite little chapel. After breakfast they would promenade on the sun deck or play a game of shuffleboard to the accompaniment of Glennon's nervous calculations about the speed of the ship. Then came a session of coaching the Cardinal in Italian — a language that he had once used with fluency but had long neglected. Now he needed conversational practice — "a brushing-up," as he put it, "so that I won't trip over any dangling participles when I speak my mind to Giacobbi."

Still harping on that string, thought Stephen. Was Glennon a prey to fantasies, or was Giacobbi really an ogre? Stephen decided to find out. One morning as they strolled on the promenade deck, he ventured to ask:

"What do you think lies behind Giacobbi's hostility?"

The Cardinal launched into a rationalized explanation. "I could say that the Lord Camerlengo has a personal grudge against me — and it's true enough, he has. The beginnings of the grudge go back to the reign of Leo XIII, when we were both domestic prelates in that great Pontiff's household. Temperamentally, Giacobbi and I never liked each other. He didn't care for my piano-playing, and I could never stomach his fondness for parrots."

"Parrots?"

"Yes, his rooms were full of nasty birds, hook-nosed like himself, always screaming in some outlandish dialect — Sicilian probably. Some people found it amusing, but my observation about parrot lovers is that they're usually queer birds themselves."

Stephen smiled. "Something more important than piano-playing and parrots must have come between you."

"Numberless things came between us. My being an American irked Giacobbi. He resented the fact that God had blessed the United States, His newest plantation in the West, with so much wealth and vigor. To put it in a sentence, Giacobbi is one of those Italians who have run the Church so long they think it belongs to them."

Glennon went off on a fresh tack: "Giacobbi was jealous of the warm friendship between Merry del Val and myself. How it chafed him when Merry and I would return from a tramping holiday through the Alban Hills! And what peasant grimaces he would make when he heard us playing a Bach toccata arrangement for four hands!" Glennon paused to relish the memory of his old adversary's discomfiture. "But the iron really entered Giacobbi's soul one day when Pius X smiled paternally at a little game called *mandarino* that Merry and I used to play."

"*Mandarino?* What kind of game is that?"

"Merry and I invented it ourselves. It was played with four small oranges, or *mandarini*, that we'd toss back and forth at each other, keeping them in the air while we capped quotations from Horace." Glennon made juggler motions with imaginary oranges and started to recite a verse:

"*Quis gracilis puer, perfusus —*" As the Cardinal's memory failed him, Stephen completed the line:

"*Liquidus odoribus, urget te, Pyrrha, in multa rosa . . .*"

Glennon glanced at his secretary in surprise. "I didn't know you were a Horatian, Father."

"I'm one of Brother Felix's boys," said Stephen.

"Ah, yes. Brother Felix had a passion for Horace, too." Promptly Glennon went back to his gloatings. "Once we invited Giacobbi to play with us. Ha-ha — you should have seen him standing there — ho-ho — with his mouth empty — ho-ha — and his hands" — Glennon was a gelatine of laughter —"*and his hands full of oranges* — ha-ha-ha!"

"No wonder he doesn't like you," said Stephen. "But there's one thing I still don't understand. If the Cardinal Camerlengo is such a boor, how did he get on in the Church?"

"He got on," said Glennon, "because no matter what you think of him personally, he happens to be one of the shrewdest men in the service of Rome. His record as papal Secretary of State proves — and I admit it freely — that Giacobbi possesses the peculiarly Italian gift of *combinazione* — a mixture of ambush and chicane best known to diplomats. Yes, my boy, the Camerlengo knows European diplomacy as you know the Lord's Prayer. How the subtle refinements of march and countermarch dwell in his thick body I can't say. But there they are."

Having enjoyed his laugh and his bit of reminiscence, Glennon turned gloomy. "Perhaps God in His infinite wisdom has willed that I shall never cast my vote at a papal election. Nevertheless, I propose to find out exactly what His intentions are in the matter."

Then came the weathervane shift, the wheedling-voiced coda: "Like a good lad now, Stephen, run up to the bridge and ask the Captain if he can't make the ship go a bit faster."

FROM Glennon's tyranny Stephen sometimes escaped to Orselli's sun deck for a chat and a game of *Mühle*. A change had taken place in Orselli; he was quieter, less eruptive. Grieving for his country's postwar misfortunes ("Italy is a bootblack, an organ-grinder among nations," he said mournfully), Orselli had lost much of his volcanic exuberance. Yet he had gained a positive magnetism thereby. The cells of his personality were charged with a profounder current, and the emotional exchange between Stephen and himself crackled with new intensity.

Orselli's Don Juanism, once the chief aspect of his character, seemed to have vanished; apparently he no longer felt the need to assert his maleness in terms of high-seas dalliance. At fifty, the Captain was still teeming with the energy that has never found a better name than love, but for some reason not clear to Stephen at first, Orselli chose not to auction his charms among the female passengers — many of them attractive — who made the usual bids for attention. Though his stargazing act was still a feature of the voyage, and though he brought his usual professional zest to the performance, he showed almost nothing of his old conquistador technique.

It was after a dullish stargazing party that Stephen and Orselli tramped the veranda fronting the Captain's quarters. From the Azores came flowering offshore airs; the sky, a tabard of midnight blue, was blazoned with spring constellations. On so perfect a stage Orselli might have strummed *dolcemente* on any of a dozen responsive lyres; instead he paced the deck with Stephen and chafed at a cigar while delivering himself of a diatribe against starshine, women passengers and the unhappy lot of a shipmaster.

"Astronomy is a science, not an aphrodisiac," he raged. "How many times can one repeat the story of Cassiopeia" — Orselli's cigar indicated an irregular W in the northern sky — "and always contrive to make her a queen in a cosmic beauty contest? What are the facts about Cassiopeia? She — *it*, I mean — is a vernal constellation of five visible stars, one of which is a sign to navigators because it forms part of the equinoctial colure. But do these languishing creatures with ermine draped over their naked shoulders — do they care about such matters?" The Captain snorted like a disillusioned bull seal. "No, they must have a tale of celestial bawdry, a titillating bit for the boudoir. And how they quiver deliciously when I serve it up to them!"

Orselli veered into the confessional. "My way of life wearies me, Stephen. In the midst of these scented seductions I am lonely." He spat out his disgust. "Had Casanova been master of a luxury liner, he would have entered a monastery at twenty-nine."

Stephen recognized the ferment churning in Orselli — the scurf of guilt and self-reproach that rises, sooner or later, in every libertine soul. Whether it was sentimental froth or the living yeast of conscience, Stephen had no way of telling. As a priest and friend he undertook to investigate.

"What you're pleading for is a miracle of growth, Gaetano. Railing against your passengers won't help. Before the miracle can happen" — Stephen baited the hook with a persuasive figure — "you must settle on a fixed love, something to steer by, like Polaris up there."

Suggestible but unconvinced, Orselli considered the stars, each shining with a separate glory: golden Dubhe, blue Denebola, Vega the pale sapphire. "They are steadfast enough. It is I who waver, Stefano. Could I choose one from among so many? No, I am a false compass, unable to hold a true course."

Stephen tried to lift the sack of self-loathing from his friend's back. "*Assurdo!* Say that you haven't tested yourself, that you need adjustment. But false? Never!" Stephen was pleading now. "You have a genius for love, Gaetano. Give yourself a fair shot of fidelity. Put a period to these saloon-deck conquests and get married." ·

"Sweet, innocent Stefano! Clearly you have no idea of my requirements. Even a marriage broker with angels as his stock in trade would be staggered by them." Orselli seemed eager to prove his point. "Shall I run over, lightly, my list of specifications?"

"By all means."

Buoyed by the oral prospect before him, Orselli nipped a fresh cigar. "You have an ear for wonders, Stephen. Life is renewed whenever I talk to you." The Captain went through the ritual of lighting his Havana. "I may soar slightly. Do you grant me full freedom of rhetoric?"

"Within limits of clarity."

"Well, then, this treasure that I seek, this most-improbable she, must have, *primo,* a serene mind already ripened on the vine of maturity. No acid grape that sets the teeth on edge. And especially, *no bubbling.* She must be a still wine of delicate bouquet, a quiet Falernian that endears itself to nostril and palate before plunging into the deep veins that flood the heart." Orselli paused to inhale his Havana from cupped hands. "Is the first specification clear?"

"Most graphically."

"Next — to explore the practical side — she must be a woman of independent means and of an accepted family. A title would help, but is not obligatory. I shun the *arriviste* trollop, the social adventuress. I might forfeit my good name. I see this paragon wife-to-be solidly established in the intimate upper set of a world city — Rome, Vienna, Paris. To a cosmopolitan like myself this makes no difference." Orselli expanded the real-estate motif. "There is, of course, the matter of a residence: I should require a house in the best quarter of town, and a country estate, not more than twenty-five miles — thirty at the most — from the city. Neither isolated nor suburban, *capisce?*"

"Perfectly. But your conditions grow a trifle difficult."

"You speak of difficulties? We have not yet touched upon the most intimate difficulty of all — the problem of beauty." A nice delicacy prompted Orselli's question, "I have your permission to develop this theme, Stephen? It will not prove — overstimulating?"

"This is *your* scenario, not mine. Write it out; you'll feel better."

"Physician seraphic, practitioner to the troubled heart — I could lift litanies to your understanding." Orselli curbed his own rhetoric. "But to the subject. As you may know" — the Captain became a man admitting a weakness — "I am addicted to the *tipo guionico*, the Juno type, with a *punta*, a mere dash of Rubens. Bluntly, I like big women. I will be candid: there is a danger here — the risk of fat. Fortunately, Italian women have the secret of keeping the flesh firm till they are well past fifty. Indeed, I knew a Milanese countess, you will not believe this, Stephen, who at *sixty-olà*, what am I doing in Milan? The point is, one must select shrewdly. Otherwise" — Orselli's cigar traced gigantic billows in the dark — "the end would be tragic."

"I hate to interrupt you," said Stephen, "but is this dream woman animated by a soul?"

"But a soul of such sensibility! It will enliven her every feature." Orselli was off on another rhetorical flight. "The eye

tranquil as it contemplates inner goodness. The mouth a spiritual enigma — Gioconda lips vibrating between a prayer and
a caress, a taunt and an invitation. The chin, despite its soft
rondure, a proud guarantee of constancy. The throat marbling
in purity to a . . ." Orselli pulled up contritely. "Forgive me,
Stephen. On a night such as this, a man should be spared
anatomical details."

"Thank you, Gaetano."

Stephen recognized easily enough the elements of Orselli's
portrait: the woman part earth, part drug, part flight. He saw
also the same components of aspiration and yearning Dante
had poured into Beatrice, transforming her thereby from flesh
into essence.

"Do you see that haze filling the heavens?" Orselli was asking.

Gazing upward, Stephen saw the glow caused by clouds of
star dust whirling through the universe. Light mysterious and
original, an aureole of loneliness shining for itself, smiling on
itself alone. The grandeur of Genesis poured down.

*And God said: Let there be lights made in the firmament of
heaven, and let them be for signs, and for seasons and for
days and years.*

"Yes, I see it," said Stephen.

"Such a glow will surround the head of the woman I seek.
Do you think I shall ever find her?"

CHAPTER 7

THE BEAUTIES of a copper-sulphate sea were wasted on
Lawrence Glennon as the *Stromboli* plowed through the
Mediterranean. His anxiety deepened during the slow business
of docking at Naples, exactly forty-eight hours behind schedule. The conclave had begun two days earlier; already eight
ballots had been cast (two each morning and afternoon), and
only the hope of a prolonged deadlock kept Glennon in the
race.

At the gangplank Orselli apologized for his broken pledge.
The Cardinal comforted him. "The fault, my dear Captain,
certainly does not rest with you or your ship. Archangels could

not have done more. *Sta bene, capitano* — my blessing on you
and your vessel."

This time, nothing could prevent Orselli from kissing the
Cardinal's ringless hand.

At the railway station Glennon was agreeably surprised
when a gold-braided official greeted him with a chin-to-knee
bow and announced that a special train would speed His
Eminence to Rome. "This arrangement," explained the stationmaster, "is necessary because a railroad strike incited by Communists is tying up the regular passenger trains between
Naples and the Holy City. Ah, these Communists! By their
machinations they will paralyze the whole peninsula."

Glennon avoided political commitment in his speech of
acceptance. "I am most gratified," he said "that the Italian
government honors me with a special train. Dare I hope that
we may board it at once?"

"*Immediatamente*, Lordship."

The stationmaster's *immediatamente* turned out to mean a
two-hour delay caused by much ceremonial, the loading of
baggage, and telegraphing to Rome for hotel accommodations.
It was noon when the train puffed out of the station. "Who do
you suppose is behind all this?" asked Glennon, as they skirted
the volcanic base of Rocca Monfina on their northward course
to Rome.

"The Cardinal Camerlengo may have had a change of
heart."

"That would be giving the devil too much due." Glennon
gazed out the window at the magnificent scenery of the Liri
Valley. Mountains, cataracts, ruined tombs, and amphitheaters
whirled past, but he saw none of them. His eye was inward,
fixed on a barrel-vaulted chamber, gloriously frescoed, in which
sixty men sitting in canopied chairs were at this moment casting a ninth ballot for Peter's newest successor. By great good
luck the Cardinal might reach Rome in time for the next
ballot . . . if there should be a next ballot!

At two o'clock His Eminence began to get hungry. "Does
the Italian government provide no box lunches for itinerant
American cardinals?" The question was snappish.

"If you can wait till Frosinone . . . the place is famous for
its fruit." To divert Glennon's mind Stephen made a practical

suggestion. "Might it not be a good idea to change from traveling attire into the robes of a cardinal-elector?"

Irritably Glennon assented. With Stephen's help he donned
the violet-colored cassock worn by cardinals in mourning for
a Pope. Then he put on his rochet, a linen knee-length garment, long-sleeved, indicating the supreme jurisdiction of a
cardinal-elector. Around Glennon's neck Stephen hung the
diamond-studded pectoral cross, also symbolic of his ultimate
authority as a member of the conclave.

"Now," said Stephen, "you're ready to enter the Sistine
Chapel as a cardinal-elector."

The Cardinal's eyes filled, overflowed a little. "One aspect
of your character baffles me, Stephen. You defy mathematical
law by increasing your enthusiasm while dividing it with
others."

IT WAS FOUR-THIRTY P.M. when they reached the Central Terminal in Rome.

Standing irresolutely on the station platform, Glennon and
Stephen were met by a purple-caped member of the Vatican
household who, after introducing himself as Monsignor Panteleoni, led his charges to a limousine bearing the papal arms.
Monsignor Panteleoni ordered the driver to make for the Vatican *a tutta velocità*. Westward across Rome they sped. Not
until they crossed the Tiber at the Vittorio Emmanuele Bridge
did Stephen get his bearings. This part of Rome he knew. As
the limousine wove through a clutter of streets rising from
the Borgo, he braced himself for the head-on view of St.
Peter's.

First appeared the stupendous ribbed dome of Michelangelo, a massive helmet crowning the most ambitious structure ever conceived by man. Then the baroque façade —
cyclopic blocks of travertine, fronted by gigantic pillars and
approached by a magnificent triple flight of steps. In the center of St. Peter's Square stood the Obelisk of Caligula flanked
by two mammoth fountains. The whole square was embraced
in the stately ellipse of Bernini's colonnades — and between
these curving arms a vast, silent crowd, possibly two hundred
thousand people, awaited the feathery puff of smoke that
announces the election of a new Pope.

Stephen remembered waiting for the dramatic signal in this very plaza when Benedict XV was elected in 1915. White smoke indicated that a Pope had been chosen, while indecisive votes were signalized by black smoke caused by mixing damp straw with the burning ballots.

"The smoke has been black for three days," said Monsignor Panteleoni. "The conclave is in a deadlock."

"Pray God I may help break it," murmured Glennon.

Through a gate guarded by Swiss Guards in blue and yellow uniforms, the car glided into Vatican City. Inside the Leonine Wall the car halted in a courtyard flanked by halberd-bearing Noble Guards wearing scarlet pompons. This entire section of the Apostolic Palace had been walled off from the rest of the Vatican; literally, the conclave was taking place behind lead-sealed doors and bricked-up walls. Once the conclave began, no unauthorized person could enter, and no one could leave except in case of death.

With Monsignor Panteleoni as escort, Cardinal Glennon and his conclavist approached a handsomely caped nobleman, Prince Chigi, head of the illustrious family that for centuries has guarded the conclave against the world's intrusion. As Marshal of the Conclave, Prince Chigi wore a mantle of black velvet, a golden sword, and a Renaissance ruff. In his cocked hat waved a snowy plume, and from his belt hung an embroidered purse containing the keys of the conclave.

Monsignor Panteleoni whispered a few words to the Marshal, who doffed his plumes and requested the honor of examining Glennon's credentials. Stephen produced the documents attesting the Cardinal's ecclesiastical rank, privileges, titles, and exemptions. While the Marshal examined the parchment and scrutinized seals and signatures, Glennon was suffering purgatorial tortures. The nerves along his heavy-soled jaw contracted involuntarily; a blue-forked vein swelled in his forehead. At length the Marshal returned the documents with a courtly flourish, opened his embroidered purse, and drew forth the key to the outer gate. He thrust the key into an iron door, opening it from his side. Within, a face appeared at a revolving grille. Formalities were exchanged. Inside, another key turned. Slowly a door swung open.

Lawrence Cardinal Glennon, Archbishop of Boston, bowed

to the plumed Marshal. The Reverend Stephen Fermoyle, conclavist to the Cardinal, bowed also. They were entering the door when a thunderous shout arose from two hundred thousand throats in the plaza.

"*È bianco, È bianco.*" (It is white, it is white.) *Then,* "*C'è un nuovo Papa!*" (A new Pope.)

Stephen, following the eager lift of Prince Chigi's eyes, saw a puff of white smoke hanging like a feather above the roof of the Sistine Chapel. The *sfumata!*

Glennon saw it, too. "No, no," he cried, piteous tears of chagrin rolling down his cheeks. For the second time, a Pope had been elected without him. Twice he had lost the transoceanic race to Rome; twice he had been thwarted in the use of his electoral franchise, and life could not promise him another chance.

Glennon paled, tottered slightly, reddened, paled again. Stephen moved to the Cardinal's side with outstretched supporting hands. He expected to touch a crumpled sack of flesh, but as his hand touched Glennon's shoulder, the Cardinal stiffened as though a heavy voltage of electricity had charged his body.

Anger exploded like a depth charge in Glennon's throat. "Lead me to Giacobbi," he bellowed at the Marshal.

Prince Chigi was startled. The Marshal, a hereditary nobleman and a millionaire, had never had such a blast directed at himself. He started to draw himself up for a ceremonious statement, but Lawrence Glennon was beyond ceremony. He pushed past the plumed Marshal, thrust aside a Swiss Guard, and strode into the conclave door.

"I beg Your Lordship to forgive him," said Stephen to the Marshal. "He is very much disturbed." Without waiting for Chigi's reply, he started after Glennon. But Monsignor Panteleoni tugged at his elbow.

"Only cardinal-electors are allowed in the Sistine Chapel," he explained. "Permit me to escort you to the Sala Ducale, where the other conclavists are waiting."

Stephen caught a last glimpse of his Cardinal storming through a large sacristylike chamber. "God of electors," prayed Stephen, "save this man from conduct unbecoming to a member of the Sacred College."

STRIDING into the Sistine Chapel, Lawrence Glennon found himself in a chamber of quelling solemnity and rich twilight gloom. Knots of venerable men wearing the uncovered rochets of cardinal-electors were congratulating each other in the satisfied manner of peers who have just completed a difficult task. Along either wall were ranged canopy-covered chairs; at the end of the chapel stood an isolated altar of white marble, and behind this altar rose Michelangelo's magnificent fresco depicting the Last Judgment, the more terrifying now because twilight obscured it in shadows. In front of the altar stood an empty armchair in which the new Pope would receive the first homage of the cardinals who had chosen him as Christ's Vicar, Patriarch of the West, Bishop of Rome, and Keeper of the Pontifical Keys.

Glennon could not help remembering happier days when he had entered this historic chamber at the side of Pius X. Then the Pope's own finger had pointed out to him the marvelously foreshortened figures of saint and sibyl immortalized on the barrel-vaulted ceiling by the perfect artist. In this very Chapel Glennon had chanted responses while the Pope himself had celebrated Mass. Now he stood in the taper-lighted gloom, an unknown latecomer searching unfamiliar faces for some ray of welcome or recognition. Where were Pillot, Ruzyna, Von Hofen, Gibbons — wearers of the red hat when the century was young? Where was Vannutelli, adviser and confident of the great Leo? Dead, all departed.

And the living — where were they? Where was Merry del Val, leal companion of his youth? Where, for that matter, was Giacobbi?

A new more terrible fear smote Lawrence Glennon. Might it be that the Camerlengo was now Pope? Who *had* been elected?

At his elbow Glennon heard an Oxford-modulated voice. "Where have you been these many days, *caro* Glennon? We had prayed, some of us at least, that you might arrive earlier."

It was the Englishman, Mourne, an elegantly garrulous prelate with the face of a Blake archangel, and a halo of silver hair floating above his forehead. "There was a moment between the second and third ballots when your vote might have turned the tide."

Anxiety charged Glennon's question, "Whom did the scrutiny reveal?"

"*Laus Deo*, Achille Ratti of Milan. *Homo liber, homo librorum*." Compulsively, Mourne explained his pun. "A free man — and a man — ha-ha — of books. The former Ambrosian librarian, you know."

"Where is Giacobbi?"

"The Lord Camerlengo assists at the *immantatio* — the robing of the new pontiff. It is rumored that Ratti will make him his Secretary of State. . . . Ah, here they come now."

A hush fell upon the assembly as the new Pope, attended on one side by Cardinal Giacobbi, on the other by Cardinal Merry del Val, entered the Sistine Chapel. Attired in a dazzling white cassock, an elbow-length cape bordered with scarlet, and red slippers embroidered with a gold cross, the newly elected pontiff walked without eagerness or false humility toward the armchair in front of the marble altar. Achille Ratti, on whom the mantle of Peter had fallen, was a stocky, spectacled man in his middle sixties, a famous Alpinist and bibliophile, destined to wear the Fisherman's ring for seventeen difficult years. Seating himself on his temporary dais, he waited with serene patience while the cardinals formed in order of seniority for the first obedience.

Assisted by chamberlains, Lawrence Glennon took his place, eighteenth in line among the cardinal-priests. Approaching the Pope's armchair, he knelt, kissed the pontiff's hand, his knee, and the cross on his slippered toe. Achille Ratti, now Pius XI, leaned forward to embrace his colleague in Christ.

"We are happy to greet our American brother," murmured the pontiff, touching his lips to Glennon's cheek. The fact that the Pope recognized him somewhat mollified His Eminence but could not wholly soothe his chafed nerves.

The first *adoratio* over, Pius XI rose and retired to the Sistine sacristy for a brief refreshment of prayer. Meanwhile the cardinals, proceeding informally to the Sala Ducale, were joined by their conclavists; Marshal Chigi and his noble attendants swelled the brilliant court.

Stephen hastened to Glennon's side. Solicitude for his Cardinal's strength prompted the suggestion, "Your Eminence must be tired. Let us go to the hotel for a rest, a bath, and dinner."

"Rest can come later," growled Glennon. "First I must speak to Giacobbi. See how he preens himself at the center of the stage."

The Cardinal Camerlengo, standing with a group of dignitaries under a magnificent chandelier, stepped forward as he saw the American approaching.

"Welcome to Rome, Brother Cardinal," said Giacobbi. "I trust that you are well, and that you enjoyed your voyage."

"I am well enough, Lord Cardinal, and I did not enjoy my voyage." Glennon unbanked his glowering anger. "Why did you not wait for my arrival?"

Giacobbi could afford to be courteous. Although he had lost the triple crown, he was still the most powerful member of the Roman Curia, and already had his reappointment as papal Secretary of State assured. Correct to coolness, he answered Glennon's question.

"I had no discretion in the matter, Your Eminence. The Apostolic Constitution explicitly states that the conclave shall begin ten days after the Pope's decease."

"The bull *In hac sublimi* gives the Camerlengo wide discretion in interpreting the Constitution," retorted Glennon.

Giacobbi countered: "That bull also stresses the necessity of choosing a new Pope without delay."

"You interpret the Constitution to please yourself. If one of your precious Italian cardinals were delayed, you would stretch a point." Physical exhaustion impaired Glennon's higher centers of judgment. "But to an American, no consideration is given."

Provokingly bland, the Camerlengo smiled. "No consideration? You are overwrought, dear Brother. Were you not met by a special train at Naples — greeted on your arrival in Rome by a member of the papal household? All was performed in accordance with usage." Giacobbi's frosty politeness was more infuriating than ill-tempered language would have been. "And now, Eminence, you must excuse me. My duties oblige me to attend the Holy Father as he gives his blessing *urbi et orbe*."

Glennon was not to be fobbed off by an excess of punctilio. "I will state my case to the Holy Father himself," he growled.

"That is of course your privilege, dear Brother." The Camerlengo bowed, and sailed off with his entourage in a flotilla of violet vestments.

Stephen took Glennon by the arm. "Come." He spoke as a wiser, older brother reminding an overtired, naughty child that it was bedtime. Fighting back angry tears, Glennon allowed himself to be led away.

CHAPTER 8

IN HIS SUITE at the Ritz-Reggia, Lawrence Glennon collapsed. The race to Rome, the cruel glimpse of the *sfumata* at the very gate of the conclave, and the frustrating interview with Giacobbi had put a terrific strain on the Cardinal's heart. His immediate symptoms — acute precordial pain and an excruciating headache — alarmed Stephen. He got Glennon into bed, put a cold compress on his throbbing forehead, then asked the hotel manager for the name of a reliable physician.

Signor Renato Mirfoglia, manager of the Ritz-Reggia, was a carefully conceived specimen of the genus major-domo. Long service to a wealthy clientele, chiefly English and American, had given him a nice appreciation of their helplessness in a foreign land. But before giving Stephen the name of a doctor, Signor Mirfoglia, a purist in matters of counsel, wished to know what kind of doctor was needed.

"This malady that attacks His Eminence — is it perhaps of the tract digestive?" he asked discreetly.

"No, it's of the system circulatory."

"Ah!" Signor Mirfoglia caressed his mustache with profound understanding. "In disorders circulatory, Dr. Velletria is the physician of choice. Indeed, in all Rome, whom else could one name?"

Dr. Velletria's black-ribboned pince-nez and the white tuft of whisker under his lower lip gave him the appearance so prized by Italian physicians who had taken their medicine from Viennese masters. He was a diagnostician of the old tap-and-ponder school, yet modern enough to confirm his findings by scientific methods. After percussing Glennon's rib cage front and back, he wrapped a blood-pressure cuff around the

Cardinal's arm and pumped a rubber bulb until the column of mercury registered 220. At this improbable figure, Dr. Velletria rejected innovation. He placed his ear to Glennon's heart, listened attentively, and came up with the pronouncement: "Your Eminence suffers from a surcharge of arterial blood which finds vent in vascular symptoms."

The language might be dated, but the diagnosis was sound. Dr. Velletria moved on to therapy. "Absolute rest in bed, massive sedation, no excitement, visitors forbidden. I prescribe an attenuating diet of herb tea and rice wafers." He wrote out two prescriptions — one of them an herb brew of cabalistic fame — and announced that he would send in a nun from a nursing order.

"No nuns," said Glennon in terror. "I don't want any women fussing around me."

Dr. Velletria's palms-up gesture hinted that vascular patients were, on occasion, eccentric. "Your Eminence will need day and night attention."

Stephen stepped into the breach. "I'll take care of him, Doctor."

"Can I get up for the coronation next Sunday?" asked the Cardinal.

"It is an inconceivability. Your heart is in the stage of prefibrillation. To natures such as yours, a papal coronation would bring on a vascular crisis."

"Stop using that word 'vascular,'" snapped Glennon, turning his plum-purple face to the wall.

At the door Dr. Velletria whispered to Stephen. "A marked case. You have a sick man on your hands."

Stephen had not only a sick man, but a querulous one. Nothing pleased Glennon; he raged at his diet, fussed at street noises, and peevishly nagged his secretary-nurse until Stephen was obliged to draw upon his last reserves of patience. Because Glennon found sedative comfort in his rosary beads, he kept Stephen kneeling at his bedside making the responses for hours at a time. These sessions of prayer were punctuated by alcohol rubs and doses of herb tea. A dull, exacting routine, but it began to bring Glennon's blood pressure down to normal.

On the Saturday before coronation, he was well enough to

want visitors. "Where is everyone?" he asked peevishly. "Don't they know I'm sick? Why doesn't someone come and see me?"

Stephen knew that the whole city was preparing for the coronation, and that the high Vatican officials had little time for visiting. Tactfully he put the case to Glennon. "Wait till the coronation's over. Visitors will come swarming then. You'll have to barricade yourself — like the Bishop of Bingen in his mouse tower on the Rhine."

Glennon groaned at the ceiling. "Will you be so kind, Father Fermoyle, as to leave off Longfellow and get me something to eat? I cannot live forever on herb tea and rice wafers. I am vascular. The Italian quack says so. Very well then, fetch me vascular food. A chop, a cutlet, a piece of steak. Is there no blood-building meat in this pontifical city?"

For dinner that evening, Stephen fed his Cardinal a juicy sirloin. The effect was magically soothing: Glennon lay back on his pillows and beamed at his caretaker.

"You might enjoy seeing the ceremonies in St. Peter's tomorrow," he suggested. "Just because I'm bedridden" — the martyrish note was still well forward in his voice — "there's no reason *you* shouldn't attend the crowning."

Stephen declined. "I've seen a coronation. Besides, I wouldn't want to leave you alone. Who'd serve you your nice refreshing cup of herb tea?"

A diagonal grin crossed Glennon's face. "If the Fermoyles ever get a coat of arms, Stephen, it will show a large red heart, rampant, aflame with loving-kindness. Kneel by my bed, Son, and we'll offer up the Five Glorious Mysteries for the Pope's special intention."

On the day after the coronation of Pius XI, a stream of visitors began to pour into Glennon's suite. Vatican officials, freed from ceremonial attendance on the Supreme Pontiff, found time to pay their respects elsewhere. The Holy Father's private physician — a knightly copy of Dr. Velletria — dropped in for a session of pulse feeling. After a learned question or two he confirmed the vascular diagnosis and advised the patient he was out of danger. Glennon began to sit up — first in bed, then, as his blood pressure fell to 160, he was permitted to lounge, convalescent style, in the sunny living room of his suite. Thanks to the tea-and-wafer diet, he was ten pounds lighter and could view the world with a more chipper, less bloodshot eye.

One morning as Stephen was getting His Eminence into a dressing gown and slippers, a commotion arose in the hallway. Opening the door, Stephen saw Signor Mirfoglia and a detachment of assistants making clear the way for a personage of sublime grandeur. Down the corridor came a tall prelate, one of the handsomest men that Stephen had ever seen. With a chamberlain's flourish, the manager presented Stephen to His Lordship, Rafael Cardinal Merry del Val.

Stephen knelt to the sapphire of the man who twice had been a candidate for the papal tiara. At sixty-five, Merry del Val was straight and spare as a Toledo blade. On his noble forehead sat the scarlet biretta of his rank, and he wore his great broadcloth cape like an admiral of St. Peter's fleet.

"Is my old friend Cardinal Glennon well enough to receive me?" he asked in a liturgical baritone.

"I'm sure he is. Will Your Eminence come in?"

The management retired backwards. Taking the visitor's cape, Stephen opened the door of Glennon's room. "Cardinal Merry del Val is here, Your Eminence."

"Rafael?" A week in bed had put buoyancy in Glennon's voice and step. He bounced from his chamber like the Biblical bridegroom in reverse, and moved toward his old friend with arms outstretched.

"Lorenzo!" The scene was too tender, too intimate for a third pair of eyes. While the old comrades embraced each other, Stephen hung Merry del Val's broadcloth cape in a closet, then discreetly vanished into his own room.

Lying on his bed, worn out by the long week of ministrations, Stephen rejoiced for Glennon's sake that the great Merry del Val had found time to make this visit. Viceregal in carriage, physically magnetic, and gently humorous (his amused smile at Mirfoglia's attentions revealed that), Merry del Val was everything that an ecclesiastical prince should be. Stephen was pondering the inscrutability of God's way with His seeming favorites when he dozed off. Glennon's voice summoned him back to reality.

"Cardinal Merry del Val has brought me a *dono*," said Glennon. "It's in his cape. Will you be so kind, Stephen, as to search the inner pocket for the Cardinal's gift?"

Stephen thrust his hand into the silk-lined pocket of the broadcloth cape, and drew out a paper bag.

"That's it," said Merry del Val. He took the paper bag from Stephen and held it tantalizingly before Glennon's eyes. "Guess what I have here, Lorenzo?"

"Animal, vegetable, or mineral?"

"Is it likely that I would be carrying diamonds — or rabbits — in a paper bag?"

"Cherries?" Glennon's delight in the game stripped twenty years from his countenance.

"You are warm. Guess again."

"Peaches?"

"In February? You sybarite! Try once more."

"Not — *mandarini?*"

Laughter filled the room as Merry del Val took some small oranges from the bag, and tossed them jugglerwise in the air. "I though you might enjoy a bout at our old game. Do you remember the rules?"

"I remember the rules well enough. But I've forgotten most of my Horace." Mischief gleamed in Glennon's hazel eyes. "Perhaps Stephen here could play in my stead."

Merry del Val took the suggestion agreeably. "Would you like to try a classical passage, Father?"

The first baseman in Stephen told him that he could catch the oranges without difficulty. Only his rusty Horace troubled him. Still, was it such a disgrace to be downed at this classic game by a distinguished Cardinal? "If you let me pick my ode, I'm willing to try," he said.

"Eminently fair. And if no one objects, we'll dispense with the orange-tossing part. To be quite truthful" — he turned to Glennon — "I haven't kept up my old sleight of hand."

"Hedging, eh? Go for him, Stephen. I'll be referee."

Of all Latin lyrics, Stephen liked best the poem in which Horace describes spring's return to a frozen world, then draws the melancholy contrast between nature's ever-cycling seasons and man's irreversible descent to ashes and shade. The poem seemed delicately appropriate now; Roman spring was in the air; rivers were at flood with melting snows, and these two

ancient comrades were renewing memories of by-gone days.
Stephen took up his stance facing Merry del Val some ten feet
away and began:

> *Diffugere nives, redeunt iam gramina campis*
> *arboribusque comae . . .*

Smiling approval at the text and delivery, Merry del Val
tossed the next line back at his opponent:

> *mutat terra vices, et decrescentia ripas*
> *flumina praetereunt . . .*

Glennon was on his feet, eager as a child. "I know *that* one,"
he exclaimed. "Try me on the next verse, Rafael. Stephen will
coach me if I break down."

Back and forth from lip to lip the golden verses flew. As
the two venerable Cardinals approached the end of the poem,
its significance touched them — especially the line, "Who
knows if Jove, who counts our score, will toss us in a morning
more?" But when, after a little bobbling, Glennon managed
to cap the final verse, they rushed toward each other laughing.

"If Giacobbi could only see us now!" Glennon cried. "How
the Sicilian would writhe!"

Tone and content told Stephen that his Cardinal was well
again. He had weathered Atlantic hurricanes, survived the
slings of ecclesiastic misfortune, and the darts of Curial
neglect. Neither separately nor altogether had they downed
him. The same surcharge of arterial blood which, in Dr. Velletria's language, "found vent in vascular symptoms" was
throbbing now with renewed vitality through Glennon's resilient, perdurable heart.

It was shortly after the game of *mandarino* that Stephen got
in touch with Alfeo Quarenghi. He addressed a note to the
office of the papal Secretary of State, and received a reply by
hand:

> Dear Stefano: Can you come to my place tomorrow eve-
> ning? Enter Vatican City through the Archway of the Bells;
> the guard will direct you thereafter. My best to your ailing

Cardinal. With lively anticipation of our reunion — hastily but affectionately yours, Alfeo.

While Glennon and Merry del Val entertained each other after dinner, Stephen set out for Quarenghi's lodgings in Vatican City. At the Archway of the Bells, the guard supplied directions that brought Stephen safely through a maze of courtyards and passageways to a masonry structure tucked into a western embrasure of the Leonine Wall. Here, in a kind of sentry box sat an ancient porter gazing Quasimodo-like at the dome of St. Peter's silhouetted against the cool young moon of Roman spring. When Stephen asked for Quarenghi, the porter slipped off his sentry stool, pointed to an oaken door halfway up a flight of stone steps, and said:

"Knock. Monsignor Quarenghi is expecting you."

At Stephen's knock the oaken door swung open and there stood Alfeo Quarenghi holding out both hands in an affectionate greeting that establishes the timeless relationship of teacher and pupil. He led Stephen into a white-walled chamber big as a tennis court and almost as bare. Except for a silver crucifix and a narrow strip of Byzantine tapestry, two sides of the chamber were unadorned. Bookshelves from floor to ceiling lined the remaining walls. In the center of the floor a glowing brazier took the chill off the air; deep in a corner lighted by an iron floor lamp stood Quarenghi's desk and two high-backed chairs. Only the dimensions of the room saved it from being the traditional monastic cell.

"Sit down, Stefano. Let me look at you." Quarenghi tilted the lampshade slightly to throw a franker light on his visitor. "How long has it been? Seven years? Yes, I see that the arch-typographer Time has traced deeper serifs on your lips and forehead. That is desirable. Otherwise, what a characterless psalter one's face would be!" He lowered the lampshade. "Do not read too curiously in *my* Book of Hours, Stefano."

Quarenghi had definitely aged. Hair that Stephen remembered as jet-black was now sprinkled with gray; an ascetic regimen had pared every ounce of extra flesh from face and body. Having passed through the diplomatic hell of a world war and harrowing nunciatures to Sofia and Belgrade, Quarenghi looked to be exactly what he was — an embodiment of the exhausting tension between the worlds of fact and idea.

The world of fact lay spread on his desk in the form of dispatches and reports from the chancelleries of three continents; the world of idea rose behind him in shelf-crowding volumes of philosophy, literature, and law. Quarenghi pulled down a book bound in gold-tooled calf and handed it to Stephen for his inspection. "This is the special binding I gave to your translation of *La Scala d'amore*. How completely you disproved the Italian proverb: *'Traduttore traditore.'* I would not have believed that a work could be carried with such fidelity — and elegance — from one language to another."

Stephen opened the handsomely bound translation of *The Ladder of Love*, and saw on the flyleaf the inscription in his own handwriting: *"To Alfeo, who labors in another part of the vineyard. Devotedly, Stephen."* Leafing through the volume, he remembered phrases and paragraphs that had cost him many a painful hour of decision. "Even a poor translator couldn't damage your ideas, Alfeo. They're timeless, indestructible. Sometimes when the job wasn't going well, I'd cheer myself by quoting Chesterton's paradox: 'Whatever is worth doing is worth doing badly.' Then I'd keep on."

Quarenghi's brown eyes gleamed with pleasure. "That is the *summa* of all wisdom, Stefano. You have learned it early. Any attempt at perfection is like a chorale in two voices — the upper cymbal of spirit clashing against the despotic metal of fact. We must accept it as the sound that life makes. An echo perhaps" — Quarenghi's eyes momentarily sought the crucifix in the shadows — "of the groan that escaped His lips at the last."

In seven years Quarenghi had not changed; his duties might be different, his responsibilities new, but he was still the teacher of the *Logos*, the utterer of consecrated truth. His purity reminded Stephen of an indestructible substance, capable of dissolving other substances, yet immune itself to dissolution.

Like distance runners settling down to a comfortable jog, the two friends lengthened out their conversational stride. Quarenghi was fascinated by Stephen's account of the obscure numberless duties in the life of a parish priest, and sat like a man listening to music while Stephen described his pastorate in L'Enclume. The felling of the pines and the distribution of the profits on a co-operative basis particularly interested him. And he was visibly moved when Stephen told of Paul Ireton's setting forth to found a new parish with only a nickel in his pocket.

"How much is a nickel?" asked Quarenghi.

"About a lira."

"Think of starting a church with one lira! What enormous courage and vitality you American Catholics must have!"

"I'm glad to hear you acknowledge it, Alfeo." Stephen spoke with the frankness permitted in any discussion between intellectual equals. "Sometimes we get the impression in the United States that Rome regards America as a sort of stepchild."

"Stepchild?" Quarenghi strove gently to correct the implication. "The Church extends her love and solicitude equally to all her children."

Stephen dared be dry. "That solicitude wasn't convincingly demonstrated in the recent conclave — or the one before it."

Quarenghi acknowledged the touch. "I can't blame you for feeling as you do, Stefano." He rose and paced thoughtfully against the backdrop of his bookshelves. "I am violating no confidence when I tell you that His Holiness is much worried about the clause in the Apostolic Constitution that makes it impossible for American cardinals to reach Rome in time for a papal election. He is eager to remedy that injustice. Has your Cardinal yet had his audience with the Holy Father?"

"No. It's scheduled for tomorrow at eleven."

"Good. Let him be prepared to mention the matter of the 'ten-day rule' when he speaks with the Holy Father *in camera.*" The cinnabar glow from the brazier threw Quarenghi's long shadow across bare walls as he strode up and down the monastic room. "I am grateful to you, Stefano, for having opened my thinking on this subject. Never before have I viewed the situation with quite such clarity. It is possible that the Holy See's preoccupation with the Old World may have been responsible for her seeming neglect of the New. And a certain provincialism in American prelates may have blinded them to the universal nature of the Church."

Quarenghi blew the fading charcoal into a brighter glow. "Our governing thought for the future should be — how can

Rome and America be brought to a closer understanding of each other's problems? Adjustments must be made, points of view reconciled. American energy, instructed and guided by Rome, may well be the decisive factor in the difficult years ahead."

Quarenghi tempered his vision of the future with a realistic awareness of the tempo at which life travels. "Mind you, this work of regeneration will not happen overnight. Decades, generations — centuries, perhaps — must pass before the task is completed." He paused at Stephen's chair as if to measure the younger man's response to his words. "Would you be willing to dedicate your life to a task that certainly will not be finished in my time — or yours?"

"Whatever is worth doing," said Stephen, "is worth doing slowly."

"You have the great temperament, Stefano. Universal enough to be Roman, outspoken enough to be American. What a joy it would be to work with you!"

Moon-blanched clouds were riding above Michelangelo's mighty dome as Stephen left Quarenghi's lodgings at midnight. Across deserted courtyards, through shadowy colonnades, he came to the Archway of the Bells. From his heart arose a chorale — echoes of his conversation with Quarenghi — the upper cymbal of aspiration ringing against the realistic metal of fact. The percussion filled Stephen with the sound that life makes at its best, and the reverberations of that sound were triumphant, selfless, slow.

BY AN auspicious union of faith and architecture, the thousand rooms of the Apostolic Palace lead inevitably to a spacious second-floor chamber overlooking St. Peter's courtyard. This, the combined library and workshop of the Supreme Pontiff, is the room nearest the tomb of the Founding Apostle. Across its threshold flows a daylong stream of personages, lay and ecclesiastical: rulers and envoys of foreign powers; cardinals prefect and Palatine assistants; heads of tribunals and congregations, chamberlains of the papal household, and canons of the Cathedral chapter — all seeking audience with the unique executive who directs the destinies of the Roman Catholic Church. They state their business, present their pleas to the white-cassocked, red-slippered man who combines in his person the triple powers of legislator, judge, and priest. Though the manner of approach is strictly prescribed, and though the pontiff employs the royal "we" in his locutions, he conducts the interviews with as much human patience and personal tact as God and experience have placed at his command. Infallible only when defining matters of faith and morals, *ex cathedra,* the Supreme Pontiff is not exempt from the possibility of error in his temporal judgments. It is this latter consideration, perfectly realized by the wearer of the triple crown, that makes his diadem a burden of grievous weight.

On the morning of February 22, 1922, His Holiness Pope Pius XI, Bishop of Rome, Vicar of Jesus Christ, Supreme Pontiff of the Universal Church, Patriarch of the West, and Primate of Italy, sat behind the long table in his private study. The scholarly, spectacled Pope was giving thought between audiences to the multiple cares of his office. Barely ten days had elapsed since the beginning of his pontificate; echoes of the solemn coronation chant, *"Tu es Petrus,"* had scarcely subsided when the groans of a distracted world broke in upon the pontiff's human ear. From every quarter of the globe, chords of misery were rising. Europe was sunk in a postwar abyss of physical and economic exhaustion; Austria, long a bastion of the Church, lay broken and starving; Ireland grappled in civil strife with England. In the Soviet north, torches of Antichrist were being lighted. In the Quirinal Palace, once the property of the Holy See, a discredited king made fumbling attempts to rescue the Italian people from pits of anarchy. And above the clash of parties, a black-shirted demagogue was bellowing his violent prescription for the ills consuming Italy.

So much for the world. And what of the Vatican itself? Still a prison, and its occupant still a prisoner. It occurred to the pontiff that his life span coincided almost exactly with the Holy See's refusal to acknowledge the seizure of its temporal domains by the House of Savoy in 1870. Voluntary imprisonment within the Vatican walls was the only weapon the papacy could use against its despoilers. Morally, that weapon had been most effective; the spiritual credit of the Vatican had never been higher than at present. But financially, the Holy See was at its lowest ebb. The Supreme Pontiff had not been surprised, on querying the Apostolic treasurer, to discover that the papal coffers were almost empty.

Billions of lire were due from the Italian government in settlement of the estates it had torn from the papacy. But not a single *centesimo* of this bribe had ever been accepted by the Holy See. Sooner or later the vexing Roman question that had plagued the relations between Vatican and Quirinal for fifty years would have to be settled. Meanwhile Pius XI would continue to remain a voluntary recluse within the Leonine Wall rather than be a pensioner of the House of Savoy.

Dark indeed was the horizon. From one quarter only, a gleam of hope appeared. America! The western star, ruddy with faith, was rising in the heavens. True, Rome had hitherto paid scant attention to that star. Rumors had reached the pontiff's ear that Vatican indifference to American affairs was beginning to be interpreted as a wanton slight to twenty million loyal Catholics of the English-speaking New World.

High on the Holy Father's calendar this balmy spring morning was a program for strengthening the ties between Rome and its prosperous provinces of the West. In a few moments the prince regnant of one of those provinces — Lawrence Cardinal Glennon of Boston — was scheduled for audience. Pius XI scanned the two sheets of memoranda, refreshing his memory on the subject of the United States in general and the Archdiocese of Boston in particular. One memorandum, containing a vast amount of usefully compressed information, was signed by Quarenghi. The other, touching more intimately upon the personal history of Lawrence Glennon, bore the signature of Merry del Val.

At the door of the papal study appeared the *maestro di camera,* traditionally ruffed and veloured. "His Eminence Lawrence Cardinal Glennon, Archbishop of Boston, is in the secret antechamber, Your Holiness."

"We are ready to receive His Eminence." The Supreme Pontiff, like any other executive easing muscular tension before an important interview, adjusted the bibelots nearest him on his desk. He moved a gilt statuette of St. Ambrose, patron of scholars, two inches to the left, and thrust a gold medal awarded him by the Società Alpinista (His Holiness had been in his youth a distinguished mountain climber) a trifle to the right. He leaned forward to bury his face in a bunch of pink and white cherry blossoms on his desk, then felt in the fob pocket of his white cassock for an article much loved but no longer needed.

As the library door opened to admit the American Cardinal, Pius XI arose to receive the homage of his visitor. From the infallible side of the table he saw the corpulent figure of a man about his own age, sinking to the full kneeling posture prescribed by papal etiquette. Through a pair of high-myopia spectacles, His Holiness watched Cardinal Glennon rise with considerable difficulty and advance to the center of the room. Before the American could begin his second genuflection the Supreme Pontiff came around the end of the table, hands outstretched, myopic eyes tender with pity.

"Let us dispense with the kneeling, dear Brother. Our joints are too old for that. Take this armchair . . . I will sit on the sofa." Pius XI could be affable; he knew every tactic of charm. Observing that Glennon's short legs dangled an inch or two from the floor, the Pope slid a gold-embroidered hassock under the feet of his guest.

"We are deeply concerned about your high blood pressure, *caro* Glennon," he began. "Did our Italian physicians succeed in lowering the column of mercury that rises in their terrible instrument?"

The Pope's solicitude soothed Glennon. The hassock under his feet gave him the double security of touching bottom and of being cared for — feelings quite different from those that Giacobbi aroused. Comfortably he folded his plump hands. Pius XI was a man one could talk to.

"Your Italian physicians are wonder-workers, Holy Father. The herb tea of Dr. Velletria began my cure, but your kindness in sending Dr. Marchiafava completed it. I am most thankful to Your Holiness."

From across the gulf of authority the Pope lifted his hand (the one bearing Peter's ring) and made deprecatory nothings in the air. "We elders must cherish each other. Can you not imagine how Moses must have grieved when one of his beloved counselors fell ill?"

The Holy Father's Biblical reference put the conversation just where Glennon wanted it. The Sacred College of Cardinals was the Roman Catholic counterpart of the seventy elders named by Moses to aid him in governing the tribes of Israel. But the Hebrew elders had this advantage over Glennon: they were not obliged to race across perilous seas in order to attend a council!

With the delicate tool that the pontiff, consciously or not, had supplied, the American Cardinal proceeded to make his point.

" The Holy Father is most flattering when he suggests comparison between a Hebrew elder and myself. Unquestionably, Moses grieved when one of his advisers, either through illness — or some other cause" — Glennon was tactfully oblique — "was unable to take part in the councils of Israel." A winning candor, tinct with dryness, seasoned Glennon's smile. "But can Your Holiness imagine the disappointment of the absent elder? How luckless, how stricken by God the poor man must have felt when the council met without him."

"A Talmudic nicety, dear Brother," said the Pope. "We are obliged to admire the finesse of your argument. Indeed, you could not have more subtly laid bare a problem that has long troubled us. The Holy See laments the injustice that has hitherto deprived American cardinals from participating in a conclave." Having acknowledged so much, the Pope paused to consolidate his position with a query. "Have you any thoughts as to how the injustice may be remedied?"

The question was fair, the answer frank. "Since Your Holiness invites suggestion, may I point out that the ten-day provision of the Apostolic Constitution is the key to the situation. Might not the time be extended, so that American cardinals may enjoy in future conclaves the solemn privilege of casting their ballots in a papal election?"

Pius XI recognized the justice of the plea. "It is within our power," he said, "to extend the period between the Pope's decease and the opening of the conclave. We will do so by altering the Apostolic Constitution. Hereafter fifteen days — eighteen if necessary — shall elapse before the balloting begins."

Moved by the generosity of the papal concession, Glennon bowed his head. The heartbreak and humiliation of his voyage had not been in vain. "I am most grateful, Holy Father.

Personally and in behalf of twenty million loyal American Catholics, lay and clerical, I thank you."

With his forefinger Pius XI tapped Glennon's skullcap lightly. "And we respond, dear Brother, by thanking *you* for your straightforward presentation of the matter. Had you failed to speak truthfully" — a teasing note entered the pontiff's voice — "you would not be worthy to celebrate the birthday of your great countryman, George Washington."

The Roman pontiff smiled at Glennon's amazement. "Did you think us wholly ignorant of American history? We can scarcely blame you. Our knowledge of the United States is slight — too slight perhaps. Yet such as it is, we sometimes find it rewarding." Pius XI removed his glasses, and polished the thick lenses reflectively. "While saying Mass this morning we were struck by a most unusual coincidence. As you know, today is the Feast of St. Peter's Chair — the day on which our Lord founded His Church on the rock Peter."

"A glorious feast, Your Holiness. May it be celebrated throughout the world till the end of time!"

The Roman pontiff slipped his gold-rimmed spectacles over his nose, and gazed curiously at Glennon. "Does it not seem a good omen that this date, February twenty-second, should also be the anniversary of your founding father, Washington?"

"An omen almost prophetic, Your Holiness. The marvel is that no one, either in Rome or America, has ever pointed it out before."

Pius XI grasped the teaching ferule of his office. "Many things must be pointed out. Henceforth, Rome and America must vie with each other in discovering elements of common strength. Is it meaningless that one of our most ancient titles is Patriarch of the West? In the time at our command, Lord Cardinal, let us speak of ways and means whereby two great Western institutions can become better acquainted."

For an hour they talked, the Italian pontiff soliciting American support in the coming years of his reign, and the full-blooded Cardinal renewing his devotion to Rome by this exchange of views with his Supreme Pontiff. The Pope spoke enthusiastically of the work being done by the North American College in Rome and agreed with Glennon's suggestion that its buildings should be remodeled. His Holiness expressed pleasure at the splendid organization of Glennon's Archdiocese, based on the pattern of the Roman Curia. "A model for the New World," were the Holy Father's exact words. Whereupon His Eminence sincerely praised the new Codex Juris Canonici as a work of amazing clarity and compression. Which indeed it was. Glennon spoke of Orselli's kindness in waiting off the tip of Cape Cod, and Pius XI made a note of the Captain's name.

With great frankness the pontiff then discussed the finances of the Holy See. "Our treasury was never more depleted," he sighed. At this point Glennon bade the Holy Father be of good courage. "America will carry an increasing part of your burden," he promised.

His Holiness, without binding himself by commitments of any kind, sounded Glennon on the subject of increasing the number of American cardinals. "In your opinion," asked Pius, "should not the Archbishop of Chicago be elevated to cardinalitial rank?"

"Such an elevation is deeply deserved, and would be warmly applauded by the entire United States," replied Glennon.

The hour being almost over, His Holiness turned to more personal matters. "We learn — no matter where or how — that the journey to Rome cost you your sapphire, dear Brother."

"Yes, Holy Father, I gave it —"

Pius XI held up his hand to indicate that details were unnecessary. "Suffice that you gave it away in a brave attempt to reach the conclave." Like a father rewarding a dutiful son, the pontiff put two fingers into a fob pocket and drew out a beveled sapphire. "We no longer have need of this ring." He pressed it into Glennon's plump hand. "It gives us great pleasure to present it to our beloved brother in Christ."

Glennon was almost speechless. "Your generosity humbles me," he managed to murmur.

"Who humbleth himself shall be exalted." To indicate that the audience was over, His Holiness arose and escorted Glennon to the door of the library. The pontiff's left hand was on the American's shoulder; his right hand was turning the chased bronze doorknob when he remembered something.

"You have as your secretary a gifted young priest named Fermoyle?"

"Yes, Holy Father. Father Fermoyle is a valued assistant, tested and proved on many occasions."

"We have had golden opinions of him from those closest to us. Monsignor Quarenghi speaks highly of his linguistic powers, and Cardinal Merry del Val describes his personal charm in glowing terms." His Holiness made a curious remark. "We are also informed that he is singularly without fear in the presence of his ecclesiastical superiors."

Glennon remembered his first encounter with Stephen. "Singularly without fear," he agreed.

"Yet — how shall we put it — not arrogant or overweening?"

A thousand memories of Stephen's docility and loving-kindness supplied Glennon's answer. "Father Fermoyle is a curious combination, Your Holiness. He has a soft heart and a hard mind. He can bend neck and knee in obedience — but for stiffness of spine, I have never met his equal."

His Holiness weighed the mixed testimonial. "*Bene, bene,* dear Brother. It occurs to us that Father Fermoyle might perform valuable liaison services in the Vatican Secretariat of State. Have you any objections to such an arrangement?"

Glennon gazed at the ring in the palm of his hand.

Gained a jewel, lost a jewel, he thought. Aloud he replied: "Your request has the force of a command, Holy Father. Sorry as I am to lose my secretary, I rejoice at the opportunity for wider service that the Holy See offers him."

A week later — almost seven years, to the day, since his ordination as a priest — Stephen received a papal brief appointing him a domestic prelate with the title of Monsignor. The appointment entitled him to wear the violet cassock and mantelletta, and assigned him to duty as a clerk in the Congregation for Extraordinary Ecclesiastical Affairs.

As a farewell gift Lawrence Glennon sent Stephen to the best ecclesiastical tailor in Rome. "Get two of everything. See that they're the finest," were the Cardinal's orders. "We'll have none of this out-at-the-elbow business among our American clergy in Rome." And when the violet capes and cassocks were delivered after many fittings, it was Glennon himself who fingered the watered silk critically and showed Stephen how the new regalia should be worn.

RICHARD CLARAHAN, summoned by cablegram, had the honor of escorting the Cardinal back to Boston via the famous shrine at Lourdes. Because Clarahan had never been to Rome, Stephen extended himself to make his classmate's visit something of a busman's holiday. To spare Clarahan the pangs of envy, Stephen refrained from wearing his new clerical outfit. Between these two promising clerics, obviously marked for advancement in the Church, a cavalier truce existed. They could afford to be generous about each other's successes. Only once did Clarahan slip beyond the bounds of good taste. After a courtesy call on Alfeo Quarenghi, Stephen's immediate chief in the Secretariat of State, Clarahan came away with a query in his fine voice and forehead.

"Isn't Quarenghi the chap whose book you did into English?"

"That's right."

Clarahan was busy aligning the edges of the new facts at his disposal. "Your translation must have helped, eh?"

"It certainly didn't hurt," said Stephen, and let it go at that.

Loading Glennon onto the train for Lourdes was the last secretarial service that Stephen performed for His Eminence. The Cardinal's farewell was a potpourri of Polonious etceteras. "Try not to make enemies . . . engage your friends with hoops of steel . . . give every man thine ear but few thy tongue" — such was the gist of Glennon's advice. At the end he lapsed into a gruff moisture of eyes and larynx. "Stay a good priest, Stephen. Don't let the dye of your cassock seep into the lining of your heart." He tugged affectionately at the ribbon of Stephen's cape. "Good-by, my Son."

"Good-by, Your Eminence." Stephen wanted to fling his arms around the old man's bulky torso. Instead, he knelt for his blessing.

BOOK FOUR

Seventh Station

CHAPTER 1

IN THE VAST and intricately geared mechanism of the Roman Curia — that ensemble of ministers and tribunals which assists the Sovereign Pontiff in governing the Church, Monsignor Stephen Fermoyle became an obscure cog. As a clerk in Quarenghi's division of the papal Secretariat of State he was given a desk in a cubbyhole on the top floor of the Vatican Palace. His office was a no-period cubicle, one of many others carved out of an attic unused until the time of Leo XIII, just before the turn of the century. Its masonry floor was covered by uncarpeted duckboards; from damasked walls originally gold-colored but now rusty and faded, two steel engravings of former secretaries of state gazed formidably at Stephen. His desk was a hand-me-down of someone's former grandeur; its rococo legs and mother-of-pearl contrasted oddly with the telephone, wire baskets, and Remington typewriter that went with the job.

A preliminary briefing by Alfeo Quarenghi instructed the new clerk in the large outlines of Vatican diplomacy. "The Congregation for Extraordinary Ecclesiastical Affairs," said Quarenghi, "devotes itself to maintaining friendly relations between the Holy See and sovereign powers throughout the world. Whether these powers be monarchies, republics, or democracies makes no essential difference to the Holy See. The Church accommodates herself to all forms of governments and civil institutions, provided the rights of God and the Christian conscience are left intact. I want to make it clear to you, moreover, that the internal politics of these governments, their commercial, military, and diplomatic arrangements with other countries, are of no interest to the Vatican unless they threaten the free exercise of the Catholic faith."

The priest in Quarenghi shone through the ecclesiastic administrator. "Supporting the entire structure of Vatican diplomacy is the frank intention to preserve and extend, through the mediacy of the Church, Christ's promises to man.

Every papal brief and encyclical, every bull and concordat, merely repeat and emphasize this motive." One of Quarenghi's rare smiles took the dogmatic edge off his remarks. "With these brief instructions you are qualified, Stefano, to begin making your share of human blunders as an attaché of the Vatican Secretariat of State."

Stephen's first assignment was to sort and distribute the huge volume of mail that poured into Quarenghi's section of the Secretariat of State. Every morning an official from the Vatican post office would deposit two or three mail sacks on the floor of Stephen's office. Dumping an armful of letters onto his mother-of-pearl desk, Stephen would slit the envelopes, rapidly scrutinize the contents and route them to the proper office. Thus, all communications from European governments (excluding Italy) were sent directly to Monsignor Quarenghi. Letters from North and South America were placed in a wire basket for Monsignor Guardiano, Quarenghi's *segretario* or chief clerk. Communications from India, China, and Japan were forwarded to the Secretary for Oriental Affairs. Finally, all documents bearing on Italian matters were bundled together and delivered to the magnificent apartment of Pietro Cardinal Giacobbi on the floor directly below.

The mere physical handling of this huge volume of mail was in itself an education. The scope and variety of Vatican contacts with other countries amazed Stephen; even his hasty scanning of the correspondence streaming into the papal Foreign Office gave him a world's-eye view of the Universal Church in action. Across his desk flowed a torrent of reports from Apostolic delegates, nuncios, and foreign envoys accredited to the Holy See. Skillfully phrased notes schooled him in the forms as well as the content of Vatican diplomacy. Opening a letter postmarked The Hague, Stephen might read: "Her Majesty's Government wishes to explore with the Holy See the implication of recent Catholic missionary activities in Batavia, with a view to defining the pre-existent rights of Protestant missions in this field." The note would go to Quarenghi, who in turn would bring the question up in his daily conference with Giacobbi. A Mexican bishop might plead for the restoration of Church property seized by the Mexican government; his plea would go to Monsignor Guardiano. The papal nuncio to Warsaw, after detailing Communist interference with a religious procession, would urge the Vatican to remind the Polish government of its engagements to the Holy See, clearly stated in the Constitution of 1919. Stephen rarely learned the final outcome of these affairs, but at least he glimpsed the nature and scope of Vatican affairs of state.

From the jigsaw puzzle of correspondence placed on his desk every morning, Stephen was able to form an over-all picture of the role played by the Church in her relationships with foreign governments. He learned that the Church, though one and indivisible, addressed mankind on two levels: by means of the sacraments she spoke to the most intimate and mysterious part of the human soul; by methods of diplomacy the Church concerned herself with such temporal arrangements as would guarantee maximum freedom in the task of preparing men for eternal happiness with God. Faced by shifting human complexities, the Vatican attempted, with varying success, to remind the world of the one unchanging, non-political, and divine truth: *God is*.

Gradually Stephen's duties were increased. Quarenghi began asking him to make condensations of diplomatic documents and to prepare lists of *dubia*, or questions that might rise in his mind concerning them. (These questions guided Quarenghi in his later discussions with the Cardinal Secretary of State or the Supreme Pontiff.) To condense and translate a report required from six to twelve hours; the preparation of carefully conceived *dubia* was even more exacting. Stephen spent long days in the Vatican library, making researches that would enable him to frame the queries that would high-light matters for his chief.

ALONG with junior attachés of other congregations, Stephen lived in the Camera di Diplomazia, a kind of ecclesiastical boardinghouse in Trastevere. It was a polyglot crew that gathered around the dinner table every evening; although Italian was the dominant tongue, an international babel always arose when the talk became controversial. At the head of the table sat Monsignor Miklos Korbay, an iron-throated Hungarian attached to the Sacred Congregation of the Fabric of St. Peter's. Korbay's duty was the maintenance and repair of the great Basilica — a task demanding special knowledge in a field lying somewhere between architecture and engineering. Long command over an army of repairmen had given the Hungarian the manners of a drill sergeant and the voice of a badly cast bell. He was animated by two notions: first, that St. Peter's dome would collapse unless he, Korbay, personally supervised its repair; second, that all nobility except Hungarian was *nouveau* if not spurious. On these two themes he was compulsive; Stephen never heard him discuss a general idea. Once, however, while making a sight-seeing tour of the Basilica, Stephen saw the Hungarian suspended on an aerial scaffolding in the vast cupola, some four hundred feet above the cathedral floor. Cassock tucked under the belt of his trousers, Korbay resembled a high-wire trapezist performing his act without benefit of a net. Then and there Stephen decided that the Hungarian had a right to brag, if he wanted to, about his special relations with the dome.

At the foot of the dinner table sat Alphonse Birrebon, a bilious little Frenchman, whose training in canon law made him a priceless secretary to the Rota, but a frightfully pedantic legalist in matters of table talk. His pedantry was offset by the Celtic wit of Padraic Logue, who sat beside him. Next to Logue sat Monsignor Carlos Mendoza y Tindaro, a gloomy Spaniard attached to the Sacred Congregation Rites. Monsignor Tindaro took a dark view of democracy, and predicted that it would one day overwhelm the twin institutions of throne and altar. He held stubbornly to the Hapsburg formula that the tide should, indeed ought to, be swept back with repressive brooms, and listened sourly when Stephen suggested that there was no necessary contradiction between the ballot box and a lively devotion to the sacraments.

Most attractive to Stephen was Roberto Braggiotti, subsecretary of the powerful Consistorial Congregation. Braggiotti was a native Roman of old family; born in an ancient palace halfway between St. Peter's and the Quirinal, he had no desire to scale the social ladder because he was already perched on its topmost rung. This captivating Roman in his middle thirties was unquestionably the best informed man at the table. His volatility and intense patriotism reminded Stephen of Orselli, but the brilliant churchman possessed intellectual and moral dimensions that the Florentine Captain lacked.

The talk that spring turned chiefly on the impending collapse of the Italian government. Events were sliding down an inclined plane; apparently nothing could stop them. The long-serviceable coalition between great landowners in the south and manufacturers in the north was cracking under pressure of popular demand for reform. Successive Quirinal ministries, unable to withstand postwar assaults on throne and lira, had crumbled pitifully. Meanwhile down the length of the peninsula, Mussolini's voice was thundering:

"Leaders, legionaries, Blackshirts of Milan and Italy! A day of glory is coming for the Italian people. We must conquer. Fascism demands power and will have it. *Viva Italia! Viva fascismo!*"

"Who is this firebrand?" asked Stephen one night at supper. "Is he demagogue or man of destiny?"

"Neither," rasped Korbay. "He is an *arriviste* . . . a man of no family. . . ."

"Whose battle hymn," added Tindaro, "merely hastens the day of rabblement."

Logue slid his thrippenny bit across the table. "God preserve the man from cross cows and rabbit holes. The Sinn Feiners will rally round his broomstick after he cleans up Italy. . . . Speaking of broomsticks, have you heard the one about the Catholic priest who caught an old woman sweeping her front steps on Sunday?"

Braggiotti quietly took charge of the subject. "Remove your spectacles of bias and blinkers of wit, gentlemen. Look clearly at this Mussolini, and you will see that he is bred of historic necessity. Italy is a bundle of loose rods lying in a quagmire of defeat. Mussolini will gather up the rods of power, bind them together with cords of discipline into the ancient Roman symbol of authority."

Patrician arrogance made Braggiotti's voice ring like a coin of imperial mintage. "At the head of a resolute elite, Mussolini will restore Italy internally, deal harshly with her foes, avenge her wrongs, and emerge as the savior of our national honor."

Monsignor Birrebon masked his Gallic fear of a strong

Italy with the question: "How would the Church fare under such a regime?"

"Better than she has fared under the House of Savoy. Could she be poorer, less honored than during the last fifty years?"

"But Mussolini is an atheist, an avowed anticlerical," persisted Birrebon.

"He is also an anti-Communist," countered Braggiotti. "I saw him quell a Communist riot in Milan with only a few lightning-forked words. But these matters are accidental. Mussolini realizes, both as a patriot and a politician, that the prestige of the Church is Italy's soundest asset." He riddled Birrebon with the shrapnel of quotation. "Did not Il Duce say in Parliament last year: 'The development of Roman Catholicism throughout the world, the fact that four hundred million people in every land have their eyes fixed on Rome — these are matters that must fill every Italian with pride, and attract the interest of every Italian politician'?" Braggiotti delivered his *coup de grâce*. "A Frenchman wouldn't understand that."

The peacemaker in Stephen sought to snatch the argument from the pit of nationalism. "How does His Holiness regard Mussolini?" he asked.

"Realistically! How else?" Braggiotti put on the dangerous mantle of prophecy. "I predict that if Mussolini knocks on the bronze gates of the Vatican, they will be opened to him."

"You are wrong, I tell you!" said Birrebon.

Braggiotti's reply blasted his opponent off the table. "*Non me lo dica, perchè io sono Romano.*" (Don't tell me, I'm a Roman.)

Only a man with two thousand years of imperial tradition behind him could have said such a thing. It was probably the most arrogant statement that Stephen had ever heard. Yet Braggiotti had not intended to be overbearing. Unconsciously he had made the assumption that the Roman habit of mind was the criterion for all other thinking.

Comparing himself with Alfeo Quarenghi and Roberto Braggiotti, Stephen was aware of their richer texture, more profound knowledge, surer touch. What mysterious gifts had made Rome the lawgiver and moral governor of the Western world?

Stephen earnestly sought an answer to this question. He did

not find it immediately or completely, but the question itself took on a sharper definition, when he collided personally with the massive bulk of Pietro Giacobbi, papal Secretary of State.

THE COLLISION took place at a Thursday-morning meeting of the Congregation for Extraordinary Ecclesiastical Affairs.

Every Thursday the Congregation met in the Cardinal Secretary's office on the second floor of the Vatican Palace. Stephen did not usually attend these conferences, but Quarenghi sometimes invited him for the experience to be gained in watching an important Vatican committee at work. The gathering reminded Stephen of Glennon's meetings with his diocesan consultors, except that Giacobbi's diocese was the world, and his advisers a corps of veteran diplomats. There were other features, too, not to be found in Boston. As Giacobbi came down the corridor from his private apartment, his favorite parrot might be heard screeching: *"Truffatore di carte"* (you old cardsharper) — a bizarre yet oddly pertinent leitmotiv for the deliberations that followed.

On this particular May morning, as Giacobbi strode across a Bruges tapestry-carpet to his desk, he reminded Stephen of a veteran matador about to dispatch his usual quota of bulls. He sat down at his huge Quattrocento desk and surveyed his assistants, violet-cassocked for the most part, seated in a semi-circle before him. Quarenghi and Guardiano, the active elements of the Congregation, occupied smaller desks at opposite horns of the crescent. Stephen, rawest of apprentices, had the end chair in the second row. The Cardinal Secretary whipped a pair of horn-rimmed bifocals onto the ridge of his beaked nose and plunged without overture into the grim business of Poland.

Warsaw, early in 1922, was a source of grave concern to the Holy See. Persecution of Catholic priests had increased in severity; since the last meeting of Giacobbi's Congregation the situation had notably worsened.

The Cardinal absorbed Quarenghi's report on Poland in three swift glances, and addressed his colleagues with a harsh-heavy voice. "I am advised by Cardinal Puzynka that during the past week three churches were burned in the suburbs of Warsaw and seven religious schools closed throughout the country. I need not tell you, *monsignori,* that the Constitution of 1919 has been torn up by Soviet anticlericalists. A crisis impends."

And what, Stephen wondered, can be done about it?

"It is the Supreme Pontiff's desire — a desire with which I heartily concur — that vigorous representation be made to Dr. Grabowitz, the Polish envoy to the Holy See. Will you, Monsignor Guardiano, be so kind as to prepare a preliminary draft of a note to the Polish ambassador, pointing out the clauses in the Constitution of 1919 that explicitly guarantee to the Church full freedom of worship and education?"

Wordlessly, Monsignor Guardiano made a notation. The draft was as good as written.

"In the event that the note fails to produce the desired result, inform Dr. Grabowitz that the Holy Father is prepared to send a legate to Warsaw."

Another nod from Guardiano.

"Keep *L'Osservatore Romano* informed of our negotiations. The full force of publicity must be employed to acquaint Europe with Soviet tactics."

Poland disposed of, Giacobbi turned to Quarenghi for new business. "You have the folder on land nationalization in Mexico?"

"Here, Eminence."

Giacobbi flicked through the dossier like a physician examining the chart of a tiresome old patient. "Hmm . . . where Cortez planted the cross, Obregón uproots it. It is one thing to nationalize the soil of Mexico, but this rascal wants the subsoil, too. Must convents be pillaged because oil is discovered a thousand feet beneath their foundations?"

"I have repeatedly put that question to the Mexican government," said Quarenghi. "To date I have received no reply."

"Brigands!" roared Giacobbi. "Gregory VII would have led an expedition against them. Today we have only our moral weapons. Well, the acoustics of the Church are still excellent, Monsignor. Have you explored the full possibilities of rousing public opinion in America?"

"Opinion is divided in the United States, Your Eminence."

"Divided?" Giacobbi brought his head up with the pugna-

cious lift of an old ram whose authority has been challenged.
"How can there be any division of opinion on such a subject?"

Quarenghi, the good subordinate, refused to lock horns with
his superior. Giacobbi's gaze traveled along the double row of
chairs and settled on Stephen. "Perhaps our American member
can throw some light on the peculiar thinking of his countrymen."

Stephen had no wish to inherit the old feud between Giacobbi and Glennon. Still, he had been asked to speak. While
the whole Congregation waited, he began with modesty:

"Your Eminence must realize that I have no special knowledge of Mexican affairs. The only contribution I can possibly
make is to refresh Your Lordship's memory on the subject of
public opinion in the United States."

Giacobbi's grunt gave Stephen a new access of confidence.
The Cardinal Secretary of State might have the rest of the
world at his finger tips, but on this American string Stephen
could teach him — tactfully, of course — where and how to
pluck. "As Your Eminence knows," he went on, "the population of the United States is predominantly Protestant. Furthermore, there exists in my country a traditional and very real
separation between Church and State. Catholics do not claim
the special position vis-à-vis the American government that
the Church enjoys in Poland or Austria." Stephen summed up.
"In view of these facts, I believe it would be impolitic — if not
impossible — to arouse American public opinion in matters
domestic to Mexico."

Giacobbi's head was down. "It is your considered judgment,
then, Monsignor Fermoyle, that the American public would
view with disfavor the Holy See's request for moral and diplomatic pressure south of the Rio Grande?"

"That is my judgment, Your Eminence."

Giacobbi gave the yearling diplomat a toss with his horn.
"How then do you account for the armed intervention of the
United States in Mexico in 1916? Have you forgotten so soon,
Monsignor, the shelling of Veracruz by American warships
. . . the landing of your gallant Marines . . . the occupation
of Chihuahua by General Pershing? What is your explanation
of these activities?"

Stephen felt the horn under his ribs. "That was a punitive expedition," he stammered. "The rights of — of American nationals had been infringed by — by Mexican bandits."

Giacobbi gave him the other horn. "Come, Monsignor. Naïveté is out of place in these councils. What are the facts? American capitalists, fearful that their oil rights were in danger, persuaded your idealistic Mr. Fourteen-Point Wilson to interfere in the domestic affairs of Mexico. I pass no judgment on the matter. I merely state it as a guiding precedent. If America could roar so mightily in behalf of oil in 1916, might it not murmur today in behalf of God?"

Giacobbi dropped his bullying tone and became the preceptor. "One final admonition, Monsignor Fermóyle. I have no desire to tread out the patriot flame burning in your American breast. But I pray you, control this preening on the subject of democracy. It is neither the ultimate nor necessarily the best form of government."

Giacobbi ended his lecture, and proceeded to consider the affairs of Peru, Ireland, British Guiana, and Spain. Stephen sat with burning cheeks through the rest of the session. No one spoke to him as he left the chamber (although Quarenghi's eyes followed him sympathetically to the door). Wretchedly, Stephen climbed to his office on the third floor and sat down at his mother-of-pearl desk. Not since Din had given him a razor-strop thrashing at the age of twelve had he taken such a beating. Snatches of the miserable argument, begun without his volition, and swept along by Giacobbi's dislike of America, played back at him from the taunting record of memory. How puny, smug, his arguments had been! Then Giacobbi's deeper analysis of the crux, "If America could roar in behalf of oil in 1916, might it not murmur today in behalf of God?"

The fugue scratched on, then branched off into searching variations. Did loyalty to the Holy See mean surrendering one's faith in democracy? Could Stephen alter his lifelong conviction that the Church and State, in America at least, ought to remain separated? Did the United States have the right to interfere in the domestic affairs of Mexico? Everything Stephen believed cried no to this last question. Yet, if intervention could be justified in terms of oil, how could it be rejected in terms of religion?

Out of the questioning fugue, out of his personal humiliation, one truth gradually emerged. Stephen saw that he was
underinformed, insufficiently educated for his duties in the
Secretariat of State. He realized, as a result of his run-in with
Giacobbi, that he could properly serve neither the Vatican nor
his country until his knowledge of both was vastly increased.
He began a systematic course of reading in history and diplomacy, with special emphasis on the concordats that had
marked the relationship of Rome with foreign powers. He saw
how patiently (and successfully) the Holy See had battled
against the nineteenth-century idolatry of the State, expressed
in Bismarck's *Kulturkampf,* Vienna's *Los von Rom,* and the
Gallicanism of France. Stephen's political reading buttressed
his realization that the Roman See was the only international-
minded organism in the modern world. He marveled at the
tenacity displayed by Rome in reminding state and peoples
that man was a spiritual as well as a political creature. And
seeing how stubbornly the links of Peter's chain had held
through mortal storms, Stephen found no alternative to the
belief that an alloy of divine metal had entered into the forg-
ing of the links.

Meanwhile, what of democracy?

After months of intense and disciplined study, Stephen came
to the private conclusion that the democratic idea with
its emphasis on tolerance and individualism was the most
hopeful manifestation of Christ's spirit in human affairs. And
despite Giacobbi's opinion to the contrary, Stephen continued
to believe that the American phenomenon of a free Church in
a free State had produced a Catholicism as stanch, loyal, and
vigorous as any that had preceded it.

He buttressed his convictions on a brace of noble statements made by two great leaders of modern Catholicism. One
was an Italian Pope, Leo XIII, who said in a pastoral letter
to the peoples of the world: "God wills that civil power and
religious power remain distinct, but He does not will them to
be divided."

The other was a statement made by the American prelate,
Cardinal Gibbons:

"The separation of Church and State in America seems to
be the natural, inevitable, and best conceivable plan — the

one that would work best among us, both for the good of religion and of the State. Any change in their relation would be contemplated with dread. The Church here enjoys a larger liberty and more secure position than in any country today where Church and State are united. There is deep distrust and strong dislike of the intermeddling of the State with concerns of religion. . . .

"As a citizen of the United States — and without closing my eyes to our shortcomings as a nation — I say with a deep sense of pride and gratitude that I belong to a country where the civil government holds over us the aegis of its protection without interfering in the legitimate exercise of our sublime mission as ministers of the gospel of Christ."

Reading and thinking, trying always to establish a realistic balance between his loyalties to Rome and America, Stephen grew in knowledge and humility. He began his day by celebrating Mass in the Chapel of St. Martha, then worked steadily at his desk until late afternoon. For exercise he took a daily walk along the Tiber or played a game of handball in the back yard of his ecclesiastical boardinghouse. Supper was followed by a cigarette and a period of conversation with Roberto Braggiotti, who, as Stephen grew to know him, was an unfailing source of personal charm and stimulation. During long Roman twilights they talked shop, sweetest of subjects. Afterwards Stephen would climb to his room for uninterrupted hours of study. Toward midnight he would read his divine Office and, kneeling beside his iron cot, pray for himself and those he loved.

Bounded without, boundless within, regular almost to the point of monotony, Stephen's life as a *minutante* seemed complete. Almost it was. And it remained so until Roberto Braggiotti invited him one evening to a social gathering at the Palazzo Lontana.

CHAPTER 2

BRAGGIOTTI had long been urging Stephen to go about socially. "If you wish to be of maximum service as a Vatican diplomat," said Roberto, "you must circulate quietly in Roman society, be seen in the best houses, become acquainted with everyone, listen to everything — including rumors, many of which will be nonsensical — and say nothing." The advice sounded not unreasonable; sponsored by Roberto, whose family connections and personal charm admitted him to the great houses of Rome, Stephen had made more than one excursion into the curious world of Black Society.

The Blacks, or *Neri,* including some of the oldest families in Rome, were the Pope's stanchest supporters. As a protest against the seizure of the Patrimony of St. Peter by the Italian government in 1870, the Blacks had severed all contacts with the royal House of Savoy. In the midst of their native city, they led an existence comparable to courtiers who had followed a deposed sovereign into exile. Politically and socially their lives were severely restricted; the men took no part in Italian affairs of state, and the women had relinquished the pleasure of attending White functions in the Quirinal Palace. To compensate for their narrow existence, the Blacks had escaped into a make-believe world of manners. They had lifted etiquette to the condition of an art — as outmoded, perhaps, as falcony — but an art, nevertheless, as Stephen discovered.

He found the system puzzling at first; only gradually did he begin to grasp its elaborate rules. He could easily understand why, in the great strongholds of Black Society, a special throne room was kept in readiness for the day His Holiness could again leave the Vatican and pay visits of honor to those who had remained faithful during his long imprisonment. (If no special room were set aside, a tapestried armchair was kept turned to the wall.) Stephen appreciated the profound loyalty and deep religious faith that buttressed these symbols, yet some of the trivia of Black Society annoyed him. He noticed, for example, that in certain houses many of the older men wore a glove only on the left hand, leaving the right hand bare. In other houses both hands were gloved, but the thumb of the right hand was exposed.

"What's this off-and-on glove business?" he asked Roberto.

"Two theoretic reasons lie behind it," explained Braggiotti. "The glove was originally a patent of nobility. You never see a peasant with gloves on, do you? Traditionally, the glove is also associated with another symbol of rank — the sword. Some believe that the right hand must be kept unencumbered, the better to draw a sword in defense of your sovereign. Another school holds that you must be ungloved in order to accept the hand of your host the moment it is offered you. Any delay might be construed as unfriendly."

"I see. But why the exposed right thumb?"

Braggiotti smiled patronizingly. "In all societies, there are degrees of intimacy. A seven-hundred-year-old family such as the Odaleschi, whose ancestors supported the Hildebrandine Popes against German brigands, cannot be expected to give their entire hand to late-comers. Anyone arriving after the seventeenth century — and that includes you, Americus — is lucky to get a thumb and forefinger."

"Do they take themselves *that* seriously?"

"Only a few of the old purists remain. The whole business of Black and White is breaking up. But it won't disappear entirely until the Roman question, involving the Pope's temporal sovereignty, is settled. Meanwhile, I advise you to lay aside your New World notions. 'When in Rome . . .'"

Stephen followed his mentor's advice to the letter. By the end of the post-Lenten season Braggiotti had taken him, with the consent of his ecclesiastical superiors, to several dinner parties. The doors of the ancient palaces flew open to the handsome Roberto and his American friend. A valuable education in the social life of Rome ran parallel to Stephen's schooling in Vatican diplomacy; his ear became attuned to the buzz of political surmise and ecclesiastic forecast rising from the salons of Black Society. He heard the usual rumors: that the royalist party of France would soon be crowning a Catholic king in Paris, and that Soviet agents were shipping vast numbers of hopeless cripples to the shrine at Lourdes with a view to discrediting its miracles. To top everything, he heard that Queen Wilhelmina was being prepared for conversion by a Carthusian confessor. Stephen's common sense discounted such rumors, but by tactfully avoiding any expression of opinion, he maintained a diplomatic tradition by no means peculiar to ecclesiastics. He watched Braggiotti and other members of the hierarchy maintaining a similar silence, and marveled at the drawing-room technique of cardinals who by a sibylline smile could at the same time confirm and deny some bit of Vatican gossip.

Women were of course present at these affairs. *Neri* hostesses, inevitably titled, mingled with wives and daughters of ambassadors to the Vatican. Invited musicians entertained the company after dinner. Because Romans "love a voice," Stephen heard a great many arias in the best *bel canto* manner that spring. He was surprised to discover that not all Italian women were brunettes; frequently he encountered blondes, exquisitely pink and gold in coloring. To sit besides some gorgeous woman in *décolletage* while a soprano poured forth Isolde's passion was something of a trial to Stephen. He mentioned it to Roberto, and Braggiotti's answer was "sensible" in both the English and French meaning of the word.

"Bothers you, does it? Well, my friend, one of the advantages of clerical life in Rome is the immunity you develop to malaria — and beautiful women."

Stephen found himself particularly at home in the Palazzo Lontana, a baroque seventeenth-century structure on the Corso. Its convex façade of pinkish-yellow travertine made the palazzo resemble a private Coliseum. One entered the palace by a side gate opening into a walled courtyard, then took a modern elevator to the *piano nobile,* and walked through a series of coldly superb chambers — each a museum of murals, marbles, and tapestries — to the warmer but equally spacious salon of the Princess Lontana. The Princess, born Loretta Kenney of Steubenville, Ohio, had brought to her titled husband (one of the four chamberlains *a numeri* to the Pope) several millions of anthracite money, a head of natural red hair that forty years had not faded, and a talent for collecting cosmopolitans. The Princess, a true multilingual, also had an ability to carry flying translations from any side of the French-English-Italian-German quadrangle to any other, and exercised her skill simply because she wanted each of her guests to understand what the other guests were saying. In a hostess less charming, this ambition might have been fatal.

Because Stephen particularly enjoyed the Princess, he gladly accepted her invitation to an after-dinner party at the Palazzo Lontana early in May. This would probably be the last party of the season; soon, everyone who could get away from Rome's wretched heat would flee to the seashore or mountains. The long oval chamber with its coffered gilt ceiling and space-creating mirrors was filled with a crush of guests as Stephen and Roberto entered. Tonight the leading figures of Black Society were out in strength: ambassadors wearing the ribbony badges of their rank; prelates in purple and scarlet; *Neri* wives and daughters, magnificently jeweled and gowned. Princess Lontana, a circlet of diamonds glittering in her red hair, came forward to meet the young monsignors. Ten feet away from Stephen and Roberto she extended both hands, addressed several guests with her green eyes, others with a private flutter of her fan, and still others with all the languages that she knew. Her salutation to Stephen was pure Ohio American, and her greeting to Roberto was Italian equally good.

"You are angels to come, both of you. Now, *everyone* is here." Her voice found the confidential level of a whisper. "This evening our *pezzo grosso* . . . *das Prachtstück* — or as we'd say in America, 'the main event' — is Cardinal Merry del Val. Pay your respects to him, Monsignors, then feel free to do what damage you can among the ladies." She accepted the "*gnädige* Prinzessin" and hand kiss of the Bavarian envoy, then turned once more to Stephen and Roberto. "Do not under any circumstance leave before supper. We have brought in *langouste* from Marseilles, Hochheimer 1911 from the *Schloss* itself, and Signora Piombino — mezzanine and all — from La Scala." With these varied injunctions and enticements the Princess began dividing herself between the Austrian Ambassador, Graf von Huntzstein, and a monocled admirer, Lord Chatscombe.

Roberto nudged his companion. "Better go easy on the Hochheimer, Fermoyle, or you'll be seeing two of everything." Laughing, he slipped into the crowd.

Braggiotti's gibe was skillfully aimed. Even without the Hochheimer, Stephen was already affected by the sight of so many unconcealed shoulders and feminine arms gloved to the elbows. He was neither prudish nor oversusceptible, yet as he watched the ever-breaking pattern of figures moving under the brilliant chandeliers he doubted the wisdom of trying to emulate Roberto's casual acceptance of mixed company.

Resolving that this would be his last appearance in Roman society, Stephen moved toward the yellow sofa from which Merry del Val was asperging charm over an attentive audience. Stephen stood on the outer edge of the circle and listened to the Cardinal's story about two clergymen — an Anglican and a Methodist — who chanced to meet each other on the way to a railway station. "No need to hurry," said the Anglican. "My watch tells me that we have plenty of time." They arrived at the station just as the train pulled out. "How vexing," exclaimed the Anglican, "particularly when I placed such faith in that watch." "Ah," said the Methodist slyly, "what is faith without good works?"

Stephen joined in the more than polite laughter that followed the theologic snapper of Merry's tale. The familiar timbre of Stephen's voice caused the Cardinal to look up in recognition. He waved a patrician hand at the American Monsignor and lifted his fine baritone in a Horatian challenge:

"Integer vitae scelerisque purus . . ."

The invitation was too tempting. Stephen responded:

"Non eget Mauris iaculis neque arcu."

Several heads turned to see the audacious fellow who could cap verses with Merry del Val. The trick was still a good one, and the Cardinal's penchant for it well known. "Go on, go on," urged the Princess Lontana. "A test, a test," cried others.

Merry del Val smiled at the commotion. "There is no need to test Monsignor Fermoyle's knowledge of Horace. I propose a *divertissement* more original. Suppose," he appealed engagingly to Stephen, "we cap the poet's verses in a language native to neither of us. What do you say to trying it in French?"

Squeals of delight rose from the ladies. Latin was beyond them; French they might understand. A space was cleared between the contestants; at one end of the gantlet sat Merry del Val enjoying the hubbub; at the other, Stephen faced him standing.

"Shall we go on with the *Integer vitae?*" asked Merry del Val.

"It's one of the few I happen to know, Your Eminence."

While the Cardinal delicately moistened his lips for the
first line, Princess Lontana gathered her linguistic skirts about
her for the hurdles ahead. Her attention at the moment was
divided between Lord Chatscombe and Baron Rumboldt; for
better or worse, these two gentlemen were about to hear in
their native languages a catch-as-catch-can translation of a
Roman lyric poet tripping off the tongue of a Steubenville,
Ohio, American.

Merry del Val began:

> "*L'homme honnête, tout pur, sans crime . . .*"

Princess Lontana whispered simultaneously from both sides
of her fan. "*Der Mann des reinen Sinnes* . . . the honest, pure-
souled man . . ."

The poetic passage at arms was interrupted by the arrival
of new guests who, sensing the unusual nature of the performance, found places along the line of fire. The Cardinal
waited serenely for the late-comers to settle down, and during
this interval of silence Stephen let his eyes range along the
aisle of listeners. He had almost completed the circuit of
faces, gowns, and coiffures when he saw quite close to him —
so close that she might have touched him with her outstretched fan — the unforgettable face and figure of Ghislana
Falerni.

More than seven years had passed since Stephen had seen
the Contessa Falerni in anything but fantasy. Now, at the
point-blank reality of her presence, a physical tremor seized
him. He heard himself finishing a line:

> "*Sans armes je rencontrai un loup . . .*"

Princess Lontana rushed in for the kill. "*Wehrlos traf Ich
einen Wölfin* . . . Unarmed, I met a wolf!"

Stephen struggled to collect himself. In the prolonged
silence he heard the Princess translating Merry's verse: "She
was an enormous creature." . . . Somehow he managed to
fake the next line; any Latinist would have recognized the
pinched injustice done to Horace; how he ever finished the
ode Stephen never knew. But when the ordeal ended, a salvo
of hand clapping greeted the performers.

"Unusual, quite," said Lord Chatscombe. "Never heard it done just that way at Cambridge."

"Remarkable show," said Braggiotti, then added, "to make it really difficult you might have *rhymed*."

For some minutes a congratulatory throng swirled about Stephen, then began to thin out as Signora Piombino made ready to sing. Stephen gazed about the enormous oval chamber, hoping to see Ghislana Falerni again.

"Here I am." The *contessa* was beckoning to him from a near-by sofa.

Stephen moved toward her, acting a great deal braver than he felt. "How did you know I was looking for you?"

Ghislana Falerni extended her hand palm downward, with the pressureless confidence of a woman who need never answer such a question. Her arm, bare between glove top and shoulder, was of a tapering roundness, ivory-pastel in coloring. Had it been the fragment of a statue, an archaeologist might have labeled it "Metaneira, fifth-century Greek," and marveled at the proportions of women in that classic age. Stephen bowed over her hand, releasing it a trifle sooner than the ritual of Black Society prescribed.

A life spent in the company of high ecclesiastics had given Ghislana Falerni an ease, rather than a familiarity, in their presence. She indicated a place beside her on the satin-tufted divan. "That was an amazing improvisation, Monsignor. Both your skill with words and the color of your habit have changed since I last saw you."

Stephen struggled against too great a forwardness. "Yours, too. Then, you wore green."

By the slightest lift of her dark lashes the *contessa* acknowledged the flattering miracle of his remembering. "That was such a long time ago." Her voice was overcast with a regret connected neither with Stephen nor herself — an impersonal sadness such as a landscape painter might feel when, in the middle of a picture, the simple light of noon becomes a more complex problem in umber.

Signora Piombino began her program with a group of mood-creating German *Lieder*. Sitting beside Ghislana Falerni, Stephen felt a skein of enchantment settling over him.

Words were unnecessary; the current of attraction flowed unspoken between them. The singer concluded with an impassioned performance of Schumann's *Widmung*.

Silence after music being so perfect, Stephen was unwilling to mar it with speech. It was the *contessa* who brought the relationship back to reality. "My cousin Roberto tells me that you are in the Vatican Secretariat of State."

"Is Roberto *your* cousin, too?"

"His mother and mine were sisters. We grew up together."

Across the room Stephen saw Braggiotti leaning languorously against a high-manteled fireplace. His head was a curly cameo; in his hands he held a terra-cotta figurine, and was evidently discoursing on its origin to a · female audience. Stephen was always puzzled by Roberto's ease in the presence of women; was he naturally immune, or had he worked up resistance by a lifetime of practice?

"Your cousin must have been a devastating boy."

"*Un demonio* . . . straight out of Raphael. Beautiful, as you see, but brimming with imagination too. Such games we used to play! Full of escapes and rescues."

"For instance? The first one that comes to mind."

"The very first? That would be 'labyrinth.' In fact, we always played labyrinth in one form or another."

"I suppose you'd take the part of the imprisoned maiden — what was her name? — the one who gave her rescuer a silken thread."

"Ariadne. Yes, Roberto would never allow anyone else to take that part. He'd make a labyrinth of brambles and hedges in the garden, and put me under a pear tree in the center. Then, after much groping about and slaying of minor characters — Roberto always insisted that they lie quite *dead* — he'd wind up the spool of silk and find me under the pear tree."

"What would he do when he found you?"

The *contessa* gave Stephen the full candle power of her eyes. "What does any rescuing hero do? The myth permits no originality in these matters, Monsignor."

Stephen felt like a man coming out of a pleasantly rarefied dream to find waking reality much more attractive. Ghislana Falerni was ten times more magnetic than he had remem-

bered. And although she had an altitude about her, she gave
no impression of being a distant star. He started to be surprised that she should have come down from her pedestal,
then realized that it was he who had placed her there.

For his own safety Stephen decided to put her back quickly.
Meanwhile, he sought to find some reassuring flaw in the
woman sitting so tranquilly beside him — some defect of
beauty or understanding that would sever the skein of
enchantment. Desperate scrutiny revealed no imperfection or
even the promise of one. Possibly the *contessa* lacked efferves-
cence, and perhaps for some tastes she was too generously pro-
portioned. A noon sun might reveal toolings of age in her
face, but in the present light no such traceries were evident.
At supper she ate creamed lobster and drank white wine with
the unaffected enjoyment of a woman who regarded food and
drink as natural goods — things to be relished and consumed.

The long evening seemed not to tire her. She gave no
impression of wishing to be elsewhere or of requiring the
attention of anyone but Stephen. After two hours of watching
Ghislana Falerni with the microscopic lens of a man praying
for disenchantment, Stephen found her singularly flawless.

On the way home Roberto said casually, "I saw you talking
to my cousin Ghislana. What do you make of her?"

Willing enough to express an opinion, Stephen found judgment difficult. "What can I say? She struck me as being lovely
and sorrowing." Unused to describing women, Stephen groped
for a metaphor. "She seems like a wick saturated with mourning. Mysterious."

"Mysterious 'Gothic' or mysterious 'Greek'?"

"Definitely Greek. There's nothing stained glass about her."

"A touch of Ceres maybe?"

"I wouldn't stress that part. But she does radiate myth.
From what she tells me of the games you used to play, she
must have always had a labyrinthine secret about her."

"She was a regular Sleeping Beauty," confessed Roberto.
"She still is. This glorious cousin of mine, for whose sake I
joyously committed symbolic acts of murder in childhood,
this creature whose emotional potentialities have never been
matched, or even tested, is still waiting — to drop the allegory
— for her emotional equal to appear."

"What about her husband?"

"A fine man . . . but much older than Ghislana. Besides, he was killed on the Piave four years ago in Italy's greatest hour."

"How has she managed to stay unattached since then?"

Braggiotti was torn between a defense of Italian gallantry and its failure to produce a prince worthy of his cousin. "Ghislana's case is unusual. She is emotionally fastidious and very caste-conscious." A note of curiosity entered Roberto's voice: "Did she strike you as being too heroically built?"

"No."

"Many men quail at a Juno. The mere prospect of encountering such a *bête énorme* — as your Horace puts it — is too terrifying."

"I can well imagine." To go on talking about this woman Stephen could have imagined anything.

"But there's more to it," continued Roberto. "You must understand that Ghislana has met only one kind of man: the *Neri* type. She married one. Not that the members of Black Society are less masculine than other men, but there is an undeniable quality of . . . of *ingrownness* about the relationship between men and women in this group. They have known each other too long, too well. Marriage verges on the incestuous. In Ghislana's case, a newcomer would be necessary." Having thought all around the subject, Roberto came out where he had gone in. "Yet how unlikely it is that any newcomer with the proper qualifications — emotional energy, social position, cultural and spiritual attainments — will ever appear."

"Yes, it *is* rather unlikely."

Stephen went to sleep that night fumbling at quite contradictory chords of emotion. He was glad that Ghislana Falerni was unmarried, sexually fastidious, and socially protected. If he could not claim her for himself, he hoped that no stranger would come scouring through the brambles to find her, whether under a pear tree or in the glass casket of *Neri* society. He simply did not want anyone else to awaken this woman. And that was strange, because just before dropping off to sleep, Stephen decided never to see her again.

THAT SUMMER Rome burned. From June to August the ther-

mometer in Stephen's office under the Vatican eaves registered
blood heat every noon, than really began to climb. Finally
Stephen threw the instrument away, and thereafter let his
drenched clothing tell him how hot it was.

The atmospheric heat was accompanied by explosive political tensions as the Quirinal regime, morally bankrupt and stra-
tegically inept, raced toward collapse. In August a general
strike paralyzed most of Italy; on farms and railways, in factories and at furnaces, men refused the questionable boon of
work at wages of seven lire a day. Riots and confusion spread
through the great cities of the north; Red "baronies" were
formed in agricultural regions, while the whole nation listened, hope dicing with terror, for the tread of Mussolini's
legions marching on Rome.

From the dust and ugliness of the Italian political bull ring
Stephen sought an interior refuge of contemplation. In vain.
Ever since the evening at the Palazzo Lontana the corridors
of his inner life had been crowded with images of Ghislana
Falerni. Through scorching afternoons he was beset — and not
too subtly — by fantasies of this woman with the Metaneira
arms and ivory-pastel flesh. Her economy of movement, which
had struck him at first as pleasing, now became painful in
retrospect. The slow extending of her gloved hand, the exquisite lift of her eyelashes, the delicate management of her body
as she rose, reached, walked — all these whirled through
Stephen's memory.

Everything she had said to him became an echo. Words
that of themselves had only the lightest of emotional content,
phrases incapable of any personal assay, thronged back now
richly freighted — not with special meaning (that would be
too absurd), but with sheer vibratory excitement. It occurred
to Stephen that the experience of listening to Ghislana Falerni,
should she ever choose to tell him anything really important,
would be unbearable. Meanwhile he found himself holding
intimate but imaginary conversations with her. On the spool
of an unsayable yearning he wound a secret thread, and when
the spool was full he always found himself on the grass with
Ghislana Falerni under a flowering pear tree.

*The myth permits no originality in these matters, Mon-
signor.*

From vassalage to these fancies, Stephen resolved to free himself. Hitherto he had always enjoyed a reasonable amount of success in his strivings for repose. He had begun to think of himself as one of those fortunate men whose natural resistance to sensual temptation was stronger than the temptation itself. Or if not *naturally* stronger, then by petitioning the Giver of supernatural grace, he had always found the extra strength that God gives for the humble asking. Until his thirty-third year Stephen Fermoyle had been let off, excused from many of the dusty and desperate concessions that most men are required to make in their emotional lives.

He was not to be let off now.

Stephen did not dare think of himself as being in love with Ghislana Falerni. Yet by no process of evasion could he deny that she had touched the central membranes of his heart and mind. Why, he asked himself, should I be so moved by this woman? Seven years ago she troubled me at sight. And now, again. What in me responds to what in her?

Answers smote him. Ghislana Falerni reveals to you, in unblurred perfection, the possibilities of an earthly happiness that you have always denied, that you never dared dream. Yet here she is: the queenly myth-mother containing all bounty within the compass of her being — aching as you do (as everyone does), for the solace of giving herself away to an emotional equal.

He supposed there were many men who spent their lives in this condition — constantly thinking of some woman, chained to the hope or memory of her person, restless without possession of it, and fearful lest she should find happiness with another. Stephen now suffered the agonizing consequences of giving one's love disproportionately to anyone but God. It shamed him to realize that Ghislana Falerni had gained entrance to the sanctuary reserved for his priesthood, and that she had advanced, during a single interview, to the very doors of the tabernacle. She must be turned away before she invaded the sacred precincts where only one love could dwell.

Stephen Fermoyle, the sworn celibate, the dedicated priest, resolved to turn her away. Without hysteria, and like a man combating a severe but curable disease, he entered upon a regime of strict self-discipline. He fasted, abstained from meat, and increased the devotional aspects of his life. Each day to the more fervent reading of his Office and the daily celebration of Mass, he added extra prayers, particularly the Litany of the Blessed Virgin. He called upon the Mother of God to intercede for him at the throne of the Father; he invoked her aid with glorious names:

> Mother most pure,
> Mother most chaste,
> Mother inviolate,
> Mother undefiled,
> Virgin most prudent,
> Virgin most renowned,
> Virgin most powerful,
> Virgin most merciful,   Pray for me.
> Mystical rose,
> Tower of ivory,
> House of gold,
> Gate of heaven,
> Refuge of sinners,
> Comforter of the afflicted.

By means of the Stations of the Cross he renewed in himself those painful intimations of mortality, of penitential suffering and atonement, that Christ had undergone as a man.

Stephen applied to Alfeo Quarenghi for heavier assignments of work and volunteered to perform Monsignor Guardiano's official duties while the latter took a month-long holiday. While Rome sweltered through August Stephen intensified his ascetic regime. Gradually the image of Ghislana Falerni began to fade; her voice grew dimmer. Like a slow, withdrawing wave she retreated down the beaches of Stephen's heart, and left him standing before the tabernacle alone.

CHAPTER 3

STEPHEN was on the verge of physical exhaustion when, early in September, Roberto Braggiotti suggested a walking trip through the Sabine Hills.

"The vines are ripe in Tivoli; new wine is being pressed on the Sabine slopes," said Roberto. "We will tramp mountain paths, lie on our backs in lemon orchards, listen to the crash of cataracts, and swim in ice-cold ponds. What do you say, Stefano?"

"I say wonderful. Guardiano is back; he can take over my work. Let's start tomorrow."

A canvas knapsack stuffed with extra socks and linen was the only luggage Stephen carried. He borrowed a denim shirt and looked longingly at some heavy-soled shoes, but the dread of breaking them in made him stick to his oldest pair of oxfords. Roberto turned up with a fine new pair of English-made walking boots, tweedy knickers, and an Alpine hat complete with feather. To get out of Rome quickly they took a train near Porta San Lorenzo and dropped off at Bagni, about twelve miles from the city.

Braggiotti, all stride and tempo, had to be kept in check. "Take it easy, Excelsior," Stephen advised. "This is a walking tour, not a steeplechase."

"But we must get into the hills tonight. There's an inn at Vicovaro, hanging on a crag over a mountain torrent."

"It'll be there tomorrow." Stephen had his own technique for cutting Roberto down to size. "Plod the first day, trudge the next — haste makes blisters — that's my text."

"You have the soul of a tortoise," grumbled Roberto. "While I" — he touched the feather in his hat — "am a Roman eagle."

They did eight miles that day, slept at the Chalet des Cascades at Tivoli, and after an enormous breakfast were off again. Now they struck slightly northward through a grape-garlanded countryside; the air was saturated with a purplish haze. Barely twenty miles from Rome they saw tiny villages unchanged since Caesar's time; in fields and vineyards peasants were gathering up the richness of earth — olives, grapes, and corn — in handmade baskets; occasionally a donkey-drawn cart with solid wooden wheels would creep past. It was all very picturesque and quite poverty-stricken.

They paused at noon for lunch at a lazy tavern, sloughed their knapsacks, ate bowls of bean soup, and drank *asciutto,* the dry wine of the country. Afterwards they cooled hands, feet, and faces in a brook, then drowsed for an hour in a grove of pines. Stephen's tensions began to vanish; Roberto's nervi- ness abated somewhat, too. He was content to plod now and began favoring the heel of his left foot where the smart Eng- lish walking boots were raising a blister. Walking, resting, they reached Vicovaro at twilight, and found the inn, as Ste- phen predicted, still on its crag overhanging the torrent. Sup- per, more wine, a cigarette on the terrace. Then too tired to talk, they fell asleep.

At breakfast next morning, Stephen asked: "How well do you know this country?"

"My family used to have a place outside Civitella, about ten miles from here. As a boy I spent my summers there."

"Then you probably know that Horace once owned land hereabouts."

"The Sabine farm? We used to picnic there. 'O fons Ban- dusiae' — you're not the only one who can spout odes, Fermoyle. But seriously now, what's this affair going on between you and Horace? How does a barbarian like you, Stephen, happen to be so fond of a Roman poet?"

"It's a long story, and I love to tell it. Wait till we get out on the road."

From the innkeeper they bought a flask of wine, some bread and cheese, then setting their sights for Monte Gen- naro, headed north. They worked the stiffness out of their muscles with a brief spurt of heel-and-toe walking, then set- tled down to a more leisurely pace. The ground was steadily rising here, and the higher altitude gave a sparkle to air and wit. Braggiotti was in a frolic mood. He wanted to run races, play games, engage in mental and physical rivalry with his companion.

"I'll bet you a dinner that I can give you the history of the Western world in one minute," he said; then added: "while running."

Stephen scoffed. "We used to do that in parochial school. Make it tougher."

"You want variations? All right — I'll give it to you back- wards."

"The history or the running?"

Braggiotti considered a moment. "Both."

"You've got a bet. Begin with the election of Warren G. Harding, analyze Lincoln's patronage policy, and discuss James K. Polk's attitude toward Mexico."

"Your country gets one sentence," said Roberto. "Here it is: 'America was discovered by an Italian who thought he was going someplace else.'"

"Thanks for mentioning us at all," said Stephen. "O.K. — here's a nice piece of road. Get going."

Roberto turned around, and beginning with the treaty of Versailles poured out a torrential account of modern, medieval, and classic civilizations. Toward the end of his recital he increased his pace and rush of language until Stephen, holding the watch on him, had to break into a run to keep up. It was a dizzying, breathless stunt of high intellectual order, and when it was over Roberto aimed a playful cuff at Stephen's head.

"You see, Americus, how the Roman mind works. It holds in focus all periods, all cultures. Time runs backward, forward, any way you want."

"Could you do it walking on your hands?" said Stephen.

"If this blister gets much worse, I may have to." Roberto was limping slightly. "Maybe the unguent of your tale about Horace will soothe it."

"Would you really like to hear the official version?"

"Yes, if you'll skip the Lord Chesterfield bromide, 'When I talked my best, I quoted Horace.' I want the real story."

Stephen shifted his knapsack to the other shoulder, offered Braggiotti a swig from the wine bottle, then took one himself. "The real story begins with a lay brother who taught Latin in a parish high school in Medford, Massachusetts. This Brother Felix was a rare and savory specimen of the genus *magister*, with more devotion to religion than many an anointed priest I could name. Why he didn't take Orders is a mystery; maybe he had the odd notion that teaching was just as important."

"This Felix interests me."

"Besides being a teacher, Brother Felix was a poet who didn't presume to practice his art. 'A poet,' he used to say, 'has no right to be mediocre.' To offset this modesty, he developed the knack of reading poetry out loud so that it made sense as well as sound. Naturally he liked the mystics: Southwell, John of the Cross, Vaughan; not for their piety — I must make this clear to you, Berto — but for their poetic energy. Brother Felix had the sense to know that all religious rhymers aren't divinely inspired, and that it takes more than a cry from the heart to make some pious nun a lark at heaven's gate."

"The Inquisition should have looked into his case. What other heresy did he preach?"

"Heresy is the word. In the midst of a culture devoted to baseball, whist parties, and sheet music, this Brother Felix taught the unpopular doctrine of *elegance*. His slightest action was the gesture of a man at ease before perfection. To see him lay a bit of store cheese on a cracker and carry it to his mouth — *to watch him drink a glass of water* — was an adventure in form." Stephen solicited Braggiotti's opinion. "Can you believe this, Roberto?"

"I've known one or two such men in my life. Both were artists; one a musician, the other a sculptor." Braggiotti's critical sense came forward. "I must say, though, that their content wasn't up to their notion of form."

"Exactly. Now you're coming right into Brother Felix's shop. He spent his life searching for the artist in whom form and content were equally balanced. And after much searching he found his man — a poet in whose work it is impossible to tell where diamond substance ends and informing light begins." Stephen halted, and took hold of the top button on Braggiotti's shirt. "Now, what would the name of that poet be?"

"Dante?"

"Good try. At his best, Dante is all luminosity. But too often his diamond purity is muddied with political and theologic sediment. Guess again."

"I hate to give credit to the nation that made these boots, but how about Shakespeare?"

"The sonnets, maybe. But the plays are overloaded with rhetoric. Mind you, we're not talking about how it feels to stand under an avalanche. We're discussing vision and design. Come on now, don't be stubborn. Say 'Horace' and get it over with."

Roberto pulled up dead lame. "I'm not stubborn." He sat

down on the grass in a hayfield and began unlacing his left boot. "But this blister is killing me."

"Let's have a look," Stephen pulled off the boot and sock, turned up the sole of Roberto's foot, and saw the chafed, swollen heel. "The skin's broken, Berto. Wait, I'll wash it off with a little wine."

Dousing his pocket handkerchief with *asciutto*, Stephen tenderly bathed the blister. "There now. A bit of adhesive will fix it."

"If we had any."

"I brought some . . . just in case." Stephen rummaged in his knapsack and came up with a spool of adhesive tape. "Lie on your back, Eagle Feather."

Leg in air, Roberto lay quietly in the grass. "Are you making the patch in the form of a cross?"

"That's right."

"Druid or Maltese?"

"The latter."

"Why? Put your answer in the form of a syllogism."

"A syllogism it shall be. How does this strike you?

In the funny papers all patches are Maltese;
Braggiotti is something out of the funny papers;
Therefore he should have a Maltese patch."

"A tissue of fallacies," cried Roberto, struggling to rise. "I'll have to beat some elementary logic into your primitive skull."

Stephen gripped Braggiotti's foot with a toehold. "Not till we finish our previous business. While I've got you where I want you" — he gave Roberto's ankle a wrestler's twist — "say 'Horace twice.' "

"Ouch, Fermoyle."

"Not 'ouch, Fermoyle.' '*Horace twice*'!"

"Horace, Horace."

"No! Can't you understand simple Italian? Say 'Horace twice'!"

"Horace twice, you damned idiot." As Stephen laughingly released his hold, Braggiotti leapt off the grass. "Twist the foot of a Roman, will you?" He aimed a blow at his companion's head. Stephen dodged it, seized Roberto by the wrist, then pivoted suddenly and levered the surprised Italian over his shoulder into a haystack.

Braggiotti came out of the hay looking like an indignant faun. Wisps of hay stuck in his curly hair; he didn't know whether to take his toss as a joke or an affront. "You spawn of guile, Fermoyle."

"*Non me lo dica . . . perchè sono Romano,*" said Stephen. The mimicry was so perfect, its application so deserved, that Roberto decided to laugh.

Watching him pull the hay out of his curls, Stephen joined his companion in laughter.

THEY CAME to the modern remains of the Sabine farm shortly after midday. Near the little village of Licenza they found a valley overshadowed by Monte Gennaro, the "rugged Lucretilis" of the odes. They climbed a knoll, crossed a rushing torrent, and came to an orchard in which men were picking fruit.

"Isn't Horace's farm around here?" asked Roberto.

"*A pie tui*" (at your feet), one of the workmen replied.

Stephen gazed down a long alley of lemon trees. Was this truly the Sabine nest that had restored the poet when, tiring of Roman heat and intrigues, he would mount his ambling mule and jog toward his mountain farm? Yes, it could be. There was the gurgling brook and the crystalline spring, most celebrated, most loved and remembered among the fountains of earth. And above, on Gennaro's slope, were the woods in which Horace had met the enormous wolf. A herd of goats cropped the grass under the trees where the poet, beguiling summer's heat, had lain with his flask of Falernian.

Across these antique recollections fell Roberto's voice. "Sorry, old fellow, but I think my blister is really beginning to kick up."

"That's serious. We must take care of it, Berto. Where's the nearest town?"

"Rocca Giovane. But there's nothing there."

Stephen was truly solicitous. "Could we get back to Rome?"

"Not till tomorrow. Say . . ." A half plan was forming in Roberto's mind: "if we could commandeer a cart . . ."

"What then?"

"The Princess Lontana has a country place hereabouts. She'd have soap and hot water at the least."

"We'll *buy* a cart."

They sat by the roadside for more than an hour until a two-wheeled *carretta* drawn by a spavined donkey came clopping through the dust. The driver was asleep. Why stay awake on such a drowsy afternoon? Stephen gently shook his shoulder, and Braggiotti did the talking.

"Where are you going, *amico mio?*"

"Two miles beyond Rocca Giovane."

Braggiotti made a proposition to the sleepy wagoner. "Would you, for twenty lire, take us a mile further?"

For twenty lire — three days' pay — the driver would have taken them to the brink of Lethe. Stephen thrust the money into the man's hand, and the two Monsignors piled into the back of his cart.

Through a bronzing countryside they jolted over ruts and boulders. It was dusk when the wooden wheels struck the graveled driveway of Princess Lontana's country place. Passing shadowy oaks, they emerged into a rolling terrain of lawn, then saw a ramble of roofs, wings, and gables gathered into country-house unity by the combined skills of architect and landscaper. On a wide-flagged terrace a half-dozen people neither young nor old lounged on wicker chairs with drinks in their hands. They seemed to be waiting for nothing more important than a cool evening. As the cart rolled up the driveway, some of them even lifted their heads.

"Get ready to hear a woman register surprise in six languages," said Roberto.

An upper servant, liveried and suspicious, came forward to ask the visitors' business. Braggiotti handled him airily. "Tell the Princess Lontana that Monsignors Braggiotti and Fermoyle are making a parish visitation among the worthy poor. Help me off this tumbrel, will you, Stefano?"

Close upon the shock of seeing two dust-begrimed prelates alight at her door, the Princess Lontana became a first-aid angel. "Umberto," she directed the liveried servant, "put your arm under Monsignor Braggiotti and show him to the bathroom in the south wing. I will come with disinfectant, salves . . ."

Half an hour later she was making pleasant chatter as she finished bandaging Roberto's heel. "Such a welcome you will receive on the terrace . . . the shortage of men has been embarrassing . . . my reputation as a hostess will be saved. Good Umberto, try to borrow other flannels with longer legs for Monsignor Fermoyle. Ask Lord Chatscombe's man to do something really fine. Does it feel better now, Roberto?"

"Much better, thank you. And, Umberto, beg a more attractive scarf from the Englishman. These polka dots do not suit me. But no, never mind. If I must hobble, I shall have to be, like Byron, elegantly daring about the throat. Name me your guests, *principessa*."

The match-making strain took charge of Princess Lontana. "There is the Marchesa d'Alessandro — without her husband, of course. The Loria sisters, Margherita and Emfilia. Lord Horrox is concentrating on Margherita. Then there is the Baroness Sigismunda."

Roberto groaned. "That Bavarian huntress? I've been dodging her for years. If you must fill your house with unattached women, Loretta, why not get attractive ones?"

"We have those, too. Your cousin Ghislana arrived only yesterday from Baia."

In the act of tying a borrowed scarf, Stephen heard the name. "Ghislana Falerni? Is *she* here?"

"In the quite radiant flesh, Monsignor. You shall see. Her skin defies sunlight in a quite unbelievable way, and her seven trunks of Parisian modes will make you glad that you are a bachelor." She gave a final pat to Roberto's bandage. "Now, *mes amis,* finish adorning yourselves and make an immediate appearance. We dine under the sky at eight-thirty." The Princess Lontana gazed up at the sky as though it were part of her decorative scheme. "With the planets in their present happy conjunction, the evening should be memorable."

CHAPTER 4

TENSIONS of overdue rain stretched the air as Stephen descended to the terrace. Candles on the glass-topped dinner table burned straight upward to a breezeless sky; the earth lay begging for a shower. It was a night for summer's-end masquing, and the players on Princess Lontana's stage were eager for the country-house revels to begin. As always, the Princess' introductions made everyone feel petted, distinguished. She displayed Stephen caressingly to her other guests, then bore him like a trophy toward Ghislana Falerni.

From a willow chair the *contessa* greeted Stephen with her usual economy of speech and movement: hand, palm downward and ungloved, lips slower to speak than smile. She expressed pleasure at seeing him so unexpectedly and remarked that men were lucky to be able to borrow random flannels from each other. "No woman could trust a stitch not made for her," she said. Stephen wanted to reply that every needleful of thread in the lemony voile confection the contessa was wearing must have been lifted in her name. But he rejected a cavalier's opening. Guard well up, he determined to give no more of himself than good manners required.

He was struggling in a net of small talk when the Princess summoned her guests to dinner. Stephen found himself between his hostess and one of the Alessandro twins — an arrangement that freed him from conversational risks with Ghislana Falerni, but exposed him to the still-greater hazard of looking at her across the candlelighted table. By the sternest discipline he tried to avoid gazing at her; even so, he felt her image forming on the sensitized film that makes pictures for memory.

The Princess was clapping her hands. "Because everyone here speaks Italian," she said, "there will be no translations tonight."

"Hear, hear!" cried Roberto.

"This leaves me only two roles," continued the Princess. "Which shall I play: the deaf duenna who has lost her ear trumpet or the wicked croupier urging everyone to play for ruinous stakes?"

"The wicked croupier . . ."

"The deaf duenna . . ."

"I shall be both." From the table decorations the Princess seized a trumpet-shaped squash and held it to her ear: "*Que dis-tu?* . . . Louder please." While her guests laughed at the mimicry, she raked in an armful of tableware — spoons, salt shakers, everything within reach. "*Faites vos jeux, messieurs, mesdames.* The wheel is crooked, but people have been known to win. Umberto, the grape! Magnums of it."

Across the table Ghislana Falerni's eyes were saying to Stephen: "Do not be afraid. This is all very innocent and harmless. Please try to enjoy yourself."

Stephen took a single glass of champagne; to the flood of wit and laughter he added almost nothing. It was Roberto who, despite his inflamed heel, sparkled the table talk. He began by giving a fantastic account of his walking trip with Stephen; drafted on a not-quite-truthful scale and colored by all the paint tubes Roberto could squeeze in three minutes, the sketch was still an amusing likeness. Lord Chatscombe responded with a half-hour account of a similar tour he had taken in the Basses-Pyrénées twenty years before. "We followed the track of Wellington's campaign against Bonaparte," His Lordship began — then in heavy-dragoon fashion proceeded to fight the Peninsular War all over again. Every gully became a British redoubt grimly fortified by His Lordship's dullness. To snatch her party from the jaws of Wellington's final victory, the Princess fluttered her eyelids in a desperate appeal to Roberto: "Head the Englishman off before he takes Italy."

At her signal, Roberto went up like a fire balloon. Without props or preparation he transformed the terrace into an enchanted deck thronging with characters swarming up from the hold of his imagination. He began by imitating a Lebanese merchant trying to sell a shipment of wormy figs to the Archimandrite of Athens, who had plenty of figs but needed a prayer rug for his chantry. Roberto seized a napkin from the table and became a Syrian rug dealer who by a singular freak of fortune had the precise article, the very thing. He invented dialects and vocabularies to describe the rug; its dimensions grew until the whole terrace was carpeted with a texture of surpassing beauty — the lifework of a hermit-artist who had blended flowers and fruits (chiefly figs) into a complex allegory of Mohammed's career on earth. This was regrettable because the Archimandrite could not entertain the idea of spreading a Mohammedan rug on the floor of an Orthodox Catholic Church. Obligingly, Roberto whipped up a new rug depicting the nine most celebrated miracles of St. Athanasius. From the Archimandrite's point of view, this theme, too, was unfortunate: "How," he inquired, "could pious feet be expected to tread upon the holy image of a great saint?" For this poser, Roberto had no reply. Stunned and grieving, he reeled out of the rug business, and became a jongleur pleading the case of a stableboy hopelessly in love with the lady of a castle high on a peak in remotest Aquitaine.

Stephen, along with the other guests, was transported by a performance so packed with imaginative energy. While the rain hung off and atmospheric tensions gathered and the party took on the aspect of a *fête champêtre,* he forgot that he was not supposed to look at Ghislana Falerni. At first he allowed himself the visual delight of framing her portrait in quick glances. Then, while a florin moon climbed the sky, he became fascinated by the portrait's detail: the medallion head (so like Roberto's), the gardenia-pastel of throat and shoulders, the opulent contours shadowing off into secrets, part myth and all mystery.

Stephen was chastening his gaze when the *contessa's* eyes engaged him at level range across the table. The glance hung, held, wavered, and caught again. He stopped laughing, and did not raise his eyes again until Roberto's comic vein ran out.

The after-dinner change of positions began. Some of the guests followed Roberto into the pear orchard to play a game composed chiefly of chasing and laughter. Couples drifted through arbors; inside the house someone was splashing lyrically at the piano. Stephen chatted on the lawn, struggling against the compulsions that drove him toward Ghislana Falerni. The moon was swimming through a gauzy bank of clouds when he finally stopped fencing with himself and sat down beside her on the almost deserted terrace.

The *contessa's* glance was a muted re-entry of the motif their eyes had struck across the dinner table. A mere phrase; no more. Then modulating into safer music, she chose exactly the right key to excite Stephen's wit, yet not alarm his senses.

"Is it my imagination, Monsignor, or have you been avoiding me?"

"Your imagination is as lively as Roberto's. The simple truth is I've been wanting to talk to you all evening."

"Let us talk then — simply at first, truthfully later." The *contessa* was a croquet hostess offering her guest a choice of mallets. "You may open, Monsignor."

Stephen included sky, earth, the *contessa*, and himself in a humorous wave of his hand. "Where shall I begin?"

"Does it matter? The first three exchanges never count anyway. Afterwards, if there is anything to say — it will be said."

Her mildly cynic mood kept the play exactly where she wanted it. Stephen was laughing now. "Well then," he asked, "where did you spend the summer?"

"At Capri, mostly. I have a house there. The bathing and boating are delightful." *See how easily it goes?* "And what have you been doing?"

"Oh, tugging at a mechanic oar."

"Didn't you find Rome unbearable during the hot months?"

At the third exchange, Stephen discovered that even talk of weather could be dangerous in this woman's presence. Memories of his rearguard action against her all summer betrayed him now.

"I survived . . ." he said, "somehow."

" 'Somehow'? The word has a melancholy fall, Monsignor. Yet I must admit" — the *contessa's* lace handkerchief occupied her eyes and fingers — "there is no other word to describe the way most lives go on."

The free moves were over: the true count could begin. But neither the *contessa* nor Stephen was willing to test the depths beneath them. In silence Ghislana Falerni stretched her lace handkerchief tambour fashion across her knees, gazing at it as an imprisoned queen might contemplate a rich and useless embroidery made by her own idle hands. The posture conveyed more clearly than any declaration, everything she wanted to say to the man beside her. Regard me (it pleaded) not as a temptress to be approached with caution, but as a woman who is weary of being decorative on garden furniture. See me, not as a threat to your priestly soul, but as a fellow creature condemned to drop day-to-day pebbles into an urn of loneliness.

The plea disturbed Stephen's mind and conscience. Twice he had misread the truth about Ghislana Falerni. In younger dreams he had cast her as the unapproachable Madonna, a

Beatrice figure on a mystical balcony. More recently he had come to regard her as a combination of high-hipped earth goddess and exquisitely girdled woman of fashion. Was he seeing her now through another veil of illusion, or was he encountering reality this time — the reality of a fastidious and lonely woman struggling to breathe in a glass casket? Stephen could not tell; he dared no longer trust his judgment about the *contessa*. He only knew that the more he saw of her, the more riddling and various she became — a profoundly feminine cipher longing to be read on many levels of meaning.

His position, both on the terrace and in the *contessa's* life, was untenable, basically false. Training and instinct urged him to walk away rapidly, but at this moment they were powerless to free him from the magnetic tensions streaming out of Ghislana Falerni. It occurred to him (as a kind of pitiful compromise) that if he gave the conversation an impersonal turn, the dread charge might exhaust itself in commonplaces.

"Wasn't Roberto a clown tonight?" His words made a doughy sound, like a child's fist beating a flabby drum. "Have you ever seen anything so comical as his rug-dealer act?"

The *contessa* came back from her tambour reverie. "You should see him in the water. He's at his best then. At Capri this summer he turned himself into a blue dolphin for a whole week. Even Cardinal Giacobbi laughed at his antics."

Stephen's surprise was genuine. "Did the Cardinal Secretary visit you at Capri?"

"Everyone visits me there." Rebuke, light as a petal, lay on the *contessa's* lips. "Had you paid me a courtesy visit in Rome last spring, I would have invited you for a holiday."

Stephen said nothing.

"And you," she went on, "would have refused the invitation."

"How could I do otherwise? I am neither your cousin — nor an aging Cardinal."

Night turned on a noiseless axle. "Does that mean you cannot be a friend?"

Ghislana Falerni's question was an honest proffer of human regard. By the timbre of her voice Stephen recognized it as a sincere bid from an emotional equal to share with her some part of his isolation and loneliness. As a man Stephen could not lightly reject the offer; as a priest he could not rise to it. He was familiar with the advice of those saintly counselors, Chrysostom and Jerome: flee relationships with unattached women. He knew, moreover, that his feelings for Ghislana Falerni were not the stuff of which friendship is ordinarily made. Yet illusion beckoned; hope soared on rosy wing. The thing was possible! Aided by the pure fires of discipline, and skill sprung of extra grace, might one not transform forbidden clay into a vessel of singular devotion?

"I should like to be your friend . . ."

A light breeze, distilling hints of rain, lifted the ends of the *contessa's* chiffon scarf about her shoulders. Her hands caught at the fluttering fabric. Too late. A loosened end of the scarf flicked Stephen's cheek and sent a shivering charge along his facial nerves.

Field scents surged across the terrace in a perfumed wave; midnight was about to dissolve in urgencies of rain. On Stephen's arm lay the unretrieved end of the contessa's scarf — gossamer testimony of a truth too heavy for denial, unerasable even if withdrawn.

From the terrace Stephen could see an orchard of pear trees in the moonlight, their low boughs heavy with fruit. To say, "Walk with me in the orchard . . . once . . . for remembering," and to hear Ghislana Falerni whisper, "Yes . . . for remembering always," would have been happiness enough. But such fulfillment was denied. The only possible relief was the utterance of her name.

"Ghislana."

"Stephen . . . I have so longed to call you by name."

"I have called you by name a thousand times."

Along the grass, tiny winds curled in rising overtures to rain. "How did I reply?"

Stephen's voice was barely audible. "In words never to be spoken — except on grass beneath a pear tree."

The first raindrop fell, a full period to their conversation.

THE EARTH lay docile under a drenching shower as Stephen waded through a field of uncut hay. Behind him the horned Adversary prowled; the wolf of midnight was abroad, seeking the ruin of souls. In the downpour Stephen came to a knoll, thinly wooded, and scrambled up its briery ascent. Branches whipped his face; thorns tore at his hands and clothing. At the top of the hill he looked back at the lights in the upper windows of the country house. Only an unwillingness to lend himself out to morbid scourings saved Stephen from the emotional luxury of throwing himself face downward and confessing to the thorny earth the nature of his desire for Ghislana Falerni. No longer could he delude himself about its moral implications. No matter how poetically one glossed the matter, Ghislana Falerni was, quite bluntly, an occasion of sin. She might be sensitive, lonely, capable of high friendship — but she was also (could he deny it?) a menace to his immortal soul.

Under a dripping oleander Stephen sat broodingly; chin on knees, he considered what he must do. He needed no angel writing in a book of gold to tell him that he was under grave obligation to guard himself from further exposure to this country-house Eve. His experiences with her had proved that she could beguile and cozen him to his death as a priest. Twice he had failed to resist her; there must be no third fall. As the rain dripped from oleander boughs, and the lights of the country-house went out one by one, Stephen reached his decision. Tomorrow he would leave quietly at daybreak; no fanfare of departure, no farewells. He would slip away after breakfast, return to Rome, make a spiritual retreat — and never under any circumstances see Ghislana Falerni again.

Resolution fixed, Stephen returned to the darkened house. In his room he removed his wet flannels and sat down to write a brief note to Braggiotti. "Dear Berto: I must get back to Rome immediately. Give my good-bys to Princess Lontana and the *contessa*. Will see you under the Dome when your holiday is over. Affectionately, Stephen."

He had folded the note, intending to thrust it under Braggiotti's door, when Roberto hobbled in, no longer the airy magician with a sackful of rugs and lutes, but a rumpled, sleepless man dragging a painfully inflamed foot.

"Take a look at this confounded blister, will you, Steve? It's getting worse. All that jumping around this evening didn't do it any good."

Stephen examined the angry inflammation. "Boy, you've got

a real infection here. You need a doctor. Tell you what: I'm
leaving for Rome early tomorrow. We'll hire a car and drive
back together."

"Back to that oven? Not Berto." He looked up questioningly. "Why the sudden departure? Don't you like the people
here?"

"Skip the inquisition. I'm leaving."

Braggiotti was indignant. "But you can't run out on me like
this, Stefano. We started out on a jaunt together, didn't we?
Now that old Eagle Feather's pulled up lame, you just can't
abandon him."

"You'll be in good hands."

"Whose? Baroness Sigismunda's? She'll paw me like a raisin
bun. And can you imagine Chatscombe's fishy mitts winding
my bandages?" Roberto was wheedling now. "I need you,
Stefano. We'll call a doctor in the morning. Please wait till
he comes."

Stephen weighed the risks. "All right," he said grudgingly.
While rain beat all night on the roof of his dormer, he knew,
by the attars of clover drifting in from drenched fields, that he
had made a mistake in judgment.

The only medical man in the neighborhood was a hunch-
backed curio, part farrier, part leech, who engaged in rustic
surgery as a side line. "Dr." Manescalco (to give him his professional brevet) lanced Roberto's heel next morning without
benefit of antiseptics, then applied a hot herb poultice "to
draw out the purulency." His instructions to Stephen were
brief: "Keep him off his feet. Change the poultice every four
hours. A young man with healthy blood should have no
trouble casting off an infection of this nature."

"But suppose it spreads?" asked Stephen.

"In that case" — the doctor explored the depths of his arma-
mentarium — "we shall poultice the entire leg."

Stephen saw that he must tread tactfully in the presence
of professional vanity. "Would you advise a return to Rome?"

Manescalco flashed a peasant wit. "Rome? Ha-ha! Later
perhaps. As yet our patient is not ready for the last sacraments.
Ten lire, please."

Stephen spent the forenoon making Roberto comfortable; it
was almost lunchtime when the Princess and her house guests

began to troop in. Standard sickroom conventions were observed. The men were bluff, false-hearty; the ladies knocked timidly and tiptoed in with pears, grapes, and nosegays. Baroness Huntzdorf went so far as to dab possessively at Roberto's moist forehead with her handkerchief. As Ghislana Falerni, crisp in orchid-colored linen, bent down to bestow the cousinly version of a kiss, Stephen turned away.

"Don't turn your head, Fermoyle," cried Roberto. "Watch me enjoy the corporal works of mercy. More corporal works, Ghislana — I'm a very sick man."

Laughter from everyone but Stephen. "Visitors outside," he ordered. "I'm changing the poultice."

It was midafternoon before Stephen permitted himself a breather. Breviary in hand, he strolled onto the sun-washed terrace to read his priestly Office — which he should have completed before noon. It was the feast of the Nativity of Mary; the prayers for the time seemed particularly appropriate and beautiful. Trying to concentrate on his holy Office, Stephen heard shouts and applause from the tennis court, where mixed doubles were in progress. Ghislana Falerni and Lord Chatscombe were outplaying Baroness Huntzdorf and her partner. Stephen had always thought of the *contessa's* beauty as essentially static; now as he watched her bend and reach for the ball he saw that she was disturbingly graceful in motion. Her game was like a silk ribbon coming off an endless spool. He forgot his breviary while she flashed in tennis whites through a long rally, and made a stunning overhead kill at the net.

This isn't helping any, thought Stephen, turning away toward the shade of the fruit orchard. Pacing down an alley of pear trees, he focused his mind on the Lesson in which St. Augustine compares Eve and Mary, the two women who run through the lives of men:

> *Eve mourned, Mary rejoiced. Eve carried tears in her heart; Mary, joy. Eve gave birth to men of sin; Mary to the Innocent One. Eve struck, and Mary healed. Let timbrels reverberate under the fleet fingers of this young mother. Mary's canticle has ended the lamentations of Eve.*

Refreshed and strengthened, Stephen went back to his sickroom duties. The condition of Roberto's foot now thoroughly alarmed him. Red streaks were shooting up the thigh; Braggiotti tossed feverishly, complaining of pain in his back and a throbbing headache. In desperation Stephen made a larger poultice, covering the leg from the knee down, a rustic remedy, powerless, he knew, to hold back the tide of infection sweeping through Roberto's body.

At cocktail time Stephen wandered miserably onto the terrace. New guests had arrived, among them a celebrity — Louis Duhamel, one of the foremost interpreters of Debussy. Busily the Princess was laying the groundwork for a performance *très intime* after dinner. At the proper time Duhamel would be cajoled to the piano and the evening would be spent listening to his exquisite renditions.

Stephen hesitated to spoil the party by telling the Princess of Roberto's change for the worse. To whom should he confide his fears that Roberto's burning forehead and wandering speech were symptoms of a generalized blood poisoning? Ghislana Falerni was the only person who would be really interested. In a low voice he told her of Roberto's condition. "I don't want to frighten the others, but I really think we should get him to a hospital."

"That means driving to Rome?"

"Yes. I suppose there are cars we could borrow."

"The Princess has several." Ghislana considered the best and simplest course of action. "I'll throw some things into a bag and meet you at the garage in twenty minutes. We'll slip away without spoiling the Duhamel show."

Stephen put in an awkward demurrer. "Will it be necessary for you to — come with us?"

Edge of realism sharpened the *contessa's* answer. "Not if you can drive a European car with a left-hand gearshift across mountain roads in the dark — and take care of a delirious patient at the same time. Can you manage these things by yourself?"

"Maybe not . . . perhaps you'd better come."

With Umberto's help Stephen prepared his patient for the journey to Rome. At twilight they carried Roberto down the back stairs and lifted him into a Fiat roadster that Ghislana had commandeered. Stealthily she eased the car down the gravel driveway in the dusk; not until the oaks screened them from the house did she slip into high gear.

"We made it!" she exclaimed. They were conspirators now.

Under the same florin moon that had shown down on the preceding evening, they drove toward Rome. Stephen had never seen a woman handle a car so competently. Over wretched winding roads Ghislana jockeyed the open Fiat. Only once did she lose her way in the labyrinthine maze. Descending from the cool mountain atmosphere, they were passing through a hamlet in the Sabine foothills. A forked road confronted them. The only visible light in the village came from a sooty lantern hanging at the door of a tavern.

"Please find out which road leads to Vicovaro," said Ghislana. "I think we turn left, but I'm not sure."

Stephen pushed open the tavern door. A group of *contadini*, bleary-eyed with smoke and wine, were still at their never-ending game of *briscola*.

"Which way to Vicovaro?" asked Stephen.

The players looked up, startled by mention of a world outside their card game. "Turn left," said one of them. The others nodded, as if to say, "Why, yes, of course. One *always* turns left to Vicovaro."

Stephen thanked the man and leapt back into the car. "Bear left," he said. In putting his arm around Roberto again, he inadvertently touched the *contessa's* shoulder.

As they passed through Vicovaro, Stephen remembered the night that he and Roberto had spent at the inn overhanging the waterfall. Blithe and footloose they had been — Americus and Eagle Feather — wrestling and laughing together on an innocent holiday. And now, three days later, both heavy with infection — one grievously stricken in body, the other morally imperiled in soul — they were retracing their course to Rome.

Only by flashes was Roberto lucid; he flung his body about and babbled in disoriented speech, mentioning names and places unknown to Stephen. "Do you understand what he's saying?" he asked Ghislana.

"He thinks we are children again." She was sobbing. "Hold him tighter, Stephen. He jostles the wheel."

It was nearly midnight when the Fiat drew up to the Fran-

ciscan Hospital on the Via Reggio. A dozing porter helped
Stephen lift Roberto from the car.

"I'll wait here," said Ghislana.

Half an hour later she was still waiting at the curb when
Stephen came down the hospital steps. "What do the doctors
say?" she asked.

"They called it 'fulminating septicemia' — the worst type
of blood poisoning." Stephen slumped into the seat beside her,
heaping self reproach on top of weariness. "I should have
brought him in yesterday."

Womanlike, she minimized, soothed. "Don't blame yourself,
Stephen. He'll get good care now." Ghislana tried to im-
personalize her voice. "You must be hungry. Would you like to
come to my apartment for a bite?"

Stephen's desire was neither food nor drink; he wanted only
the solace of being alone with Ghislana Falerni. Impossible.
By definition, an occasion of sin.

"It's late. You'd better drop me off at my place."

Through the steaming city she drove slowly as if trying to
prolong the few moments remaining to them. The shared
,experiences of the past two days, their common love for
Roberto Braggiotti, gave them the illusion that they had spent
years together, and that by some miracle they would continue
to go on doing so. But the miracle failed to materialize. At the
gate of Stephen's lodging he opened the door of the car and
took the first step in his lifelong journey away from Ghislana
Falerni.

IT WAS two o'clock when Stephen fell into an exhausted sleep.
At nine next morning he was awakened by a telephone message from the Franciscan Hospital, telling him that Roberto
was sinking rapidly. In tears and prayer Stephen knelt beside
Roberto's bed while the last rites of the Church were administered.

At noon, the most promising of the Vatican's younger diplomats sank into a final coma. Two hours later, this gay, attractive human being died of an acute generalized septicemia.

That week marked the end of Stephen's youth. A phase of
his life ended when the vault door clanged shut on Roberto
Braggiotti's clay.

CHAPTER 5

Except for its bell tower and cross, the Benedictine monastery on the rim of the Roman Campagna might have been a powder magazine, a military prison, or a pesthouse for contagious diseases. At various times it had been all of these. Inside its bullet-pitted walls Garibaldi's enemies had languished; against its walls they had been shot. And in its gloomy cemetery, now filled with frightful examples of baroque statuary, their bones lay in sterile dust alongside the victims of cholera, smallpox, and other epidemics no longer in fashion. After 1870 the building had fallen into shunned neglect, but around the turn of the century a group of Benedictines had taken it over as a monastery. By diligence and skillful management the disciples of St. Benedict had rebuilt the moldering pile, dispersed the unwholesome vapors surrounding it, and given the place a quiet reputation in the fields of science and religion. The present Superior, Dom Arcibal Tedesco, was both a noted seismologist and a cunning restorer of souls. From all parts of Europe visitors came to the Benedictine monastery, either to inspect Dom Arcibal's wonderful new instrument for recording earthquakes or to make a spiritual retreat under his saintly direction.

Monsignor Stephen Fermoyle had little interest in seismology as he approached the monastery on a September afternoon shortly after the death of Roberto Braggiotti. The dust of a three-mile walk from the nearest village lay on Stephen's black coat as he tugged at a bellpull dangling from the front door. He was dubious, depressed, about making this retreat. Dom Arcibal might be able to detect a temblor at the bottom of the China Sea, but could he lay his finger on the fractured foundations of a human soul?

Stephen yanked the bellpull again. A little wicket opened, and the tonsured head of a young man popped out as from a cuckoo clock. The young man had a soup-bowl haircut and a cast in one eye — a combination that made him look not too bright.

"I wish to see Dom Arcibal," said Stephen.

The tonsured one revolved this idea in his head like a child rolling a marble in a cup. "Dom Arcibal is in the observatory. He is having a hard time with Stromboli today." Evidently the young man thought Dom Arcibal's instruments kept the volcano in check. "Is your business important?"

"Not particularly. I've come to make a spiritual retreat."

"In such cases" — there was an inner rattling of bolts — "Dom Arcibal's orders are to let the retreatant in and show him courteously to his cell."

The door swung open, and Stephen saw a lubberly lay brother who had outgrown his coarse, brown tunic. Red wrists projected from short sleeves; he was barefoot, and a blast of kitchen odors gushed from him as he reached for Stephen's suitcase. Stephen dubbed him "Fairhands" on the spot, and followed his guide down a stone corridor to an iron-hinged door. Fairhands bunted the door open, then with courtesy more gracious than manners motioned Stephen to precede him into the cell.

"When Dom Arcibal comes in, I shall tell him you are here. There is fresh water in that jug." With these advices Fairhands seemed to run out of ideas. Mysterious occupations awaited him elsewhere; he was off to perform them.

Stephen surveyed his cell, furnished with standard anchorite gear: an iron cot, a straw mattress, one blanket, two clothes hooks, a rush-bottom chair, a kneeling bench, and a crucifix at eye level hanging slightly askew on a rough plaster wall. Stephen's first act was to straighten the cross; the next was to gulp three large swallows of water. He then removed his collar, hung his dusty coat on a hook, and gazed out the curtainless window at the ornate monuments in the cemetery. When Italian taste falters, he thought, it really falls on its face. Unable to pray or meditate, he rolled the rough blanket into a bolster, lay down on the straw mattress, and gave himself up to thoughts of two people, one dead, the other throbbingly alive, whom he could not drive from his mind.

Again he knelt with Ghislana Falerni beside Roberto's coffin and prayed for the repose of his friend's soul. Once more, and for the thousandth time, he underwent the pitiful, dumb ordeal of riding back to the city with Ghislana after the funeral. Through a veil of black chiffon her face was a grieving cameo. Comfort of physical endearments was denied them; their suffering must be shared without a caress.

"What will you do now? Where will you go?" Stephen had asked.

"There are always places, things, friends — eager to help one forget. And the pity of it is, they succeed. The dead are so defenseless. Other voices drown them out; other images overlay their memory. After the first grief passes, the problem becomes how to remember."

"Do you really believe that?"

"The evidence is strong — so strong that Italians have made a proverb of it: 'Love makes time pass: time makes love pass.' There is wisdom in that proverb, Stephen."

Wisdom perhaps, but of a kind not provable (as Stephen discovered) in a month or year. His daily routine became a meaningless squirrel wheel; tasks once light as straws took on the heft of teak logs. A malaise coupled of grief and desire seized him. Days were saltless; at night the nether world of dreams, bubbling up in scarcely disguised form, shook him with waking sweat. The imperious voice of duty could not drown out a single syllable that Ghislana Falerni had ever spoken.

Stephen realized that he needed guidance not to be found in the ordinary confessor-penitent relationship. Once when Quarenghi made some mild comment on a poorly handled assignment, Stephen almost confessed his inner turmoil. But he was ashamed to tell the ascetic Quarenghi of his love for Ghislana Falerni; instead, he contrived to make it appear that his wretchedness stemmed solely from Roberto's death. It was Quarenghi who had finally advised the spiritual retreat under the direction of Dom Arcibal Tedesco.

"This Benedictine is a true physician of the spirit. Put yourself completely in his hands for a month," counseled Quarenghi. "He will skim the froth of misery off the surface of your soul. But more important, he will search the springs of confusion that seep into . . . ah, every life. I shall write him a note."

And now, tossing on his monastic cot, Stephen waited for the wonder-working Dom Arcibal to appear. At intervals he heard male voices chanting the liturgical hours — Vespers, Compline. The bronze leaves of the graveyard oaks deepened into purple, then lost all color as Stephen, lying face downward on his mattress, prayed to be released from servitude to Ghislana Falerni.

Clearly enough he saw the nature of his attachment to her. There it stood, third in the list of capital sins — lust, a virus tide inflaming the membranes of his heart. But how treat the disease? The keenest instruments of self-scrutiny, the severest physic of discipline, had failed him. Sincerely Stephen wished to be cured, yet he was weary, too, of flogging himself with whips of remorse. *That* wasn't the remedy. . . .

What was?

Dark the cell, darker yet the storm of guilt and confusion in Stephen's soul. Hideous voices were taunting him, when he heard the sound of footfalls, one slightly heavier than the other, coming down the corridor. Stephen sat up as a cowled monk carrying a lighted candle entered the cell. The visitor, a compact, roundheaded man in his late fifties, placed his candle on the window sill and seated himself in the rush-bottom chair.

"I apologize for this delay in greeting you," said Dom Arcibal in a bass rumble somehow pleasant to hear. "You must blame my tardiness on Stromboli. The Passy savants claim that the old volcano has been quieting down lately, but if today's indications mean anything, we shall see a pretty show of fireworks within twenty-four hours." Frank glee at the prospect of confounding a rival school rose in Dom Arcibal's throat. He quelled the uprising. "But let us speak of you, my friend. Monsignor Quarenghi's note was a masterpiece of discretion. It gave me no hint as to the nature of your difficulties. If you care to discuss them" — Dom Arcibal spread his hands in a savory, wholesome gesture — "I am free to listen."

Dom Arcibal's casual opening was the skilled maneuver of a serenely confident soul. It reminded Stephen of an incident of which Orselli had once told him. An Italian officer, taking command of sullen troops after Caporetto, had lined up his regiment in parade formation. Drawing his sword, he tossed it high in the air. The steel blade glittered upward, hung suspended for an instant, then began its downward plunge. At exactly the right moment the officer reached out, seized the falling weapon, and thrust it wordlessly into its scabbard.

"Can you imagine," Orselli had asked, "what would have happened if the officer's eye or nerve had failed?"

It occurred to Stephen that Dom Arcibal had taken an even greater risk. A fumbling approach, a single false note, would have aroused distrust or hostility. But the Benedictine's friendly overture combined just the right mixture of scientific detachment and professional interest. His reference to Stromboli said, in effect: "Two things fascinate me: the disturbances deep in the earth and similar upheavals in the secret places of the soul. Both can be recorded — the one, by a needle scrawling indicative ink on drum-turned paper; the other, by words discharged under pressure of buried emotions. I have listened to Stromboli's story all day, and now I am prepared to spend the night listening to yours."

Load-weary, Stephen began to unpack his heart. Tentatively at first, then with increasing confidence, he traced the course of his relationship with Ghislana Falerni. During the recital, Dom Arcibal watched the younger man's lips as a seismologist might watch a jagged graph reporting a fracture in the earth's crust. At times, the line grew faint, retraced itself hesitantly, then stumbled forward again. Not until it had stopped altogether did Dom Arcibal make his first comment.

"Everything you have told me thus far, Monsignor, has occurred within the past few months. I should like to hear about your earlier life. Suppose we go back a bit. Tell me something of your youth, your family, and your general background."

"As you wish," Stephen took a deep breath, then shot down the foaming rapids of memory. "I am the oldest of six children; my father and mother are devout Catholics who brought me up in a home of great piety and warm parental love. My outstanding recollection of childhood is the early sense of responsibility I developed while taking care of my younger brothers and sisters. I was a kind of — of lieutenant father to them, and exercised a natural authority over their actions. I dressed, fed and bathed my brothers and sisters till I was fif-

teen years old. The only privilege denied me was the right to
punish them when they were disobedient."

"Did you resent this curtailment of your authority?"

"Sometimes. But when my father explained to me that parents received this authority directly from God, and could not
delegate it to anyone else, I accepted his explanation without
question."

"Go on."

"During adolescence I felt a strong urge to be first in everything: studies, sports, popularity. I wanted to lead my classes,
be captain of all the athletic teams, go with the prettiest girls.
I burned to excel. When competition threatened, I put forth
greater energy, prayed harder for success. When it came, I
accepted it as my due. I always had the feeling that I was one
of God's special favorites."

"As I remember," said Dom Arcibal dryly, "Lucifer cherished a similar illusion. How do you account for such a grotesque notion on your part?"

"I never thought of it as grotesque. I saw that God had
blessed me with special gifts, and believed I must demonstrate
His favor by the excellence of my performance."

" 'Performance' is a word used by actors. Are you a strolling
player or a priest?" Without waiting for an answer, the monk
continued: "Come, let us get into deeper material."

Stephen took the plunge. "From my fourteenth year — the
age at which I felt my first call to the priesthood — I liked
girls. My mind throbbed with fantasies circling about the
female secrets. I felt the need to enter upon and explore these
mysteries. Between the ages of fifteen and eighteen I was
strongly tempted to do so."

"But you did not?"

Stephen's voice was very low. "I dared not."

"An interesting locution. I gather that you developed a profound sense of guilt about these sexual temptations."

"I did. This guilt increased when I entered the seminary.
Dedicated to the priestly life, I found myself torn between an
ideal of chastity and a yearning for women. The conflict was
so great that at one time I was deeply concerned as to whether
I should continue my studies for the priesthood."

"By what means did you solve this conflict?"

"By the means I always used when the going was hardest. I increased my devotions, prayed for the gift of supernatural grace, held on somehow from day to day. . . . It was never easy."

Dom Arcibal gently rubbed his tonsure: "Avoid smugness, my son. Returning now to your handling of this deep conflict. Were there any other factors present in your solution of it? Any incident, encounter, or event that influenced you? Do not hurry with your answer."

Stephen thought a long time. "I can't remember anything."

"Did your mother bring pressure of any kind?"

"Not unduly. I knew she was praying for my vocation, of course."

"Your father, then?" Dom Arcibal permitted a note of personal curiosity to enter his voice. "What kind of a man was he?"

Stephen launched into a tribute to Din the Down-Shouter. "My father was an uneducated workingman, but I have never met his equal in strength of mind or goodness of character. From childhood he was my model and guide. I think he has always been the dominating influence of my life."

"Did you ever cross swords with him?"

"Not openly. I tried to be an obedient and docile son. But underneath, there was a constant competition between us. In this competitive struggle I always felt that I was wrestling with someone stronger than myself. This led me to ever greater effort to surpass my father. It has never been clear to me why I should contend, except in loving-kindness with one who was always so good to me."

"We shall come to that later," said Dom Arcibal. "Meanwhile I think we have struck something of great importance. In the period when you were torn between chastity and desire for sexual pleasure, was there any significant passage between you and your father?"

"I can't remember anything."

"It's not a question of remembering. Let your mind range freely over the whole field of your relationship with your father, and tell me the first thing that comes to mind."

"Car tracks," said Stephen, surprised at his answer.

"Why car tracks?"

"My father was a motorman. He drove a trolley car between Boston and Medford. As a boy I liked to stand with him on the front platform and watch him handle the controls. He seemed godlike to me as he drove the car along the steel tracks that have turned up many times in my later life as symbols of discipline and duty."

Associations came crowding now. "The car tracks ran past a Catholic church — the Immaculate Conception, it was called — and my father always lifted his motorman's cap as we passed the center door." Stephen began to talk rapidly. "One day — I was about nineteen and a seminarian at the time — I took a ride with my father for old time's sake. As we passed the church, he lifted his cap as usual. No perfunctory touching of hand to visor, but a real off-the-head obeisance to the Presence on the altar, accompanied by the ejaculation, 'Blessed be God, Maker of heaven and earth.' I have never seen a more pious action. Afterwards he turned to me and said, 'Stephen, when I think that one day my son will stand at the very door of the Tabernacle, I am overcome by the Lord's goodness and mercy.'"

"What effect did your father's statement have on you?"

"I was deeply touched by it. To justify the faith he had in me, I determined to be a priest."

Dom Arcibal shook his head in mild amusement. "That's like saying that Dante wrote *The Divine Comedy* to justify the faith the Italian language had in him. Surely, there were other elements in your decision."

"I don't quite understand," said Stephen.

Tartness of quince puckered the Benedictine's lips. "You don't understand because your remarkable talent for self-delusion won't let you. Come now, Monsignor — didn't your father's remark open a whole new world of possibilities? Didn't you see your chance to overtop this godlike figure at the controls by celebrating mysteries forbidden to him? I put it to you flatly: didn't you realize that as a priest you could hold in your hands the actual body and blood of Christ while your father must be content with a passing act of adoration from the street?"

The enormity of such motives shocked Stephen. "Are such things possible?"

"Your whole life has shown it to be so. One aspect of your priesthood — I do not say all of it, because a priestly vocation is a complex work of God — is based on a desire to outrival your father. This unconscious rivalry is the key to your present difficulties. Proceed with your account."

Omitting nothing, Stephen poured out the history of his love for Ghislana Falerni, and his struggle to stand free of it. From the sponge of memory he pressed the mixed sweetness and gall of their meetings, the joy of gazing at her across the table, the magnetic tide of sympathy that flowed between them, and the fearful backwash of remorse that buffeted him after each encounter. At the end, more confused than when he began, Stephen lifted perplexed eyes to Dom Arcibal in a plea for guidance.

"The thing that frightens me most is the force and recurrence of my feelings for this woman. Three times I've tried to tear her from my heart, three times I've failed. Will the old misery start all over when I see her again? Must I spend the rest of my life running away from Ghislana Falerni or flogging myself with whips of conscience for having talked with her?" His voice rose in anger and perplexity. "Why should she afflict me? I was proof against all others. Why am I defenseless against her?"

Sympathy for perplexed mortals charged Dom Arcibal's reply. "Millions of lovers have found depthless joy in asking that very question. Ordinary men and women never cease to marvel at the biologic attraction (unique, they think) that they exert upon each other. We admit that such love exists in the world" — Dom Arcibal's voice snapped — "but by our priestly vow of celibacy we renounce it."

"I will not indulge in homiletics with you, Monsignor," Dom Arcibal continued. "I merely remind you that as a grown man you took a vow of eternal chastity. In language unambiguous and solemn you entered upon a sacred contract with God. To break that contract, or even trifle with it, means moral death . . . this is all quite clear?"

"Quite clear."

"Yet, realizing as you do that your sacerdotal purity is in danger, why do you persist in this deadly dalliance?"

"I don't know . . . I wish I did."

Like a Greek chorus cleansing a tragic stage with chants of far-off ancient things, Dom Arcibal changed his mood. "Do you remember the passage from the *Confessions* in which St. Augustine laments pillaging a pear tree?"

A *pear tree?* "Yes, I remember."

"As you will recall, then, Augustine asks: 'What did I love in that sin?' And he tells us that his pleasure was not in the pears — which he barely tasted and afterwards threw to the hogs — *but in the offense itself!* Augustine stole those pears because they offered a childish opportunity to pit himself against God. Not merely to displease Him by breaking the Seventh Commandment, but as Augustine says: 'I wished to mimic a maimed liberty by doing things unpermitted me, in darkened likeness of God's omnipotence.' In pain and humiliation the saint afterwards acknowledged that his offense at bottom was the colossally malicious sin of pride."

Laying back his cannon-ball head, Dom Arcibal filled the cell with Augustine's lamentations. "'So doth pride imitate exaltedness . . . thus doth the soul commit fornication when she turns from Thee. Thus we pervertedly imitate Thee who lift up ourselves against Thee. Behold Thy servant fleeing from his Lord and obtaining a shadow. O rottenness, O monstrousness of life and depth of death, that I loved when I might not — *only because I might not.'*"

Revulsion at the linking of Augustine's "O rottenness of death" with the living beauty of Ghislana Falerni; unwillingness to loosen his fingers in complete renunciation, and the belief that his love was not entirely rooted in disobedience crushed sore words from Stephen.

"It isn't true that I loved her only because I might not."

Contempt that the elect in wisdom sometimes employ on the ignorant for their salvation twisted Dom Arcibal's smile. "You still hug that delusion, do you? Well, we must take that childish toy from your arms without delay." Dom Arcibal became the cross-examiner moving in to trip the witness on his own testimony. "This *contessa* is a woman of virtue?"

"That is true."

"And being such a woman, she would disdain to enter into any relation other than marriage?"

"That is also true."

"I ask these questions," said Dom Arcibal, "merely as a prelude to the main inquiry, which is this: would you abandon your priesthood to marry her?"

Stephen uttered a weak and desolate "No."

The Benedictine inveigler of souls placed his finger on the secret flaw in Stephen's character. "What we are dealing with here, Monsignor, is the case of the half offender who carefully selects a sin that can never materialize. A would-be Lucifer who dares not take the consequences of open revolt against either the earthly or the Heavenly Father. Can you deny the pitiful mechanics of this plot against yourself?"

"I have no wish to deny anything," said Stephen abjectly. "Only tell me what I must do to salvage my priesthood."

Dom Arcibal's voice returned to its normal register of kindliness. "First of all, Monsignor, you must stop pillaging pear trees. Give over contending with God. You are no match for Him, anyway. I suggest also that you revise your idea of the priesthood as a courtly tournament — half joust, half miracle play — in which you have cast yourself as a knight at arms, alone and palely loitering. Perhaps the Church needs cavalier priests. Well, let others tread that stage. A man carrying your impost of conscience would be split wide open by such a role."

Reassuring warmth rayed from the monk's bulky person. "There is much love in your heart, my son. God wants all of it, else He would not so relentlessly pursue His fleeing servant. . . . We will discuss these matters frequently and at length in the days ahead. I suggest, for the present, that you make the Stations of the Cross daily while you are with us here. Meditate particularly upon the seventh station, Christ's second fall. Let it be a symbol of the special temptation that may crush a man midway in this mortal life."

"I shall do so, Father." Humbled by the new understanding that Dom Arcibal had given him, Stephen slipped to his knees beside the Benedictine's chair. "I should like very much at this time to make a general confession covering my entire life."

Silently Dom Arcibal drew a purple stole from his pocket. By the act of placing it around his neck he was transformed; the human counselor became the divinely commissioned looser of sins. Clinician and seismologist vanished. A priest took their place.

"I shall be glad to hear your confession, my son."

Kneeling on the stone floor, Stephen Fermoyle endeavored to fulfill the conditions required of anyone, layman or priest, who hopes to receive the sacrament of penance. He confessed his sins fully, neither mitigating nor extenuating them; he made a firm resolution nevermore to offend God, and he accepted the penance his confessor laid upon him.

At the end, Dom Arcibal lifted his right hand to exercise the priestly power of absolution. "Cleanse your heart now in the springs of pure contrition." His *Ego te absolvo* blended with Stephen's "O my God, I am most heartily sorry for having offended Thee." Together their voices rose in affirmation of the boundless love that taketh away the sins of the world.

DAY BY DAY, Stephen entered more deeply into the life of the monastery.

There were no drones in this monastic hive; each member of the community, whether a full-habited monk, a lay brother, or a postulant, had his assigned task. Some toiled in the gardens and vineyards stretching far out onto the Campagna; others tended goats and made an excellent cheese from their milk. The repair and upkeep of the old monastery required the constant attention of masons and carpenters. There were stablemen, kitchen helpers, cooks, launderers, and wielders of mop and broom. And finally there was the scientific work of the laboratory, where, under Dom Arcibal's direction, a group of monks kept the seismograph adjusted and watched its needle scrawl a tremulous record of upheavals and displacements in all parts of the earth's crust.

The entire life of the monastery pivoted on St. Benedict's Rule — a remarkable document written fourteen hundred years ago, and still a model of wisdom and reasonableness in directing man's attention to his eternal destiny. The rule barred extraordinary asceticism; St. Benedict — and Dom Arcibal after him — held surprisingly moderate views on fasting, mortification, and prayer. Although the use of flesh meat was forbidden, two meals a day were permitted. Idle chatter was discouraged, but conversation on profitable subjects might be pursued. Public prayers were brief; there was no limit, however, to the length of one's private devotions. Studying the rule, Stephen found it to be singularly perceptive in gauging the capabilities and limitations of human nature. Benedict had shrewdly appraised the distance that a well-disposed soul could travel in its day-to-day progress toward God.

The chief spiritual activity of the Benedictines was the recitation of the Divine Office or *Opus Dei* — "to which," as St. Benedict urged, "nothing is to be preferred." Seven times daily — at Matins, Prime, Terce, Nones, Sext, Vespers, and Compline — the entire congregation gathered in the choir to chant the canonical hours. As a retreatant Stephen was permitted to be present, but could take no part in these exercises. Longing to lift his voice in the noble strophes of psalms and antiphon, he stood humbly mute while others praised the Creator's name and works. After the first pangs of rejection had passed, he learned to console himself with Paul's counsel to the Corinthians: "Sing with the spirit . . . sing also with the understanding."

As a retreatant (and, therefore, a guest), Stephen might have claimed exemption from physical labor. On Dom Arcibal's advice, however, he entered into the work of the community by helping in the kitchen for two hours before each meal. If vegetables were to be peeled, bread pans greased, or a fire built in the baking oven, Stephen performed these menial duties under the preoccupied eye of Brother Alphonsus — who turned out to be the short-jerkined, not-quite-bright oaf that Stephen had nicknamed "Fairhands" on the day of his arrival.

Brother Alphonsus was kitchen boy, dishwasher, and, by his own election, slavey-general to the monastery at large. A clumsier piece of clay had never whirled off the potter's wheel. At stumbling, falling, bumping into chairs and tables, Brother Alphonsus was a virtuoso. As he staggered across the kitchen with an armful of hot loaves or a pile of plates, his lack of co-ordination seemed pitiful. Halfway across the floor it became ludicrous. When he finally reached his goal with the bread still in his arms, Stephen knew that by some miracle the God of falling sparrows had marked Fairhands for special protection.

Brother Alphonsus displayed an inexhaustible cheerfulness at whatever work he was doing. After the day's cookery was

over he would wash and iron the linen for the entire monastery
— with great inner serenity and much exterior banging. As a
lay brother he made no aspirations to the priesthood; while
other members of the community chanted, performed devotional Offices, or helped Dom Arcibal with his seismographic
work, Fairhands was content to remain in the kitchen.
Although he could read well enough, he found no satisfaction
in books. Evidently he feared that too much learning would
make him vain.

It soon became clear to Stephen that every act of Fairhands'
life was a devotional exercise — offered privately when others
were present, openly when he was alone. Coming into the kitchen one morning, Stephen found him prostrate before the
stove. At the risk of prying, Stephen asked, "What are you
doing on the floor?"

Fairhands got up sheepishly. "I am not able to offer great
things to God," he said, "so I make what offerings I can. While
waiting for my little pancake to cook, I sometimes prostrate
myself in adoration of Him who gives me the grace to make it
— as well as the flour to make it with."

Stephen had known dedicated souls — his sister Ellen and
Ned Halley among them — but he had never seen, or even
heard of, a humility equal to that of Brother Alphonsus.

One day as Stephen helped Fairhands dice the onions and
potatoes for the soup that was the main meal of the day, he
thought he heard the lay brother call him by name. "What did
you say?" asked Stephen above the clatter of knives. Fairhands shook his head: "Nothing." A minute later Stephen
again heard his name. "Whom are you talking to?" he
demanded. Brother Alphonsus continued to hack away at
great risk to his thick fingers, and said:

"I am merely asking God to accept my work as an act of
love . . ."

"Fine. But how did my name get into it?"

"I was begging Him to protect your fingers."

"*My* fingers? What about your own?"

Fairhands began whacking at another onion. "If God wills
that I cut myself, I shall accept it as a mark of His favor. But
since I have placed the whole matter in His hands, it is not
likely that any accident will befall."

Since I have placed the whole matter in His hands . . .

All Dom Arcibal's wisdom, all Stephen's meditations on humility, all the devotions of the *Opus Dei*, were summed up in the crystal simplicity of Fairhands' faith. Instead of trying to outrival the earthly father or dazzle the Heavenly One, you merely surrendered yourself, trustingly, completely, to His will. Whatever happened thereafter was a mark of special favor. . . .

As simple as that. And as difficult. . . .

STEPHEN stayed a month at the monastery. In prayer and contemplation the hours wheeled past, each a reminder of God's timeless plan. When the month ended, Stephen's problems were by no means settled, yet he had become aware, temporarily at least, of his true position as a finite and very humble segment on the compass of infinity.

He returned to Rome on October 29 to find the city ominously quiet under the hand of Mussolini. Il Duce had marched on Rome at last, not with flashing banners but in a sleeping car. The dictator who was to lead the Italian people through an era of seeming triumph, and fearful degradation, had descended on the Eternal City while its citizens were all asleep.

CHAPTER 6

THE NEXT THREE YEARS were for Stephen a time of tempering and growth. He weathered that critical period in the midthirties when a man discovers that either he must generate new energies or lie down in the living grave of mediocrity. He reorganized his life on a basis of rigid economy. Attitudes and activities that did not buttress the temple of his priesthood were ruthlessly lopped off. He refused all social invitations, smiled less often, lost some of his fresh coloring; for impact he depended not so much on personal charm as on his basic deposit of character. In spite of an ascetic way of life (his only indulgence was an occasional after-dinner cigar), he became heavier about the neck and shoulders; at thirty-eight his hair began to show tufts of gray. Three years in Rome transformed Stephen into a stern, unglittering administrator of the Universal Church.

Gradually, the wisdom of Ghislana Falerni's proverb began to come true. "Time makes love pass." Under the rasp of day-to-day duties, Roberto's faunlike profile became less sharply etched. Occasionally Stephen would turn to share a transport of happiness, only to find a fading ghost where once a living friend had stood. He added Roberto's name to the list of people for whom he prayed. Ghislana Falerni's name was on the list also, but he saw or heard from her no more.

Stephen's relations with his Vatican colleagues and superiors had long ago passed through the apprentice phase. He was firmly entrenched now in the confidence — and confidences — of Quarenghi and Guardiano. Even Giacobbi changed his matador tactics in dealing with the American Monsignor. The Cardinal Secretary's brusque manner could never entirely disappear, but after Stephen had completed several difficult assignments, Giacobbi began to put brakes on his peevishness. In its place, a twitting humor emerged. It pleased the Sicilian to rally Stephen on the subject of American dollar diplomacy. When in 1924, the United States lent Germany two billions under the Dawes Plan — hailed at the time as a great marvel of finance — Giacobbi burst into guffaws:

"The Vatican's monetary troubles are over," he roared. "This very day I shall advise His Holiness to declare war on the United States. Then, after our Household Guard takes its trouncing, we shall apply to our conquerors for a fat loan. How much do you advise us to ask for, Monsignor Fermoyle?"

"As much as the traffic will bear. Don't hold back on *my* account, Your Eminence." Two years ago Stephen would have flushed with anger; now he could let the barb bounce off harmlessly. Giacobbi noted the difference and murmured something about a thick skin being one of the ultimate gifts of the Holy Ghost.

From his tiny cubicle Stephen was summoned with increasing frequency into the presence of Pius XI, either to brief the Holy Father on some aspect of the American scene or to act as interpreter for distinguished English-speaking visitors. The Pope was actively seeking to strengthen the ties between

Rome and the United States; as an earnest of his purpose, he bestowed red hats on Archbishop Mundelein of Chicago and Patrick Hayes of New York, thus increasing to four the number of American cardinals in the Sacred College. His Holiness laid himself out to be particularly gracious when bishops from the United States made their ad limina journeys to Rome. In long, cordial audiences Pius XI would question the visitor about his administrative problems and American affairs generally. What was the seating capacity of the parochial schools in the bishop's jurisdiction — the number of beds in his hospitals? Were the seminaries and religious orders thriving? Had the bishop noticed any falling off in the number or quality of candidates for the priesthood? Consulting a memorandum, His Holiness might inquire: "Do the foreign-language minorities in your diocese appear to be contented with their English-speaking pastors?"

At the end of the audience the visiting prelate would be deeply impressed by the pontiff's precise and specific information. "How does the Holy Father know so much about my diocese?" was a question the bishop would inevitably ask when he found himself alone with Stephen after the interview.

"His Holiness has many sources of information," Stephen would say, tactfully omitting to add that he himself had drawn up the memorandum for the pontiff's guidance.

Increasingly close contacts with the Holy Father's person and office gave Stephen a profounder insight into the organization of the Universal Church. He was amazed by the volume and variety of business that flowed across Vatican desks; by every instrument of communication — telegraph, telephone, air post, and wireless (not to mention dog sled, dory, kayak, shank's mare, and word of mouth) — reports flowed in from every part of the world. The baptism of an obscure African tribe by Dominican missionaries, the laying of a convent cornerstone in Wales, or a squabble between an Australian bishop and his cathedral chapter, was reported as soon as it occurred. Twelve major congregations, each governed by a Cardinal Prefect, acted as nerve ganglia relaying impulses from all parts of the mystical body to the visible head of the Church. Each congregation sent voluminous reports to the

Holy Father; no matter how carefully the chaff was sifted out, or how fine the good grain was milled, a huge stack of documents — involving delicate matters of faith, diplomacy, and finance — always lay awaiting the final disposition that only the Pope could give. Merely to read the material was a crushing labor that kept a light burning till long past midnight in the Pope's private apartment on the third floor of the Vatican.

The core of the pontiff's character, Stephen discovered, was his unyielding stubbornness in matters affecting the spiritual prerogatives of the Holy See. He regarded as basic and inalienable the right of the Church to teach, extend, and conserve the faith. In bull after bull he proclaimed this position; by means of concordats with Germany, France, and Poland, he secured spiritual rights for Roman Catholics in those countries. And with Mussolini, Pius XI arrived at a *modus vivendi* guaranteeing freedom of worship and religious education to Roman Catholics in Italy.

Under the robes and ritual of his office, Pius XI emerged clearly as a human being. Stephen found him to be wonderfully patient about long-range objectives but apt to be flash-tempered on the short haul. Stupidity, slowness of speech, or carrying water on both shoulders irked the Holy Father. He liked men who could crack the nut of a problem quickly and serve up its meat without shells. Stephen once heard him exclaim irritably: "Must we spend our life listening to things we already know." Yet he made no claim to omniscience and could be on occasion quite humorous about the gaps in his knowledge. Once during an audience with Bishop John T. Spraker of Indiana, His Holiness became expansive on the physical grandeur of the United States. "Your snow-spiked Rockies — how I should love to see them! What a challenge for climbing! And those enormous stretches on which you grow your wheat" — he turned to Stephen — "how do you call them — pampas, savannas?"

"We call them prairies, Your Holiness."

"Prairies, of course. 'Pampas schooner' wouldn't sound quite right, would it?" The pontiff beamed myopically on Bishop Spraker. "You see, dear Brother, how geography limits our infallibility."

In his strictly mortal aspects Achille Ratti was a man who

ate sparingly of fruits, cheese, and vegetable soup, drank
nothing stronger than cocoa (which he liked), and slept about
five hours a day. His schedule began with daily Mass in his
private chapel at six-thirty A.M., followed by breakfast consisting of a buttered roll and bowl of cocoa. From eight to ten
he handled his enormous correspondence. Then followed a
series of conferences with his chief cardinal advisers; later
came audiences with bishops, abbots, and distinguished personages lay or clerical. At two P.M. the Pope lunched alone
(by tradition he was never permitted to break bread at the
same table with others). Then came a short siesta and more
official business till five. After a solitary walk in the Vatican
gardens, he took a supper of consommé Romana — a broth
enriched with eggs — followed by pears, cheese, and more
cocoa. He then picked up the *Osservatore Romano,* the Vatican newspaper, and read every word in its pages. Around nine
P.M. he entered his private study and began on the pile of
documents and reports on his desk. Feast days added a tremendous weight of religious ceremonial and public blessings
to this man-killing schedule. Under the burden of his office,
Pius XI developed the gnarly strength found in lone firs that
have plunged their roots into some rocky cleft at the edge of
the snow line. No man could have been higher in personal
asceticism, deeper in devotion to his Vicarate, lonelier, more
isolated as a human being.

EASTER MONDAY, 1924. The Paschal feast had been marked
with services of extraordinary beauty at St. Peter's; now in
green vestments both Church and nature entered upon the
joyous cycle of resurrection. Stephen sat at his inlaid desk,
examining a petition of certain French-Canadian fishing parishes — alleging invasion of their lobster-trapping rights by an
American syndicate. The matter was complicated: a dozen
international treaties had been broken, and Stephen was preparing to study the law covering the subject when his telephone rang.

It was Gaetano Orselli; the Captain's voice gurgled with
excitement. "I must see you, Stefano. There is news of the first
importance — news that can be related only over a bottle of
wine. Meet me for dinner tonight at the Café Sorrento on the

Via delle Botteghe Oscure. You'll recognize me by the flower in my mouth!"

The flower in Orselli's mouth was a blossoming grin that spread uncontrollably over his face as he greeted Stephen. They sat down to a tureen of excellent soup, and a cutlet *parmigiana*. The first bottle of Falerno had disappeared before Stephen had a chance to ask:

"What's your news? Political? Have you been offered the Navy portfolio in Il Duce's government?"

"Portfolio? Il Duce? Trivia! Stephen, my news is of the heart. I am Romeo, and you are Friar Lawrence." Orselli lifted a glass, struck his breast in a mock *mea culpa*. "Shrive me, Father, that I may be worthy to touch the hem of an angel become woman."

"Riddling confession gets but riddling shrift. What's this Romeo business? The last time we talked, you were off women for life."

"Women in the plural, yes. You now behold a man who thinks and speaks only of the Woman — singular and unique. Stephen, I've *found* her!"

"Not the 'impossible she' with the town house, the country house, the title, the income, and — oh yes, I almost forgot — the star dust in her hair?"

Orselli was dead sober. "You have every right to be skeptical, Stefano. I admit I've sailed a zigzag course; my love log is full of lying entries written in a careless hand. But now I know how the compass needle feels when the polestar grips it. Compulsion, surrender, peace. And not the peace of passivity!" Orselli chose a marine simile: "It is like the dreaming quietness at the center of a turbine whirling at full speed."

"You're in sad shape, Captain. Where did you meet this female turbine?"

"At Capri, barely a month ago. At the first exchange of glances I felt my soul slipping out of me. At the next exchange, it was returned to me doubly charged. I was almost prostrated. Until I met Ghislana Falerni I could not believe that such intensity of emotion existed. You stare? You doubt me?"

"Am I staring? I . . . I happen to know the Contessa Falerni."

"How you clerical rogues get about! Then you can understand what I'm trying to say. Don't you agree that she resembles a Corneille heroine — Phèdre, perhaps?"

"She is a woman of unusual charm."

"Come, this is lukewarm, Stefano. Speak freely; you have taste and judgment in these matters. Did you ever hear such a voice? A brook, silver-pebbled. And where but on the Attic frieze could one find such a torso? Forgive me, my friend, for mentioning such matters — but she is mortal flesh, this promised bride of mine. Do you wonder at my happiness? Congratulate me, Stefano."

An inward agony was beginning in Stephen as he clasped Orselli's hand. "Has the marriage date been fixed?"

"We are to be wed early in June. I would ask you to perform the ceremony, but Cardinal Merry del Val is an old friend of the family. You understand how these things are?"

"Quite."

"But you'll come to the nuptials, of course? The privilege of kissing the bride is being limited to a few trusted friends."

Stephen's agony was mounting. *Am I still not free of her? Must I go bound forever?* He felt cornered as Orselli went into lyrical transports about Ghislana Falerni's person and accomplishments. *How can I get out of here without exposing myself? If this gloating libertine continues to smack his fat lips . . .*

Orselli nipped an after-dinner Havana between his fine square teeth, lighted it leisurely. Its oily fragrance drifting across the table suggested a plan of escape.

"I've acquired a new vice," Stephen heard himself saying. "If your cigars are very mild, I'll celebrate the occasion by smoking one with you."

"Forgive me, dear friend." The Captain extended his case. "Try this Vuelta. I recommend it for body and aroma. Ah, the solace of tobacco. As your Kipling says — 'A woman is only a woman. . . .' "

Stephen lighted up, simulated the appreciative puff of the connoisseur. "Tell me your plans, Captain. Will you give up the sea?"

"Yes, my sailing days are over. My bride is a land creature; hereafter, her element will be mine. Fortunately, I have been offered a shore berth, the post of Examiner-General for the Italian Line."

"I suppose you'll entertain a great deal." (Keep the talk impersonal.)

"I dare say. Ghislana is a born hostess. Her services should be valuable in bringing Quirinal and Vatican closer together. How do you like that cigar?"

"Excellent. It seems a trifle strong."

"You are burning the tobacco too fast. Most Americans smoke that way. Of course we shall manage to steal away for a summer of honeymooning at Capri. Ghislana has an estate there. An estate — what am I saying? — an Eden, rather." Orselli's tongue caressed the Vuelta. "Doesn't it seem a miracle to you, Stefano, that after my lifelong furrowing of the sea, I should find this perfect haven in marriage?"

"Miraculous, as you say." Drops of sweat began to form on Stephen's forehead. He wiped them away ostentatiously with his handkerchief. "Am I imagining, or is it warm in here?"

"No, it's rather cool."

Stephen took an enormous drag at the Vuelta. "Perhaps it's this cigar."

"Relish it more slowly. Your ash is an inch longer than mine already. Here, drop it in this tray." Orselli picked up the ash tray at his elbow, and slid it across the table. It was a common enough piece of native Roman pottery — pink clay, cheaply kilned and bordered with an egg-and-dart design. Dizzied by the fumes of his cigar, Stephen leaned forward to flick its ash when his eye caught the motto painted on the tray.

L'AMORE

FA PASSARE

IL TEMPO;

IL TEMPO

FA PASSARE

L'AMORE

Love makes time pass; time makes love pass!

"Tell me now," Orselli was saying, "when and where did you meet my Ghislana?"

Napkin to his lips, Stephen rose limply. "Sorry, Gaetano,

I'll have to get out of here. Your cigar has made me feel greenish." Unsteadily he started for the door. Outside, in the Street of Dark Shops, he leaned against a brick wall and was wretchedly sick.

Orselli, all solicitude, hovered near by. "Shall I take you home, Stefano?"

"No, no. Just call a cab. I'll be all right soon as I can lie down quietly." He attempted a sickly grin. "I guess I'm not the cigar smoker I thought I was."

Convulsions of nausea racked Stephen all the way home. Between seizures, the egg-and-dart design on the ash tray whirled like a pinwheel pivoting on a cruel nail:

Il tempo fa passare l'amore. . . .

By IMMEMORIAL custom and papal decree, the Holy Door in St. Peter's Basilica is opened every twenty-five years. The origins of this ancient tradition go back to the times of Boniface VIII, who, in 1300, caused a section of St. Peter's wall to be broken open as a token of sanctuary to men of all faiths. The custom persists. At quarter-century intervals the reigning pontiff taps a certain brick (previously loosened by stonemasons), and the brick tumbles to the ground. Other bricks are removed; the door remains open all during the Holy Year, and through its portals, a multitude of the faithful — shawled, kilted, hooded, caped, sandaled, and veiled — pours into the great basilica.

During the Holy Year 1925, one million two hundred thousand pilgrims journeyed to Rome for the festivities, solemn and joyous, that mark the opening and closing of the Holy Door. They came to obtain the Jubilee indulgence granted to all who fulfilled the prescribed conditions. Rather mild conditions they were. The pilgrim was required only to visit each of the four major basilicas in Rome: St. Peter's, St. Paul's Without the Walls, St. John Lateran, and St. Mary's Major, reciting in each three Our Father's, three Hail Mary's, and three Glory Be's. Then having made a good confession and received Communion, he received a plenary indulgence.

In 1925 the streets of Rome were thronged with pilgrims bearing flowers and statues to their favorite shrine. Among them was Celia Fermoyle. Five years of scrimping on her "house money," together with a few sundry oddments wheedled out of Florrie, plus a hundred dollars sent by Stephen, had enabled her to buy a round-trip ticket from Boston to the Eternal City. She wanted to see, particularly, the building in which her priest-son worked, and to hear the Sistine Choir singing High Mass. Celia's other ideas concerning Rome bordered on the shadowy side — as Stephen discovered when calling upon his mother at the Cenacle of the Blue Sisters, where he had made a reservation for her two weeks' sojourn in the Holy City.

At sixty, Celia still had much of the birdlike quickness of movement that Stephen remembered from childhood. Her once-black hair was ivory white, but her eyes still sparkled with shoe-button brightness, and the tonic of the sea voyage had renewed her lightness of foot and spirit. Stephen had expected to find her exhausted; instead, she was so excited that she could scarcely sit still in the little parlor of the Cenacle. Stephen finally quieted her down to the point where she could bring him abreast of family history.

"The old house at 47 Woodlawn isn't the busy place it used to be, Son," said Celia. "Sometimes I sit alone in the kitchen of an afternoon, remembering the times when school got out and you'd all come rushing in the back door for your bats and skates or footballs, then rush out again till supper. What a commotion! The evenings are quieter too, now that Florrie and Al have moved out. They've got a nice place of their own in Roslindale. A baby or two would blend them together, but I don't see any coming."

"How's Ellen?"

"Happier than I've ever seen her. It was God's blessing that sent Father Ireton to Medford with work for her. Ah, the goodness of Father Paul! In three years he's won everyone's heart. He's started a new church — it's only a basement yet, but he's planning to build on top of it."

"He'll make it. And Bernie? I hear he's on what they call 'radio.'"

Celia bobbed a puzzled head. "He sings the same songs they wouldn't pay a dime to hear in the cafés. The 'Irish Thrush' they call him now. Would you believe it, Bernie's been making fifty a week — come Murphy, go Murphy — for the past six months?"

It was hard to believe. Then came the question that Stephen had been longing to ask. "What's little Regina like?"

"She's an angel. Pretty — like Mona was. A little darker-complected maybe. Rita and Dr. John take wonderful care of her." Celia rummaged in her bag for a handkerchief to wipe her eyes. "I never get over the goodness that God puts into people's hearts. But tell me now, Son, is it true, like you said in your letter, that you work in the Vatican on the same floor with the Pope?"

"Yes . . . except that he's in another wing."

"Are there many others that come as near to him as that?"

Stephen laughed. "Quite a few. It's a big place, you know — over a thousand rooms."

"Will you have time to point it out to me?"

"Point it out to you? I'm going to take you all through it. You're going to see everything — the Sistine Chapel, Michelangelo's great frescoes, the Clementine Hall — and if I can arrange it, you're going to have a private audience with the Holy Father himself."

Stephen arranged it. Dressed in black, veiled, with her son at her elbow, Celia slowly climbed the great staircase, waited tremulously in the papal antechamber, then knelt to the Fisherman's ring on the pontiff's finger. Six hundred thousand people had already kissed the ring that year. Buffeted as he was by the tidal wave of pilgrims, Achille Ratti, fourth son of a silk weaver, was still able to give an individual touch to the audience. And that touch was a surprise to Stephen. His Holiness spoke to Celia in English!

"God has blessed you with other children, my daughter?"

"Yes, Your Holiness. I am the mother of three boys and four girls."

"Has your heart a favorite among them?" asked the pontiff teasingly.

Celia's eyes rested on her first-born standing violet-cassocked beside her. "I am very proud of my oldest son, Your Holiness. He has brought me great joy and never caused me a moment's sorrow." She started to check a mother's garrulity, then let it slip again. "When Stephen was a little boy, he used to beg me to say that I loved him more than the others. I wanted to tell him then, and I wish I could tell Your Holiness now, that he always was first in my heart. But I can't say something that wouldn't be fair to the others. A mother must make all her children feel that she loves them equally. Anything else would be displeasing to God."

Of the many words Pius XI heard that year, Celia's moved him more poignantly than most. The pontiff recalled his own childhood plea: "Mama, say you love me best. Whisper it, Mama, so that the others won't hear." That plea had never been requited. His Holiness gazed curiously at Stephen, linked with him in the common fellowship of rejection. Would it really be displeasing to God, he wondered, if mothers should murmur: "Dear son [dear Achille, dear Stephen], it is you that I love beyond all others." Yes, doubtless it would be unwise, for if such words were uttered, the sons of women would perish in too much earthly bliss.

A chamberlain's signal reminded the harried pontiff that others were waiting in his antechamber. From a rosewood box Pius XI took a medal of the Virgin and presented it to Celia.

"This Mother, too, loves all her children equally," he said, lifting his hand in papal benediction. It was the pinnacle of Celia Fermoyle's life; the gold bar of heaven seemed very near as Stephen led her out of the pontifical chamber.

In SEPTEMBER of the Holy Year, Lawrence Cardinal Glennon sailed from Boston on the *Canopic* with a band of pious New Englanders, six hundred strong, and landed at Naples on the feast day commemorating the Jesuit saints of North America. The delegation was officially greeted by Monsignor Stephen Fermoyle arrayed in mantelletta, ring, and cross befitting the Pope's personal representative. What a troop of dignitaries streamed off the *Canopic!* First came the Cardinal in full ecclesiastic regalia, followed by three venerable bishops, one of them so infirm that he had to be carried down the gangplank in a chair. Then debarked a purple squadron of monsignors, followed by a regiment of pastors and curates — the infantry of the Church. The laity was nobly represented by His Excellency the Governor of Rhode Island, four Catholic Congressmen, seven mayors, a spate of aldermen, and a generous sprinkling of lawyers, doctors, businessmen, and contractors. Among the latter was Cornelius J. Deegan, who came — gilt chain, velvet cape, and all — to assume his duties as honorary chamberlain to the Pope.

The staff work for this huge expedition had been handled by Right Reverend Michael J. Speed, the rapidly rising Chancellor of the Archdiocese, on whom Cardinal Glennon leaned with increasing dependence in administrative affairs. The Cardinal knew well enough that his monopoly on Mike Speed's services was drawing to an end. By seniority and deserts, the Chancellor was first in line for the next vacant bishopric. And the diocese that got him (everyone said) would be lucky indeed.

Glennon embraced Stephen with a frank hug; Mike Speed's greeting was kind speaking to kind. After an hour of introductions to the Catholic nobility and gentry of New England, Stephen began to look around for a certain high-marbling forehead.

"Where's Dick Clarahan?" he asked the Chancellor.

Mike Speed laughed. "Someone had to run the Diocese. It's Dickie's big chance to practice up. Say, Steve, here's an old friend of yours. Claims he knew you when."

The claimant was Dollar Bill Monaghan, Stephen's first pastor. Ten years had not taken the steely curl out of Monaghan's hair; at sixty-six he still had the shoulders of a champion mortgage lifter, and the appraising squint of a rector on the lookout for a serviceable assistant.

"Welcome to Rome, Father," said Stephen, gripping Dollar Bill's hand. "How's the milk route in Malden?"

"We're still making house-to-house deliveries, Stephen. Curates aren't what they used to be, though. Rome skims off the cream." Monaghan fumbled with paternal admiration at the ribbony knot of Stephen's cape. "Handsome rig you're wearing, Monsignor."

"I'd swap it this minute for a parish somewhere north of Boston," said Stephen. "Can't you use your pull with His Eminence to get me transferred?" In the milling throng on the pier, they talked of St. Margaret's and its old parishioners. What was Jeremy Splaine doing? Why, Jeremy was in his final year at the Brighton Seminary. Head of his class. Had the makings of a fine priest.

And whatever became of Milky Lyons, Stephen wanted to know. "Ah, poor Milky," said Monaghan, "he went melancholy on us."

In strength they stood who stood. In weakness they fell who fell.

The Cardinal's descent on Rome was the progress of an ecclesiastical lord accompanied by his retinue. Bishops, Congressmen, and a crush of distinguished pilgrims drifted in and out of Glennon's compartment as they sped northward on a special train. Stephen was unexpectedly homesick; the sight of so many American faces and the sound of his native tongue hit him with all the subtlety of a brass band playing "The Stars and Stripes Forever."

"Send me home," he prayed secretly, as the train whirled toward the Holy City. "Not my will but Thine. Only send me home."

Stephen's work really began when the delegation reached Rome. Acting as liaison officer between the Vatican and his countrymen, he arranged group visits to the four principal basilicas and side trips to venerated shrines. The Holy Father graciously consented to say a special Mass for the Americans and — rarest of honors — gave them Holy Communion with his own hands. In the audience following the communion breakfast, Pius XI referred to Cardinal Glennon as "our noble, valiant brother." Speaking in Italian, with Stephen standing beside and slightly behind him as interpreter, His Holiness praised the New Englanders for their stanch piety and hailed them as the largest, most loyal, and certainly the most generous band of New World Catholics ever to visit Rome.

The pilgrimage was a roseate triumph for everyone concerned. The Governor of Rhode Island was made a Knight of Malta, and eleven other New Englanders received the insignia of papal nobility. Meanwhile Cornelius Deegan was taking his chamberlain service most gravely. Every morning, attired in cloak and sword, he presented himself for assignment to the Vatican Major-Domo. And because there was always need for a certain number of gentlemen in waiting, the Knight of St. Sylvester walked in many processions or stood ornamentally about whenever he was bidden. His tour of duty over, he gave an enormous dinner party at the Ritz-Reggia to a hundred guests lay and clerical. An emblazoned invitation was propped beside the plate of each diner. "You are most cordially invited," the invitation ran, "to be the guest of Cornelius J. Deegan on his specially chartered yacht, the *Santa Croce*, on a pilgrimage to the shrine of Our Lady of Lourdes. R.S.V.P."

Acceptances were heavy. On All Souls' Day a merry company of American Catholic gentlemen sailed out of Naples Harbor on the largest yacht that Corny could charter. Old Glory fluttered from the main truck of the *Santa Croce*, and just below it rippled the pennon of the Order of St. Sylvester. Corny's orders to the captain were: "Proceed northward with dignity and dispatch to Marseille." An Italian man of war, mistaking the *Santa Croce* for a royal barge of some kind, fired a twenty-one-gun salute as she cleared the harbor.

Standing on the dock, waving his countrymen off, Stephen could have wept with loneliness and longing for America.

ON CHRISTMAS DAY the Holy Door was bricked up for another twenty-five years. After the elaborate ceremonies were over, and the last pilgrim had departed, life in the Vatican settled down to its normal tempo. Stephen was gathering up the scattered threads of office routine when, during the Octave of Epiphany, Alfeo Quarenghi dropped in on him. Visits from Quarenghi were rare; he had little time for chatty calls. The Secretary for the Congregation of Extraordinary Ecclesiastical Affairs took a chair and plunged immediately into the subject of his visit.

"The Holy Father," he began, "is deeply concerned about the Apostolic Delegate at Washington. The present incumbent, Archbishop Rienzi, is an extremely learned and able man, but according to advices from Cardinal Glennon and others" — Quarenghi was phrasing the matter with a diplomat's tact — "it appears that Rienzi is somewhat out of touch with the American temper."

What's he getting at? Stephen wondered.

"For some time now," continued Quarenghi, "the Holy See has felt the need of a fresh approach to the relationships between the Vatican and the United States. Rienzi is to be recalled and will of course be elevated to the cardinalate. Meanwhile His Holiness has honored me with the Washington assignment." Modesty lowered Quarenghi's eyes. "The post carries the title of archbishop."

Stephen was on his feet. "Congratulations, Alfeo. Apostolic Delegate to the United States! What an honor! Think of the tremendous job you can do there."

"There's certainly a job to be done. The task carries almost frightening responsibilities." Quarenghi's quite unfrightened gaze met Stephen's at level range. "The Holy Father has granted me the privilege of choosing my own staff. Will you come to Washington with me, Stephen, as my assistant and special adviser in American affairs?"

Choked with joy at the prospect of returning to America, awed by the dimensions of the task ahead, Stephen could not speak. Like a man touching the haft of a sword in pledge of liege devotion, he laid his hand on Quarenghi's shoulder.

A week later Pius XI invested Alfeo Quarenghi as Archbishop of Mytilene and embraced him affectionately as he sailed for the United States. The pontiff's parting words to his legate were: "It is our most prayerful wish that you show all men how perfectly an embassy of the spirit may be carried into a country of mixed religious faiths and free political opinions."

STEPHEN'S FIRST VIEW of his homeland was the battlements of Manhattan emerging through gray flurries of snow as the Cunarder zoomed hoarsely into the North River. Headed by Patrick Cardinal Hayes, a detachment of overcoated American prelates met the papal delegate at the pier. During the formalities of introduction, Quarenghi's teeth began chattering with unaccustomed cold. Cardinal Hayes whispered to a mufflered aide, "The dear man will freeze entirely in another minute. Let's get him up to the house." In three black limousines, preceded and flanked by police motorcycles, the little procession whirled to the Cardinal's residence on Madison Avenue, colloquially known as "the Powerhouse."

While Quarenghi was resting in his room before dinner, a curly-haired Monsignor named Fergus Carroll took Stephen in tow. Monsignor Carroll was a former Holy Cross boy now attached to the Cathedral chapter. "Is there anything particular you'd like to do in the next hour or two?" he asked.

"That's a fine question to ask a man who's never been in New York before," said Stephen. "What I'd really like to do is stretch my legs — walk around the city a bit."

"I'll borrow a pair of overshoes for you," said Fergus. "There's a lot of snow outside."

The air was tingling at seven or eight degrees above zero as they crunched along the still uncleared pavement of Fifth Avenue. Late-afternoon traffic was in a typical New York snarl. While snow swirled like a dotted muslin curtain in a stiff wind, a crawling paralysis seemed to grip busses and taxis. Horns, the roar of motors, and the whistles of traffic cops made a strident confusion as Stephen and Fergus dodged in and out along the crowded sidewalk. Yet it was exhilarating too, this New York tempo so markedly different from the languid Roman beat. Snow nipping his cheeks, Stephen was glad to breathe the air of his native north-temperate climate.

A specific craving for something he had dreamed about for a long time broke out in Stephen now. "Are there any drugstores around here?" he asked Fergus Carroll as they neared Forty-second Street.

"Sure. The Grand Central district is full of them. What do you want?"

"Don't laugh," said Stephen, "but I want a strawberry icecream soda. And bad. It's been coming on for years."

"Will you take it in a booth or on a stool?"

Stephen had his strawberry ice-cream soda on a stool. When Fergus Carroll handed him two straws, he knew that the heart of the country was sound.

They walked up Madison Avenue to Fiftieth Street. "How'd you like to make a little visit before dinner?" asked Fergus.

Stephen knew what his companion meant. Together they entered a side door of the Cathedral, stood for a moment in the candlelighted shadows of the south aisle. Kneeling at the epistle side of the main altar, he said a short prayer of thanksgiving, then made his wish. A simple one: that Alfeo Quarenghi's mission would succeed.

Shortly after seven, Quarenghi and Stephen were escorted

to the dining room by their Cardinal-host himself. The classic
protocol (which decrees that twelve is the proper number for
a bachelor dinner or some unconscious observance of an even
older tradition) had led to the seating of an even dozen guests.
All ranks of the hierarchy were present: the Cardinal sat at the
head of the table, with Archbishop Quarenghi on his right
and the Auxiliary Bishop of New York at his left. Simple hos-
pitality rather than high ceremony was the note. His Eminence
murmured grace, then picked up a spoon and began operations on a thick vegetable soup. Afterwards there was roast
lamb, gravy, and plenty of pan-browned potatoes, but no
salad. For dessert, apple pie and coffee; cigars for those who
smoked them.

The table talk was neither exalted nor commonplace. No
philosophic observations were offered and only one clerical
story was told. The company discussed the approaching
Eucharistic Congress in Chicago, the grave troubles of the
Church in Mexico, and the overemphasis on football in certain Catholic colleges. Quarenghi made inquiries regarding
the health of Cardinal Dougherty, and praised the remarkable
work the Philadelphia prelate had done in the Philippines.

Knowing the range of Quarenghi's mind, Stephen thought
that his friend might have talked more brilliantly. Yet as the
dinner progressed he began to realize that the Apostolic Delegate was purposely letting his host set the conversational pace.
Since Cardinal Hayes neither was a great intellect nor pretended to be one, Quarenghi accommodated himself to the
prevailing gait. It was no part of the papal legate's plan to
overwhelm the Americans either with personal charm or his
knowledge of Roman affairs. Frankness and courtesy marked
his answers to whatever questions were asked, but he initiated
no topics and disclosed nothing that could not have been
gleaned by any thoughtful reader of *L'Osservatore Romano*.
Long before the dinner ended, Stephen could see that Quarenghi's modesty and reserve were creating a quietly soothing
effect on the diners. Yet they were waiting for something, too.
When the party moved into the Cardinal's library for coffee,
Stephen whispered to his friend: "I think they're expecting
you to open up a little."

A glance from the Apostolic Delegate's brilliant brown eyes said: "I'll try not to disappoint them."

The book-lined shelves, open fire, and deep leather chairs of the library made a perfect setting for the performance that followed. In the relaxed mesmeric voice that Stephen remembered from classroom days, Quarenghi began drawing the American prelates into the field of his personality. He spoke of the Holy Father's grief at the melancholy posture of human affairs. Then, as was his habit when developing a line of thought, Quarenghi arose and paced quietly before the open hearth. A huge global map of the world flanked one side of the fireplace. As Quarenghi talked, he spun the globe gently, then braking its motion with his hand, brought it to a stop with Italy under his palm.

"Italia," he said, "progenetrix of law, womb of culture, mother of the arts, awakener of Europe! That awakening, my friends, has had unforeseeable results. For today Europe is a grid of contesting races, so riddled by anxieties, military and economic, so cluttered with nationalist debris, that the stanchest soul can scarcely find kneeling space." Alfeo Quarenghi shook his head sadly. "I am a European. I love the cultures of Italy, Germany, France. They are the priceless yeast that will leaven new loaves. But I cannot honestly say that the future of civilization dwells in the fatigued and battered continent of Europe."

Quarenghi's hand moved north, eastward. "And here is Russia — 'All the Russias,' as we used to say. A vast expanse in which the light of God's word has been officially extinguished. Last year His Holiness sent fifty missionary priests into this area — candle flames in the darkness. Their tongues of light were discovered, snuffed out. Not a man of that heroic company now lives. A hundred more will be sent this year. They, too, will suffer martyrdom." The Roman legate put a question in the Latin form that expects a negative answer: "Can the world look hopefully to Russia as a champion of religion while the atheism of Lenin endures?"

He gave the globe a fresh spin. "Here is the New World. Concerning South America, what can be said? Though the dominant faith is strongly Catholic and most ardent, these loyal children of the Church are plagued by economic and political problems. They will be fortunate if they can preserve their pristine faith — a good fortune that has not been permitted their Mexican brethren."

The Apostolic Delegate now laid his open palm on the shield-shaped curvature of the United States; seemingly he experienced the tactile pleasure of a man rubbing a ruddy apple. "This is the land I have so often envisioned in fancy. What may we not expect from a country so boundlessly blessed by God? I speak not of the iron in your hills, the carbon in your mines, the torrential power generated by your rivers and machines. I speak rather of the spirit generated by your people — the spirit of American fortitude and resourcefulness, tinged by an almost mystical trust in its own destiny."

The arch of Quarenghi's discourse became a bridge between present and future. His hearers saw nations and religions crossing that bridge in a vast migration toward a divine goal. Quarenghi made the toiling progress seem possible, real. And in closing he revealed both the nature of his mission to American Catholics and their responsibility to the future.

"The Holy Father has sent me to your country not in the spirit of authoritarian conquest. I come as neither a meddler nor an overseer, but merely to remind you that the world looks to the Catholics of the United States for a rekindling of the spiritual flame that is now almost extinguished in the world. If your light fails, there is danger of universal darkness."

No one in that room had ever heard such a declaration of faith and hope. During a long silence each man sat before the council fire of his private thought; then Patrick Hayes voiced with characteristic simplicity the hesitation and fears of all:

"You lay a heavy burden upon us, Archbishop. Our strength may falter, our light may fail."

Quarenghi was too realistic to deny the truth of the Cardinal's statement. "That is possible," he replied. "But as Socrates pointed out long ago: 'No one can come to harm in contemplating ideals of love, government, or education.'"

THOUGH PHYSICALLY TIRED, Stephen slept poorly that night. The excitement of being home again, the stimulus of Quarenghi's eloquence, and the knowledge that a new chapter of relationship was opening between Rome and America made him restless, eager for the new day to begin. Around three o'clock he rose to gaze out his window at the great metropolis silently receiving its sacrament of snow. From the window sill he picked up a handful of the precious substance that gave rigor to the American climate, fortitude to the American character. A gleam of light from a street lamp made the snow sparkle with crystalline fire. Stephen praised the glinting flakes — frozen sparks of the flame that Quarenghi had invoked against darkness.

He made a snowball with his bare hands and sponged his forehead with its grateful cold. Then, moved by some overhang from boyhood, he felt the need of heaving the snowball at something. At what? The lamp-post stood at a too-difficult angle of fire. No chance of hitting it. Peering through the gauze transparency of snow, Stephen saw the apse of St. Patrick's looming to the west. For a moment he enjoyed the boyish fantasy of having an arm strong enough to hit one of its pinnacles. What a wing that would be!

The fantasy vanished like a grace note in a song. Stephen tossed his snowball out the open window, watched the arc of its flight as it fell harmlessly to the sidewalk. He threw two more snowballs, drank in a lungful of the frosty air, then, tensions released, he leapt back into bed and fell asleep.

IT WAS February 17, 1926. Not a date to be remembered in history — but typical perhaps of the era in which it fell. Mayor James J. Walker, ill with a cold, was snatching a vacation in Atlantic City. Senator Fernald of Maine had pledged a lastditch fight against American entry into the League of Nations. President Coolidge was opposing an outlay of half a million dollars for repairs on the White House roof. A certain Reverend Mr. Empringham, having made a tour of New York speakeasies, was declaring Prohibition a bleary failure. The "Spanish Trunk" fraud was being revived; a bill limiting the working hours of women and children to forty-eight hours a week had just been introduced in the New York State legislature. Samuel Insull was buying control of the Chicago, Aurora, and Elgin Railroad; two obscure gentlemen named Hoffman had taken out a six-million-dollar insurance policy on their collective brains. A seat on the New York Stock Exchange would sell that day for $148,000, and real estate in Miami was being snapped up at a hundred dollars per running foot. In the sovereign state of Delaware the whipping post had just been revived to check the mounting wave of burglary; and in McKeesport, Pennsylvania, Seventh Day Adventists were predicting the end of the world.

CHAPTER 7

THE RESIDENCE of the Apostolic Delegate to the United States was, in 1926, a three-story limestone building at 1811 Biltmore Street, N. W., Washington, D. C. American bishops, drawing on diocesan funds, had underwritten its construction, then in token of their loyalty and devotion had presented it to the Holy See. By means of cornice and entablature the architect had given the Delegate's residence the unmistakable exterior of a legation, which indeed it was. A purely ecclesiastical legation, to be sure; an embassy dealing not with civil government but solely with the hierarchy of the Catholic Church in the United States.

In May, 1926, Archbishop Alfeo Quarenghi, for the past few months Apostolic Delegate to the United States, sat in the oak-paneled study on the second floor of his residence, writing a letter to His Holiness Pope Pius XI. It was a personal letter, not a report, combining respectful intimacy, grave matter, and literary style in fairly equal proportions. He had already covered five pages of crested stationery with the small script of the practiced writer; before the letter was done he would cover five more. Halfway down the sixth page he wrote:

The secret of the American temperament still eludes me. These people teem with a physical and nervous vitality for which (I am beginning to think) they have as yet found no complete or satisfactory expression. Their outstanding achievement appears to be a vibrant and highly perfected technology; with breath-taking machines they have developed a remarkable system of production and exchange capable of creating incredible wealth. Yet this very technology has bred deep conflicts in their personal lives and national polity. Unless these conflicts can be solved, I fear that the collective American soul will suffer a rude shock in the not-too-distant future.

Alfeo Quarenghi read what he had written and started a fresh page:

I am beginning to understand the difficulties that beset my distinguished predecessor. Daily it becomes more apparent that the Holy See faces a special problem vis-à-vis the bishops of this democratic, intensely national, and very prosperous country. Not that the American hierarchy is stiff-necked or rebellious. Quite the contrary; the prelates who have thus far paid their respects to your legate are animated by the liveliest devotion to Rome. Their orthodoxy is unimpeachable, and I have been deeply touched by their material generosity. But I have also been struck by the spirit of independence that has made these amazing people what they are. In a word, Americans.

On one point particularly — the absolute separation of Church and State — the American hierarchy is most emphatic. Their attitude is best expressed perhaps in the words of the late eminent Cardinal Gibbons: "American Catholics rejoice in the separation of Church and State . . . it seems to us the natural, inevitable, and best-conceivable plan." Without necessarily accepting this viewpoint, I am at present exploring its foundations in American character and history. My search has been aided by the study of several works, among which I may mention Lord Bryce's *American Commonwealth*, Woodrow Wilson's *Congressional Government*, and, of course, all documents and publications touching upon American synods and plenary councils.

Thoughtfully, Quarenghi began his seventh sheet.

My position here is one of extreme delicacy. I must, by definition, maintain an "office of vigilance" over the health and progress of the Church, while striving always to leave unimpaired the authority of American bishops. What is lacking here is any well-founded corpus of precedent and practice that will serve both sides in their dealings with each other. My constant effort will be directed at casting the core of such precedent — an armature (so to speak) that will stand up under the highly charged energies flowing between Rome and the Catholics of the United States.

The Apostolic Delegate rested his eyes momentarily on the excellent copy of Luini's *Christ Disputing in the Temple* hanging on the wall opposite him.

Already I am beginning to see that the absolute separation of the two powers has many practical advantages. Though the Federal government grants no subsidies to the clergy, neither does it meddle in the appointment of bishops or the religious education of the young. Religious and political freedom walk hand in hand here, guarded by a clause in the American Constitution which declares: "No religious test shall ever be required as a qualification to any office of public trust." While it would be naïve to think that bigotry is nonexistent, I find that the clause operates effectively in many sections of the country. For example, the present Governor of New York State, His Excellency Alfred E. Smith, is a Roman Catholic, thrice elected to his high office by the combined suffrage of Jewish, Catholic, and Protestant voters.

Speaking of Protestants, Your Holiness will be interested to learn of their current attempt to weld their numerous sects (some 250, I understand) into a common front. Tomorrow an Inter-Faith Convocation begins, under avowedly nonsectarian auspices, in New York City. Representatives of all faiths have been asked to attend. I received a cordial invitation to be present in person and was in somewhat of a quandary about accepting. I shall observe the amenities by sending Monsignor Stephen Fermoyle to the Convocation as an envoy, so to speak, without portfolio.

While on the subject of Monsignor Fermoyle, may I tell Your Holiness what a bulwark of strength he has been during these first difficult weeks? As my equerry, courier, and counselor, he has proved himself the perfect liaison buffer between me and an unfamiliar world. When newspapermen clamor for interviews, it is Monsignor Fermoyle who gives them their "story." He has accompanied me on my round of courtesy calls to the State Department and the embassies of foreign powers. Most valuable of all, he coached me on the personal and geographic idiosyncrasies (striking in some instances) of the fifteen American bishops who have thus far paid their respects to your legate. I scarcely know what I should have done without his brilliant assistance. . . .

And where, at this moment, was Archbishop Quarenghi's adviser, equerry, and liaison buffer, Monsignor Stephen Fermoyle? Why, he was in an adjoining office patiently listening to the complaints of Father Peter Morkunas, a Lithuanian pastor who was having trouble with his German-born superior, Franz Josef Schwabauer, Bishop of Steubenville, Ohio.

Father Morkunas wanted to build a social hall behind his church and listed a dozen reasons for building it, including basketball games, card parties, charity bazaars, and communion breakfasts. But in ticking off his needs, he had somehow failed to mention prior financial obligations. Under the pressure of Stephen's cross-examination it appeared that the roof of Father Morkunas' church was sagging under a little mortgage — a mere nothing at all — well, to be exact, something in the neighborhood of thirty-three thousand dollars. "And what," asked Father Morkunas, "is thirty-three thousand dollars in boom times like these?"

"I wouldn't trust the times too much, Father," said Stephen, glancing at his wrist watch. In less than an hour he must catch the Congressional Limited for New York. "But good times or bad, the Apostolic Delegate has no authority to intervene in this affair. The matter is one of diocesan jurisdiction. Bishop Schwabauer is the sole and final judge of whether or not you may build your social hall."

"But can't an Apostolic Delegate overrule a bishop?" asked Father Morkunas, somewhat puzzled.

"No. In the spending of diocesan funds, the Apostolic Delegate has no voice."

The Lithuanian pastor began to get apprehensive. With a not-quite-clean handkerchief he mopped a far-from-dry brow.

"You won't tell Bishop Schwabauer that I've been here — that I tried to go over his head?"

"You didn't try to go over anyone's head, Father," said Stephen. "You came here to find out what your rights were. Or perhaps you came just to make a call on His Grace. Would you like to pay your respects in person?" Stephen added an enticing coda. "He speaks Lithuanian, you know."

In the brief interview between the Apostolic Delegate and the obscure pastor from Steubenville, nothing of world-shaking importance was said. Quarenghi asked Father Morkunas what town in Lithuania he came from. When the pastor replied: "Siauliai," Quarenghi recalled having heard the church bells there. "One was bronze, with an excellent throat. The other two were, as I remember, a trifle on the tinny side."

"The Prussians stole two of our best bells in 1914," said Father Morkunas. "The chimes you heard were poor replacements. Ah, Your Grace should have heard the original trinity."

Fifteen minutes later the Apostolic Delegate was back at his personal letter to the Pope; the Lithuanian pastor was standing on Connecticut Avenue, marveling at the God-tuned ear of a man who could hear church bells once, then describe them ten years later. And Monsignor Stephen Fermoyle, having taken an affectionate farewell of his superior, was boarding the Congressional Limited on his way to the Inter-Faith Convocation in New York.

THE PULLMAN CAR was barely half filled; in 1926 the tidal flood between Washington and the rest of the nation had not yet begun. Relaxing in his parlor chair, Stephen felt like a seminarian on a holiday; for the first time since his return to America a free afternoon stretched ahead. While the car wheels clicked soothingly, he watched the scenery flash past, then in a pleasantly eupeptic state he began paging through the *Times*.

There was a mixed bag of news. The stock market was soaring into the empyrean blue; Herbert Hoover, Secretary of the United States Department of Commerce, had announced that the production of automobiles had touched a new high. President Calvin Coolidge was being scolded by a group of Middle Western Senators for his refusal to aid the farmers, struggling through the worst agricultural depression since 1845. Coolidge advised the farmers to rotate their crops a bit more, then went on to praise the exploits of General Custer. Gertrude Ederle was preparing to swim the English Channel. Bishop Leonard of the Methodist Episcopal Church snapped both barrels at Al Smith's eligibility for the Democratic nomination. "No candidate who kisses a papal ring can come within gunshot of the White House," declared the bishop. Imperial Wizard Evans, presiding at a Klan Kloncilium, announced that the sheeted brotherhood would parade (without masks) in Washington, D. C. A dispatch from Illinois described the utter collapse of Prohibition enforcement in Cook County; with leaden ballots the Capone gang had taken over virtual control of Chicago's municipal government.

A photograph on the religious page showed Aimee Semple McPherson garbed in long white raiment, ecstatically preaching her Four-square Gospel to a packed Temple in Los Angeles. From Agawam, R. I., came news that Otis Cubberley, aged fifteen, had just descended from a flagpole on which he had sat for ten days, eleven hours, and nine seconds. At his descent a brass band gathered and gave music. In Philadelphia, members of the rapidly growing Water Cult sat in hot water with cold towels around their heads, concentrating on difficult questions for the Water Master to answer.

Stephen laid down his paper and tried to fit the jigsaw pieces of the day's news into some comprehensible pattern. What had happened to the country? Either the *Times* hadn't printed the right news — or else (a disturbing alternative) the American people were frittering away their energies in infantile nonsense.

Stephen picked up *The Saturday Evening Post*. Here was substance: two hundred pages of glossy-coated paper, containing a serial, several short stories, and inspiring articles by America's leading writers — all for a nickel. He skipped the literature, and turned to the advertising pages — a glowing world of pearly-toothed smiles and almost intolerable satisfactions. Into a candlelit dining room gleaming with crystal and silver, a liveried butler proudly bore aloft on his salver a can of baked beans while the diners repressed jets of saliva with politely lifted napkins. A female with exquisite bosoms peeping through her French nightgown lay back with an ecstatic smile on a snow-white bed and beamed: "My Yumsutta sheets are satin-smooth at a ridiculously low price." In gleaming kitchens, unperturbed housewives whipped up a Sunday-night snack for an unexpected party of eight by reaching for a tin of Five-Star Deviled Ham and a can opener. A high-powered executive type pointed his finger straight at Stephen and cried: "I am looking for a man I can pay five thousand a year. Are *you* equipped to accept my offer?"

Stephen was mulling over the proposition when a glossy-napped individual entered from the dining car and sat down in the next chair. Quite successfully the newcomer proceeded to give the impression that he was a director not only of the Pullman Company, but also the Pennsylvania Railroad, American Telephone and Telegraph Company, United States Steel, and sundry other blue-chip enterprises. His finest directorial effect was achieved when he summoned the porter in an "I-mean-you" voice and ordered him to produce a table immediately so that some highly important work could be done on papers involving figures of the eleventh power. From his calf-skin brief case he drew out a sheaf of documents and began marking them with a patent gold pencil containing red, blue, and green leads. He made at least twenty marks before holding up the pencil for Stephen's inspection:

"Neatest little invention since the coaster brake," he announced with considerable breeze power. Without waiting for Stephen's comment, he began to demonstrate. "Suppose you're breaking down a list of clients into their Dun and Bradstreet ratings. AAA customers — that means a credit rating over a million dollars — get a blue check mark. Anything between a million and five hundred thousand — that's a prospect of another color. So you just give this little knob a quarter twist, and out pops a green lead. See the point, Dominie?"

"A pun my word I do," said Stephen.

"Not bad, not bad, Padre." In his best board-room voice, the gadget lover summoned the porter again. "George, bring me a bottle of Poland Springs water. Not Vichy, not Saratoga, but Poland Springs, hear?"

When the water came, Stephen's companion tapped the label on the bottle and said: "Beauty of advertised trade names. Be sure of what you're getting when you ask for what you want. Almost good enough for a slogan, eh, Reverend?" Modestly he withdrew the claim. "Guess I'll leave ad writing to the other fellow. Not my territory." Solicitude larded his query. "How's business in your line, Doctor?"

"We're doing all right, thanks."

"Glad to hear it. No reason why religion can't be put on a paying basis in the United States. You a Catholic or Episcopalian, Father?"

"Catholic. Roman Catholic."

"Cozy outfit. Plenty of organization and showmanship all the way down the line. Course there's a lot of people with funny notions about importing religion from Rome — but that's bigotry stuff. Believe and let believe, I say. Only the other day I was lunching at the Willard with a big Catholic client. Happened to be a Friday, and he ordered pompano. Had to respect the man."

Next thing he'll say, thought Stephen, is: "Catholic, Jew, Protestant — what's the difference?" The man said exactly that, then added: "We're going to have a long ride together . . . might as well get acquainted. I'm Horace F. Stoner, sales manager of the Hearthstone Security Corporation. Home office in Dayton, O. — branches all over. He handed his business card to Stephen. "Ever need any investment advice, just give me a ring."

"Thank you very much," said Stephen. "It's not likely I'll ever be in a position to make any investments."

"Never can tell. Client of ours in Detroit — pastor of a big parish — salts down a regular amount every month in Hearthstone. Got a Methodist bishop in Wilkes-Barre — shrewd operators, these divines — all loaded for the next big rise."

"Will there be another rise?"

"Will there *be!* Padre, let me put it in conservative terms — Hearthstone terms. Inside of three weeks there's going to be a touch-off that'll send our national economy right through the ceiling. Don't take *my* word for it." Horace Stoner clicked open his brief case. "Just cast your clerical optics over this statement by the U. S. Commerce Department."

Stephen glanced at the mimeographed release, complete with graphs and pie charts. "The recent advances in stock

prices," he read, "may be considered the first insistent reading
of the new and greater prosperity for which the people of the
United States have been consciously preparing. These
advances (see graph, page 2) are based on an unprecedented
increase in national wealth, ascribable chiefly to (1) assembly-line production; (2) more efficient methods of distribution; (3) a new attitude toward investment on the part of the
general public."

"Sounds pretty convincing," said Stephen.

"Convincing! I'm sold up to here." Mr. Stoner held a rigid
forefinger under his nose like a man trying to stop hiccups.
"And the things that sell me hardest are the magic little
words 'assembly-belt production.' Ever see a belt in operation?"

"Can't say I ever did."

"Then, Mister, I mean Padre, you've got a treat coming.
When that old conveyor belt slips into high, she purrs like a
dynamo throwing off sparks of pure gold. Finest flower of
American ingenuity. Do anything on a belt — stamp, cut, drill,
saw, spin, polish — cheaper and better, too. Funny thing, it
turns out stuff in ever-*increasing* quantities at ever-*decreasing*
costs. Get it? Means more cars, refrigerators, vacuum cleaners,
washing machines, and coffee percolators for more people."

"I understand the theory," said Stephen. "But does it work
out in practice? How can the average wage earner afford to
buy all the goods whirling off the production line?"

Mr. Stoner disposed of the question as a surgeon disposes
of a soiled dressing. "Installment buying fixes all that." He
waved a deprecatory hand. "Oh, I know — five years ago,
people thought there was something immoral about buying
things they couldn't pay cash for. My old man, for instance —
he'd rather be caught *flagrante delictu* (excuse the expression, Doctor) than coming out of an installment house.
But the new generation is different. These days people want
immediate possession, and industry's smart enough to let them
have it. Anyway, it's not called 'installment buying' any more.
You 'exercise your credit,' buy a car on 'deferred payments.'
Budget as you go. More dignified."

So. Wishes had become horses, and beggars could ride. In

dignity, too. "Sooner or later," said Stephen, "everyone will have everything. What'll happen then?"

This gruesome idea found a "No admittance" sign nailed to the portals of Mr. Stoner's mind. He spent the hour between Wilmington and Philadelphia explaining just why American purchasing power could expand forever. Tinctures of poesy tinted his argument. Under the guidance of the American businessman (pictured by Horace Stoner as a combination of daring navigator and benevolent captain), the bark of private enterprise was sailing into the palm-fringed harbors of a permanent Utopia. Or, to change the figure, the airtight infield of installment buying, advertising, and salesmanship was performing the miraculous triple play by which that snide base runner, Poverty, would never again reach home plate. As he talked, the luxurious train whirling northward through an industrial gantlet of factories seemed to corroborate his predictions. Maybe he was right.

Only after Stoner had left for bigger operations in the smoking car did Stephen have a chance to test the investment broker's argument against the logic of fact. Shocking rebuttals lay near at hand. Behind the façade of factories in Pennsylvania and New Jersey manufacturing towns, Stephen saw the gray wasteland of tenements and mean streets. No flight of business rhetoric could make the scene anything but what it was: a wretched landscape of substandard dwellings peopled by the workers who kept the production line whirring. Was this the palm-fringed Utopia that Horace Stoner had painted with such glowing colors?

Crossing the Jersey marshes, the train halted for a moment while waiting for the block signal's permission to plunge into the Manhattan tunnel. Harsh fumes seeped into the waiting cars: the acrid stench of industrial chemicals — sulphur, chlorine, and ammonia — mingled with the odors of decay rising from the stagnant marshes. As the train entered the dark tunnel, Stephen could not help thinking that the approaches to Dante's city of Dis were scarcely more ominous or terrifying.

STEPHEN had dinner that evening with his brother George on the glassed-in roof of the Lawyers' Club atop one of the recently built skyscrapers in the Grand Central district.

George was making a name for himself in the field of work-men's compensation — a new branch of law stemming from the social legislation of Governor Alfred E. Smith. At thirty-two, an inch taller and ten pounds heavier than Stephen, George rather resembled Gene Tunney. There was about him, how-ever, a truculence that Tunney always lacked. Definitely, George was cast in the crusader mold, with a pugnacity of mind and a jut of jaw inherited from Dennis Fermoyle. In the four years since Stephen had seen his brother, George had channeled his energies into the cause of social reform — noth-ing radical, of course; merely a practical wage-and-hour pro-gram for labor. Apparently he was taking an active part in the political push behind Al Smith. His enthusiasm for the Brown Derby fell just short of idolatry.

"The Governor's twenty years ahead of everyone else in his legislation for the comman man," he told Steve. "If he keeps moving forward, he'll have more than a chance for the Demo-cratic nomination in 1928."

"But Smith's a Catholic. . . ."

"Well? There's nothing in the Constitution that says a Cath-olic can't be President, is there?" George simmered down. "I know what you mean, Stuffy. Any R.C. candidate for the presidency has two and a half strikes against him. But aside from the religious angle, Smith's program should appeal to a lot of ordinary working stiffs who aren't getting their share of Coolidge prosperity. This boom stuff is caviar for the few, not meat and potatoes for the general."

To support his statement, George began laying down a fac-tual barrage. "Did you know, Stuff, that steel puddlers are still getting twenty-seven dollars for a sixty-hour week? And that coal miners average twenty-four-fifty — when they work? I'm not inventing these figures; they're in the Department of Com-merce report, if anyone wants to look them up."

How would Horace Stoner's patent gold pencil check *that?* thought Stephen. "Funny, George, I said something like that to a man on the train today. Investment salesman. He blasted my ear off, telling me how wrong I was."

"Don't be fooled by their canvass, Stuff. Those salesmen are so busy blowing four-colored bubbles, they don't know what's going on in the country."

"What *is* going on, George? In the four years since I've been away, something's changed. I sensed it the minute I stepped off the boat. The papers, the very air, seem full of snarling contradictions and frightful discords. You're the social student — what's the clash all about?"

George pondered the question. "Everyone has a different theory. Some say it's the emotional backlash of an unfinished war. The energy we generated for high martial adventure never got used up on the Germans, so now we turn it on ourselves in gang wars, race riots, lynchings, and floggings. There's something to it." George stirred his coffee gloomily. "Others say we're afraid to accept the challenge of world leadership offered us at Versailles and are seeking infantile substitutes in bunion derbies and goldfish-swallowing."

"Those are only surface symptoms," prodded Stephen. "The disease itself must lie deeper."

"It does. The real cause of our trouble — well, let me put it this way: in the last five years American technology has developed a remarkable system of industrial production. Agreed?"

"That's what the man on the train said."

"What he *didn't* say is that our oh-so-wonderful technology has become a runaway juggernaut, leaving the rest of our social institutions far behind. An enormous, unlovely gap has opened between our technical achievements and our cultural ideas. The gap widens every day, and no plan is being devised for bridging it. Whole sections of the population, *people,* Stuffy, are falling into the chasm, while our so-called leaders don't even know that it exists."

"Your theory isn't exactly new," said Stephen. "Leo XIII stated it thirty-five years ago in his encyclical *Rerum novarum.*"

"I know. Leo made a powerful plea for social justice. But he didn't offer any practical methods for obtaining it. I hate to say this, Stuffy, but the Catholic Church — along with education, Congress, and everything else — hasn't kept pace with the needs of people in a machine age. I wish she'd draw up with the times and really get interested in the plight of troubled human beings."

"The Church is so interested in troubled human beings that she can't be interested in anything else. Whom do you suppose

Christ was talking to when He said: 'Come unto me, ye who are heavy laden'?"

"When Christ said that, He was talking to fishermen, laborers in the vineyard, hewers of wood, and drawers of water — men who lived and worked in a simpler age." George spoke with moving sincerity. "I'm not just trying to win an argument, Stuff. All I'm saying is that technology has made life so fearfully complex that the old premachine formulas don't work any more. Can the ordinary working-stiff — the steel puddler at his open-hearthed hell, for instance — find support in a 'Come-unto-me' religion? Can such a religion bring emotional and economic security to the assembly-line robot or bridge the widening gap between man and technology? Don't be blithe, Steve. *Answer* me!"

Stephen Fermoyle was in no mood to be blithe. He had been through quite a day. He had listened to Horace Stoner's selling line, read the news in the *Times* and the ads in the *Post*. He had run the gantlet of factories between Wilmington and New York, seen the festering slums behind them. He had smelled the mingled odors of chemical waste and natural decay blowing across the Jersey marshes. And now he had heard his brother's indictment of an archaic culture that included the Catholic Church. The effect of all these sights, sounds, smells, and ideas disturbed Stephen as he began his reply.

"We've always differed about the part the Church should play in human affairs. I think I know why." Stephen chose his words carefully. "You, as a layman, see the problem in terms of this world. I, as a priest, see it in terms of the next. You're interested in the cure of social disorders; I'm interested in the cure of man's immortal soul."

"Can't the two programs be combined?" asked George.

"Some hard thinking has been done on the subject by Catholic theologians. The outlook is hopeful. But get this, George." Stephen was teaching now. "It's not the mission of the Church to work out practical methods by which the just state is brought into being. The function of the Church is to form public men who *will*. Men of Christian conscience and moral purpose, who believe that human beings have a right to live on the plane of morality, dignity, and security intended by God."

Stephen hammered out the final link — part definition, part apology — in his argument. "When you accused me of being blithe a moment ago, it stung. I had to tell myself, and I have to tell you now, that a priest is not a sociologist or politician or labor organizer. He is simply a mediator between God and man. He must keep his function pure, even though, as Leo XIII has shown, the Church is not indifferent to economic ills."

Then, in summation, Stephen Fermoyle stated the priest's reason for being. "Only poets can write poetry; only women can bear children. Only a priest can remind men that God forever was, is now, and — come hell, high water, or technology — always will be."

CHAPTER 8

THE INTER-FAITH CONVOCATION began early next day with a luncheon in the Grand Ballroom of the Waldorf-Astoria. The Right Reverend Alfred Cartmell, Episcopal Bishop of Long Island, invoked the blessing of God on the assembly, ending his prayer with the plea: "Let Thy light so illuminate our hearts that we may see eye to eye those common truths vouchsafed unto all peoples through Christ our Lord. Amen."

Stephen, seated on the right wing of the speaker's table, found himself between Rabbi Jonas Mordecai, patriarch of orthodox Judaism, and Hubbel K. Whiteman, Ph.D., lay author of *Protestantism on the March*. The dubious droop of Rabbi Mordecai's beard bred more interest than Dr. Whiteman's chin-up militancy. After exchanging amenities with both luncheon partners, Stephen turned a sympathetic eye on the Rabbi as the latter gazed mournfully at the lobster cocktail heading the menu. Rabbi Mordecai went so far as to lift a small-tined fork, then laid it down again with a four-thousand-year-old smile of resignation.

"I'm out of the running already," he whispered to Stephen. In the Rabbi's voice were melancholy echoes of Leviticus: "Whatsoever hath not fins and scales shall be an abomination unto you." Properly interpreted, the Rabbi's observance of the

ancient code of Jewish holiness was no mere dietary whim;
rather a reverberation of Sinai's thunder: "I, the Lord your
God, am holy, and have set you apart from the peoples that
ye should be Mine."

Across Stephen's meditation fell the voice of Dr. Hubbell
K. Whiteman, "What hopes do you entertain, Monsignor, for
the success of our Inter-Faith movement?" The question, legitimate enough, had the quality of a skirmisher's shot. Dr.
Whiteman was merely finding his range.

"Protestantism may benefit," said Stephen. "But quite honestly, I can't see what Roman Catholicism stands to gain."

Dr. Whiteman was affable with a difference. "Suppose you
change 'Roman' to read 'American.' Wouldn't certain changes
flow from such a shift in emphasis?"

"For example, Doctor."

Hubbell K. Whiteman launched into a demonstration of the
benefits that might accrue to Catholics if they organized, as
he put it, "on an American basis." During the mulligatawny
soup (which Rabbi Mordecai did not taste) the author of
Protestantism on the March made the point that American
Catholics, divested of "foreign allegiance," would be regarded
"less suspiciously" in many quarters. Consequently, they
would be eligible, he argued, "for a larger role in American
political life." Stephen replied that American Catholics were
bound by no foreign allegiance — unless, possibly, God could
be regarded as a foreigner. While the assemblage hacked away
at broiled chicken, and Rabbi Mordecai clasped his wrinkled
hands in resignation, Dr. Whiteman suggested that a stronger
and really beautiful Christianity would result if *all* American
faiths would federate, loosely perhaps, in the manner of the
several states. He was pumping three hundred words a minute
on this federation idea when Chairman Quincy A. Howson,
professor of moral philosophy at the Manhattan Theologic
Seminary, arose and said:

"The Convocation will now hear grace after meat, offered by
that distinguished exponent of orthodox Judaism, Rabbi Jonas
Mordecai."

Everyone felt very democratic, very fine, when the puzzled
Rabbi, not having touched a morsel of the luncheon, intoned
the ancient Hebrew prayer of thanksgiving after food.

Professionally swift on the uptake, Chairman Howson now introduced the keynoter of the occasion, the Reverend Bradbury Towne, D.D. (Cantab), LL.D., Harvard, and rector of St. Barnaby's New York City. Handsome and erudite in the high-Anglican manner, Bradbury Towne had worn the surplice of special grace for so many years that it now hung quite easily from his fine shoulders.

In diction and content, Dr. Towne's address was a thing of frank charm. "We are met to honor God and ourselves," he said, "by considering those things which ought to be done, indeed which must be done, if His kingdom is to prevail in our midst. Although the imperfect arcs of existing (and sadly enough, *competing*) faiths are not capable of being wholly fused, as the poet Browning suggests, into a 'perfect round,' yet a beginning can be made. With a little less insistence on dogma perhaps, not quite so much emphasis on differences of ritual, and a more sincere attempt to understand the purely *historical* nature of those differences, the work of unification could be greatly advanced." Dr. Towne went on to say that advantages both spiritual and temporal would flow from such a consolidation of faith. The Church United — "federalized" was possibly a better word — would be in a more strategic position to combat the materialism of the day. Sectarian rivalries at an end, less prosperous churches could merge with congregations more — ah — substantially founded. Harassed rectors would find themselves (a benign humor accompanied Dr. Towne's descent into the idiom) using not quite so much red ink. And lastly, the miasmas of bigotry and intolerance having been blown quite away, religion in the United States could soar on new-found pinions into clear American ether.

Without ever saying so, Dr. Towne implied that he was both willing and ready to lead the wandering denominational tribes into the Promised Land of Unification.

Prolonged applause and a grim benediction by the Most Reverend Timothy Creedon, Catholic Bishop of Newark, followed the keynoter's remarks.

Stephen could almost hear Tim Creedon muttering to himself, "What in God's name am I doing here among these psalm singers?"

With the amiable aroma of Dr. Towne's speech still hanging

about them, the delegates proceeded to various seminars and forums to consider specific problems. Stephen was assigned to a discussion of "Religious Tolerance as an Instrument of Democracy." With five other clergymen, including Rabbi Mordecai, he sat at a table facing an audience of probably a hundred laymen. The panel moderator, a white-eyebrowed veteran of the sectarian wars, explained that each speaker had ten minutes, and that a question period would give the laymen their chance later on. Meanwhile, no heckling, please.

The discussion was opened by the well-known Methodist preacher, John Fort Newcomb. "Tolerance," he said, "is the virtue by which liberated minds make conquest of bigotry and hatred. It implies more than forbearance. Properly conceived, tolerance is the positive and cordial effort to understand another's beliefs without necessarily sharing or accepting them. In the words of Phillips Brooks, 'Tolerance expresses a perfectly legitimate and honorable relation between opposite minds.' I disagree with my friend. I want him to be true to his convictions, yet I claim the right and duty of trying to persuade him to my belief." The speaker wound up by pointing out that tolerance is the basic ingredient of democracy, "the meeting in perfect harmony, or earnest conviction and high personal privilege."

The next speaker, a Presbyterian minister named Alonzo Runforth, made the nice point that tolerance should not be confused with pallid indifferentism. He quoted John Morley: "Much that passes for tolerance is only a pretentious form of being without settled opinions of our own." Danger lurks in this form of slothfulness, said the Reverend Dr. Runforth, "because tolerance, a fragile plant, has to be diligently tended, else it withers and dies. As it fades, another growth — the poisonous mushroom of *in*tolerance — takes its place. A privilege is shorn away here, a censorship is erected there, hatreds take root, and soon we are living in the black forest of intolerance, sunless and fearsome for all."

Thus far the discussion had gone forward on a high level of decorum. Now arose the Reverend Twombly Moss, a Southern fundamentalist, who slammed his open palm onto the table and exploded sulphurously. "Tolerance my necktie! What this country needs is a good five-cent stick of brimstone!"

The shocked moderator lifted white eyebrows. Who had put this zealot on the program? Whereupon Twombly Moss ripped off his necktie and brought the rod of Aaron down on the backs of the unrighteous.

"How can anyone be tolerant to violators of the Eighteenth Amendment?" he bellowed. "Take a man who says he has the *right* to sozzle in rum and use tobacco in all its forms — pipe, chew, and cigarettes. Isn't *license* what he means? License to befuddle his brains and stunt his body with poison? And if you don't believe tobacco is poison, just try this experiment. Tuck a plug of chewing tobacco under your armpits, then sit down in a rocking chair and try to be comfortable. Just you try! Inside of three minutes you'll be sicker'n a gangrened beagle pup with the collywobbles." The fundamentalist Savonarola raged on. "And another thing! There's too much bunnyhugging going on to suit the Reverend Twombly Moss. This cheek-to-cheek dancing has got to stop. Clean house, I say. Cut out this tolerance twaddle and let's put an end to booze, cigarettes, dancing and cardplaying, or the country'll wake up some Tuesday morning and find itself raking ashes in hell."

An astonished hush settled over the hall. The hush was broken by the voice of some nameless wit in the back benches.

"What's your stand on popcorn, Reverend? Agin that, too?"

A wash of laughter cleansed the sulphur-laden air. In the deluge Twombly Moss sat down, his five-cent stick of brimstone very much dampened.

It was hard to get the forum on the track again, but the white-eyebrowed moderator finally succeeded. Two more speakers gave their views on religious tolerance. Then it was Stephen's turn. This is what he wanted to say:

My dear friends, I find myself in agreement with most of the vague agreeabilities proposed in this forum. I would be lacking in frankness, however, if I did not tell you that the Catholic Church takes a most uncompromising stand in matters of faith and morals enjoined upon it by God. You will find the Church notably lenient in contemplating human frailty; but you will find it grimly unyielding when asked, in the name of tolerance, to deviate from the divine revelations and theologic dogmas on which Catholic doctrine is based. We hold

Quarenghi laid his finger tip on a wall map of the United States. "I want you to make a tour of this region," he said, indicating the area between the Great Smokies and the Mississippi River. "Find out, if you can, what is happening to the Roman Catholics in the South and Southwest. Take three months, more if necessary, and make a report of your findings."

In three months Stephen traveled ten thousand miles through a part of the United States he had never seen before. On muleback, in jerking day coaches and battered Fords, he traversed a terrain clothed with fernbrakes and pine — a land desolate at best, but made uglier where ruthless logging had pimpled the landscape with stumps. It was a region of starveling scarcity, where even the razor-backed shoat could not prosper and the blacksnake whip cracked loudly in the hands of invincibly ignorant men. Stephen entered counties that had never seen a priest; in some states, paintless churches were supported on a vaguely missionary basis or not at all. White families traditionally Catholic were losing their faith by default, and the spiritual neglect of the Negro had permitted nearly ninety per cent of the colored population to fall uncontested into Protestant hands.

Stephen was shocked to see the linkage between economic poverty and religious hatred. In counties where the Church was poorest, the Klan flogged Roman Catholics relentlessly. But wherever a bold bishop thundered — though his altar might be hundreds of miles away — there, Catholics were least molested.

DEEP IN the desolate bayou country, far beyond the protection of any bishop, Stephen ran into serious trouble. He was returning (via the one-track Gainesboro & Pitney R.R.) from a solitary Josephite mission school for Negroes, when the train halted in the middle of a swamp. At the sound of drawling profanity Stephen looked out the window and saw the engineer mopping his neck with a blue bandanna.

As the only passenger of the train, Stephen had a personal interest in the proceedings. It appeared that number 9, a cow-catcher locomotive of Stonewall Jackson vintage, had snapped an eccentric rod. According to Lem Tingley — engineer, fireman, and conductor on the G. & P. — the repair of food that sustains you is denied me. Your words are kindly intentioned, yet they do not fill my heart with gladness. Phillips Brooks is good, John Morley is good" — the Rabbi contemplatively rubbed the blue vein at his temple — "but because I have spent my life hearkening to Moses and Isaiah, I have lost my ear for prophets less majestic."

Stephen wished that his brother George could have heard and seen Jonas Mordecai. The Rabbi was neither modern nor near to modern; he had made no concessions to contemporary culture. Outmoded but modeless, appearing rarely yet constantly among men, Jonas Mordecai was the very pattern of the dedicated priest. Out of the bickerings and doctrinal differences, the Rabbi's voice emerged in beauty and wisdom as he went on:

"But now lest you go away saying what a cynical, weary old man this rabbi is, I will speak to you in a parable. There was once a king who owned a wonderful diamond. He was proud of his jewel, but one day by accident it was deeply scratched. The king called in gem cutters to repair his stone — yet try as they might, they could not polish away the scratch. At last there appeared in that kingdom a lapidary artist of surpassing genius. With skill and patience he carved a beautiful rose on the part of the stone that was flawed. And by his cunning art, he contrived to make the deepest part of the scratch the rose's stem."

Rabbi Mordecai turned his palms outward in a gesture that might have had several meanings. All of which, in the tradition of parables, he left unstated.

The Inter-Faith Convocation ended next day. In none of its sessions did a lapidary artist of sufficient skill step forward to carve a rose on the scratched diamond of faith. In fact, during the forums on divorce, birth control, and religious education, the diamond received several new scratches.

Acrimonies were hushed, but not ended, by adjournment. The formal resolutions of the Inter-Faith Convocation, published some months later, were unanimous only in agreeing that bigotry and intolerance, like the grade crossing and the man-eating shark, must be eliminated.

ANNUS MIRABILIS 1927. The Book of Calvin was drawing to a

close. Over the strayed homespun in the White House the Delphic mantle of double talk had descended; whatever he said or did was undiluted paradox. His fame rested on six words: "We must have law and order." Yet during his presidency the law of the land was in a virtual state of suspension while mobsters proclaimed the statute of the tommy gun and rival beer kings dealt out the leering justice of the ride. Thrift was Cal's religion; he could save fifty thousand a year on his salary and haggle about the number of hams to be served at an official dinner. But he made no protest against the orgy of stock gambling and financial thimblerigging that went on under his codfish eye. He sounded no trumpets, tilted at no windmills, and dodged every problem that could not be solved on an abacus. Having made the nasal announcement that the business of America was business, he sat back in his rocking chair and watched his countrymen engage in a breakneck scramble for the prosperity that still bears his name.

Given the fatness of these years, what happened in the United States? Was there a renaissance of the arts, a quickening of religion, a tranquil deepening of thought? No. Living under conditions nearly perfect (according to the advertising pages) for the expression of man's nobler self, the people abandoned themselves to diversions, which, though not out of place at a Shriners' convention, were scarcely creditable to a great nation at the peak of its material fortunes. While millions of children developed rachitic knobs from malnutrition, and the League of Nations floundered impotently without Western support, the American people gave themselves up to marathon dancing, pole-sitting, and kindred freak contests, each dizzier and more meaningless than the last.

Stephen Fermoyle, observing the Washington scene at close range, found little that was instructive. Only his intuitive belief that millions of private citizens were living lives of unproclaimed nobility and goodness saved him from outright pessimism. His state of mind was shared by many of the ecclesiastical friends he had made in the Cathedral chapter of St. Matthew's and at the Catholic University, where he was preparing for his doctorate in philosophy. Whenever this set gathered for an evening, a single overwhelming question arose: "At what point might the Catholic Church legitimately draw

America's attention to the fact that 'business morality' and a laissez-faire theory of economics were forcing men into practices criminally at variance with divine and natural law?"

The question was neither academic nor theologic; it carried grave reality for employers and wage earners at every point where economics touched upon morals. Pope Pius XI described the struggle as one "in which only the strongest survive; and the strongest, often enough, means those who fight most relentlessly, who pay least heed to the dictates of conscience."

Had the administration chosen to fulfill Leo XIII's ideal of a Christian state, it could have done much to prevent the landslide of mischief that was about to be loosed upon all classes of society. But the government, impervious to spiritual influence, displayed the typical weakness of a state that excludes God from its deliberations.

As ASSISTANT to the Apostolic Delegate, Stephen was learning a great deal about the Catholic Church in America. Most of his information came by way of diocesan reports clearing through Quarenghi's office en route to Rome. From the study of these documents two facts emerged: in great centers of population, Catholicism was vigorous and thriving; under the guidance of competent bishops and hard-working pastors, large city parishes were expanding; new churches were lifting crosses and bell towers to the sky. But when one turned to outlying areas, the picture was less encouraging. Here and there, an energetic bishop managed to keep roofs on the shabby churches in his diocese. Generally speaking, however, the Roman Catholic faith was not prospering in the poorer agricultural regions of the United States. In fact, it was barely holding its own.

Quarenghi's "office of vigilance" bound him to investigate this laggard condition; yet his manifold duties in Washington made a personal visitation impossible. Early in March, 1927, he looked up at Stephen from behind a rampart of official documents and casually asked:

"Would you be willing, Stefano, to undertake a mission above and beyond the call of paper work?"

"Try me."

our teaching to be the only true teaching. We will not alter
any part of it; indeed we cannot, because man is powerless to
alter the truth of God. In view of these facts, I see no point in
extending my remarks.

Had Stephen been attached to an American diocese or
speaking under the jurisdiction of an American bishop, he
would have said these things (very probably Bishop Creedon
was saying them this minute in another room). But because
Stephen was attending the Convocation as a representative of
the Apostolic Delegate, he felt obliged to protect Quarenghi
from the controversy that certainly would result from such a
forthright statement. Discretion rather than expediency
prompted Stephen to temper his utterance as follows:

"Mr. Moderator, respected colleagues: It occurs to me that
in our discussion of tolerance we have somehow overlooked
its spiritual origin. No one has yet mentioned that tolerance is
an extension of God's great commandment, 'Love thy neighbor' — an injunction that all of us, irrespective of creed, are
bound to obey."

At this acceptable Christian doctrine the moderator beamed.
Stephen continued:

"May I point out that tolerance has two meanings: to *suffer*
and to *bear.* Both meanings were combined into a single act
when the Son of God became man in order to bear His cross
and suffer on it for our redemption. It is my thought that we
shall best fulfill God's commandment when we imitate the
tolerance of His son."

There was a genteel patting of hands as Stephen sat down.
Rabbi Mordecai was the last to speak. He rose slowly, his
bowed figure emaciated with advanced age, and gazed about
the hall with eyes dimmed by seventy years of poring over the
Torah and Kethubim. He fingered his beard, as if amused by
what he had heard from the clean-shaven ministers of younger
faiths. Then on the withered parchment of his forehead, bewildered wrinkles appeared.

"What can I say that will be helpful here?" he began. "It is
not that I am old or tired, or wish to heap ashes of self-pity on
my beard. But we are so far apart that not even the wisdom of
Maimonides could bring us together in understanding. The

eccentric rods was a complicated business. First you walked to Racey, the nearest whistle stop four miles down the track. From there you called up Gainesboro, the southern terminus of the G. & P. If anyone answered, you asked him to send up a new eccentric rod on a handcar. "Ought to get here tomorrow noon," said Lem. "Then allowin' three or four hours for fittin', we'll be on our way by suppertime on Friday."

The prospect of idling for thirty hours in a mosquito-ridden swamp was scarcely inviting. Quarenghi's orders had been: "Find out what's going on in the South," and the time might be more profitably spent by visiting near-by towns. "Is there anyplace around here I could stay?" asked Stephen.

Yep, there was the Crescent House in Owosso, eight miles down the line. Decent enough place, but from the depths of his conscience, Lem Tingley couldn't rightly recommend it to Stephen. "Folks hereabouts are apt to get ugly when they see a Roman collar."

"I'll take my chances." Leaving his luggage on the train, Stephen started down the track. To prevent the sun from wilting his collar, he took it off; not until he reached Owosso three hours later did he observe the priestly amenity of putting it on again. The white badge of his office created a minor disturbance among the rocking-chair brigade seated on the rickety veranda of the Crescent House. Seven or eight loungers, looking for all the world like an unemployed posse, were apparently engaged in some kind of contest involving the production of tobacco juice. The volume, distance, and accuracy of the spitters fell off for a moment, then increased noticeably as Stephen mounted the steps.

A clerk who might have served as a Confederate drummer boy in the battle of Chickamauga reluctantly produced a register. "That'll be two dollars — in advance," he said, as Stephen signed his name. "Here's your key, Mister. Room Four. Up them stairs, last door on the left."

Room Four smelled like the bottom of a fish barrel. An iron bedstead swarming with leprous scabs supported a sway-back mattress. Moldy straw matting covered the floor. On the wall hung a fly-blown religious calendar, the yellowed memento of a Full Gospel convention held long ago in Owosso. Stephen read the text for the month of August, 1912.

What is man that Thou art mindful of him, or the son of man that Thou visitest him?"

The only plumbing in the Crescent House was a lavatory on the first floor. To this, Stephen descended. He was washing his face and hands, thinking pleasantly of the supper of fatback probably awaiting him, when a delegation of quid-and-chaw contestants lounged into the lavatory. One of them sluiced a half pint of tobacco juice into the washbowl and inquired: "What you all doing in Owosso?"

"Minding my own business," said Stephen cheerfully.

"What sort of business might that be?"

"I'm a priest, making a survey of Catholic churches in this part of the country."

"Fixin' to start a Catholic church in Owosso?" A cheekful of brown liquid splashed off the cap of Stephen's shoe.

"Look, Mister," said Stephen, "you've either lost your aim or your manners."

"'Tain't his aim he's lost," snickered one of the trio. "Jeff can drown a fly at twenty paces."

Unmoved by this home-town flattery, the fly-drowner came to the nub of his argument. "Us folks in Owosso ain't in favor of strangers wearin' collars hindside foremost. We-all intend, friendly-like, to let them get out of town without causin' no trouble. But if they-all don't leave peaceable, why, we got ways of persuadin' 'em."

"I'm getting out of here as soon as I can," said Stephen. "Will tomorrow morning suit you?"

"Right now'd suit us better," said Jeff.

"Sorry I can't oblige." Stephen shouldered his way out of the lavatory.

Supper was an early-evening affair at the Crescent House. The menu was simple: pork chops, grits, black-eyed peas, and rain-water coffee. Exhausted by his eight-mile walk that afternoon, Stephen went directly to his room, removed his outer clothing, and lay down on the sway-back bed. It was dark when he was awakened by the sound of a heavy boot kicking at his door.

"Open up."

Stephen jumped out of bed, pulled on his trousers and

shoes, then opened the door. The corridor was filled with sheeted figures wearing conical hoods.

"You didn't git out of town your way, so we're gittin' you out ours. Put your clothes on, collar and all. This is goin' to be a full-dress affair." Three pairs of hands jerked Stephen across the threshold. Other hands blindfolded him. He was tumbled down the stairs and into the back seat of an automobile that grunted painfully under the weight of its occupants. No one spoke during the long drive into the country.

When the blindfold was taken from his eyes, Stephen saw that he was in the center of an open field. In the light of three burning crosses, white-sheeted men were ominously grouped. Directly in front of him a hooded man was caressing the lash of a blacksnake whip. Another hooded figure held a small glinting object in the palm of his hands.

"Know what this is?" he asked.

Stephen looked at the object in the man's palm. "Yes."

"What do you Catholics call it?"

"Catholics and Christians everywhere call it a crucifix," said Stephen.

"Danged if you ain't right. That's what the whining nigger called it when we took it away from him. Funny the way he begged to kiss it when we strung him up."

"Many men have begged to kiss it at the moment of death," said Stephen.

The whip-handler took over. "Well, this ain't no 'Come to Jesus' meetin'. There'll be no cross-kissin' here tonight. What we're aimin' to see you do, stranger" — he cracked the flexible lash past Stephen's ear — "is *spit* on it."

The values of the proposed ordeal by saliva seemed unreal to Stephen. That grown men should suggest such a thing nauseated him.

"What will it prove?" he asked.

"Why, it'll just prove that no white-kidneyed priest can stick his nose in where he's not wanted."

Stephen saw his opening. "It's all clear to me now," he said. "I thought for a minute that you men came out here to see Christ's image defiled. I was wrong. You don't really want to insult your Saviour. You just want to scare a Catholic priest."

"That's about it, I reckon."

"Well, start scaring."

The whip-wielder expected a showier display of cringing. "You mean you ain't going to spit on this here object?"

"I couldn't possibly." Stephen reversed the proposition. "*You* spit on it."

The suggestion alarmed the master of ceremonies. He held the crucifix at arm's length, gazing at it curiously like a man seeing something for the first time. "Don't rightly know how's I could."

"How about some of you other chaw artists?" asked Stephen.

A tremor of negation passed over the group. "Throw the damned thing in the bushes," someone muttered.

"No, give it to me," said Stephen. He held the crucifix between thumb and forefinger, lofting it like a lantern in darkness. "Let's get on with the whipping."

"Jes' 's you say, Mister." The hooded leader curled a python lash around his victim's ankles. "Ef you won't spit — *dance!*"

Ancient strength of martyrs flowed into Stephen's limbs. Eyes on the gilt cross, he neither flinched nor spoke.

"Mebbe he needs a little music. Give him 'Dixie' on your harmonica, Lafe."

The metallic wheeze of a mouth organ rose above the blacksnake's thud. Joyless voices took up the refrain. Calloused hands beat out the rhythm. Higher around Stephen's body, past knee and thigh, the whip climbed.

> *Den I wish I was in Dixie,*
> *Hooray! Hooray!*

Land of the quid and chaw. Forgive them, Lord, they know not what they do.

> *In Dixieland I'll take my stand . . .*

One had to take a stand somewhere. Dixie, Roncesvalles, Tyburn Hill — what matter where? Stephen prayed silently that no drop of spittle, no whimpering plea for mercy, would fall from his lips before the end.

Now, seeking a gayer tempo, the harmonica switched to "Turkey in the Straw," but, for some reason not understandable to the audience, the show wasn't coming off as scheduled. Murmurs of dissatisfaction began to arise:

"He don't squirm proper."

"Losin' your touch, Jeff?"

The whipmaster was apologetic. "I can't crack her in *nacheral* while he holds that thing in front of him. Anyone else want to try?"

There were no takers. All sadistic relish had evaporated by now. With a grunt of disgust, Jeff folded up his whip. "C'mon, let's get back to town. The muskeeters'll finish him off."

Glum as hunters who had treed their coon but couldn't get him down, the sheeted men clambered into their cars. Not until the last taillight had disappeared did Stephen lower the crucifix.

Alone, on a midnight terrain utterly strange to him, he knew that it would be foolhardy to wander about the countryside. The wisest course was to sit down and wait for morning. To the embers of the fiery crosses, Stephen added brushwood and broken branches, thereby gaining the companionship and protection that a fire offers. Sitting in its smoke, he kept the mosquitoes at bay, and by the firelight examined the welts on the lower part of his body. In several places where the skin was broken, dark trickles oozed and coagulated. Not a full baptism of blood — but close enough.

Through the little eternity between midnight and dawn, he pondered the mystery of the gilt crucifix. Even on souls shrouded in darkness, this glinting symbol of the perfect sacrifice had proved its power to moderate, however slightly, the passions of men.

At sunrise Stephen made a rough calculation of his position, then struck a course in a general southeasterly direction, hoping sooner or later to strike the G. & P. tracks. He breakfasted on water from a clear stream, bathed the dust and blood from his body, then continued his way across eroded fields too poor to support animal or human life. Hunger began to sap his strength. It was nearly midday when he struck a humpbacked dirt road sparsely rutted with wheel tracks. Exhausted, he lay down in a dry ditch by the roadside and fell asleep in the blaze of noon.

He was awakened by a foot poking at his shoulder. Looking

up, Stephen saw a lantern-jawed man, his cheek bulging with the inevitable quid, gazing down at him. In appearance and costume, the stranger was a composite of all the loungers on the Crescent House veranda. Frayed straw hat, butternut jeans torn at the knees and sagging at the end of stretched-out suspenders. Unshaved chin, big Adam's-apple. The posse type again, complete, except for shotgun and bloodhounds.

"Appears like you fell among thieves, brother," the man was saying.

The Biblical cast of the remark was something of a novelty. Without answering, Stephen watched the stranger rummage in the haversack hanging from his bony shoulder. The man drew out a square of cornbread, added a slab of fat-back to it, and offered the food to Stephen.

"Work up your strength on this," he advised.

Stephen devoured the cornbread, then ruefully surveyed the appetizing bit of pork. No dodging the issue now. "Thanks," he said, "but I don't eat meat on Fridays."

"Catholic, eh?"

Might as well get it over with. "Yes, a Catholic priest."

The announcement caused no change of facial expression other than a ruminant sideslip of the tobacco chewer's jaw. "Don't see many of your kind in these parts. Where're you bound?"

"I'm trying to reach the G. & P. track four miles south of Racey. Do you know the place?"

The man spoke pridefully. "Racey? Got a molar there. Figured to yank it tomorrow, but I guess Pa Crumps wouldn't object if it came out this afternoon."

"Are you a dentist?" asked Stephen.

The man plunged his hand into his haversack and pulled out a pair of forceps. "Carry the tools, anyway," he grinned. "Painless Tatspaugh's the name. Antiseptic methods. Prices reasonable. Bicuspids and molars, two bits. Wisdom teeth, half a dollar."

The itinerant dentist narrowed a diagnostic eye at Stephen. "You look all beat up, brother. What they been doin' to you?" Without specifying who "they" were, Painless Tatspaugh drew a cocoa can from his haversack and scooped out a fingerful of salve. "Tatspaugh's Sovereign Elixir," he explained. "Guaranteed to heal cuts, ringworm, harness sores, and" — he spat mightily — "whip welts. S'pose I rub some of it over the painy spots."

Stephen accepted the ministrations gratefully. Refreshed by the combination of cornbread, Sovereign Elixir, and Samaritanism in general, he rose stiffly to his feet.

Walking toward Racey at the terrific pace set by Painless Tatspaugh, Stephen revised his estimate of the Southern character considerably. Ben Tatspaugh chewed just as much tobacco and spat it as accurately as any man on the Crescent House veranda. He was unwashed, illiterate, and reasonably addicted to profanity. But he possessed that unpurchasable asset peculiar to no economic class or geographic region — the truly gentle soul. His gentleness came out when he stooped to gather a clump of foxglove which, he explained, would do Gran'ma Fugitt's heart a world of good. It was revealed in his manner of adjusting the rope harness that was galling a mangy mule. Watching him extract a tooth from a sharecropper's swollen jaw, Stephen realized that Painless Tatspaugh's reputation sprang not alone from skill, but also from the almost hypnotic confidence he inspired in his patients.

Through a broiling dusty afternoon, Ben Tatspaugh's long legs ate up incalculable mileage. Worn almost to exhaustion, Stephen finally panted, "How much further to Racey?" Without missing a stride, the itinerant dentist clucked encouragement. "Bear up, Reverend. We ain't got fur to go." From his haversack he pulled a black oval object, placed it to his lips, and blew a tentative note. "Mebbe a marchin' tune'll put sperrit into your legs. Ever hear a sweet pertater?"

Stephen admitted that he never had.

"Then you got a treat comin', brother." On the crude instrument, kin to the gourd, Ben Tatspaugh displayed his virtuosity as they crossed gullies, swamps, and unfenced fields. From a long repertory of hornpipes, jigs, and reels, he chose the liveliest. Then, his narrow chest pumping at full pressure, the sweet-potato player burst triumphantly into "Dixie."

> *Way down south in de land of cotton,*
> *Old times dar am not forgotten,*
> *Look away, look away, look away, Dixieland.*

Full circle. Same melody, same words, same landscape. *Da capo al fine* — only this time different fingers were searching the stops of Stephen's heart. Dust-grimed but jubilant, he joined in the chorus.

Coming out of a pine grove, Stephen almost stumbled over a rusty railroad track. "Racey," announced Painless Tatspaugh. He pointed south. "You'll find Number 9 down thata way." Solicitude was in his final question. "Want me to walk along?"

The man had already walked ten times the Biblical mile, and was willing to go still further. "No, thanks," said Stephen. "I can make it from here." In parting, he tried to press a five-dollar bill into his guide's hand, but Ben Tatspaugh's essential gentility waved aside more ready money than he would see in a month of molar-pulling.

"Keep your money, Reverend," he said. "When I can't help a neighbor out of a ditch, I better close up shop."

A four-mile walk down the track brought Stephen into the presence of Lem Tingley, twisting a final nut onto Number 9's eccentric rod.

"How'd you find things in Owosso?" asked the engineer.

"Pretty much like most other places." How comment otherwise on the alternate threads of good and evil woven into the fabric of life?

No one ever knew that the assistant to the Apostolic Delegate had been flogged in the performance of his mission, or that his wounds had been anointed by a passing stranger. Stephen never mentioned it to Quarenghi or anyone else. The only memento of the affair was a cheap gilt crucifix that Stephen always tucked in his bag whenever and wherever he traveled.

HIS BRIEF CASE bulging with materials, Stephen returned to Washington and began writing a special report for the Apostolic Delegate. He spent a week describing the condition of the Church in the South, and ended his report with urgent recommendations for Catholic action in that neglected part of the United States. "To preserve and extend the faith in this region," he wrote, "two things are needed: money and bishops. Funds must be raised by voluntary contributions from more prosperous areas. New bishops must be created in Georgia, Mississippi, Louisiana, and Alabama. The incumbents must be vigorous, young men, able to cope with the double challenge of economic want and religious bigotry."

Stephen's report, approved and signed by Quarenghi, was sent to the Congregation of the Consistory in Rome. The Cardinal Prefect of that Congregation, impressed with the urgency of the report, promptly recommended to His Holiness the creation of four new bishoprics in the United States as requested by the Apostolic Delegate.

The selection of these (as of all) bishops was no random procedure. To obtain the best possible men for the posts, the Church utilized its time-proved method of scrutiny based on the terna. Every two years the bishops of an ecclesiastic province come together in a meeting; at these meetings each bishop submits a terna — the names of three men in his diocese whom he considers most eligible for episcopal rank. These lists are then sent to the Apostolic Delegate, who forwards them, along with much collateral material, to the Congregation of the Consistory in Rome. Here the names and records of the candidates are carefully examined; all but the most promising are weeded out, and the remaining names are subjected to still more searching scrutiny, consisting of additional letters of information, and comment from Church officials. The opinion of the Apostolic Delegate carries enormous weight here. This mass of material, sifted through an almost microscopic screen, produces at length the outstanding candidate. The name of this candidate is placed before the Holy Father, who, in the exercise of his power as Supreme Pontiff, makes the final choice when a vacancy occurs.

In the 1927 terna forwarded by Cardinal Glennon to the office of the Apostolic Delegate, Stephen saw his own name, bracketed with those of Michael Speed and Hubert Silvera of New Bedford. A shiver of apprehension ran along Stephen's spine. The day was nearing when he would be called upon to defend, judge, interpret, ordain, confirm — and rule!

The call did not come at once. When bishop Shields of Maine died that summer, the Right Reverend Michael Speed was named as his successor. Stephen attended Mike Speed's consecration; with sixty-five other members of the American hierarchy, he watched his old friend prostrate himself before the altar, then rise to receive the miter and crozier, symbols of episcopal authority, from the hands of his consecrator, Lawrence Cardinal Glennon. Afterwards, at the reception in the new Bishop's residence, there was much handshaking and felicitation all around. Not a man present begrudged Mike Speed his advancement; it was agreed that of all the younger clergy in the United States, the ex-Chancellor of the Boston Archdiocese best deserved, and would most eminently fulfill, the honors and responsibilities of his new post.

Scarcely a month later, the Most Reverend John T. Qualters, D.D., Bishop of Hartfield — a man heavy with years and riddled by five contending diseases (heart, kidney, liver, arthritis, and gallstones) gave up the ghost. To honor the deceased Bishop, whose diocese was the second largest in New England, the Apostolic Delegate accepted an invitation to attend the funeral and deliver the eulogy in person.

"I shall be gone a week or more," said Quarenghi to Stephen shortly before he left. "In my absence, you will act as temporary chargé d'affaires. If matters of special importance arise, you can get in touch with me at the residence of Cardinal Glennon in Boston."

The Associated Press put the full text of Quarenghi's eulogy — a moving oration in the highest tradition of sacred eloquence — on its wires. Letters and telegrams poured in from all parts of the country; even non-Catholic commentators hailed Quarenghi's speech as the fruit of a new understanding between Rome and America.

When the Apostolic Delegate returned to Washington, his mood was quietly jubilant. "Well," he said, "I've made my little swing around the circle. Isn't that the idiom used by campaigners in this country?" Quarenghi went on: "I saw many remarkable things and people, but perhaps the most remarkable of all was your Lawrence Cardinal Glennon. Why, he's a monument — a phenomenon."

"I'm glad you discovered his real stature," said Stephen. "In Rome he was overshadowed. But in this country people regard him as the ideal of what a prince of the Church should be."

Quarenghi was going through the mail on his desk, apparently searching for a special envelope. "His Eminence thinks highly of you, Stefano. In fact, he sends you a gift."

"A gift?"

"Yes." Quite casually, Quarenghi handed Stephen a small box tied with an amethyst ribbon, then returned to the business of scanning his mail. Stephen snipped the amethyst ribbon, removed the outer wrapping of Glennon's gift, and saw a ring case of faded blue velvet. He snapped the lid open, and there, in a groove of white satin, lay a ring — a beveled amethyst with a bezel of seed pearls.

It was the Dolcettiano ring that Orselli had given him years ago. The ring that Stephen had sold to defray the expenses of Ned Halley's final illness. The ring that Glennon . . .

He looked up wonderingly at Quarenghi, who, having found the envelope he was looking for, was slicing its seals with an ivory-handled knife. "Si, si, Stefano." The Apostolic Delegate was nodding and smiling. "Cardinal Glennon believed that you'd be needing your amethyst again," he continued, glancing at the heavy fold of vellum he had taken from the envelope. "And my mail from Rome tells me that he was right."

Quarenghi handed Stephen the vellum sheet bearing the personal crest of Pius XI. Stephen glanced at the document: three paragraphs in Latin covered the page. The first paragraph set forth the regrettable fact that His Excellency the Most Reverend John T. Qualters was deceased. The second paragraph recited that the See of Hartfield had consequently fallen vacant. The last paragraph read:

By virtue, therefore, of the authority transmitted to us in unbroken descent from Peter the First Disciple, we declare and publish our desire that the Right Reverend Stephen Fermoyle be consecrated Bishop of Hartfield in the United States of America, and that he shall enter at once upon the powers, duties, and obligations laid upon him by the solemn oath of his office. In testimony whereof we give this Apostolic mandate on the 14th day of July, anno Domini 1927.

The letter was signed Pius XI, and underneath the signature was the imprint of the Fisherman's ring.

BOOK FIVE

The Crozier

CHAPTER 1

ATHENAEUM AVENUE is not one of the chief thoroughfares
of the United States, but few American streets are handsomer.
From the circular hub of Hartfield Common, the broad maple-
shaded avenue runs due south through the most prosperous
quarter of the second-largest city in New England. For the
first few blocks Athenaeum Avenue is flanked by imposing
semipublic structures: here in pillared grandeur stands the
Phoenix Mutual Assurance Company; beside it rises the cool
white spire of the Congregational Church, one of the purest
examples of meeting-house architecture in America. Opposite
them are the Hartfield National Bank, St. Alfred's Episcopal
Church, and the Greek-porticoed Athenaeum, which gave the
avenue its name. Alongside the Athenaeum is St. Philip's
Cathedral, seat of the Roman Catholic Bishop of Hartfield.
That these structures, together with the Hiram K. Weatherby
High School and the Central Fire Station, support and preserve, each in its own way, an existing order and a desirable
mode of life has never been pointed out to the four hundred
thousand citizens of Hartfield. The fact itself is either too
self-evident or has become too deeply unconscious for comment.

It was not always so. Time was when only property holders
were allowed to enter the shadowy bookstacks of the Athenaeum — and none but worshipers at St. Alfred's or the Congregational meetinghouse could become directors of the Hartfield National Bank. That era was already on the way out
when, shortly before the turn of the century, Bishop John P.
("Desperate") Desmond bought the two-acre lot on Athenaeum Avenue and broke ground for St. Philip's. "Overweening," "cheeky," "riding for a fall," were some of the kinder
things said about Bishop Desmond. The only fall the Bishop
feared was the aesthetic tumble one might easily take while
building opposite the chill white perfection of the Congrega-

480

tional meetinghouse. What he said to his architect will never be known, but his directions went something like this:

"Design a Cathedral that will translate Chartres, Strasbourg, yes, and St. Peter's, too, into American terms. Use native freestone; it weathers best. Besides, our local quarries need the business. Build out of the eternal past, into the industrial present, for the unforeseeable future. *Give Catholicism and Hartfield a monument they can be proud of!*"

How an architect could manage to translate the symbolism of rose window and flying buttress into an idiom acceptable to a Yankee community is only part of the secret that clings to the Gothic. Undeniably, this architect had succeeded. St. Philip's massive strength seemed to spring from the unshakable rock of Peter; its stone poetry, ascending in twin magnificent spires, suggested the devotional dream that nourishes the lives of men. On September 7, 1927, both the strength and the dream were renewed in the profoundly mystical ceremonies accompanying Stephen Fermoyle's consecration as Bishop of Hartfield.

At ten o'clock that morning, while four thousand worshipers knelt inside the Cathedral and an exterior multitude clogged traffic on Athenaeum Avenue, a procession of richly vested clerics, preceded by cross-bearer, acolytes, and choristers, entered the center door of the great church. A full organ swelled jubilantly into *Ecce sacerdos magnus;* bourdon, *Doppelflöte,* and open diapason hurled triumphant thunder down the long nave as the ecclesiastical train approached the altar. Soon the sanctuary was a pool of crimson and gold; throughout the Cathedral softer blocks of color marked the presence of religious orders: Carmelites and Dominicans in white, Paulists in black, Capuchins in coarse brown. Kneeling in the first pew, Dennis and Celia Fermoyle scarcely dared lift their eyes to the solemn pageant in which their son was playing the central role.

Tall tapers wavered in vagrant drafts as Lawrence Cardinal Glennon, flanked by Alfeo Quarenghi and Michael Speed as assistant consecrators, moved in the slow tempo of ceremony to their positions at the Epistle side of the altar for the reading of the Apostolic mandate. Meanwhile, Stephen had put on his amice, alb, cincture, stole, and cope. Kneeling before his con-

secrators, the Bishop-elect took a solemn oath of obedience
to the decrees and ordinances of the Church. He pledged himself to defend it from evil men, promised to visit the tombs of
the Apostles Peter and Paul in Rome at five-year intervals,
and render during these visits a full accounting of his steward-
ship to the Pope. Examined briefly regarding his orthodoxy in
matters of faith and morals, Stephen declared his firm belief
in the fundamental doctrines of the Holy Roman Catholic
Church.

While choir and organ burst into Haydn's *Kyrie eleison,*
Solemn High Mass began with Cardinal Glennon as celebrant.
Stephen meanwhile put on the stockings and slippers proper
to a bishop. Taking off his cope, he received the pectoral cross
together with the dalmatic. Attired in these traditional vestments, each symbolizing the powers and duties laid upon
him by the Church, Stephen was again brought before his
consecrators. Mitered, they knelt while Stephen prostrated
himself at full length before the altar. In the position of the
meanest suppliant, he lay flat on his face, humbly entreating
God not to mark his iniquities as a man or his unworthiness
as a priest. No jubilant music now; no supporting ritual. Only
a whispered plea for grace — the sanctifying gift by which
God bestows on men some part of His nature.

Muffled in his robes, Stephen heard the choir chanting in
Latin the Litany of the Saints — that roster of names blessed
in heaven and venerated on earth:

*St. Michael, St. Gabriel, St. Raphael . . . All ye holy
patriarchs and prophets,*
Pray for us.
*St. Peter, St. Paul, St. John . . . All ye holy Apostles and
evangelists,*
Pray for us.
*St. Benedict, St. Dominic, St. Francis . . . All ye holy monks
and hermits,*
Pray for us.
*St. Magdalene, St. Agnes, St. Cecily . . . All ye holy virgins
and widows,*
Pray for us.

The note changed; the plea for protection and mercy ascended directly to God:

> *From Thy wrath,*
>> Deliver us, O Lord.

> *From anger and hatred and ill will,*
>> Deliver us.

> *From the spirit of fornication,*
> *From lightning and tempest,*
> *From plague, famine, and war,*
> *From everlasting death,*
>> O Lord, deliver us.

Again the note deepened; became somber with fear of the Lord:

> *In the Day of Judgment,*
>> We beseech Thee, hear us.

That Thou wouldst spare us, that Thou wouldst pardon us,
>> Lord, we beseech Thee.

That Thou wouldst vouchsafe to govern and preserve Thy
> *Holy Church,*
That Thou wouldst vouchsafe to confirm and preserve us
> *in Thy holy service,*
>> We beseech Thee, hear us.

Lamb of God, who takest away the sins of the world,
>> Spare us, hear us, have mercy on us, O Lord.

The Litany ended. No human voice or action seemed worthy to break the hush that followed. Worshipers, choir, consecrators, the muffled figure lying prostrate before the altar, were motionless, silent. For a moment the ritual passed into a realm of mystery as the sense of the Apostolic succession about to take place hung over the Cathedral.

Stephen rose to a kneeling position. Assisted by coconsecrators, Lawrence Glennon laid the open Book of the Gospels on Stephen's neck, murmuring as he did so, "Receive the Holy Ghost." In the name of the Holy Trinity, the Cardinal then anointed Stephen's forehead with a chrism composed of precious oils and resin blessed for the purpose. The anointing disarranged Stephen's hair; Glennon smoothed it back with a gold-handled ivory comb. He anointed Stephen's hands that he might labor for God, then gave him his crozier, saying: "Receive the staff of the pastoral office, so that in the correction of vices thou mayest be lovingly severe, giving judgment without wrath, softening the minds of thy hearers whilst fostering virtues, not neglecting strictness of discipline through love of tranquillity." Blessing the episcopal ring, he slipped it onto Stephen's finger as a sign that as Christ is wedded to the Church, so the bishop is wedded to his diocese.

In return Stephen presented his consecrator with two votive candles, two small loaves of bread, and two tiny gold barrels of wine.

Not until the Mass was over did the new Bishop receive his miter. When Glennon placed the gold-embroidered crown on Stephen's head, choir and organ burst into the *Te Deum* of St. Augustine. Turning for the first time to his people, Bishop Fermoyle descended the altar steps and moved down the aisle, showering benediction on his flock as they bent before his upraised hand.

The first to receive his blessing were Dennis and Celia Fermoyle. They took their son's benediction with bowed heads and hands clasped, right thumb over the left. When Stephen passed on, they brought their heads close to each other, as dumb creatures sometimes do when sharing knowledge not communicable to others.

THE PUBLIC RECEPTION on the Cathedral lawn combined the best features of a civic holiday, a Hibernian picnic, and a family reunion. From refreshment tables set up by the Knights of Columbus, eight thousand sandwiches and two hundred gallons of grape-juice lemonade vanished in forty minutes. A uniformed K. of C. band gave music while notables of all sects and politicians of both parties shook Stephen's hand. The governor of the state (Repub.-Episc.) ended his address of welcome on the elegant note *gloria virtutis umbra,* which meant, he was careful to explain, "Glory is the shadow of virtue." The Mayor of Hartfield (Dem.-Cath.) presented a scroll illuminated in Book of Kells style; into his address he worked

a Gaelic phrase meaning "plow deep." The Protestant clergy
sent a noble delegation headed by the patrician Bishop Forsythe of the Methodist-Episcopal Church. Rabbi Joshua Felshin of Temple Beth Israel shook Stephen's hand. A bevy of
little girls from St. Rose's Academy tendered Stephen a spiritual bouquet. Prelates of the Cathedral parish and heads of
religious orders filed past, each kneeling to kiss the episcopal
ring; some seven hundred pastors, curates, and nuns from all
over the Diocese did likewise. Flash bulbs snapped; reporters
begged for statements, and traffic through Hartfield Square
had to be rerouted.

At one-thirty P.M. the last sandwich had disappeared, and
the band played its final number — a medley of *"Adeste
fideles"* and "My Country 'Tis of Thee" composed for the
occasion by Professor Valentine Mullaney, principal of the
Hartfield Academy of Music. As the crowd drifted away,
Stephen turned to greet his family and friends gathered in the
parlor of the episcopal residence.

The parlor, furnished in what might be called Irish Vic-
torian style, was trying hard to preserve the museum atmosphere that Mrs. Goodwin, the "old Bishop's" housekeeper, had
stamped upon it during her long reign. The windows were
lace-curtained, with beige overdrapes caught up in a swirl
of silver knots so admired by undertakers. Though the
deceased Bishop had not been addicted to dressing his hair
with bear's grease, Mrs. Goodwin had taken no chances —
every chair was protected by an antimacassar. A crystal chandelier hung from the ceiling like a frozen stalactite, outpropor-
tioning everything else in the room but the Ivers and Pond
piano, a claw-footed walnut monster that Mrs. Goodwin had
seemingly tried to conceal with a triangular lace throw. In
the cēnter of the room a glass bell stood on a marble-topped
table, and under the glass bell was the missal used by the first
Bishop of Hartfield. Empty, the parlor would have been a
tomb. Now, filled with Stephen's family and friends, it buzzed
with quite untomblike gaiety.

Having changed his robes for a black broadcloth suit given
him as a consecration gift by his parents, Stephen stood in the
doorway. "Alone at last," he said, and plunged shoulder-deep
into the laughter caused by his remark. Here, gathered in a

single room, were the people who, by blood or love, were most nearly part of himself. One by one he greeted them: Din and Celia, givers of life itself; Din, painfully barbered and wearing a baggy blue serge suit, undistinguishable — saving the arm stripes — from his motorman's uniform; Celia, almost comely in the silk print and chic new hat her daughters had urged upon her. With awe and curiosity Celia fondled her son's amethyst ring. "Handsome, Steve, handsome," she murmured. Then a touch of mischievous humor lighted Celia's once-pretty face. She held out the third finger of her left hand on which she wore the thin gold band that Din placed there thirty-nine years before.

"This had to come before *that,"* she said with mimic hauteur. And not all the theologians between Origen and Mercier could have refuted her.

The happiest event of the day took place when Stephen presented his father to Cardinal Glennon. Proudly he led Din to the armchair that Glennon had transformed into a throne by the simple act of sitting in it. Din, the earthly father, and Glennon, the spiritual sponsor, both aware of their equity in the young Bishop of Hartfield, shook hands as equals. Tutored by natural dignity, Din bowed over the Cardinal's sapphire; Glennon, moved by the knowledge that in one respect at least this grizzled motorman was his better, drew Din close, locked him for a moment with a half embrace, and said:

"This must be a proud day for you, Mr. Fermoyle."

"It is, Your Eminence."

Glennon's imperious hazel eye scrutinized Din's massive head. "Stephen once said I reminded him of you. Can you see the resemblance?"

Visible evidence told Dennis Fermoyle that the resemblance was not physical. He had all his hair; the Cardinal was bald as an egg. Din's midriff and hands were hardened with toil: Glennon was paunchy, soft. A life of command had given the Cardinal a viceregal carriage; drudgery had bowed Din's head and shoulders. Could a likeness exist between these two men? Dennis saw that it could. Lacking courtier skill, he uttered the simple truth:

"I think I know what Stephen meant, Your Eminence. I taught my son to prize fearlessness. If he finds a resemblance between us, it is because he sees my teaching magnified in you."

Din's compliment fairly took the wind out of Glennon's purple sails. "You Fermoyles," he murmured, then recovered himself sufficiently to add: "The most striking resemblance that *I* note in this room, Mr. Fermoyle, is the notable likeness between you and your son."

The blue vein in Glennon's domed forehead was throbbing violently — the outward sign (Stephen knew) of a splitting headache brought on by strain and excitement. "Would Your Eminence like to lie down a bit?" he asked tenderly.

"And miss the jollification? No, Steve boy, no. I can have a headache any day — but how often can I enjoy a family party like this? So much prayer and ceremony today! Let us be people for a little while."

Pressing around their Bishop-brother were the Fermoyles: Bernie, resplendent in morning jacket, ascot, and suède spats — no longer the touch artist, but a rising radio star, billed nationally as "the Irish Thrush"; George, the political lawyer, and adviser to Alfred E. Smith, correct in the not-to-be-imitated New York manner of selecting and wearing clothes. Here was shy Ellen, unwimpled descendant of St. Theresa, the frail candle of her body still flaming with scarlet devotions and tireless labor in the sacristy. *In all thy orisons remember me, Ellen.* Childless Florrie, trying to yield a little under her heavy corset as Stephen embraced her Next, Rita and Dr John Byrne, weaving an oak-and-ivy pattern of Catholic marriage, their four children budding around them. And gazing up at Stephen, the dark-curled fosterling, Mona's child, that the Byrnes had adopted as their own.

"Regina, this is Uncle Stephen," said Rita.

Nothing bashful about Regina. "Hello, Uncle Stephen," she said, making a little curtsy. Delicate face turned upward, she accepted his kiss with a matter-of-fact comment: "You smell like a church."

General merriment: "Out of the mouths of babes," remarked Glennon.

In the doorway Mrs. Goodwin was announcing luncheon, served buffet style in the dining room. Diligent thumbing through the pages of her *Marion Harland Cook Book* had led the housekeeper to choose scalloped oysters, stewed tomatoes, Parker House rolls, Washington pie, pistachio ice cream, and coffee as the opening salvo in her campaign to "stay on" with the new bishop. She had brought out the Spode china, Gorham silverware, and double damask napkins, all of which created a proper sense of awe in Celia Fermoyle. In a private conversation with Mrs. Goodwin, Celia ticked off her son's favorite dishes: creamed codfish on Fridays, beef and kidney pie, hot gingerbread, well buttered, and clam chowder, *without* tomatoes. "Before he goes to bed," continued Celia, "he sometimes likes a glass of milk with a slice or two of home-made bread and a small pitcher of molasses." All of which Mrs. Goodwin noted for future reference.

While an edifying clatter of forks went on in the dining room, Stephen foraged for laggards in the parlor. There he found Dollar Bill Monaghan, failing somewhat in eyesight but otherwise in good repair, discussing the high costs of construction with Cornelius Deegan. Mike Speed and Paul Ireton, seminarians together at Brighton, were catching up on the lost years. Stephen shunted them toward the table. Hanging back, too, was Father Jeremy Splaine, a chestnut-haired young curate with electric blue eyes and the chrism of ordination still wet on his forehead. "Jemmy, you remind me of the Italian peninsula," said Stephen. "You're too long for your width. Into the dining room with you."

From her discreet station in the butler's pantry, Mrs. Goodwin watched the provisions vanish like so many rabbits at a magicians' convention, while waves of merriment creamed up the walls of the dining room. She decided that the stoutish man in the morning coat and ascot tie must be quite an entertainer, else why should tears of laughter be streaming down the Cardinal's face at some story or other about a piccolo player?

BACK in the parlor, Bernie Fermoyle was gradually taking over the party. Good food, and the even headier stimulant of Glennon's laughter, had brought out Bernie's biologic compulsion to sing and play. Sooner or later he would sit down at the piano and cast his warbling spell over an audience quite ready to be entertained. His opportunity came sooner than he had expected. Sipping coffee, crony fashion, with the Cardinal and Stephen in a curtained bow window, Bernie fingered the silver knots on the beige overdrapes.

"Such grandeur, Steve," he said. "Quite a bit different from 'Shanahan's Ould Shebeen.'"

Lawrence Glennon pricked up his ears. "'Shanahan's Ould Shebeen'? My father used to sing it. I didn't know anyone remembered 'Shanahan' these days."

"Show His Eminence how good your memory is, Bernie," suggested Stephen.

Thus persuaded, Bernie strolled over to the Ivers and Pond, twirled the piano stool a couple of times, and sat down with the easy seat of the born performer. He vamped a few bars, then, laying back his head, sounded off with his own variant of the all-but-forgotten ditty describing the forlorn plight of one Cassidy, longing amid wealth, for the old carefree days in Shanahan's Ould Shebeen.

In me bran'-new brownstone mansion — lace curtains
hangin' fine,
The Cathedral round the corner and the Cardinal in to
dine —
Sure I ought to be stiff with grandeur, but me tastes are
mighty mean,
And I long for a mornin's mornin' at Shanahan's Ould
Shebeen.

That's why, as I sit on me cushins, wid divil a thing to do,
In a mornin' coat of velvet and a champagne lunch at two,
The mem'ry comes like a banshee, meself and me wealth
between,
An' I long for a mornin's mornin' in Shanahan's Ould
Shebeen.

'Tis fit I mix with the gentry — I'm a laborer now no
more —
But ohone! those were fine times, lad, to talk of them
makes me sore,
An' often — there's times, I tell you, when I'd swap this
easy chair,

> *An' the velvet coat, an' me footman wid his Sassenach*
>   *nose in the air,*
> *An' the Cardinal's elegant learnin' too — for a taste o' the*
>   *days that ha' been,*
> *For a glass o' a mornin's mornin' in Shanahan's Ould*
>   *Shebeen.*

Lawrence Glennon struck his plump hands together in hearty applause. "More, more," everyone cried.

"Any request numbers?" asked Bernie.

Din spoke up. "Like a good boy, Bernie, give us 'Drill, Ye Tarriers, Drill.'"

"Sure thing, Dad." Again Bernie was off in song — this time his own version of a railroad chantey sung by Irish immigrant laborers who had made straight the transcontinental way for America's steel tracks.

> *Oh, every morn at seven o'clock*
> *There are twenty tarriers on the rock.*
> *The Boss comes along and says: "MacGill,*
> *Put all your powder in the cast-steel drill."*
>
> *(Voice of Boss: spoken) "Stand out there with the*
>   *warnin' flag, Sullivan. Look sharp, O'Toole. Blast!*
>   *Fire! All over."*
> *Then drill, ye tarriers, drill;*
> *Drill, ye tarriers, drill.*
>
> *Oh, it's work all day with no sugar in your tay*
> *When ye work beyant on the railway.*
> *So drill, ye tarriers, drill.*
> *Blast away that hill,*
> *Crack those ledges with your I-rish sledges.*
>   *Drill, drill, drill.*
>
> *(Voice of Boss: spoken) "Stand out forninst the fence*
>   *with the flag, McCarthy. Where's the fuse,*
>   *McGinty? What? You lit your pipe with it? Stop*
>   *the handcar coming down. Stand back! Blast!*
>   *Fire! All over."*
>
> *Just as the terrible blast went off,*
> *A mile in the air went big Jim Goff;*

When payday next it came around
Jim's pay a dollar short he found.
"What for?" said he. Came the boss's reply:
"You were docked for the time you were up in the sky."

Operating on the vaudeville formula, "Always leave them laughing," Bernie retired. Stephen hoped the Cardinal would volunteer to play, but His Eminence made no movement toward the instrument. Instead he gazed paternally at the little girls clustered around Rita Byrne. "Will any of you young ladies favor us with a selection?" he asked. While Louise and Elizabeth Byrne snuggled blushingly into their mother, Regina piped up:

"I'll play."

"Good girl. What pieces do you know?" asked the Cardinal.

"*Für Elise* and *Le Secret*."

"Why, those are quite hard. Especially *Le Secret*."

"Not really. Sister Veronica says it's only the sharps and flats that make it *seem* hard." Regina twirled the piano stool till it teetered up to its last spiral groove, then climbed aboard and sailed through the chromatic narrows of *Le Secret*. It was a sprightly, though by no means prodigious, performance for a six-year-old child. After absorbing the last drop of applause, Regina followed with *Für Elise*. "It's by Beethoven," she explained, then proceeded to gather up the gently melodic phrases into her little basket of music. Her assurance and beauty fascinated Stephen. He was sorry when Regina, her repertory exhausted, started to climb off the stool.

Obviously, Glennon was sorry, too. "Have you any other pieces?" he asked.

"Sister Veronica says my Chopin won't be ready till next week."

"Chopin?" Glennon pretended to rack his memory. Then hoisting himself out of his armchair, he walked to Regina's side. "Does it go like this?" The Cardinal fingered the first four measures of the Prelude in A major.

"Yes, yes!" Regina clapped her hands. "How did you know?"

"Oh," His Eminence was suitably vague. "Sister Veronica tells me things. Do you think you can play it now?"

Regina began bravely enough, then bobbled hesitantly over

a wrong note. Violet eyes sought the Cardinal's help. "That doesn't sound right," she said.

Glennon agreed. "How many sharps in the key of A major?"

"Three. F, C, and G."

"Sharp your F and see what happens."

Regina sharped her F, smiled gratefully at His Eminence, and went on. Toward the end she broke down. "I don't remember how it goes from here." Arms around the little girl on the piano stool, his hands on the keyboard, Lawrence Glennon finished the prelude.

Afterwards he sat down at the piano and improvised a theme from Scarlatti.

Almost a quarter of a century before, he had embroidered this very theme in the presence of a Pope long dead. Sadness wove a golden thread through the Cardinal's music; meditatively his fingers explored the nostalgic shadows enshrouding departed days and friends. A triumphant note emerged as he recalled the power and the glory that had been his; honors of place and preferment — he had known them all. An unwonted melancholy returned to his music; he had missed something, too — something that Dennis Fermoyle had enjoyed in fullest measure. The rewards of family life, the pride of gazing at a powerful son, a taller, nobler projection of oneself! How did it feel to be surrounded by earthly immortality in the shape of beautiful children repeopling the world with others like themselves? The power to consecrate bishops lay in Glennon's hands, but he could never fondle as his own a dark-haired little girl with violet eyes who could tell you fearlessly, and quite correctly, that the key of A major had three sharps.

Glennon's music took on a more buoyant voice as he glanced across the room at his spiritual son, who, hearing the sadness in the Cardinal's playing, gazed back at him with unspoken sympathy. Glennon smiled, nodded: "It has passed. All is right again." Breaking off his musical meditations, the Cardinal ended his little recital with a showy arrangement of Elgar's *Pomp and Circumstance,* a selection perfectly suited to the taste and understanding of his audience.

Homage and affection saluted him as he left the piano. Both were comforting to His Eminence, but more comforting yet was the fact that his headache had entirely disappeared.

CHAPTER 2

SURVEYING his Diocese, Bishop Fermoyle was obliged to acknowledge that a substantial vineyard had been entrusted to his keeping.

The see of Hartfield, southernmost diocese in New England, covers an area of fifty-five hundred square miles in one of the oldest and most prosperous sections of the United States. At the center of the Diocese lies the city of Hartfield, capital of the state, a traditional stronghold of mercantile and industrial wealth. The home offices of great insurance companies give an air of solid permanence to its business district; a huge railway terminal makes Hartfield a nexus between New England and the rest of the United States. North and east of the capital, populous manufacturing cities produce fine metal goods: locks, tools, clocks, watches, building hardware, firearms, and precision instruments. West of the Hartfield River lie rich agricultural counties whose chief crop is an excellent grade of shade-grown tobacco. In 1927 — the year that Stephen took up his duties as Bishop — the population of the state was one million five hundred thousand; of this number approximately one third were Roman Catholics.

Stephen's spiritual authority over his people was virtually unbounded. Canon law made him an ecclesiastic king, answerable solely to the Pope and limited only by the common law of the Church. He had the power to judge, teach, interpret, censor, ordain, and confirm. But if his powers were large, his obligations were heavy. Upon him fell the responsibility of preserving in his Diocese the purity of Catholic doctrine and the vigor of Catholic faith. He must maintain constant vigilance over the conduct and training of the clergy, oversee the education of youth, and protect the sick and destitute within his jurisdiction. At regular intervals he must make a personal visit to every parish in his Diocese, audit the parish accounts, inspect the physical property of the Church, and ascertain the moral condition of pastors and people. The office of bishop has always demanded enormous physical strength, rare executive ability, vast prudence, superhuman tact, and (in a diocese the size of Hartfield) the ability to collect and administer large sums of money. Dangers surround a bishop's throne. He must resist the temptation of letting financial and administrative activities become ends in themselves. To remind him of his chief function, he is obliged to celebrate every Sunday and feast day the *missa pro grege* — the shepherd's Mass for the flock given to his keeping.

And finally, like any other man, the bishop must somehow find time to cultivate and preserve his own soul.

Stephen spent the first few days familiarizing himself with the organization of his Diocese. Chancery maps and records told him that he had jurisdiction over some two hundred pastors, four hundred curates, forty-seven parochial schools, six hospitals, three orphanages, eleven convents, and a seminary. To acquaint himself all at once with these various institutions and their personnel was impossible. Stephen turned for further information to the quick intelligence of Monsignor Ambrose Cannell, administrator of St. Philip's Cathedral.

Culturally, Ambrose Cannell was a type new to Stephen. British-born, and a convert from Anglicanism, Monsignor Cannell had inherited from his Dorsetshire forebears the country-squire ruddiness that one associates with tweeds and fox hunting. In addition to one of the best classical degrees that Oxford could confer, Ambrose Cannell possessed a marked interest in liturgy, church music, and architecture, as well as a most practical sense of how far the silk threads in a goldback could be stretched without breaking. Besides being the perfect administrator of a large Cathedral, Amby performed the still more difficult feat of remaining quite British and making his Celtic-American colleagues rather like it.

Stephen's first interview with Monsignor Cannell (it was really an informal conversation) took place in the Bishop's study on the second floor of the episcopal residence. Stephen was poring over a diocesan map when the administrator's fresh-colored countenance emerged through a cumulus cloud of pipe smoke, which in turn rose from the handsomest meerschaum Stephen had ever seen. The sherry-colored bowl of

Amby Cannell's pipe was a counterpart of the man himself —
nutty-flavored, aromatic, humorous, and reliable.

Stephen sniffed appreciatively at the smoke nimbus surrounding his colleague. "What's the name of that Elysian
blend you're burning?"

Ambrose Cannell removed the curved amber bit from his
mouth. "You may think I'm overplaying the part," he said,
"but it's a mixture of Three Nuns and Parson's Pleasure."

"You give it a Trollope flavor," said Stephen. Ambrose Cannell, who had heard all too few literary allusions since leaving
Oxford, appreciated the donnish touch. Between great billows
from his meerschaum, the administrator piled a hayrick of
facts and figures onto the bishop's desk.

"St. Philip's is not the richest cathedral parish in the United
States, Your Excellency," he began, "but its revenues are
steady and substantial. During the last fiscal year, parish collections amounted to one hundred and ten thousand dollars;
special gifts and contributions added another thirty thousand.
These are boom-time figures, you understand. Ordinarily, I
think you may safely count on an income somewhere in the
neighborhood of one hundred and twenty-five thousand dollars."

One hundred and twenty-five thousand dollars! Since, by
canon law, cathedral revenues accrue to the bishop, this sum
would be at Stephen's personal disposal. After deductions, of
course. "How do expenses run?" he inquired.

A flawless smoke ring haloed up from Amby Cannell's pipe.
"Heat, light, upkeep, and repairs on the Cathedral — twenty
thousand dollars. Salaries to clergy, choir, and organist come
to an equal amount. Ecclesiastical supplies, new vestments,
and so on — oh, I should say, seventy-five hundred. Then
there's the episcopal household. Bishop Qualters, a frugal
man, spent somewhere between ten and twelve thousand a
year on servants, food, and other domestic expenses."

Sixty thousand dollars gone in a puff! "How about the
parochial school?" asked Stephen.

"Never less than thirty-five thousand dollars, Your Excellency."

"Is the seminary self-supporting?"

Last year there was a deficit of ten thousand dollars."

"And St. Andrew's Hospital?"

"Depends on contributions. Bishop Qualters was always digging down for it." In the glowing bowl of Amby Cannell's meerschaum, the Bishop's fine income was being consumed to a still finer ash.

"Why, we'll be lucky to keep out of the red!" exclaimed Stephen.

"It will require some management," agreed Monsignor Cannell. Blandly, he went on to explain certain capital outlays long put off by Stephen's predecessor. The entire Cathedral needed sandblasting; its roof and buttresses could stand a structural overhauling. The new outpatient clinic of St. Andrew's Hospital was only half financed. Amby Cannell waved his amber pipestem at the shabby furnishings of the Bishop's study. "Naturally you'll want to make some alterations in your own house . . . Mrs. Goodwin concurring, of course."

Stephen smiled. "By stretching my canonical authority I may be able to get rid of the antimacassars."

Humorous resignation was in Amby Cannell's sigh. "That's more than Bishop Qualters was ever able to do."

Curiosity inflected Stephen's voice. "I never knew him. What kind of man was he?"

"In his prime, he ran a splendid shop here in Hartfield. He was a methodical man, an able organizer, scrupulous in his accounting, both fiscal and moral." Monsignor Cannell stuffed a palmful of ribbon cut into his meerschaum. "Towards the last, it was the old story of prolonged illness. *Ex pede Herculem*," he concluded cheerfully.

Loyalty to his departed leader and present colleagues prevented Amby Cannell from saying more. Nor did Stephen press for details. He was content to let the facts, whatever they were, advertise themselves at the first meeting of the diocesan Curia.

THE OUTSTANDING FACT about the Hartfield Curia — the board of ecclesiastics that acted as Stephen's aides and advisers — was the extreme age of its members. Every man at the council table was several years older than the Bishop. Vicar-General Mark Drury, an imposing oak of a man at seventy, had become intellectually blanched by standing for twenty-five years in the nobler shade of Bishop Qualters. Like that earlier cleric, Dean Swift, the Vicar-General was beginning to go from the top. A noticeable tremor agitated his head and voice as he greeted his superior and took the seat at his right hand. At Stephen's left sat Chancellor Gregory Shane, currant-dry after too many years on the vine. He had hoped to succeed the "old Bishop" at the latter's demise; obliged to step aside while a younger man grasped the crozier, Gregory Shane suffered the all-too-human pangs of those who serve well, wait patiently, and watch the prize go to another. Ranging down the table were other members of the council: Joseph Drumgoole, a dun-colored cleric, head of the charitable bureau; Edward Rickaby, chief of rural deans; and Thomas Kenney, of the marriage tribunal.

Never one to cut butter with a cleaver, Stephen knew well enough that butter did not cut itself. Assuming that everyone else knew it too, he moved without preliminaries into the business that had piled up since the last meeting. Decisions on many points had apparently been hanging fire for months. The docket of the marriage tribunal was badly clogged; the tempo of its hearings on annulments would have to be speeded up. Monsignor Drumgoole's reports on Catholic charities indicated a failure of grasp somewhere; expenditures were being made without proper investigation. He could not, for example, answer Stephen's direct question: "Has the herd of Guernseys at St. Brendan's Home for Boys proved to be a profitable venture?" Dean Kenney's recommendation that Polish-speaking priests be obtained for the tobacco-growing parishes in the Hartfield River Valley was excellent, yet the Dean had no idea where such priests could be obtained.

Stephen's decisions in these matters were tactful and conservative. Hundreds of similar meetings under Glennon's chairmanship, followed by four years in Rome and two in Washington, had given the new Bishop a tremendous background of judgment and experience in the handling of ecclesiastic affairs. For fifteen years he had studied under able masters; now, his apprenticeship over, his journeyman service behind, Stephen's touch was steady, his voice sure, as he disposed of the council's business. Feeling his strong hand, the diocesan consultants, familiar with the mysterious rule which decrees that some men must lead while others follow, were content, for the most part, to fall into line behind their young Bishop.

The only clash occurred when Chancellor Shane finished reading his report on the financial position of the Hartfield see. The report itself was encouraging: there existed a working capital of four hundred and fifty thousand dollars — not a vast reserve when checked against annual expenditures. Half of this sum was in cash, and the remainder in Grade A common stocks. Both cash and securities were held, of course, in the Bishop's name as a corporation sole.

"Should we not," the Chancellor was asking, "divert a larger portion of our cash into the purchase of common stocks?"

Stephen fingered the typewritten sheets of Monsignor Shane's financial report, which included a portfolio of the securities owned by the Diocese. He scanned the list: Aluminum Corporation, Carbon and Carbide, Pennsylvania Railroad, International Nickel, Standard Oil, United States Steel. Blue chips all. "What is the history of these investments, Monsignor Shane?" asked Stephen. "When were they purchased, on whose advice, and at what cost?"

Chancellor Shane had the matter at his finger tips. "Bishop Qualters bought them in 1922, at the suggestion of his brokers, Demming, Condit, and Hughes. Steel was picked up at eighty-five, Aluminum at one hundred and fifty. In the past six years all the diocesan holdings have more than doubled in value. The best financial opinion is that they will go higher." A litmus test of Monsignor Shane's voice would have indicated the presence of acid. "Very much higher."

Stephen pondered his reply. "One hundred per cent would seem a reasonable profit. Suppose we sold now?"

Drawstring muscles tightened the Chancellor's lips. "Why sell, Your Excellency? These are boom times."

Boom times! The expression was tripping off everyone's tongue. Yet beneath the rising tide of Wall Street prosperity, one felt an ugly undertow. Last year the Florida bubble had burst; rumors of overproduction and layoffs were gaining currency. Now and then, even the stock market would stumble ominously. Stephen remembered his ten-thousand-mile trip through the starveling South. No boom times in Dixie! He recalled a caustic remark by his brother George: "If yachts were selling for ten dollars apiece, most people couldn't afford to buy a cake of Lifebuoy Soap." Totaling the sum of all these parts, Stephen was reminded of the trick question in arithmetic. "Add six apples to five pears, and what do you get?" Answer: "Nothing."

"I don't pretend to any special knowledge of the stock market," said Stephen. "Doubtless these shares will go higher. Yet I'd feel safer if we held onto our cash, and converted these common stocks" — he tapped the portfolio with his finger — "into less hazardous securities."

The Bishop solicited opinions from his consultors. "Feel free to speak, gentlemen. Remember, it's diocesan money that's involved."

Father Drumgoole led off. "I see in the *Times* this morning that Steel went up four points. If we ride along with the market another six months, we might get enough to finish the outpatient department of St. Andrew's."

Whether Vicar-General Drury's head was nodding assent or merely shaking with age, Stephen couldn't tell. Monsignor Drury said nothing. Tom Kenney volunteered, "A friend of mine in Wall Street tells me we haven't seen anything yet."

Chancellor Shane took the candid role. "Why not consult with Harry Condit down at Demming, Condit, and Hughes? He'd give us the professional slant."

Briefly, Stephen considered the proposal. "We all know what that would be, Monsignor. 'Load up.' 'Double your holdings.' 'Don't sell America short.' Maybe it's smart professional advice." The Bishop of Hartfield studiously kept the iron out of his voice. "But we're not going to take it. Monsignor Shane, I want you to sell these stocks at the market opening tomorrow. Deposit the proceeds in the Hartfield Trust Company, and tell Hammond, their vice-president, that we want to put our money into the safest, solidest bonds he can buy for us."

No one at the table made an audible murmur of dissent. The Bishop had spoken. Gregory Shane did exactly as Stephen bade him, and for a whole year had the unbearable satisfaction of seeing United States Steel and Aluminum Corporation climb steadily into the blue. The Chancellor's cup of satisfaction overflowed when Steel touched two hundred and fifty and Aluminum five hundred dollars a share. As a matter of fact, Monsignor Shane was — until a certain unforgettable day in October, 1929 — as smug and difficult a clergyman as one could find in the entire Western world.

AUTUMN'S SEPIA SCARF went down the wind; winter covered earth's nakedness with an ermine stole. This was the season Stephen loved best; temperatures that made ice and snow were kindest to his blood, driving it in a full tide to heart and brain. In judgment and action he grew steadily surer; yet he made few actual changes in the diocesan picture, preferring to give his advisers and pastors the secure feeling that their tenure depended on ability and performance rather than on the Bishop's whim. Human errors of judgment were overlooked. "It could happen to anyone" was Stephen's favorite expression in letting a subordinate off the hook. The unspoken inference was "Don't let it happen again."

Only when a man was clearly incompetent, as in the case of Father Frank Ronan, did the Bishop intervene.

Frank Ronan, a middle-aged priest whose mercurial temperament quite outmatched his intellect, was the supervisor of St. Brendan's Home for Boys. St. Brendan's had started out as a run-of-the-mill orphanage, then, following a nice puff in a national magazine, had become for a time one of those "boytown" schools that never fail to grasp the popular imagination. Father Ronan installed an honor system in the classroom; he let the boys police themselves while they hoed vegetables in the St. Brendan truck garden and turned out crude furniture in the model carpenter shop. During the early twenties, St. Brendan's was a laboratory for social workers alert to the trend of the times; it received an enormous amount of publicity and a few medium-sized bequests. All of which became fatal wedges that opened up the flaw in Father Ronan's character. He fell into the dangerous habit of spending a hundred dollars for every fifty he collected, and became so busy paying interest that he quite neglected his human charges.

Finding himself mired in a financial bog, he attempted to

jack himself onto solid ground by purchasing a herd of Guernsey cows. The idea, as presented to Bishop Qualters six months prior to his death, had two brilliant features: *primo,* every orphan and invalid in Catholic institutions throughout the Diocese would grow fat on Guernsey milk; *secundo,* the St. Brendan herd would be paid for by monies formerly handed over to commercial dairies. *Quid pro quo* and *quod erat demonstrandum* — except that the plan didn't work. The cows had been in operation for almost a year, and the flow of butter fat was disappointingly meager.

With the money he was getting and expected to get, Father Ronan had built a model dairy farm: silos, milking machines, cream separators, all very expensive. Then he brought his boys into contact with his cows. The carnage was ghastly. Being neither a farmer nor a disciplinarian, Frank Ronan didn't know what to do. And while he scurried around for fresh funds, neither the cows nor the boys made any progress with each other.

Inklings that all was not well at St. Brendan's reached Stephen through various channels. Twice he referred the matter to Father Drumgoole, hoping that the director of charities would straighten things out. Then shortly after Christmas a paragraph appeared in "Pickles and Chowder," a peppery column conducted by Jake Mabbott in the Hartfield *Item.* The paragraph ran:

No one who values his job would dream of criticizing the conduct of affairs at a certain orphanage not a thousand miles from the state capital. Only kids and cows are involved, anyway. If worst comes to worst, the kids can always hit the road. But what can you do if you're a cow?

Stephen called in Father Drumgoole, showed him the "Pickles and Chowder" paragraph. "What's behind this, Father?"

The director of charities struck the newspaper with the back of his hand. "Just what you'd expect from a booze-fighting agnostic like Jake Mabbott. He hates the Church and everything it stands for."

"I'm not interested in Jake Mabbott's personal habits or theologic background," said Stephen. "He isn't discussing faith and morals here. He's talking about orphans and cows. Stop beating the devil around the bush, Father. What's going on at St. Brendan's?"

The gist of Father Drumgoole's answer was that Frank Ronan had been in squeezes before and had always worked himself out of them. It seemed that he had one of those sunshine-and-shower temperaments. Cloudy today, rosy tomorrow. If the Bishop would only have patience . . .

"I've got the patience of Bruce's spider," said Stephen. "But I don't want to see any more digs at us in 'Pickles and Chowder.'"

The next day Stephen had a phone call from Mayor Aloysius Noonan. "Sorry, Bishop," said the Mayor apologetically, "but my health commissioner says he'll have to tack a notice on Father Ronan's barns. Things are that bad up there."

"Can you hold your commissioner off for twenty-four hours, Mr. Mayor, till I take a look for myself?"

"Sure thing, Bishop."

Early next morning Stephen made an unannounced call at St. Brendan's Home for Boys. He left his car at the gate and walked into an Augean mess. The dormitories were filthy; the kitchen worse. Little boys were underclothed, big boys were underfed. But the real shock came when Stephen entered the stables. Manure piles, bales of hay, bags of feed, and assorted dairy equipment were inextricably tangled. After much climbing and detouring, Stephen discovered Father Ronan surrounded by a group of shivering boys, trying to make an AC electric separator work on DC current — a miracle that would defy the full powers of a first-rate saint.

Stephen beckoned to Frank Ronan. "I wish to speak to you privately, Father."

Through snowdrifts they trudged in silence to the office of St. Brendan's, a curtainless clutter of broken furniture and disordered files. Stephen closed the door and faced the collarless, haggard priest. "You have exactly ten minutes to tell me what you're trying to do here," he said.

In ten years Father Ronan couldn't have told. His unshaven face sank between dirty-nailed hands. Sobs of shame and relief shook him; shame at his failure, relief that the ordeal was over at last.

Sorry as Stephen felt for the man, he felt infinitely sorrier for the boys and the cows. His first act was to relieve Father Ronan of all responsibility and send him to a rest home. Next he summoned the frightened lay brother in charge of St. Brendan's kitchen and dormitory. "Clean up your departments in twenty-four hours," he ordered. "I'll be back this time tomorrow for an inspection." A phone call to a commercial dairy brought in a cattle expert to supervise the feeding and care of the Guernseys. None of these temporary measures, however, solved the deeper problem of setting St. Brendan's Home in order.

Stephen took the problem back to his office and talked it over with Amby Cannell. The administrator stuffed a half ounce of shag into his meerschaum, and said:

"I've never been in the milk business, but if I ever did go into it I'd call in the Xaverian Brothers to help me. They're wonderful with boys and farm animals."

"Unfortunately, we haven't any Xaverian Brothers in the Diocese."

"Your friend Bishop Speed might send down a flying detachment from Maine," suggested Monsignor Cannell.

"Amby, you think of everything. Get Mike Speed on the phone, will you, please?"

Forty-eight hours later a squad of Xaverians were in full charge of St. Brendan's. Within two weeks the Guernseys were streaming with milk. The little boys were clothed, the big boys were fed, and Catholic institutions throughout the Diocese of Hartfield began receiving regular shipments of milk, butter, and cream.

The stirabout at St. Brendan's had several consequences: Father Joe Drumgoole lost his job as director of charities and was quietly transferred to the small parish of Denham; Amby Cannell received a pound canister of Parson's Pleasure from his Bishop and took over Vicar-General Drury's office when the latter succumbed to a stroke. As for Father Frank Ronan, he wandered out of the rest home and was last seen hitchhiking along the Boston Post Road toward New York.

Despite all of Stephen's efforts to find him, no trace of Frank Ronan ever turned up. He became one of the ten thousand souls who each year slip their moorings and drift by rudderless courses into the port of missing men.

THE PART of his episcopal duty that Stephen enjoyed most — and labored hardest at — were the diocesan visitations.

Chauffered by Peter Tuohy, he would start off without breakfast (even a bishop must fast if he expects to say Mass) for an inspection of some parish in his domain. The purpose of these visits, as defined four hundred years ago by the Council of Trent, was to "maintain orthodox doctrine; to defend good and correct bad manners; to incite the people to religion, peace, and innocence by sermons and warnings; and to arrange all things according to the prudence of the bishop for the good of the people." Notified well in advance of the Bishop's visit, rectors would have their books ready, their churches in order, and often enough their hearts in their mouths as Stephen, attired in rochet and mozzetta, alighted at their door.

A strictly observed ceremony then took place. The rector, accompanied by cross-bearer, thurifer, and acolyte, would extend a small crucifix for his Bishop to kiss. Removing his biretta, Stephen would kneel for a brief prayer in the doorway. Rising, he would receive the aspergil from the rector, sprinkle his own forehead with holy water, then sprinkle those around him. Preceded by a thurifer, altar boys, curates, and pastor, Stephen then would go up the aisle, blessing the congregation. Mass might now be celebrated, or the sacrament of confirmation administered. Stephen would address the people briefly, then, seated on his faldstool — a kind of movable throne — he would hear the pastor read, first in Latin, then in English, the indulgence granted by the visiting bishop:

The Right Reverend Father and Lord in Christ, Stephen Fermoyle, by the grace of God and of the Apostolic See, Bishop, gives and grants to all persons here present fifty days of true indulgence, in the customary form of the Church. Pray to God for the good estate of His Holiness, Pius XI, by Divine Providence Pope, of his Lordship the Bishop, and of Holy Mother Church.

Afterwards (and this was the part that Stephen liked best), the Bishop stood at the main entrance of the church to receive the people. In theory, this was their opportunity to air grievances, if any; in practice they shook the Bishop's hand or kissed his ring (either was considered good form), then went home and spent a good part of the next year telling their neighbors, families, and each other what a handsome, young, stern, holy, and democratic man the Bishop was. And with reason they might. For, at thirty-eight, Stephen Fermoyle's lean figure, his dark hair parted on the side and rising above his grave, ascetic face, his powder-blue eyes, and vibrant low-pitched voice — all combined to make him an endearing human being and an inspiring leader of his people.

The physical inspection of the church property would now begin. Attended by the rector, Stephen walked about the interior of the church, examining the altar, confessionals, pulpit, fonts, and pews. In the sacristy he inspected the sacred vessels, vestments, and stock of holy oils. A bit of lunch might be taken at this point to give the rector strength for the financial audit and scrutiny of the parish register that followed. On the last used page of the account books and register, Stephen wrote the word *visum*, accompanied by his signature and the date. The Bishop now made whatever remarks, complimentary or otherwise, that the state of affairs called for. Then, after a final visit to the Blessed Sacrament, he was off.

Stephen's manner during these visitations was a blend of personal cordiality and ecclesiastical reserve. Coming in as a steward-general to inspect morale, supplies, and fortifications, he discovered that he must repress much of his natural warmth. One simply couldn't play the good-fellow role; undue geniality might lead to a fatal weakening of discipline. On the other hand, hard-working rectors must not be chilled by a too-frosty demeanor. Stephen chose the middle path; he was liberal with praise, firm and constructive in criticism, and particularly alert to avoid being taken in by the deference that he encountered during his visits.

The rectors fell into two groups: graying field veterans who, after long years of service, found themselves in charge of important city parishes; and younger men (around Stephen's own age) enjoying their first taste of parochial command in smaller towns. Though few geniuses appeared among them, they were solid administrators, the steel vertebrae that supported the physical body of the Church. Their financial accounts and parish records were usually well kept, their churches tight, trim, and in good repair. It would be easier, Stephen sometimes thought, to wrest Hercules' club from his hands than to criticize the pastoral labors of such men.

Still they had their troubles. For some mysterious reason, collections weren't what they should be. "People are buying hooch and gas with the money they used to put in the plate" was the explanation advanced by Dan O'Laughlin, rector of the biggest church in Fairhaven. Other pastors told similar stories of dwindling collections -- of dimes and quarters taking the place of heavier silver and folding green. Then, too, pastors were finding it difficult to weld a mixed population of Yankee aborigines with second-generation Irish and first-generation Italians and Poles. "It gets harder every Sunday to give a sermon they can all carry away with them," complained Father Matt Cornish, rector of the Sacred Heart in Bridgeton. Worst of all, the Catholic population seemed to be falling off slightly. "Five years ago we'd have fifty or sixty kids in a First Communion class. This year we had twenty-nine," was the way Andrew Brick, Pastor of Waterville's Star of the Sea, put it.

These waning rays of financial, moral, and procreative energy gathered themselves into a perfect focus, one cold February day in 1928, as Stephen was inspecting St. Anselm's in Springfield, a medium-sized manufacturing city on the eastern border of his Diocese. He was greeted at the door by Father Peter Mendum, a tense wiry man who gave the impression of running while standing still. After the usual ceremonies, Stephen went over Father Mendum's accounts; revenues were checked against expenses, and both were diligently compared with those of preceding years. The audit showed that the parish income had fallen off by almost a thousand dollars. Stephen asked why.

"I don't quite know, Bishop." Father Mendum's knees and elbows were tensed like a relay racer waiting for the baton. "Your Excellency realizes, of course, that people are losing their jobs every day. Take Eagle Hardware, for instance — they make locks and hinges, everything that builders use. I was talking to their sales manager, Ben Mackey, the other day

— Ben's one of my parishioners — and he told me that Eagle's cutting down on production. Building hardware just isn't moving."

The man needed motor release. "Let's take a walk around the church," suggested Stephen. With Father Mendum well in front, the physical inspection of the church property began. First, the outside: yellow firebrick, granite trim, slate roof — a triumph of no-period design. Inside, St. Anselm's was stucco-plastered and oak-timbered, like so many of the smaller suburban churches built since World War I. Its stained-glass windows were standard items purveyed by ecclesiastical-supply houses. Altar and stations of the cross, ditto. Neat enough and scrupulously clean, yet without a single touch of distinction.

Why do they make them look so much like *bungalows,* thought Stephen. "I'll glance through your parish register," he said aloud.

Scrutiny of the marriage and birth records brought out the interesting fact that marriages were up and christenings down. "How do you account for this, Father?"

"Birth control, Your Excellency," said Peter Mendum, striding up and down the sacristy.

"Have you pointed out to your people that birth control is a mortal sin?"

For a moment, Father Mendum stood still. "I might just as well talk to the east wind, Bishop. It's not that people don't want children. It seems that this birth-control business is all tied up with their jobs and way of life. I'll illustrate: say a nice Catholic couple get married and make their down payment on a little home. They have two children — three seems to be the limit. Anything over that — well, what with the payments on the house, and a car, perhaps — they feel they can't afford to risk having any more. Someone tells the wife she can buy a tube of jelly that'll do such and such." Father Mendum tapped the cover of his parish register. "No more christenings in *that* family."

Riding back to Hartfield, Stephen concentrated upon the social and economic aspects of the birth-control problem. He knew well enough that the decline in the birth rate was most noticeable among the upper and middle classes; the very people who could afford to have children weren't having them. Why? Did a genuine feeling of insecurity threaten these people, or were they merely using the economic argument as a false front for the murderous practice of contraception? Stephen decided that mere pulpit thundering wouldn't solve the problem; it needed fresh and realistic examination from every point of view.

He began his investigation by looking up the state laws regarding the sale of contraceptives and the dissemination of birth-control literature. Rigid statutes existed against both; State as well as Church had set its official countenance against criminal tampering with the life stream. But the laws were weakly enforced; every drugstore sold contraceptive devices, and recently a new organization — the Planned Motherhood League — had begun passing out birth-control pamphlets at street corners. Stephen obtained and studied one of these pamphlets, entitled, with unconscious humor, *What Every Free Woman Should Know*. He was puzzled by the morbid, whining tone of the pamphlet:

American women! [it began] Your health is being destroyed, your happiness wantonly laid waste, by a conspiracy on the part of the priest-ridden legislatures, a backward medical profession, and a gagged press. This cruel triumvirate keeps you in a condition of debased ignorance regarding your true nature and function. Not until birth-control literature and contraceptive devices can be placed in the hands of every woman who has suffered the wracking torments of childbirth, not until American women and mothers are armed with knowledge of the risk and dangers accompanying unwanted children, will they shake off the chains of this vile bondage.

What a blast! Maybe, thought Stephen, I've underestimated the pangs of labor and the ruinous effect of childbearing on a mother's health and happiness. He compared the martyrish tone of the pamphlet with the tender cooing sounds he had heard Celia make while she nursed and bathed her babies. Against the neurotic statements of *What Every Free Woman Should Know* he placed the joyous testimony shining from the eyes of a thousand young mothers whose infants he had baptized. Someone was maltreating the truth. . . .

Stephen's impulse was to ask the Honorable Aloysius

Noonan, Mayor of Hartfield, why the statutes against the dissemination of birth-control literature weren't being enforced. Testing the idea on Ambrose Cannell, he got thirty seconds of meditative pipesmoke and a well-considered "I wouldn't do it, Bishop" from his Vicar-General.

"Why not?"

"Because," said Ambrose Cannell, "your vestments would get all chewed up in the interlocking gears of Hartfield politics, industry, and finance. They *do* interlock, you know. And some of the most important levers are thrown by the delicately gloved hand of Mrs. F. Dennison Towle, president of the Planned Motherhood League."

"Should I be impressed? Frightened? Tell me more."

"I'll tell you all I know," Ambrose Cannell turned portraitist. "Mrs. F. Dennison Towle (born Imogene Barlow) is that not-unusual combination of wealth, blood, energy, and social position often encountered in American cities of the second magnitude. She's a *Mayflower* descendant, a personage in the D.A.R., and a prominent alumna of Bryn Mawr. As you might suspect, she's unhappily married — and childless. What you *mightn't* suspect is that she's not unattractive in a pince-nez sort of way."

Amby Cannell selected a fine brush for the next detail. "Lady Imogene, as we call her, is full of gushing kindness to insects and animals. With my own ears I've heard her call them 'wee beasties.'"

"No!"

"Yes."

"Anything else?"

"Two years ago she brought out, privately, a puce-colored volume of verse entitled *Rustlings from a Quiet Garden*. It was reviewed in *Horticulture, Opera Lore,* and, of course, the *Hartfield Item* — in which Lady Imogene owns considerable stock. With the editors of these periodicals she keeps up a spirited, chatty correspondence about the gay bright faces of her petunias, the haunting melodies of *Parsifal,* and the wretched condition of the childbearing American woman." Amby Cannell concluded his sketch with an interesting bit of information. "Under the rose, Your Excellency, *What Every*

Free Woman Should Know dripped from the pen of Imogene Barlow herself."

"Has our well-placed Mrs. Towle a special dispensation to break the laws? A court test might cut her down to size."

Tact, courage, and a British distaste for unedifying spectacles were in Amby Cannell's reply. "Legal action would be . . . messy. Why not fight her with moral weapons — a pastoral letter, perhaps — exposing the fallacies and roundly condemning the dangers of birth control?"

The Bishop of Hartfield was able to recognize a good idea even when it came from a subordinate. "Thanks for the suggestion, Amby. I'll think it over."

To LAY BARE the moral and psychologic errors of birth control and to rebut them in a pastoral letter was no casual weekend task. Stephen's first step was to familiarize himself with the best medical opinion on the subject. Much of it was contradictory, yet with curious unanimity doctors of all schools agreed that four, five, or even a half a dozen children would not jeopardize the health of a well-nourished, properly cared-for American woman of the middle or upper class.

Still, such women were in the minority. What about homes blighted by poverty and already overcrowded with children? What of wives whose ill-health made further childbearing dangerous? To cover these cases, the Church prescribed one of two courses: the admittedly difficult practice of continence or the newly discovered rhythm system based upon careful calculation of female periods of fertility.

Lastly, Stephen studied the papal utterances celebrating the sacramental nature of marriage and advocating economic measures that must be taken to protect the family. In Leo XIII's *Arcanum* he followed the closely reasoned argument that the vigor and welfare of civil society depend upon the "domestic society" of the home. When the home is weakened by laxity, licentiousness, or economic want, said Leo, the State is in grievous danger. In the encyclical *Casti connubi* of Pius XI, the reigning Pope exalted children as the prime blessing of marriage, and a source of compensation for the sorrows of life. Pius XI restated Leo's teaching that "the State should adopt economic measures enabling every head of a family to earn as much as is necessary for himself, his wife, and the rearing of his children. . . . To deny him this wage, or to pay him less than is equitable, is a grave injustice, placed by Holy Scripture among the very greatest of sins."

Collating his material in the light of Catholic morality, medical science, and human happiness, Stephen wrote his pastoral letter on the subject of birth control. He made several drafts, trying always for greater clarity of thought and simplicity of language. On the second Sunday in Lent the following letter was read from every pulpit in the Hartfield Diocese:

Beloved Brethren:

The special grace conferred by God on the sacrament of matrimony perfects human love and makes both husband and wife holy. In the excellent mystery of wedlock the married partners joyously yield themselves to each other for mutual solace and the propagation of mankind. To tamper with these mysteries is an offense against God, an affront to nature, and a defeat to conjugal love. Yet the partisans of birth control criminally propose such tampering. In defiance of moral and natural law, they disseminate theories of marriage contrary to Catholic teaching, hurtful to the individual, and ruinous to the State.

It is my duty, as Bishop, to counsel you against the errors set in motion by the advocates of birth control. They will approach you with arguments unfounded in medical science or economic truth. You will be urged to thwart, by means of drugs and devices, the deepest instincts of parental love. In exchange for the jubilant promise of the Catholic nuptial Mass, *"Thy children shall be as olive plants about thy table,"* you will be offered the barren husks of a Planned Motherhood pamphlet.

By stressing the physical risks of childbearing, birth-control literature conveys a false and morbid picture of maternal fruition. Labor is indeed a heavy ordeal, yet as our Saviour Himself has said: *"A woman when she has brought forth a child remembereth no more the anguish for joy that a man-child is born into the world."* Physicians will tell you that women who refuse to accept children as the crowning fulfillment of life pay a penalty more prolonged and infinitely heavier than the temporary pangs of childbirth. No frustration is deadlier than that of the woman who deliberately evades the responsibility of motherhood.

Exponents of birth control often ask: "Why should more children be brought into a world plagued by economic insecurity?" To these the Catholic Church sternly replies: *"Our duty is not to prevent life from entering the world, but to make the world a better place for life to enter!"* Squalor, disease, and undernourishment are caused not by large families, but by social inequities condemned long ago by Leo XIII. Pinching off the life stream is not the cure for poverty and unemployment. These are evils that must be remedied by economic, not criminal, measures.

It is not the mission of the Church to frame legislation. It is, however, the duty of the Church to warn society that unless these problems are solved, fearful dangers will engulf our people and destroy our State.

I remind Catholics in particular that the practice of birth control is a crime not only against the body and the State, but, more importantly, against the immortal soul. As Pius XI has said in his encyclical on Catholic marriage: "Since the conjugal act is destined primarily by nature for the begetting of children, those who in exercising it deliberately frustrate its natural power and purpose sin against nature and commit a deed which is shameful and intrinsically vicious."

Let no one tell you that the Catholic Church exhorts her people to rear families beyond their economic means or the strength of the mother. Illness and want may make it inadvisable for a married couple to have more children. But the only lawful method of avoiding parenthood is abstinence, either total or periodic. It is the particular glory of Catholic marriage that many husbands and wives practice self-restraint rather than indulge in practices contrary to moral and natural law.

I urge you to remember that matrimony is a sacrament instituted by Christ. It is administered not by a priest, but by the husband and the wife, each of whom confers the sacrament on the other. By the purity and strength of your mutual love, shown in lifelong acts of tenderness, devotion, and forbearance, you will confound those who would threaten the happi-

ness of your marriage, the vigor of your country, and the salvation of your immortal soul.

                    Devotedly in Christ,
                        STEPHEN FERMOYLE, Bp. Hartfield

Stephen's pastoral letter touched off a nation-wide controversy. The Associated Press picked it up, and the battle was
on. In an article entitled "Miter over Mind," *The Statesman*
led the attack with a typical blast: "The Catholic Bishop of
Hartfield refurbishes some moldy and discredited arguments
against birth control in a pastoral letter to his gaping flock.
How any contemporary mind can believe such nonsense passes
comprehension. Isn't it high time that the Catholic Church
took off the blinkers of ignorance and caught up with the
march of social science?"

An editorial in the New York *World* viewed the matter from
quite another angle: "To Bishop Fermoyle's timely and sensible letter we would add the following facts. (1) Seventy-one
per cent of divorces in the United States occur between childless couples. (2) Today there are a million fewer children
under ten years of age in this country than there were five
years ago. Regardless of what the Planned Motherhood crowd
says, marital discord and race suicide seem to be the prime
products of birth control."

Crank letters poured in: "Your recent utterance clearly
reveals the contempt and hatred of womankind that is festering in your heart. I pity you." "What does a celebate (?) know
about childbearing? Stick to your incense and flummery." "It's
your kind that keeps Mexican women ignorant and priest-
ridden. As an American clubwoman and mother of two, I
despise the sexual peonage you would foist upon us."

Other letters came in, too. One from the Governor of New
York, himself the father of a family: "Thanks for sending that
beam of light up the alleyway where economics and morals
grapple in the dark." Quarenghi wrote: "Sounds of cannon-
ading reach here. Your pastoral grapeshot is cutting the enemy
to pieces." But the best letter of all came from a woman who
said: "I take my pencil in hand to thank you for the fine things
you said about big families and the joy they bring. You must
of come from one yourself, no one else would know. Some-

times my friends tell me I ought to stop having children but I can't, I love them so. If God sent me a hundred, I'd still pray for more."

The letter was signed, "Mother of Thirteen."

CHAPTER 3

MARCH was flaunting the usual false promises of spring. Under a tattered cape of snow, one caught an occasional glimpse of green on Hartfield Common; umbrellas blew inside out, rubbers leaked, overshoes were too heavy to wear, and fifty thousand practicing poets touched off lyric fusees to forsythia, the first robin, and other vernal harbingers. Among the poems that actually got published, Jake Mabbott's *March Troth*, heading the "Pickles and Chowder" column for March 16, 1928, was probably one of the tenderest and most original. The sonnet ran:

Tart trollop March, of bouncingest whims and weather,
Half winter's still, yet half seduced by spring,
Trapping more lovers with a snowy feather
Than summer gets with all her emeralding;
Show me, who loves your beauty next to autumn's
(Yes, I am spousaled to a tawnier queen)—
Show me, along your lakes and valley bottoms,
Those silver secrets spring will turn to green.

Can I but love, March, without taint of treason,
A younger mistress or a bolder bride,
I should abandon to your wantoner season
My autumn peace; and by this mountainside
Rutted by thaws (and for a budding reason)
We could swear faith, March, even though we lied.

Stephen was savoring the craftsmanship of the poem when his desk telephone began jingling.

"New York calling Bishop Fermoyle," said the operator. Then a familiar voice: "Stuffy? This is me, George."

"Who else would be calling me 'Stuffy'? How's the campaign going, Gug?"

George sounded worried. "We need some advice about an article coming out next month in *The North American Monthly*. The Governor's just received galley proofs of an 'Open Letter to Al Smith,' written by a fellow named Hubbell K. Whiteman. Know anything about him?"

Stephen remembered his luncheon companion at the Inter-Faith Convocation — the chin-up chap who had unsmilingly suggested that American Catholicism "break" with Rome. "Hubbell K. Whiteman? Why, he's made himself quite a reputation as a militant Protestant. What does he say in his article?"

"Well, underneath the whiskered verbiage he asks what Al would do if his loyalties as a Catholic came into conflict with his oath as President."

"That's absurd. No such conflict could possibly arise."

"A lot of voters don't know that. And the Democratic Convention probably won't know it either. That's why I'm calling you, Stuff. Can you take a day off to come down here to advise us? If anyone knows the answers, you do."

Stephen hesitated. "You realize, Gug, that as a Catholic bishop I can't allow myself to get mixed up in politics."

"You're allowed to talk to your brother, aren't you?"

"Tell you what I'll do," said Stephen. "Mail me the galley proofs, special delivery. I'll look the piece over before committing myself."

Whiteman's "Open Letter to Al Smith" turned out to be a frank piece of anti-Catholic propaganda skillfully put together on a seeming plane of candor and dignity. The opening paragraph was particularly disarming:

The American people take pride in viewing the progress of an American citizen from the humble estate in which his life began toward the highest office within the gift of the nation. It is for this reason that your candidacy for the presidential nomination has stirred the enthusiasm of a great body of your fellow citizens. They know and rejoice in the hardship and the struggle which have fashioned you as a leader of men. They know your fidelity to the morality you have advocated in public and private life, and to the religion you have revered; your record of public trusts successfully and honestly discharged; your spirit of fair play and justice even to your political opponents. Partisanship bids fair to quail before the challenge of your personality, and men who vote habitually against your party are pondering your candidacy with sincere respect.

At this point Dr. Whiteman laid aside his ponderous affability. "A basic, irrepressible conflict exists," he said, "between Roman Catholic teaching and the principles of civil and religious liberty on which American institutions were founded." To support his argument, Whiteman quoted from Pope Leo XIII's encyclical on the Christian constitution of states: "The Almighty has divided the charge of the human race between two powers, the ecclesiastical and the civil — the one being set over divine, and the other over human things."

The quotation sounded familiar, but how incomplete! On looking up the reference, Stephen discovered that Whiteman had omitted the next sentence of Leo XIII's statement, which ran: "Each power in its kind is supreme; each has fixed limits within which it is contained — limits which are defined by the nature and special province of each."

According to Whiteman, the Roman Catholic Church claimed "sovereign and paramount powers" over the civil government of the United States. Furthermore, said Whiteman, in any conflict between Church and State, the Church must prevail! The Pope was represented as a foreign suzerain with the final word over American affairs.

Whipping these fallacies into a fine froth of patriotism, Dr. Whiteman now asked Al Smith how he proposed to reconcile this "basic and irrepressible conflict between the two powers." If, as President, Mr. Smith encountered such a conflict, would he, *could* he, be loyal to the oath of his high office? Rather, wouldn't he be obliged to place Catholic doctrine and the authority of the Pope above his oath to support the Constitution?

Startled by these interrogations, Stephen could scarcely curb his anger; his impulse was to refute, passionately, and at once, Whiteman's insinuations. Al Smith's fortunes faded into the background of his thought; whether Smith won the Democratic nomination or was elected President became matters of

remote concern. First in Stephen's mind was the scalding
injustice that had been poured over the Church.

Part of his wrath sprang from a sense of futility in debating
with adversaries who kept on reviving the ancient clichés
against Catholicism: "implacable threat of the papacy,"
"divided allegiance between Church and State" — arguments
dragged from the rubbleheap of other centuries. How long
would these men persist in regarding the Church as a band
of conspirators plotting against the Constitution? Would such
men never realize that Catholicism in the United States was a
cornerstone of civil order, a bulwark against the corrupting
forces of anarchy and decay? To those who accused the
Church of undermining American freedom, Stephen wanted
to cry out: "Our sole aim is to inculcate patriotism founded
upon divine law. Our only objective is to help men keep alive
the light of their souls, the hope of heaven, the love of God."

Arrows of sleet were breaking against the windowpanes of
Stephen's study; arrows of grief and anger were splintering in
his heart. Hopeless to combat such prejudice. Inconvenient,
too, at this busy season of the year. Stephen strode back to his
desk, leafed through his calendar, solidly booked for the next
two weeks with conferences, diocesan inspections, confirmations in distant parts of the state. Why add the burden of futile
polemics to an already overcrowded schedule? To draw up
counterarguments against Whiteman would mean several
days' work in the library. Let someone else sweat over the
source books and dig out the answers that Al Smith needed.

Stephen was attempting to phrase a "Sorry, count me out"
telegram to George, when his indecisive eye fell upon the
motto on his desk pad, one of those text-a-day appointment
calendars given away by ecclesiastical supply houses. The
text for March 20 happened to be St. Paul's exhortation to
Timothy, written almost two thousand years ago, when the
Church was struggling to establish herself in the midst of
enemies:

"Preach the Word: be instant in season, out of season;
reprove, entreat, rebuke in all patience and doctrine."

Paul to Timothy, Bishop of Ephesus? No, Paul to all bishops
everywhere — then, now, and always — counseling them in the
supreme tactic of the Word.

Not in anger or arrogance, but in all patience, must Catholic doctrine be preached, in and out of season, personally convenient or no. In loving severity, error must be reproved, the enemies of the Church rebuked over and over again till the Word prevailed.

Stephen sent his telegram to George:

NORTH AMERICAN ARTICLE FILLED WITH GRAVE ERRORS OF FACT AND INTERPRETATION. REBUTTAL IMPERATIVE. MUST SPEND A COUPLE OF DAYS IN LIBRARY LOOKING UP REFERENCES. WILL MEET YOU WEDNESDAY P.M. CAMPAIGN HEADQUARTERS NEW YORK AFFECTIONATELY STUFF.

GEORGE FERMOYLE was standing under the big clock of the Biltmore when Stephen entered the lobby. Seeing his brother first, George enjoyed for a moment the pleasure of observing him with a secret eye. Attired in the habit of a working priest, the Bishop of Hartfield needed no insignia to mark him as a full-powered male. In build, he approximated the life-insurance ideal of how much a six-foot man should weigh at the age of forty-one. Though Stephen's blue-black hair was prematurely streaked with gray, and his coloring a touch too pale for outdoor taste, in motion he seemed younger, more elastically muscled than senior prelates have a right to be. By some private management of head and limbs he appeared to be treading a slight incline — whether the tilted deck of a clipper ship or the broad steps of a dais or tabernacle, George could not decide. Curiously mixed hints of an ascetic philosopher, a renaissance prince, and a field officer of general rank hung about the Bishop of Hartfield as he crossed the lobby to greet his brother.

"Good of you to come, Stuffy," said George, leading the way toward the bank of elevators. "I've taken a suite for you on the seventeenth floor. How long can you stay?"

"It'll have to be just overnight, I'm afraid. My Hartfield franchise expires unless it's renewed every twenty-four hours."

George took his brother's bag, hefted it questioningly. "What've you got in here?"

"Pajamas, toothbrush — and a portable library. We must talk by the book, else we're ruined."

"Does Whiteman really know his stuff?"

"He's been around theologically." In the suite Stephen opened his bag and drew out a manila envelope crammed with notes. "Here's the whole dossier. Glance through it while I wash up."

Like a fact-hungry prosecutor George devoured the notes. "What a lawyer you'd have made!" he said as Stephen came out of the bathroom, rubbing his face with a towel. "The Governor will stop chewing Perfectos when he sees this brief. Ready to go?"

Walking down the corridor to Al Smith's headquarters, George brought up a little matter of protocol. "It's a minor point, Stuff, but both you and the Governor rate the title 'Your Excellency.' How does a master of ceremonies introduce two Excellencies to each other? Who gets presented to whom?"

"The old problem of Church and State," said Stephen. "A good rule to remember is that the visiting team bats first."

Introduction offered no real problem when George brought his two Excellencies together. "Governor Smith, may I present you to my brother Stephen, Bishop of Hartfield?" he said simply. Al Smith, already halfway across the room, extended both hands: "You honor us by coming, Bishop Fermoyle." Reverence for Stephen's office took nothing from the Governor's dignity or the human warmth of his greeting.

Stephen appraised the fabulous "Brown Derby," the ex-fishmonger of Fulton Street who had emerged from the shadows of Brooklyn Bridge to become the first four-time Governor of New York. The most noticeable mark of that rough-and-tumble passage appeared in Al Smith's speaking voice. It was a brusque, inelegant organ, seemingly contemptuous (at times) of those who spoke with a more cultured diction. The Brown Derby's too-florid complexion and rather bulbous nose were offset by a spacious forehead and a pair of ocean-blue eyes honest as a carpenter's level. Close up, the "barefoot boy of the Biltmore" was better-looking, Stephen decided, than his campaign pictures indicated.

The Governor laid his hand on an armchair and kept it there until Stephen sat down. "A cigar, Bishop? . . . Do you mind if I smoke?" Under his deference the Brown Derby was tensing himself for an overwhelming question.

"Well, Your Excellency," he asked, "what do you think of Dr. Whiteman's little essay in understanding?"

"Judging the motive from the deed, I'd say he was out to ruin you. The article is very polite and quite sinister."

"That was my feeling." The Brown Derby leveled a point-blank query at Stephen. "Can it be answered?"

"It can."

The ash that Al Smith flicked from his cigar seemed to take a ten-ton weight from his shoulders. Vocal harshness disappeared as he explained his problem to Stephen. "You understand, Bishop Fermoyle, that I'm no theologian. I didn't get my Catholic faith from books, and I'm at a disadvantage when an opponent like Whiteman here jumps out from behind a hedge, and cross-examines me on doctrinal points that never even entered my mind. Could you help clear the ground for me by answering one or two questions about this matter of Church and State?"

"I'll be glad to try, Governor."

Al Smith's first question was as frank as his ocean-blue eyes. "Is there anything in our religion that might, by some wild stretch of imagination, bring a Catholic officeholder into conflict with the Constitution of the United States?"

"The answer," said Stephen, "is no. Flatly, unequivocally, no. Catholic doctrine teaches that the civil government and the Church derive their separate and quite distinct authority from the same divine source. God did not intend that the two powers should clash. Legitimately exercised, they cannot. When anyone declares or even insinuates otherwise, he's either ignorant or malicious."

"Good! Now one more question. Suppose the Pope were to issue a command in some purely civil matter? As an American citizen and officeholder, what would my duty be?"

"The Pope will not issue such a command," said Stephen. "But if he did, your duty would be to disobey him. Cardinal Gibbons treats the matter explicitly in his essay. 'The Church and the Republic.' " The Bishop consulted a note he had made on the galley proofs: "This is what Cardinal Gibbons says: 'If the Pope were to issue commands in purely civil matters, he would be offending not only against civil society, but against God, and violating an authority as truly from God as his own.

Any Catholic who clearly recognized this would not be bound to obey the Pope; rather his conscience would bind him absolutely to *disobey*, because with Catholics, conscience is the supreme law which under no circumstances can we ever lawfully disobey.' "

Al Smith smacked the heel of his hand down hard on the desk. "That does it. We'll rake Whiteman with the facts. How do you think we should begin?"

"Why not use your favorite. Let's look at the record approach?" suggested Stephen. "Start off by disclaiming Whiteman's imputations, then chop his fallacies to matchwood, one at a time."

"I can do the disclaiming all right," said the Brown Derby. "It's the fallacy-chopping part that bothers me."

George came in with a practical suggestion. "Suppose the Governor dictates an opening paragraph or two — just to set the tone of the piece. Then you, Stephen, could take it from there. After you finish your draft, the Governor could give the whole thing his personal touch." George was up to his old trick of pleading, not arguing, his case. "It would be *such* a lift, Stuffy."

Al Smith neither presumed nor thought it politic to second George's urging. There was a dead silence while the Governor looked at Stephen, Stephen looked at the Governor, and everyone looked at each other.

The Bishop of Hartfield broke the silence. Genuine regret was in his voice as he addressed the Brown Derby: "I'm sorry, Your Excellency, that I can't fall in with the suggestion George has made. In the first place, I'd be overstepping ecclesiastic bounds. Second, I lack the ability to cast theologic material into popular form. The only help I can offer is my unofficial opinion on matters touching the relationship between Church and State."

Al Smith met Stephen's frankness with candor of his own. "I understand perfectly, Bishop Fermoyle. My reply to Whiteman, whatever form it finally takes, must be the product of my own conscience. I wouldn't want your help — and I know you wouldn't give it — on any other terms."

SIX WEEKS later, Al Smith's reply to Dr. Whiteman told the

American people exactly what a great Catholic officeholder felt about his religion, his country, and his duties as a public servant. In forthright colloquial language, very much his own, the Brown Derby met every point in the "Open Letter." Reading the article, Stephen was proud of Smith's logic and dignity. In particular, the last three paragraphs struck him as being the perfect statement of a man who had kept faith with the ideal of free worship in a democratic state.

"I summarize my creed as an American Catholic. I believe in the worship of God according to the faith and practice of the Roman Catholic Church. I recognize no power in the institutions of my Church to interfere with the operation of the Constitution of the United States. I believe in absolute freedom of conscience for all men and in equality of all churches, all sects, and all beliefs before the law as a matter of right and not as a matter of favor. I believe in the absolute separation of Church and State and in the strict enforcement of the provisions of the Constitution that Congress shall make no law respecting an establishment of religion or prohibiting the free exercise thereof.

"I believe that no tribunal of any church has any power to make any decree of any force in the law of the land other than to establish the status of its own communicants within its own church. I believe in the support of the public school as one of the cornerstones of American liberty. I believe in the right of every parent to choose whether his child shall be educated in the public school or in a religious school supported by those of his own faith. I believe in the principles of noninterference by this country in the internal affairs of other nations and that we should stand steadfastly against any such interference by whomsoever it may be urged. And I believe in the common brotherhood of man under the common fatherhood of God.

"In this spirit I join with fellow Americans of all creeds in a fervent prayer that never again in this land will any public servant be challenged because of the faith in which he has tried to walk humbly with his God."

AL SMITH's forthright reply to Whiteman was a decisive factor in his winning the Democratic nomination. Higher the

Brown Derby could not go. In the presidential campaign that followed, he was frightfully smeared. The nation became a wallow of prejudice and partisanship; Protestants revived the old libel that if Smith were elected, he would set up a Vatican annex in Washington; Republicans warned that he would pitch a Tammany wigwam on the White House lawn. The drys screamed that Smith was a creature of the whisky ring. All three — Protestants, Republicans and drys — said he was a drunk.

Meanwhile, on the other side of the campaign fence, nothing but long-stemmed American beauties, thornless and deliciously scented, were growing. Herbert Hoover had only to cut the choicest blooms and offer them in armfuls to the voters. His speeches were nosegays of complacent prophecy. "The poorhouse is vanishing from among us," he said in his speech of acceptance. "Given a chance to go forward with the policies of the last eight years, we shall soon be in sight of the day when poverty will be banished from this nation."

Hoover believed it; the people believed it, too. On November 6, 1928, the voters, beguiled by promises of two-car garages and a chicken in every pot, gave the Republican party a mandate to continue the policies of the last eight years.

Eleven months later a dazed people watched their golden dreams of prosperity dissolve in the sizzling acids of panic. The bell that announced the cessation of trading on October 24, 1929, tolled the knell of an era departed forever. The circus philosophy that national well-being could be achieved by jumping through paper hoops of margin came to an abrupt end, and the clowns who had believed it lay stunned and bleeding on the tanbark floor.

CHAPTER 4

Now began the long and tragic travail of depression, lightened only by the fortitude and forbearance of the American people. As the extent and nature of the disaster grew slowly upon the nation, it became apparent that many innocent bystanders were going to be hurt.

Over the Diocese of Hartfield the blight ran its typical

course. Banks began to fail, factories slowed down, workers were laid off, sales dwindled, mortgage foreclosures and evictions turned people out of their homes. Torments of hunger and cold ravaged the country; the pallor of underfed children, and the despair of jobless fathers, deepened. Middle-class families, having spent their savings, drew their curtains and starved with genteel resignation; men and women tramped the streets in search of work, crowded into churches and police stations, seeking relief; stood in lengthening bread lines or begged at the doors of charitable institutions. Instead of two-car garages, Hoovervilles of tin and tar paper rose outside industrial cities.

On the basis of sheer humanitarianism the President was urged to make Federal appropriations for relief. Such proposals ran counter to Hoover's economic philosophy. "I am opposed," he said, "to any direct or indirect government dole." Then he added:

This is not an issue as to whether people shall go hungry or cold. It is solely a question of the best method by which hunger and cold shall be prevented. It is a question as to whether the American people will maintain the spirit of charity and mutual self-help through voluntary giving and the responsibility of local government, as distinguished from appropriations out of the Federal Treasury. My own conviction is strongly that if we break down this sense of responsibility, of individual generosity and mutual self-help, and if we start appropriations of this character, we have not only impaired something infinitely valuable in the life of the American people but have struck at the roots of self-government.

Admirable as political theory, Hoover's pronouncement put no bread in hungry mouths. Although the President sincerely believed that the sum of individual effort would overcome the depression, he did not realize that the individual, no matter how rugged, was powerless to combat the cumulative and gigantic disaster that had overtaken society. Individualism had caused the damage, but individualism could not cure it.

Like every other American community, Hartfield tightened its belt and attempted to combat the depression by local charities and institutional care of the needy. The first winter was a time of hit-or-miss distribution of cash, food, and fuel, as religious and municipal agencies tried to take care of their own. The resulting waste and inefficiency was so deplorable that the honorable Aloysius P. Noonan, Mayor of Hartfield, summoned a civic conference to remedy the evils of piece-meal welfare.

Around the Mayor's table rallied Hartfield's community leaders; State and Church, bench and bar, banking and commerce — all the buttresses and ornaments of society were there. In cutaway, piped vest, and gray-striped tie came Governor Webster Turnbull; as candidate for U. S. Senator the Governor thought it possible that a political plum or two might lurk in the welfare pie. Beside him sat the silver-haired dean of Hartfield's clergy, the Right (and truly) Reverend Tyleston Forsythe, a Methodist-Episcopal in doctrine, a very great Christian in practice. Next down the table was Public Layman Number One — Harmon I. Poole, president of the Hartfield Trust Company, whose initials HIP on a ninety-day note told the borrower exactly who had him — and where. Between Banker Poole and Major Tom Overbaugh, state commander of the Salvation Army, sat the Most Reverend Stephen Fermoyle, D.D., Roman Catholic Bishop of Hartfield.

Stephen nodded to other community figures ranged about the table. Justice Rigg of the appellate court bowed in acknowledgment of the Bishop's cordial headshake; Courtney Pike, chairman of the Excelsior Bolt and Screw Corporation, did likewise. No such response, however, came from Mrs. F. Dennison Towle, president of the Planned Motherhood League, who appeared to be polishing a mote in her pince-nez every time Stephen glanced in her direction.

His Excellency expected trouble from Mrs. Towle before the meeting ended. So did His Honor Mayor Noonan, who rapped for order and opened the meeting with a brief exposition of the dangers boiling up from the vat of hit-or-miss relief. "We must pool our resources in a community fund," said the Mayor, "otherwise, to mix a figure, this thing will cut us to pieces."

A civic babel rose from the conferees. Governor Turnbull wanted to know who'd administer the funds. "Will it become"

— he minted a phrase —"a political football?" Harmon I. Poole made a pointed inquiry: "What bank will get the deposits?" Reverend Gilbey Dodds, rector of St. Alfred's, offered the suggestion (tentative, to be sure): "Shouldn't proof of church affiliation be required of all persons applying for aid?" Industrialist Courtney Pike took the position that no union member had the right to expect public relief while the union treasuries were loaded — "yes, and I mean *loaded*." Mrs. F. Dennison Towle asked beamingly, "Isn't this a good time to intensify our birth-control activities among the poor?" These and other questions embroiled the meeting; friction threatened the bearings of the community machine. Honest warmth was degenerating into spitting bad temper when Bishop Stephen Fermoyle rose in his place.

"No one at this table," he began dryly, "can accuse my Church of lightly regarding her prerogatives in matters of faith or doctrine." A humorous grunt from Banker Poole and an appreciative smile from Tyleston Forsythe greeted his remark. "In ordinary times I would take the position — with all humility and great firmness — that my Church should not yield one iota of her spiritual primacy, or suspend for an instant her right to extend her primacy in every legitimate manner." Bishop Fermoyle paused to freight his words with emphasis. "I feel, however, that in this hour of common peril, no religion, no civic group, should think in terms of creed or preferment. We must lay aside our sectarian differences. Help must be extended to human beings on the simple basis of need. As Bishop of the Roman Catholic Church in this Diocese, I shall require no proof of religious affiliation from any man or woman who requires assistance. And I pledge, further, that no attempt at proselytizing will be made by any individual or agency under my control."

Stephen's eyes circled the table. "If the members of the committee can make similar guarantees, I shall be glad to contribute one hundred thousand dollars from diocesan monies to the Hartfield Community Fund."

The committee loosed its collective breath in a sigh of relief. This was the kind of leadership — backed by the kind of cash — that everyone at the table was waiting for. Everyone? Not Mrs. F. Dennison Towle. The president of the

Planned Motherhood League, who had been gunning for
Stephen ever since his birth-control letter, planted her pince-
nez firmly on the bridge of her nose and aimed a battery of
exceptions at her powerful foe.

"I'm sure we all appreciate Bishop Fermoyle's generous
offer," she began. "What he says about laying aside religious
differences is just splendid. But since the Planned Motherhood
League is a nonsectarian organization, I must insist — I really
must — that it be allowed to carry on its program, especially
among the deserving poor."

Mayor Noonan slapped his forehead with a despairing
hand. That woman was in again! Webster Turnbull adjusted
his gubernatorial cravat: "Now look here, Imogene," he began
placatingly. The Governor had to use that tone in speaking to
Imogene Towle because she pulled a hefty oar in the Republican committee boat. Others at the table used other tones,
according to their private convictions or theories of public
welfare. When the fracas subsided, they all found themselves
waiting for Bishop Fermoyle's verdict. Would he withdraw
his offer, excoriate Mrs. Towle, or — as so many others had
done in the past — knuckle under to her demand that the
Planned Motherhood League be allowed to continue its work?

Stephen fingered an assortment of barbed answers — any
one of which would have destroyed Mrs. F. Dennison Towle.
The ugliest retort might have been: "Madame, since your
Planned Motherhood League is operating in defiance of law,
your hands, legally speaking, are not quite clean. One more
peep out of you, and I'll slap criminal charges against you
and your outfit." Such a remark would have embarrassed both
Governor Turnbull and Mayor Noonan; Stephen rejected it.
Again he might have said: "Since Mrs. Towle cannot find in
her pocketbook enough cash to match the contribution of the
Catholic Church, won't she try, in the goodness of her heart,
to match its forbearance?" But this smacked too much of the
Pharisee. Adroitly, Stephen chose the one argument that
would take the most skin off Mrs. Towle's patrician nose and
at the same time apply soothing unguents to everyone else's.

"Is it possible," he asked, "that so distinguished a citizen
as Mrs. Towle has forgotten the most salient lesson of our
American tradition? May I remind the lady member that when

her Pilgrim ancestors signed their mutual-safety pact in the cabin of the *Mayflower*, no one claimed special rights or exemptions? The common welfare was uppermost then; it is my belief that the common welfare is uppermost now." Stephen turned to the Mayor. "I am willing, however, to abide by the majority decision in this matter. I move, Mr. Chairman, that we put the lady member's proposal to a vote."

"Second the motion," said Appellate Justice Rigg.

In the vote that followed, the lady member's proposal was defeated, eight to three.

Briskly now, the committee proceeded to set a goal of $1,500,000 for the Community Fund, to be administered by a nonsectarian, nonpolitical board consisting of the Mayor, the Reverend Gilbey Dodds, H. I. Poole, president of the Hartfield Trust Company (who had to be satisfied with half the deposits), Major Overbaugh of the Salvation Army, and the Bishop of the Roman Catholic Church. A firm of professional fund raisers offered their services gratis. In the door-to-door campaign that followed, the giant thermometer on Hartfield Common climbed from zero to boiling point in ten days. A sum of $1,650,000 was collected, every penny of which went into food, fuel, and clothing for the needy citizens of Hartfield.

Mrs. F. Dennison Towle continued privately to bring jellied broth, concert tickets, and contraceptive devices to the deserving poor.

IN FEBRUARY, 1930, Stephen learned that unauthorized nuns were begging in the factory towns of his Diocese. The method and scale of the begging suggested that a resourceful mind was behind the operation. On payday in various cities, two or three gray-habited nuns would stand at factory gates, basins in hand, soliciting alms of the workers. After skimming off a thin collection of dimes and quarters, the nuns would disappear, only to pop up next week in another town.

From several sources Stephen got the same details: gray habited nuns, agate basins, quick fadeaway, and sudden reappearance at some distant point. He wrote letters to all the convents in his Diocese, requesting further information, but no one knew anything about the gray nuns. The mystery came down to this: who was begging, and for what purpose?

Stephen determined to investigate the matter personally. Knowing that Thursday was payday in one of the large electrical plants near the Rhode Island border, he drove out alone in his Buick one sleety afternoon and sat in his car, waiting for the mendicant nuns to appear.

Ten minutes before closing time, a trio of gray-habited women took their places at the factory gates; as the workers streamed out, Stephen saw the sisters holding out their basins in dumb, piteous appeal. The sight of holy women standing in the snow was too much for the workers; from thin pay envelopes everyone dropped a small coin into the basin. The whole procedure was beautifully timed and staged. When it was over, the nuns dumped their coins into a canvas bag carried by their leader, and caught an outgoing bus by the handles.

In the sleety twilight, Stephen followed the bus several miles through a semirural section lying between Lancaster and Hopedale. It was dusk when the nuns alighted and started walking down an unplowed road. Stephen parked his car at a gas station and trailed them on foot until they disappeared through an arched gateway. He approached the gate and read a small sign bearing the single word: *Misericordia.*

Pushing open the gate, he entered a desolate courtyard. A low rambling house, dormered and wide-verandaed in an outmoded style of architecture, stood under melancholy pines. Unshoveled snow clogged the steps. The falling sleet, a low wind moaning through the trees, and a single dimly lighted window on the second floor created an almost sinister atmosphere. What was going on in this gloomy house? Stephen opened the front door and walked in. Stale deodorants lay on the cold air. A candle stuck in a baking-powder tin threw flickering shadows on a number of closed doors on the drafty lower floor. Listening at the first door, Stephen heard a sepulchral groan. From the second came a gasping low cry; from the third, frightened whimpers.

A nun glided out of the shadows, carrying a sickroom utensil.

"May I see the Sister in charge here?" asked Stephen.

His priestly garb was passport enough. "You will find Sister Martha Annunziata on the second floor. Last door on the left."

The smell of deodorant became heavier as Stephen mounted the creaking stairway. He found himself tiptoeing down an uncarpeted corridor dimly lighted by a single taper burning before a plaster figure of the Virgin. At the last door he listened to a strange antiphon; one voice soothed, the other answered with weak retchings.

Stephen rapped gently, then opened the door. A blasting stench of putrescence struck his nostrils. The odor of death came from a ghastly yellow-fleshed human being — whether man or woman, it was impossible to tell — propped up on pillows. The eyes were staring in pain, the lower jaw sagged uncontrollably as greenish bile poured across from its broken dam.

Kneeling by the bedside, a gray-habited nun gazed with infinite tenderness at the horrible face on the pillow. In her hands she held an agate basin to catch the fetid trickle oozing from the death's-head. The nun was not praying or exhorting. From her lips came a laving murmur, the sounds a mother might whisper to a feverish child. Only one voice in the world could speak like that.

Lalage! Lalage Menton.

The nun lifted wet-shining eyes to Stephen, recognized him, and made a little signal, part headshake, part finger to her lips. The gesture said: "In a moment it will be all over. Please wait outside."

Stephen was glad to close the door. In the drafty hallway, he knelt before the Virgin's statue, and prayed for the soul that Lalage Menton was leading toward release.

The end must have been peaceful. Candle in hand, Lalage came out of the sickroom and beckoned Stephen to follow her down the dim hallway. At the top of the stairway, she faced him tranquilly. In the taper-light he could see that Lalage's face had lost the contour of youth and the radiance of its first beauty. Her hands were roughened by menial labor; at thirty-two the nut-brown maid was prematurely old. But her eyes were illuminated from within, and a trace of old mischievousness curved her lips.

"I have been expecting your visit," she said. "Scold me if you wish."

"I have no wish to scold you, Sister Martha."

"It was wrong to beg in your Diocese. Especially when I got your letter telling me to stop."

"We'll go into that later, Sister. Tell me about the work you're doing here. What kind of place is this — a hospital?"

"No. Misericordia is a house of last breathings — a refuge for destitute incurables, who would otherwise die uncared for."

"But these are medical cases. Doctors, hospitals, should look after them."

Lalage's work-roughened hand swept a row of closed doors. "Misericordia is filled with people who have been given up by doctors and hospitals. Our patients are dying of last-stage cancer and tuberculosis. Even morphine is powerless to ease their pain. Nothing can be done for their bodies. We try at the end to give them what comfort we can."

"How long have you been here?"

"Not quite a year. We chose a bad time to start our work."

"Have you no regular source of income?"

Sister Martha Annunziata shook her head in a proud negative. "Geraldines are always poor. The Mother House sends us all it can spare."

"Why did you not apply to me for assistance?"

"By the rule of our Order we make no financial claims on the Diocese." Lalage pinched a drop of melting wax from the candle's edge. "We live on drippings, Your Excellency."

A Sister whom Stephen recognized as one of the nuns he had seen at the factory gates approached. Her shoes and the lower part of her habit were still wet from snow.

"The throat case in Room Five is sinking, Mother Superior."

"I will come, Sister." Lalage Menton turned to Stephen. "Is there anything more you wish to say to me?"

"Yes." Stephen firmed his voice. "I want you to stop begging in the Diocese of Hartfield. It is not fair to the workingmen."

He waited for the female plea, "What else can I do?" It did not come, and Stephen knew that Lalage Menton intended to go on begging until she could find some surer source of income. To prevent this fearless, determined woman from committing the sin of disobedience, Stephen made a voluntary offer of assistance.

"I shall make a financial contribution to your work here. As of today, Misericordia House will be allotted five hundred dollars monthly from diocesan funds."

"That is most generous, Your Excellency." Faint suggestions of a tease were in Lalage's voice. "You won't chop down our pine trees, will you?"

Stephen smiled. "No, that won't be necessary. But I must receive regular reports covering your expenditures, the number of patients admitted, and the treatment they receive. Is this quite clear, Sister?"

"Yes, Your Excellency."

They were walking down the creaky stairs. "When money eases up a little," continued Stephen, "we must think of making a few repairs. This place is a barracks, and a drafty one at that. I shall send one of my assistants out to inspect it in detail — foundations, furnace, plumbing, roof, everything." In trying to be severe, Stephen found himself imitating Glennon's executive voice and manner. "Simple piety isn't enough, Sister. I must consider the physical well-being of the religious establishments within my Diocese."

"Of course, Your Excellency." Sister Martha Annunziata darted off to lay her ear against a door, the better to interpret the whimpering moans within.

Watching her come toward him again, the candle flame shielded with her hand, Stephen softened his official demeanor.

"Are you happy in your work here?"

"It is the work I was born to do," she said simply.

Echoes of Lalage's reply accompanied Stephen all the way back to Hartfield. She had answered his question as Theresa or Francis might have answered it. In fact, everything that Lalage Menton had ever said, everything she had ever done, was a perfect manifestation of the thing she was. All needy creatures claimed her, and in making a dedicated response to their needs, she had found the perfect fulfillment of her being.

AS THE DEPRESSION DEEPENED, Stephen's parish visitations became grim affairs. Every church had its local difficulties; the

Bishop's antechamber swarmed with rectors and heads of religious orders begging for outright aid or for a reduction of the Cathedral tax expected of them. Stephen went over their parish accounts in detail, suggesting economies, short cuts, a trimming of sails to the economic hurricane. Yet, quite early in the depression, the Bishop of Hartfield had discovered that many economies were double-edged. If, for example, you discontinued building a school or called a halt to repairs, more men were thrown out of work. The wisest course (it took courage as well as wisdom) was to make prudent expenditures, dig into your cash reserves, and hope that they would hold out.

Meanwhile from the White House came an amazing series of pronouncements, denying at first that disaster had befallen the country, then later switching to a dogged reiteration that the crisis had passed. "There is nothing in the situation to be disturbed about"; "The crisis will be over in sixty days"; "Prosperity is just around the corner." Despite these bland proclamations, the country sank deeper into the quagmire until at last the White House bulletin was greeted with derisive laughter.

Stephen marveled in those dark days that the great mass of the people, abandoned by their political leaders, did not rise in some violent outburst of fury. That they remained calm and well disciplined under the withering fire of disaster was a reassuring sign of the basic stability of the American character.

AT THE PEAK of his career, and at a time when his high office required the utmost expenditure of physical and nervous energy, Stephen Fermoyle was stricken by a crippling disease.

A sharp bout of pneumonia, induced by the strain of chronic fatigue, sent him to bed early in October, 1930. The good medical care of Dr. Howard Gavigan, plus the prayers of Stephen's congregation, were apparently speeding the patient to uneventful recovery. After two weeks, he was able to walk about his room; already he had begun to plague Dr. Gavigan with the restless convalescent's question: "When can I get back to work?"

"You'll be able to celebrate Mass on All Saints' Day," promised the doctor. "Be grateful for the cure the Lord has worked upon you, and don't test His patience or mine by any more questions."

Then, on the morning of All Saints', Stephen noticed a curious swelling of his right leg — a distension so marked that he could not tie his shoe. "I'll say nothing about it, try to walk it off," he resolved, and managed to struggle through High Mass without revealing the condition of his leg to anyone. After lunch he was glad to get back into bed. The next day his leg was swollen to the knee. Alarmed, he called in Dr. Gavigan.

The old physician made a thorough examination of the swollen limb. He pressed the calf, put his fingers under the arch of Stephen's knee, and asked humorously: "Been in any jungles lately?"

"No."

"Then it's probably not *Wuchereria bancrofti*."

"What are they?"

"The parasites that cause elephantiasis." Dr. Gavigan was off on another diagnostic tack. This time he applied a stethoscope to Stephen's heart, listened long, and brought his grizzled head up reassuringly. "Well, it's certainly not cardiac, Your Excellency."

"That's fine. It's not my heart, and it's not elephantiasis. What is it?"

"I'll be asking the questions today, Bishop. Anyone else in your family ever have trouble with their legs?"

"My father had varicose veins."

Dr. Gavigan went into a ponder, and came out on the tentative side. "The Mayo Brothers might call it one thing," he said, "and Elberfeld's Calculating Horses might call it another. Meanwhile, I'll call it phlebitis."

"Is that good or bad?"

Dr. Gavigan began putting away his stethoscope. "It's a common thing after pneumonia. No one ever died of it."

"But it might prevent a man from crossing the street? Is that what you're trying to say, Doctor?"

"Now don't start painting the devil on the wall. We'll keep you off your feet for a couple of weeks, and see what happens."

"A couple of weeks! That's impossible: I've got a Community Chest drive, an ordination, two confirmations" — Stephen flung out his hand impatiently — "and pecks of other business."

"They can wait. Bed rest is nature's best remedy."

And bed rest it was, for two trying weeks. Dr. Gavigan bandaged the swollen leg, kept it elevated, and put his patient on a bland diet. Contemptuous of slow treatment, the swelling increased; Stephen's leg was now enormous; it throbbed painfully and would not sustain his weight when he attempted to walk.

"I think we ought to call in a specialist," admitted Dr. Gavigan finally. "A consultation is indicated here."

"Get Dr. John Byrne," said Stephen. "He's specialist enough for me."

John Byrne's examination included laboratory tests of Stephen's blood, urine, and a specimen of fluid drained from his swollen leg. Then, laboratory reports on hand, John Byrne sat down beside Stephen's bed.

"My diagnosis agrees with Dr. Gavigan's, Steve. You've got phlebitis — that is, an inflammation of the veins deep in your leg. The picture is complicated by a lymphatic involvement" — he started to explain what the involvement was when Stephen interrupted with a taut question.

"Is it curable?"

Dr. Byrne was strangely evasive. "Very little is known about lymphatic disorders. Cannon and Drinker are doing experimental work on the subject at Harvard. Sooner or later, something may come of it."

"Meanwhile my leg will continue to look and feel like a sausage. Is that the story?"

"The acute stage may pass. Spontaneous cures have been reported." John Byrne was encouraging. "We'll try everything: arsenicals, drainage, heat . . ."

"And more bed rest." Stephen was disconsolate.

"That's about all we can do. You must have patience, Steve."

Patience! Medicine easiest to prescribe, hardest to take. Patience! The calm enduring of catastrophe or pain. Patience! One of the moral virtues — a special gift of the Holy Ghost.

"I'll try," promised Stephen.

LIKE most men who have enjoyed the blessing of health all their lives, Stephen was a poor patient. Flat on his back, legs propped up on pillows, he passed through irritability to bitterness, through bitterness to desperation. For the first month he felt like a torture victim strapped to the floor of a belfry while monstrous chimes tolled "doom, doom" above his head.

Meanwhile diocesan business accumulated — and lapsed. Some details he handled from bed, some he delegated to assistants, but the more important duties — such as confirmations and parish inspections — demanded the Bishop's physical presence. Stephen put whip and spur to his aides, all of whom responded with selfless devotion. Vicar-General Cannell strained the seams of his cassock to accomplish tasks that Stephen laid upon him; Mark Drury (a much-humbled man since the Wall Street crash) flogged both himself and his subordinates over the Chancery hurdles. Still, neither the Vicar-General nor the Chancellor possessed the canonical authority to administer confirmation or ordain new priests. Amby Cannell solved this problem by tracking down a retired missionary bishop, the Most Reverend Fabian Coxe, D.D., living with his sister in the outskirts of New Haven. Rickety and aging though he was, Bishop Coxe forgot his own infirmities and traveled about the Diocese confirming and ordaining in Stephen's stead.

Unexpected strength developed in Owen Starkey, Stephen's stripling secretary. To the handling of an enormous correspondence and an ability to sift the essential grain from mountains of chaff, Father Starkey added various roving assignments. He became a mobile foreman in charge of building projects, the upkeep of cemeteries, and the inspection of the model machine shops that Stephen had established before his illness. Only a youthful diffidence in dealing with older clerics kept Father Starkey from being the perfect lieutenant.

"It's hard for me to crack down on men who were celebrating Mass before I was born," he confessed to Stephen. "Sometimes I feel like a buck private trying to tell a top sergeant how to lace his shoes."

The mention of shoelaces brought a rueful groan from Stephen. Suddenly, shoes became the most beautiful things in the world; would he ever again enjoy the almost sacramental privilege of wearing them? Grumble and grin mingled in his

warning to Owen Starkey: "The next man who mentions shoelaces around here will have to eat his own, *boiled*." The
Bishop's tone softened: "Don't let these top-sergeant characters frighten you, Ownie. Just remember you're my auxiliary
legs, and step out accordingly."

By means of auxiliary legs, hands, and eyes Stephen managed to keep the diocesan machinery rolling. He could not,
however, do much about the depression. Like a merciless glacier it ground onward, crushing factories, banks, parishes, and
human beings to economic flinders. Sources of private charity
dried up, parishes plunged deeper into deficit; the diocesan
treasury sank lower, and the Bishop of Hartfield lay in bed
with a heavy leg and still heavier heart.

Visitors came — friends and family — each bearing some
leaf of comfort to lay on Stephen's coverlet. Glennon urged a
trip to the Mayo Clinic for the best obtainable diagnosis and
treatment. Corny Deegan drove down from Boston with two
characteristic gifts: a carton of S. S. Pierce's tinned brown
bread and a powder-blue check for five thousand dollars.
"Something for church mice to nibble on," he said cryptically,
folding the check between the pages of Stephen's breviary.
Bernie Fermoyle lugged in the newest thing in radio: a six-
tube affair bristling with knobs and dials. "If you want to hear
me, just turn this to six-sixty every night at eight o'clock. It's
the Jelo-Pud Hour, bringing you the jiffy dessert with the
extra tremble." Every evening, thereafter, Bernie's chamois
voice rubbed away some part of the day's tarnish.

These and many other visitors — Alfeo Quarenghi, Paul
Ireton, and Jeremy Splaine among them — were beacons
that helped light Stephen's passage across seas of illness. Their
friendship was immeasurably sweet, a temporary prop to his
loneliness, a corporal proof of love. Gradually, however,
Stephen began to realize that mortal friends, with all their
sustaining strength, could not float him over the sunken ledges
of despondency. Only one Friend could do that. And where
was that Friend now? Once in a midnight hour of querulous
misery, Stephen cried out: "*Deus meus, Deus meus, ut quid
dereliquisti me?*" (Lord, Lord, why hast Thou forsaken me?)
To his anguished cry no answer came God's silence was
stony. His face was turned away

For five bedridden months Stephen's condition did not change. John Byrne came down from Boston every week to drain off accumulated fluids or try an experimental drug. His skill and medicines were unavailing; Stephen's leg remained a swollen useless thing suspended in a leather harness. A fever hung on, too. Three times a day the waxen fingers of Sister Frances Veronica placed a thermometer between Stephen's lips, then after a tranquil reading of the mercury (how maddeningly composed the woman was!) she would make either a spike or a trough on her patient's chart. The spike meant 100.2; the trough 99.4 — a monotonous graph indicating the presence of a chronic low-grade infection that resisted both diagnosis and treatment.

One day while John Byrne was trying out a new heat lamp, Stephen asked him bluntly:

"Do you think I'll ever be able to walk again, John?"

" 'Ever' is a vague word. Suppose I said 'no.' How would that affect the situation?"

"I'd know what action to take about the Diocese. I could resign . . . let a well man take over the job. It's not fair to serve six hundred thousand Catholics from bed."

"Have you had any complaints about your administration?"

"No. Everyone is so — touchingly loyal."

John Byrne brought the heat lamp closer to Stephen's leg. "Then why don't you develop a little loyalty yourself?" he asked in his quiet way.

Nerves frayed, patience in tatters, Stephen burst out irritably: "What do you expect me to do? Lie here for the rest of my life, hands folded in cheerful resignation, while my Diocese falls apart and my leg hangs from the ceiling like a piece of condemned pork?"

John Byrne turned off the heat lamp and sat down beside his brother-in-law's bed. "What's happened to you, Steve?" he asked sharply. "I know you've been flat on your back for six months. Agreed, it's tough. From an ordinary man I'd expect the usual writhings — bootless cries to heaven and all that. But coming from you, it's out of character."

With scalpel words Dr. Byrne stripped his patient to the pelt. "Lately, I've been asking myself, 'Is this peevish rebellious Bishop of Hartfield the fine priest I used to know? Has Steve

Fermoyle lost his gift of humility? Has he forgotten that suffering is God's physic to swollen pride?' "

Crimson shame tinged Stephen's cheek as he gazed into the mirror that his brother-in-law's honesty held up to him. Defenseless, he took John Byrne's chastisement, then reached out for the surgeon's bony hand. "Thanks for the bitter medicine, John. Dose me again if I need it."

Now began the desperate struggle for acceptance of the Father's will. In daily communion, by incessant prayer, and from pages of saintly works, particularly Thomas à Kempis' *Imitation of Christ,* Stephen earnestly sought to place his life in God's keeping. Almost he succeeded. For an hour or two he would recapture the power of accepting tribulation. A blessed repose would permeate his heart and mind. Then Ambrose Cannell or Owen Starkey would come in bearing news of parish hazards or some leak in the diocesan dike that only a bishop's clenched fist could plug. Harnessed to his bed, Stephen would issue a fighting directive. Then the whole structure of his interior life would sway and crumble again.

Inching progress always ended in a stunned retreat. How difficult to find solace in the serene pages of Thomas à Kempis:

"Thy way is our way, and by holy patience we walk to Thee who art our Crown. If Thou hadst not gone before and taught us, who would care to follow? What would become of us if we had not such a light to help us follow Thee?"

While Thomas nestled in the very bosom of the Lord, Stephen could not even catch His eye. Desperation was claiming him, when Dennis Fermoyle journeyed down from Boston to visit his son.

After forty years of service on the cars, Din had been put out to pasture on a meager pension. Age had melted down his once heroic torso; his baggy blue suit hung about him in folds; gun-flint sparks no longer leapt from his eyes. As old men will, he talked of his youth — the earlier years in Dublin before he had come to America.

"You know, Son, there used to be a Dublin legend that said every clan living on the banks of the Liffey carried some special mark of God's favor. With the O'Donnells it was hair — men and women of that tribe had yards of silky gold falling around their shoulders. With the Flatleys it was all voice

When a Flatley sang or spoke, the lardy richness of it would drown you. The Desmonds had wonderful muscles. Every tribe had something."

"What did the Fermoyles have, Dad?"

Din's voice was tremulous with memory. "The Fermoyles were marvelous at games of leaping and running. A proud way of walking they had, too. People used to look out the window to see my father come swinging down Vico Road. It wasn't a strut or a swagger — no." Din tried to describe the legendary mark of the Fermoyle bearing. "Corny Deegan once said that my father looked like Adam striding across the first bog."

To the loom of recollection Din added the dark thread. "There was a penalty attached to the possession of these gifts, Son. The legend ran that Liffey men were always stricken in the place they were proudest of. And somehow, it always turned out that way. The O'Donnells went bald young, Desmond muscle turned early to fat. . . ."

"And the Fermoyles?" asked Stephen.

"Well, like every other clan — they were given their little cross, too."

Little cross! From his pillow Stephen saw for the first time the tragedy of the proud-walking Dennis Fermoyle. Sprung of a clan famous for leaping and hurling, Din had early and obediently put on the harness that shackled him for life to the platform of a trolley car. Never a murmur all those years while his leg veins knotted and broke on the job. Could no lesson be learned from this godlike, uncomplaining man?

In the days that followed Din's visit, Stephen searchingly examined the nature of his own "little cross." Whether his illness was an outcrop of the Liffey legend (he smiled at the idea) or whether it was a harsh purge to his pride made little difference. The essential lesson that had to be learned over and over again (how many times, O Lord?) was that no man could understand the agony of Christ until he had suffered a similar agony in his own heart. Only then would he be able to bear his cross with fortitude; only then would he be worthy to hear the Father's comforting promise: "Behold I am with you all days, even unto the consummation of the world."

On these foundations Stephen began to build anew. The wisdom of à Kempis, once so shadowy, became luminously clear in the light of Din's example. From the chapter entitled "Temporal Sufferings" Stephen read:

Lord, because Thou wast patient in Thy life, herein most of all fulfilling the Commandment of Thy Father, it is well that I, miserable sinner, should patiently bear myself according to Thy will. For although the present life seemeth burdensome, it is nevertheless made very full of merit through Thy grace; and to those who are weak, it becometh easier and brighter through Thy example and the footsteps of Thy saints.

My own father high among them, thought Stephen.

His fever hung on; the calf of his inflamed leg now measured thirty inches, more than twice its normal size.

Meanwhile the economic wheels of the richest nation in the world ground to a virtual halt as swarms of panhandlers shuffled along the streets muttering the refrain of the year's theme song: "Brother, can you spare a dime?"

From his bed a stricken bishop administered such aid as he could to his people. The diocesan coffers were almost empty now. The depression, settling over the nation like a blight, might have crushed the Bishop of Hartfield had he not accepted with perfect trust the teaching of à Kempis:

A man may give away all his goods, yet that is nothing; and do many deeds of penitence, yet that is a small thing. And though he comprehends all knowledge and has great virtue and zealous devotion, yet much is lacking unto him, yea, one thing which is the most necessary of all. What is it, then? That having given up all things besides, he give up himself and go forth from himself utterly, and retain nothing of self-love.

IT WAS on a man who retained little of self-love that Dr. John Byrne performed a surgical operation in mid-April, 1931.

John Byrne came in quietly that spring morning, took the latest copy of *The New England Medical Journal* from his pocket, and showed his brother-in-law an article entitled "Surgical Management of Chronic Lymphatic Disorders." "The Harvard people have come through," he announced, the veriest minim of excitement in his voice. "I've studied their results, Steve." John Byrne was professionally candid. "Three out of eleven cases died on the table; the risk of postoperative infection is great. . . ."

"I'll take my chances," said Stephen.

Adhering closely to the Harvard technique, Dr. Byrne made a long incision on the outside surface of his brother-in-law's leg. From these areas the surgeon removed an affected mass of lymphatic tissues and fasciae. He then placed the patient's skin in direct contact with the leg muscles, sewed up the wound with "interrupted sutures," and bound the leg tightly with surgical bandages.

Blood transfusions, intravenous injections of sugar, and nurses on three shifts helped Stephen survive this pioneer adventure in plastic surgery. Three days after the operation *The Hartfield Item* carried an encouraging headline:

"Bishop Fermoyle Improves Steadily."

On an inside page of the same edition, the *Item* ran a short news story reporting some rather odd goings-on in Topswell, fifteen miles southeast of Hartfield.

"It appears," said the report, "that events of a miraculous nature are taking place at one of the graves in the Gates of Heaven Cemetery. Many cures have been effected, and afflicted persons in great numbers are flocking to the burying ground."

CHAPTER 5

ON THE MAPS given away by gasoline companies, the town of Topswell is indicated by neither a circle nor a star, but by the merest decimal of a dot. And the macadam road that winds down from Hartfield becomes a dusty soft-shouldered thing long before it reaches a dead end at the Gates of Heaven Cemetery, two miles east of town. In ordinary times not a hundred cars a year make the trip to the burying ground. But on a certain May afternoon in 1931, the road was so snarled with traffic that Father Owen Starkey had to park his Ford a half mile down the road, and make his way on foot to the iron gates of the cemetery.

Bright drops of perspiration beaded Father Owen's forehead, and buttercup pollen made a yellow dust on his shoes when he reached the entrance. Around the open gates surged a tide of automobiles; a dozen cars were parked inside. Disapproving wrinkles corrugated Father Owen's brow. As overseer of cemeteries he felt a certain responsibility for this undignified traffic. Joe Dockery, the grounds keeper, should have kept the gates closed. The man would have to do some tall explaining.

But where was Joe Dockery? Father Owen rapped at the door of the grounds keeper's lodge. "Joe . . . Joe Dockery," he cried. No answer. Must be down at the grave, thought the young overseer. Maybe I'd better go down, and take a look.

He fell in with the stream of foot traffic winding down an alley of copper beeches — dark, good-looking trees that were the only distinguishing feature of the cemetery. For the rest there was little of quality: the plots were small, unfenced; the monuments, if they could be called by so grand a name, were markers of no style or period. On the headstones were carved proud tribe names borne by former kings of Ireland: Flaherty, Dignan, Boyle, and O'Connor. "*Requiescant in pace aeterna,*'" murmured Father Owen. "If," he added, "they'll let you."

In the lee of the tool house — a low green shed with a Dutch door — he saw Joe Dockery. A clay pipe, black with age, jutted from the grounds keeper's mouth, and his legs were crossed in the relaxed manner of an Irish squire surveying his estate. He arose as Father Owen approached and touched the visor of his leather cap with easy respect.

"A good afternoon to you, Father. A good warm afternoon to you. Sit down out of the heat here, while I draw a cooling draught from the spring of Tubber Tintye." He turned the faucet of a pipe at his elbow, and handed the priest an iron mugful of tap water.

"Thanks, Mr. Dockery." Owen Starkey needed that drink. He had another, then sat down on the bench beside the grounds keeper.

"What do you think of the crowd we're gathering, Father?" asked Joe. "Eighty-two cars yesterday. Ninety-six so far today. They're beginning to come in now."

Father Owen started to choose stern words and ended by uttering characteristic mild ones. "I scarcely know what to think, Joe. Before I can form an opinion, I'll have to hear more. All the Bishop gets is rumor — and he wants very much to learn the facts." Stephen's secretary waved a hand at the dusty procession. "How did all this start, anyway?"

Joe Dockery's smile had a benign "all-in-good-time-if-you're-patient" quality about it. "You've heard the beginning of it . . . about Tom O'Doul's arthritis, that is?"

"I've heard nothing."

"Would you have the tale from O'Doul himself?"

"If you think he can tell it better than you, yes."

Joe Dockery put two fingers in his mouth and whistled the first three notes of "The Hearty O'Doul." "That'll rouse him."

The vibration had scarcely died when a sepulchral male came out from behind a grassy mound. The brush hook in his hand predicated weed cutting of some kind, but everything else about him suggested chronic fatigue. He stepped charily as if begrudging his joints the drop of oil they needed for movement. The hearty O'Doul touched his cap to the cloth, and waited for Dockery's instructions.

"Tom," said the grounds keeper, "tell Father Starkey just how all this began. Start with the Friday I put you on the lawn mower."

Thus briefed, O'Doul entered upon his tale: "Like Joe says, he took me off the sickle that Friday and put me on the lawn mower, cutting grass on some plots under the blasted elm. I was a sufferer from arthritis," explained O'Doul in the voice of a professional testifier. "Untractable pain it caused in my principal joints — ankle, knee, elbow, shoulder, and hip socket."

"It was that bad," said Joe, "his fingers were caking up with chalk."

"On this particular Friday, after I cut the grass on a certain grave, I felt queer. *Good* queer. I said to myself, 'Tom, the pain's gone.'"

"Flew," said Joe Dockery, opening his hand as if releasing a bird. "But it came back, Tom?"

"It did, Joe. A day or so after."

"Tell Father Starkey what you did then. You don't mind, Father, if Tom sits down on the tub?"

"Not at all . . . sit down, Tom."

Gingerly, O'Doul settled his bony posterior on an overturned tub, and proceeded wth his tale. "In a spare hour I went back to the grave, trimmed it a little around the edges, and sure enough . . ."

Joe Dockery opened his hand in the bird-releasing act. "Off it flew again," he said.

"Like a crow off a pine tree," testified O'Doul. "And it hasn't come back since."

They both looked at Father Starkey. "Whose grave was it?" he asked.

"Tell him, Tom."

"There was a headstone on the grave all cracked and weathered. When I scraped away some of the moss I could make out the lettering, 'Here lies the body of Reverend William J. Flynn, 1805-1877, a priest forever according to the order of McChisideck.' "

"*Mel*chisidec," corrected Father Starkey absently. He turned to Joe Dockery. "Did you check it in the records?"

"I did, Father. The cemetery books show that a Reverend William Flynn was once pastor here. My mother, God rest her soul, used to speak of him with awe."

Owen Starkey wet his handkerchief under the faucet of Tubber Tintye and cooled his face and hands. "I'd like to see more," he said. "Let's go down to Father Flynn's grave."

"RESTING COMFORTABLY," ran the official bulletin on Bishop Fermoyle's condition four days after his operation. "The patient is doing as well as can be expected," said the bulletin three days later. "Some improvement noted." "Surgeon hopeful." "Bishop recuperating slowly." "Temporary setbacks to be expected." These and other canting medicalisms were handed to the press in lieu of the sad truth that Bishop Fermoyle was having a rugged postoperative time.

The pain wasn't so bad; morphine could control that, and since no well-established mortality figures existed for this type of operation, one had to face the possibility of death with Christian resignation. The thing that bothered Stephen most was the gaunt tension in Dr. John Byrne's facial muscles. Having done all that a creative surgeon could do, John Byrne was now undergoing the special torment of waiting for nature to do the rest. He had made a gambler's throw. Stakes?

Stephen's power of self-locomotion. At the end of a week the coin was still in the air.

When the bandages came off, the coin would fall.

Till then, in some suspended fashion, life had to go on. With complications, of course — financial, administrative, personal, and disciplinary judicial. Money complications first, as always. In the second year of the depression, with sixteen million unemployed persons in the United States and two hundred thousand of them in Hartfield, dollars were scarcer than ox bile. Ill-housed, ill-clothed, ill-nourished, the people were pleading for food, shelter, and medical attention that only local charity could provide.

From the heap of documents on the low table beside his bed in St. Andrew's Hospital, Stephen selected a long cardboard tube, unscrewed the metal cap, and examined a roll of blueprints. The plan for a new wing on the Diocesan House of Refuge. Good plans, too. Father Jed Boylan's plans. Father Jed would be in pleading for them again tomorrow. Stephen could hear him now. "But, Bishop, where'll we *put* the people? They're broke, sick, hungry — and bitter. We've got to take care of them. Let's start building anyway . . . we'll get the money somewhere."

Hard-working Jed, a wonderful director of charities. Too bad he'd have to take no for an answer. "Sorry, Jed. The Diocese is strapped. The banks won't lend us the money. Next spring, perhaps. Jed, you heard me. I said '*no*.'"

It would be no to Mother Alicia, who was tired of shoveling coal into the firebox of the Poor Clares' worn-out boiler. It would be no to Brother Gregor Potocki, who needed fertilizer for his tobacco co-operatives. Always no. Stephen rolled up the blueprints, slipped them back into the cardboard tube, and wondered whether two legs would really be better than one in begging or borrowing money for his down-at-the-heel Diocese.

He picked up *The Hartfield Item*. The usually melancholy grist of news. Banks failing all over the country, people jumping out of windows in New York, marathon dancers entering their thirty-second day. Would the papers ever print good news again? A front-page box caught his eye:

"New Miracles Reported at Topswell Cemetery"
Grounds Keeper Dockery Makes Statement

Almost, this Dockery persuadeth me, gritted Stephen, flinging the paper aside. If Owen Starkey's report warranted disciplinary action, Dockery would be relieved. And what, incidentally, was delaying Father Starkey? The usually punctual secretary should have been back an hour ago. Bishop Fermoyle opened his mouth to accept the clinical thermometer from Sister Frances Veronica's cool, waxen fingers. Her noncommittal glance at the column of mercury told him he was running a temperature again. She was expostulating on the folly of trying to manage a diocese from a sickbed when Father Starkey, dust-grimed and sweaty, came through the half-open door.

"What news from the miracle mart, Ownie?"

"A tale of great wonder, Your Excellency. It will make your hair stand up like the porpentines." Without prologue Owen plunged into his report. Rapidly condensing the Dockery-O'Doul dialogue, he came to his inspection of Father Flynn's grave.

"It's an ordinary single plot with a thin slab of marble for a headstone. Nothing to distinguish it from a thousand other graves — except . . ."

"Except what?"

"Except," said Owen Starkey, "that a hundred people, mostly cripples of one kind or another, came to kneel around it today. If Dockery's estimates are correct, there'll be two hundred tomorrow and two thousand next week."

"How are they behaving themselves?"

"Not very well, I'm sorry to say. They've ripped all the sod off the grave and now they're carrying away little bags of earth." From his pocket Owen drew a cheesecloth affair somewhat resembling a tea bag, and handed it to his superior.

Stephen fingered the earth-filled packet. "Whose idea was this?"

"Dockery's. He calls it a soil-conservation measure. His point is that everyone gets the same amount of earth, no matter how much money they throw into the tub."

"Money?" Stephen sat bolt upright. "Tub?"

Father Owen struggled for lucidity. "Well, you see, Bishop, people were tossing coins and bills all over the grave, so Joe Dockery put a washtub by the headstone. Not counting the coins, about eighty-five dollars was thrown into it yesterday."

"What becomes of this money? Does Mr. Dockery pocket it personally?"

"No. He realizes that the money isn't his. He seems to think, though, that it should be spent in building a shrine — like Lourdes or St. Anne de Beaupré." At the incredulous lift of his Bishop's eyebrows, Owen Starkey went on. "Something's got to be done, Your Excellency. The crutches are piling up fast."

This piece of information sent Stephen's eyebrows still higher. If the lame and the halt were discarding crutches, walking away under their own power, the events taking place at Father Flynn's grave must be viewed in a new light. He fingered the cheesecloth bag thoughtfully. Did the dust of this obscure priest, dead for fifty years, really have miraculous power? Or was the whole affair another example of mass hysteria?

Stephen's self-addressed questions were interrupted by the appearance of Amby Cannell in the doorway. The Vicar-General, buffer and liaison officer between the Bishop's cot and the outer world, removed his meerschaum from its customary station. "The gentlemen of the press are here," he announced. "A.P. and U.P., complete with photographers. They want a feature story on the 'Gates of Heaven Miracles.'"

"I'll give them features, Amby — bedside features. Bring them in and have a stenographer take down what I say. Free press means free fancy to some of these chaps."

The leader of the press delegation, a veteran correspondent named Hotchkiss, made a frank opening. "Bishop Fermoyle," he began, "miracles are news. This Gates of Heaven business looks like a Grade A miracle — and, you'll pardon me for saying so — a gold mine. Before things get off on the wrong track, won't you, as Bishop of Hartfield, make a statement?"

"The only statement I can make," said Stephen, "is that I can't make a statement until every aspect of the Gates of Heaven situation is carefully investigated. Until the findings are sifted, weighed, and interpreted, I must be silent." Stephen smiled. "I trust, gentlemen, that you will respect that silence."

The press spent a glum five seconds. Then a cynical voice spoke up. "That's fine, Bishop. But who gets the money? There's going to be boodles of it."

Stephen was candid. "By canon law, the bishop has sole responsibility for, and title to, all monies collected in his diocese."

They wrote that down. Then the U.P. man piped up. "Grounds Keeper Dockery says there's going to be a shrine at the Gates of Heaven. He's given out a story that Father Flynn's skeleton will be dug up and put in a glass casket."

"Mr. Dockery has an active imagination and persuasive powers of speech," said Stephen. "As a private citizen he may give free rein to both. As grounds keeper of the Gates of Heaven he is not, however, the final voice in diocesan matters."

A flash bulb snapped. "No pictures," said Stephen.

"Aw, Bishop, what's the harm in a little picture?"

Stephen disregarded the plea. "Monsignor Cannell, get that plate," he said firmly. "I don't mean to be arbitrary, gentlemen, but this is not a circus. If pictures are needed, my office will give you glossy proofs of the official photograph."

"One more question, Bishop Fermoyle." Hotchkiss was speaking. "What form will your investigation take?"

"The usual form prescribed by the Church. My assistants will interview persons allegedly cured and take written testimony from them. If miraculous cures are discovered, competent medical authority will pass upon the facts. The process may take some time."

Hotchkiss was a ferret for news. "You say it'll take some time, Bishop. Pending the outcome of your investigation, mightn't it be wise to *close* the cemetery?"

The query was fair enough; Stephen answered it thoughtfully. "If the events taking place at the Gates of Heaven are truly miraculous — if God in His wisdom has bestowed the power of healing on the dust of this obscure priest — I would be guilty of a great sin in opposing His intentions. Not until all the facts have been studied can I risk a decision."

"May we quote you on that?"

"You may. I'm afraid you won't get it right, and that many of your readers won't understand. But you may quote me."

The reporters filed out. Amby Cannell had barely closed the door behind them when Stephen issued a general directive. "Round up a dozen of the smartest, most active priests in the Diocese," he ordered. "Get them in here immediately; I'll brief them myself. We're going to dig and dig, sift and sift, weigh and weigh, till the facts give us something to go on."

Stephen turned to his secretary. "You're in charge of field operations, Ownie. Your first assignment is to tell Joe Dockery that I shall hold him personally responsible for the maintenance of order and a full accounting of all monies collected at the Gates of Heaven Cemetery."

FIFTEEN DAYS after the operation, Dr. John Byrne removed the bandages from Stephen's leg. Two things were obvious; the long, curving incision showed no signs of infection, and the circumference of the leg was normal. Stephen uttered an aspiration of thanksgiving and gripped the surgeon's hand. "Physician most worthy!" The neat sutures fascinated him. "What a dressmaker you'd have been!"

No smile relieved the tension at the corners of John Byrne's eyes. "It looks fairly clean to me, Steve, but we're not out of the woods yet. The real test will come when you put your weight on it."

"When will that be?"

"No telling. We've got to be sure that the lymphatic processes between skin and muscle are re-established. Meanwhile, immobility. bed rest — and no cheating on either for another two weeks."

"Afraid I'll spoil your case if I get out of bed?"

Dr. Byrne shook a sober jaw. "The only thing I'm afraid of, Steve, is the danger of infection. You see, the lymphatic system is the body's chief defense against bacterial invasion. If a single streptococcus gets into that wound, your leg comes off at the groin."

"I'll stay in bed," promised Stephen.

Diocesan activities took a bullish turn for the next ten days; Stephen's hospital room became an executive chamber as heads of departments swarmed in with wire baskets of unfinished business. On his crowded calendar of appointments Stephen made a special place for progress reports brought in daily by Owen Starkey. The Gates of Heaven investigation had taken Owen and his assistants into all parts of the Diocese. By May 15 the list of completed interviews, signed and attested by lay and medical witnesses, numbered well over two hundred.

Stephen glanced at the mass of papers in Owen Starkey's brief case. "Pick me out a typical case, Ownie," he said.

Father Starkey selected a neatly typewritten sheet from his collection, and handed it to his superior. "Here's about the way they run, Your Excellency."

The document consisted of two parts: a description of the interviewee and a signed affidavit reciting the facts of the case. Stephen read the following:

Agnes Leenan, widow, age 46, occupation part-time domestic. Type of illness: persistent backache dating from birth of sixth child, 14 years ago. Other ailments: dizziness, spots before eyes, palpitations, ringing in ears, hot flushes [sic], swelling ankles, nightmares, rash on back of hands, distress after eating greasy foods. Subject wept throughout interview, apologized for odor of liquor on breath, quoted "wine for the stomach's sake," then offered interviewer bottle of beer "for his parch."

Résumé of statement made by Mrs. Leenan: has always been a churchgoer, never misses Mass, contributes generously to the support of the pastor when there is any money in the house. Special devotions: Rosary and Stations of the Cross. Treated by several physicians without beneficial result. Got some relief from a chiropractor in 1929. First heard of cures at Gates of Heaven five weeks ago. Visited grave of Father Flynn, said Rosary kneeling on grass beside grave, took a small bag of earth home after leaving fifty-cent piece on grave. Felt "airy" for a week; pain in back seemed to decrease. Now wears earth-filled bag around her neck. Says it gives "blessed relief." Intends to make another visit to cemetery because back pain is gradually returning. Has no doubt the grave has miraculous powers, or that she will ultimately be cured.

I have read the above and declare it to be a true and accurate statement made by me.

(Signed) Agnes Leenan

Attached to the statement was a note on the letterhead of a Hartfield physician. "I have examined Mrs. Agnes Leenan on two occasions in my office and diagnosed her principal ailment as a low back-pain syndrome, probably due to displacement of internal organs."

Stephen looked up in wry dismay. "Are they all like this, Ownie?"

"Pretty much, Your Excellency."

"It's not the stuff that miracles are based on, would you say?"

Owen Starkey turned optimistic. "There's one pretty good case here. Harold Trudeau's the name." He handed Stephen the paper containing Trudeau's history. "Infantile paralysis at age of ten. Wore braces and crutches; unable to work for livelihood. Visited grave March 15, threw down crutches, and walked home. Now gainfully employed by the Hartfield Telephone Company."

"This *is* something," cried Stephen, examining the medical affidavits attached to Trudeau's statement.

"I'm glad you think so, Bishop. The man is sober, fairly intelligent, and quite obviously cured. One leg is shorter than the other, but he gets around on it."

Stephen curbed his enthusiasm. "He might be a hysteric. . . ."

"It's possible, of course."

"Could you bring him in here? I'd like to see the man personally."

Harold Trudeau turned out to be a sallowish young man whose simpering diction and gaudy taste in cravats were clear compensations for the orthopedic boot he wore on his right foot. At the Bishop's invitation he sat down and recited a fairly straightforward story of childhood paralysis and partial atrophy of the lower limbs. During adolescence made painful by his deformity he had worn leg braces, but had discarded them at the age of twenty. Thereafter he had depended wholly on crutches for support and locomotion until the day he visited Father Flynn's grave.

"I went to the cemetery to visit my mother's grave — she died last spring," said Trudeau. "While there, I saw a number of people kneeling around Father Flynn's grave. I knelt down, said three Hail Marys, and rubbed a handful of earth onto my knee. When I got up I didn't need my crutches."

"And you haven't used them since?"

"That's right, Bishop. I can even dance now."

"Splendid," said Stephen. "When did you start dancing?"

The witness flushed. "Well, you see, Bishop, I've been kind of crazy about a girl for a long time, but she wouldn't have anything to do with me on account of — of my crutches. Soon as I got rid of them, I began to make time with her."

"I see." Stephen tried not to glance at Owen Starkey. "And how are things turning out?"

"Swell. We're getting engaged as soon as I can save up enough for a ring."

"My congratulations, Mr. Trudeau," said Stephen. "And thank you very much for coming."

When Harold Trudeau had limped out, Stephen fingered a dubious lip. "I wouldn't call him a convincing peg to hang a miracle on, would you, Ownie?"

"Scarcely. It was keen of you to pick up that dancing clue."

Amby Cannell came in with the latest edition of *The Hartfield Item.* "Latest communiqué from the miracle front," he said humorously. Stephen glanced at the front-page photographs of Joe Dockery, showing newsmen the site of the new Gates of Heaven shrine. "Estimated cost to run into six figures" was the caption under the picture.

"I hate to snap the axle off Joe Dockery's dream cart," said Stephen, turning toward his secretary. "But tomorrow morning, Ownie, I want you to go down to the cemetery and tell our enterprising grounds keeper that the show's been called off. Bid him lock the gates and put up a sign, 'No miracles till further notice.'"

NEXT FORENOON (it was a Saturday), Father Owen Starkey battled his way on foot through the disorderly mob swirling about the gates of the cemetery. Overnight, the miracle rush had taken on a carnival aspect. Popcorn vendors cried their wares; at hastily constructed booths one could buy balloons, apples on sticks, gilt rosary beads, conch shells bearing decalcomania likenesses of Father Flynn, and any quantity of holy pictures and hot dogs. Between the entrance pillars, two currents clashed in a fierce tide rip as incoming miracle seekers collided with the outgoing horde that had already visited Father Flynn's grave. Buffeted by these eddies, Owen Starkey reached the cemetery tool house, arranged his disheveled clothing, and rapped at the Dutch door.

"Enter without knocking," cried a voice from within. Father Starkey pushed open the upper half of the door and saw Joe Dockery engaged in the pleasantest of all tasks — the counting of money. His occupation had transformed him: gone was the clay pipe and leather cap. On the grounds keeper's head a derby was tilted, and a gold-banded cigar jutted not too aromatically from his mouth. Sickles and lawn mowers no longer concerned Mr. Dockery. Metal more attractive dripped from his fists as he scooped double handfuls of silver coins from a washtub and poured them into a burlap bag on the table.

Proprietary magnificence streamed from his person. He was ducal as he offered Father Starkey a cigar, viceregal as he tied the neck of a money sack with a twist of twine. "It comes in so fast, we bag it raw," he explained to his visitor. "If this keeps up, I'll have to hire someone to count it."

Owen Starkey let the news fall. "It's not going to keep up, Joe. The orders are to close the cemetery gates."

"Orders?" Dockery started filling another bag with coins. "*Whose* orders?"

"Bishop Fermoyle's." Father Starkey was trying hard to be firm. "The whole business has gotten out of hand, Joe. You must close the gates at once."

Exceeding pelf had made Joe Dockery bold. And jocular. "You're kidding, Father."

"I'm not kidding, Joe. Bishop Fermoyle doubts the authenticity of these cures. . . ."

"He can't doubt the authenticity of *this* — can he?" Joe pointed to the tubfuls of hard and soft money lying about the premises.

"The money's secondary. The important thing is to stop the unseemly brawl going on here." Father Owen spoke as sharply as his temperament permitted. "Start clearing the grounds; we're locking the place up."

Torn between respect for the clergy and still greater respect for cash literally in hand, Joe Dockery temporized. "Orders are orders, Father, but I can't lock the gates just on your say-so. It'd be like" — he struck a happy simile — "like your telling me to set fire to a barnful of twenty-dollar bills. I've got to see the orders in writing, with the Bishop's signature and seal at the bottom of the paper."

"You're laying yourself open to charges of disobedience, Mr. Dockery."

"Oh, I wouldn't call it that, Father. Just get some little sign of authority from the Bishop — and *click*" — Joe made a turn-key motion with his hand — "I'll lock up the place like that."

"You're risking the wrath," warned Owen Starkey.

FIERCE AMAZEMENT gathered like thunderheads in Bishop Fermoyle's eyes as Father Starkey tried to explain the grounds keeper's *lèse majesté*.

"Do I hear you correctly, Father?" Stephen sat upright in his hospital bed. "Are you trying to tell me that Joe Dockery *refused* to close the cemetery?"

"He didn't actually refuse, Your Excellency. He just wants written confirmation of your order. 'Some little sign of authority,' as he said."

Anger exploded in Stephen's voice. "I'll give him a 'sign of authority.'" He tossed aside the coverlet, leapt out of bed. "Is there no one who can execute an order in this Diocese? Hand me my crutches, Father. Fetch me my clothes. This man Dockery must be curbed."

A much-shaken secretary was rummaging in the closet for his Bishop's trousers when the wax-lily face of Sister Frances Veronica appeared in the doorway. At the sight of her patient hobbling about on his bandaged leg, she lost her composure for the first time in twenty-three years. "Bishop, Bishop," she pleaded. "You mustn't pound about so. Get back into bed. Dr. Byrne will be very angry when I tell him."

"Not so angry as I'm going to be for the next hour or two," said Stephen. "Will you kindly get out of here, Sister, while Father Starkey helps me get dressed?"

Sister Frances retired like a figurine folding backward into a Swiss clock. "The Bishop's mad," she whispered to Sister Humilia in the corridor.

"Angry mad?" asked Sister Mercedes.

"No, the other kind. If he walks on that leg" — the idea undid her — "O merciful saints, protect him. Ssh — ssh, here he comes now." The nuns cowered into an alcove as the Bishop, trailed by Father Starkey, hobbled past on his crutches.

It was not quite madness of "the other kind" that possessed the Bishop of Hartfield. True, the blaze of anger, touched off by Joe Dockery's disobedience, crackled toward the powder keg that all Fermoyles kept locked in their endocrine system. Stephen doused it just in time — not, however, until he found himself riding with Amby Cannell and Owen Starkey on a disciplinary tour of duty to the Gates of Heaven Cemetery.

Police outriders, summoned by Monsignor Cannell, cleared the Bishop's way on motorcycles. And fortunately, too, because the dirt road between Topswell and the cemetery was clogged with a tooting tide of curiosity seekers inching toward the grave from whence sprang dangerous hysteria and unwarranted hope. Father Starkey, noting the tight seam of disapproval sewing the Bishop's lips, wondered what would happen when His Excellency saw the gimcrack booths at the entrance to the cemetery. As the episcopal Buick slowed down to a crawl, dirty-aproned vendors began leaping onto its running boards. "Hot franks? Peanuts? Holy pictures, Mister? Get your sacred clam shells . . . only a quarter."

Sacred clam shells! The seam in Stephen's lips grew tighter. Disobedience compounded into sacrilege! Ecclesiastic discipline scorned, and the majesty of death defiled!

"Roll up the windows," said Stephen.

When the Bishop's car halted at the granite pillars of the cemetery, the hysterical throng witnessed something of a spectacle. They saw a tall pallid man robed in vestments customarily worn by a Bishop making a canonical visitation step gingerly to the ground. On his head sat a biretta; from his shoulders fell the *cappa magna* in brocaded folds. Before him walked a cross-bearer; at his side, supporting his elbow, was the Vicar-General of the Diocese.

The Bishop himself was on crutches.

Seeing the robed figure, the pious rabble made a natural mistake. They thought the Bishop had come to get his share of the miracle-working dust. As he hobbled through the gates of the cemetery and proceeded down the tree-lined path, an impromptu procession fell in behind him. This was the genuine thing in piety — the Bishop himself leading his flock to the healing shrine.

Marchers in the procession were somewhat surprised when the Bishop stopped at a low green shed, obviously a tool house, and beat upon the door, first with a crutch, then with a long curved staff that one of his clerics handed him. The staff was, in fact, a crozier, the supreme sign of episcopal authority, and the watchers thought that either the door or the staff must break under the Bishop's pounding.

"Enter without knocking," said a voice inside the shed. "Come in, I say! I'll lose my count if you keep up that racket."

The knocking persisted. "Must I come out and get you?" roared Dockery. He flung open the upper half of the Dutch door, and stood framed there: an opulent figure, derby hat tilted backward, a canvas bag of silver in one hand, and a cigar in the other.

As to what next followed, no two accounts agree. Eyewitnesses say that in trying to remove his hat, hide the silver, and dispose of the cigar, Joe Dockery got all three inextricably mixed. Others aver that he froze rigid with terror and could make no move of reverence, defense, or flight. Some contend that he took off his derby, put the bag of silver on his head, and swallowed his cigar. But whatever he did, his actions dwindled into unimportance when compared with the answers he made to the Bishop's questions.

"You are Joseph Dockery, grounds keeper of this cemetery?" asked Stephen.

"Yes, Your Excellency."

"You have given unauthorized interviews which in part are responsible for the present undignified and un-Christian status of affairs here?"

"Yes, Your Excellency."

"And this morning you refused to obey my orders to shut the cemetery gates?"

"Y-yes, Your Excellency."

"At that time you demanded some little sign of authority?" Stephen paused for the answer that Joe Dockery could not choke up. "I hereby produce for your benefit, Mr. Dockery, this crozier, this ring, and this pectoral cross. You recognize these, do you, as symbols of the episcopal authority vested in me?"

Joe Dockery found his voice again. "I do, Your Excellency."

"Good." Stephen felt sorry for the man. "I have no wish to persecute you, Mr. Dockery. All I want you to do is to obey such legitimate orders as I may give you in the future. Will you promise me that?"

Tears were making quite unmagnificent runnels down Joe Dockery's face as he nodded, "Yes."

"Go to the gates," said Stephen, "and wait there till I come."

The Bishop turned to his people. "I beg you all to leave these precincts of the dead in dignified and orderly fashion. To those who have come here sincerely hoping for a cure, I urge no weakening of faith in God's power to suspend miraculously the operation of natural law. I ask that such persons be patient until God's intention be clearly shown here. At the proper time, and in accordance with ecclesiastic law, you will learn the meaning of what has happened at the grave of Father Flynn."

Stephen edged his voice with contempt. "And to those who have come through idle curiosity or to vend inappropriate wares, I say — leave this holy place before I invoke action by the public authorities."

At four o'clock the dead were resting in peace again. Joe Dockery closed the gates in person; news bulbs flashed as he handed the key to his Bishop. And next morning every paper in the United States carried a headline:

Bishop Fermoyle Disavows Gates of Heaven Miracle
Leaves Sickbed to Restore Order in Cemetery

Dr. John Byrne came in around noon next day to find his patient walking about with no sign of limp or hobble. The surgeon's clinical eyes and fingers searched Stephen's leg. "Everything clean and healthy." He bent the leg at the knee. "Good flexure." He popped a thermometer into Stephen's mouth. "Temperature normal." Whereupon Dr. Byrne exulted in the manner of surgeons who have obtained what is known to the trade as "a satisfactory result."

"Wait till the Harvard people hear about this," he exclaimed.

"Twenty-one days after a major lymphoidectomy the patient puts his entire weight on the leg, walks a quarter of a mile, exposes wound to dangerous infection . . ." John Byrne broke off his scientific dithyrambics and grinned wonderingly at his brother-in-law. "You can disavow all the graveyard miracles you want, Steve, but you're standing on one right now. For heaven's sake, man, get back into bed before God changes His mind."

A FEW DAYS LATER, while gathering together his personal belongings before leaving the hospital, the Bishop of Hartfield came upon two apparently unrelated articles. One was a little cheesecloth bag containing a spoonful of earth from the grave of Father Flynn. The other was a copy of *The New England Medical Journal* containing an article entitled "Surgical Management of Chronic Lymphatic Disorders."

What, if anything, was the relationship between the bag of earth and the scientific article? Must they (Stephen asked himself) necessarily stand in opposition to each other? Was it not conceivable that each in its own way expressed some syllable of the healing Word — that both were manifestations of God's wondrously inscrutable love for His creature, man?

Offhand, the Bishop of Hartfield was unable to answer these questions. But the more he thought about his own cure, the more he was inclined to distribute credit equally. After some weeks he settled the problem in a manner befitting his financial means and condition of soul. From the money turned over by Joe Dockery (who was allowed to keep his job) Stephen contributed one thousand dollars to the Harvard Medical School for the study of lymphatic disorders. And he spent an equal sum in erecting a modest fieldstone grotto over the dust of Father William J. Flynn.

When the Gates of Heaven Cemetery reopened, all unseemly hysteria had evaporated. A few people came to pray at Father Flynn's grave; departing, they left an occasional coin or crutch behind. The dead slept in majesty under their copper beeches, and in the outside world the miracle of daily life went on.

BOOK SIX

The Red Hat

CHAPTER 1

Y ES, life went on. Meanly and grandly, by the knife and the Word, with sinister stroke and valiant counterstroke, the world spun round. In Munich a terrible man was shouting *"Wir wollen wieder Waffen"*; along Manchuria's eastern marches, the spear of Japanese aggression sank (with appropriate regrets) into the vitals of China. On the balcony of the Palazzo Venezia, a latter-day Caesar vowed to Romulus, Remus, Horatius Cocles, *et alii* that the eagles of Rome would again swoop in imperial squadrons against Italy's foes. *Avanti Fascismo . . . Viva il Duce!*

In dustier parts of the vineyard, ordinary men toiled daylong, each for his penny. Specifically:

IN NEW YORK, not far from Carnegie Hall, a coffee-dark young man carrying a scuffed violin case pushed open a door bearing the brass plate: W. PFUNDT — VIOLINS BOUGHT SOLD AND REPAIRED. Against a showcase containing instruments insured for half a million dollars leaned Wilhelm Pfundt — uninsurable himself because of fatty heart and Buerger's disease, but otherwise in good repair. The violin dealer was, in fact, a very triumph of repair work: a nine-pound truss kept his tripes in place, and a leather harness did likewise for his wobbly sacroiliac. These supporting devices, together with a hearing aid, a double row of dental crockery, and a pair of improbably convex eyeglasses made Herr Pfundt the living proof that anything — including the human frame — can be wired, clamped, glued, braced, and strapped together again, long after its first sweet integrity has disappeared.

"Nu, nu, Junge" — molasses and vinegar were mixed equally in Herr Pfundt's greeting — "what have we in our little box today? A left-handed Cremona, or an Amati by way of the woodpile?"

Rafael Menton opened his leatherette case, marveled privately at the perfection of the Eve-shaped instrument he had created, then held it up for the dealer's inspection.

"My Bergonzi model," he announced, plucking the A string as a lover might caress a lobe of his sweetheart's ear.

Herr Pfundt's approach to the fiddle was rather more clinical; indeed, his whole manner suggested a pediatrician examining a baby with rickets. He tapped the slightly swollen belly curve of the violin, peered at its tawny amber varnish, then, observing the first rule of successful dealership, handed it back to the maker. "Stradivarius will not turn over in his grave today," he grunted. "Well, *nu . . . wieviel?*"

"Three hundred dollars."

"For a baseball bat with strings you ask three hundred dollars? Take it out to Yankee Stadium. Or better yet" — Herr Pfundt modulated into a Dutch-uncle role — "look at a real Bergonzi." The dealer indicated a pale orange-colored instrument in his showcase. "A true masterwork made by a pupil of Stradivarius. It is for instruments with a golden voice like this that fiddlers pay money."

The young luthier stood his ground. "Play both violins in Carnegie Hall — mine will outsing yours in everything but reputation. Please, Mr. Pfundt, just draw a bow across the open strings."

The dealer picked up a bow and made scraping noises vaguely resembling *Träumerei.* Then blowing into his hearing aid as if to clear away static, he peered again at the purfling and F-holes of the violin.

"You are a promising workman. *Vielleicht,* you could make a good umbrella stand. . . . One hundred dollars."

Angry protests met the offer. "Listen, Mr. Pfundt, it took me two hundred and fifty hours to make this violin. The back is curly maple, cut from a special tree. The varnish is a secret formula — no other American maker has it. I'll take two hundred and fifty dollars — that's only a dollar an hour for my labor — and not a penny less."

He was putting the violin back in its case when Herr Pfundt's sense of dealercraft prompted a new tack. "Patience makes everything possible," he soothed. "If you won't sell, so perhaps you will swap. I have something here that may interest you."

The dealer opened a cupboard and produced the shattered skeleton of a violin. "A lost Cremona," he said, placing the instrument in Rafe's hands. "*Ganz verloren* for two hundred years. Last week it comes to me — legally, you understand — from a source I cannot reveal. Repaired by a man of your skill, it should be worth" — Herr Pfundt made indefinite, large gestures — "who knows how much?"

Rafael examined the decrepit violin. Its neck was broken, the top badly cracked, and the back entirely missing. Yet across its grandeur of proportion and delicate carving, the master's hand still moved.

Few men in the world, perhaps only the two bending over the ruined instrument, would have dreamed of restoring it. But here they were, the necessary ingredients conjoined: Rafael Menton, the artist-luthier, sick for the feel of greatness, and Wilhelm Pfundt, the living proof that patchwork reigns, though Parthenons crumble.

"Put a back on that, and you'll have something with a voice *and* a reputation," said the dealer.

"I'll swap you even, Mr. Pfundt. My Bergonzi for your Guarnerius."

"Not so fast, young man. For this Cremona I must have your Bergonzi — *mit* two hundred dollars."

"I haven't got that much money, Mr. Pfundt." It was the somber truth. After ten years as a full-fledged luthier, Rafe Menton could not lay his hands on fifty dollars in cash.

Lardy benevolence greased Herr Pfundt's next proposal. "So work it out in repair jobs for me. If fiddle dealers cannot trust each other . . ."

That very afternoon, returning to his murky shop under the Second Avenue El, Rafe Menton began piecing together the fragments of a three-hundred-year-old masterpiece.

REGINA BYRNE was nine now, and nine was different from eight. At eight you thought of boys as cat drowners and bird stoners. At nine there was another reason for boys' existence: they either noticed you or they didn't, and it desperately mattered which.

To solve the mystery of why boys noticed girls, Regina took to gazing in the mirror.

"I am gruesome," she told herself.

Regina's Spanish-dark braids and olive skin weren't gruesome at all; they simply were not the most popular combination at St. Bridget's Parochial School. If Regina could have written her own beauty ticket, she would have ordered an ensemble like Vivian Bursay's: golden-blond hair, baby-blue eyes, and strawberry pink complexion. No wonder the boys rassled on the sidewalk for the privilege of strapping Vivian's roller skates onto her dainty feet. None of the young gallants who streamed out of the boys' side of St. Bridget's had ever struggled for the privilege of strapping on Regina's skates. Gladly she would have exchanged all the love she got at home, all the acclaim showered on her when she played the piano at school concerts, for some overt proof of Charlie Dunne's devotion.

Heavy with the impossibility of such hope, Regina turned for comfort to her cancellations. The ritual worked like this:

$$\cancel{R}\cancel{E}G\cancel{I}\cancel{N}\cancel{A} \ \ B\ Y\ R\ \cancel{N}\cancel{E}$$
$$C\ H\ \cancel{A}\cancel{R}\cancel{L}\cancel{I}\cancel{E} \ \ D\ U\ \cancel{N}\cancel{N}\cancel{E}$$

Counting the letters that didn't cancel, you got nine. According to the rules, you now subtracted one—and you had the enigmatic result, H, the eighth letter in the alphabet, Hate or Happiness—which did it stand for? L clearly meant love, and M betokened Marriage. But H demanded a deeper reading. If it truly meant Happiness, Charlie Dunne would have to co-operate a little more actively. Pull a braid maybe, throw a snowball at her—anything to show that he was aware of her existence. The first step, then, toward lifelong bliss with Charlie Dunne was to attract his attention by some compelling deed.

The nature of this daring deed sprang full-blown into Regina's mind when she saw the tortoise-shell cat in the window of Miss Fifield's thread-and-needle shop.

Around the cat's neck was a red-leather circlet of tiny bells.

Just what I need, thought Regina. With criminal coolness she entered Miss Fifield's little shop and said: "I want a spool of Number Forty Clark's O. N. T. black thread." While Miss Fifield turned around to pull out a tray of spools, Regina leapt at the cat's collar. She unfastened the tiny buckle and whipped the red-leather circlet into her pocket. Shrugging a puzzled shoulder, the cat dozed once more.

"That will be five cents," said Miss Fifield, putting the spool into a paper bag. Regina paid her nickel and minced out of the store, a perfect little lady. Outside the shop she started to run; not until she was home did she pull the collar out of her pocket. She shook the bells. "Lovely, lovely," she said, stirred by the beauty of their sound. "Just the thing to make H come truly true."

Regina's bid for Charlie Dunne's attention was somewhat delayed by the strict separation of boys and girls in St. Bridget's School. Her moment came, however, on the last day of preparation for Holy Communion. Boys, herded into the Gospel side of the basement church, girls ranged on the other, were rehearsing under the direction of Sister Superior herself, who had come in to coach her angelic little charges in the proper manner of approaching the sacrament.

"Clasp your hands as though carrying a spiritual bouquet," said Sister Superior. "Wait until the boy or girl in front of you takes six steps before you leave the pew. Walk with grave piety to the feast our Lord has prepared for you, then kneel at the altar rail. Now let's try it one at a time."

Simultaneously from the first pews, a boy and a girl filed to the altar. "No giggling, Eustacia . . . hands higher, Frederick. . . ."

When Regina's turn came, she started for the altar. There was a slight quiver of bells about her as she walked. A titter ran along both sides of the aisle.

Sister Superior whirled sharply. "Who is jingling bells here?" she challenged. No answer. No need of one. The source of the unholy tinkling was clearly evident as Regina knelt at the rail.

Sister Superior approached the suspect. "Regina Byrne," she asked grimly, "are you shaking any bells?"

Innocence itself creamed Regina's voice. "No, Sister." (They certainly were *all* looking at her now.)

"Then where did that jingling sound come from?" Sister Superior laid hold of Regina's shoulder and shook her experimentally. A muffled carillon emerged from somewhere under

Regina's clothes. The sound was so unbelievably shocking that Sister Superior did not shake the child again.

"Step into the sacristy," she said. "I propose to find out where this indecent noise is coming from."

With a proud little swagger Regina walked towards the sacristy, tinkling her bells as she went. Walking past Charlie Dunne, she smiled; big-eyed, he stared at her, grinned back.

Regina floated into the sacristy in a haze of triumph. She was glad of all that had happened, and only slightly afraid of the consequences. "They won't *dare* do anything to me," she told herself. "My Uncle Stephen's a bishop — he'll *ostracize* them."

Sister Superior and Sister Marcella, a pair of wimpled inquisitors, stalked into the sacristy.

"Where are the bells, Regina? Are they on your dress?"

"No, Sister Superior."

"On your — petticoat?"

"No, Sister Marcella."

Deeper than this, the nuns were not prepared to plunge. They glanced at each other as if to gain strength for the next step. Then Sister Marcella bent over swiftly, and thrust her hand under Regina's clothes. There was a faint jingle, and the amazed nun straightened up as if she had touched a charged wire.

"Sister Superior," she declared, "Regina Byrne has sewn bells onto her garters!"

JAMES SPLAINE, better known to his intimates as "Gillette" (Gillette me have a ciggie? . . . Gillette me have two bits?), nipped at his dwindling pint and addressed a scrawny bay gelding tethered to a nearby tree. "Sarge," he said, "we gotta start now with the bandages. You done your part O.K. Now, hol' still an I'll do mine."

Gathering up some handfuls of steaming manure, Jimmy Splaine applied it like a poultice to the bay gelding's knee. "Ol' vet'inary trick, Sarge. Never fails. Jes' eases lil' ol' osselet back into place." He bound the poultice with a piece of burlap and admonished the mangy beast. "They'd a shot you, Sarge, sure'n Christmas — you'd be soap by now, on'y I said: 'Look, here's a sawbuck I made on the third race.' For that dough,

Sarge, them crum-bums'd stop makin' soap out of their gran'-mother."

Jimmy Splaine fumbled compulsively at the neck of his pint. "You ain't no Man o' War, but if that popped osselet pops back, we'll play the county fairs all summer. . . . Clean up at Marshfield, Barnstable, yeh, 'n maybe Rockingham. Win, place, or show. Settle f'r anything."

Gargling for the relief of his chronic dryness, Jimmy Splaine went on. "On'y one thing we hafta do first. Gotta change your name. Never liked sergeants in the army. All basserds, same as cops. *Basserds!* We'll latch onto a name with class to it . . . sump'n people can trust . . . de*pen'*able." Jimmy Splaine aimed his empty bottle at a rock and burst into laughter. "Sa-ay, how 'bout namin' you after my brother Jeremy? Then there'd be two monsignors in the Splaine family — one a cardinal's seketary 'n the other — ha-ha-ha — a bay gelding! *Ominus nabiscum.* Didn' know I was an altar boy once, eh, Sarge, I mean Monsignor? . . . Plenny Latin. *Hominy nonsum dinkus.* Whoa, boy. Oats, is it?" The owner-trainer of Monsignor surveyed a dime, two nickels, and a penny, drawn from his pocket. "Sorry, pal, hafta feed you grass awhile. Jes' pop that osselet an' you get plenny of oats. On'y make it so's I don't have to kneel down when I feed 'em to you, Monsignor."

IN THE VATICAN PALACE a hook-nosed Secretary of State gathered up his parrots and prepared to retire.

Pietro Giacobbi's work was done. The old matador, who by a species of homeopathic magic had taken on the burly truculence of the thousand bulls he had vanquished, was leaving the arena. Never had the fame of Vatican diplomacy stood higher than in Giacobbi's hour of retirement. As Secretary of State under two Popes he had guided the foreign policy of the Church through the mine field of a world war; in the turbulent decade following Versailles he had swept away, by means of concordats and treaties, every visible or suspected danger swimming in the dark waters of European affairs. The last and greatest of his triumphs had been the Lateran Treaty, a prolonged and delicately balanced negotiation with the Duce, hailed at one time as the diplomatic coup of the century.

By the Lateran Treaty the Pope renounced all claims to the

temporal powers and properties seized from him by the House
of Savoy in 1870. In return he received a cash indemnity of
seven hundred and fifty million lire, plus another billion in
government bonds. The papacy was to enjoy sovereignty over
Vatican City — a tiny state of one hundred and ten acres.
Religious societies were to be recognized; the sacramental
nature of marriage was reaffirmed; Catholicism was to be
taught in the schools. God had been restored to Italy, Italy
restored to God. Having brought the estranged parties
together, Cardinal Pietro Giacobbi retired.

His successor, Eugenio Pacelli, was probably the only man
in the world whose diplomatic skill and experience matched
Giacobbi's. From earliest childhood the new Secretary of
State had dedicated himself to the service of the Church.
Sprung from a family of canon lawyers — Eugenio's father was
a consistorial advocate, his grandfather had served as Undersecretary of the Interior to Pius IX — the Roman-born youth
had at the age of ten declared his intention to become a priest.
At fifteen he entered Capricana College in Rome, the oldest
and most distinguished ecclesiastical school in the world.
After precocious triumphs in scholarship (doctorates in philosophy, theology, and law were his at twenty-two), Eugenio
Pacelli received the sacrament of Holy Orders on April 2,
1899. The next day — it was Easter Sunday — he celebrated
his first Mass in the basilica of St. Mary's Major, then accepted
the chair of law in the Pontifical Institute of the Appollinaire
at Rome.

A career in canon law seemed to be indicated for Eugenio
Pacelli. But destiny had other plans for the young priest. Monsignor Pietro Giacobbi, then Secretary of Extraordinary
Ecclesiastical Affairs, persuaded Father Pacelli to resign his
chair of law, and give all his time to the Vatican Secretariat.
The future Pope became Giacobbi's protégé and pupil; he
assisted the Cardinal Secretary in the prodigious feat of recodi-
fying the entire body of canon law. In World War I he had
become Apostolic Nuncio to Bavaria — a post of utmost importance, for Germany was at that time the diplomatic pivot of
Europe. Unmatched political insight, the gift of tongues, and
extraordinary personal charm made Cardinal Pacelli at fifty-
five a power in the chancelleries of Europe. What more

natural, when Giacobbi decided to retire, than that his brilliant protégé should succeed him as papal Secretary of State?

Scarcely had Pacelli taken up his new duties when ominous birds, winging from Mussolini's headquarters in the Palazzo Venezia, began lighting on St. Peter's dome. In two short years the Lateran Treaty had broken down. Il Duce, who had beamed triumphantly for world cameras when the treaty was signed, began to scowl when its provisions went into effect. His promise that Italian children should receive religious education clashed violently with the Fascist program of *giovanezza* — State control of youth from cradle to combat training. Black-shirted police began roughing up Catholic Youth Clubs as they marched to church on feast days. Street fighting between Catholic student societies and armed Fascist bands became commoner, rougher. When Il Duce declared that despite the Lateran Treaty, the Church was subject to the State, Pius XI branded him as an oath breaker.

Shortly thereafter, the Fascist press accused the Vatican of plotting to assassinate Mussolini. Cardinal Pacelli denied the charge; demanded proof. The only answer was official silence and squads of Fascisti crying: "Death to the Pope," as they clubbed schoolboys belonging to Catholic Youth Societies. Again Pacelli protested. His protests were ignored; worse, they were strangled when Mussolini seized all telegraph and cable stations communicating with the outer world.

Such was the melancholy posture of events when Bishop Stephen Fermoyle arrived in Rome, by special dispensation, for his ad limina visit in June, 1931.

Five years had wrought noticeable changes, seemingly for the better, in the Italian scene. There was a spanking new pier at Naples; the train for Rome left on the dot and arrived on time. Driving from the modernized central station to his hotel, Stephen noted the face-lifting improvements on the public buildings and felt the accelerated tempo of a city trying to regain imperial status. Because it was a great feast day, Stephen expected to see the usual processions — flower-decked statues and banners being carried to church. Not a sign of holiday-making anywhere!

"Where are the processions?" he asked the taxi driver.

The man lifted a "How should *I* know?" shoulder, glancing

from side to side as though the curbstones had ears. Mystified, Stephen saved the question for someone who wouldn't be so obviously afraid to answer it.

At the Hotel Ritz-Reggia a new manager greeted him with a Fascist salute. Behind the desk, where formerly a bucolic painting of Lake Maggiore had hung, a portrait of Mussolini glowered. The porters, once so leisurely, moved with exaggerated military bearing; they wheeled Stephen's modest luggage to his suite as though manning a gun caisson.

It was all very bewildering, and became more so when Stephen phoned his old superior, Monsignor Giuseppe Guardiano, to learn the time of his audience with the Pope. The telephone service was excellent; Monsignor Guardiano's voice came through clearly, but with puzzling caution. In response to Stephen's joyous salutation, the Undersecretary's tone was almost brusque:

"Greetings, Your Excellency. The Holy Father will receive you tomorrow at ten."

"Fine, Seppo. Thanks for arranging things. How've you been, old fellow? What goes on, generally?"

"Tomorrow at ten, Your Excellency." The telephone clicked. What *does* go on? Stephen wondered.

Weary with travel, he dined alone in his room that evening. Finishing his coffee, he was momentarily tempted to phone Princess Lontana and hear her exclaim: "Come over at once, Your Excellency; but *now, immediatamente!* My party needs a good-looking Bishop." No, that phase of life was past— buried with Roberto Braggiotti and Ghislana Falerni. Dangerous to awaken sleeping echoes; even a single reed-thin vibration might bring the avalanche of memory roaring down.

To discipline himself, Stephen pulled out a white-and-gold bound copy of the ad limina report that he would present to His Holiness on the morrow. Leafing through its pages, he became slightly apprehensive. Set down in bald pica, the five-year record of his Diocese was not particularly impressive. His cash position, itemized in Schedule A, was woefully weak; of the quarter-million-dollar legacy left him by Bishop Qualters, barely fifty thousand dollars remained. To offset this slender balance, Stephen could point to three new churches and four new schools he had built during the depression. On the credit

side also were the farming co-operatives he had helped finance
in rural areas. Among the intangibles not appearing in the record was his curial organization staffed with energetic young
men.

Troubled by misgivings, Stephen laid the report aside.
How would the Pope comment on his servant's stewardship?
With filial resignation, tinged by the knowledge that he had
done the best he could, the Bishop of Hartfield went to sleep
on a trusting prayer.

NEXT MORNING, entering the Vatican Palace through the
familiar courtyard of San Damaso, Stephen presented himself
to a plumed *maestro di camera* in the papal antechamber.
There was a period of waiting, a ceremonious progress to the
Pope's study — then the opened double door and the sight of
the Holy Father seated at his long worktable. Emotion welled
up in the American Bishop as he beheld his spiritual leader,
terribly worn by the burdens of his office. Stephen dropped to
his knees, arose, advanced, knelt again. For some inexplicable
reason, his eyes were moist. Now the pontiff's arms were
around him, and the Holy Father was murmuring:

"*Caro figlio,* Stefano. Five years . . . such a long time!"

Stephen dashed his tears away. "Forgive me, Holy Father,"
he said. "I didn't come all the way from America to weep on
your shoulder. Just a sudden case of *lachrymae rerum.*"

The tears of things! Through the fog in his spectacles Pius
XI gazed clinically at Stephen. "What was this famous surgery
we heard of?" (Achille Ratti, conqueror of Monte Rosa, knew
the value of a leg.) "Are you quite recovered? Sit down, dear
son. Take this armchair."

Settling himself on a damask sofa, the Pope cheerfully
waved aside Stephen's inquiry about his health. "The entire
matter," said His Holiness, "is summed up in a Neapolitan
proverb. 'A century from now, we shall all be bald.'" The
pontiff pointed to his white skullcap. "As you see, we are still
blessed with a few hairs." Sunlight, bouncing off the tessel-
lated pavement of St. Peter's Square, twinkled along the gold
rims of Achille Ratti's spectacles. "You yourself have grown
gray at the temples, Stefano. Pastoral cares?"

"No more than my share, Holy Father." The Bishop of

Hartfield placed his ad limina report in the pontiff's hand.
"Here is the detailed account of my episcopate. Not exactly
a chaplet of roses — as Your Holiness probably knows."

Pius XI fingered the document thoughtfully. "We have
studied the copy sent us by Archbishop Quarenghi. Considering the state of the world, it is an encouraging report. We
are particularly proud of your pastoral letter condemning the
sin of birth control, and are deeply honored that you buttressed your argument by quoting from our encyclical on
marriage."

The Holy Father leafed through the pages till he came to
Schedule A. "We are pleased, also, that you gave so generously to the community fund in your Diocese — even though
you — ah — depleted your reserves to do so."

The pontiff commended Stephen for the churches and
schools he had built during the depression. "That took courage," he murmured. "But even more courageous, in our opinion, is the establishment of the farming co-operatives in your
rural areas. As you may recall, this is a matter stressed by us
in *Quadragesimo anno*."

"I undertook the venture, Holy Father, because — as you
pointed out in *Quadragesimo anno* — rural dwellers have been
fearfully neglected in this industrial age. I must confess that
results in Hartfield have not, thus far, come up to my expecta-
tions."

Pius XI leaned forward to give his words emphasis. "Do
not be disheartened by a meager harvest, dear son. The fruit
will ripen slowly. Meanwhile, the Church must encourage
young priests to forgo brilliant urban careers in order to serve
neglected millions who spend their lives tilling the earth. Will
you carry back to your country and your diocese our special
prayer for Catholic action in rural parishes?"

"I shall do everything in my power, Holy Father, to further
the teachings of *Quadragesimo anno*," said Stephen.

"Thank you for that promise, dear son." The Pope gazed
broodingly through a tall window overlooking St. Peter's
Square. "We are much moved by the filial constancy and
obedience of our children in the New World. It is the eldest
of our daughters, Italy, who causes us most pain. Treaties
signed in good faith are disregarded. Our zeal for the Chris-

tian family is scorned. God Himself is subordinated to the pagan notion of State."

The pontiff's agitation mounted. "With the House of Savoy, we at least knew where we stood. But in this stucco Caesar — this self-idolater" — Achille Ratti spat the words out like fishbones — "there is neither constancy nor truth. His throat is an open sepulcher, his tongue trafficks in deceit."

Pius XI strode to his worktable and snatched up a fistful of handwritten sheets. "Il Duce thinks to dislodge us by bullying." The old Alpinist dug the soles of his red slippers into the carpet like a mountain climber feeling for a firm foothold. "He forgets that we are part mountain goat, and that our *pou sto* is the Rock of Peter."

Pou sto. A place whereon to stand! The foothold that Archimedes sighed for — and that Pius XI possessed!

"We are preparing an encyclical, *Non abbiamo bisogno,* which will condemn Il Duce's errors, expose his broken promises." As Pius XI read aloud from his manuscript, Stephen realized that the Pope's message was a mighty pry bar, a moral lever capable of moving the world.

Thou art indeed Peter, thought Stephen, and the gates of a totalitarian hell shall not prevail against you.

LEAVING the Holy Father, Stephen was in a state of tonic exhilaration. He scarcely heard the *maestro di camera* saying to a chamberlain: "Escort Bishop Fermoyle to Cardinal Pacelli's apartments." He followed a ruffed chamberlain through a series of antechambers to the Cardinal Secretary's suite on the floor below. Descending a grand staircase, Stephen was awakened from his cloud trance when his guide thrust out a sturdy leg in a mimic attempt to trip him flat on his face.

"*Furfantino!*" cried the chamberlain. The voice was oddly familiar. It was, in fact, the voice of Captain Orselli.

"Gaetano!" Stephen flung his arm around the velvet-caped shoulder of his old friend. "What blaggardry goes on here? Trip me, would you?" He clapped a headlock onto the ex-captain. "Your ruffs and capes fooled me, you false-bottomed Florentine."

Gaetano Orselli's beard — oiled, perfumed, but grizzled now — was brushing Stephen's cheek. "Most Excellent Excel-

lency — most air-treading Prince of Clerics! Fooled you, did I?
Ha-ha-ha. You were walking on clouds coming out of the Holy
Father's presence. Had I been a coalhole you'd have fallen into
me. *Gesù*, but I'm glad to see you, Stefano."

Stephen laughed. "How did a fearful Ghibelline like yourself ever break into these sacred precincts? Don't tell me *my*
prayers got you here."

Orselli blessed himself like a pious cutpurse standing before
a magistrate. "I am the victim of a woman's heaven-storming
wiles, Stefano. Novenas, rosaries, tons of the finest beeswax
candles, all have ascended in my behalf. Did I know this
would happen? Could one believe that a pirate Turk would
be converted into a papal gentleman — veloured, caped, easy
about the knees" — Orselli bounced in and out of a genuflection — "and *like* it? It is a miracle, Stefano, performed by that
most beautiful of creatures, Ghislana, my wife."

The name still hurt. Stephen covered the wound with a
question. "Did she convert you from Fascism, too? When we
last met you were showing me starry marvels in the constellation of Il Duce."

Orselli's beard was a drooping burgee. "I was gulled, like
so many others, by his promises of a greater Italy. He dazzled
us with trinkets of brass and glass. Ah, the misery this false
leader has poured over our people. Corruption, murder, degradation — these are his stock in trade." Orselli shook a disillusioned head. "Among my friends who dared protest, some
are rotting in Sardinian dungeons; others, luckier — are dead."

Stephen was genuinely puzzled. "Why do we hear so little
of this in America, Gaetano? Almost everyone there thinks of
Il Duce as Italy's smiling benefactor."

"Is it news that a man can smile and still be a villain?"

"Hamlet suggested that it *wasn't* news."

Orselli's snort was the Italian equivalent of "faugh." "What
would an English-speaking Dane know about such matters? In
the art of double-dealing, we Florentines lead the world. Our
methods are classic — yes, but adaptable, too. In Lorenzo's
time we affected the cloak and dagger" — Orselli gave his
cape a Borgia flourish. "Today — we merely add airplanes."

"What's so devilish stealthy about an airplane?"

From heights of pity, the Florentine smiled down. "Of itself, a plane is a fairly obvious piece of machinery. It is the *deployment* of the pieces that counts. Remember our little game of *Mühle*, Stefano? A feint here — an ambush there? Well, so it is with our planes."

"Whose planes?" asked Stephen.

Hand at mouth, Orselli whispered: "A company of patriotic gentlemen with whom I am leagued — incidentally, I assure you that neither the Holy Father nor anyone in the Vatican knows of our undertaking — decided some time ago to take countermeasures against Mussolini. We operate, in our small way, a kind of air ferry to whisk out poor devils that Il Duce would like to get his hands on."

Relishing the sauce of his own duplicity, Orselli went on. "We have two planes. One, a single-engine De Havilland, stands fair and free in the Municipal Airport for all to behold. The other, a ten-seater Caproni, lies hidden under a hedge on the Campagna. While Ovra agents nose about the cockpit of the De Havilland, the Caproni is over the Alps and far away."

"Devious chaps, you Florentines. And where do you land your passengers?"

"Paris, Brussels — London in a pinch."

Approaching the entrance to Cardinal Pacelli's suite, Orselli suddenly realized that official custody and private enjoyment of his old friend must soon end. He begged for a renewal of their loves. "So much to talk of, Stefano — so little time left in life. Can you not dine with us this evening? There will be just three of us. You and Ghislana may chat, while I drowse *en pantoufles* before the fire."

The permissive-proprietary quality of "you and Ghislana may chat" put a barb in Stephen. "Thanks for the invitation, Gaetano. If I am free . . ."

At the Cardinal Secretary's door, a chamberlain bowed. "His Excellency the Bishop of Hartfield," Orselli announced to a fellow functionary, who now led Stephen into the presence of the Cardinal Secretary of State.

MEETING Eugenio Pacelli was one of the outstanding experiences of Stephen's life. In physical appearance the Cardinal Secretary of State resembled an El Greco version of Abraham Lincoln. Lanky, almost gaunt, he combined the asceticism of a greater Quarenghi with the charm of a shrewder Merry del Val. At fifty-six his flesh stretched with taut virility over the bony structure of his face and body. Stephen had never seen eyes quite like Pacelli's. They had the uncompromising quality of a surveyor's transit; when they fixed on an object, that object had better be in plumb.

The Cardinal had heard many favorable things about his American visitor, and now proposed to test with eye and intellect everything he had heard. His outstretched hand said, "No protocol, please. More important business awaits us." Pacelli had learned of Stephen's operation. "Was there a miracle or not?" he asked smilingly.

"*Et mihi mirum est*" (I wonder myself), said Stephen. His light play on the Latin root of "miracle" delighted Pacelli. Neither his position as Archpriest of the Vatican Basilica nor his responsibility as Secretary of State had blunted his Roman love of wit. Himself a *maître d'escrime*, he valued a quick wrist in another.

Leading Stephen across the priceless tapestry carpet covering the floor of his workroom, the Cardinal Secretary paused at his desk. He had intended to bestow on his visitor some gift at the end of the interview — a medal, rosary, or precious relic — but the foil-like quality of his first exchange with Stephen demanded a gift more edged and instant. From among the many objects on his desk, Pacelli selected an especially beautiful letter opener. The handle was ivory, carved in the Byzantine manner; the shaft of the instrument was damascened steel; a delicate basketry of silver wire formed the guard. The letter opener was part poignard, part cross. Laying it across his wrist, handle toward Stephen, Pacelli said:

"We shall be writing often to each other in the future, dear Brother. When you open my letters with this gift (which contains a relic from the pectoral cross of Gregory VII), let it remind you of our first sparkling passage at arms."

Stephen accepted the accolade humbly. "I shall treasure this gift, Your Eminence. It is curiously, beautifully made" — he flexed the blade — "and your words give it a special temper."

Smiling, the Bishop of Hartfield reached into his pocket. "In my country when one is presented with a sharp-pointed gift, we give in return — a penny."

Pacelli took the coin, smiled *gratias,* then, placing the penny in the fob pocket of his cassock, led his guest to a luxurious divan. Pacelli's curiosity concerning American affairs was insatiable; the coming presidential election particularly fascinated him.

Seated against a backdrop of Pinturicchio's murals, Pacelli began: "I am always amazed," he said, "at the fury of your political campaigns and the peaceful manner in which your people accept the decision at the polls. How do you account for this seeming contradiction?"

Actually, the Cardinal Secretary was asking for a nutshell explanation of the American character. Not an easy assignment! How clarify, without taint of chauvinism, the secret of democratic government? How demonstrate to this European-trained diplomat the unique mintage of faith and energy struck off in the United States?

Inspiration served the Bishop of Hartfield. "If I may have my penny back for a moment, Your Eminence, I think it will help me answer your question."

Two heads bent over the penny in the Bishop's open palm. "This, our commonest coin, is a whole gallery of Americana," said Stephen. "As Your Eminence will note, one side bears the image of Abraham Lincoln and the word 'Liberty.' Image and word are synonymous. Both serve to remind my countrymen that government of, by, and for the people is their heritage — and responsibility."

"A noble conception," said Pacelli. "But is it not commonly misinterpreted? Do not many Americans hold that democracy derives its authority from the people rather than from God?"

"Doubtless such error exists in some minds, Your Eminence. But may I call your attention to the four words over Lincoln's head? *'In God We Trust.'* Deeply — unconsciously, perhaps — Americans know that God is the source of our trust in democracy."

Eugenio Pacelli was beginning to understand why the Holy Father regarded the Bishop of Hartfield so highly. He listened attentively as Stephen went on: "Your Eminence asks why Americans struggle so violently to elect a candidate, then accept the popular decision with so much composure." Stephen turned the penny over. "I think the answer is to be found in the motto on the reverse side of the coin."

" '*E pluribus unum,*' " mused Pacelli. "Out of many — one. Why, the words are open to mystical interpretation!"

"True, Your Eminence — though I think few understand it that way. In actual practice it means that out of many conflicting views, out of deep and grievous difference, springs our hard-won ideal of unity."

The talk lengthened out. Pacelli, guiding the conversation, led it inevitably to the subject that was disturbing all Rome.

"As the Holy Father has doubtless told you," he said, "we are confronted by a breakdown of negotiations between the Quirinal and the Holy See. It is, I must confess, a painful situation. No honorable solution presents itself. Our protests are ignored . . . diplomatic measures have been exhausted."

Stephen ventured a question. "Is there no way of enlisting the support of the people? Surely the majority of Italians must disapprove of Mussolini's tactics."

Pacelli's fingers nursed a bony jaw. "Police methods have terrorized the population. Every medium of communication is controlled. Strange as it may sound to an American, there exists no means of sounding opinion inside Italy."

"Il Duce is sensitive to world regard. Might not foreign correspondents report the Vatican's plight to their papers?"

"Fascist censorship is ironclad," said Pacelli. "Several courageous men are now in prison for trying to break it. The only dispatches emanating from Italy are what my journalist friends call 'sugar pieces.' "

Both men knew that the encyclical lying on the pontiff's desk on the floor above was no sugar piece. Pacelli's ingrained sense of diplomacy prevented him from mentioning the encyclical; Stephen, on his part, did not feel at liberty to disclose his knowledge of the manuscript. Instead, he chose to ask a hypothetical question:

"Suppose the Holy Father were to frame a vigorous indictment of the Fascist regime? Would Mussolini dare block its publication?"

Pacelli, recognizing Stephen's tact, acknowledged it with a smile. "I can inform Your Excellency that His Holiness is preparing such a statement. And I may add that Il Duce has threatened to execute the chief of his secret police — a creature named Maranacci — if a syllable of the Pope's protest reaches the outer world."

"Suppose someone were entrusted with the task of delivering the Pope's message to the London *Times* or *Le Soir* in Paris?"

Pacelli had heard much of American resourcefulness; now he saw it personified in the Bishop of Hartfield. "The person carrying such a document would run certain risks. If caught, he'd be tied to a chair and shot in the back."

"A macabre touch," said Stephen, "but one that wouldn't particularly frighten two men of my acquaintance."

For the next five minutes the Bishop of Hartfield outlined a course of action — simple, swift, and reasonably certain — that would enable the Pope to present his case to the court of world opinion. The end of the interview found Pacelli's lanky figure leading the way, without benefit of papal chamberlains, to the Holy Father's study. There was another conference, at which Gaetano Orselli found himself surrounded by high-ranking prelates. That night, and for three nights thereafter, lights burned in the pontiff's workroom.

At dawn, four days later, a double-engined Caproni took off from a lonely spot on the Roman Campagna. It crossed the Alps, landed at Le Bourget. At noon, an American bishop handed a copy of *Non abbiamo bisogno,* to the managing editor of *Le Soir.* English copies of the text were wired to the *London Times* and *The New York Times.* Next morning, newspapers of the world published Pius XI's stinging condemnation of a Fascist philosophy that exalted the State above God, the Christian family, and the individual soul.

Il Duce, reading all about it at breakfast, sent for the head of his secret police, and watched the man grovel till shot. Fourteen Ovra agents were banished to Sardinia. But the damage had been done. World protests crashed so violently against the balcony of the Palazzo Venezia that negotiations were reopened between Quirinal and Vatican. The last act of the diplomatic drama saw Il Duce and King Victor Emmanuel riding in state to the Vatican. The King knelt, and Il Duce uncovered to a red-slippered figure standing on an invisible rock.

Il Duce never learned, and Victor Emmanuel never cared, that a link existed between the publication of *Non abbiamo bisogno* and the new honors bestowed by Pius XI upon Bishop Stephen Fermoyle. Possibly no such link did exist. Perhaps the Holy Father, talking matters over with his brilliant Secretary of State, thought that the See of Hartfield, with its teeming cities and resourceful leader, should become an Archdiocese. At any rate, Stephen Fermoyle was named Archbishop of Hartfield on January 2, 1933. The appointment was announced to the nominee by a papal brief dated the eighth and preconized in the consistory of January eighteenth.

At forty-four, Stephen found himself the youngest Archbishop in the United States.

CHAPTER 2

MERELY TO BE ALIVE in the spring of 1933 was, for most Americans, a gloriously exciting business. An inspired leader was telling his people: "We have nothing to fear but fear. This great nation will endure as it has endured, will revive and prosper." Demoralized young men who had rarely seen a pay check were taken off street corners and put to work clearing forests, building dams and levees. There was an upsurge of creative energy as musicians, painters, and writers exercised talents that had been crumbling to decay. Some called it "boondoggling," but the President defended these projects on the simple ground that they kept human beings — American citizens — from economic and moral ruin.

While hope fermented throughout the nation and juke boxes played *Happy Days Are Here Again*, the Archbishop of Hartfield — ineligible for New Deal aid — watched his cash reserves dwindle to the vanishing point. Temperamentally Stephen was not given to worries about money. His training as a curate under Ned Halley had inoculated him against the financial cares that infest the days (and ruin the nights) of many priests. Yet as overseer of an important ecclesiastical domain, and as co-ordinator of some three hundred parishes, Stephen could not ignore the fact that some parts of his Archdiocese were more prosperous than others. Rectors of industrial parishes had comparatively large sums at their disposal, while many rural pastors existed on a hand-to-mouth basis. How might these economic peaks and valleys be leveled off into a somewhat fairer plane?

Feeling the need of counsel, Stephen made a flying visit to Alfeo Quarenghi. At dinner, and during the long discussion that followed, the Apostolic Delegate made many helpful recommendations but steadfastly refused to cast a deciding vote. "The problem is yours, Stefano. By canon law you have the authority to make whatever financial arrangement will most benefit your Archdiocese. Why not thrash the matter out in a diocesan synod?"

Quarenghi's suggestion was the one that Stephen followed. He returned to Hartfield, and in the manner prescribed by Church law convoked a synod for the purpose of adjusting the financial inequalities that were hampering his Archdiocese.

As defined by Benedict XIV, a diocesan synod is "a lawful assembly convoked by the bishop, in which he gathers together the priests and clerics of his diocese for the purpose of doing and deliberating on matters concerning the pastoral care." On the feast of the Epiphany — January 6, 1934 — Stephen's decree of convocation was affixed to the doors of the Cathedral, and thereafter published on three successive Sundays in the parish churches. Early in February, some two hundred rectors assembled in the Cathedral to hear Mass and prepare themselves spiritually for the deliberative councils about to take place.

Although the decrees of a synod are proposed by the bishop and receive their authority from him alone, it is in consonance with the mind of the Church that all interested voices be heard. And at this synod they *were* heard — so thumpingly that the chandeliers in the auditorium of St. Joseph's Seminary (where the business meetings took place) tinkled like glass mobiles in a high wind. Aided by Ambrose Cannell, Stephen had prepared comprehensive agenda. Minor business opened the meeting; there was to be a new architectural advisory board with powers of reviewing all building plans. Because Hartfield had no Catholic newspaper, a committee canvassed ways and means of establishing one. All was harmonious until the reorganization of diocesan finances came up for discussion. Whereupon, touched in their pocketbook nerve — probably the most sensitive part of their anatomy — several prosperous rectors emitted screams of genuine pain.

Stephen was far too clever to go into open synod without holding some preliminary talks on the new bookkeeping system he had in mind. At an informal meeting in his study he frankly laid the problem before a picked group of diocesan leaders. "We are all aware," he began, "that serious inequities exist in distribution of diocesan monies. Under the present system, the Bishop receives from individual parishes a cathedral tax amounting to less than ten per cent of their total income. Under this arrangement, some of the older, more financially favored parishes have accumulated sizable bank balances, while in other parts of the Diocese, actual poverty cripples the work of the Church."

The rectors listened, each in character. Dan O'Laughlin, pastor of the richest parish in Fairhaven, pulled his ear lobe pugnaciously; the wattle under Michael ("Cozy") Kernan's chin quivered perceptibly. What was the Archbishop about to propose?

"The time has come," continued Stephen, "when the overall welfare of the Diocese must be our guiding consideration. At tomorrow's meeting I plan to introduce a resolution which I trust will not seem too arbitrary." He turned to Ambrose Cannell: "Will the Vicar-General please read the proposed decree?"

Amby Cannell's Oxford intonation never fell more gratingly on Hibernian ears. "On and after July 1, 1934," he began, "all parish revenues from whatever sources shall be payable on a monthly basis to the diocesan treasury. . . ."

"Payable — *where?*" Dan O'Laughlin went gray about the gills.

"Do I hear what I hear?" Cozy Kernan asked in consternation.

"Please permit the Vicar-General to continue," said Stephen.

Amby read on: "The rectors of the several parishes shall accompany their monthly remittances with a complete statement of expenses. The term 'expenses' is here construed to mean the salaries of the rector and his assistants, the upkeep of the parish church, school, and other institutions within the pastor's jurisdiction."

Dan O'Laughlin broke in sarcastically: "Would that include, now, a cup of tea for the cop on the beat?"

"It would," said Stephen. "It would also include tea for the rector's sisters, cousins, and aunts, as well as side trips to Florida and other little perquisites similar in nature. Read on, Ambrose."

The Vicar-General proceeded: "The total of such expenses shall be deducted from the monies forwarded to the archdiocesan treasury. The remainder shall accrue to the Archdiocese of Hartfield, a corporation sole, to be expended at the discretion of the trustee, Stephen Fermoyle."

Groans . . . a pushing back of chairs . . . cries of "Your Grace" . . . "I must protest."

"One at a time, gentlemen," said Stephen. "Everyone will have a chance to be heard. I think I saw Father O'Laughlin's hand first."

Dan O'Laughlin made a blunt statement to the effect that the proposal was "confiscatory," socialistic, unheard-of, and not in accordance with canon law. His remarks were vigorously seconded by Michael Kernan, who declared that he would carry the case to the Apostolic Delegate for a ruling.

"That is, of course, your privilege, Father," replied Stephen. "I must inform you, however, that the Apostolic Delegate assures me my proposal is quite in accordance with canon law. . . . Are there any other speakers?"

As the discussion went forward, younger men arose to defend the Archbishop's proposal. Most eloquent among them was Father Gregor Potocki, Polish-speaking pastor of St. Ladislaus', a poverty-stricken parish in the tobacco-growing region west of the Hartfield River. "The proposed change will enable the Archbishop to pump life-giving funds through the outlying, almost atrophied veins of the Diocese," declared Father Potocki. "In no spirit of hostility to city parishes, but with a simple plea for fairness to all, I believe that the decree should be accepted."

Inevitably, but with much opposition from senior rectors, the decree was accepted by the synod on the next day. The resolutions of the synod were published; bound copies were deposited in the chancery archives, others were sent to the Apostolic Delegate, who forwarded them to Rome. In due time Stephen received a letter from the Cardinal Prefect of the Congregation of the Council congratulating him on the introduction of a fiscal system so well adapted to the needs of his Archdiocese.

UNTIL the new money actually began coming in, Stephen was desperately pressed for cash. In mid-Lent, 1934, he was obliged to borrow fifty thousand dollars from the Hartfield Trust Company to meet current expenses. A week later, half of this money had been spent on urgent needs. Then, quite unexpectedly, Stephen was confronted by an extraordinary opportunity.

The Argus Press was for sale. Cheap!

Owen Starkey brought in the news with the morning mail. "I hear Ollie Greenleaf wants to sell his press," said Father Owen.

Stephen knew of the Argus Press, of its fully equipped plant quite capable of printing the Catholic newspaper acutely needed in Hartfield. Private attempts to provide such a paper had failed, either through lack of capital or dimness of editorial vision. Of the half million Catholics under Stephen's jurisdiction, few had the vaguest idea of what was going on outside their own parish.

Stephen tried to keep his voice casual. "Why does Greenleaf want to sell? Losing money?"

"No, asthma. This climate's killing him. He's got to get away."

Momentarily Stephen brushed aside the publisher's crown, then decided to try it on just for size. "Call him up, Ownie. Say I'll be down to look at the place after lunch."

The printer's ink in Stephen's blood caused him considerable suffering that afternoon. With Ollie Greenleaf wheezing at his side, he inspected presses and equipment that had originally cost well over seventy-five thousand dollars. There were two linotypes, a job press, a guillotine-style papercutter, saddle binders, tons of type in all fonts and sizes. And in the middle of the shop stood a flat-bed press that could easily handle a weekly edition of an eight-page newspaper. Stephen could see Vol. I, No. 1, of *The Hartfield Angelus* (not a bad name, at that) coming off the press right now.

Choking with asthma and grief, Ollie Greenleaf said he was willing to let the whole thing go for twenty-five thousand dollars.

Supreme self-restraint kept Stephen from closing the deal then and there. "I'll sleep on it, Mr. Greenleaf," he said, tearing himself away from the shop. As he left, two other prospective buyers were on their knees examining the flat-bed press.

Little sleep came to the Archbishop that night. Fantasy wrestled with fact as the circulation of *The Hartfield Angelus* mounted from fifteen to forty thousand between midnight and two A.M. At that point, a temporary cooling process set in. Undoubtedly the Diocese needed a newspaper; undeniably the Argus Press was a bargain. But to spend one's last twenty-five thousand dollars on a printing press! What would the Holy Father say about that?

Stephen came out of his bedroom next morning with the question still unanswered. At the Secret of the Mass he prayed for guidance. At breakfast, reading the *Item* headlines: "Legislature Opposes Bus Transportation for Parochial Students," he felt anew the necessity of having a diocesan newspaper to state the Catholic side of the case.

Stephen had practically decided to buy the Argus Press when Father Gregor Potocki, drawn and haggard about the eyes, entered the Archbishop's study for the day's first conference.

"Your Grace," said Father Potocki, "the tobacco co-operatives are falling apart. Something must be done about them."

It wasn't an ultimatum; merely a statement of fact. Father Potocki had valiantly undertaken the tobacco project during the early part of the depression. His plan — a bold one — envisioned a shift of Polish Catholics from industrial city slums to the tobacco-growing counties west of the Hartfield River. Clear advantages, human and economic, stood to be gained by such a migration. The Poles were natural farmers; gainfully employed at tobacco-raising, they would become self-sustaining citizens. Furthermore, as Father Gregor pointed out, Polish-speaking pastors moving about their rural parishes could give their compatriots the personal and sacramental attention certainly not given to them in large cities. On paper the plan was most attractive; in practice it had worked out disappointingly.

Stephen knew exactly where the hitch had occurred. Tobacco greedily drains phosphates and potassium from the soil; to produce a marketable crop, tons of commercial fertilizer must be poured back onto every acre each year. The price of these chemicals, rigidly maintained by a fertilizer combine, was a barrier that Father Potocki had never been able to hurdle. His optimism and eloquence had persuaded about a hundred Polish-American families to settle in the rather bleak fields comprising St. Ladislaus' parish. But tobacco would not grow on optimism alone. Fertilizer, curing sheds, and modern tools were needed. Unable to buy these, the tobacco co-operative had languished. And now, as Father Potocki had said, they were falling apart.

To hearten the courageous young priest, Stephen asked for an itemized statement of what was actually required to keep the St. Ladislaus project afloat.

"State your minimum needs, Father," said the Archbishop, "and, mind you, I mean minimum."

Father Potocki consulted no memorandum. "We need one thousand tons of commercial fertilizer, two hundred thousand feet of shiplap for the repair of curing sheds, and a tractor for plowing and cultivating. The total is twenty-one thousand dollars."

Can't anything be had for less than twenty thousand dollars these days? thought Stephen. To avoid the scrutiny of Father Potocki's haggard eyes, Stephen walked to the window of his study. He knew that unless planting began immediately, discouraged Polish farmers would drift back to city slums. He also knew that if he didn't close with Ollie Greenleaf that afternoon, the Argus Press would be snapped up by someone else. Stated in simple terms, the Archbishop's problem came down to this:

Was a diocesan newspaper more important than a few Polish families? *Honestly now, how about it?*

Stephen had little knowledge of Poles. They gibbered in an outlandish language, ate cabbage, and quite successfully resisted American ideas of sanitation. In the choir of Stephen's affections, the Poles trolled most unmusical staves.

On the other hand, how simply wonderful to have a newspaper! How very much in keeping with the time spirit — how desirable ("imperative" was not too strong a word) to record the daily activities of the Diocese, to link parish with parish — to inform, educate, publicize — and, quite incidentally, be publicized in return! There would be a literary column, a sports page (*mens sana in corpore sano*), aggressive editorials condemning birth control, Communism, and improper movies. Other papers would quote from the columns of the *Angelus*. All over the United States, people would hear about Archbishop Fermoyle's progressive program in matters of — ah, well, read all about it in *The Hartfield Angelus* . . . Subscribe now.

Very enticing.

Against such enticements Stephen heard only one voice of protest. It came from a bespectacled, white-skullcapped man whose picture hung behind his desk.

"*We must encourage young priests to forgo brilliant urban careers in order to serve neglected millions who till the earth.*"

Well, here was a young priest begging for an opportunity to help his neglected flock of earth tillers. Multiply Gregor Potocki by ten, then by ten hundred, and the problem of Catholic action in rural America would be solved.

Stephen remembered his promise to Pius XI. "*I shall do everything in my power, Holy Father, to further the teachings of* Quadragesimo anno."

Thrusting aside the publisher's crown, Stephen put his hand to the co-operative plow. He sat down at his desk, wrote a check for twenty thousand dollars, and handed it to the Polish priest.

"Buy fertilizer and equipment with this, Gregor. And when the tobacco crop begins to come in, I hope you will take me through your fields."

ON EASTER MONDAY, under the rays of an auspicious sun, spring planting began in the parish of St. Ladislaus.

Tractor-drawn plows turned over gleaming furrows. By hand the seeds were sown and covered with loamy earth. Fertilizer spreaders scattered rich chemicals between the furrows. April rains and May sun brought green shoots peeping. Now before the beaming sun became too hot, vast tents of gauze netting were spread over the tobacco fields. Through June and July the broad leaves flourished. When Stephen visited St. Ladislaus' in August, a bumper crop of fine shade-grown tobacco was being harvested. Men were cutting the tender top leaves. *"Bogo Pomorzek"* (God gives), they would say, as Stephen and Father Potocki passed. *"Pomorzek bogo"* (Give to God), replied Father Potocki.

Women and children carried the leaves to the curing sheds, where they were bound into bunches and suspended from rafters. Charcoal braziers glowed upward from earthen floors; ruby gleams rising to meet the overhanging green bathed the interior of the curing sheds with light that changed from aquamarine to amber as the tobacco dried out.

Early in September, buyers from the cigar factories came to St. Ladislaus'; the entire crop was auctioned at excellent prices. Thirty thousand pounds of prime shade-grown tobacco were bought as wrappers for domestic cigars. Another ten thousand pounds, cheaper in grade, were sold as "filler."

After paying part of its loan to the Archdiocese, and setting aside five thousand dollars for next spring's fertilizer, the St. Ladislaus cooperative distributed profits amounting to $13,200 among ninety-one Polish families.

No great matter for jubilation, one might say — four months' hard work at a day-labor wage. But the people of St. Ladislaus' parish seemed to think otherwise. On October 1, they held a harvest festival to praise the Giver of earthly bounty, and invited their Archbishop to attend the festivities.

In the largest of the curing sheds, a long table was heaped up with salami, sauerkraut, and loaves of black bread. From a huge kettle simmering over an open fire, women ladled cabbage soup enriched by ham bones. With Ambrose Cannell at his side, Stephen blessed the steaming caldron, then took his place at the head of the long table. A fifteen-year-old boy, his golden hair brass-colored by sun, offered bread to the Archbishop. The boy was slender, strong; his hands beautiful as fragments of Phidias.

"What is your name?" asked Stephen.

"Conrad Szalay, Your Grace."

"Do you work in the tobacco fields, Conrad?"

"Yes, Archbishop. In summer I help with the curing. In winter I go to high school."

Father Potocki spoke up proudly. "Conrad is an excellent violinist, Your Grace. Later, he will play for us."

The harvest dinner began. Stephen's preconceptions of the Polish race vanished with the cabbage soup. He had never seen human beings so spontaneously gay as Father Potocki's people. They devoured Gargantuan quantities of sausage, sauerkraut, and black bread, laughing, gesticulating all the while, not like Americans, Irishmen, or Italians, but in the barbaric, half-Eastern manner of Slavs. Then, instead of falling asleep like Germans or Swedes, they leapt from the table to tread out bouncing krakowiak measures to the accompaniment of flute, fiddle, and accordion.

As the moon climbed they leapt higher. After an hour there was a pause while the dancers flung themselves on the ground to get their breath. Then a cry went up: "Conrad . . . Conrad Szalay. . . . Play for us, play, Conrad."

Gregor Potocki leaned toward his Archbishop. "Now Your Grace will hear something."

The golden-haired lad who had offered Stephen bread stepped into the circle of firelight by the soup caldron. Tuning his instrument, he was a modest, unassuming boy; tucking the cheap violin under his chin, he became a gypsy baron playing for an encampment on the edge of the steppes between Poland and Russia. Taking a krakowiak theme, Conrad improvised on it with pyrotechnic skill. The sadness of a dismembered nation, the grief of a passionate, melancholy people, wailed through his improvisation. Then, as if remembering the presence of cultivated men, he broke off abruptly and bowed to Stephen.

"Variations on *The Scarlet Sarafan*, by Wieniawski," he announced.

Amby Cannell leaned toward his Archbishop. "A concert piece, full of technical difficulties."

The technical difficulties of the Wieniawski showpiece troubled Conrad Szalay not at all. Accompanied by an accordion, he shook *The Scarlet Sarafan* like a boy rifling a plum tree; double stops and harmonics were thrown off in a prodigious display of virtuosity.

"Good Lord!" breathed Amby Cannell. "That technique! Where does it come from?"

At the end of the impromptu concert, Stephen arose and walked toward the young violinist. The Archbishop's knowledge of music was far from professional; he could only express his pleasure and gratitude by shaking the boy's hand.

"You have a tremendous gift, Conrad. Will you come and play for me some time?"

The boy blushed. "Whenever Your Grace wishes," he said simply.

Ambrose Cannell's compliment showed more musicianship. "You play beautifully, Conrad. I don't know which I liked better: your improvisations on the krakowiak theme or your masterly handling of Wieniawski. Who taught you to play?" he asked curiously.

The boy glanced at Father Potocki, who in turn beckoned to a gnarled, bent creature standing behind the young virtuoso.

"May I present Max Lessau?" said Father Gregor. "This is the teacher who has perfected Conrad's talent."

"Perfected he is not yet," said the gnarled one, who seemed quite unimpressed by the hierarchy's presence. "All through the *Sarafan* I heard pigs squealing. Half the blame must be put on the instrument. What is it but a varnished cigar box?" In the dimming firelight Max Lessau resembled a musical Vulcan criticizing the smithy work of a promising apprentice. "Still, time and hard work may choke the pig-squealing with butter — eh, Conrad?"

With a decently courteous nod to Stephen and Bishop Cannell, the gnarled maestro limped off.

"And who is Max Lessau?" asked Stephen, as Father Potocki accompanied his superiors to their car.

"It's a strange story, Your Grace. Max is a Jewish peddler who comes among our people, selling holy pictures, statues — you know the kind of thing — from a black oilcloth pack. Only he wasn't always a peddler. As a young man, Max was a child prodigy — gave concerts in Warsaw, Paris, Berlin. Then at twenty-seven, arthritis stiffened every joint in his body. Career, fame, mode of support, all vanished. He came to this country around 1915. Couldn't speak English, so he turned peddler. One day he heard Conrad scraping on a three-dollar fiddle and offered to teach him how to play. For the past ten years, Max has hammered dáily at his pupil. You heard the results tonight."

Sorrowfully, Father Potocki shook his head. "The sad part of the story is that Max Lessau's getting old. Peddling saps his strength. It's only a question of- time before he's completely crippled."

On his way back to Hartfield with Ambrose Cannell, a quiet happiness — the afterglow of his evening with Father Potocki's people — warmed Stephen's heart and mind. Laughter, dancing, music — were not these timbrel thanksgivings acceptable and pleasing to the Giver of all bounty? And what a paean of praise the young violinist had drawn from his instrument. Not perfect yet, as the gnarled Max Lessau had said . . .

Stephen spoke to his companion: "Amby, what would you say if we established a scholarship in music — called it the St. Cecilia Prize — and gave it to some deserving student?"

"I'd say it was God-marked, Your Grace."

That was the beginning of an award for musical study granted annually by the Archdiocese of Hartfield. For three years it went to Conrad Szalay, who practiced seven hours a day under the direction of his crippled teacher, Max Lessau. The pig-squealing (heard only by that savage perfectionist) was drowned in the melting butter of Conrad's flawless technique. After a year, his varnished cigar box was replaced by a two-hundred-and-fifty-dollar German trade fiddle, but Max Lessau still grumbled.

"Could Kreisler make music on a packing case?" he would moan. "*Lieber Gott* . . . sooner or later, the boy must have a real violin."

CHAPTER 3

To STEPHEN the passing years brought a predominance of good. His Archdiocese flourished, his plans marched, his friends prospered. Judiciously, he brought forward younger men to assume key posts in chancery and parish; by 1935 his principal aides were — with the exception of Ambrose Cannell

— all under forty. Owen Starkey no longer trembled at the
scowl of clerical top sergeants. When he said to a grumbling
pastor, "Thats the way His Grace wants it" — that's the way
it was. Gregor Potocki's farm program attracted more Poles
from urban to rural parishes; his thriving tobacco co-operatives proved that spiritual as well as material fruits can be
grown when the seed falls on good ground.

Ambrose Cannell, now an auxiliary bishop, was developing
into the combination of executive and field officer that every
ecclesiastical general prays for. He took responsibility without
usurping power. Plain chanting and liturgical responses from
the congregation — dreams that had slipped through Milky
Lyons' feeble fingers — became realities under Bishop Cannell's vigorous hand. Putting his architectural ideas to work,
Amby planned and supervised the building of three modern
churches, clean-lined adaptations of the Gothic. In the magazine *Liturgy* he expounded the startling theory that an altar,
being the stage on which the drama of Calvary is re-enacted,
should be clearly visible from any seat in God's house.

"Keep the interior of the church uncluttered," urged Bishop
Cannell. "Let the altar stand forth like a jewel in the simplest
of settings." In certain quarters these ideas met traditional
resistance — a matter of small concern to Amby, who knew
that his chief was solidly behind him.

With money flowing in from all parts of the Archdiocese
(the new bookkeeping system was in full swing now), Stephen
was able to apportion funds where they were most needed.
To Misericordia House he allotted ten thousand dollars
annually; no longer were the Geraldine nuns obliged to beg
with basins at factory gates. Though Sister Martha Annunziata's refuge was treated to major repairs, it still remained a
drafty, under-equipped barracks. A real hospital where incurables could receive medical and spiritual comfort in their last
agonies would cost upwards of three hundred thousand dollars. To find such a sum became one of the Archbishop's long-
range goals.

In the depression-charred cities of Hartfield's industrial
plain, Stephen continued to maintain diocesan machine shops.
Hundreds of young artisans were trained in the key skills of
casting, die-cutting, and toolmaking — trades that underlie the

whole structure of America's industrial system. As the assembly line of economic production began to whir again, graduates of these crafts schools found jobs as foremen and skilled machinists in the metalworking factories north of Hartfield.

Late in 1935, Stephen allayed the printer's itch that had long troubled him, by publishing the first edition of *The Hartfield Angelus*. On Amby Cannell's advice, he had rejected several opportunities to buy a press; it was easier and cheaper, the Archbishop discovered, to have the actual printing done by someone else. Carefully he assembled a small staff — mostly laymen — then put the whole operation in charge of Father Terence Malley, a young priest with a flair for journalism. Stephen's instructions to Father Malley were simple:

"Bear in mind, Father, we're not competing with the Associated Press or the New York tabloids. Coverage of world events is impossible. Just give Roman Catholics in Hartfield some idea of what's going on in the Archdiocese and their own parish. Play up legislation or any other news that affects the Church. Consult me if you're in doubt about the official angle."

Father Malley followed his Archbishop's instructions to the letter; the paper filled a need, caught on. At the end of a year, with the *Angelus* going into twenty thousand Catholic homes, Terence Malley could report: "If we can pick up another five thousand readers — and sell a few more ads — we'll be self-supporting."

Across the bright sky of Stephen's personal life, occasional dark clouds began to run. He was reaching that age when the older men who had played decisive roles in his life were beginning to fail or pass away. Dollar Bill Monaghan had died, leaving an empty chair in the council of elders who had tutored Stephen's youth. Lawrence Glennon was ailing, too; his climbing blood pressure brought cruel headaches, dizziness, and occasional blackouts. When on the Cardinal's seventy-seventh birthday, Stephen inquired: "How does Your Eminence feel?" Glennon replied with the grim *mot*: "As well as I ever did — for about ten minutes a day."

Inoperable cataracts were forming on Corny Deegan's eyes. Doomed to blindness, and no longer able to play his favorite role of *deus ex machina*, the contractor-Knight sat miserably idle in his magnificent home on the banks of the upper Charles. During one of Stephen's visits, Corny attempted — not too successfully — to accept his fate with Christian resignation.

"They tell me, Steve," he said, "that a man marooned on an iceberg dreams mostly of tropic seas. Well, as the shadows drift in on me, I find myself remembering the wonderful eye power I used to have. Would you believe that when I was a hod carrier I could tell how much a brick weighed just by *looking* at it?"

The bitter present engulfed him. "Today I couldn't tell the difference between a brick and a gray goose's wing, unless" — he blinked a rheumy eye at his visitor — "unless it fell on me."

"The only thing that's going to fall on you, Corny, is God's peace — gentler than any goose feather. Lie back in the gloaming of a good life — and let it waft down on you."

Corny's gloom did not lighten. "Before I can feel that gentle waftery, Steve, there's spadework to be done on a buried corpse — my conscience." The Knight of St. Sylvester took off on one of his notorious circlings around O'Houlihan's barn. "You mightn't suspect it, Steve, but a contractor is open to fearful temptations. Many's the time I've cut a corner here or there, shaved a specification while the architect wasn't looking, dumped a shovelful of sand where cement ought to go, or passed off a ton or two of shale for honest traprock." Dolor and shame mingled in the Knight's confession. "Things like that come back to plague me now."

Without condoning the practice of short measure, Stephen tried to comfort his old friend. "Stop worrying about it, Corny. None of your buildings ever caved in, did they?"

"Oh, it was never that bad, Steve. 'Tis only that now and then — I — I skimped a bit, and the memory of it presses sore on my heart."

The priest in Stephen came forward. "What would you like to do about it? Restitution is always good for the soul."

"That's what I knew you'd say, Steve. But since I never kept books on my skimpings — I wouldn't know exactly where to send the cement, the crushed stone, or the money." Corny lifted his dimming eyes hopefully. "I was thinking, Your Grace, that perhaps I might heap up all the skimped material into a noble building somewhere. My mind turns to a hospital or an institution for the aged and decrepit. Would you be knowing where such a building is needed?"

"I might, Corny." Visions of a new Misericordia House flashed upon the Archbishop's inner eye. The better to ease his friend's conscience, Stephen drew a desolate word picture of the Geraldine retreat for incurables, then touched up the facts with a brush of rhetoric. "The place is little more than a stable, Corny. You should hear the wind rattling the loose clapboards! A heavy fall of snow would snap the rooftree entirely."

The wind and snow did it. At a stroke, Corny could clear his conscience and assume his loved role of fixer. Off the penitential mat he bounced, swinging both arms.

"Send your architect to his drafting board at once, Stephen. Let him specify nothing but the best. Granite foundations, steel and firebrick construction throughout. Copper roof, marble trim — nothing's too good for those poor souls passing away in agony. I'll talk to my lawyer about conveyances this very afternoon."

Corny Deegan never saw the handsome new Misericordia House that he gave to the Archdiocese of Hartfield, but he was very much present when the cornerstone of Vermont granite settled into place. His hodlike hand passed over the quartz-speckled rock, felt the huge I-beams standing in place, and fingered the cement pouring out of the giant mixers.

"No skimping here, Stephen," he murmured. A gray goose feather settling over a field at twilight could not have fallen more peacefully than the syllables of Corny Deegan's atonement.

DIN FERMOYLE was failing. He carried a cane now, a blackthorn that gave him the look of an ambulatory tripod whenever he walked abroad. Mornings were spent in "getting his strength up"; then, after Celia had fixed him a bite of lunch, the retired motorman would hobble down to the carbarns for a pipe and a chat with Bartholomew ("Batty") Glynn, likewise retired. On sunny days the pair sat on a bench outside the octagonal dispatcher's box that had once been Batty's domain. Too old for dispatching, Glynn was just coming of age as a Biblical commentator. What a knack he had for

expounding the sublime truths of Ecclesiastes and Isaiah —
one ear cocked to the Red Sox games on his portable radio!
"Hark, Din, to the majesty of this," Batty would say, tracing
the verse with a heavy fingernail. " *I have seen all things
under the sun, and behold, all is vanity and vexation of spirit.*'
Was ever such wisdom uttered by man?" In the midst of
Batty's exegesis, the Yankees would score a run. "Vexation, is
it? What would them Old Testament buggers know about it?
. . . If Tris Speaker were in center field now, his throw-in
would have nipped that runner at the plate."

When the game ended, or the flow of Batty's wisdom grew
thin, Din would start for home. The gradient of Woodlawn
Avenue steepened every day. At the first hydrant, Din would
pause for a lungful of breath; his next stop was Pat Creedon's
gatepost, where Pat's children (or were they his grandchil-
dren?) were playing hopscotch. Leaning heavily on his blackthorn, Din would take eighteen or twenty steps more; then
halfway up the steep ascent he would turn to gaze backward
at the vale of all his yesterdays. The crest of the hill was
gained by a dogged foot-by-foot climb till he reached Number
47 — still boxy, brown, and graceless, but mortgage-free now,
thanks to the generosity of his sons and daughters.

On June 2, 1935, Din climbed the hill more slowly than
usual, took a longer look at the vale behind him, and entered
the back door of his home. He greeted his wife with a pleasant
word or two, so as not to worry her, then went into the parlor
and lay down on the sofa for a bit of rest.

A few moments later he cried: "Ceil, Ceil," in an odd gasping sort of voice. Five minutes later he was dead.

Celia Fermoyle told her son Stephen the manner of his
father's passing.

"He came home from the carbarns where he sometimes
spent an hour or two puffing at his pipe and listening to Batty
Glynn explain the whole world from the beginning. 'The gift
of tongues was on Batty, this afternoon,' said Din, coming in
the kitchen door. 'At one time there, just before Gehrig hit a
homer with two on, Batty had the Book of Psalms in pieces
all over the carbarn floor — but when the game ended, he put
them together like one of your patchwork quilts, Ceil.' 'Did
you stand up and give him an argument, Din?' I asked. 'I did

not,' said Din. 'The language was pouring out of the man, so I let it pour.'

"Well, with that, Son dear, your father went into the parlor to take off his shoes and lie down while I went on getting supper. Beans, brown bread, and tea we were having, just the two of us. I was taking the bean pot out of the oven when I heard him call, 'Ceil, Ceil,' in a stranglish voice. I ran in, and there he was lying on the sofa, struggling for breath, his hand at the buttons of his balbriggan undershirt, and a glazy look in his eyes. 'What is it, Din? I'll call Dr. Hardigan.' 'No,' he said, 'by the time the doctor gets here, it'll be too late. Kneel by my side, Dubhe.' '"

Celia buried her face in Stephen's arm. "That was the name he used to call me when first we met, Son — the name of a wondrous star it is. . . ."

Stephen knew the star. Below Polaris it burned in high magnitude, a sign to navigators, pointer nearest to the Pole. Had this gray, withered woman in his arms once been the particular bright star in love's firmament?

" 'Kneel by me, Dubhe,' said Din, 'and put your cheek on mine. 'Twill make it easier, and harder, darling, to break the promise I made you.' So I knelt by him, Son, knowing the promise he meant — the only one he ever broke in all our married life. Then 'Cumhyll,' I cried, 'O my proud-walking one, let me go first, as you always promised. . . .' "

Celia dried her eyes. "But he went without me, saying a very strange thing."

"What did he say, Mother?"

"I didn't catch the exact words. Something about a 'watch in the night.' Do you know what he meant, Son?"

"Yes. It's a verse from the Eighty-ninth Psalm, and it goes: 'A thousand years in Thy sight are as yesterday, which is past. And as a watch in the night.' "

God grant I may die, thought Stephen, with such grandeur on my lips.

Assisted by Paul Ireton, Stephen said the funeral Mass for his father. The Most Reverend Richard Clarahan, Auxiliary Bishop of Boston, delivered the eulogy. In a moving tribute to the deceased, Bishop Clarahan pictured Dennis Fermoyle as the perfect pattern of the Catholic husband and father. The

imprint of his character and the power of his righteousness
were to be found, said the Bishop, in the lives of his children.
It was an excellent oration. But above and beyond the rounded periods of eulogy, Stephen heard a man and a woman whis-
pering before he was.

"Dubhe, guide star, glisten for me always."

"Life-leaper, Cumhyll, leave me never."

. . . As yesterday which is past. And as a watch in the night.

ARCHBISHOP FERMOYLE'S Thursday dinners were becoming
famous. Intimate and exclusively masculine, His Grace's table
was considered something to get your legs under. Lawyers,
artists and authors would come, and physicians, judges, publishers, politicos, and financiers — to exclaim at the pheasant
chasseur or flash a knowing eye at a cobwebbed vintage. "It's
the kind of a dinner," Senator Bates Furnald explained to his
wife, "that you don't feel heavy after." Alec Surtees, British
lecturer-novelist, could write chattily in his journal: "Dined
with Archbishop Fermoyle tonight. The man has a positive
flair for serving wines. With the duckling he introduced a full-
bosomed Nuits-Saint-Georges, quite trim about the ankles. A
really superb Oporto followed the sweet. Damned good talk
during and afterwards. He makes one *give off*, without chattering like a fool."

At the head of his own table, *primus inter pares,* Stephen
entered upon one of the chief joys of life: stag company. He
was fleshing up slightly, but the additional weight served to
insulate his nervous system against the jarring assaults of public office and private pain. A broad interpretation of his function as a Catholic prelate enabled Stephen to accept the friendship of the men who ruled society, created its opinions, and
took its praise or blame with Jovian unconcern. His ear was
sought, his favor solicited, his judgment valued in matters
extending far beyond the administration of his Diocese. Seven
years in Hartfield had, in fact, given the Archbishop a function not unlike that of the municipal water supply — something that everyone unconsciously depends upon for purity
and volume at a constant rate of pressure.

On a particular Thursday evening in October, 1935, Judge
Seth Feakins, an ornament of the Hartfield bench, sipped some

of Stephen's V.S.O. brandy and flicked an anecdotal ash from his cigar. "Odd case in court today," he said to the dinner company. "It's a prosecution for attempting to defraud the Columbia Indemnity Company. Defendant is an obscure violinmaker. 'Luthier,' he calls himself. Appears that the luthier insured an instrument for twenty-five thousand dollars. Claimed it was an Italian masterpiece. Insurance experts appraised the instrument, the premium was paid, and the policy was duly issued."

Judge Feakins inhaled his brandy. "Barely a week later, an accident befalls."

"The fish leapt right out of the milk bottle, eh, Judge?" Harmon I. Poole, President of the Hartfield Trust Company, had a keen nose for rogues like this luthier chap.

"Nothing so transparent, H. I.," said Judge Feakins. "The defendant wasn't directly involved in the accident. Seems he loaned the instrument to Mossel Pola, the concert violinist, in the hope that Pola would buy it. Pola was actually carrying the instrument to a concert, when a cab knocked him down. He suffered only minor injuries, but the violin was smashed to splinters."

Judge Feakins continued: "I use the word 'splinters' literally, gentlemen." The State's case turns on an analysis of the shattered wood that once was a violin. Under the microscope it appears that the maple back of the violin isn't Italian at all — but a piece of American curly maple about twenty years old."

"What does the luthier say?" asked Stephen.

"His defense is interesting. He admits that the back of the violin is a piece of American maple. Says he carved it himself and glued it onto the original frame."

"He must be a man of unusual skill."

"Undoubtedly, Your Grace. But that's not the point at issue. The question before the jury is: Can a three-hundred-year-old violin with an American back honestly be called an Italian masterpiece?"

"Of course it can't," grunted H. I. Poole. "The man's a trickster."

Stephen focused morals and law into a single beam. "To commit a mortal sin, *intent* must be present. Theologically, such intent is shown by 'sufficient reflection and full consent of the will.' The question I'd like to ask is: 'Did the man intend to deceive?' "

"An excellent point, Your Grace. Counsel for the defense admits that his client did not tell the insurance company about the full extent of his repairs. On the other hand, perhaps the insurance appraisers should have been more alert. Again, that's a question for the jury."

Banker Poole applied the J. P. Morgan test. "Is this violin-maker a man of good character? What's his past reputation?"

"No one knows much about him," said Judge Feakins. "He runs a hole-in-the-wall shop in New York — does repair work for a living. Swarthy French-Canadian type. Came from Massachusetts originally."

"What's his name?" asked Stephen.

"Menton, I believe."

"*Rafael* Menton?"

"That's it. Do you know the man?"

A strange agitation stirred the Archbishop. "I knew him as a boy in my first pastorate. He was about sixteen, very talented. His one ambition was to become a luthier."

"He became a luthier, all right." The jurist's tone suggested that Rafael Menton might very well have become a crook, too.

Stephen chose to ignore the implication. "Would it help if I appeared for him in court as a character witness?"

Judge Feakins lighted another cigar. "I'm not the young man's lawyer, but if I were, I'd consider it a stroke of rare good fortune to have Your Grace appear in behalf of my client."

Next morning, as Rafe Menton and his lawyer gloomily waited for court to begin, Stephen volunteered his services as a character witness. There was a moment of joyous recognition, followed by deep emotional release as Rafe grasped the Archbishop's hand.

"Aren't you taking a chance testifying for me?" asked Rafe.

"What chance am I taking? I knew your mother and father. I know your sister. The Menton character is something this court should hear about."

Sitting in a packed courtroom, Stephen listened to Wilhelm Pfundt give expert testimony. "*Ja*, the violin was a genuine

seventeenth-century Cremona, but badly broken," said the
New York dealer.

The District Attorney put a searching question. "Is it considered good practice in your profession, Mr. Pfundt, to make
major restorations of this type — to put a whole new back on a
violin — and call it an old master?"

"Excellent practice — if one has the skill to do it," said
Herr Pfundt. "*Natürlich*, carpenters cannot shake these things
out of their sleeve."

Mossel Pola's testimony followed. "The violin had a voice
of amazing purity and power," said the virtuoso. "I was planning to buy it from the defendant when the accident occurred."

The Archbishop of Hartfield, called to the stand as a character witness, said that he had known Rafael Menton for fifteen years, that he came from a good home, and that his sister
was head of the Geraldine Order in Hartfield. At this point the
Archbishop turned to Judge Feakins. "May I tell the court of
a conversation I once had with the defendant on the subject
of violinmaking?"

Because of the distinguished position of the witness, the
D.A. made no objection; whereupon the court ruled that such
a recounting would be in order.

Gazing across the years, Stephen re-entered a tar-paper
shack clinging to the rocky hillside of L'Enclume. At a workbench cluttered with shavings of spruce and maple, a serious-
faced boy was turning the pages of an illustrated folio. That
same boy — older now, his face straining with anxiety — listened to the Archbishop's recollection of things past.

"When Rafael Menton was about sixteen years old," said
Stephen, "I gave him a book entitled *L'Art des luthiers italiens*.
The more he studied the book, which contained many plates
and illustrations of master violins, the more discouraged he
became. At the time to which I refer, the boy asked me a
question I shall never forget."

Stephen paused to give his words the authentic flavor of
memory. " 'Do you think, Father,' the boy asked, pointing to
the illustrations, 'that instruments as beautiful as these will
ever be made again?'

" 'Yes, Rafe,' I replied. 'American craftsmen, combining
New World materials with Old World designs, will produce

violins — and many other things — more beautiful than any yet made by man."

The Archbishop concluded his testimony. "I do not presume to comment either on insurance law or the art of violinmaking. I can only tell the court of my great happiness that Rafael Menton — with single-hearted devotion and under enormous difficulties — has tried to fulfill my prediction."

The District Attorney hastily conferred with counsel for the insurance company. There was a nodding of heads; together they approached Judge Feakins and requested permission to settle their differences with the defendant.

"Step into my chambers," said the Judge. He beckoned the defendant. "You, too; I want all parties to be satisfied with the final disposition of this case."

Case or no case, prior business claimed Rafael Menton. He crossed the courtroom; with reverence and gratitude, he kissed the Archbishop's hand. "How can I ever thank Your Grace?"

"By coming to see me often, Rafe. We must never lose track of each other again." Stephen put his blessing on the younger man's head. "Now go into that Cremona conference and fight for every penny your violin was worth to you."

LEAVING COURT, Stephen felt a tug at his clerical coattail. It was Max Lessau; the arthritis-gnarled teacher was quivering with excitement. He drew the Archbishop into privy conference on the courthouse steps and asked indignantly: "Why didn't you tell me this violinmaker was a friend of yours?"

"I had lost track of him for several years, Max. It's wonderful to find him again. From the fine things that Mossel Pola and Herr Pfundt said, he must be a marvelous craftsman."

"Let him be only half so marvelous," said Max Lessau, "and he is still the man sent by Providence to make a violin for Conrad."

"The idea never occurred to me," said Stephen.

"It didn't occur to you, because every day you don't hear Conrad scraping his heart out — and mine, too — on that cheese-box fiddle of his." Max came down to business. "A Cremona violin worthy of Conrad's talent would cost thousands of dollars — too many thousands. But now, while this luthier is aching with gratitude in every joint, why not ask him to make a violin for our protégé?"

"I couldn't take advantage of him, Max."

"Advantage?" Bargaincraft, born of a peddler's hagglings, oiled Max's voice. "Forgive me, Archbishop, but this would be the opportunity your luthier friend is looking for. Arrange a meeting, I beg. Let him hear Conrad play. Will you do that, Your Graciousness?"

"Yes," Stephen promised, "I will."

A few evenings later, the Archbishop invited a small company to an informal concert in his home. Among the guests was Rafael Menton — ten thousand dollars richer now as the result of his out-of-court settlement with the Columbia Indemnity Company. Scarcely knowing what to expect from the young violinist tuning a quite ordinary German fiddle, Rafe sat back contentedly, his eyes fixed on Stephen rather than on the artist of the evening. He applauded mildly as Conrad Szalay rose to play the Bach *Chaconne* for unaccompanied violin.

Neither Rafael, nor Ambrose Cannell, nor anyone else in that small audience had ever heard such music.

Standing alone near the piano, Conrad, a golden eighteen, intoned the first measures of an ancient ceremonial air. In a series of stately minor chords his bow swept austerely over the strings, seeking but never demanding the source of Bach's somber purity. Pursuing its almost bleak way, the musical line began to create from within itself a house of many mansions. Broken chords and superlative double stopping supported the temple that Conrad was building with lean, tremendously disciplined fingers. Arpeggios invited him to fly a little; he left the ground in a flurry of undulating scales, always returning with gratitude to the opening theme. Rejoicing in its steadfastness, he uncorked a brightly colored phial, scented faintly with incense. Full blown and resonant, the theme mounted a broad triumphant staircase till it reached a high altar where, in cool subdued light, the now-familiar motif chanted in ecclesiastical vestments.

Stirred by the impact of Conrad's artistry, Stephen glimpsed St. Cecilia deep in the shadows of a choir loft. The patron saint of music was listening, a smile of approbation on her face.

Fourteen-year-old Regina Byrne, sitting beside her uncle,

identified herself with the woman-shaped instrument swept by cruciform strokes of Conrad's bow.

Ambrose Cannell forgot the young violinist's technique long enough to marvel at the profundity of his musicianship. This was no gypsy fiddler, dependent on one-fingered slides, vibratos, or left-handed pizzicati. Rather, it was musical sensibility of the first order, drawing its power equally from tradition and life. The Bishop glanced at Max Lessau, the strange peddler genius who had endowed his pupil with the fearful ability to transform human experience into the serene beatitude of art.

Hunched almost double on his chair, Max Lessau grieved as he gloried in his pupil's performance. "I can teach the lad no more," Max mourned. "He must study with a greater than I. But first, I will get him a violin."

Toward the last section of the *Chaconne*, Conrad's contemplative eye turned inward for a moment of ascetic renunciation. Then, as if rebuking himself for this too-facile escape, he described an assertive outgoing gesture that embraced finite and infinite reality. On a strong foundation note of D (*Dominus?*) he concluded his experience, ending as he had begun, austerely and starkly alone.

Afterwards, there was applause, cries of "bravo," "encore," "Play again, Conrad." This time, accompanied by Regina Byrne, Conrad began the last movement of César Franck's Sonata for Violin and Piano.

An air of quiet serenity descended upon the young musicians, the pianist stating a tranquil, nearly resignational theme, which the violin repeated. Conrad and Regina had found the motif of peace. Having found it, they began interweaving and mingling their voices. The calm reassurance of the canon never left them, except for a short passage in which the violin and piano engaged in a divine questioning. The final episode found them enunciating a strongly punctuated note of triumph with increasing strength in each voice, gathering overpowering momentum in the magical questionings and answerings of the canon.

More could not be expected. Only one thing more remained to be asked.

At precisely the right moment, crafty Max Lessau called attention to the wretched inadequacy of Conrad's fiddle.

Standing between the Archbishop and Rafael Menton, the old peddler tapped the instrument with a contemptuous hooked forefinger. "Could Heifetz himself make music on a rattrap like this?" he asked.

Eagerly, joyfully, Rafe Menton stepped into the gambit. "Let me make a violin for Conrad," he volunteered. "It will be a Stradivarius model, conceived in the great tradition." He was looking at Stephen now. "From American spruce and maple, patterned on the Italian design, perhaps we may fashion a violin that will outsing any instrument yet made by man."

CHAPTER 4

In the great hall of Mappamondo, late in March, 1937, the Prime Minister of Italy sat reading a most inconveniently timed document. Entitled *Mit brennender Sorge* and addressed to the German people, the document — an encyclical letter — was a scathing indictment of the Prime Minister's dear friend, Adolf Hitler. It had been written by an ailing, supposedly moribund old mountain climber named Achille Ratti, more widely known as Pius XI. Little evidence of waning energy appeared in the encyclical; phrases, sentences, indeed whole passages, leapt from its pages to chafe Il Duce's sensibilities, especially tender just now because Herr Hitler was about to honor Rome with one of his rare visits.

Guttural acid would drip from Der Führer at this latest failure to hold the Vatican in line. "In Berlin we manage these things better," he would sneer. True enough, Der Führer *did* manage things better. Much better. In a brief four years he had armed his people, remilitarized the Rhineland, threatened Austria, humbled England, intimidated France, and, bitterest of all, thrust Italy under his yoke as the weaker member of the Axis.

How awkward, how downright galling, to stand before this all-conqueror and apologize for your inability to curb the maunderings of an unarmed old man!

To discharge some part of his wrath, Il Duce had summoned the Vatican Ambassador into his presence for a good dressing down. The victim was in fact being admitted at this

very moment through the heavily guarded doors of Mappamondo. For the next sixty seconds his clerical boots would
squeak across Mappamondo's polished acre, an ordeal calculated to shake even the composure of veteran diplomats.

It so happened, however, that Alfeo Cardinal Quarenghi,
Vatican Ambassador to the Quirinal, wore boots that did not
squeak. Furthermore, he carried under his scarlet cassock a
quite unshakable composure. He knew well enough what he
was going to hear, and with equal surety knew what he
was going to say. Il Duce would bellow: "I." Quarenghi would
murmur: "The Holy Father." Il Duce would thunder: "The
Axis." Quarenghi would say: "The Church." In a final
exchange, Il Duce would invoke the dread name: "Hitler." To
which Quarenghi would reply: "God."

In much the expected fashion, the interview began. Mussolini greeted his visitor with icicle courtesy, then launched
into a tirade against the Holy Father. "Will this tiresome old
man never die?" he fumed, waving a copy of the encyclical in
Quarenghi's face. "Or if that is too much to ask, hasn't he the
common decency to stop pouring out these senile effusions
against Der Führer?"

Il Duce whipped through the pages, quoting fearful examples of *lèse-majesté*. "Listen to this: 'Whoever transposes Race
or People, the State or Constitution, from the scale of earthly
values, and deifies them with an idolatrous cult, utterly per-
verts and falsifies the divinely created order of things.' " He
slapped the encyclical peevishly against his desk. "Divinely
created moonshine. Doesn't the Pope know what's happening
in Europe?"

"The Holy Father knows very well what is happening,"
replied Quarenghi. "That is why he spends his declining
strength protesting Hitler's frightful program of spiritual corruption."

"It is not the Pope's duty to criticize internal arrangements
of a foreign government. Herr Hitler has strengthened Germany, unified his people against their enemies."

"The Holy Father makes no objection to the unification of
the German people. But he cannot remain silent while Christ
and His Church are attacked."

Having beetled to no purpose, Il Duce now attempted the

man-to-man wheedle. "When I first entered politics, the Church was content to side with established governments. She was willing to be a sister arm, a supporting prop to the *status quo*. For my information, Eminence, instruct me in the nature of the change that has taken place. Does the Holy See aspire, perhaps, to a more dominant role in world affairs?"

Il Duce's seeming frankness failed to cozen Quarenghi. "The Holy See is not concerned with temporal dominance," he said. "But it does not propose to play a passive role while totalitarianism threatens the immortal soul of man. Twice within the past month the Supreme Pontiff has lifted his voice against the cynic godlessness of leaders who deny that man is a creature made in the image and likeness of God." Quarenghi pointed to the encyclical on Il Duce's desk. *"Mit brennender Sorge* warns the German people that Hitler's crooked cross means death to the soul. In *Divini Redemptoris*, the Holy Father lays bare the terrible fallacies of atheistic Communism, exposes its false messianic claims, points out that Communism strips man of human dignity, and denies his origin in God." Quarenghi ended his brief demonstration of the Holy See's attitude to totalitarianism. "In the coming struggle between the State and the soul, the Church ranges herself on the side of the soul."

The Cardinal's reference to *Divini Redemptoris* gave Il Duce a handle for argument. "If Communism triumphs, there will be no soul. Der Führer is Christianity's champion against Soviet atheism."

Again Quarenghi knew the answer. "At the moment, Your Excellency, it suits Der Führer to play such a role. The Holy See happens to know, however, that Herr Hitler is shipping machinery, tools, and ammunition to Russia in a desperate attempt to arrange a nonaggression pact with Moscow. If it suited Hitler's purpose, he would melt down the sacred vessels of every church in Europe to buy Soviet quiescence while he unleashes war."

The Cardinal-diplomat had no need to add: "Your Excellency, being a realist, knows this as well as I."

Being a realist, Il Duce knew this and a great deal more. He knew he had become the most abject foot swallower in history. Since this is not a pleasant thing to know about one-self, Mussolini tried to forget the whole business.

"My purpose in inviting Your Eminence here today," he glowered, "is to inform the Holy See that Herr Hitler will soon honor Fascism with a visit to Rome. I will not permit the visit to be marked by incidents. I must have your assurance that Catholic Youth Societies will refrain from unmannerly demonstrations while my guest is in Rome."

The merest whisper of a smile accompanied Quarenghi's question: "With ten thousand secret police lining the streets, how could anyone demonstrate?"

"It has happened before," snapped Il Duce. "Fascist honor requires a positive guarantee that it will not happen again."

So Caesar has come to this, thought Quarenghi. Aloud, he said, "I shall lay Your Excellency's request before the Cardinal Secretary of State." The interview apparently over, Quarenghi rose, bowed, and started to recross Mappamondo's barren expanse when Il Duce called him back.

"One thing more, Your Eminence." Mussolini consulted a memorandum on his desk. "I take this occasion to protest the treacherous activities of one Gaetano Orselli. The man is a zealot, a turncoat. He has repeatedly snatched political ene-mies from my grasp and transported them by airplane to France and England."

"Why does Your Excellency bring these activities to my attention?"

"Why? . . . Orselli is a papal chamberlain, is he not?"

The Cardinal shook his head in the negative. "Signor Orselli no longer serves in the Vatican. I am uninformed as to his present whereabouts or activities."

"In that case," said Il Duce grimly, "you will be in no posi-tion to object when my agents catch up with this elusive traitor."

WHILE the crescendo of European events rose in a brutal scream, the city of Hartfield prepared to celebrate the tercen-tennial anniversary of its founding.

Civic pride (and there was a great deal to be proud of) mounted steadily during the spring of 1938 and reached its peak on the Fourth of July. The great day went off in traditional American style; there was a parade in the morning, a baseball game in the afternoon. Home-town fans were delighted when the Hartfield Tomahawks scalped the Fairhaven Pioneers in a free-hitting 14-9 contest. Cokes and hot dogs, supplied gratis by the Chamber of Commerce, were enjoyed by all. Then along toward eight-thirty P.M., four thousand citizens crowded into the auditorium of Symphony Hall for a mammoth rally.

The meeting opened with community singing of the national anthem. Immediately thereafter, Mayor Quincy P. Jenkins undertook the oratorical task of reviewing Hartfield's growth from a frontier stockade to its present commanding position among the industrial cities of America. Other speakers roared like Kiwanis-Rotarian lions. "Hartfield's municipal credit is A-Number One . . . our streets are broader . . . our water supply larger . . . our public buildings handsomer." Thus spake the civic oracles in periods most pleasing to the Hartfield ear.

Seated on the speaker's platform, Archbishop Fermoyle thought that the tone of the meeting was too aggressively secular. He wanted to remind his audience that Hartfield might profitably model itself a bit more closely on Augustine's *City of God* than on Chamber of Commerce press releases. He had hoped to take his text from the Psalm beginning: "Unless the Lord keepeth the city, he watches in vain that keepeth it." But since the Right Reverend Tyleston Forsythe and Rabbi Joshua Felshin had trimmed their sails to the nonsectarian breeze, Stephen felt obliged to do likewise. Because honor among clergymen frowns on proselytizing at a public gathering, the nub of Stephen's problem, as he sat waiting his turn to speak, was this: "How can I lift the spiritual tone of this meeting without mentioning Roman Catholicism?"

A solution presented itself when a platoon of grade-school children saluted Old Glory. "We pledge allegiance to our flag," they piped, "and to the Republic for which it stands. One nation indivisible, with liberty and justice for all."

The words struck associative nonsectarian sparks in Stephen's mind. Republic . . . Plato. Plato? . . . justice. *Justice for all!*

Ideas older than Hartfield, more durable than public buildings of granite, more important even than municipal credit.

Justice! A covenant made between God and man, a virtue passionately discussed by the Athenians, a blessing persistently sought by nations and individuals. While Mayor Quincy P. Jenkins introduced him, Stephen decided that a few remarks on the subject of justice would be very much in order.

"Dear Friends and Fellow Citizens," he began. "Others have spoken this evening of Hartfield's glorious history and material achievements. The record is excellent, the story inspiring. But both would be meaningless were they not founded upon the immortal ideal of justice celebrated by our school children in their salute to the flag. May I therefore, as an American citizen, speak tonight in praise of that ideal?"

By the mechanics of a brief silence Stephen set the scene for his discourse. "Twenty-three hundred years ago, a little group of Athenians were engaged in a discussion of justice — the crowning virtue of the citizen and the supreme guide of the State. We know precisely how that discussion ran, because Plato — a member of the group — made a transcript of the conversation. It has come down to us as *The Republic*, one of the most influential treatises on politics and morality ever written by man.

"Socrates, the antique forerunner of Christ, is guiding his disciples along an ascending path of argument. This man, whose physical ugliness is only less arresting than the beauty of his thoughts, turns to one of his young companions and says:

" 'Glaucon, we have been speaking earnestly about justice for some time, yet I must confess I do not know the nature of this virtue. Can you tell me, Glaucon, either in your own words or in the language of any poet, what is justice?'

"Glaucon tries bravely, but cannot tell Socrates what justice is. Thrasymachus, the bully and sophist, swaggers into the argument to define justice as 'the interest of the stronger.' But Socrates rebuts his argument by showing that although the physician is stronger than the sick man, it is in the patient's interest that the doctor practices his healing art.

"Driven by Socrates, the talk climbs steadily upward, until at length justice is defined as being — both in the State and the individual — *the harmonious balance between all the other virtues*. Curiously enough, the Republic that Socrates describes is, in its system of harmonious balances, not unlike our own ideal of government. . . ."

There was a commotion in the auditorium. A man rose to his feet and shouted bitterly:

"That's a lot of eyewash, and you know it."

Members of the audience cried: "Shame . . . hire a hall . . . throw him out."

To quell the disturbance Stephen held up his hand. He had never been heckled before; the experience was unpleasant, but it must be met. "Let our friend speak. I'm sure we all want to hear what he has to say."

"Maybe you will, maybe you won't," said the heckler, his tone and manner revealing the professional haranguer of crowds. He addressed the audience as though warning them of a plague. "Can't you see through this Catholic hocus-pocus?" he asked. "Wise up to Reverend Mr. Applesauce. All he's saying is: 'See how liberal the Catholic Church can be — get a load of what wonderful Americans we are. Allegiance to the flag. Sure. America the beautiful, *Dominus vobiscum.*' It's the Rome line, and our speaker has got it down pat."

Boos from the audience failed to muffle the heckler, who now addressed Stephen directly. "Mr. High Priest of the *status quo,* I'd like to ask you a simple question."

The eternal Thrasymachus. "Ask," said Stephen.

"O.K. Can you give one specific example of how, when, or where the Catholic Church ever contributed to the idea of justice?"

The man, whoever he was, deserved an answer — the best that faith and logic could provide. To phrase such an answer, Stephen took his stand on the highest possible ground.

"This meeting began as a civic gathering," he said. "I had intended — all had intended — to keep it so. But the query from the floor illustrates the impossibility of separating eternal values from human affairs. I say then, in reply to the question, that the Catholic Church makes its chief contribution to human justice by reminding men that God, and God alone, is its source and perfect expression. I go further. I say that our American courts, our laws, our democratic way of life, are manifestations of that justice. And I am happy to add" — the Archbishop bowed gravely to the Reverend Dr. Forsythe and

Rabbi Felshin — "that my Church claims no monopoly of this teaching."

With outstretched evangel arms Stephen turned again to the audience. "Nowhere have we yet seen God's justice perfectly revealed in this world, nor are we ever likely to see it with our mortal eyes. But I profoundly believe that the system under which we live comes nearer to realizing justice than any state of which I have ever heard. We are permitted, in America, to approach the ideal expressed by Socrates: 'To grow as much like God as man is permitted to.'"

Part proselytizer, all priest, Stephen unloosed the eloquence within him. "It is toward this ideal that American life is irresistibly drawn. As in the oak germ there dwells, potentially patterned, the storm-loving and leafy citadel that is to be, so in man there resides a similar imperative to approach as nearly as possible the stature and form of divinity. The whole duty of society is to permit men to attain this form and stature. It must aid them not only to satisfy their material needs, but to actualize their spiritual possibilities as well."

Prophecy and realism mingled in the Archbishop's voice. "At present, in many souls and in many states, the battle goes against the forces of good. Some say the conflict will be fatal, but I have no such fear. Gazing at our country, I am not cast down. Our people are the throbbing proof that the Adversary makes but little headway in our midst. Thus far we have achieved much that an older world of hate and cruelty thought impossible. What future impossibilities need be feared? If we have come thus far by reason of the divinity within us, may we not, impelled by the same force, struggle yet higher toward the Face of Light?"

Forgetting that the audience was not his congregation, Stephen lifted his hand to bless them.

"*Procedamus in pace et justitia*," he said, and from the auditorium there arose an affirmative roar, each voice crying in its own accent, "Amen."

IN AUGUST of that year, Dr. John Byrne made a routine checkup of Stephen's physical condition. With stethoscope, blood-pressure machine, and a tiny instrument that threw a gimlet beam of light into his patient's eyes, the physician went over his brother-in-law. At the end of the examination he asked: "How do you feel generally, Steve?"

"Not exactly teeming with vigor. My appetite's off, and I can't get to sleep at night." Stephen glanced questioningly at Dr. Byrne. "Find anything wrong with me?"

"No, no. Your blood pressure's a trifle high, but within normal limits for a man pushing fifty."

Pushing fifty! (Almost Monaghan's age, thought Stephen, when I first knew him.) Getting on, getting on.

With thumb and forefinger, Dr. John took a clinical pinch at Stephen's bare arm. "Your muscle tone isn't quite what it should be, and you're as pale as a flounder's belly. You've been working too hard, Steve. You need a layoff — a couple of weeks outdoors. Let the sun get a whack at your skin. Treat those lungs of yours to a whiff of fresh air."

"Fine medicine, Doctor. But where's this rest cure going to take place? I hate resorts — and traveling's no joy. When people discover I'm an Archbishop, they're all over me with questions: 'Will I meet my non-Catholic wife in heaven?' 'Can you fix me up for an audience with the Pope?'"

John Byrne grinned. "I know how it is, Steve. Why don't you ask George to take you for a trip on his boat? Rita and I had a wonderful two weeks on Lake Ontario with him last summer."

The idea of taking a holiday jaunt with his brother was most appealing to Stephen. That afternoon he put in a call to New York. George, it turned out, was planning a trip to Lake Champlain, and eagerly fell in with Stephen's suggestion that they take a vacation together.

"Meet me at the Red Wing Boat Club, East River and Fiftieth Street, next Saturday morning," said George. "Look for a cabin cruiser with a flying bridge and *Flotsam* painted on her chubby stern. Bring some old clothes — not too many of them. We'll spend most of the time in bathing trunks."

Glimpsing the *Flotsam* tied up at the Red Wing dock was a case of love at first sight. Freshly painted and broad of beam, the thirty-foot cruiser had the confident look of a boat that would go anyplace her owned dared take her. At Stephen's cry, "Reporting on board," George's head popped out of the cabin. Forty-five, an SEC lawyer, and still unmarried, George was the perfect specimen of the fresh-water boatman — a creature happiest when wearing a Breton jersey and white duck shorts. Barefooted, he leapt onto the dock to greet his brother.

"Stuffy!" he cried joyously. "I expected to see you pull up in an archiepiscopal barge, scattering benedictions. Lost your touch?"

"Just laid it aside for a couple of weeks, Gug." Taking in the brass and mahogany details of the trim craft bobbing at anchorage, Stephen already felt his ecclesiastical cares slipping away.

"The crew sleeps forward," announced George, taking Stephen's bag. "You'll find yourself sharing the fo'c'sle with a sea cook who doesn't know a sextant from a folding anchor."

The sea cook turned out to be Bernie Fermoyle, the "Irish Thrush" himself, thirty pounds overweight, but obliged to carry the extra "custard," as he called it, to keep his pipes sweet. The three brothers contrived, with the aid of a finger's worth of Scotch, to cast the *Flotsam* loose. With George at the wheel, she slipped through Hell Gate, maneuvered under the Harlem River bridges — then pointed her bow up the broad Hudson.

Somewhere north of Yonkers Stephen discovered how tired he really was. Lolling on the forward deck, he let the river begin its nerve cure with massive doses of sunlight and scenery. All that afternoon and most of the following day he dozed. Largo was the beat of the ancient waterway, a tempo quiet as the pulse of a drowsy woman. Myth simmered in its valleys, legend echoed from its low hills, unchanged since the Iroquois ranged through its passes. Sometimes the channel would broaden into a wide lake edged with rushes, abandoned icehouses, or stagnant towns. No two aspects of the river were identical; hour after hour it played infinite variations on a fluminal theme.

Occasionally Stephen would waken from a nap to hear Bernie warbling "The False Bride of O'Rourke" or "Bendemeer's Stream." Unmistakable odors of corned-beef hash would rise from the galley ventilator to remind Stephen how good it was to be hungry again. Drenched by sunlight, and drugged by the river's peace, he secretly praised John Byrne's wisdom and the patron saint (whoever he was) of little boats.

On the second day out, he saw George loading a small brass cannon. "What are you doing, Gug?"

George pointed to a grove-screened mansion standing high on the east bank of the river. "That's F.D.R.'s place. I'm getting ready to fetch a salute to a great guy." He jerked the lanyard, and a Lilliputian bang bounded off the riverbank.

As the echoes died away, George asked:

"Ever meet him, Stuff?"

Stephen nodded evasively.

"What's he like?"

"Pretty much as you said: 'A great guy.'"

"Don't be so damn mysterious. What did you talk about?"

"I'm sorry if I seem mysterious, Gug. But I can't let even you into the secret. You'll be reading about it in the papers one of these days."

By the time the *Flotsam* nudged into the first lock of the Champlain canal, Stephen had completely relaxed. George and Bernie were perfect companions; the three brothers spent whole days fishing off the side of the *Flotsam* or splashing about in birchy coves. In the evening, wonderful conversations sprang up; they would discuss the state of the world, or argue some point of law, metaphysics, or morals. But because blood is thicker than ideas, and because no flesh is sweeter than that clinging to the bones of one's own family, they talked oftenest of the Fermoyle tribe, its fortunes and vicissitudes.

Again they searched for Mona in the dark byways of the South End; again they tried to find a reason for Florrie's incurable nagging. They recalled the time that Din saved Ellen's life with his heaven-storming prayers. Together they laughed at Celia's habit of "putting away" towels and table linen against a day that would never come. From Bernie, who still lived at 47 Woodlawn, Stephen learned that Celia retained much of her old bounce. "She goes to Mass every morning, cooks dinner for me, and still says 'A hungry man is an angry man' when she hands me my plate."

During one of these family talk fests, George posed a searching question. "Why did so few of us marry, Stuff? Rita's the only one who ever took to the idea. You, Bernie, Ellen, and

I are still single. Do you suppose anything's wrong with us?"

Stephen shook his head. "The Church holds that a person has the right to marry or stay single, just as he pleases. You don't feel guilty about being unmarried, do you?"

"I wouldn't call it guilty. Still, there's something odd about the three of us being bachelors."

Stephen turned to the Irish Thrush. "Why didn't you ever get married, Bernie?"

Very simply, like one of Bernie's songs, the answer came. "I guess I never met anyone that I loved better than myself."

And I, thought Stephen, met One I loved better than myself or anyone else.

Under Champlain's red-gold moon they canvassed the subject of the celibate strain in the Fermoyle stock. Heredity? No, both Din and Celia had joyously embraced marriage and each other. Reluctance to take on obligations? Bernie admitted as much, but both Stephen and George could point to heavy responsibilities they had laid upon themselves. Fear of women? Blessed with a loving mother, why should this be so?

George came nearest to suggesting an answer. "Maybe Din had something to do with it."

"In what way, Gug?" asked Stephen.

"It's hard to say exactly — but the old boy was a curious mixture of patriarch and bull walrus. He could speak to Jehovah, and knock off any yearling challenger with a sweep of his tusks. God forgive me for saying it, but I think he frightened us, Steve."

"He always scared me stiff," admitted Bernie.

Lying awake in his bunk that night while a gale swept down from Canada, Stephen pondered the testimony of his brothers. Could it be that the tip of Din's walrus tusk — no matter how clipped by domesticity or velveted by affection — had somehow frightened his children, and shunted them off the feeding grounds of married love?

If true, how strange! Stephen fell asleep, saying a prayer for the repose of Din's patriarchal soul.

Next morning, the rising gale made further northward progress impossible. With the wind at her stern, the *Flotsam* scudded south. Both cruiser and crew were glad to huddle into the protecting lock at Whitehall.

The journey down the Hudson was a placid coda to Stephen's holiday. Rested, tanned, hungry for work and food, he arrived back in Hartfield on September 1, and plunged into his archiepiscopal labors.

ADVENT, 1938. With a letter opener that was part poignard, part cross, the Archbishop of Hartfield slit a long envelope with the Vatican crest, and drew out two sheets of note paper covered with the familiar handwriting of Alfeo Quarenghi.

CARO STEFANO:

I have a mixed bag of news for you. The Holy Father is again quite ill; his latest heart attack frightened us terribly. Yet stricken as he was, he rose from his bed when he learned that Hitler was coming to Rome. "I cannot remain in the same city with Antichrist," he said, and took off for Castel Gandolfo, where he remained all during Hitler's stay.

Since your last ad limina visit, the Holy Father asks for you constantly in tones of longing and affection. He refers to you as his "American Benjamin," a term of endearment that shows by chapter and verse the Old Testament nature of his affection for you.

The Cardinal Secretary of State is immensely pleased by the results of your discussions with the President, which have served admirably to achieve a closer *rapprochement* between Vatican and White House. Your phrase "parallel endeavors for peace" expresses with great exactness the thought that we hope will govern the President's appointment of a personal representative to the Vatican. Your suggestion that the appointee be a Protestant has been warmly received here We all agree that sectarian considerations must be subordinated to the greater purpose that the President and the Supreme Pontiff hold in common: the avoidance of war, if humanly possible.

Although the Holy See addresses all its prayers and actions toward this end, it is our conviction here that we are dealing with a paranoiac in the person of Herr Hitler. That he wants a war of extermination, and intends to force it upon the world, becomes increasingly clear. No one here knows exactly when it will come; the precise date depends wholly upon the nonaggression pact that Ribbentrop is arranging with Molotov.

Brace yourself now for hard personal news, Stefano. The body of your friend Gaetano Orselli was found under a hedge in a lonely spot on the Campagna. When discovered, he had been dead for some time. He had been shot in the back — clearly the work of Ovra assassins. His death is one of a thousand murders that will go unpunished so long as the colossus of Fascism bestrides this unhappy country . . . .

STEPHEN dropped the page and covered his face with both hands to blot out the image of his friend lying alone on the desolate Campagna. Orselli dead! Living images and echoes returned in a whirring montage of sight and sound: Orselli as Stephen had first seen him, pointing out the stars on the bridge of the *Vesuvio;* his ringed forefinger, scented beard, and rakish cap; his haughty arrogance in blasting a British warship off the ocean with a cool: "It is I, Gaetano Orselli, who defy your orders."

Other pictures, other phrases. "Astronomy is a science, not an aphrodisiac." *"Furfantino,* are you a Bishop yet?" Orselli nipping a cigar between his strong white teeth. "Relish it more slowly, my friend." "Ah she is an angel, Stefano." *"L'amore fa passare il tempo. . . ."*

How Gaetano's throat had thirsted for life! "The corkscrew, Torino. We must drink as we talk." Slaked now that thirst. Dust-dry forever those passionate, generous lips. *"Il tempo fa passare l'amore."*

Tears streamed from Stephen's eyes as he prayed for the repose of Orselli's soul.

His private mourning continued throughout the joyous season of Christmas, and weighed heavily upon him as he embarked for Rome with Owen Starkey early in mid-January, 1939.

A double motive underlay Stephen's journey. He wished to inform Cardinal Pacelli of his most recent discussions with the

President. And with filial sadness, "the American Benjamin" yearned to look on Jacob's face for the last time.

CHAPTER 5

No LONGER able to hold audiences in his study, Pius XI lay propped up on pillows on a four-poster bed in an upper room of the Vatican Palace. The pacemaker of his heart (that mysterious node which normally sends seventy-two electrical impulses a minute across the cardiac muscles) was failing. Yet, through his wasted body the flame of intellect and resolve still burned fiercely. In daily conferences with Cardinal Pacelli, the pontiff kept an unyielding grip on the policy of the Holy See — a policy that sought, now as always, the primacy of God in the affairs of man. The only concession His Holiness would make to Dr. Marchiafava, his attending physician, was to limit each conference to a half-hour, then take fifteen minutes of rest before plunging into the next interview.

Pausing at these little oases of refreshment, he would close his eyes, and drink from springs of memory. Sometimes these springs were fed from conscious sources: he would recall his long quiet years in the Ambrosian Library, or his youthful ascents of snow-capped mountains, when no cliff was too steep, no path too rugged, for his alpenstock. Sometimes he would plunge into deep reveries. Here, in the shadowy region where dream and wish meet in confluent streams, he became the shepherd king leading his flock through green pastures. Old Testament identifications colored these patriarchal fantasies; on Sinai's peak he heard Jehovah's great commandment: "I am the Lord thy God: thou shalt not have strange gods before me." With Jacob he dreamed of a ladder standing upon the earth, the top thereof touching heaven.

Once, opening his eyes to see Dr. Marchiafava bending over him, the pontiff murmured inaudibly: "Has Benjamin come yet?"

The physician, unable to catch his patient's words, said soothingly: "He is here, Your Holiness." Turning to Stephen, the doctor whispered: "Try not to prolong the audience, Your Grace. Conversation overtaxes the Holy Father."

Stephen nodded and knelt beside the pontiff's bed.

"Benjamin . . . I have been waiting for you," murmured the Pope. The dream mist cleared. Reality disclosed an equally welcome presence. "Why did you not come sooner, my son?"

"I did not wish to burden you, Holy Father. Grave bulletins reached us in America."

Wan humor flickered across the Pope's face. "How could doctors gain a reputation unless their bulletins kept a patient *in extremis?* We have twice contributed to the fame of our physician. With God's help, we shall do so again."

"Many prayers bear you up, Holy Father."

"And heavy malice bears us down, Stefano. How desperate, how bitter is the constant struggle in the world between the forces of love and the powers of destruction! When we were younger, better armed with strength, the battle seemed not at all hopeless." Pius XI made tired pluckings at the coverlet of his bed. "The final test of faith is to believe, in moments of weariness, that the powers of darkness will not triumph in the world."

"Your Holiness has no fear that they will?"

Onset of energy vibrated in the pontiff's voice. "Our remaining task is to make certain that they do not! It is for this reason we have summoned you, dear son. In the struggle soon to begin, the Vicar of Christ will be called upon to vindicate his great title. To do so, we must fortify ourself with the strength of fresh minds and younger hearts."

Metaphor framed the Pope's thought. "Old trees cast a noble shade, but when the *uragano* rages, tough heartwood, deep tap roots, are needed." The forest image branched out toward the New World. "Ah, how I should have loved to see America, climb its magnificent mountains, hear the wind stampeding across its prairies!" His smile had mischief. "Do you remember, I once called them 'pampas,' Stefano?"

"I remember, Holy Father." Tears welled into Stephen's eyes.

The Pope's breathing was stertorous; he struggled for each word. "We are not fated to visit America, but it is within our power to draw upon its magnificent strength for the greater glory of God and His Church. It is our desire that you stay in

Rome, Stefano, to add New World strength to Vatican councils."

"Your wish commands me, Holiness."

Allegory and dream had quite vanished from the Pope's mind. "Your duties will consist chiefly of liaison work between the Holy See and the White House. You have opened new doors of understanding for all of us, Stefano. To provide you with the necessary authority to carry on your noble work" — Pius XI sat up among his pillows — "and as a sign of our limitless confidence in you, we have named you Cardinal in our recent secret consistory."

Had Stephen been standing, he would have dropped to his knees. But because he was already kneeling by the Pope's bedside, and because the Holy Father's words, "We have named you Cardinal," lamed his tongue, Stephen could neither move nor speak. No words could discharge his feelings of astonishment and unworthiness. Involuntary mechanisms far below the level of consciousness took possession of him. A fine sweat broke from the roots of his hair; the blood momentarily withdrew from his face, then climbed again in a hot tide. He knew that if he spoke he would stammer; if he continued to gaze at the wasted, propped-up figure on the pillows, he would dissolve in tears.

There was only one thing for Stephen Fermoyle to do — a common thing that he had already done ten thousand times in his life. He folded his hands, right thumb over the left, bent his head in the manner of one who had just partaken of the Blessed Sacrament, and murmured: *"Domine, non sum dignus."*

"Your humility is pleasing, Eminent Son. But come now," Pius XI rallied his newest Cardinal affectionately, "you must really begin assembling a vestiary. We bestow only the red hat, you know. Everything else — scarlet cassock, ermine cape — you must find for yourself. You will barely have time to piece together a wardrobe for our public consistory, to be held, God willing, a week from tomorrow."

On January 25, 1939, Pius XI added fresh luster to the fame of his physician by rising from his bed to bestow red hats on three new cardinals. In the presence of the Sacred College and the entire papal court, the cardinals-elect prostrated themselves before the papal altar in St. Peter's, then arose to receive the ceremonial red hat with its tassels of gold, signifying that the wearer is a prince of the Church.

Ermine-caped, his long train borne by attendants, Stephen knelt before the Vicar of Christ and kissed the Fisherman's ring in token of submission. Then descending the altar steps he embraced one by one the members of the Sacred College, henceforth to be his spiritual brothers. With the eminent lords Pacelli and Quarenghi, with the Palatine Prelates Pignatelli di Belmonte and Caccia-Dominioni, Stephen exchanged the kiss of fellowship. Afterwards, at a formal reception held in the Chigi Palace, he was greeted by ambassadors and envoys of world powers. Listening discreetly, saying little (little, that is, which might lend itself to misconstruction or distortion), Stephen moved among them, newly conscious of — but not overcome by — the hazards that a cardinal-diplomat encounters in ordinary conversation.

On February 10, 1939, Stephen had his *audience de congé* with the Holy Father. "Against our will, we are permitting you to leave us for a little while," said the Pope. "We realize that the affairs of your Diocese must be set in order before you return to take up your duties in Rome. Go quickly that you may come back sooner. Will you travel by boat or plane?"

"By plane, Your Holiness. My reservation is made for tomorrow. I shall return within the month."

Pius XI seemed wretchedly worn when Stephen left him Later that day the pontiff took to his four-poster and, unable to add further glory to Dr. Marchiafava's reputation, sank into a coma from which he never awakened.

Next morning, just as Stephen was starting for the airport, a papal chamberlain appeared at the door of his hotel suite. The chamberlain's mien was melancholy as he made his announcement:

"Eminent Lord, the Holy Father passed away last night. The chair of Peter is vacant. It is the wish of Cardinal Pacelli that Your Eminence remain in Rome for the approaching conclave."

THE NOVENDIAL, the nine days of mourning for a deceased

Pope, now began. While the body of Pius XI lay in state, daily Masses were celebrated; incessant litanies arose as high prelates kept constant vigil at his bier. The government of the Roman Catholic Church passed into the hands of a "particular Congregation," composed of three senior Cardinals, headed by Eugenio Pacelli as Camerlengo. This committee now set in motion the machinery for the assembling of a conclave.

From all corners of the globe, cardinals began their pilgrimage to Rome. Among the ecclesiastical princes to receive notification of the Pope's death was the octogenarian Archbishop of Boston, Lawrence Cardinal Glennon. In the tower room of his residence, he read over and over again the cablegram placed in his hands by his secretary, Monsignor Jeremy Splaine. By an almost incredible combination of longevity and fate, His Eminence was about to fulfill an unsatisfied ambition. He was going to Rome to participate in the election of a Pope! After humbling His Eminence on two previous occasions, God was giving his aged servant another chance.

Lawrence Glennon addressed his secretary in a voice that, though it still bit like an emery wheel, was not the old double-forte organ it used to be.

"Jeremy, round up my diocesan consultors. Flush them out of their cubbyholes, or wherever they hide themselves when important business is afoot. While they're in here palavering, I want you to arrange for a letter of credit — make it ten thousand — then get a couple of reservations on the Transatlantic Clipper. Tell the press that 'Gangplank Larry' is flying this time."

Monsignor Splaine absorbed the first barrage of orders. The second salvo caught him unprepared.

"Run over to the chancery office, and pick out a good smart priest who can write English with a crunch to it," said Glennon. "Instruct him in the details of your job here. I'm taking you to Rome with me as my conclavist."

As Monsignor Splaine withdrew, His Eminence called after him. "Send a cablegram to Cardinal Fermoyle at the Ritz-Reggia Hotel. Tell him to get me a suite adjoining his own."

Seventy-four hours later, an exultant old Cardinal was letting himself be hugged by a still more exultant young one.

"You made it, Eminence," cried Stephen. "After fifty years you managed to reach Rome in time for a conclave."

"Conclave! Why, that's two weeks off," said Glennon. "I came for the Novendial, Steve. When a man reaches my age he likes to feel the grandeur of death's wing as it brushes past."

Except for a loss of ruddiness and the natural tissue shrinkage that takes place after eighty, Glennon seemed almost as hale as ever. He turned to his secretary. "Jemmy, let me present you to Cardinal Fermoyle. Study him, Jeremy — he's a compass for American prelates to steer by. What? . . . You two know each other?"

"From long ago," said Stephen. "Monsignor Splaine was my first altar boy. Remember that performance you gave with the Book and bells, Jemmy?"

"I'll never forget it, Your Eminence. Or how kind you were afterwards."

"And I'll never forget the lacing I got from Dollar Bill Monaghan." Stephen imitated his old pastor's disciplinary voice and manner. " 'I hear that you and your server did some fancy juggling with the Book this morning. Is that the latest thing with the American College crowd at Rome?' "

To Glennon's way of thinking, his juniors were having too good a time. Never the one to take a scene downstage, Glennon reclaimed Stephen's attention. "Will any of my old friends be at the conclave?"

A diligent racking of memory produced not one name of Glennon's contemporaries. Giacobbi, Merry del Val, Mourne, Vannutelli — all departed. Next to Cardinal Pignatelli di Belmonte, Glennon would be the oldest member of the conclave. The realization saddened Number One.

"All of them shall grow old like a garment; and as a vesture Thou shalt change them," was the sustaining wisdom that he took with him into the obsequies of Pius XI and the ensuing conclave that began on March 1, 1939.

On the morning of that day, sixty-two cardinal-electors attended a Missa Solemnis sung by Cardinal Pignatelli di Belmonte in the Pauline Chapel, the "parish church" of the Vatican. Attentively they listened to an eloquent sermon delivered in Latin by Monsignor Antonio Bacci, Undersecretary of Letters to Foreign Rulers. Begging the sufferance of his listeners,

Monsignor Bacci stressed the solemnity of the occasion, the mournful state of the world, and the fearful responsibility that rested upon the electors of a new Pope. He exhorted his hearers to bear in mind that the man they were about to choose as Keeper of the Pontifical Keys must be the ablest, most saintly among their number.

"You must ask yourselves, Most Eminent Lords," said the speaker, "which among you has the character to resist the new paganism of State that is even now preparing to engulf the world with blood and force? You must search your hearts to discover which of your noble fellowship is best fitted by knowledge, experience, and God's grace to bring the Church — nay, civilization itself — through the hazardous pass ahead."

Monsignor Bacci paused for rhetorical emphasis. "Do I say 'hazardous pass'? Permit me, Most Eminent Lords, to employ an apter figure drawn from the art of navigation. The man elected by you will be called upon to pilot St. Peter's bark through seas infested by ice floes that even now are breaking loose from the fearful glacier of barbarism."

Ornate? Perhaps. Yet when the orator rounded into his peroration, Stephen thought that Monsignor Bacci's sermon was as fine a combination of form and substance as he had ever heard.

In the afternoon, the cardinal-electors again assembled — this time in the Sistine Chapel — to take the customary oath governing their actions in the coming conclave. One at a time they swore to safeguard the best interests of the Church and permit no coercive factor to sway their judgment. Then, "with minds free and consciences bare" (as Gregory XV had prescribed), they retired to their cells for meditation and prayer.

At eight o'clock that evening, a hushed bell rang thrice in the courtyard of San Damaso. Inside the conclave, completely walled off from the outer world, Swiss Guards walked through tapestried corridors, crying: "*Extra omnes*"—All out. Now, with lighted torches, a committee of three cardinals, led by the tall, pallid Camerlengo, searched the conclave for the presence of unauthorized persons. None were found. Whereupon, the task of officially closing the heavy bronze gate of the conclave fell upon two men. Three outer locks were turned by Prince Chigi, hereditary marshal of the conclave, who had already taken his ancestral oath to watch over the Vatican Palace during the election of a new Pope. Through a wicket, the Camerlengo watched Prince Chigi turn three outer bolts and place the key in an embroidered purse. Then, in the presence of Cardinals Glennon and Pignatelli di Belmonte, the Camerlengo turned a key controlling the three inner bolts. Thus locked up, from within and without, the cardinal-electors partook of a light supper and retired to their cells for prayer and rest.

Stephen was awakened next morning by a guard crying outside his door: "*In capellam, Domini*" (Into the chapel, Lords). He arose, celebrated Mass at one of the portable altars that had been set up in the Sala Ducale. Then, after a light breakfast of coffee and rolls, he summoned Owen Starkey to assist him in robing for the conclave. He put on a violet-colored cassock fastened by a hook and eye across the chest, the train caught up in back. Over this was placed a lace rochet; on his breast lay the pectoral cross, openly exposed as a symbol of his authority as a papal elector.

Owen Starkey's hand trembled slightly as he handed Stephen his biretta; the trembling ceased when the Cardinal gripped his hand. "Pray for me, Owen," said Steve, then took his place in the silent procession filing into the Sistine Chapel.

Overnight, Vatican architects had transformed the chapel into a sacred polling place. Along both sides of the vaulted chamber stood a row of thrones, a canopy over each. In front of every throne was a desk, green-covered for cardinals created by earlier Popes, violet-covered for those named by Pius XI. Pens, inkwells, blotters, sealing wax, and a small pile of ballots had been placed on each desk by secretaries. On the altar at the further end of the chapel stood a huge gilded chalice into which the cardinal-electors would deposit their ballots. Beside the altar a small stove had been set up, its long pipe extending upward through the roof. In this stove, the ballots would be burned at the conclusion of every vote.

The older cardinals, Glennon among them, sat nearest the altar. Stephen, youngest of the electors, took his place near the door. Gazing obliquely down the row of thrones opposite him, he could see Cardinal Faulhaber of Bavaria, destined to suffer for his outspoken opposition to Hitler. Beside the Ger-

man Cardinal sat Kaspar of Czechoslovakia, whose country
had already been trampled by the Nazi boot. There was Ver-
dier of Paris, his face a worn ledger carrying tragic entries
soon to be balanced against his country. Halfway down the
row of thrones sat Pacelli, heir, by pre-election consensus, to
the triple tiara. From a purple-covered desk almost opposite
Stephen, Alfeo Quarenghi smiled.

"Most Reverend Lords," Cardinal Pignatelli di Belmonte
was saying, "we shall proceed to the scrutiny."

Stephen examined the ballot on his desk. It was an oblong
sheet of vellum, divided into three sections. At the top was
printed in Latin:

> *I, Cardinal* ————

In this blank space Stephen wrote his own name. On the
middle section appeared the words:

> *I elect Cardinal* ———— *as Sovereign Pontiff.*

Stephen knew that on the initial ballot a certain number of
votes would be cast for purely honorary reasons. Faulhaber of
Bavaria and Kaspar of Czechoslovakia would doubtless
receive such tributes of regard from a scattering of the
assembled electors. How Lawrence Glennon's heart would
dilate with happiness if even a single ballot bore his name!
Moved by a love that contained no trace of political or nationalistic significance, Stephen wrote the name "Lawrence Glennon" on his first ballot.

The lowermost section of the ballot was completely blank.
Here, each elector was supposed to write a brief scriptural text
for purposes of identification should his vote be challenged or
questioned in any way. In this section, to commemorate the
last words of Dennis Fermoyle, Stephen wrote the fourth verse
of Psalm Eighty-nine:

*"A thousand years in Thy sight are as yesterday, which is
past. And as a watch in the night."*

He folded this section under and away from himself, sealing
it flapwise over the top section, so as to conceal his own name.
Then he awaited his turn to deposit the ballot in the gilt chalice on the altar.

One by one, in order of seniority, the cardinals walked to

the altar and placed their ballots in the uncovered chalice. Presiding at the altar were three cardinal-scrutineers. When all the ballots had been cast, the senior scrutineer placed a silver paten over the chalice, shook it thoroughly, and deposited it again on the altar. He now drew the ballots from the urn one at a time, and handed them to a second scrutineer, who placed them face upward on the altar, counting aloud as he did so. Meanwhile a third teller counted the number of cardinals present. Sixty-two cardinals sat in their chairs; sixty-two ballots lay on the altar. Since the two counts tallied, the election could proceed to its next phase.

Placing the ballots in a second chalice, the scrutineers carried it to a table in the center of the chapel. Singly, the ballots were withdrawn by the senior teller, who read aloud the name of the candidate inscribed thereon, then passed the ballot to his colleagues for verification. During this process, the seated cardinal-electors made their own tabulation of the votes cast for each candidate.

On the first ballot, Eugenio Pacelli received thirty-five votes, seven short of the necessary two-thirds majority.

At this point in the proceedings, one member of the conclave got the shock of his life. When Lawrence Glennon heard his name read by the senior scrutineer, Number One's head came up in blinking startlement. An astronomer, seeing his own face gazing back at him from a distant star, could not have been more bewildered. In the long history of the papacy, it was the first vote an American Cardinal had ever received.

Again the voting began. On this second scrutiny, Cardinal Pacelli received forty votes — two short of the required majority. Only the formality of a third ballot stood between the Camerlengo and the Throne of Peter. After a noon recess, pens scratched once more against parchment; for a third time the ballots were deposited in the gilt chalice, shaken up, and tallied by scrutineers. When the count for Pacelli passed forty-two — the number required to elect — the Camerlengo covered his face with his hands. Still the count went on — forty-three . . . forty-four . . . forty-five — until an all-but-unanimous majority of sixty-one votes was announced. Every one but Eugenio Pacelli himself had voted that the Camerlengo should be the 262nd successor to Peter.

Now entered (on summons) the Prefect of Papal Ceremonies. Aided by assistants, he began lowering the canopies over all the thrones except the one occupied by a tall, ascetic man who had sat down a Cardinal and would arise a Pope.

Before the election could be duly notarized, one ceremony remained. A trio of venerable Cardinals — Pignatelli di Belmonte, Glennon and Caccia-Dominioni — gravely approached the throne where Eugenio Pacelli sat. It was their duty to put the traditional question:

"Acceptasne electionem de te canonice factam in Summum Pontificem?" asked Pignatelli di Belmonte, spokesman for the trio.

Literally the question could be translated: "Do you accept your election to the office of Supreme Pontiff?" Actually, what the aged Cardinal asked Pacelli was this: "Will you take upon yourself the burdens of the loneliest, loftiest, most exacting office in the world — will you stand patiently beneath its avalanche of drudging detail, and concern yourself from this moment until death with the spiritual leadership of four hundred million souls who look to you for guidance?"

Other men confronted by a similar question had burst into tears, begged to be let off, actually declined the crushing burden. Visibly disturbed, Pacelli hesitated.

"I am not worthy of this office," he said. Then, bowing his head, he murmured: *"Accepto in crucem"* (I accept it as a cross).

In commemoration of the first Pope, whose name Christ changed from Simon to Peter, Cardinal Pignatelli di Belmonte asked: "What name do you wish to assume?"

"I wish to be called Pius, because most of my ecclesiastical life has taken place under great pontiffs of that name." Tears were streaming down Pacelli's gaunt face. "And particularly because I am indebted to Pius XI for his personal kindness to me."

At five-thirty that afternoon a plume of white smoke rising over the roof of the Sistine Chapel told the multitude in St. Peter's Square that a new Pope had been elected.

While Pius XII retired for the *immantatio,* Lawrence Glennon sought out Stephen. "Eminent rascal," he chided, "confess your wickedness. Why did you cast that vote for me on the first ballot?"

"I?" Stephen feigned innocence.

"Who else?" said Glennon tenderly. "Who else would pour such balm on an old man's soul? I won't live to return the compliment" — Number One tinged prophecy with affection — "but mark me, Steve, the others will."

The bells of Rome's four hundred churches, led by *il camponone,* the eleven-ton master of St. Peter's, were tolling the Angelus when Cardinal Caccia-Dominioni appeared in the central balcony overlooking the Piazza. Loud-speakers carried the traditional announcement in Latin:

"I announce to you a great joy. We have a Pope. He is my Most Eminent and Reverend Lord, Eugenio. . . ."

A tremendous shout rose from half a million throats. Everyone knew who Eugenio was. Cries of *"Viva il Papa"* drowned out the pealing bells. But the real ovation occurred when the Pope himself appeared on the balcony of St. Peter's to give his blessing *urbi et orbi.* When the thunderous tumult had spent itself, all knelt in silence while the Pope blessed the city and the world.

Watching the pontiff's hand lifted in benediction, Stephen understood the serene truth of the Italian proverb: "The Pope dies, the Pope lives." Two hundred and sixty-one wearers of the triple tiara had faded from the earthly scene, but the papacy itself—now embodied in the lean and fearless person of Eugenio Pacelli—was deathless and eternal.

THE WEEK between the election and the coronation of a Pope is traditionally festive. In courtyards of great palaces, medieval torches flared while noble hostesses vied with each other in the splendor and gaiety of their parties. As befitted her rank, Princess Lontana (born Loretta Kenney of Steubenville, Ohio) was planning the gayest party of all. Her carefully selected guest list, elaborate supper menu, and the originality of her *divertissement* would, she hoped, add fresh luster to a social coronet long brilliant in Roman society.

The years had not been kind to the Princess. They had dulled the flame in her once fiery red hair without quenching it in her blood and had sluiced some of the wonderful green of her eyes into her envious soul. At sixty-one the Princess suggested withered ivy—not the ivy that softens storied walls, but the poisonous variety that brings an itching rash to all who touch it.

Even the gift of resignation had eluded the Princess. It was a source of particular anguish that the years that had filched away her charms had put a riper bloom on the beauty of her once dear friend, Ghislana Orselli. Still worse, Princess Lontana's husband continued to sink into senile dotage, while Captain Orselli had been gentleman enough to die a heroic death, thereby conferring the priceless freedom of widowhood on the handsome Ghislana.

On a kidney-shaped divan in her boudoir, an intimate rose-lighted room, the Princess was discussing her entertainment plans with Ruggiero Bari, once the leading dramatic actor of Italy. Signor Bari had outdistanced his first youth but had never quite succeeded in outrunning his creditors. He suffered from the two commonest ailments of the acting profession — a chronic lack of cash and a tendency to recall his earlier triumphs. For the past five years he had been something of a fixture in the Lontana ménage — part pensioner, part confidant, and a most serviceable friend. He listened now almost attentively as the Princess ticked off the arrangements for her party.

"I am offering my guests a *Leipziger Alleolia* by way of entertainment," she said, peering through her bifocal lorgnette at a sheet of blue note paper. "In the earlier part of the evening there will be music, of course. I have invited a young American pianist to play."

"An American pianist? Do such things exist?"

"You'll be pleasantly surprised, Ruggi. Signorina Byrne plays very well. She has been studying with Lugoni for more than a year. Surely you remember hearing her at one of Ghislana Orselli's evenings last winter. The child has quite a talent."

Bari's smile was meant to be inscrutable. "But that's not why you're feting her."

"Don't be so dashed penetrating, Ruggi." The Princess laid her cards face downward. "As a matter of fact, I'm asking her to play so that her uncle will come to my party."

"All this hugger-mugger for a mere uncle?"

"Cardinal Fermoyle is no 'mere uncle'; he's a Palatine counselor. To snare him, I was obliged to use the most attractive bait." The aging Lucrezia proceeded to unfold the rest of her plot. "I have something really original in mind, Ruggi. You can help me — on a professional basis, of course. Together, we can create an evening that will be the talk of Rome." She placed her fingers skillfully on the stops of Bari's vanity. "You will have an audience — and I — well, I shall have satisfactions of quite another kind."

"Clarify and expand, dear conspirator."

In the next few minutes the Princess outlined the details of her plan. Listening, Signor Bari alternately preened his thespian plumage and shuddered at the ferocity of feminine revenge.

"If you bring this off for me, Ruggi," the Princess concluded, "I shall write you a check *immediatamente* for ten thousand lire."

Signor Bari pressed his lips devotedly to the corded blue veins on the back of the Princess' hand. "For ten thousand lire Madame, I would declaim publicly from the works of Rudyard Kipling."

"*Bene.*" The Princess scribbled a check. "This is merely the first payment. Put your soul into it, Ruggi, and you will have a bonus of five thousand more."

HALFWAY THROUGH the evening, Princess Lontana knew that her party was a huge success. A crush of the inimitably right people, lay and ecclesiastic, moved about her oval-shaped salon, sipping champagne. Of ambassadors with ribbony badges, the hostess could count nine first-class specimens. Papal chamberlains? Ten, eleven, twelve. Knights of Malta were satisfyingly in evidence, and of distinguished laymen, a goodly spate. Among the last was the Scots scientist, Lord Eltwin, the noted seismologist, accompanied by Dom Arcibal, Superior General of the Benedictines. An odd pair, apparently interested in nothing but earthquakes. Among her female guests the Princess noted six diamond tiaras almost as valuable as the diadem blazing in her own artfully titianed hair. At ten o'clock the party was ticking like a jeweled Swiss watch —

a watch, to continue the figure, that lacked only an hour hand. The principal guest of the evening, Stephen Cardinal Fermoyle, had not yet arrived.

Keeping one eye on the entrance to her salon, the Princess circulated in her fan-fluttering multilingual way among her guests. Never once did she loosen her grip on the brunette eighteen-year-old beauty she had in tow. Approaching a knot of champagne sippers, the Princess would say:

"Permit me to introduce Signorina Byrne, our artiste of the evening. Do not be dazzled by her beauty. *Le vrai éblouissement* will occur when you hear her at the piano. Regina has another distinction, too . . . she is a niece of Cardinal Fermoyle. I am expecting His Eminence at any moment."

Having repeated this hostess rigmarole thirty times, the Princess could finally add at ten-fifteen: "And here he is now!"

Tugging Regina by the hand, Princess Lontana advanced to greet Stephen. The seventeen years since she had last seen him had subtracted no fraction of male vigor from his features. Deeper through the heart perhaps, and certainly more grizzled under his scarlet skullcap. Sterner, too, about the eyes and chin. Still long of flank, and still preserving the head carriage of the dedicated priest, the American Cardinal wore his watered silk as a cup defender wears its complement of sail.

The Princess curtsied, kissed the sapphire on Stephen's extended hand, then became intimate-exclamatory. "Seventeen years is too long a time to stay away from old friends, Your Eminence. Another such disappearance" — she drew Regina into her little tableau — "and we shall be feting your grandniece."

"You make the future seem almost as attractive as the present," said Stephen, bending to kiss Regina's cheek. "Been practicing hard, widgeon?" (How easily his old nickname for Mona fitted this lustrous-eyed girl smiling up at him.)

"Hours and hours, Uncle Stephen. Signor Lugoni says — guess what he says I have?"

"Talent? *L'esprit? La fiamma?* It all depends on the language your teacher was speaking that day. What does Signor Lugoni say you have?"

"He says I have *industry*." Regina laughed at the dubiousness of her teacher's compliment. "I should hate to be known as an industrious piano player."

Princess Lontana had no intention of letting Regina monopolize the guest of the evening. "*Verve* is the word for your niece," she whispered, leading Stephen trophy fashion down the gantlet of her salon. At every step there was a presentation, carried off with prestissimo fan flutterings and an afterthought introduction of Regina. Having come for the express purpose of hearing Regina play, Stephen was about to suggest that the social circuit be closed, when his hostess whispered:

"Prepare yourself, Eminence, for the pleasantest moment of all. You are about to meet an old friend." Though the quivering timbre of her voice suggested excitement, Stephen was not prepared for the Princess' next remark:

"Look, Ghislana, at the surprise I have arranged. Stephen has come back to us. Our American Monsignor returns a glittering Prince of the Church."

The Princess' triumphant manner disclosed an element of trickery, planned in advance and suddenly sprung. The touch of chicane struck Stephen as being definitely in bad taste. His hostess need not have staged this meeting so dramatically or announced it with such fanfare. Yet, in spite of his displeasure, Stephen was glad to see Ghislana Orselli again.

Time had sifted impalpable dust-of-pearl over her face and hair, hushing the cry of her loveliness, as a harpist mutes toovibrant strings with his hand. Though traces of her earlier mystery remained, he saw that she was, at fifty-two, a serenely matured woman with the same slow smile and quiet manner of lifting her eyes.

"Felicitations, Your Eminence," said Ghislana. "I congratulate you on your elevation" — her violet glance rested on Stephen's cross of diamonds — "and on your niece. The first, I could have predicted. The second" — she smiled at Regina — "I had to discover for myself."

"I am happy that you and Regina found each other," said Stephen. It was an accurate statement of his feelings. Could he have chosen a single friend for Mona's daughter, he would have named Ghislana Orselli as custodian and tutor of all that was enduringly feminine in the world.

Princess Lontana's awareness that her grand salvo had

somehow misfired brought an itch of irritation into her voice. "Gina dear," she said, "I think that everyone is waiting for you to play. Come, let me make a little speech telling them who you are."

In the expectant hush that followed Princess Lontana's introduction, Regina took her place at the piano. With seeming simplicity she played a Chopin nocturne. To Stephen, as to the rest of the audience, it was apparent that the pianist had the unusual gift of letting the music deliver its own message. Chopin was followed by *Reflets dans l'eau*, a Debussy tone poem, delicately nebulous under the artiste's hand. Taking her meed of applause gracefully, Regina moved into the grandly styled Bach-Tausig Toccata and Fugue in D minor — a work that emerged in appropriate sweep and strength.

Happiness, differing in kind and intensity from any he had yet known, filled Stephen as he watched Regina at the piano. This was Mona's daughter, more beautiful, more gifted than Mona — a soul obviously at ease before perfection, capable of loving and growing in its light. This was the child the white-coated doctor would have destroyed in routine fashion. In eighteen short years, the curve of God's circle had been revealed. From the broken arc of Mona's life, He had shaped this perfect round.

Sea-deep, haunting, Regina's music filled the salon. Men and women rose to applaud as she left the piano. Stephen stood, too, eyes brimming with pride and happiness. At his side, he felt Ghislana Orselli sharing Regina's triumph with him. Secretly they smiled at each other; together they waited for Regina to join them. But the Princess evidently had other plans, for she led the artiste to a little court of admirers at the other side of the salon.

Now appeared Signor Ruggiero Bari, florid, self-assured, and curiously mesmeric, "Our hostess, self-sister of the Muses and patroness of poets," he began, "has asked me to present for your entertainment a few scenes from dramatic literature. I shall begin with an interpretation of D'Annunzio's *Francesca da Rimini,* in which, creating the part of Paolo" — he bowed with affected modesty — "I have had the honor to support the immortal Duse."

Without props or costume (Signor Bari wore tails and white

tie), the actor proceeded to demonstrate the naked power of his art. Setting the stage in a few majestic strophes, he re-enacted D'Annunzio's version of the illicit love between Paolo and Francesca da Rimini. His portrayal of the tragic lovers won well-deserved "bravos" from the audience.

Much taken by the man's art, Stephen wondered why Signor Bari had chosen this particular theme. It was, of course, older than Dante; undeniably, too, it furnished the actor with histrionic material of a high order. Still, from the entire range of literature, guilty love was scarcely the subject one might have expected on such an occasion.

Ruggiero was making his next announcement. "I shall now render Alfred de Vigny's *La Colère de Samson,* depicting the eternal struggle between man's vision of God and woman's unremitting attempt to divert him from that goal. Samson, shorn of his strength, laments the treachery of Delilah — *la ruse de la femme* — by which man is constantly betrayed."

Bari's rendition of the poem was superb. But why this pre-occupation with the pathology of mortal love? Somewhat puzzled, Stephen turned to Ghislana: "Surely there are other poems he might have chosen. Am I suspecting a motive where none is intended?"

"I think the intention is strongly marked, Your Eminence."

"But what is behind it?"

"*La ruse de la femme,*" said Ghislana quietly.

The depth and malice of Princess Lontana's plot seemed almost unbelievable to Stephen. Yet of the hundred or more persons in the audience, the Princess alone had private knowledge of the old passion that had existed between Ghislana and himself. Could it be that the Princess was purposely contriving to awaken echoes of the past? Or was she taking a perverse, malignant delight in saying (under cover of Bari's declamation), "See how much I know about you two?" It was unthinkable that anyone, even a faded old harridan, could devise such torments for herself, or impose such cruel embarrassment on onetime friends. Yet it was clear now to Stephen that the Princess had baited her trap with Regina's innocence, then arranged matters so that he and Ghislana would sit together during Bari's performance. Shocked and angered by the ugliness of the plot, he turned in agitation to his companion:

"Princess Lontana must be mad!"

Ghislana's answer came in a soothing whisper: "Don't give her the satisfaction of seeing that you are disturbed."

It was good advice. Powerless to fight or run, Stephen was preparing to follow it, when a bass rumble, very pleasant to hear, came from a member of the audience. Dom Arcibal was addressing the actor. "Are you familiar, Signor Bari, with the passage in Dante's *Paradiso* that describes the poet's last vision of Beatrice? I think the scene occurs in the thirty-first canto."

Stephen saw petulant displeasure cloud the Princess' face. Evidently Signor Bari saw it also. To protect his five-thousand-lire bonus, the actor began an elaborate apology. The passage was familiar to him, of course, but unfortunately the lines were not quite fresh in his memory.

Dom Arcibal was not to be shaken off so easily. "Surely our hostess, self-sister to the Muses, has a copy of Dante in her library. It would give an old monk extreme pleasure to hear the passage read by so great an artist as Signor Bari."

Overreached, Princess Lontana sent a servant for a copy of *The Divine Comedy*. Book in hand, Bari was glancing desperately through its pages, when Dom Arcibal gave the screw another twist.

"For the benefit of my friend, Lord Eltwin — whose only cultural deficiency is a sorry lack of Italian — might we have a running translation in English?" Beaming innocently about the salon, the monk finally glanced at Stephen. "Cardinal Fermoyle's felicity with tongues is remembered by many in this room. If it is not too great an imposition, Your Eminence, will you exercise your skill for us tonight?"

A meaningful wink from Dom Arcibal's off-eye accompanied the request.

The cunning instrument placed in his hands by Dom Arcibal — the only other person in the world who knew of Stephen's former attachment to Ghislana — gave the American Cardinal an unexpected weapon. Human enough to enjoy using it against his deceitful hostess, he arose, smiled at Dom Arcibal, and said: "I shall be glad to translate for the benefit of your friend. You must forgive me, though, if I stammer in the presence of Alighieri's genius."

The reading began with Dante's glorious apostrophe to the divine light that penetrates the universe:

> *O trina luce, che in unica stella*
> *scintillando a lor vista si gli appaga,*
> *guarda quaggiù alla nostrà procella*

Stephen rendered the lines freely:

"O triune light, which in a single star contents all upon whom it shineth — gaze down upon our mortal storm."

Bari continued with the stanza in which the poet recounts his rapture at beholding Beatrice shining near the center of sempiternal light:

> *. . . gli occhi su levai,*
> *e vidi lei che si facea corona,*
> *riflettendo da sè gli eterni rai.*

Stephen felt the poverty of his translation:

"Lifting my eyes I saw her, crowned, reflecting the light of those eternal rays."

> *. . . chè sua effige*
> *non discendeva a me per mezzo mista.*

How recreate the unsayable vision? Stephen tried:

"Her image unsullied by baser atmosphere, descended upon me."

At the lines immortalizing Dante's gratitude to Beatrice, Stephen translated in shining verses the essence of his own regard for Ghislana Orselli.

> *By virtue of love's power,*
> *From servitude to freedom thou hast drawn me . . .*
>
> *Preserve in me thy pure magnificence,*
> *So that my spirit, cleansed of all desire,*
> *May, praise to thee, be loosened from my body.*

Moved either by the elegance of Stephen's translation or by some secret knowledge that the audience — enthusiastic though it was — could never share, Dom Arcibal rose to lead the applause. His bass *"bravissimo"* rolled toward Stephen on a special wave, as if echoing words uttered years ago in a penitential cell on the Campagna: "There is much love in your heart, dear son. God wants all of it. *Bravissimo*. By grace and self-conquest you have offered Him the nearly-perfect gift He demands from His anointed servants."

HIGH in the dome of St. Peter's, silver trumpets sent echoes of the Papal March flying. Seventy thousand persons stood inside the church, half a million more jammed the Piazza outside, as the coronation procession of Pius XII entered the central doors of the Basilica.

No external sign of pomp and pageantry was lacking. First came an Auditor of the Holy Rota, holding aloft a spearheaded cross, surrounded by seven acolytes of noble birth. Came papal gendarmes in towering black busbies and white breeches, followed by chamberlains in lace ruffs and chains of gold. Knights of Malta advanced in solemn phalanx, their white cloaks emblazoned with crimson crosses; behind them at the slow pace of pageantry came sandaled monks, bearded patriarchs, mitered bishops, and purple-robed archbishops. Now the princes of the Church appeared, cardinals regally-caped, walking solemnly two by two, the younger men first, the more venerable elders nearer the papal *sedia* directly behind them. Between the cardinals and the Pope a band of heralds and mace-bearers guarded the triple tiara, a beehive in shape, studded with precious stones, and borne on a red velvet cushion.

On the shoulders of twelve throne-bearers, attired in crimson damask liveries, the Pope's *sedia gestatoria* floated above the throng. His cloth-of-gold cape was caught at the throat by a jeweled clasp; over his head a cream-colored canopy swayed. On either side, prelates waved the traditional *flabelli*, magnificent ostrich-plumed fans. While the Sistine choir chanted *"Tu es Petrus,"* the Pope ceaselessly made signs of the cross, blessing the multitude with white-gloved hands.

At the chapel of the Most Holy Trinity, the procession halted while Pius XII descended from his throne to adore the Blessed Sacrament. Like any other priest he knelt, head bowed, in prayer. No music now. Hushed all. From the enormous vault of the dome, silence fell like a tapestry.

Finishing his prayer of adoration, Pius XII rose from his knees and prepared to seat himself again on his throne. A cowled monk approached. In one hand he carried a lighted taper; in the other, a tuft of wax-impregnated hemp. Bowing to His Holiness, the monk brought flame and hemp together. Fire flashed momentarily, then vanished in smoke.

"Sic transit gloria mundi," cried the monk.

As the procession moved at the tempo of high ritual past the statue of St. Peter, the symbolic act of earthly consummation was re-enacted. In sepulchral tones, *"Sic transit"* reverberated through the Basilica.

At the central altar, reserved for the Sovereign Pontiff alone, Pius XII vested for solemn Pontifical Mass. At the conclusion of the Mass he would be crowned with the triple tiara, symbolic of the Church Suffering, the Church Militant, and the Church Triumphant.

Princes would bow to the wearer of this crown; panoply would surround his person; a semblance of divinity would clothe his words. Only a forehead proved against personal vanity could bear so flaming a burden. To remind the Pope of the fearful jeopardy in which he would live, and the ultimate dust to which mortal glories return, the hooded monitor approached him for the third time. Again flame met hemp, again the lugubrious warning sounded: *"Sic transit gloria mundi."*

The Mass began. Stephen, sitting among his compeers, watched the changeless sacrifice unfold. As in all other Masses, whether celebrated in vaulted temple or thatched hut, the priest re-enacted the Passion suffered by Christ that men might gain life everlasting. As Pius XII extended his hands over the oblation he was about to consecrate, Stephen silently joined him in the *Hanc igitur.*

"We therefore beseech Thee, O Lord, mercifully to accept this oblation of our servitude, as also of Thy whole family: and to dispose our days in Thy peace; and bid us be delivered from eternal damnation, and to be numbered among the flock of Thy elect. Through Christ our Lord. Amen."

The grandeur of earthly pomp, the gauds of fame, the baubles of power, and the transient adulation of men — all,

all would vanish as a spark amid darkness, a yesterday which is past. But the oblation would remain. The eternal sacrifice would live on, concelebrated by priest and people, fellow partakers of His promise: "Behold I am with you all days, even to the consummation of the world."

EPILOGUE

Between Two Worlds

LIKE that better-known English captain before him, Sir Humphrey Grylls, K.C.B., master of the luxury liner *Oriana,* was never, never sick at sea. As a younger man he had been slightly apprehensive of icebergs — a pardonable fear, perhaps, in view of that rather bad show on the *Titanic.* But now in his middle fifties, the only remainder of that earlier dread was a tingling in Sir Humphrey's nasal membranes whenever his vessel came within a hundred miles of a berg. In the trade, Sir Humphrey was regarded as a captain's captain. He ran a spit-and-polish, loyalty-up, loyalty-down ship; in 388 transatlantic crossings, not a flake of paint had been scraped from any of his commands.

With military brushes Sir Humphrey coaxed an ebbing tide of collie-colored hair across a widening beach of scalp, adjusted his hat to the slant prescribed by Beatty of Jutland, and surveyed himself in a double-hung mirror. Imperially slim, the Captain might have been thought handsome except for pallid blue eyes, too narrowly set for some tastes. His numerous decorations, with the Victoria Cross as a pendant, hung from the left breast of his dress jacket. Having won the cross as a reserve lieutenant in World War I, Sir Humphrey now wondered whether he would be eligible for command of a battle cruiser in the coming struggle. If not a cruiser, then a destroyer. Anything. *England expects . . .*

Sir Humphrey filled his cigar case, nipped down the points of his waistcoat, and went on deck. The night was moonless, clear; acid stars etched brilliant, geometric patterns in the heavens. By Polaris and the Bear, Captain Grylls approximated the position of his ship. Thirty-two hundred miles out of Liverpool on a rhumb-line course to New York. With luck, landfall by daybreak.

He felt a curious tingling in his left septum. Ice? The indication was not definite. To a junior officer saluting him at the saloon-deck companionway, he murmured: "Station lookouts in the eyes of the ship, Mr. Ramilly. Have the searchlights play about. If the temperature drops another five degrees, notify me at once."

Having virtually insured the safety of his vessel (Sir Humphrey's lightest utterance was like a turret lathe cutting wax), the Captain entered the Regency Lounge, bestowing at regular intervals that special inclination of the head reserved for distinguished landsmen. The lounge was unusually crowded this evening; a cosmopolitan buzz, incited by predinner cocktails, rose from the tables. It occurred to Sir Humphrey that the wave of European refugees — titled, wealthy, or talented — had reached a new high on this voyage. Seemingly, everyone who could get out of Europe with a whole skin (and enough capital) was traveling first class aboard the *Oriana*, seeking life, liberty, and the pursuit of happiness in the New World.

Not only was the passenger list swollen. The *Oriana* herself was bursting with valuable cargo — works of art, crown jewels, rare brandies, furniture from ancestral castles, priceless manuscripts, family plate, and costly fabrics. Not to mention thirty million dollars in gold bullion stowed in steel compartments below the waterline. A whole civilization was being transported across the Atlantic to the barbarian, but infinitely safer shores of the United States.

At the entrance to the dining room, Sir Humphrey gave his hat to the steward and walked, every inch a baronet, to his oval table in the center of the dining room. On a French ship, part of the captain's duty is to pause at least once and inquire: "The *moules marinières*—you find them exciting?" The master of an Italian ship is expected to admire, momentarily at least, the beauties of an especially handsome corsage. No such obligations devolve upon a British captain. Therefore, Sir Humphrey proceeded straightway to his own table, bowed to the seated ladies, prayed the gentlemen not to rise, and took his place between two comely women. On this, the last night of his 388th crossing, the Captain was prepared to enjoy the nigh-onto-forty charms of Lady Adela Bracington (blonde), at his right, and the budding promise (brunette) of Regina Byrne, at his left.

Similarly situated, the master of a German ship might have smirked: "*Eine Dorne zwischen zwei Rosen.*" Coming from

Sir Humphrey, the remark would have sounded fatuous. Not that the Captain was immune to feminine allure. Quite the contrary. Lady Adela Bracington had heard (as who had not?) of the notorious "Humphy-Bumphy" letters, bought up at a devilish steep price on the eve of their publication in *The Mayfair Tatler*.

About to join her diplomat husband in Washington, and prepared to hate every minute of it, Lady Adela had her twitting cap on tonight. In the shrill, abrasive tones that only English gentlewomen are permitted to use in public, she rallied the Baronet.

"Where do you keep yourself all day, Sir Humphrey? I've been rummaging about the boat for hours. Looked for you everywhere except the buttery."

"That's precisely where I was, Lady Adela. Who do you suppose prints these little crests on the butter pats?"

In the laughter following this bit of *esprit anglais,* Sir Humphrey nodded to his more important guests: the Archduke Rollo, second in line to the defunct throne of Hungary, and his Archduchess Helen, forlornly beautiful in a wickless-lamp sort of way. To the chap with the Académie-Française whiskers — André Girardot, Prix Goncourt novelist — he gave a respectful glance. Slightly more chill was his recognition of Professor Kurt Gottwald, author of that massive tome, *Welt-Politik und Zeitgeist,* reputedly the philosophic basis of Nazism. Unlike Cassius, Professor Gottwald's thinking had not made him thin. The Captain would be glad at journey's end to say: "*Auf Wiedersehen*" to Herr Gottwald, his messy table manners, and his ugly sarcasm.

Sir Humphrey exchanged smiles with His Eminence, Stephen Cardinal Fermoyle, newly elected to the Sacred College. Most exclusive club in the world, Sir Humphrey had been told. Cardinals were a doddering lot generally, but this American prelate seemed terribly fit. Youngish, too. Been mentioned as the first American Pope. Reasonable enough. With everything else crossing the Atlantic, why not the papacy?

"I am sorry to hear," said Sir Humphrey to Stephen, "that illness confines my old friend Cardinal Glennon to his quarters. His Eminence has proved an excellent sailor on previous journeys."

"Your compliments will cheer him, Captain," said Stephen. "We hope to have His Eminence up for the concert later in the evening."

Lady Bracington's carborundum voice gritted against the general ear. "Question for you, Sir Humphrey. Came up this afternoon after a beastly bit of impertinence from one of your stewards. The fellow actually mumbled under his breath." With this upper-class prelude, Lady Adela put her question: "Could a captain shoot down a crew member who refused to obey an order?"

Sir Humphrey's reply was a model of conservatism: "If the captain were an Englishman, Lady Adela, the answer would be: 'He could, but wouldn't.'"

Teutonic whimsy caused Professor Gottwald to make choking sounds with his soup. "You say 'wouldn't,' Captain. Has England, in her orgy of appeasement, entirely renounced discipline?"

Sir Humphrey kept his voice within the bounds of the declarative. "British crews simply don't disobey a properly given order."

Gottwald dropped the mask of amenity. "You forget the *Titanic* incident."

"I do not forget the incident. I happened to be one of the *Titanic's* junior officers when she went down."

Pressing hard now, the author of *Welt-Politik und Zeitgeist* lapsed into a German locution. "Crew members were on that occasion shot, *nicht wahr?*"

Sir Humphrey's narrow-set eyes converged sharply on his guest. The man was hectoring him. Gratuitously and with ghoulish enjoyment the Nazi philosopher was exhuming pitiful events long buried by the sea. Sir Humphrey's nostrils quivered. More than a quarter century ago, in this very latitude, at about this time of year, he had been hurled from his bunk by the collision of rushing steel with solid berg. There had been a desperate scene of confusion as twenty-five hundred passengers charged the lifeboats. Half naked, pistol in hand, Lieutenant Humphrey Grylls had supervised the lowering of No. 4 life raft — one of the few constructive actions performed on that fateful night — and had paddled 109 hysterical passengers out of the liner's fatal down draft.

"If guns were drawn on that occasion," said Sir Humphrey, "it was to guarantee that women and children should have first places in the lifeboats."

"Really?" Gottwald reminded Stephen of an entomologist about to pin a rare butterfly to his specimen board. "Then how did you happen to survive, Captain?"

Stephen had never seen a man on a crueler spot, yet there was no wriggling from the Britisher as he took the pin through his High-Anglican viscera. "If you are sufficiently interested, Professor, to read a detailed account of what happened, I recommend the British Admiralty report, published by the official board of inquiry."

Gottwald's satisfaction was almost unbearable. "These reports you refer to, Captain. As a professional historian, may I point out that they were written by Englishmen, about an English disaster, as described by English — shall I say? — survivors."

Having permitted his guest the pleasure of bidding a grand slam, Sir Humphrey summarily took all the cards away from him.

"History will always be written that way, Professor," he observed. The Baronet spread a bit of personally printed butter on a biscuit, and turned to the young lady at his left. "I am looking forward to the pleasure of your concert later in the evening, Miss Byrne. Will you include any English composers in your repertory?"

Something about the Captain's question and his droll-dry manner of asking it brought a bubble of laughter to Regina's lips. "Which English composer would you like to hear, Captain?"

"Bless me if I can remember any of their names," said Sir Humphrey. "Of course," he added, "one can always find a tune in *H.M.S. Pinafore*."

AT THEIR VARIOUS STATIONS aboard the *Oriana*, plowing across the North Atlantic toward the New World, men and women advanced the pattern of destiny.

In his suite on A deck, an octogenarian Cardinal thrust one leg out of bed, and cried: "Jeremy! These walls bore me. Must I lie here counting rosary beads forever? Clap some clothes onto me prestissimo, Monsignor. Fetch me my gold-headed cane. I want to have a front seat when Regina begins the opening movement of the Brahms Sonata."

In a stateroom on B deck, Conrad Szalay released some of his mounting tension by bowing a spiccato passage on the strings of a violin presented him by his patron, Cardinal Fermoyle. The instrument, a perfect replica of the Cremona school, bore the signature "Rafael Menton, 1937" on the parchment glued inside its maple back. In two years the violin had ripened marvelously, keeping pace with the prodigious development of its owner. Tonight, a cosmopolitan audience gathered in the music room of the *Oriana* would hear the young virtuoso present the fruits of eighteen months' study with Georges Enesco, one of the greatest teachers in Europe.

Ordinarily, the program offered at a shipboard concert is of the musical-meringue variety. This evening, however, the fare would be somewhat more substantial — and for two reasons. First, Cardinal Fermoyle must be given audible proof that his support and encouragement had not been bestowed unworthily. Second, the American concert manager, Frederick C. Schang, would be in the audience, checking personally on reports of Conrad's wizardry that had reached him from Paris and London. If "Schangoni," as many of his artists endearingly called him, were sufficiently impressed, a concert contract would be forthcoming. And with such a contract in his pocket, Conrad could ask Regina Byrne to marry him.

In a cabin adjoining her Cardinal-uncle's suite, Regina Byrne sat at a dressing table, clipping a pearl onto the lobe of her ear. Uncle Stephen had given her the pearl earrings in Rome, and had kissed the places where they would be worn. Odd? Not at all. What was odd about being kissed by a man you loved more than anyone else — Conrad excepted — in the whole world?

Gazing at herself in the mirror, Regina no longer sighed for blonde curls and china-blue eyes. She knew now that her ivory-pastel coloring, with its violet underhue repeated in the shadows of her eyes and hair, was the dark beauty that Conrad loved most. He had said so, sometimes in his own words, sometimes in language borrowed from the poet who had sworn that dark was fair.

Regina rose from her dressing table, pivoted on the toe of her satin slipper till her chiffon evening gown swirled like a ballerina's. No music she would make this evening could accompany the saltarello bounding in her heart.

AT A CORNER TABLE of the men's bar, André Girardot was engaged in the typically French pastime of laying his intellectual doubts against a sympathetic ear. Born a Roman Catholic and educated by Jesuits, M. Girardot had, at the age of sixteen, slanted off on one of those agnostic tangents so dear to the Gallic mind. Now, a world-famous novelist at fifty-five, he was circling back to the faith — and making a very circumstantial tale of his experiences to Cardinal Fermoyle.

"The only hurdle that blocks my wholehearted acceptance of the sacraments," he explained to Stephen, "is the emphasis that Rome places on its institutional trappings. I should be so much happier, Your Eminence, if the Church would forsake temporal considerations, and return to the pristine simplicity of the catacombs."

Always the fisher of souls, Stephen angled cautiously for this intellectual carp. "One can always make the return privately," he suggested. "Christ is just as accessible in the Eucharist today as He ever was."

M. Girardot clung with tenacity to his argument. "True. But might not Rome make a more powerful appeal if it laid aside political weapons, picked up the cross, and went forth crying: 'Under this sign, and this sign *alone*, we conquer.'"

Stephen was framing his reply when the bulky figure of Professor Kurt Gottwald waddled toward the table. Behind the Professor — erect, head shaved, and very soldierly in bearing — came Major General Piotr Kolodnov, military attaché to the Soviet Embassy in Washington.

By the freemasonry existing in a ship's bar, Professor Gottwald felt he had the right to interrupt any conversation he pleased. By the same code, Stephen and M. Girardot were bound to accept the interruption. The French novelist would have preferred to continue his revelations to the American Cardinal, yet the prospect of insulting Herr Gottwald was also attractive. To state the case exactly, M. Girardot, a highly articulate Frenchman, longed for the pleasure of talking the German deaf, dumb, and blind.

No sooner was Professor Gottwald seated when M. Girardot began making fancy shots on the pistol range of wit. He would have juggled wineglasses, even performed match tricks, for the sheer delight of keeping the Professor muzzled. Stephen was enjoying the spectacle of two professional talkers jostling each other like six-day bicyclists competing for a sprint prize. Girardot, all pace and vivacity, held his lead; Gottwald stubbornly pedaled behind him, while the Russian General, brooding over his cognac, brought up the rear. Suddenly there was a change of position. Girardot, having told the cynical fable (then current) of four authors — an Englishman, an American, a German, and a Frenchman — who displayed their national characteristics in a treatise on elephants, waited too long for laughter that did not come. Writhing on his fat haunches, Gottwald shot ahead of his Gallic rival.

"Your tale is amusing, Monsieur. Instructive, too, since it leads us directly into the theme of nationalism — a subject developed exhaustively by the German philosopher, Hegel."

Triumphantly out in front now, Professor Gottwald proceeded to explain Hegel's dynamic of history. "In every age," he said, "there emerges a nation charged with the mission of carrying the world through its present phase of development." Herr Gottwald held up his hand like a fat semaphore to keep the Frenchman and Russian at their sidings while the Hegelian express roared past. "Hegel tells us that the State is pure spirit embodied in the person of a leader whose actions reveal the unity and meaning of history. To those who have read my *Welt-Politik und Zeitgeist,* is it not three times clear that Der Führer is the perfect embodiment of the time-spirit?"

Major General Kolodnov bristled. As military attaché to the Soviet Embassy, he could do no less.

"Stalin has destroyed Hegel's bourgeois conception of history," he said. "History is the outworking of the class struggle, demonstrated in the Marxian triad: feudalism, capitalism, the soviet. The first two phases are already dead." Kolodnov lifted his glass of Napoleon brandy. "I drink to Stalin, spokesman of the future."

"*Quel sentiment!*" murmured Girardot. He turned to Stephen. "Is Your Eminence content to be outdone in this court of orthodoxy? The champions of Hitler and Stalin have lifted their glasses. What? No toast to His Holiness Pius XII?"

Stephen took the tease lightly. "I didn't want to appear *arriviste*," he smiled. "The two hundred and sixty-second successor to Peter needs no clinking of glasses to bolster his position."

"A very palpable hit," said Girardot gleefully.

Strains of music, unmistakably Brahms, entered the *Oriana's* bar. Teutonic satisfaction relaxed Herr Gottwald's features. "An encouraging sign, gentlemen. The ascendency of German music appears to be acknowledged even on British ships."

"Let's see who's playing the German music," suggested Stephen.

The four men strolled into the adjoining salon, where an audience of about two hundred persons sat listening to Brahms' A-major Sonata. At the piano sat Regina Byrne, quarter-profiled. Facing the audience, Conrad Szalay, violin lofted, was attacking the first movement of the sonata with confident mastery. There was no chamber-music humility about his playing, yet no stridency either. The large singing tone of his violin filled the salon.

"Resonant without grease," said Herr Gottwald approvingly. "Just the way Brahms should be played."

At the end of the sonata, Conrad stepped aside to let Regina take the major share of applause.

"Technique by the fistful," said Kolodnov. "He plays like a Russian."

Stephen did not think it worth while to point out that Conrad was an American, born of Polish parents.

"Our next selection." Conrad was saying, "will be the *Introduction and Rondo capriccioso* of the French composer, Saint-Saëns."

"Now we shall hear something," said Girardot.

Regina's hands descended into silence and brought forth a subdued carillon. The violin entered, singing plaintively. Elegant legato tones resolved suddenly into a burst of droplets, shaken from Conrad's bow as he broke the harmonic spectrum into scintillating fragments. The plaintive air returned,

and was again put to flight by a miniature explosion of spiccato notes in the lowest register of the violin.

From the G string Conrad began subtly climbing until he
reached the highest register of his instrument, poised there a
moment, then descended in a parabolic cadenza. Regina
bolted suddenly. Brisk, measured chords from the piano began
beating the motif for a saltarello. Into a circle of clapping
hands the violinist entered, capering gaily on the gleaming
E string.

Lawrence Glennon, his chin resting on the knob of a gold-
headed cane, exhaled in sheer unbelief. Schang, the American
concert agent, reserved judgment until the next section — the
stumbling block of all but a few exceptional violinists. Stephen
Fermoyle, listening to the flood of music pouring from Conrad's violin, wished that Rafe Menton might have heard his
instrument singing this night.

A sudden magical impulse at the tip of Conrad's bow sent
it skipping upward in a rollicking staccato. With unerring
mechanical precision, the fingers of his left hand drove like
pistons propelled by the ignited fuel of his temperament. Hand
extended to the very top of the fingerboard, he plummeted
downward in a shower of sparks.

Until this moment Herr Gottwald had always sniggered at
the idea of French music. He was not sniggering now.

Deserted momentarily by the pianist, Conrad executed a
cadenza of triple-stopped chords with hammerlike strokes of
his bow. Now the two instruments entered the home stretch
together. Fingers beating like hoofs, Conrad hurdled the final
arpeggios with effortless strength; he swept up the pianist in
his exuberance, and ended on the swift gleam of a harmonic.
Carried by the impetus, Regina crashed powerfully into a
finale of majestic chords.

The audience went up like a rocket. Gottwald, Girardot,
and Kolodnov joined voices for the first time that evening:
"Bravo! . . . Encore!" they cried, while Lawrence Glennon
pounded the floor with his cane, and "Schangoni" made an
involuntary clutch at his fountain pen. Even the Victoria Cross
on Sir Humphrey's dress coat shook visibly as he applauded.
Flushed and happy, Conrad and Regina bowed to the audi-

ence and each other. Then, leaning close to Conrad's ear, Regina whispered something. The young violinist smiled and nodded.

"By special request," he announced, "we shall now play a melody from *H.M.S. Pinafore*."

The Captain of the *Oriana*, enjoying himself enormously, was humming: "And when the breezes blow, I generally go below," when a junior officer edged through the salon to his side. Evidently the young officer's communication was grave, for Sir Humphrey left the salon and, instead of "seeking the seclusion that my cabin grants," took up his station on the bridge of the *Oriana*.

A gold St. Christopher medal in the fob pocket of his waistcoat warmed the Captain's High-Anglican heart as he took personal command of his ship.

To WARD OFF the bone-piercing chill in the air, Stephen put on his ferraiolino, the great cape worn by Peter's admirals, and stepped on deck. He drew his cloak cowl fashion around his head, and walked toward the bow of the vessel. Braced against the rail, he let his mind rove like a planchette across the events of the evening. How mixed, how blent of joy and grief, love and hatred, a few hours could be! The dominant note of the evening had been, of course, Conrad's superb performance. His amazing virtuosity, his personal magnetism, and the obvious love that existed between him and Regina had struck a joyous yea-saying chord for every listener. Yet under the triumphant themes of art and love, Stephen heard the fearful discords jangling aboard the *Oriana*. That flareup at dinner between Sir Humphrey and Herr Gottwald! Ostensibly about an ill-fated ship, the encounter had in reality disclosed black hatreds squatting in the chasm of national rivalry. That rivalry had received grim underscorings from Gottwald and Kolodnov in the ship's bar. Their bitter wrangling had drowned out the plea of a gentler Voice: "How often would I have gathered together thy children, as the hen gathereth her chickens under her wings, and thou wouldst not."

On the darkened bridge above him, Stephen heard a series of paired chimes. Eight bells. By landsman reckoning, midnight. Day's nadir, the deepest pit of darkness from which the day-star must climb wearily to the uncertain shelf of dawn. Never had the world's midnight been more chill with dread. Never would the little hours climb more perilously to cock-crow.

Stephen lifted his eyes to the stars glittering in the hard blue arch of heaven. True north, Polaris glowed. Pointing in constancy at the polestar was Dubhe of lustrous magnitude, guide to shepherds, navigators, and occasionally, to drivers of trolley cars. Low on the sea rim burned the planet of many names — Lucifer, Venus, Hesperus — always the same star, fiery, threatening, and peculiarly linked with events in Stephen Fermoyle's life.

He remembered Orselli's dandyish forefinger pointing at it from the bridge of the *Vesuvio.* "Why do you wish to know Lucifer's position?" Orselli had asked. "Do you fear his fate?" Across a quarter-century Stephen recalled his own answer: "I fear, you fear, we all fear." In the years intervening between that westward passage and this one, not a single word of Stephen's answer could be altered. Now, as then, nations were careening toward war. Arrogant and unheeding, men still rejected Christ's commandment: "Love ye one another."

A patch of mist blurring the horizon blotted out the fiery star. Other patches floated in. Stephen thought it strange that fog should be gathering on such a night. Usually, fog was caused by currents of warm air crossing a colder sea. But here the air itself was frigid. What, then, was causing the fog?

Off the *Oriana's* port bow loomed the answer — a gigantic mountain of ice, its base obscured by wraiths of mist, its pinnacles glittering in the starlight. The glacial invader, drifting into a sea warmer than itself, was generating the double hazard most dreaded by shipmasters. Icebergs alone were perilous enough: wrapped in self-created fog, they compounded danger at a fearful ratio.

A lookout posted in the eyes of the ship had seen the danger; he signaled the bridge:

"Iceberg off the port bow!"

On the bridge, coolly watchful, Sir Humphrey Grylls spoke to his engine room. Stephen felt a slackening throb of the *Oriana's* propellers as the vessel slowed to quarter speed.

Another signal ascended: "Iceberg off the starboard bow!"

Peering ahead, Stephen could see the drifting archipelago of icebergs through which the *Oriana* must pick her way. Rising from the ice field, a ghostly fog embraced ship, stars, all.

Alone, mist-wrapped, an American Cardinal, approaching the shores of his homeland, meditated.

Possessor of a mind seasoned by reality and fortified by long experience of men and affairs, Stephen Fermoyle was the ripe product of religious faith, spiritual discipline, and intellectual energy. Courage to speak and discretion to keep silence were equally balanced on his tongue. A quarter century of priestly obedience had not impaired his independence as a man, nor had the instinct for authority blunted his still deeper instincts to worship and love. Now at fifty-one, tender of heart, stanch of soul, and well conditioned in body, he was being called upon to exert his full powers in the service of the Holy Roman Catholic Church.

How best should those powers be used? Stripped of accidentals, what was the essential function of the Church? What position, what *action*, should it take in a world beset by wars and evil men?

Should the Church retreat, as Girardot had suggested, to the catacombs? No. That was naïve, romantic, even frivolous. Such a withdrawal would be contrary to the injunction Christ had laid upon His Apostles: "Go ye, and teach all nations." *All* nations! None to be favored, none neglected, none exempt. The divine mission to preserve and extend the faith was universal, constant, binding upon all. If this mission were to be performed, the Church must manifest itself clearly, actively, *militantly*, in a world sorely needing some accent of the Holy Ghost.

By what instrumentalities should the work of the Church be carried on?

Primarily by the sacraments — the seven outward signs instituted by Christ to give grace. To administer these sacraments, a tremendous organization was necessary. The Visible Church, with its ceremonial observances, its laws and revenues, its spiritual head, the Pope, and under him the bishops — successors of the Apostles — must be vigorously maintained.

Of necessity this visible organization must work within the existing pattern of society. It was legitimate therefore, by means of concordats and other diplomatic measures, to arrive at agreements with civil governments that recognized the rights of God and the claims of Christian conscience. But with powers that did *not* recognize these rights — with governments that exalted the State or any individual leader above God — no intercourse was possible. They were the enemy, the Dark Adversary wandering through the world, seeking the ruin of souls. Now more than ever it was imperative that the Church make common cause with those governments which recognized the right of worship and the primacy of God in men's lives.

For the present, since the structure of human society was nationalistic, the Church in its human aspects must function within that frame. Eventually, in God's time, the Church would disclose the larger design of His plan. In some future age, men would pick up the cross and go forth conquering under that sign alone. But they would pick up many other things first — national banners, terrible weapons, false symbols, and blasphemous words. In clashing dissonance their tongues would cry down the gentle admonishments from the Mount:

Blessed are the poor in spirit, for theirs is the kingdom of heaven.
Blessed are the meek, for they shall possess the earth.
Blessed are they who mourn, for they shall be comforted.
Blessed are they who hunger and thirst for justice, for they shall be satisfied.
Blessed are the merciful, for they shall obtain mercy.
Blessed are the clean of heart, for they shall see God.
Blessed are the peacemakers, for they shall be called children of God.
Blessed are they who suffer persecution for justice' sake, for theirs is the kingdom of heaven.

Had men entirely forgotten these counsels of blessedness? Would the meek ever possess the earth, or mourners be comforted? The *Oriana's* foghorn, braying at two-minute intervals, cast terrifying doubts on the matter. Traveling outward from the vessel, the sound waves would strike a berg, then rebound in vibrations cruelly deformed by ice and fog. The mocking antiphon, pitched in the key of foreboding, chilled Stephen with its hoarse restatement of human discord. Counterpoint of chaos, struck by man and re-echoed by the elements! Was this the sound that life made wherever one listened — the reverberations of cruelty and despair that would drown out His voice at last?

Stephen dared believe that, under the strident accents of brutality, men were listening for the first faint promises of the human *concordia* to be. Not given to modeling human clay in images contrary to fact, Stephen entertained (even at this dread hour) a realistic hope for such concord. His hope had been powerfully strengthened by Conrad Szalay's performance at the concert earlier in the evening. Properly viewed, Conrad's violin was a kind of *lyra mystica* creating harmony out of diverse, even hostile elements. The violin had been made of American maple and spruce, carved by the skill of a French-Canadian luthier, on a pattern of Italian design. It had been played by a youth of Polish-American descent, taught in childhood by a Russian Jew, and later by a Rumanian. On a British liner, Conrad had played the music of Brahms and Saint-Saëns to international listeners, who had temporarily laid aside their differences to applaud his universal art. Accompanying the violinist was a girl sprung of American, Irish, and Spanish stock who would soon blend not only her music, but her bone and blood, with the man she loved.

Stephen did not wish to tack the allegory down too firmly. He could not foretell the political form that the human *concordia* of the future would take. But his faith told him that one day all nations would lift their hearts and voices in similar unity. With all his profoundly affirmative strength, he believed that the process by which Spirit infiltrates and purifies creature substance was slowly taking place in the world.

And who would advance this process? Who would hasten and guarantee its fulfillment? Leaning over the *Oriana's* rail, Stephen heard the primal sounds of ocean far below. Unbidden, the lines of John Keats sprang to his mind:

> *The moving waters at their priestlike task*
> *Of pure ablution round earth's human shores . . .*

Priestlike task! How better describe the office divinely

entrusted to the Church? Heaven's beach might be far away, but round earth's human shores the labor of purification would constantly go on. Across the desolate shingle of the world, priests would move among erring, afflicted men and women, comforting their sorrow, counseling them against despair, teaching them to support each other in acts of loving-kindness, pleading with them to accept some fragment of grace or receive — amidst scenes of mortal decay — some intimation of their immortality.

Memories of Ned Halley, Bill Monaghan, Paul Ireton, Dom Arcibal, Gregor Potocki, and Alfeo Quarenghi warmed Stephen with knowledge of priestly good. He uttered their names, a litany of familiar saints. To these names could be added thousands of others unknown to Stephen — pastors, curates, confessors, binders of wounds, obscure filesmen in the army of the Church Militant, washers of weary feet and pourers of sacramental oil, exhorters, sustainers, whippers-in along the dusty line of march.

"Father," men called them. O most trusting of names — an echo of the Name uttered by circling choirs of seraphim, by souls clinging to the cliffs of purgatory, by bereaved children of Adam weeping and wailing in this valley of tears. A Name repeated ceaselessly in monodies of praise by lynx and leviathan, by inchworm, wind, and wave. A Name trumpeted by the hurricane, flashed in the lightning's code — a Name boiling at the volcano's heart, and roaring above the avalanche . . .

The pinnacle of an iceberg toppled like exploding thunder alongside the *Oriana*.

. . . A Name terrible in wrath, fearsome in its commandments to men, icy with anger when those commandments were broken . . .

Stephen gripped the rail as the vessel lurched, faltered.

. . . A Name hurling death at mockers . . .

Foghorn waves, resounding from the cliff of a monstrous iceberg, screamed like tormented souls in hell.

. . . A Name breathing forgiveness to those who humbly implore its mercy . . .

As the ship entered the narrowing defile of ice, Stephen lifted that Name in utter dependence and trust:

"Our Father Who art in heaven, hallowed be Thy name . . ."

Above all other names of nations, rulers, dynasties, and powers.

"Thy kingdom come; Thy will be done on earth as it is in heaven . . ."

In Thy will is our peace, and our hearts are restless till they find rest in Thee.

"Give us this day our daily bread . . ."

Grant this humblest of invocations rising from Thy children earning their bread by honorable toil.

"And forgive us our trespasses . . ."

This most particularly, O Lord. For if Thou markest iniquities, who shall stand?

"As we forgive those who trespass against us . . ."

Yes, even those who condemn, injure, and most despitefully conspire against Thy Church.

"And lead us not into temptation . . ."

Through a rift in the fog, Stephen could see the dull glow of Lucifer, ominous, blood-colored, constant in the lives of men.

"But deliver us from evil . . ."

From sudden and unprovided death; from plague, famine, and war; from lightning, ice, and shipwreck; from false leaders; from the ultimate ruin of Pride — and mercifully from Thy wrath, O Father in heaven, we beseech Thee, deliver us!

The little hours began to climb from the pit of darkness. Faint musks of earth, borne seaward on vernal winds, scented the air with melting promise. Overhead, the Dipper spilled septentrional glory down. New World spring was breaching the fog barrier. Vigilance, wrought of hope and faith, would bring the vessel through.

Night and ice floe, tide and planet, ship and world — irresistibly drawn by a love that blends all wills and desires to Himself alone — moved on their destined courses as Stephen murmured, "Amen."